Since 2004, internationally bestselling author **Sherrilyn Kenyon** has placed over sixty novels on the *New York Times* bestseller list; in the past three years alone, she has claimed the No.1 spot seventeen times. This extraordinary bestseller continues to top every genre she writes within.

Proclaimed the pre-eminent voice in paranormal fiction by critics, Kenyon has helped pioneer – and define – the current paranormal trend that has captivated the world and continues to blaze new trails that blur traditional genre lines.

With more than 25 million copies of her books in print in over 100 countries, her current series include: The Dark-Hunters, League, Lords of Avalon, Chronicles of Nick, and Belador Code.

Visit Sherrilyn Kenyon online:

www.darkhunter.com
www.sherrilynkenyon.co.uk
www.facebook.com/AuthorSherrilynKenyon
www.twitter.com/KenyonSherrilyn

Praise for Sherrilyn Kenyon:

'A publishing phenomenon ... [Sherrilyn Kenyon] is the reigning queen of the wildly successful paranormal scene'
Publishers Weekly

'Kenyon's writing is brisk, ironic and relentlessly imaginative. These are not your mother's vampire novels'
Boston Globe

'Whether writing as Sherrilyn Kenyon or Kinley MacGregor, this author delivers great romantic fantasy!'
New York Times bestselling author Elizabeth Lowell

Styxx

SHERRILYN KENYON

piatkus

PIATKUS

First published in the US in 2013 by St Martin's Press, New York
First published in Great Britain in 2013 by Piatkus
This paperback edition published in 2014 by Piatkus

A CIP catalogue record for this book
is available from the British Library.

ISBN 978-0-349-40066-2

Printed and bound in Great Britain by
Clays Ltd, St Ives plc

Papers used by Piatkus are from well-managed forests
and other responsible sources.

MIX
Paper from
responsible sources
FSC® C104740
www.fsc.org

Piatkus
An imprint of
Little, Brown Book Group
100 Victoria Embankment
London EC4Y 0DY

An Hachette UK Company
www.hachette.co.uk

www.piatkus.co.uk

AUTHOR'S NOTE

Writing about history is always a difficult prospect. To begin with historians themselves are extremely argumentative on anything that cannot be proven or that is not carved in stone ... which is the vast majority of human history. Years ago, Norman Cantor wrote an amazing book called *Inventing the Middle Ages,* which goes into how a historian's views and opinions and background greatly color their research and conclusions. I spent many years in the history field, and in professional groups of historians, and have defended enough papers and opinions/conclusions to know firsthand just how much our opinions differ and how virulently we will all defend them.

That being said, the first part of this book exists outside of any current hard archeological evidence, and before the majority of human recorded history. There are thousands of archeological sites that are hotly debated as to their age and how advanced they were when they were thriving. Sites we, honestly, know very little or nothing about that can be interpreted numerous ways. And the historical record is written and rewritten every year as new evidence and discoveries and interpretations are introduced.

In the realm of Dark-Hunters, at the time this book takes place, the ancient world is much more advanced than the accepted human record we currently have. It doesn't make it wrong. It simply makes it fiction.

In my series, after the death of Acheron, Apollymi blows the entire world back into the Stone Age and that is why the ancient Greece we're taught about in school isn't as advanced as the one I write about for Acheron and Styxx. It is not historical inaccuracy on my part, or lack of research, but rather it's the fictional world I have created.

The Greece and Egypt of Acheron and Styxx predate our current histories for those countries. They had to, since we don't have written records for the time of Atlantis (other than Plato's mention of the doomed city many centuries after it'd been destroyed), never mind the thousands of years before Atlantis that made up the world of Bathymaas and Aricles.

Some of the city-states and countries in the book, such as Didymos, are fictitious while others, such as Athens and Thebes, were real. However, since we don't have written records for this time period, and given the way cities and countries can change (sometimes very quickly), I have taken liberty with them.

Also, the Greek that Styxx and Acheron would have spoken is not the same as modern Greek or even traditional written ancient/Classical Greek. Languages are a living entity and the meanings for words are constantly changing. Such as twenty years ago to say something was "sick" would be negative. Today, it can be negative or positive depending on context. Language is always evolving. To give my fictional world a sense of realism, I incorporated that human tendency into the books.

Likewise there may be words or phrases that might be construed as modern that really aren't. Ancient man was highly creative with their vocabulary and insults. In some cases, I have used their recorded creativity and in others, I've shortened it to things such as "fuck you," which will sound current. It doesn't mean it is strictly a modern phrase (we have numerous historical examples of its written use). In the past, they would have said it and usually embellished on the specifics. Meanwhile words such as "moron" that may sound modern are actually Greek in origin—μωρός— which was written in text as far back as the fifth century BC and has the modern meaning of the word. We don't know how old such words really are, as we can only gauge their age by when they are written. But usually words and phrases are around for a long time before they make it into the written records, especially in historical times.

The only truly anachronistic term in the book is "hell," but they did have the modern concept of hell in the ancient world, they would have just used the words *Dozakh* or *Pyriphlegethon*. For simplicity sake, I kept our modern term. Much of our current concept can be traced to ancient Zoroastrianism some 3,500 years ago. Which again means the concept was around far longer than we can prove, but that it was popularized by that religion as it spread through recorded history. The word "hell" itself goes back to medieval Norway. I have chosen to use it in the book to simplify things for modern readers and to convey the proper meanings without having to explain and give the history of every ancient, unfamiliar word. While the people of the characters' time period would have used other words for everything they say and do, I have kept my language more modern to not bog down the reader with constant history lessons that detract from the characters and story.

My personal belief, given my extensive years of research, is that people are people and have always been people. The more things change, the more they stay the same. Back when I taught courses on ancient societies, one of the things I began the class with was the following quote from Aristophanes's play *The Clouds* (423 BC):

Yet certainly these are those principles by which my system of education nurtured the men who fought at Marathon. But you teach the men of the present day, so that I am choked, when at the Panathenaia a fellow, holding his shield before his person, neglects Tritogenia, when they ought to dance. Wherefore, O youth, choose with confidence, me, the better cause, and you will learn to hate the Agora, and to refrain from baths, and to be ashamed of what is disgraceful, and to be enraged if anyone jeer you, and to rise up from seats before your seniors when they approach, and not to behave ill toward your parents, and to do nothing else that is base, because you are to form in your mind an image of Modesty: and not to dart into the house of a dancing-woman, lest, while gaping after these things, being struck with an apple by a wanton, you should be damaged in your reputation: and not to contradict your father in anything; nor by calling him Iapetus, to reproach him with the ills of age, by which you were reared in your infancy.

Yet certainly shall you spend your time in the gymnastic schools, sleek and blooming; not chattering in the market-place rude jests, like the youths of the present day; nor dragged into court for a petty suit, greedy, pettifogging, knavish; but you shall descend to the Academy and run races beneath the sacred olives along with some modest compeer, crowned with white reeds, redolent of yew, and careless ease, of leaf-shedding white poplar, rejoicing in the season of spring, when the plane-tree whispers to the elm.

If you do these things which I say, and apply your mind to these, you will ever have a stout chest, a clear complexion, broad shoulders, a little tongue, large hips, little lewdness. But if you practise what the youths of the present day do, you will have in the first place, a pallid complexion, small shoulders, a narrow chest, a large tongue, little hips, great lewdness, a long psephism; and this deceiver will persuade you to consider everything that is base to be honourable, and what is honourable to be base; and in addition to this, he will fill you with the lewdness of Antimachus.

His rant against the children of his day and lack of respect and decorum is one found time and again for as long as humans have had written stories and histories. From all my readings of ancient works, in all countries and in many ancient languages, the one thing I always find is that while our toys and civilizations and laws change, the basic human animal never does. While some may try and hope for better, others do not.

People will be people, and we are all very complicated beings who are the summation of our pasts and emotions, and our sensory intake.

With every book, I strive to do justice to the characters and to show the complexity of human motivation and emotion. But more than that, I try to show that while some cave to bad situations, not everyone does. And that the tragedy and trauma that can destroy one person can also be what gives another the ability to overcome and build a better future.

We do not have to become or remain the victims that life sometimes makes us all. With enough strength and courage, all of us can overcome and learn to thrive in spite of the horrors and tragedies we've survived.

As Plato said, "Be kind to everyone you meet, for we are all fighting a fierce battle." That is the one motto of my life and it is what has seen me through my own hell and dark hours. I believe in the beauty and the power of the human spirit because I know how hard-won the battle for sanity and safety can be. And I know how hard it is to leave behind a brutal past that should have never existed.

Every day is a new battle and while I may lose some of those fights, I will never lose my war. I couldn't control the past or some of the nightmares forced upon me, but I can and do control my present and I will not let those vultures steal another moment of my life.

We all have moments of weakness, but with that comes the strength of knowing that we're still here. And we still matter.

All of us.

With that, I dedicate this book to all of the soldiers in the world, past and present and future, who take up arms every day and stand at the wall of humanity and refuse to see it fall to the vicious onslaught of those who would destroy us for no reason whatsoever, other than they are so malcontent with their own existence that they can't bear to see anyone else happy. Don't let them win.

We are all survivors and we are all beautiful human beings who deserve our dreams and our sanity.

Styxx

The gods make kings, fools and pawns of us all ... In equal turn, but not in equal length.

—SAVITAR

JUNE 19, 9548 BC

"You missed, moron. My son still lives, and one day, we are going to bathe in your blood."

Dressed in Greek cavalry armor to hide his identity, Archon, the king of the Atlantean gods, froze in the middle of the dark hallway as he heard the taunting voice of his angry wife in his head. A sick feeling of dread clenched his stomach tight. "What say you?"

"Well," Apollymi projected mentally to him, drawing the word out. "Lord High King God Intelligent, ye who knows all, I am still imprisoned in Kalosis and that baby you hold in your arms is quite dead. What does that tell you?"

That he'd slaughtered the wrong infant.

Damn it! He'd been certain this was the right child . . .

Wincing in utter agony over what he'd done, Archon heard the screams of the Atlantean queen from where he'd left her in her bedroom as she cursed them all for the death of her newborn son. It was an unforgivable act, but Apollymi had given him no choice. She had refused to hand over her son and had hidden the infant here in the mortal world so that Apostolos would live in spite of Archon's order that the boy be killed.

If her infant son grew to manhood, *all* of them would die. The Atlantean pantheon and their people. But Apollymi didn't care. So long as Apostolos lived, the rest of them could burn.

Heartbroken over the innocent life he'd mistakenly taken, Archon handed the baby's body to a guard on his right so that it could be returned to its grieving mother.

"Where is your son, Apollymi?" he demanded in his head.

She laughed at his anger. "Where you will *never* find him. Go on, slaughter every pregnant queen and her brat in the mortal realm. I *dare* you!"

1

Archon glanced at the three gods with him, who were also disguised as he was—in cavalry armor. The Atlantean queen believed them to be vengeful Greeks sent to assassinate her child. Since they were the gods she and her people worshiped, they couldn't afford for her to hate them. Not when the worship of the Atlantean people fed their powers.

And if they searched through the mortal realm where other gods ruled to find Apollymi's son, they would have to do so very carefully. Especially if the mission was to slaughter princes. The humans would call out their own gods, who would then demand retribution for their followers, and it would be a divine bloodbath between feuding pantheons.

Been there. Done that.

And it hadn't been the least bit enjoyable.

No doubt that was what Apollymi craved as much, if not more, than the return of her child. Born of the darkest powers in the universe, the first goddess of destruction lived only for such warfare. It was the very air she breathed.

Disgusted and furious over his mistake, Archon flashed himself from the human world to the main temple hall on Katateros, where the Atlantean gods ruled their people. The three gods who'd gone with him to Atlantis followed.

The moment the four of them were corporeal in their ornate temple, the other Atlantean gods stared at them expectantly.

"Well?" Misos, their god of war, asked. "Did you get him?"

Archon shook his golden head and narrowed his gaze on Basi. Beautiful and seductive, the drunken goddess of excess was the one who had taken Apollymi's son and hidden him out of their reach. Unfortunately, the sot had no recollection of where she'd put the baby, other than in the stomach of an already pregnant human ... maybe. Maybe not.

Big help that, bitch. Thank you.

That was why Apollymi had chosen the drunkard and forced her to do this deplorable deed. When it came to giving up any kind of useful information, Basi was worthless.

2

Archon shed the hated Greek armor and skin in favor of his true form—that of a perfect blond male in his mid-twenties—and donned his dark blue Atlantean formesta robes. "Can you remember anything else?"

Fear darkened Basi's beautiful brow. "No, Archon. I just remember Polly telling me to hide it in a queen ... Yes. It was a queen. I think I was in Greece, but I can't remember. Maybe Sumer ... Akkadia or Egypt? I think the queen had dark hair ... but it might have been blond or red ... Maybe."

It took everything he had not to kill her for her stupidity.

His brother, Misos, sighed heavily. With black hair and a full beard, Misos was as different in appearance from Archon as he was in his divine warring powers. "So what do we do now?"

Archon growled at the only option they had. "We go out and we hunt that bastard down. Whatever it takes."

Chara, the plump redheaded goddess of joy and happiness, scowled at him. "If we venture into the domains of other pantheons to search, we'll have to hide our powers from their gods. How are we to find Apostolos without them?"

It wouldn't be as easy, but ... "I know my wife. There will be something about him different from other mortals. You won't mistake Apostolos when you *see* him, and I doubt our powers will help anyway since she has him shielded so carefully. In the meantime, those of us who remain in Katateros while the others search can call out to him and drive him insane. That, too, should help us find him. He'll be the mortal prince who hears the voices of the Atlantean gods even when he doesn't worship us."

Bet'anya Agriosa stood up from where she'd been sitting next to her mother, Symfora. With flowing black hair and perfect caramel skin, she stood out from the other Atlantean gods. "For the record, I want to state my displeasure over all this. I may be the goddess of wrath and misery, but I find it distasteful and wrong to hunt down an innocent child and kill him because of the accidental prophecy of three little girls."

Archon glared at her. "My daughters may be young, but they

hold the power of two pantheons in them. You better than anyone know how powerful that makes them." While his daughters were born of him and the Greek goddess Themis, Bet'anya was Atlantean and her father the Egyptian god, Set—one of the most powerful beings in existence.

Some even claimed Set held more power than Apollymi, and *that* was something Archon never wanted to test.

Bet'anya arched a brow. "So? You don't fear *me*."

That wasn't true, but Archon wasn't dumb enough to let her know that. Bet'anya held a lot of dark power herself and he wasn't about to cross her. No one with a brain would. The last time a god had taken her on, the world had almost ended over it. "You don't draw the same powers Apollymi does. And we don't know what powers her son holds."

Misos nodded in agreement. "As the son of Apollymi and Archon, he could easily be the mightiest of any pantheon."

Archon inclined his head to his brother. "We have twenty-one years to find this boy and kill him. We *cannot* fail. The sooner he's destroyed, the better for us all."

Bet'anya clenched her teeth as they began to divide the world between them. Apollymi had always been one of her allies. And Bet hadn't been here when the other Atlantean gods had united their powers to trap her in Misos's hell realm, Kalosis. Personally, she couldn't blame Apollymi for her anger. Had they ganged up on her and locked her away while calling for the life of her child . . .

She, too, would show them exactly how dark her powers ran.

But like it or not, Bet'anya was part of this pantheon and would be honor bound to hunt for the child.

She'd just do so leisurely.

Her great-grandfather, Misos, approached her. "What are you thinking, child?"

"That it's a sad day when a mere baby can threaten a pantheon so powerful."

4

"While I concur, I would remind you that pantheons have fallen for a lot less." He kissed her brow.

"Fine, Tattas." She used the Atlantean term for grandfather. "I'll take southern Greece and Egypt where I can use my powers to find him . . . if he's there."

She looked back at the leader of this cursed quest and spoke to him. "I have one question, Archon . . . you slaughtered an Atlantean citizen and prince by mistake. How is it that here at home, where you have full power, you couldn't tell the baby was mortal?"

"The queen's son stank of a god's powers. Not to mention, her husband died well before its conception and to our knowledge, she's had no other lovers. That smacked of Basi's interference." He growled low in his throat. "Obviously, I was wrong. I should have known Apollymi wouldn't make it that easy on us."

Bet'anya arched a brow at that. There was only one god from outside their pantheon it could possibly be. "It was Apollo's son?"

"Most likely."

She cringed inwardly. While she wasn't afraid of the Greek gods, she didn't want to be in another bloody war with them. Every time she went up against their rampant stupidity, she felt like it sucked a portion of her own intelligence out of her. "And you think the Greek god will be all right with your actions?"

Archon wasn't concerned in the least. "Why would he care? He has bastards aplenty he ignores. Besides, he doesn't dare rattle our cage since Atlantis is the only place his Apollites can live and thrive. No other pantheon will tolerate them among their people."

And the warring Apollites had been a constant source of grief in Atlantis, but Archon didn't see it that way. To him, they were another set of beings to honor the Atlantean gods and feed their powers.

To her, they were creatures who were as likely to turn on them as they were to continue to worship them. Anything Greek made her skin crawl. She hated them above all races.

Out of the corner of her eye, Bet'anya saw Epithymia slinking out a side door. Tall, beautiful and golden, she was the goddess of all desires.

Curious about what had her so skittish, Bet'anya followed after her. "Epi?"

Outside the hall, she froze instantly. "Yes, Bet? What I can do for you?"

"What have you not confessed?"

Epithymia stiffened. "That which I *will* not confess."

Unwilling to play this game, Bet'anya gestured toward the hall they'd just left. "Then perhaps I should tell Archon about this?"

"Don't you dare!" Epithymia grabbed her arm and hauled her to a corner so that they couldn't be overheard by anyone. "I have to do something I don't want to do."

"Kill a baby?"

Epithymia scoffed. "I wish. *That* would be easy." This from a goddess of light powers? If Epithymia was so quick to kill, it explained so much about Bet'anya's proclivity for violence.

"Apollymi has enlisted me in her scheme and I have to do it. If I don't . . . I can't even tell you what she holds over me because I can't afford for anyone to learn it. That bitch!"

Bet'anya frowned. "What has she asked you to do?"

"Birth her child."

Bet'anya sucked her breath in sharply at that implication. "He's not born yet?"

She shook her head. "And if you tell a soul, I swear I'll join Apollymi against you."

Rage clouded her vision as Bet'anya glared at her. "Do not threaten me. God or not, I will feed on your entrails. But in this, you don't have to fear. I have no desire to kill a defenseless baby."

Epithymia released her. "Good. Because I have a plan. Apollymi wants me to oversee his birth to make sure nothing goes wrong with it, and I intend to deliver him myself."

Bet'anya's stomach clenched at what the goddess was telling her. "You intend to touch a babe who will be born without god powers?"

She nodded.

That was so cold . . .

"The humans will tear him apart in their desire to possess him. And they will hate him for it."

Epithymia winked at her. "I'm just following my orders from Apollymi. To the letter."

"Why not tell Archon—"

"She'll rip out my heart and devour it if I do. I wouldn't cross that bitch for anything. I cannot even hint at where that child is or anything else about his birth. She wrung an oath from me."

And Atlantean gods could never breach their oaths. As such, they tried their best to never make any.

"It would be kinder to kill him on delivery than to leave him with your touch and no protection."

Epithymia held up her hands. "Apollymi won't let me. So I'm doing this her way. And if you breathe a word . . . "

"My oath, I will *never* tell the ones hunting him where he is or what it is you do." No sooner had those words left her lips than she realized what she'd said. It was just such a slip that had cursed poor Apostolos.

Epithymia glared at her.

"I didn't mean . . . " There was no need in explaining. "Fine. I can still kill him if I find him."

Epithymia relaxed. "Good luck, Agriosa." She left to go to her own temple down the hill.

Bet'anya sighed at Epi's parting shot that referred to the fact that she was also a goddess of the hunt. She absolutely hated the thought of harming a child.

Any child.

And yet . . .

What she'd said was true. Death would be the kindest act. Otherwise, that child would live a life of absolute agony. No one should be condemned to such a horrific fate.

"I'm sorry, Apostolos."

As in all battles, when a soldier's wound was mortal, no matter his age, and there was no doubt he would die from it, the kindest thing was to end his suffering with a single fatal blow.

She would commit this mercy killing and pray that one day Apollymi could understand and forgive her. It was for the good of all.

Especially the boy.

Her only hope was that she found the child first. The other gods would not be so merciful to him.

JUNE 23, 9548 BC

King Xerxes stared down at the infant boy who peacefully slept in his arms. How could his joy have turned so bitter so fast? For a moment, he'd believed himself to be the most blessed of all kings. That the gods had granted him two sons to rule his vast empire.

Now . . .

Did he even have one?

There was no doubt that the firstborn, Acheron, was born of the gods. That his wife-queen had whored herself to them and birthed it.

But Styxx . . .

The king studied every inch of the perfect, sleeping child nestled against his body. "Are you mine?" He was desperate to know the truth.

The infant appeared to be a mere human babe. Unlike Acheron, whose eyes swirled a living silver color, Styxx's were vivid blue and perfect. But then the gods were ever treacherous.

Ever deceitful.

Could it be that Acheron was his son and this one was not? Or that neither child belonged to him?

He looked to the elder wise woman who'd proclaimed Acheron

a god's son just after his birth. Decrepit and wizened, she wore heavy white robes that were richly embroidered in gold. Her gray hair was wrapped around an ornate gold crown. "Who is the father of this child?"

The woman paused in her cleaning. "Majesty, why do you ask me something you already know?"

Because he didn't know. Not for certain. And he hated the taste of fear that scalded his throat and left it bitter. Fear that made his heart pound in trepidation. "Answer me, woman!"

"Truth or lie, will you believe whatever answer I give?"

Damn her for her sagacity. How could the gods have done this to him? He'd sacrificed and prayed to them his whole life. Devoutly and without blasphemy. Why would they taint his heir in this manner?

Or worse, take his heir from him?

He tightened his grip, which caused the baby to wake and cry out. A part of him wanted to slam the child into the ground and watch it die. To stomp it into oblivion.

But what if this one *was* his son? His own flesh and blood . . .

The wise woman had said it was.

However, she merely relayed what the gods told her, and what if *they* lied?

Angry and betrayed, he went to the woman and shoved the infant into her arms. Let someone else solace it for now. He couldn't bear the sight of either child.

Without another word, he stormed from the room.

The moment she was alone with the babe, the old crone transformed into a beautiful young woman with long black hair. Dressed in bloodred, she placed a kiss to the boy's head and he instantly calmed down.

"Poor, poor Styxx," the goddess Athena whispered as she rocked him in her arms to soothe him. "Like your brother's, yours will be an unpleasant future. I'm sorry I couldn't do more for either of you. But the human world needs its heroes. And one day, they will all need *you*."

MARCH 10, 9543 BC

Five years later

"You wretched little thief!"

Styxx looked up at the shrill cry of his older sister. Ryssa towered above him and his twin brother Acheron as they played with their wooden horses and soldiers on the floor.

Why was she always so cross at him? No matter what he did to try and please her, it was never enough.

Ryssa hated him. She always had.

"I took nothing."

Curling her lip, she closed the distance between them and yanked him up from the floor by his arm. "Where did you put it, you worthless little worm?" she demanded, shaking him so hard it felt as if she'd rip his arm off.

Styxx tried to break free, but she was too strong for him. "Put what?"

"The toy horse Father gave me for my birthday. I know you collect them and I know you stole mine. Where is it?"

"I haven't touched it."

"You're such a liar!" She threw him toward the ground then went to search his things again. "Where have you hidden it?"

Styxx met Acheron's gaze. "Did you take it?" he whispered to his brother.

Acheron shook his head.

Then who?

"What are you doing in here?"

All of them froze at the sound of fury in their nurse's voice. Before Styxx could explain that he'd invited Acheron in to play with him, the nurse snatched his brother away.

Acheron cried out as the nurse's grip bit into his small arm. "How many times have you been told to stay in your own room?"

Styxx panicked as he realized Acheron still held one of the soldiers in his hand. Even though he'd given them to his brother, he knew what would happen if anyone saw it in Acheron's possession.

His brother would be punished. Again.

Wanting only to protect Acheron, Styxx launched himself from the floor and grabbed it out of Acheron's hand.

Acheron offered him a small smile of gratitude before he was taken away.

"You!" Ryssa sneered as she glared at the toy he held. "You're so selfish. You never think of anyone but yourself. What would it have hurt to let him keep one toy? Huh?" She gestured to the others scattered on the ground. "Nothing's ever enough for you, is it? You always want more and you don't care who you take it from."

She jerked the toy from his hand, cutting his palm in the process, and stormed from his room.

Heartbroken, Styxx stood alone. He hated being by himself with a passion that made no sense. Ofttimes, he wondered if it came from being born a twin. Surely the gods wouldn't have given him a brother if they meant for him to be forever by himself.

And yet, he spent very much of his life alone.

Sighing wistfully, Styxx glanced around the room that was littered with toys. He would gladly give them all away if he could only have one person to play with. Ryssa refused because she didn't like him and he was a smelly boy, and, according to her, he was too stupid to follow the games she played with Acheron. The other children ran away from him because their parents were afraid they might hurt him, either by accident or on purpose, and incur his father's wrath.

Acheron was the only one who welcomed him as a playmate. But their father demanded they stay separated.

Styxx looked down at his brother's toy and wished with everything he had that it was different for them both. Rather they'd been born poor farmers than have to endure the burden of this wretched family and its meanness.

He set the toy aside. Later, after everyone was asleep, he'd return it to his brother.

"Acheron?" Styxx whispered, nudging his sleeping brother awake.

Slowly, Acheron blinked his eyes open. Rubbing them with his fist, Acheron sat up in bed. Styxx shoved the loaf of sweet bread in his face, making Acheron smile the moment he saw it.

"I didn't bring the honey, sorry. But ... " Styxx opened his small cloth bag to show the sugared figs he'd taken. "I managed to pilfer your favorite."

Acheron's silver eyes lit up. "Thank you! But you shouldn't have. You could have been caught."

Styxx shrugged. "I wouldn't have been hurt over this." At least not physically—those beatings were reserved for other offenses. Though there were times when he'd prefer being hit to listening to them call him worthless or other names.

Glad he'd helped his brother, Styxx watched as Acheron tore into the bread. Since they'd sent them both to bed with no supper, Acheron was starving. But as usual, Styxx had been unable to sleep and so once the palace quieted down, he'd snuck to the pantry.

"What did you eat?" Acheron asked.

"Bread ... with your honey." He grinned wide with his guilt.

Acheron laughed. "That was wrong of you."

Styxx indicated the small bag. "I thought you'd rather have the figs."

"You could have given me the choice."

"And I would have had my belly not been cramping. It smelled so good, I couldn't take it anymore. I had to eat some on my way here. Sorry."

"Then I shall forgive you." Acheron held the bread out. "Would you like more?"

He shook his head, declining it. Even though he was still hungry, he knew Acheron was even more so.

Frowning while he ate, Acheron cocked his head. "Can you not sleep again?"

"I tried." Morpheus held a grudge against him for reasons only the gods knew. No matter how hard Styxx tried, sleep forever eluded him.

Acheron scooted back on his pallet, making more room.

Grateful beyond measure, Styxx accepted his unspoken invitation and lay down by Acheron's side.

Within a few minutes, he was sound asleep. Acheron finished his food then tucked the bag into Styxx's chiton. Licking the last of the sugar from his fingers, he curled up behind Styxx, back to back, and placed the bottoms of his feet flush to his brother's. As far back as he could remember, they had slept like this whenever they could. Neither of them liked to be alone or apart, and yet their family seemed determined for them to be so. It was something neither of them understood.

How they both wished they could be left alone together.

And Styxx was the one he loved best.

His brother was the only one who treated him like he was normal. Styxx didn't hate him like their parents did, nor dote on him like he was a god incarnate as Ryssa was prone to do.

They were brothers. They played. They laughed. And they fought for everything they were worth. But whenever the fighting was done, they would dust off and be friends again.

Always and forever.

Closing his eyes, Acheron heard the voices that were continually in his head. Styxx heard them, too. But while Acheron only heard those of the gods, Styxx heard those and many, many more. It was one of the reasons his brother had such difficulty sleeping. Whenever they were together, the voices in Styxx's head stopped shouting at him and left him free to rest. Styxx could only hear Acheron's thoughts then, and Acheron was very careful of them.

But the moment they were apart, the voices returned to Styxx with a vengeance. The constant lack of sleep made his twin irritable most days and gave him terrible headaches. Headaches so ferocious that at times his nose bled from them, and he was often sick to his stomach.

No one else understood that. They accused Styxx of faking the pain. And both of them were terrified of telling others what they heard. Everyone but Styxx hated him enough already. Acheron had no desire to give them another cause.

When Styxx had tried to tell others about the voices, he'd been ridiculed and punished for lying. Even Ryssa had accused him of making it up for attention. So both of them had learned to keep the secret and tell no one. Ever.

There were many secrets the two of them shared.

And they had promised each other that one day, when they were grown and no one could stop them, they would leave this place and go somewhere else where people didn't treat them so badly.

Like his twin brother, Acheron couldn't wait for that day to come.

MAY 9, 9542 BC

"Sit up straight! You slouch like a fishmonger's son."

Styxx flinched at his father's angry tone and straightened himself immediately in his uncomfortable gold chair where his legs had gone numb from dangling over the edge of it. But if he folded them under him, it would anger his father even more than his slouching. While his father often doted on him, especially whenever they were in public, there were other times when his father would be so cross that nothing he did pleased him. Times when his father seemed to begrudge him every breath he took.

Today was definitely one of those days.

14

"Are we boring you, boy?"

Styxx shook his head quickly, resisting the urge to groan out loud as pain split his skull with absolute agony. He'd always hated his headaches and the one today was more excruciating than normal. It made it impossible to focus. Worse, he felt as if he would vomit at any moment. *That* his father would find unforgivable.

What? Are you a pregnant woman, boy? You vomit as such. Learn to control your stomach. You're to be a man, for the gods' sakes. Men don't throw up every other minute. They control themselves and their bodies at all times.

His stomach heaved violently, sending more pain throbbing through his head, which then sickened him all the more. The constant seesawing between his head and stomach was enough to make him want to scream in agony.

"Might I be excused, Father?"

His father turned to glare at him furiously. "To what purpose?"

"I don't feel well." That was a substantial understatement.

"Come here."

Styxx scooted off his small throne and resisted the urge to wince as a thousand needles stabbed at his sleeping legs. Knowing better than to let his father see the pain it caused him, he crossed the dais to his father's huge gilded throne. It was so massive that the top of his blond head barely reached the arm of it. Dressed in a white and purple stola and chlamys that matched Styxx's chiton, the king gave him a suspicious glower. His father's blond hair and beard gleamed in the light beneath the gold-leaf crown that would one day be Styxx's.

As they always did on this day of every week, they'd spent all morning dealing with the problems and concerns of the nobles and people who wanted an audience with their king. Since this was something Styxx would have to do once he ruled this kingdom, for the last year his father had made him stay and listen so that he could use his father's wisdom once he inherited the crown. While Styxx was here, he was never to move or speak. Only observe.

The "privilege" of attending these sessions and the "joy" of a drill instructor who lived to knock him around had been his sole birthday gifts last summer when he'd turned five.

With a fierce frown creasing his forehead, his father touched Styxx's brow. "You have no fever. What are your symptoms?"

"My head aches."

He rolled his eyes. "And?"

I want to vomit and I'm terribly dizzy. But he knew from experience that his father would only ridicule those complaints.

"That is all, Father. But the pain is ferocious."

His father glared at him. "You will one day be king, boy. Do you think they will stop a war or an uprising because you have a meager headache?"

"No, Sire."

"That is correct. The world does not stop for something so trivial. Now sit and listen. Observe your future duties. Your people are far more important than your boredom and they deserve your full attention."

But it wasn't boredom. Every shred of light or hint of sound pierced his head with a pain so foul that he wanted to bash his own brains in. Why could no one *ever* understand his headaches and how much they hurt?

Tears of pain and frustration formed, but he quickly blinked them away. He'd learned long ago that while his father would console Ryssa whenever she cried, he would never tolerate tears from his son. Styxx was to be a man, not some mollycoddled girl . . .

Trying not to jar his head while he moved, Styxx returned to his seat.

"Sit up!" his father barked instantly.

Styxx jerked upright then winced in pain. *Don't show it . . .*

But it was so hard not to. Swallowing in agony, he glanced out the window to see Ryssa in the garden with Acheron. They were laughing as they chased each other and played. What he wouldn't give to be outside with them in the beautiful sunshine.

Not that it would matter. Even if his head didn't hurt, Ryssa

16

would never swing him around like that. She'd never laugh with him or tickle him. Her love was reserved solely for Acheron.

Turning his head, he tried not to think about it as another wave of misery pierced his brain.

Styxx leaned forward at the same time blood poured from his nose. *No! Please, not now . . . Please, gods.* He pressed his hand to his nose, trying to stanch it before his father took note.

"Majesty? Is His Highness all right?"

Styxx panicked at the guard's question that brought his father's full attention back to him.

Rage darkened his father's brow. "Did you do that apurpose?"

Yes, I purposefully cut open my nose with no means whatsoever just to spite you, Father. I'm truly *talented that way.*

"No, Father. I shall be all right. It's just another nosebleed. It will stop in a few minutes."

The king curled his lip in disgust. "Look at you! You're filthy. You don't dishonor those around you or your divinely given station with such sanguinariness." The king jerked his chin at the guard who'd ratted him out and Styxx's valet who was charged with keeping him immaculate and presentable any time he was in public. "Take the prince to his room and see that he's cleaned and changed."

Great, I sound like an infant or puppy.

They bowed low before crossing the room to stand before Styxx.

Already dreading what this would mean for him later, Styxx kept his nostrils pinched together and slid off his seat then headed for his room upstairs. As he crossed the atrium from the throne room toward the main palace, he paused again to watch Acheron and Ryssa laughing and playing in the back garden. The bleeding in his nose worsened as did the voices that shouted even louder than before.

Tears filled his eyes. He wanted to scream from it all, and when Acheron fell and scraped their knees, Styxx couldn't take it anymore.

He hit the ground, clutching his leg and crying out as his pain finally overwhelmed him completely.

Please, gods, please just let me die . . .

Acheron came running to his side. "Styxx? Are you all right?"

No. I live in a state of constant physical pain no one understands or has mercy for. And he was tired of it. Dear gods, could he not have one single hour where something didn't hurt?

"Styxx?"

He couldn't respond to his brother, not while he ached so badly and in so many ways. Instead, he stared at the blood on Acheron's ravaged skin. He felt the same exact injury on his own knee and yet he knew that if he looked at his leg, he'd have no wound to explain the throbbing ache he felt there.

"Don't get hurt again, Acheron," Styxx finally breathed. "Please."

Acheron frowned as Ryssa came forward. She knelt on the ground by Styxx's side. "Why are you lying here?"

Styxx pushed himself up before she could mock his pain, too. "I fell."

She glanced around the path. "There's nothing for you to trip over. What? You saw Acheron fall and couldn't stand him getting five seconds more of attention than you?"

Styxx glared at her as more agony split his skull. "Yes, that's exactly what happened."

"Have you another headache?" Acheron asked.

Styxx nodded then winced.

Ryssa scoffed. "Father says you only pretend to have them to get out of your responsibilities."

He gestured toward his soiled chiton. "What of the blood that covers me?"

"You probably injured yourself for sympathy. I know you. You're not above doing anything for attention."

That was so him . . . never.

Unable to deal with her criticism, Styxx cradled his aching skull in the palm of his right hand and continued on to his room with his valet and guard trailing in his wake.

Acheron started to follow after him, but Ryssa held him back.

"Let him go, Acheron. He'll just get you into trouble like he always does. Come. Let us play more."

Hours later, Styxx lay in bed, trying his best not to move or breathe. Suddenly, he felt a gentle hand in his hair. He knew instantly who it was. Only one person was that kind or caring where he was concerned.

"Acheron?" he whispered.

Without answering, his brother crawled into bed behind him. "Is your head any better?"

"Not really. Yours?"

"It hurts but not as much as yours, I think. I can still function with mine." Acheron touched the fresh bruises on Styxx's bare back that throbbed even more than his head did. "Why were you punished?"

"I left the court sessions early. Like Ryssa, Father didn't believe my head hurts. He thought I was trying to avoid my responsibilities." Something their father had absolutely no tolerance for.

Acheron put his arms around him and held him close. "I'm sorry, Styxx."

"Thank you." Styxx didn't speak for several minutes as the voices in his head finally grew fainter and the cranial ache lessened enough that he could almost breathe normally again. "Acheron? Why do you think I can feel your pain, but you don't feel mine?"

"Ryssa would say it's the will of the gods."

But why? Styxx suspected that he must not be as important to the gods as Acheron. Why else would he feel his brother's wounds while Acheron was impervious to *his* pain? It was as if the gods wanted to ensure that Styxx protected his brother from all harm. As if he was Acheron's divinely chosen whipping boy . . .

"What do *you* believe, Acheron?"

"I don't know. Any more than I understand why the gods have abandoned us to such awful people while they speak so loudly in our heads. It doesn't make sense, does it?" Acheron turned over and pressed his back to Styxx's then his feet. As they lay quietly in the darkness of Styxx's room, Acheron reached to take Styxx's hand into his. "I'm sorry Ryssa is so mean to you. She just thinks that you're doted on and spoiled while they treat me badly."

"What do you think?"

"I see the truth. Our parents are suspicious of you, too. And while they are nice to you at times, they're also very, very mean."

Yes, they were. And unlike Acheron, he couldn't complain about it. No one believed him when he did so. They accused him of being spoiled and then disregarded his pain as insignificant, or worse, they took perverse pleasure in his suffering as if he deserved it because he was a prince while they were not. Sometimes he thought it would be better to be Acheron. At least his brother knew what reception he'd receive whenever their parents were around. Styxx never knew until it was too late.

Sometimes his father was loving, and then at others . . .

He lashed out as if he hated Styxx even more than he hated Acheron. It made no sense and was terribly confusing to his young mind. For that reason, he didn't want to be around either of his parents or his sister.

It was best to avoid them and the confusion they caused.

Sighing, he squeezed Acheron's hand and let that touch silence the voices that urged him to kill himself. They were merciless in their taunts.

You are poison. So long as you live, you will suffer!

But if he died, Acheron died, too. The wise woman had proclaimed it so when they were born. Their lives had been joined together by the gods themselves and there was no way to undo it.

Maybe that is why you suffer.

The gods were trying to make him kill Acheron. To hate his brother so that Styxx would murder them both. It made sense in a way. Maybe they thought that if they tortured Styxx enough, he'd grow so tired of it that he'd be desperate enough to kill Acheron to end his own agony. Was that why their eyes were different? So that if he killed his brother, he wouldn't be looking into his own blue eyes when he did it?

Yet he couldn't make himself hate the only person who loved him. The only person who could comfort him and quiet the evil in his head.

Gods or no gods, misery or happiness, Acheron was his brother. Forever and always. He was the only real family Styxx had.

And the one thing he'd learned in his short life was that he couldn't trust anyone. Not even the gods. People lied all around him. Constantly. Even about the little things. Only Acheron was trustworthy and honest. Only his brother didn't try to harm him or seek to betray him to his father. So how could he hurt the only person in his life who treated him as something more than an object to be despised? The one person who didn't smirk in silent satisfaction whenever he was harmed?

"I love you, Acheron."

"I love you, too, brother."

Styxx leaned his head back until it rested against Acheron's and finally let the tears fall that had been misting his eyes all day. He could show them to Acheron. His brother understood and would never mock him for them. "Do you think we'll ever be able to leave this place and find peace?"

"No. I think we were born to suffer."

The saddest part? So did he. "At least we have each other."

Acheron nodded. "Brothers—always and forever. They'll never be able to take that away from us."

AUGUST 30, 9542 BC

"He's coming through the gates right now!"

Styxx looked up from his lessons to see Acheron in the doorway with a huge smile on his face. He didn't have to ask who Acheron was talking about. It would be their uncle Estes who always came to visit them this time of year. It was the one event all of them looked forward to with equal pleasure.

His heart pounding with the same excitement Acheron felt, he glanced up at his tutor, Master Praxis. "Might I be excused, sir? Please?"

"Of course, Your Highness."

Styxx set his scroll aside and ran to Acheron. Hand in hand, they rushed through the hall and down the stairs until they were at the front door where servants were assembling to greet their uncle. Ryssa was already outside on the stone steps, a few feet from their father.

His smile withered as cold dread filled every part of his body. How would his father greet him? For some reason, he couldn't hear his father's thoughts and the king's rigid stance gave him no clue as to the old man's mood.

Acheron let go of his hand and sidled over to Ryssa so that their father wouldn't notice him. How Styxx wished he could go to her for protection, too, but Ryssa never welcomed his company. Only his absence.

The musicians began their fanfare as his father turned in his direction. Styxx braced himself for his father's derision.

Instead, his father smiled warmly and held his hand out to him. "There you are, my precious boy. I was just about to send a servant to fetch you. Come and greet your uncle."

Maybe his father was in a good mood . . .

Smiling even while his stomach knotted harder, Styxx took his father's hand and allowed him to pull him up into his arms.

You better remember this. There's no telling when he'll embrace you again.

It was true. He'd taken to trying to hold on to any memory of his parents' kindness toward him. It was what saw him through their vicious attacks and periods of hateful words.

Styxx laid his head on his father's shoulder and closed his eyes.

How he wished it could always be like this. Most of all, he wished Estes lived with them. His father was much kinder and happier whenever his brother was around. Like him and Acheron, Estes and their father had a special bond. One that was evident as his father rubbed Styxx's back and held him close, like he treasured him.

His father didn't release him until Estes's procession stopped at the drive below. Gleaming with gold armor and bright red cloaks and banners, his uncle's men were as impressive as his uncle himself. But what never failed to amaze Styxx was how much his uncle favored his father. At first glance, they, too, could pass as twins, even though Estes was three years younger. Identical in height, they had the same build, curly blond hair, and beards.

In full military regalia, Estes stepped down from his chariot and, laughing, rushed up the stairs to embrace his father. "Xerxes! How much I've missed you!"

"And I, you, little brother! How was your journey?"

"Any journey that brings me to my family is a good one, indeed." Estes stooped then gaped at Styxx. "Is that my little squirrel all grown and looking like a short adult? What are you now, child? Ten-and-eight? A score?"

"I'm six, Uncle!" Styxx smiled in delight then launched himself at Estes, who caught him with a laugh and held him close to his chest. "I'm not as big as you are. But one day——"

"You shall tower above me, little squirrel. No doubt." Estes kissed his cheek and squeezed him so hard that Styxx groaned from it. His uncle carried him up the stairs to where Ryssa and Acheron waited. His sister's blond hair fell to her waist in bright golden curls. Dressed in purple, she was truly the most beautiful girl in all Greece—if only she had the personality to match. "Ah ... my fairest Ryssa, you are a vision. More beautiful every time I see you."

She blushed then moved to hug him. "It's so good to see you, Uncle."

Estes set Styxx down as he saw Acheron. "And little Acheron ...

23

look at how much you've grown, too. I barely recognize you and Styxx. Come and embrace me."

Acheron jumped into his arms and hugged him tight. "Have you been fighting the Atlanteans again?"

Their uncle always regaled them with the stories of his glorious battles against their enemies. A legendary, undefeated *strategos*, Estes was one of the most respected soldiers in all the world.

"Not lately, dearest. Unfortunately, we are trying for peace with them."

"Peace?" their father scoffed. "Such is not possible where *they're* concerned."

"So say you, brother, but the other Greek kings are trying, and I've been named as an ambassador to Atlantis while they negotiate the peace terms."

That seemed to please their father a great deal. "Well, if anyone can make peace with those jackdaws, it is you. Now come and let us catch up for a while."

Estes kissed Acheron's cheek then set him down beside Styxx. "Remind me later, boys, I have special gifts for both of you."

Their father curled his lip. "Why do you dote on that one when it's obvious he's not one of us?"

Estes caressed Acheron's cheek. "He's a fine, handsome boy, Xerxes. But for his freakish eyes, you'd never know he wasn't Styxx's brother."

Acheron winced at words Styxx knew cut his brother to the bone. He started to comfort him, but Ryssa picked Acheron up and cradled him to her. Acheron laid his head down on her shoulder and closed his eyes. Before Styxx could move, she headed back inside with Acheron while his father and Estes withdrew to his father's study.

Alone, Styxx watched as everyone dispersed. He'd been completely forgotten.

Again.

Sighing at the common occurrence, he headed inside so that he could return to his solitary studies. Other boys his age met together to learn, but his father didn't want him held back by those who were slower. It was far more important that Styxx, as a future king, commit to memory as much as he could as fast as was possible. Therefore, he had the best, most learned tutors his father could procure and he was required to fully utilize them and not waste their time. Failure to advance at the rate his father set was met with the harshest of punishments for both the tutors and for Styxx. So his tutors, fearful of the king's wrath, were brutal with their expectations, and Styxx had to keep up or be punished first by them and then by his father. The king had given all his tutors and trainers full rein to make his life miserable if he did anything they didn't approve of.

You will be responsible for everyone in this kingdom, boy. You must learn to focus and think through every complicated matter and obstacle. I will not leave my throne to a senseless fool.

Because his father had inherited the throne so young, he didn't care that Styxx was still a child. Should anything happen to the king, Styxx would advance to the throne immediately. It could happen twenty years from now, or tomorrow. In the event of the latter, it was crucial that he was trained and ready to accept his responsibilities as king.

There's no place in the heir's life for foolish childhood pastimes or pursuits. Every man, woman, and child of this kingdom is looking to you for their welfare and future. For thousands of years, Didymos has stood as the greatest of the Greek city-states. Undefeated. The House of Aricles is the oldest in the land and we have a glorious history of renowned heroes spanning untold generations. Gods willing, we will continue to be the greatest of them all. I will not allow you to taint our empire or tarnish the names of our esteemed Ariclean ancestors. When they look at you, they do not see Prince Styxx, they see the son of Xerxes of the House of Aricles. Every word you say or action you take reflects on me and I've worked too hard to achieve my stellar reputation to have it tainted by you or anyone else.

Acheron and Ryssa were lucky. Their father didn't view them as an extension of himself. Whenever they did something wrong, the king didn't consider it an affront to his good name. They were tutored together and at a much more leisurely pace by the women in Ryssa's retinue. Sometimes Styxx could hear them laughing through the walls while his tutors mercilessly drilled him.

But at least Praxis wasn't overly harsh. He was far more patient and understanding than the others.

You are still a young boy, Highness. I know it's hard for you to sit for hours on end and focus. Let's take a brief break and let your lessons sink in before we start the next session.

Sometimes he'd even bring sweets for Styxx to snack on while they worked.

As Styxx neared the stairs, he saw his mother waiting in the shadows. An older version of Ryssa, she had been a celebrated beauty in her youth. But too many years of overindulging alcohol had aged her beauty so that she now appeared older than their father.

For a moment, he thought she might be sober. But as he drew closer, the stench of excess stole his breath.

"Which bastard are *you*?" she sneered.

"Styxx, Mother."

Angrily, she narrowed her gaze as if she didn't quite believe him. "Where's the other one?"

"With Ryssa."

A smile finally curled her lips. "My precious Ryssa . . . she was supposed to come visit with me this morning." She started for the staircase then stumbled. Styxx moved to help her. At first, she recoiled from his touch, but after a moment she relaxed and allowed him to give her his shoulder so that she could climb the stairs without falling and hurting herself.

"Who came just now?" she asked as they walked down the hall, toward her chambers.

"Uncle Estes."

"Good. That'll make the old *skatophage* happy for a while."

Styxx didn't comment, but he was glad his father wasn't around to hear his wife call him a dung-eater. No doubt it would upset him greatly.

He led her into her room and deposited her on her dressing stool. As he started away, she reached out and grabbed him by the hair then yanked him closer to her.

"Please, Mother. You're hurting me." He tried to pull her hand away, but she held him fast and with the strength of all the Furies.

She snorted derisively. "You don't know what pain is. Try birthing an ungrateful bastard from your loins, followed by another of his kind. Then watch as your husband's love turns to hatred for you because of them. *That's* pain. But *you* . . . you're the precious, beloved heir he adores. You're all he loves now."

Funny, it didn't feel that way to him. Not while his father censored everything he did. For every bit of praise he received, his father made sure to give at least three criticisms to accompany it.

She gentled her grip in his hair, but didn't let go. "You have hair like your father. I used to love to run my hands through it at night. Back then, he was mine alone and he loved me so. He would have done anything for me . . . At night, he couldn't wait to bed me." Tears filled her eyes. "Why did *you* have to be born?" Sobbing, she pulled his hair then slapped him. "Get out of my sight! You disgust me!"

Styxx ran from the room as fast as he could. His cheek burned from her blow, but he knew better than to leave his mother alone like this. His father would be very angry should he learn that Styxx had abandoned her when it was obvious she needed someone to watch over her. Wiping at his tears, he went to the small antechamber where her maids were gathered to sew and gossip.

"What are you doing here?" the eldest maid snapped as soon as she saw him in the doorway. "I was told by Her Majesty that you were not allowed in this part of the palace. She has no desire to see *you*."

He disregarded her venom. "The queen is in her room and summons you."

She brushed rudely past him without a word. The others stared at him as if he were the filth that sullied their shoes. They were forever looking at him like that whenever he was without his father and he hated it. Most of all, he hated how it made him feel like he *was* the filth on their shoes.

Lifting his chin, he glared back at each one in turn. "I am your prince and heir. You are not to meet my gaze without my permission," he reminded them. "Or I should have you whipped for it." He slammed the door and turned to find Ryssa in the hall behind him.

She raked him with a look that made him feel even lower than the maids had. "You wretched little tyrant. You think you're so much better than everyone else. You're not, you know. You're just a spoiled little pig who's nothing without his father. I hope one day you get *exactly* what you deserve."

The sincerity of her gaze and cruelty of words shredded his heart. Why could she not, just once, say something kind to him? What had he ever done to her? Nothing, and he was tired of her insults. "Shut up, *kuna*! I hate you! I wish you were dead and burned!"

Ryssa grabbed his arm and shook him. "How dare you talk to me like that and use such a filthy word!"

"Styxx!"

He cringed at his father's furious tone. Knowing what would follow, he pried her harsh, bruising grip from his arm and walked past Ryssa to the top of the stairs so that he could see his father below, standing beside Estes.

Fabulous. Now his father would show off for his younger brother.

"Come here, boy!"

His heart pounding in fear he didn't dare let show, Styxx descended the stairs. "Yes, Father?"

"What have I told you about respecting your sister?"

She is the sole princess of this realm. As such, she is to be treasured above all . . .

It was so unfair. If he were Ryssa, he'd be able to whine and tell his father what had happened. But he knew from experience that it would only make this worse. Men did not complain, and most especially not kings. They took the repercussions for their actions and held their heads high no matter what.

Still, he wasn't king. Not yet. And he definitely wasn't a man. "She started it, Father."

He grabbed his arm in the same place Ryssa had twisted it, causing Styxx to grimace. "How dare you! You do not disrespect your father and you damn sure do not disrespect your king," he snarled. "Ever!"

His father yanked his arm and hauled him toward the guard room until they reached the Royal Scold's station. The scold came to his feet immediately and bowed low.

His father flung him at the tall, beefy man Styxx hated with every part of himself.

"Twenty lashes, and ten more if he whimpers or cries."

The scold nodded respectfully. "Am I to be given immunity, Majesty?"

"Aye, of course."

The scold turned his dark eyes to Styxx. "Your Highness?"

It galled him so that he was forced to grant immunity to the person who was about to cane him. But since it was death for anyone to strike a member of the royal family, it had to be done before the scold could carry out the king's orders against a prince. And if he didn't grant it, his father would only make it worse on him.

"Aye. I grant it," he whispered.

"When you're finished, take him to his room and see to it that he's kept there until morning with no comforts."

"Yes, Your Majesty."

His lips trembling from his pent-up tears, Styxx watched as his father left him alone with the giant mountain of a man. For lesser offenses, which he never seemed to commit, he had a whipping boy who would take his punishments for him. But for anything that was deemed a personal insult to his family, Styxx, unlike Ryssa, had to bear it all himself. The princess was never whipped for anything. *She* was too precious and dainty for such. Most of all, she wasn't being groomed for manhood and kingship.

And now that the scold was granted immunity by the two of them, he would take a great deal of pleasure in hurting him. He always did. Even if Styxx didn't cry or whimper, he would still receive the harshest punishment his father had called for. And all because the scold, like Ryssa, thought him to be a spoiled, undeserving brat who needed to be humbled.

You think you're so much better than the rest of us. You're not, dog. You're just a rich man's son. A drunken god-whore's whelp.

Laughing in greedy expectation, the scold pulled him into the small room that was reserved solely for Styxx's private punishments, and bent him over the caning bench. He shoved a piece of leather into Styxx's mouth for him to bite down on and muffle his cries so that his pain wouldn't disturb others or embarrass his father. He tied Styxx's hands to the front of the bench to hold him in place and make sure he didn't try to run then bared his buttocks for the beating.

Styxx placed his cheek against the cold stone and tried to be brave. He did. But when the scold lightly brushed the wood cane against his naked thighs to let him feel how thick and hard it was, he wet himself in fear of the coming pain.

"Some worthless king you'll make," he mocked then he lashed him with every ounce of his massive strength.

Horrified and in pain, Styxx held his screams in for as long as he could, but in the end, he was as worthless as they all thought. He couldn't help it, especially since the scold didn't hurry it along. Rather he dragged it out, waiting for the numbness to pass before he struck again.

At least it took Styxx's attention away from the bruises on his arm and cheek. He should probably be grateful for that.

When it was finally over, the scold dragged him to his room and locked him inside. The servants had already come in and stripped his bed of its linens and pillows. Everything except his bed and chamber pot had been removed.

Tired and aching, Styxx limped toward his bed, but he hurt too much to climb into it. Rather he lay down on the stone floor and wished that he was the son of anyone else. He hated being a prince. Too much was expected of him and everyone despised him for it.

Even his own sister and mother.

Just once he wanted to be free to go outside and play like other children did. To have them welcome him as another playmate and not run away in fear or hatred. While they frolicked with carefree abandon, he had to learn how to speak, read, and write Atlantean, Greek, Akkadian, Egyptian, Sumerian, and a million other languages he didn't care about. Other children got to participate in fun games and friendly competitions, while he had to master swordplay and military tactics taught to him by instructors who detested him even more than the others. Instructors who knocked him to the ground and delighted whenever he bled.

Get up, Highness. In battle, you'd be dead or taken already. You have to fight the hardest of all so that your men will respect you and be willing to lay their lives down at your command. No one follows a coward, no matter what crown he wears . . .

Don't laugh, boy, it isn't kingly. Don't smile or they'll think you're soft or stupid. You must be composed and dignified at all times. Never let your guard down. They are your subjects, not your friends, and you are their future king. You mustn't ever forget that.

On and on it went until it rang in his head alongside the voices of the gods and horrible thoughts of other people.

He didn't see a single perk to being king. Not if it meant you couldn't enjoy laughter or . . . well . . . anything.

I wish Acheron was the heir . . .

But as soon as he had that thought, shame filled him for it. He would never wish this sort of misery on his beloved brother. Acheron had enough to deal with.

"One day I *will* be king," he sobbed, slamming his small fist against the floor. And when he was, things would be *very* different for both of them. No one would ever make either him or Acheron feel like this again.

Not even his sister.

FEBRUARY 3, 9541 BC

Long after midnight, Styxx lay abed, trying to sleep, yet it was impossible. If the pain in his skull wasn't excruciating enough, Acheron had been beaten earlier for the high grand offense of meeting their father's gaze as they passed in the hallway.

His back burned in sympathetic pain for his brother's wounds. He still didn't know how he'd made it through dinner without crying or screaming from the agony, but now that he was alone, he could writhe and moan in peace.

Why can't I just die already?

Surely death would be better than living like this. How could one head hurt so much and not render the victim dead or brain damaged?

How?

Sucking his breath in sharply between his teeth, he heard someone at his door. He froze in panic. It couldn't be Acheron. They were both in too much pain to leave their beds.

The door opened to show his father in the dim firelight. This couldn't be a good thing. His father never disturbed him at night.

What have I done now?

That was a stupid thought. He'd done nothing. *Rather, what does he believe I've done?*

Styxx squeezed his eyes shut, feigning sleep and praying that his father would leave him in peace. Instead, his father sat on the edge of his bed. Styxx held his breath, terrified of what this meant. Why was he here? What could he possibly want with him at this hour?

I didn't do anything . . .

He'd been on his best behavior for weeks now. Only Acheron had been acting out lately. Not that he blamed his brother. They were both tired of how they were treated.

His father sank his fingers into Styxx's hair. His hand was so large that he was able to cradle the whole of Styxx's head in his massive palm.

Styxx's eyes flew open as he waited for the pain he was sure would follow.

Yet his father began running his hand through Styxx's blond curls, toying with them, brushing them back from his face. Maybe he wasn't angry with him, after all. Hoping for the best, he met his father's gaze in the firelight, but didn't dare speak a word. There was rare tenderness in his father's gaze, mixed with concern.

"You remind me much of Estes when he was a boy. Things you say and do ... It makes me think of our childhood together and how much I miss it. Even this was his room back then ..." His father brushed his thumb over Styxx's brow and smiled at the memories. Suddenly, the smell of alcohol on the king's breath hit him hard. His father was terribly drunk.

Biting his lip, Styxx prayed that his father wouldn't fly into one of the legendary rages that his mother had whenever she fell too deeply into her cups.

"He was my only friend. He still is. You've no idea what it's like to have a brother like him. One you can trust who would never do anything to betray you."

His father was wrong about that. Acheron was the best friend anyone could ask for. Not even Estes could equal him.

Leaning closer, his father squinted at him while he held his chin in his hand. He turned Styxx's head so that he could study his face from different angles. "You look like us ... but are you really my son?"

"Father—"

"Don't speak to me!"

Styxx clamped his jaw shut as another wave of terror washed over him. What would his father do?

His father pulled the blanket back so that he could rudely inspect every inch of Styxx's entire body. "You look so human ..."

Styxx wanted to scream as pain racked him hard whenever his

father touched the areas of his small body bruised by Acheron's beating. But he didn't dare let his father know he was hurting when there was no obvious reason for it.

His father rolled him onto his back. Styxx's jaw quivered as tears filled his eyes. There'd been a good reason why he'd been lying on his stomach. His breathing labored, he watched as his father pulled the knife from his belt.

Is he going to kill me?

"But are you human? I have to know." Before Styxx could move or react, his father seized his forearm in a merciless grip then he violently slashed it open. Unable to hold back, Styxx cried out as blood covered his arm and soaked his sheets.

"Sweet Hera," his father breathed. "What have I done?" He clutched at Styxx's wounded arm, trying to stanch the blood flow. "I'm so sorry, Styxx. Forgive me, child."

His hands shaking, his father wrapped Styxx's arm with cloth he tore from Styxx's sheets then he pulled him into his arms and rocked him while Styxx silently sobbed. "Shh, little one. It's all right. It's all right . . ."

But it wasn't and Styxx knew it. From the moment of his birth, his father had questioned his parentage. If not in words, then by the unguarded glares Styxx would see whenever they were alone.

"It's not your fault, child. It's that demon bastard. He's to blame for all of this. He's the one who makes me doubt you. Every time I see his face . . . It fills me with such violence."

Not just Acheron's face. It was his face, too.

His father cupped his head in his large hand and kissed his brow then his cheek. "You are my baby boy. The heir I prayed and sacrificed to the gods for. I know you are. I know it." Tears filled his eyes as he cast a suspicious glare at Styxx. "Aren't you?"

How could he answer a question when he wasn't sure either? His father sensed the very thing he knew for a fact. That he wasn't right. He wasn't normal. While Acheron had the eyes of a god, Styxx was the one who felt phantom pains from wounds given to his brother. *He* was the one who heard stray thoughts of random

34

people. Heard the voices of gods much louder than Acheron did. He sensed other people's emotions and intended actions, even when they tried to conceal them, and he knew the weather without fail.

But the worst were the merciless headaches that plagued him all the time.

Maybe I'm not human . . .

In all honesty, Acheron seemed to be far more normal than he did.

"Answer me!" his father growled. "Are you my son?"

There was only one answer to give. Right or wrong. "Y-y-yes."

His father placed Styxx's head under his chin and wept while he continued to rock him. He didn't let go again until well after dawn. Then, he laid Styxx down on his bed and tucked him into his bloodstained sheets as if nothing had happened. Kissing Styxx's brow, he gave his shoulder a light squeeze then left him alone.

Scared and hurt, Styxx stared at the makeshift bandage his father had wrapped and knotted around his forearm. His hand shaking, he peeled it back to see what he'd suspected . . . he was already healing from the vicious wound. By the end of the day, it would be almost completely gone, with only a scar to mark its location.

I'm not human any more than Acheron is.

And his father would absolutely kill him if he ever learned the truth of it.

AUGUST 30, 9541 BC

Styxx opened his bedroom door to find Acheron on the other side of it. He let out a relieved breath. "Thank the gods it's you."

"Why is your door locked again?"

He shrugged, not wanting to tell Acheron or anyone else about the midnight visit from the king. Since February, he'd made sure to lock and block his door every night lest he receive another unwelcomed surprise.

"What are you doing here?" Styxx asked, trying to deflect his brother's attention away from a question he had no intention of answering.

"I brought your present to you from Estes. You left it downstairs. After what happened last year, I wanted to make sure you got to keep this one."

Styxx took the wooden horse from Acheron's hand and offered a smile he didn't feel.

You deserve nothing until you learn how to conduct yourself civilly and with honor. His father's cruel words still haunted him.

"Thank you, Acheron." Styxx moved to place the horse on the chest by his window where he kept his collection of them. After last year's nightmare, he hadn't felt the same about his wooden horses. Instead of being a source of pride and pleasure, all they reminded him of was his father forcing him to burn the beautiful Atlantean horse Estes had brought him while his legs had ached from his beating and his ego from wetting himself. And all the while Ryssa had smirked in pleasure of his being forced to destroy his gift over his "insult" to her.

Sighing, he moved away from the chest. "A set of beads from us both."

Acheron scowled. "What?"

Styxx met Acheron's deep frown. "What what? You asked me what I got Mother for her birthday."

"No, I didn't. I only thought about asking you."

Styxx ground his teeth as he realized that he'd read Acheron's mind. *You better be more careful.* Such a slip around someone else could be fatal. "It must be our twin blood." That was always a safe bet whenever he was with Acheron. His brother accepted that explanation without question or malice.

36

Grabbing the small wooden box from his table, he took it over to Acheron. "You want to give it to her?"

He shook his head. "You better do it. She'd prefer it from you, I think."

And he'd prefer not to see her at all. Most of the times he was with their mother, she looked at him as if she could go through him. "Shall we get this over with?"

"I'm game if you are."

Honestly, I'd rather have my eyes gouged out and fed to me.

But part of being a king was doing things you didn't want to without complaint or hesitation. Head high. Back straight. Show no emotion. *Even if you were only seven years old.*

Styxx clutched the box to his chest, dreading it already. "Maybe she'll still be passed out and we can leave it with her maids."

Hoping for the best outcome, he took Acheron's hand and led him through the back hallways of the palace to their mother's rooms.

At the door, Styxx hesitated for so long that Acheron moved around him and knocked in his stead. A few seconds later, the oldest maid opened it to stare down her nose at them.

Styxx ignored her disdain. "We've come to wish the queen a happy birthday. Is she awake?"

Without a word, the maid stepped back, opening the door wide enough to allow them to enter the room. Their mother sat in a chair near the window, staring out it.

Unsure of her mood, Styxx hesitated. Why did his powers always fail him when he needed them most?

"Is she sober?" Acheron whispered in his ear.

"I don't know."

Their mother let out an exasperated sigh. "Will you two stop whispering. Either come in or leave. Preferably the latter."

Styxx started to go.

Acheron pushed him forward.

Thanks, brother . . .

Crossing the room, Styxx held the box out toward her.

She frowned at it. "What's this?"

"Happy birthday, Mother," they said in unison.

A rare smile lit her face as she took the box and opened it to find the shell bead necklace Styxx had bought in the marketplace. Hoping to please her, he'd traded one of his carved horses for it.

"Thank you." She pulled him into a cold, mechanical hug.

Bug-eyed, Styxx met Acheron's gaping stare. Before he realized what Acheron was doing, his brother stepped forward.

"Happy birthday, Mother." Acheron moved to hug her.

Shrieking in outrage, she slapped him hard across his face. "Get away from me, you repulsive monster!"

Styxx's nose exploded with blood as pain permeated his cheek, skull, and eye. Damn, for a sot, his mother could pack a wallop.

She continued to rail against them as they ran for the door and then down the hallway. They didn't stop until they'd reached the bottom of the stairs.

His breathing labored, Acheron turned to face him. "Why do they do that to me?"

"I don't know. They're crazy."

"What in the name of Zeus happened to you?"

Styxx flinched at the sound of his father's angry voice as he wiped at the blood on his face. He cringed over the sight of blood droplets on his white chiton. Few things upset his father more than for him to be disheveled in public.

"Did you hit him?" he accused Acheron.

Acheron shook his head.

"Liar!" He moved to take his arm.

"Father, no!" Styxx blocked him from attacking his brother.

Acheron ducked then ran like mad up the stairs and out of sight.

His father started after Acheron, but Styxx grabbed his arm and held him in place. "He didn't do it, Father. It's just another nose-bleed. I get them all the time."

"Xerxes?"

Styxx glanced past his father to see his uncle closing the distance between them. "Uncle, please tell him that Acheron didn't harm me. It's nothing."

Estes passed a skeptical look from Styxx to his father. "It doesn't look like nothing to me, child. Rather, that's a severe injury on your face. It's obvious *someone* hit you."

"It wasn't Acheron." Styxx let go of his father so that he could hold his nostrils together to contain the bleeding. "I shall be fine, Father. I'm sorry for the mess." Hoping he'd given Acheron enough time to hide, he left them and went to his room to clean his nose and change his clothes.

He'd barely finished dressing a few minutes later when he heard Acheron and Ryssa yelling. What in the name of Olympus?

Normally, he was the one screaming with Ryssa. It wasn't like Acheron to get crossed up with her for anything. But as he left his room, he realized it was something far worse than a fight between siblings . . .

Soldiers were dragging his brother down the stairs, toward the front door. Terrified, Styxx ran after them. He didn't catch up until they were in the drive outside. He tried to reach his brother, but his father held him back while Estes carried Acheron away in his arms.

Styxx glared at his father. "What's going on?"

"Estes is taking him to live in Atlantis."

That was an even harder blow than the one that still stung his face. "What? No! No!"

Styxx tried to break out of his father's hold to get to his brother, who was fighting Estes every bit as hard.

"It's for the best. He's a danger to all of us, especially you."

How could they be so stupid? His brother was the only one who would *never* intentionally hurt him. "Acheron! Please, Father! Don't take my brother from me! Please!"

"Styxx!" Acheron held his hands out toward him while Styxx did everything he could to get to him.

No one listened to them. Nor did they take pity or mercy on the boys.

Heartbroken, Styxx fought his father's hold and watched as his uncle and brother rode out of sight. And as they went, he knew that Estes hadn't just taken his brother from him.

He'd taken everything . . .

Completely devastated by the loss of Acheron's company, Styxx pushed the door open to Ryssa's room. Her sobs had been relentless. For hours now, he'd listened to her give free vocal rein to the same emotions that flogged him. But if he cried as she did for Acheron, his father would have him beaten for it.

The desolate loneliness was terrible. It was as if someone had cut off his arm and thrashed him with it. He felt bereft and betrayed. Without Acheron, he had no one to turn to. No one to talk to. No one who would hug him or make sure he was all right when he hurt.

He was all alone and completely desperate for something to hold on to, even if it meant embracing the big sister who hated him.

"Ryssa?"

She pulled away from her nurse who'd been holding her, trying to comfort her pain. Drawing a ragged breath, she glared at him as if it was his fault Acheron was gone. "What do you want, you selfish little beast?"

Styxx bit his lip in indecision. Her mood was extremely volatile. But what did he have to lose now? "I could be your little brother, too . . . like Acheron."

She curled her lip as more tears fell down her face. "You? You're the reason they took my brother from me. Just because you look like him, it doesn't make you what he is. You could *never* be my Acheron. You're just a poor copy of him. Get out of my sight. You sicken me." Wailing, she buried her head against her nurse's shoulder. The old woman patted her lovingly while they ignored him entirely.

"But I could love you, too, sister. If you'd let me."

Shrieking, she shot from her nurse and grabbed his arm. "I don't want your love, you brat. You know nothing of loving others.

Only yourself." She shoved him out the door and slammed it shut in his face.

Styxx's lips quivered as he stared at the closed door with tears in his eyes. "I could learn to love if only one of you would teach me how," he whispered.

But none of them wanted to love him and he knew it. The only person who'd loved him was gone now. Stolen away from him.

I have no one. And he hated being alone. Twins weren't born to be apart. He was only one half of a whole.

Brothers, forever and always.

That had been their pact. Styxx wiped at the tears in his eyes as he went to Acheron's room. But there was nothing here. Like his heart and soul, it was empty. The only possession left behind was Acheron's flat, worn pillow.

With tears streaming down his face, he went to the bed and pulled the pillow into his arms then went to his own room. He held his fist to his mouth to stifle his sobs as he placed Acheron's pillow on the floor next to the wall. Lying down on it, he pressed his spine to the wall and then his feet, trying to pretend it was his brother at his back. But the wall was so cold, and while the pillow smelled of Acheron, it just wasn't the same.

It couldn't hold his hand or speak to him with comforting words. It was just a pillow.

His brother was gone from his world. The grief and agony were so fierce he couldn't bear it. It felt as if someone had reached into his chest and yanked his heart out.

"What am I to do?"

Styxx glanced at his wooden horses and saw the one Acheron had brought to him earlier that day. Rage clouded his sight. How dare Estes give him that and then take Acheron. Did he think a stupid horse could replace his brother's love?

Did he?

Unable to stand it, he ran to the chest and smashed all of the finely carved horses to pieces. He stomped them on the floor until they were splintered. He didn't want to see them again. Ever!

When he came to the last whole one, he stopped. It was the horse Ryssa had given Acheron for their birthday two years back.

Will you keep it for me, Styxx? I would weep if it were lost.

Pulling it toward him, he cradled it to his chest. "I won't let it be harmed, Acheron. It will be here for your return. I promise."

No matter where they lived or how far apart, they were still brothers.

Forever and always.

JUNE 18, 9537 BC

Four years later

Sighing heavily, Styxx picked through the merchant's wares, trying to find something his sister might like for her birthday gift. Unfortunately, Ryssa had everything imaginable.

He hesitated at a necklace.

"You don't have enough money for that, Highness."

Styxx cringed at the resonance of his valet's snide tone that gloated at being able to say that to him. Loudly. There were several snickers from nearby patrons over the comment.

Growling low, he moved away from the necklace. He hated being embarrassed. He suffered enough of that from his sister, mother, father, tutors, and trainers. The last thing he wanted was for another servant to publicly mock him, too.

Even though Styxx had asked his father for a loan, his father had adamantly refused. *If you want more money, work harder for it.* Something difficult to do given the magnitude of the study load he carried, the court sessions he had to attend, his war training, strategy sessions, and temple obligations.

And the small fact that he already worked an average of twenty-two hours a week . . .

They just rarely paid him for it.

"They have cheaper items over here that I'm sure you can afford, Your Highness." Styxx cringed even more at his valet's snottiness.

Unwilling to be embarrassed further, Styxx left without a word.

His valet followed with the same smug stare. "Highness? You're—"

"You're dismissed," Styxx snapped at his valet as soon as they were outside the shop. "Return to the palace immediately, *servant*. I've had quite enough of you for one day."

"Styxx!" Ryssa barked as she happened by at just that precise moment.

Why, gods . . . why?

Styxx ignored her as he refused to give in on this. It was bad enough others berated and embarrassed him all the time. He wasn't about to tolerate it in public for others to laugh at him, too. "I have my guard. You are to leave. Now!"

The valet glared at him, but he had no choice except to obey.

Ryssa grabbed Styxx's arm, sinking her nails into his flesh until he was certain he'd have half-moon cuts from it. "That was rude!"

And grabbing his arm in front of everyone wasn't? "Let me go," he growled.

She tightened her hold. "Father will have a fit if he sees you here without your valet."

"I have my guards."

She shoved him back. "Fine. I hope he catches you, you little beast. You deserve it." Without a word, she spun toward her guard and escort and left him.

Styxx rubbed at the small cuts she'd left behind on his flesh. He definitely didn't feel like getting her a present now. But if he didn't, his father would be furious.

It was expected, after all.

I better be quick. Ryssa would run to tell on him. He had no doubt. She always did. His heart pounding in fear of being caught in public without his manservant, he went into the next store, where he often bought gifts for his father.

He was rather surprised to find Master Praxis inside. But since this was usually Styxx's allotted study time with him, it made sense that Master Praxis would also be running errands.

His tutor inclined his head to him. "Prince Styxx . . . How has your pursuit of a gift gone?"

"Futile so far, sir. But I'm hoping to find something here."

"Perhaps I could be of service?"

Styxx smiled at him. "I hope so, Master Praxis. Otherwise I won't have time before her banquet."

His tutor returned his smile. "Then let us count this as a lesson in economics."

Styxx was more than grateful for the help.

The owner came out from the back with a ring for Master Praxis. "Greetings, young prince."

"Greetings, Master Claudius." Styxx wandered about to look at the necklaces while his tutor finished his purchase.

"I take it you're not shopping for His Majesty," the owner asked as soon as he came over to assist Styxx.

"No, sir. My sister."

"Ah . . . Her Highness was in here earlier." He pulled out a pair of pearl hair combs. Intricately engraved, they were very pretty. "One of a kind. She was quite taken with them, but said she'd have to ask your father for the price."

Styxx bit his lip. "How much?"

"For you, Highness, a tetradrachm."

"That's a bit steep, is it not?" Master Praxis asked the owner.

"These are the finest quality pearls available, as is the silver and gold. And the workmanship is in a class of its own."

Styxx sighed as his face warmed from even more embarrassment. "I'm afraid I don't have that much."

"How much do you have to spend?" the owner asked.

"Half of that." He'd brought all his savings, including the money he'd set aside for a set of dice he'd wanted to buy himself for his birthday next week.

"Would you be interested in a trade?"

Styxx hesitated then nodded.

"What you have, plus . . . your fibula."

His heart clenched at the price. The king had given the brooch to him last year and it was one of his most prized possessions. He bit his lip in indecision.

Master Praxis frowned. "That's a dear cost, Highness. Perhaps she'd like a bracelet?"

She had drawers full of those . . .

"Did she really like it?" he asked the owner.

"She did, indeed."

Styxx glanced around, but didn't see anything else as pretty . . . and if he didn't make her happy, his father would be furious. *A king must sacrifice for the good of his people.* It would always be expected of him.

He looked up at Master Praxis. "The good of the many is always better than the good of the few." Still, he really loved his fibula.

His sister not so much.

Styxx fingered the brooch that was his sole piece of grown-up adornment.

We must spoil our women, boy. A happy woman makes a happy home. An unhappy one makes us drink.

His stomach aching for the loss, Styxx nodded and unpinned his brooch. He handed it and his coins over to the jeweler, who had his apprentice box the gift.

"She will be thrilled, Highness," Claudius said.

Master Praxis appeared as thrilled about the purchase as Styxx did.

"Thank you." Styxx took the hair combs and left.

Master Praxis followed him outside. "Would you like me to walk home with you, Highness?"

"Yes, please. Thank you, Master Praxis."

And while they walked, his tutor went over the philosophy

lesson that had been suspended for the day so that Styxx could attend his other duties.

By the time they reached the palace, his father was waiting for him in the foyer with a glower on his face that wrenched Styxx's stomach hard. "Where is your valet?"

"I sent him back early."

"And look at you. Out in public . . . an embarrassment to me." His father snatched Styxx's chlamys where Styxx was holding it in place with his hand. "Where's your fibula I gave you?"

Styxx exchanged a glance with Master Praxis and begged him with his eyes not to tell his father what he'd done. To know Styxx had bartered with a merchant like some penniless fishmonger would only anger his father more. "It's lost, Father."

"Lost!" His father cursed. "Get upstairs and put yourself in order."

Styxx headed up the steps to find Ryssa smirking in the hallway. He wanted to throw the gift at her.

But the cost for it was too dear.

Styxx ignored her and went to his room where the valet was waiting to snatch him around and "accidentally" pinch and bruise him while he righted Styxx's attire.

Tsking over the missing brooch, his valet dug the old tin childhood fibula out of Styxx's wooden chest. The valet had just returned the chlamys to its proper drape when his father joined them.

"Leave us."

Styxx held his breath in fear of his father's sharp tone.

"Since you've proven yourself so irresponsible, I'm sending *your* birthday gift back to the merchant. There's no need in giving you anything until you learn to appreciate the cost of things."

Styxx opened his mouth to protest then caught himself. His father wouldn't listen. "Yes, Father."

"Master Praxis is in your study. I suggest you don't keep him waiting."

Taking care not to run because only peasants did so, Styxx went to his room down the hall where his tutor sat with a stern glower.

46

"Why didn't you tell your father what happened to your fibula, prince?"

Because a lost brooch would cost Styxx a birthday present. A bartered one would mean a harsh beating. "Only peasants barter. He would have been furious had he learned that I went shopping without sufficient coin."

"That was hardly insufficient, Highness. The cost was extravagant and I'm baffled why you didn't get her something else."

Styxx let out a weary breath of frustration as he explained his dilemma to his tutor. "Had my father gone in to buy them—which he would have, given Ryssa's propensity for extreme nagging—and been told that I passed on them for something less expensive even though Ryssa had clearly and dearly wanted them—which Claudius would tell him he told me—I would have been in a lot more trouble. While my father expects and accepts that Ryssa will have to ask about purchasing jewelry, it's not acceptable for me to do so. A prince must always be seen as affluent and respectable. This," he pointed to his cheap fibula, "was the lesser evil."

His brow furrowed, Master Praxis sighed. "Our lesson today was about Scylla and Charybdis, but I think we shall move on. You are already well versed in being caught between a rock and a hard place, Highness, and having to successfully navigate the treacherous waters that divide them."

JUNE 21, 9537 BC

Styxx sat in the study with his father and Master Praxis, reviewing his weekly progress, when Ryssa came storming into the room. At first, he feared she was angry. But as she came closer, he saw the bright smile on her face.

"Father! Look what a messenger just brought!" she gushed as she opened her hands to show him the combs Styxx had purchased. "Acheron sent them to me! Is he not the best brother ever?"

Master Praxis gaped as he met Styxx's gaze.

Subversively, Styxx touched his finger to his lips to implore his tutor not to out him. "They're beautiful, Ryssa."

Scoffing at him, she put them in her hair and turned back to their father. "I shall wear them tonight at banquet! And at every banquet from now on. How did he know I wanted them? Are they not gorgeous, Father? I can't wait for Matisera to see them!" She rushed out of the room to show their mother.

His father glowered at Styxx. "What did *you* get your sister?"

"I didn't have time, Father. I'm sorry."

The look on his father's face promised him the retribution of the Furies. "Then I suggest you find something. Fast! And we will talk about this later."

Euphemism for a beating to come. "Yes, Father."

"Go. Get out of my sight."

Styxx gathered his scrolls as Master Praxis escorted him from the room.

"I am extremely nonplused, Highness."

Styxx jerked his chin to where Ryssa stood showing off the combs to one of her maids. "Had I given them to her, she wouldn't be so excited, I promise you. She would have placed them in a box and never worn them again. They mean much more to her coming from my brother."

"But you paid dearly for them, and not just in coin . . ." His tutor's gaze dropped to Styxx's side where his chlamys had fallen away and exposed his bruised skin.

Styxx jerked it back into place before anyone else saw it. "Gifts are for the delight of the recipient, not the giver, Master Praxis. And if I have to pay such a dear cost, I'd rather see her enjoy her combs than not."

"You're a good boy, Highness. And I hope her gift to you is half so noble."

Styxx bit back a derisive snort. Ryssa had already given him his present . . . a scalding lecture on why he wasn't worthy of one this year.

But that was fine by him. Unlike his sister, he placed no value on objects that, sooner or later, would be taken away or destroyed as punishment.

AUGUST 30, 9536 BC

One year later

"Get up, you worthless *suagroi*!"

Styxx saw red at the insult that accused him of molesting pigs. Pushing himself up from the ground where he'd been violently thrown, he glared at Galen, his *hoplomachos*—fighting instructor. He lifted his blank, bowl-shaped shield and wooden sword, and readied himself for their next round of Stomp the Prince into Oblivion. "*Suagroi*? Sorry, Master Galen, but your wife's far too old for me."

That got the desired reaction. Galen went crazy on him as he attacked.

Fast and furious, raining down lethal blow after lethal blow, Galen rendered Styxx's xiphos blocks useless as the older man shattered the inch thick wood backing and bent the metal part of Styxx's hoplon around his arm with strikes that would fell a thick tree. Something that said it all about Galen's legendary strength. It was all Styxx could do not to die. He finally gave up and dropped his xiphos, which wasn't helping him hold his ground even a little then used both of his arms to angle the shield to keep from being murdered by the ancient soldier who was more than a foot taller and six times his weight. For that matter, one of Galen's beefy arms was the same diameter as Styxx's waist.

So much for his hoplon being more of a weapon than a source of protection . . .

His weakened left arm that was still healing from when Galen had broken it during practice several months back ached and threatened to give way under the vicious assault.

Bellowing in rage, Galen kicked him so fiercely it lifted him from his feet and slammed him to the ground, flat on his back. Styxx hit the dirt so hard, his breath left his lungs with such force that it felt as if both lungs had collapsed.

Stunned from the pain, Styxx stared up at his trainer through the cheek guards of his bronze helm. Galen painfully wrenched the hoplon from his arm and threw it aside then started kicking him mercilessly in the ribs with all his stout strength.

His arms were so numb and battered from the earlier blows, Styxx couldn't even begin to protect himself from the kicks.

"Is that your answer, boy, when you're attacked? Drop your xiphos and then cower behind your hoplon like a cornered mouse? What do you think an enemy would do to you in battle?"

If I'm lucky, kill me.

"Tell me, where's your smart mouth now?"

It wasn't his mouth that was damaged. Rather he had yet to draw enough air into his lungs to speak.

"Enough!"

Galen delivered one last stomp to Styxx's groin before he heeded the king's shout.

Cupping himself, Styxx saw stars as bile rose in his throat. Damn, that hurt. The old man kicked like a stampeding rhinoceros.

His *hoplomachos* bowed low to his father while Styxx writhed in absolute misery. "Majesty. To what do I owe this honor?"

"I wanted to check my son's progress, such as it isn't . . . Now leave us."

With a vicious glare at Styxx that promised him retribution for making him look incompetent before the king, Galen inclined his head then made a hasty retreat.

Still coughing and wheezing, Styxx rolled over and forced himself to his feet. He let go of his groin and straightened even though all he wanted to do was lie down until he could breathe again.

His father's revulsion and disdain hit him even harder than Galen's last kick. Styxx spat the blood from his loosened teeth to the ground.

"What was that I just saw?" his father growled.

Me getting my ass kicked by your retired polemarchos. Was the man blind? There was a reason why Galen had once led the entire Didymosian army. Stronger than Atlas, the old buzzard had never been defeated by anyone.

And definitely not by a skinny boy.

His father struck his cuirass so hard, it forced Styxx to take a step back. "You threw down your xiphos?"

"I was trying to protect myself," Styxx explained.

His father jerked the helm from Styxx's head and threw it on the ground in disgust. He hit him in the chest again. "You're not worthy of armor this fine. You disgrace it." His blue eyes blazed with fury an instant before he backhanded Styxx so hard his head snapped back. "Coward!"

Facing him without fear, Styxx licked at the blood on his lips then wiped it away with the back of his hand. "I'm just a boy, Father. Not a grown soldier."

Only ten-and-two . . . Galen wore sandals that were older.

His father grabbed his hair and jerked him forward. "You have shamed me with your effeminate fear," he shouted in Styxx's ear. "I thought I was raising a king and not a queen. I should make you fight in one of your sister's peploses and earbobs." He shoved him away, toward the direction of the dressing rooms. "Change your clothes, go to your mother and placate her then you are to be whipped for your cowardice and insolence. Understood?"

Styxx gave him the most sarcastic salute he could manage. "Understood . . . my king."

Pain in my ass.

The repugnant expression on his father's face promised severe

51

retaliation later. So be it ... He'd failed to meet the king's high expectations.

There's a fucking surprise.

Disgusted with himself and his father, Styxx retrieved his helm and hoplon. When he went to pick up his sword, his father kicked him to the ground.

"You haven't earned the right to touch a Didymosian xiphos, even a training one, and I won't have your weak, effeminate hand defile it." The king retrieved it, and left. He handed the sword off to Galen on his way out of the arena.

Sighing, Styxx rose to his feet and again picked up his damaged hoplon and helm then limped off to change clothes.

Galen met him just outside the dressing room.

Without a word, Styxx handed the veteran soldier his extremely bent blank shield. A hoplon that would remain unpainted until Styxx proved himself worthy of a battle symbol.

At the rate he was going, that would be never.

Sick at the thought of what was waiting for him, Styxx placed his helm on the straw armor mannequin then moved to undress. He wiped another round of blood off his mouth with the back of his hand, before he licked the wound his father had given him.

Galen paused a few feet away. "What did the king say to you?"

"I'm to be whipped for my cowardice."

To his shock, Galen winced. "I should not have lost my temper with you, Highness."

Styxx snorted. "My enemies won't hold back. Why should you?"

Shaking his head, Galen's gaze fell to Styxx's arm as Styxx removed his bronze vambraces. "Sweet Hera!"

Styxx looked down to see that his left arm was terribly swollen. It was now even larger than Galen's massive forearms. The laces from the vambrace had left impressions so deep, bruises had already formed around them.

"Did you re-break it?"

Styxx clenched and unclenched his fist then rotated his wrist and bent his elbow. It hurt, but he had total mobility. "Nay. It's fine. Just swollen from the fight."

"It must pain you and yet you act as if it doesn't. How can you stand it?"

"What can I say, Master Galen? The agony of my crushed testicles distracts my attention."

To his shock, Galen laughed for the first time since Styxx had met him. "Come, young prince. Let me help you out of your armor."

Styxx frowned as his trepidation rose. He wasn't used to people being nice where he was concerned. It actually scared him. "Why are you being kind to me?"

"Guilt, Highness. It's a potent thing."

"Why should you have guilt?"

"I have misjudged you, and I don't do that often."

Styxx was even more confused than before.

Galen placed his hand on Styxx's shoulder in the manner of respect and solidarity. Only Acheron had ever touched him thus. "If you were the brat I had thought you to be, my lord, you'd be whining about how unfair it is that you're to be punished later for my unwarranted attack. But it occurs to me in the last two years that I've been training you, you have never once complained nor cried foul about anything I have done to you during practice. Not even when I broke your arm."

"That was my fault. You told me not to hold my shield that way and I forgot." Styxx glanced down at his arm, which was four times its usual size. "It's a lesson I shan't forget ever again."

Galen's gray eyes softened. "As I said, Highness, if you were the royal brat, you wouldn't think that. You'd still be blaming me for it and calling for my testicles on your gilded platter." Galen unlaced Styxx's cuirass and lifted it over his head then placed it on the mannequin for him.

Unsure of what to say to that, Styxx untied his pteruges and handed it to Galen.

His teacher grimaced at the swelling which was even more

severe, and the bruising that was more prominent than before. "We should bind your arm."

Shaking his head, Styxx moved to unlace his greaves. "It would anger my father."

"How so?" Galen pulled Styxx's white linen chiton and purple wool chlamys from where Styxx had stored them then placed them on the bench beside his foot.

"He already considers me weak. If we bind it, he'll think I'm doing it to postpone or lessen the severity of my punishment. Trust me, that won't go well for me." Styxx set his greaves and shoes on their shelf then removed his red practice chiton. He folded it and placed it next to them.

Turning, he caught the fierce scowl on Galen's face as he stared at Styxx's bare side.

He glanced down to see the red and purple bruises along his ribs and over his chest that were already forming where the older man had kicked him after he'd fallen. And that wasn't counting his other, faded bruises from things he would rather forget.

Galen lifted his gaze to Styxx's. "Did I ever tell you about the first time I fought in battle, Highness?"

Styxx quickly washed himself off in the large basin of water. "No, sir."

Galen took a deep breath as Styxx toweled himself dry then pulled on his chiton and fastened a belt around it. "I was so scared that I soiled my armor. It slickened the stones so that when my commanding officer went to attack the enemy, he slipped and fell on it."

Aghast, Styxx stared at him. He wanted to laugh, but didn't dare.

"He was so angry that after battle, he had me given twenty lashes for it."

Styxx wasn't sure how to react to that. He was both amused and horrified. And the last thing he wanted to do was offend the man who routinely beat the crap out of him.

Galen handed Styxx his royal chlamys. "What I'm trying to tell you, Highness, is that all men, no matter how well trained or brave, have moments of profound fear. No man should ever be judged for the one and only time he throws his sword down to protect himself when he's facing a much larger and more ferocious opponent. Rather he should be seen for all the times he doesn't."

He inclined his head respectfully to Styxx. "Even though I have retired and swore I'd never war again, I would be honored to ride by your side into battle, young prince, and to fight beneath your banner. Even if we had to fight this day." His gray gaze intensified. "I no longer see the boy you are, but rather the man you will one day be ... And that man will be *fierce* indeed."

That was the kindest thing anyone had ever said to him. "Thank you, Master Galen."

Striking his fist to his shoulder, Galen saluted him. "Take heart, good prince. One day the king will see in you what I do."

He appreciated the words, but he knew better. His father would never see him as anything other than a horrendous mistake. "Again, thank you."

Galen offered him a tight-lipped smile. "Rest well tonight, Highness. Tomorrow I shall not take mercy on you."

"I look forward to it," he said sarcastically.

Galen's laughter followed him out of the building.

Sighing in sudden dread of his duties to come, Styxx headed up the hill to the palace with his guards trailing in his wake. Since they were such a permanent fixture of his life, most of the time he didn't even notice them.

Not until their thoughts overrode his, anyway. Gods, how he hated the voices that gave him no quarter.

Without stopping, he entered the palace and went to his room to retrieve his mother's birthday gift from his chest by the window. He paused as he accidentally uncovered Acheron's wooden horse. Pain hit him hard as unshed tears choked him.

How he missed his brother. There wasn't an hour in the day that he didn't wonder what was happening to Acheron. If he was well and happy.

Trying his best not to think about something he couldn't change, he wrapped the horse back in its cloth and retrieved the gold bracelet he'd bought for his mother. It'd taken him three months to save up the money for it.

Because his father wanted him to appreciate what it took for their citizens to make a living, Styxx wasn't given a stipend like other noblemen. Rather, he was required to donate labor to the temple priests and record keepers. And, if he really made his father angry, the stable master who hated him passionately. His father paid him an hourly wage for his work, provided the ones he worked for spoke highly of his labor. That was fine by him, except for when they lied to his father out of petty spite. Since they didn't know how his father was with him in private, they thought it funny to belittle his efforts with offhand comments such as, *He is a pampered prince after all, Majesty. What can you really expect from one such as he?* They had no idea that his father took any report of his "laziness" as a personal criticism and embarrassment. Nor did they know that Styxx, unlike Ryssa, who was given everything she desired, received no other coin from his father. So for every ten hours he worked, he was lucky to be paid for two.

Yes, his father clothed and fed him as befitted his station, but all the charitable funds a prince was expected to give, as well as all gifts for his family and servants, came out of what Styxx earned. Gifts that had to be on par with what a king would give or his father would also view that failure as a personal insult.

We are known by the gifts we give . . .

Styxx snorted as he thought of the presents his father had "bestowed" on him, such as the "honor" of attending boring senate meetings and court sessions.

Then I guess you're a cheap fucking bastard, Father.

But Styxx was never allowed to be so "thoughtful." Irritated, he touched the bracelet that had the face of Artemis, his mother's patron goddess from her homeland, stamped in the center. It was dainty and intricately cast. He'd never seen anything prettier.

Maybe this time she would smile at him.

Just don't throw it in my face like you did last year and have lashes added to what's already coming to me.

And after this most charming meeting with his maternal host, he had that beating to look forward to . . .

Khalash!

Pulling his chlamys down to hide his swollen arm, he headed for her chambers to get it over with.

He knocked on the door and waited for her maid to answer. Per her normal routine, the maid didn't speak to him—the bitch who'd been attending his mother since his mother was a girl held him responsible for his mother's ruination and she despised him passionately for it.

With a curled lip, Dristas opened the door wider and allowed him to enter while his guards remained outside.

His mother was pacing in front of the window that looked out onto the back courtyard. She was more agitated than usual.

Men! I hate them all. They're worthless, faithless pigs who should be slaughtered and gutted. Every one of them! May they all rot in Tartarus for eternity!

Styxx drew up short as her enraged thoughts rang in his head. This was definitely a bad time.

As he started to turn around and leave, his mother caught sight of him.

"What are you doing here? You're not my Ryssa."

That was a definite affirmative. Her grand powers of observation never ceased to stun him.

He lifted the small wooden box up so that she could see it. "I was bringing you your birthday gift, *Matisera*. But I can see it's a bad time."

She raked a sneer over him. "Another cheap trinket . . . Meaningless tribute from a worthless ingrate."

Not really. The cost had been rather dear. *I should have spent the money on the horse I wanted.* At least he would have gotten some joy out of that.

And a little affection to boot.

57

"I'll leave it here on your table for you." He set it down, his heart aching for the hatred his mother bore him. "Happy birthday." Wishing he could make her smile, just once, he turned to leave.

The moment he did, she shrieked in outrage.

Before Styxx could see what was wrong with her, he felt a sharp bite in his right shoulder. All her maids began screaming. Their voices, both in his head and out, were so shrill that he couldn't understand any of them. As he twisted around, there was another vicious pain in his arm, followed by another and another. Unable to comprehend the source of the sensation, he looked at his tiny mother and saw the bloodied knife in her hand as she pulled it out of his body.

She moved to stab him again.

Styxx caught her wrist and held it with his injured arm. The tip of the knife hovered directly over his heart which was what she'd have stabbed had he not stopped the blow. "*Matisera?*"

"I'm not your mother, you whoreson!" She snatched her hand out of his weakened grip. Then, cradling the knife in both of her hands, she fell against him, using her full body weight to bury the knife deep in his chest.

Styxx sank to the floor as his guards finally rushed into the room to seize her. Stunned and in shock, he stared up at the ceiling in horror of what had happened.

His mother had stabbed him.

Repeatedly.

The knife was still buried in his flesh . . . all the way to the hilt. Biting his lip, he reached for it and jerked it out. Warm blood soaked his clothes as he waited to finally die. A sharp buzzing in his ears drowned out the sound of all the voices in his head, filling him with an unexpected sense of peace.

"Styxx?"

He heard his uncle's voice from far away. But he had no desire to go back to the hell he lived in. Instead, he closed his eyes and waited for Hermes to take him to Charon so that the ancient god could ferry him to his final resting place.

JUNE 21, 9535 BC

Styxx rubbed at his brow as boredom threatened to kill him while his father conferred with the musicians over what would be played during his sister's coming-of-age banquet later tonight.

In spite of what Ryssa thought, she was by far their father's favorite. Even though his birthday was in two days, all preparations for his had been postponed in favor of hers. His father had even taken him aside three months ago to tell him as much.

You understand, boy. She reaches her full majority and it's not that important for you this year.

Truthfully, he didn't want any kind of celebration, ever again. Birthdays had never boded well for him, anyway. Neither his nor anyone else's.

At best all they did was remind him that he shared his birthday with a brother he was forbidden to see. And it wasn't like he had any friends to invite. Only users trying to curry favor with his father or with him.

Even if he had the delusion that someone might actually like him as a person, his ability to hear other people's thoughts quickly squelched that idiocy.

Princes had no friends.

Although, here lately, he had plenty of girls, and even full-grown women, from all social classes, who made numerous advances toward him. But they didn't care about him either. Rather they wanted to hold the bragging rights of being his first lover. Or better yet, become the mother to one of his bastard children so that he'd have to support them for their rest of their lives. He could barely move without one of them cornering him and stripping off her clothes or trying to fondle him, and while most men would welcome it, the fact that he heard their thoughts made him steer clear of their heartless traps. It was a total lust-kill when you knew beyond a doubt that the woman couldn't stand you, and that she'd be talking about you as soon as it was over, and not in a favorable way.

He'd rather die virgin than suffer any more ridicule for his ineptitude.

"Father!"

Styxx cringed at Ryssa's angry shriek as she ran into the room, holding one of her elaborate himations in her arms. *Whatever it is that ails her, please don't let it be directed at me.* Ryssa blamed him for everything—including his mother's brutal attack on him last year.

She wouldn't have stabbed you had you not deserved it! My mother is a gentle woman who wouldn't harm a soul. I know you, Styxx. You had to have said something awful to her to provoke it! She would never have attacked you otherwise. Admit it, you threatened or insulted her, didn't you?

Zeus help him, but if it rained tonight during her banquet, somehow that, too, would be *his* fault.

His father stepped away from the musicians to greet her.

"Look!" She shoved the garment at him. "They've crushed the embroidery on my himation! What am I to do?"

Go naked, dear sister. Oh wait . . . better yet, wear one of your two million other gowns. Not like she didn't have a dozen chests bulging with them.

Their father cupped her cheek in his hand. The tender look on his face was enough to made Styxx's lip curl. If he dared to complain over something so trivial, he'd be publicly embarrassed at best, beaten at worst.

"Don't fret. They can fix it, kitten."

"No, Father. It's ruined." Huge tears fell down her cheeks. No wonder his father despised them. "I just won't attend. I can't. They'll all laugh at me." She narrowed her icy blue eyes on Styxx, who stiffened as his gut clenched.

Here it comes . . .

"You distracted my maid, didn't you?"

He had to struggle to keep the venom from his voice. "No."

"You're lying! I've seen the way you watch her. It's revolting."

"I don't watch your maid, Ryssa. I don't even know which one was responsible for your dress."

"Then you don't know if you've distracted her or not, do you? Do you!"

Styxx would throw his head back in exasperation, but he didn't want his father jumping all over him for disregarding her pain. Besides, Ryssa's hysterical tantrum was enough for anyone to deal with.

"You've probably destroyed my sandals, too. You'd love for all of them to laugh at me tonight, admit it." She stomped her foot at him.

"I don't want anyone to laugh at you, lamb-head. I just don't care." Styxx turned to walk away.

But Ryssa wouldn't let it go. She grabbed his arm and jerked him around to face her. "Why can't you ever learn to be happy for someone else? Huh?"

Honestly, I'd be thrilled if I could just learn to be happy for myself. "Unlike you, Ryssa, I don't waste my time worrying about other people."

"Exactly my point. You're so selfish and cold, it's disgusting."

"That's not what I meant," he said, but she was already gone. He started to fling his hands out in an obscene gesture then caught his father's angry glare and disturbing thoughts over the fact Styxx wasn't giving his sister due respect.

Instead, Styxx held his hands up in helpless surrender while Ryssa cornered their father with her complaints against her brother who could do nothing to please her.

Except die.

"You see, Father! You see how he treats people with such blatant disregard of their feelings? How can someone so cold and heartless be king? Zeus help us all with him on your throne."

I know. I'm not fit to breathe your precious air and I should be killed where I stand.

He was surprised she didn't come after him with a knife like his mother had. *Gods save me from hysterical bitches.*

Styxx started to turn away, but just as he moved, a fierce, unbelievable pain went through his tongue. It was so bad that he couldn't breathe for it, and it sent him straight to his knees as his head reeled.

What in the name of Hades?

He felt like he was choking on blood, and instead of easing, it worsened. Unable to stand it, he cried out in utter agony.

Oh gods, Acheron . . . what are they doing to you now?

It was the only rational explanation. Over the years, he'd learned to hide the phantom pains that came when he wasn't expecting them. Most he understood. They were canings or beatings. Hair-pulling. Burns. Hunger pangs even though he'd just eaten . . . But others, like this, he didn't comprehend what caused them. All he knew was how bad it hurt.

"Styxx?"

He heard his father's voice, yet he couldn't respond. His tongue was too swollen. While he didn't often show the physical traces of Acheron's injuries, he would at times have peculiar handprints or swollen places on his body. But never had anything like this happened before.

Arching his back, he tried to focus on something else. Yet it was impossible. Tears streamed down his face as his vision swam.

"He's faking." Ryssa snarled, kicking at his legs. "He's jealous that I'm getting all the attention and he can't stand it."

His father's senior advisor knelt on the floor beside him so that he could inspect Styxx's damaged mouth and swollen tongue. "Majesty, it's the *bakkheia*." A type of insanity caused by Dionysus that was said to infect those who had offended the god of wine. "I think he's possessed."

No! Styxx tried his best to say the word.

Nothing came out.

His father knelt down on his other side. "What do we do?"

"We must get him to the Dionysion and let the priests tend him."

Styxx shook his head, trying to stop them. While working at

the temples, he'd heard too many stories about what befell those deemed mad. Or anyone who was believed to have offended a god.

But no one listened. They couldn't understand him. Nor did they try.

Before he could stop them, his father called for his guards and had him carried to the Dionysian temple in the middle of the city.

Helpless against his inexplicable pain, Styxx listened as his father explained to the high priest how he'd been stricken for no reason. How he had a history of headaches, vomiting, and "imagined" ailments. That he seldom slept. And that his mother had gone mad shortly after his birth, and succumbed to her cups, that in a fit of rage last year, she'd stabbed Styxx and then tried to kill herself in front of him.

"It's a good thing you brought him here, Majesty. You are right. He is possessed and we can definitely make him better for you."

Styxx shook his head as terror held him tight to her bosom. "F-f-f-fa-fer?"

"Shh, boy. The priests will help you."

Styxx clutched at his father's palla, desperate to go home, but his father pried his hands off his clothes while the priests came forward and put chains on him.

The last words he heard from his father before they dragged him away sickened him the most.

"I grant you and your priests full immunity. Do whatever you must to heal him."

JUNE 21, 9535 BC

Styxx choked as the priests forced a gag into his mouth. They'd already stripped him naked and hung him in the center of the temple so that they could begin "treating" him.

One of the priests drew symbols in lamb's blood over his body while another brought out a pair of shears and a ceremonial dagger. They lit incense and candles while they chanted for the god's forgiveness for whatever sin Styxx had committed against him. Then to his complete horror, they started cutting off pieces of his hair and then burning the locks in a gold bowl.

Screaming around the gag, he tried to stop them, but with his arms spread out and chained, there was nothing he could do.

"Don't fight us, Highness. We're not the ones possessing you, and causing you this trouble and agony. We're only trying to help you."

The oldest priest nodded as he painfully sawed off a handful of Styxx's hair. "We have to make you less appealing for the demons who inhabit your body. They have no need for an ugly host and they will flee you once you no longer attract them."

Dear gods . . . what are you planning to do to me?

Piece by piece, they removed all the hair from his head then shaved his scalp before painting more symbols there. The scent of burning hair made him ill.

Look on the bright side . . . You won't have to worry about your father pulling at your hair now.

Or any more women coming on to him.

"Should we bleed him first?"

Styxx tried to shrink away from the priest who asked that question.

"No. His case is too extreme. Light the rods. We'll have to scorch the demons from him."

Scorch? What the Hades was that?

Two massively huge priests unlocked his hands. Styxx fought against them, doing everything he could to break free. But they held him fast and dragged him to a smaller room where he was placed on a cold stone table. His hands were stretched out and chained so that he couldn't move them at all. Next they locked cuffs around his ankles then spread his legs so wide that it felt as if they were breaking his hipbones.

The oldest priest came forward and placed a hand to Styxx's head. "Shh, Highness. Stop fighting us. Accept what's being done. This is for your own good, after all."

Styxx's eyes widened as he saw them wheel in a cauldron of coals that had a dozen pokers in it. *Please gods, no!* He didn't even want to know where they intended to put those.

A younger priest stepped forward with a long piece of white cloth.

"Bind him tight," the oldest priest said. "We don't want to geld him by accident."

Geld? Geld!

"While the king has given us immunity to treat him, he is our prince, we can't leave any marks that will show when he's dressed."

"If we leave no visible marks, how will that keep the demons from possessing him again?"

"They see all marks. Even with them hidden beneath clothing, the demons won't want a scarred host."

In spite of the fact that it made his head pound more, Styxx screamed for them to stop this insanity. But the gag and his swollen tongue kept his words from being intelligible, which only made the priests believe all the more that evil daemons had control of him.

Please! I'm not possessed. It was Acheron's pain he'd felt. And it hurt bad enough. He didn't need this added to it.

They paid him no attention as the young priest used his cloth to tie Styxx's cock flush to his body.

"There," the old priest said, moving the younger one aside. "We need access to the tenderest parts of his body, where it'll hurt most. Demons hate pain."

Well, there you go then . . . He had enough that no demon should ever bother him.

The priest went to the cauldron and pulled a thick leather glove onto his left hand. He stirred the coals with the tip of a poker before bringing it over. Whispering a prayer, the priest placed his hand against Styxx's scrotum, moving it aside before he laid the rod down on the uppermost inner part of Styxx's thigh.

Styxx screamed so hard from the pain that it caused a vocal fold hemorrhage. Tears streamed down his face as the searing burn drove all other pain from his attention. It was the most excruciating thing he'd ever felt. The smell of his burning flesh made him heave as the priest pulled the poker off his leg.

"That's it. Fetch me another rod."

Styxx tried to fight, but it was no use. All he could do was lie here and take whatever they did. And with every poker placed on him, he hated his father. But most of all, he hated the gods who had done this to him.

And deep in his heart, he hated Acheron. If not for his brother, none of this would be happening. It was Acheron's silver eyes that betrayed their origins. Acheron who couldn't hide among people.

Acheron's pain that had made him fall today.

Banging his head against the stone, Styxx wished himself dead. Why hadn't his mother killed him last year? Why?

But no matter how hard he prayed, the gods refused to take mercy on him. Prince or not, his sole purpose in this life was to suffer and to bleed.

And he was sick of it.

Please, gods . . . please someone help me!

JUNE 22, 9535 BC

"Apollo?" Dionysus popped into his brother's open golden temple on Olympus to stand in front of him. "I know how much you love things of great beauty so I *must* show you this." He flashed out of the room.

Sighing in deep aggravation, Apollo set aside the lyre he'd been strumming when his half brother Dionysus had decided to annoy him. "Where are you, Dion? I have no intention of playing this game."

With short dark brown hair, Dionysus returned to stand in front of him. "Don't take that tone with me, brother. Trust me. You *want* to see what I have in my Didymosian temple."

This time, Apollo followed, and drew up short as he saw the beautiful young man someone had thoughtfully chained to the wall. Even with his hair sheared off, the boy had features that appeared to have been chiseled by the gods themselves. Never had he seen such handsomeness in the mortal realm.

"Is he part god?"

Dionysus shook his head. "Purely human. But look at those amazing eyes. Couldn't you stare at them forever?"

Truly. They were a perfect, riveting blue. The same intense blue of the Aegean that Apollo had always favored.

The young man's condition, however, was deplorable. "Why is he tied and bleeding?"

Dionysus took a deep drink of his wine then passed the kylix over to Apollo. "The idiots think I've possessed him."

"Have you?"

"No, but I was thinking *you* might want to." Dionysus gave him a lecherous grin.

Smiling, Apollo swallowed his drink before he returned the cup and approached the human male. It was quite true that he was attracted to any beautiful human, male or female. They each had their advantages and fun.

And even scarred by the priests, this one was still well beyond the beauty of any Apollo had seen in a long time.

Dionysus moved to stand next to him. "I know he's still a bit young, but—"

"He's the age of Ganymede." Like this one, Ganymede had been born a human mortal. A prince of Troy. His flawless beauty had attracted Zeus, who'd brought him to Olympus to serve as their cupbearer . . . among other things. Yet Ganymede was nowhere near as handsome as this boy. Even bleeding and in need of a bath, he made Apollo's mouth water for a taste of that golden skin. And those lips . . . Full and perfect, they'd been made for kissing.

Dionysus moved to the opposite side of the boy. "He's the prince and heir to Didymos. I figured if nothing else, we could tag him for later use."

Apollo snorted. "Tag him? Dear brother, I want to nail him."

Dionysus slid his gaze down the prince's body. "He does have the nicest ass you'll ever see, and the priests were kind enough to secure his important parts from harm." He drained his kylix. "And you'll be happy to know he's hung like a god . . . Should I leave you two alone?"

"Unless you wish to watch."

Dionysus arched a curious brow. "Will you share?"

Styxx scowled as the air around him stirred. One second he was alone. In the next, there were two men in the room with him. Tall and dark-haired, they were clean-shaven and dressed as noblemen and not priests.

"Do you know who we are, prince?" the one on his right asked.

Unable to speak past his raw and sore throat, Styxx shook his head.

"You should. You've been summoning us for quite some time now."

Gods? Styxx tried to say the word, but nothing came out.

The one on his right leaned in to whisper intimately. "Have you a name?"

It took him several heartbeats to muster a sound. "Styxx." It came out as a hoarse croak.

"So, Styxx," the other one said, leaning in on his left side. He ran his hand down Styxx's chest, raising chills all over him. "You've been calling out to all the gods on Olympus for rescue . . . Would you like us to free you?"

Desperate to be away from the torture, he nodded.

The other god began stroking his undamaged nipple. Licking his lips, he smiled down at Styxx. "For every favor you're granted, young prince, you have to give us something. But you don't appear to have anything to offer . . . other than yourself." The god covered Styxx's lips with his own and kissed him passionately.

Crying out, Styxx turned his head away and did his best to get free.

The other god tsked at him. "Would you really rather be tortured than to have us free you?" It was his turn to kiss him.

Styxx gagged.

Offended, the god pulled back to glare at him. "Now that was just rude." He jerked the linen off Styxx's hips, leaving him completely naked.

Terror consumed him at what they intended. "Please don't," he breathed.

The one who'd exposed him slid his gaze to the other. "Rape is your thing, not mine. Although, at the moment, I can see the appeal. Still . . . " He returned his attention to Styxx. "Your last chance, dearest. Who would you rather have play with this luscious body of yours? Me or the priests?"

Styxx glared at him and answered without hesitation. "The priests."

"Very well. You have chosen." He handed the cloth to the other god. *"Troo to peridromo." Eat a bellyful* . . .

Then he vanished.

Apollo bit his lip again as he ran his gaze down the length of the prince's bare body. He let it linger at the hipbone . . . one of his favorite things to nibble. "You would really rather be tortured than spend a day in my bed?"

The prince nodded vigorously.

Offended, Apollo sighed. "I should warn you. Bad things happen to those who deny me." He pressed his body against the full length of the prince then buried his lips against his neck.

Styxx fought him like a lion.

Too bad. "Fine then, human. If I can't toy with you one way, I'll have you another."

Styxx's eyes widened as he saw the god's canine teeth elongate into a set of sharp fangs. The god lowered his head so that he could bite Styxx's jugular. Pain tore through him like fire. He would have cried out, but no sound came as the god drank from his blood. The room spun as wave after wave of dizziness consumed him.

Time hung still as Styxx felt his willpower drain out.

After a few minutes, he was so weak from blood loss that he could barely hold his head up. The bite left him panting and in excruciating pain. Smiling down at him, the god cupped his cheek and angled his head until their gazes locked. The god licked Styxx's blood from his lips then leaned in to lick the remnants from Styxx's neck.

He nipped Styxx's chin. "I own you now, little human. You are forever bound to me." He brushed his hand over Styxx's chest. "I could make you beg me to take you. But I think as punishment for your rejection, I'll let the priests do it for me. I shall leave you to their tender care, and when you tire of it, call to me for rescue and I'll grant it." He kissed him again, only this time it was rough and extremely painful. "Just remember what the payment is for your release. You will willingly come to my bed for a week. And you will gladly take my cock wherever it is I wish to put it."

Sucking his breath in sharply between his fangs, he gave Styxx's body one last once-over. "I'll be waiting, little prince. But don't make me wait too long. Otherwise, you will regret it. I promise you." Then he was gone.

Even more horrified than he'd been before, Styxx hung by his arms, hating everyone, and everything about his life. So, the Olympian gods had answered him with something far worse than what he was facing.

I can't believe it.

Either way, he was going to have a rod shoved up his ass . . .

If he was smart, he'd accept the god's offer and be done with this place. Surely being a god's concubine would be better than the torture they'd been putting him through.

Then again, given his father's careless disregard for *his* lovers . . .

70

Styxx definitely didn't want to be one of those. While the priests would scar his body, they did have fear of his father's wrath should they deform him too much.

The god would fear nothing. And while the Olympian wouldn't leave physical scars, he'd leave them on Styxx's heart and in his soul. Something he knew would never heal.

So be it.

Like everything else in my life, I can suffer this in silence.

He had no choice.

AUGUST 26, 9535 BC

Mentally numb and cold, Styxx stared at the wall before him while he lay on his side, aching all over. It even hurt to blink his eyes. He had no idea how long he'd been undergoing his "treatments" for madness. The torture sessions had long ago blurred together as the priests sought to drive the demons from him.

In the end, it had done nothing except scar his body and make his headaches even more severe than they'd been before. Most of all, it made him hate every single member of his family. And every god who lived on Olympus.

The door behind him opened.

Tears filled his eyes as he waited for them to drag him back to the room he'd learned to despise with every part of his being. "Come, Highness. You have a visitor."

Visitor? Could his father have finally come to get him?

Styxx tried to stand, but his legs were too weak to support his weight. The priest moved forward and covered his naked body with a rough cloak then pulled him up by his arm. Styxx let out a groan as his blistered side contacted with the priest's scratchy stola. Ignoring it, the priest helped him walk down the hall to the last room on the left. The priest opened the door then pushed him through it.

His legs buckled as the door was shut behind him.

"Styxx?"

He lifted his head to find his uncle moving closer.

"Dear Zeus, what have they done to you?"

Styxx couldn't answer. His throat was too raw from the screams his treatments had wrung from him.

Estes cradled him in his arms like an infant. "Can you speak?"

Styxx shook his head, wincing as more pain went through him.

"Here." Estes pulled a small skin of wine from his belt and held it for him to sip.

It burned, but tasted wonderful. He hadn't had anything but spoiled milk, fouled water, and other disgusting things that were designed to drive the demons from his body. Swallowing hard, he licked his dry, cracked lips. "P-p-please, Uncle," he whispered. "Take me home."

Estes ground his teeth as his eyes flared with anger. "I can't, little squirrel. Xerxes said that you have to stay here until you're healed. He would be furious if I took you home without his consent."

A tear slid down Styxx's cheek at those words, burning the wounds that were left from blows he no longer felt when they were given. So much for Estes's boasts of bravery in battle. In the end, he, who lived in a foreign country, was as scared of his father as everyone else.

Fucking coward.

"I'll speak to your father on your behalf. Has he been here to see you?"

Styxx shook his head.

"I will get you out of here, I promise. Gods, I can't believe Xerxes has condoned this." Estes laid him back on the floor. "I'll be back as soon as I can."

Don't leave me. Please, Uncle. I can't take any more. I can't.

I'm just a boy . . .

But his uncle was gone before he could get one word out.

His breathing labored and pain-filled, Styxx realized that for the first time in months he wasn't locked up. If he could get to the door Estes had used, he might be able to escape. Seizing that hope, he forced himself to ignore the agony of his bleeding burns and wounds to crawl across the ragged cobblestone floor. It took several minutes, but he finally reached the door.

Joy spread through him as he rose to his knees and touched the latch.

Almost there . . .

Styxx was so close to freedom now that he could taste it on his parched tongue.

He'd just freed the latch when the door behind him opened. Terrified, he shoved against the wood and forced himself to stand. As he tried to run, someone slammed into him, knocking him to the ground.

No!

Roughly, a priest rolled him over and crashed Styxx's bruised body against the stone. "Where do you think you're going, Highness?"

Back to Tartarus.

Styxx turned his head so that he saw rays of sunlight through an open window in the temple hall. He hadn't seen the sun since his father had dumped him here. Without a word, he reached for it, wanting to feel it just one more time. But the priest seized him and dragged him back to his dark cell where he left him alone.

Closing his eyes, Styxx did his best to remember what the sun had felt like on his skin as he heard the door lock him in his misery. He hadn't been crazy when they'd put him here, but with every passing day, he felt his sanity slipping. He did his best to hold on to it, yet what was the use?

"Why? Why can't you kill me or take my mind?" Styxx silently asked the god who came so often to torment him.

"All you have to do is say the magic word, little prince. You know my price."

Tears filled Styxx's eyes. *"I will not be your whore. My freedom's not worth it."*

"No?" the god mocked. *"Well then have fun with your priests."*

AUGUST 30, 9535 BC

"We've had progress. But the evil daemons are attracted by his great beauty and wealth. They are fighting us hard."

Styxx opened his eyes as he heard the priest entering his torture chamber. For a full minute, he couldn't breathe as he saw his uncle and father with the old man.

His lips quivered as hope went through him. Was it finally over? Surely his father couldn't leave him like this . . . Not if he loved him.

Estes rushed to his side and placed a tender hand on his bald head. "Styxx? Can you hear me?"

He gave a weak nod.

A tic started in his jaw as Estes looked back at his father. "See what I was telling you? They've ruined him."

Styxx met his father's gaze, but the lack of feeling there hit him harder than the priests' blows. How could his father not be indignant or horrified?

Something . . .

But the king stood there, stoically. Unsympathetic to his pain. "It's for his own good, brother."

For his own good . . .

Styxx would laugh if those words didn't bite so deeply.

"How can you say that? Look at him. They've scarred him abysmally. He'll never be the same."

"The scars are necessary, Highness and Majesty. They keep the daemons from coveting his young body."

But they didn't keep the gods from coveting it. The irony of that sickened him even more.

Estes cursed. "This is insane, Xerxes. The boy needs to go home."

I don't want him home again until he's normal. Burn it all out of him. Styxx winced as he heard his father's cold, brutal thoughts.

"Do you still suffer from headaches?" his father asked him.

He knew better than to say anything other than what his father wanted to hear. "No, Majesty."

"You're lying."

Styxx panted in desperate panic. "Please, Father. I'll do anything you ask. Please don't leave me here."

"That's the daemon in him talking. Hear how his voice has changed, Majesty? How hoarse and deep?"

Daemon? Was the old man as crazy as he accused him of being? He was hoarse from months of screaming.

His father was pitiless. *Now you understand what it means to be king. You can't allow your emotions to cloud your actions or judgments. You do what you have to.* His father's thoughts made him ill. "You need to stay until the priests clear you of your daemons."

Styxx sobbed aloud at the horror his father was relegating him to. He couldn't help himself. The agony was too brutal for him to bear anymore.

The king turned toward the priests with a curled lip. "And for the sake of all the gods, can you stop him from bawling like a woman? I'm sick of it and he's too old to weep like that." *How could I sire something so weak and pathetic?*

Styxx glared at him, hating everything about his father. *Let me chain you to a stone and burn you to the marrow of your bones, you skatophage. See then if you cry or not . . .*

Furious at Styxx for crying, his father stormed out with the priests trailing behind him.

Estes touched his bruised cheek. "I'm so sorry, Styxx. I'll keep trying to convince him to release you. I will do my best for you, I promise."

And then Estes, too, was gone.

Styxx's gaze fell to the old scar on his forearm where his father had cut him years ago. The king still didn't really believe he was his son. How could he leave him here to suffer if he thought it?

I am alone in this world.

Except for Acheron. That lucky bastard was with Estes, who had some love for them. Surely his uncle was taking better care of his brother than *this*.

But the phantom pains he felt at times in horrifying places on his body made him wonder. Something caused injury to Acheron . . .

And it, too, was highly unpleasant.

The door opened again. "Time to be bled again, Highness."

Styxx slammed his eyes shut so that he wouldn't see the leeches they were about to cover him with. His stomach heaved in revulsion as all reason abandoned him.

I'm never going home. Unless he agreed to be a god's whore, this was his lot. He might as well learn to accept it. Hope was nothing more than a fickle bitch who mocked him daily.

Grinding his teeth, he tried to block out the pain and the priests. To dream of a place where someone might learn to love him.

But he knew such a place didn't exist. He had been damned from birth and there was no comfort for those the gods had damned. No peace.

No haven.

Bitter, and filled with hatred, he laughed out loud. "Go on and bleed me, you *suagroi*. Take all my blood." If he was bloodless then maybe the god who kept coming to him would leave him alone.

"Don't look at him. It's the demon taunting us. We're finally making progress."

No, they weren't. They were turning him into something he didn't want to be.

His father.

Cold. Callous. Unfeeling.

Years ago, he'd begged his sister to teach him how to love. She'd rebuffed his pleas with her coldness. Aphrodite had spit on him that day and turned her back to a child who'd only wanted to belong to someone.

It was Odia and Lyssa who now took him to their breasts and suckled him. He drank the warmth of their venom in and let it strip the pain away. His family had failed to teach him love, but from the world and their callous arms, he'd finally learned how to fully hate.

JANUARY 2, 9534 BC

"I have to admire your strength, little prince. While I find it appalling, I do have to respect it. Especially given everything you've suffered." The god brushed his hand against Styxx's neck.

Styxx quickly jerked away then grimaced in pain.

"In that regard," the god continued, "I think I should be insulted and highly offended that you'd rather be so abused than lie with me . . . but you're young so I will forgive you . . . For now."

Lying on the floor of his cell, Styxx didn't bother to look at the god who'd returned to torture him again. He was used to his visits. The Olympian came often to flog Styxx's spirit and will while the priests flogged his body.

"Am I really so repugnant to you?" Well aware that Styxx wouldn't answer, he shoved Styxx onto his back then ran his hands over the burns and scabs on Styxx's skin. "I could heal all of these."

"I won't be your whore. I won't be anyone's whore."

The god smiled. "Spoken like a true prince. But here's the thing. Sooner or later, everyone whores themselves for something. And I am tired of watching you be hurt."

Then stop it, you bastard!

"It's not that easy. You want out . . . "

Styxx shook his head, refusing to pay the price the god demanded.

The god growled at him then grabbed his jaw in a fierce grip. "All right. Fine. I know that one day, there will be something you are willing to whore yourself for, and then you *will* come to me on your knees. And you *will* receive me. In the meantime, before they do any more damage to your beauty, I will amend my terms. If you want to go home . . . remove your clothes and lie here with your arms open and your knees parted. I will leave my clothes on, but you will cradle me like a lover while I feed from you."

Styxx cringed at the very thought of it. But given the other things he'd been put through these past months, that didn't seem so bad. Besides, the god would feed from him anyway. He knew that for a fact. The Olympian had tied the two of them together and there was nothing Styxx could do to stop it.

"I have your word you won't rape me," Styxx breathed through his hoarse throat.

"I swear on the River Styx that this one time, I will not rape you. But only so long as you hold me and let me feed until I'm full."

I can go home then?

"I will have you sent home on the morrow."

Styxx nodded in consent.

The god withdrew from him and watched as he slowly pulled his coarse stola off. Naked, Styxx lay back on the floor and did as the god had asked. Turning his head so that the god would have access to his neck, he closed his eyes and waited.

Apollo took a moment to savor this one small victory that he knew had cost the prince much of his pride. Honestly, he'd expected Styxx to refuse. "Remember the terms of our deal, human. Until I'm sated. If you fail to cradle me like a lover, I can have you any way I want."

Styxx nodded again.

The god approached him slowly. Styxx slammed his eyes shut,

waiting for the familiar bite. Only this time, the god didn't use his jugular. Rather, he sank his fangs into the femoral artery in his thigh.

Styxx barely caught himself before he shoved the god away. Any breach of their agreement . . .

It would be a lot more humiliating than this.

His jaw quivering, Styxx forced himself to sink his hand into the god's dark hair and cradle his body as if he enjoyed the god's touch. Bile rose in his throat. Biting his lip, he tried to focus on anything else to get him away from this moment of absolute horror.

Tears pricked at his eyes. The only good thing was that whenever the Olympian was around, the voices in his head stopped. He heard nothing. But right now, even that distraction would be welcome.

When the god finally finished, he crawled up his body then pressed himself against Styxx. Styxx had to force himself not to curl his lip or fight as he felt the god's erection on his blistered thigh through the cloth of the god's stola. He took Styxx's chin in his hand and forced him to meet his gaze. "One day, prince, I will have you fully."

"Will you at least give me your name now so that I know whom to avoid?"

The Olympian laughed. "When I'm deep inside you, prince, I will give you my name so that you know who honors you."

JANUARY 3, 9534 BC

"Welcome home, boy."

On the palace steps, Styxx inclined his head to his king as he drew his chlamys tighter around his body. Not because he was cold, but because he didn't want to be touched by anyone ever again. "Thank you for your magnanimous benevolence, Majesty."

He was lucky his father was too stupid to pick up on his sarcasm.

Swallowing the bitter hatred he felt for all of them, Styxx swept his gaze over the servants who'd gathered to receive him. Not that they had missed him or cared. Rather his sire had ordered them to be here. But the worst were their voices in his head.

He's as mad as his mother.

Why would they release him when it's obvious he's no better?

What a wasted life.

How can that ever be our king?

Styxx did his best to block their thoughts, but it was impossible. And the more he heard them, the more the hatred inside him built. How dare they look down their noses at him. He wasn't a pathetic waste. He couldn't help being born the way he was and he damn sure hadn't asked for it.

It took everything he had not to curse them. But the last thing he wanted was for his father to return him to the Dionysion for more treatment.

If he could learn to ignore the depravity and horrors he'd witnessed and suffered these last months then he could certainly ignore *them*.

"I see you've returned." Ryssa's frigid tone definitely didn't help his mood. *You don't look as if you've suffered any. You look fine and healthy, except for that stupid bald head.*

Ignoring her cruel, childish thoughts, Styxx met her cold gaze. She was beautiful, he'd give her that. But he pitied whatever man was stuck with such a heartless bitch in his bed.

"Come, Ryssa," their father said, smiling at her. "Embrace your brother."

The loathing in her eyes turned his stomach. *I'd rather hug a snake. And grow your hair back. It doesn't make you look manly. You're sickening without it. And what's with that voice? Trying to sound more mature? Please . . .*

Styxx forced himself not to touch his head as her internal comments cut him to the bone. He couldn't help the damage done to his voice. Unlike his hair, that was a permanent reminder of the months he'd spent screaming in agony and begging for a mercy that never came.

"It's all right, Majesty," he said to his father. "I'd rather go to my room . . . if I may?"

He scowled. "Of course."

Styxx lowered his head and didn't look up again until he was locked in a place where no one could harm him.

Even so, he didn't feel safe here. He'd never feel safe again. How could he? At any moment, his "patron" nameless god could find him and feed on or grope him.

All the priests had taught him was a brand new hell. In the past, he'd detested being alone. Now he despised being with people, too. And while the pain and voices continued to torment him, he now had frequent panic attacks that assaulted him whenever he let his guard down.

His unidentified god could be lurking in any shadow . . .

Worse, he'd learned that he was as disposable as Acheron. If he displeased his father in any way, he'd be sent back and left there. Then he'd have no choice except to turn to the Olympian who wanted to own him.

Styxx removed his chlamys then hissed as his palm began to burn for no reason whatsoever. It felt just like one of the hot irons they'd tortured him with. Shaking his hand, he tried to get it to stop, but it wouldn't.

Damn it, Acheron!

What in the name of Hades was he doing? Why couldn't his brother behave and not get hurt?

Styxx blew cool air across his palm as tears blinded him. *Please don't do this to me again. I don't want to go back to that damn temple.*

Next time, his father might never allow him to return home.

Cold fear gripped his heart. "I will be perfect. I swear." Whatever his father wanted him to be, he would be without argument. Yes, he hated them, but he hated that temple most of all.

Styxx froze as he caught sight of himself in the mirror on his dressing table. Ryssa was right. He was hideous.

He ran his hand over his scalp, where only the tiniest bit of hair was growing back. Turning away, he lifted the hem of his short chiton. Though mostly healed, the blisters and scars were even more appalling than his head. While he healed faster than humans, it didn't mean he wouldn't scar. In fact, his entire left side from his armpit to his thigh was a solid line of vicious scars. They went along nicely with the ones in his shoulder and chest where his mother had stabbed him.

"What difference does it make?"

Scarred or not, women would still clamor to bed him. Men would still cater to his ego.

And each would despise him as much as his sister and mother did, and their insults would ring in his ears. In all honesty, he had to give credit to his family. At least they didn't bother to hide their true feelings. They openly insulted him every chance they got. He could almost respect them for that.

Sick and angry over his fate, he reached for the wine on his desk and carried it to his bed where he intended to get drunk enough to drive every last bit of it from his mind. "I *finally* understand you, Mother."

AUGUST 16, 9534 BC

"Greetings, Uncle." Styxx gave a formal bow to Estes as he met him on the palace steps.

Estes arched a brow at his aloof formality. "No hug for your uncle, little squirrel?" *What has happened to you, boy?*

Refusing to react to his uncle's thoughts, Styxx glanced to his father before he quickly complied then stepped back out of Estes's reach. He still didn't like being touched by anyone.

"He's becoming quite the dignified man, isn't he?" his father asked, clapping Styxx on the shoulder.

It was all he could do not to cringe or grimace. Only his father would be stupid enough to mistake diffidence for dignity.

"Uncle!" Ryssa ran forward to hug and kiss him.

Grateful for her distraction, Styxx took three more steps away from them and folded his hands behind his back.

Estes glanced at him over Ryssa's shoulder while she chattered on about nonsense. Styxx averted his gaze. It was hard to get past the fact that the last time his uncle had seen him, he'd been lying broken and naked on a table and sobbing like a woman.

An event his father never hesitated to throw in his face. *I should leave my crown to Ryssa. At least when she cries, it's understandable.*

But more than that was Styxx's anger over Estes not helping him when he'd needed him most. For all his promises, his uncle had gone home to Acheron while Styxx had spent another four months on that table being bled and tortured. He was only now getting back to his full strength and filling out again.

I wish all of you were dead.

Styxx cleared his damaged throat, which still sounded as if he had a severe cold even when he didn't. He'd lost a full octave range courtesy of the priests. "Father? May I be excused? I'm to meet Master Galen for practice."

Ryssa curled her lip at him. "How thoughtless are you? You're going to practice with Uncle just arriving?"

His father held his hand up to silence her. "Your brother's quite right with his priorities, Ryssa. And I'm glad to see him showing some ambition for once." He inclined his head to Styxx. "You're excused."

Styxx gave them a curt bow before he headed down the drive, toward the gymnasium with his guards in tow. While he didn't enjoy battle practice as a rule, he would much rather have Galen knock him around for a bit than face the shame and horror he felt whenever he remembered begging his uncle not to abandon him to his tormentors.

And then watching as the bastard left him.

Twice.

It was the same atrocious feeling he had any time he was required to attend *any* temple celebration.

His aversion to the gods at this point should be legendary. And he despised the fact that he had to publicly worship the same gods who'd damned him to this existence. To the nameless one who'd preyed on him.

Meanwhile everyone told him how lucky and privileged he was to be born prince.

The stupid, blind bastards could have it all.

Rage darkened his gaze as he entered the small gymnasium that had been built for the royal family's private use. It was identical to the public gymnasium further in town except for the size. While the other nobles trained and were educated in the public gymnasium, this one was reserved for Styxx. Like everything else to do with him, he trained alone when most boys his age trained with friends.

Of course, it would help if he actually had some of those . . .

Galen met him at the entrance to his dressing room. "You're early, Highness."

Styxx hesitated. "If you have something else to do—"

"No, it's all good. You're welcome here any time, you know that."

Styxx inclined his head to him. "Am I to dress or undress?"

Most of their skill training was done in the nude, but actual battle training required him to wear his armor so that he could become accustomed to the extreme weight of it. And hopefully to build enough muscle that he could use it in battle.

"What does His Highness favor for the day?"

Blood.

"Armor."

"Then dress, my lord, and I shall meet you on the field."

Styxx stepped past him and went to where his armor was stored. As soon as he opened the upright chest, he paused at the sight of the cuirass he'd bought for himself a month ago to replace the one he'd outgrown to the point he could no longer lace it closed. When he'd foolishly asked his father for the money, the king had curled his lip in disdain.

The way you cower when you fight, you deserve nothing but my contempt and your old child's armor. When you prove yourself worthy of a man's armor, I'll replace it. Until then, do without.

But the bastard didn't know how he fought. He hadn't seen him train in years. So Styxx had pulled every bit of his savings to buy it, with Galen being kind enough to offer him a loan for the matching helm and greaves.

For an old grizzly war dog, Galen could be incredibly kind. He was the closest thing to a friend and father Styxx had ever known.

Suppressing a smile at his beautiful armor, Styxx ran his hand over it. Black as his soul, the cuirass was molded into the shape of a perfect muscled adult male chest. The hinges were gold leaves and the golden head of Athena rested in the center, just below his neck. On either side of her face were dragons facing each other. Two small gold circles rested over his nipples. And five gold dragon heads were studded into each leather strap of his pteruges.

It was the only thing of beauty he owned.

Maybe one day, I'll be worthy of it.

Pushing that thought aside, he removed his chiton and chlamys, and replaced them with the thick black wool chiton that padded his armor.

He tied on his pteruges before he lifted the heavy cuirass. Though most soldiers had shield-bearers to assist them, Styxx had been trained to dress without one. The thought being that in war, no one could be trusted at a king's back. It was too easy to bribe servants to sabotage equipment or to slip a knife into your ribs while he dressed you. Even bodyguards had been known to assassinate their charges. And given Styxx's past, there was no way in Hades he would ever allow someone that close who could harm him.

Not after his own mother had attempted to end his life.

Trying not to think about it, he reached for his greaves and laced them on then his vambraces. He took a moment to savor the heavy weight of the hammered bronze that covered his body. His armor was the closest thing to a mother's embrace he'd ever known. There was something extremely comforting about it.

A rare smile curled one corner of his lips as he remembered trying it on for the first time with Galen by his side.

"How does it feel, Highness?"

"Incredible. I feel invincible in it."

A slow, wry grin had spread across Galen's face. *"Don't,"* he'd said with his usual curt sagacity.

If Styxx loved anyone in this world, it was Galen. While Galen was harsh at times, his trainer at least had some regard for him.

Styxx touched the stiff black and white horsehair plumage on his black helm. The same head of Athena that embellished his cuirass rested above his nose guard, and matching dragons ran down each side of the helmet.

He placed it over his head then reached for his plain sword and unpainted shield that quickly reminded him he wasn't really a soldier or a man.

Just an incompetent boy, playing at war and getting his ass kicked by an old, retired soldier.

In one heartbeat, every ounce of pride he'd temporarily gathered drained out of him. *Time to get my brains bashed in.*

Strangely, he was looking forward to it.

I am a masochistic bastard. Sighing, he headed out to the arena, where Galen was already dressed and waiting.

Galen saluted him as soon as he entered the field. Styxx returned the gesture.

"Ready, Highness?"

"Give me your best."

Galen laughed. "That's the spirit, young prince. I love when I hear the fight in your voice. It warms me." He lunged at him.

Styxx barely blocked his thrust and staggered back from the force of it. His whole arm stung and was numbed. Damn, for an old man, Galen had a surprising amount of strength.

Biting his lip, he rolled his shoulder, hoping to alleviate some of the misery.

Galen pulled up short to allow him time to recover. "Are you coming in injured, Highness?" His instructor's euphemism for asking if he'd been beaten for something. Because they often trained in the nude, Galen alone knew how harsh the king could be with his heir whenever Styxx displeased him.

Which he did a lot. Sometimes by doing nothing more than breathing in the same room.

"Nay, sir. Just clumsy. I'm still not used to the weight of the new armor. It's throwing off my center of balance."

"It makes a big difference, doesn't it?" Galen flipped his sword up, caught the blade of it then offered the hilt to Styxx.

He frowned.

"You need a man's sword to fight with and not that unbalanced toy you hold." Galen gently touched the pommel to Styxx's cuirass. "Go ahead, Highness. It's time."

Styxx threw his iron sword aside and took Galen's into his hand. While he tested the heft and made a few practice swings, Galen went to retrieve another one from his headquarters.

The old man was right. There was a huge difference in how this xiphos felt compared to the iron one Styxx had been using. Right down to the worn leather grip. He stared at the leaf-shaped, serrated edge blade that had probably taken dozens of lives in Galen's masterful hand. The words *To the Glory of Pallas Athena* were etched into the bronze, and the circle pommel held the same emblem of the goddess's head that Styxx's armor had.

"Is something the matter, Highness?"

Styxx looked up from the sword to Galen as he returned with a matching one. "What is it with you and Athena?"

"Every man chooses a god to invoke in battle. Ares, Apollo, Deimos, Phobos, Zeus, Nike, Poseidon . . . For me, it will always be the Pallas Athena." Galen glanced down to his own pommel where her face stared up at him. "Anyone can battle for pride, power, vanity, greed, or hate, but war should always be approached with an equal measure of wisdom and strength. It's not just enough to know when to fight, but to know when to lay down the sword and negotiate. Not everything in the world is worth fighting for."

Styxx considered that for a moment. "Is *anything* worth fighting for, Master Galen?"

"Of course."

For his life, he couldn't think of a single thing he'd shed his blood to protect. "What?"

"Love and family."

Styxx bit back a snort. He knew nothing of love and what he knew of family he could do without. "Not country?"

"Countries come and they go, good prince. They're only worth preserving when the loss of them would cause harm to the people you cherish."

So as Styxx had said, there was nothing to fight for. But he was curious about one thing . . .

"Who do you fight for, Galen?"

"At one time, I fought for my beautiful and gentle wife, who left this world at far too young an age." He winced as if someone had struck him. "Even after all these years, I feel her absence as a physical pain, and hope that you will one day find a woman so fine and decent . . . One whose face fills your heart with pride and love." He offered Styxx a gruff smile. "These days, I would fight for my daughter and grandchildren. And I will always fight for you, Highness."

Those words warmed him. Since Galen seldom said anything tender, or even kind, Styxx knew he meant them.

Galen lifted his sword. "Now, shall we get on with this lesson or continue to chat like old women?"

Styxx raised his shield. "By all means, let my ass-beating commence."

Laughing, Galen swung at his head. Styxx jerked back and countered with a down stroke of his sword, followed by an attack with his shield. Galen blocked his attack then advanced with a barrage of blows that were hard to deflect. That was the one thing about Galen, he taught Styxx to use every part of his body as a weapon, and to hold nothing back. In war, all that mattered was surviving it . . . preferably with all body parts attached.

But as they fought, something inside Styxx burst. A flood of . . . Strength? Power?

He wasn't sure what it was. But an inner door opened and with it came an ability to know the exact move Galen would make right before he did it. Styxx had sometimes been able to do that in other situations, yet never in battle.

Today, that changed.

All of a sudden, Styxx could deflect or block every thrust and stroke. For the first time ever, Galen was forced to back up from his attacks and to protect himself.

Styxx's vision turned dark until he no longer saw Galen as a man, but rather a target to be destroyed. He lost all sense of where he was or why he trained. Or even the fact that he trained at all. Instead, he rained blow after blow with both hoplon and xiphos across Galen's shield until he broke through the thick wood lining and bent the bronze out of shape.

With no choice, panting and weakened, Galen threw the useless hoplon aside then buried the tip of his sword into the ground before kneeling in front of Styxx. "I yield, fair prince!"

Applause rang out.

Lowering his sword, Styxx frowned until he located the source of it. Estes and his father stood just off the main gate. His uncle opened it and came inside with his father trailing two steps behind him.

"Impressive, little squirrel." Estes paused to retrieve a fresh hoplon from the wall bank of them. "But let's see how you fare against a warrior in his prime and not an old man."

He took the xiphos from where Galen had planted it then used it to salute Styxx.

A slow, evil smile curved his lips. "Are you sure, Uncle? I'd hate to injure you on the day of your arrival. Perhaps you should rest first?"

Estes laughed. "Arrogant . . . I love it. But prepare to see your ego debased."

That would be different than normal, how?

Styxx returned his salute, and waited for his uncle to make the first move.

He did. The sound of metal clashing echoed off the stone walls surrounding them. This time, not only did Styxx see the moves before his uncle made them, he gained strength with every blow. It was like he was siphoning off Estes's life force. As his uncle grew weaker, he became stronger. In a matter of minutes, he had his uncle disarmed and flat on his back with the tip of his xiphos pressed against Estes's throat.

His breathing ragged, Estes held his hands up in surrender. "I yield, good Styxx."

Styxx buried his sword into the ground and removed his helm and placed it on the hilt. He extended his arm to his uncle to help him to his feet.

Estes was incredulous. "By the gods, you're not even breathing hard. Oh to be so young again . . ." He looked over at Galen. "My highest regards to you, Master *Hoplomachos*. You've done an amazing job with my nephew's skill. It's been an incredibly long time since anyone disarmed me, never mind knocked me to the ground." Then he glanced to the king. "Brother, if we'd had Styxx on our side in the war, we'd have never had to enter talks with Atlantis. We'd have buried her."

His father finally closed his gaping jaw. "I had no idea he was so skilled. The boy has hid it well." He turned to look at Styxx. "No wonder you sought new armor."

And you denied it to me with mocking disdain . . .

Asshole.

But there was no trace of that now. His father actually appeared almost proud.

The king jerked his chin at Styxx's shield. "It's time we decorated that aspis of yours, boy, and forged you a warrior's xiphos and kopis. You're finally ready to defend my throne."

Those words should make him happy. Instead, Styxx felt only emptiness. There was no pride or satisfaction inside his heart. In truth, he didn't want his father's praise anymore. It no longer mattered to him what the bastard thought. Not when he knew how his father really felt where he was concerned.

Unless he was perfect, he was garbage to be thrown aside and ridiculed.

Or worse, forgotten.

All the months he'd been gone for torture, his father hadn't even missed him. For that matter, his father had barely looked at him or talked to him since his return. The only reason the king was here now was because Estes had wanted to see him train.

Why bother wasting our time . . . ? The boy fights like a methusai. *I'd rather watch the grass growing in the yard.*

His father narrowed his gaze on his *hoplomachos*. "Galen, fetch a scribe and have him design a royal emblem for my son. Something worthy of a princely champion. An eagle or a lion, perhaps."

Estes shook his head. "I'm thinking a pegasus or trident."

"A phoenix," Styxx said. There was nothing more fitting for him. Forged by the flames of Hades's Pyriphlegethon River, he emerged. And like a phoenix, he wouldn't really exist until his father was good and dead.

The king inclined his head to him. "You heard my son, Galen. Phoenix it is."

"I shall see it done, Majesty, and deliver his new hoplon within a month."

While Galen and his father walked away to discuss the matter, Estes came forward.

"Your father's right, Styxx. You *are* becoming quite a fine young man."

Styxx didn't comment as he retrieved his helm and sword. "How does my brother in your custody, Uncle?"

A strange tremor went through Estes that Styxx couldn't define. And even though he tried, he couldn't discern his uncle's thoughts on the matter.

"He's very well. Happy. Healthy. Looks just like you."

"Except for his eyes," Styxx reminded him.

"Except for his eyes."

And the brand scars . . .

Trying not to think about that, Styxx returned his hoplon to the wall then entered Galen's headquarters with Estes one step behind him. "Does Acheron ever ask after me?"

"He does. Often. One day, I should like to have the two of you together. I think we'd all enjoy that greatly." There was something even odder in his tone. Something that sent a shiver down Styxx's spine.

Still, he couldn't hear one single thought from his uncle. How was that possible?

Disturbed by the anomaly, Styxx placed Galen's xiphos on the rack where his trainer normally kept it.

"So tell me, young Styxx. Has any woman caught your attention or heart yet?"

It was all he could do to not curl his lip in revulsion of that question. Between his mother and Ryssa's hateful lunacy and the faithless, mercurial women who threw themselves at him constantly, tying one to him was the last thing on his mind. "No."

"No?" Estes was aghast as if he couldn't fathom such. "How can you be so young and handsome, and not in love?"

It might help if he wasn't a complete stranger to that emotion. "I find women tedious and demanding. Boring and unappetizing. I've no interest in them."

Estes arched a brow at that. "You prefer the bed of men, then?"

This time, he did screw his face up in disgust as memories assailed him. "Gods, no. Hardly. I find the bed of neither one appealing."

His uncle gaped then choked. "Virgin still? At *your* age?

Inconceivable. Both your father and I had bastards aplenty by the time we were ten-and-five. And your brother has long since found the pleasures to be had in the arms of others. I can't even begin to count the lovers Acheron has had."

"I guess I'm not the man my brother is." Of course it helped to not spend the better part of a year being tortured for demons you didn't have.

After that . . .

He had no desire to be touched by anyone, for any reason.

Styxx left Galen's headquarters and walked toward the dressing room.

Estes followed after him. "Hey now, I didn't mean to offend you with my shock. I spoke out of turn."

Yes, you did, asshole. Why else mention it?

Still angry at the insults, Styxx said nothing as he unlaced his cuirass. Estes helped him remove it. While his uncle took it to the mannequin, Styxx removed his black chiton and reached for his white one.

As his uncle turned back toward him, Estes sucked his breath in sharply at the ugly sight of the numerous scars on Styxx's body. Reaching out, his uncle laid his hand over the ones marring Styxx's left rib cage. "I'm so sorry for what happened to you."

His fury mounting at the useless sympathy, Styxx stepped away from his uncle so that he could unlace his greaves.

"Styxx . . ."

"Please, Uncle. I've no wish to talk about it. What's done is done."

And you said it yourself at the time. I've never been the same. The whole experience, combined with his mother's unwarranted and brutal attack, had robbed him of any sense of security or value.

At best he felt like an unwelcomed intruder with his family, at worst, a despised bastard stepchild. He just wanted to be away from them all.

Estes grimaced as he saw the additional scars that lined his back and groin. "Is that why you haven't taken a lover?"

In part, but not for the reasons Estes was thinking. He wasn't ready to answer questions about those scars and why a prince who'd never been to battle would carry such. "All of my equipment is fine and in proper working order. That has nothing to do with my decision. The priests took great precaution to ensure they didn't leave me impotent or sterile." His tone was as frigid as the anger in his heart over it.

And Estes finally realized how volatile this subject was with him. "All right. It's none of my business. But I am here for you, Styxx. If you need me."

No, you're not. You're a chicken-shit bastard. And that was the problem he had with his uncle. Like everyone else, Estes lied to his face. His brave, noble uncle whose heroic deeds had been told and retold by historians, poets and scribes had been too scared of his father to bring him home against his father's wishes and save him from his torment. Instead, the war hero had tucked his tail between his legs and walked out and left a child to suffer. How could he ever forgive that?

Styxx's gaze went to the five-inch scar on his forearm his father had given him, and the pain of the past racked him hard. He was so tired of it all. The lies, the duality. The hatred.

Failed expectations on everyone's part.

He moved to wash himself. "If you don't mind, Uncle, I should like to be alone for awhile."

"I thought you hated isolation."

That was before he'd been forced into it and had learned to make a bitter peace with the voices that shouted and whispered in his head. "People change."

"So they do." Estes clapped him on the back. "I shall leave you to your own company. But know that I do love you, nephew."

If love meant abandoning someone when they were helpless and being victimized, then he could do without it. But what did he know of Aphrodite's charms?

That bitch hated him like everyone else.

A tic worked in his jaw as he glanced to his helm and the image of Athena that mocked him, too. He should pry that badge off and replace it with Eris or Odia. They were the only residents on Olympus he could relate to.

Styxx toweled himself off and dressed then swirled his chlamys around his shoulders. He made a hood to shield his face. The last thing he wanted was to go home where his father would make more demands of him. Ryssa would revile him with her rancid tongue, and some random whore would grab his cock and try to pull him inside her.

I just want five minutes of peace . . .

There was a new play in town. If he hurried, he wouldn't miss more than a few lines. At least there he could forget this world for a short time and live in another. And so long as he sat in the common seats, no one would bother him. He could be just like everyone else . . .

At least for a little while.

Lifting his hand, he held the cowl in place as he all but ran to the paltry haven he had.

"Estes?"

His brother looked up from the scroll he was reading at Xerxes's desk across the room. "Yes?"

Folding his arms over his chest, Xerxes leaned against the wall behind him. "What do you honestly think of Styxx?"

Estes gave him an arch stare. "How so?"

Xerxes hesitated and debated with a matter that plagued him constantly. One he didn't dare breathe a word of to anyone other than his brother. While he might doubt Styxx's paternity in private, the boy was the only heir he had. Publicly, he must always act as if there was no question about his loyalty to Prince Styxx. If Styxx didn't inherit, civil war would tear his kingdom apart and there was no one else strong enough to put it back together.

And while Estes would be strong enough to hold it in his lifetime, he would never father an heir. Which would ultimately destroy the proud House of Aricles.

Xerxes could never allow that.

Didymos had to have a strong, uncontested king on her throne. Even if it meant putting a man there he hadn't fathered.

"Does he seem . . . odd?"

Estes leaned back in his wooden chair and thought about the question. "He's at that awkward point where he's neither boy nor man, but a combination of the two, brother. His body is changing and growing faster than he can keep up with and he's being assailed with potent desires he's never known. He's also facing the reality that one day, after you're gone, he will rule and be responsible for the largest Greek city-state and her army and people. Honestly? We were all odd at his age. You more so than I."

Xerxes laughed. "No one was odder than you, brother." But Estes was right. At Styxx's age, Xerxes was terrified every day of losing his father and being saddled with a throne he wasn't ready to ascend. He'd been so nervous about it that he'd driven his father to madness with his constant concern for his health.

And he'd barely been ten-and-seven when his father had succumbed to a sudden illness.

Yet he didn't sense that from Styxx. The prince was extremely distant and withdrawn from him and everyone else. At times, he even feared the boy might make an attempt on his life.

Xerxes sighed. "Perhaps. But he doesn't really favor us, does he?"

"Are you mad? He has the same blond hair and blue eyes. The same broad shoulders."

"His features—"

"Are his own. Granted. Still, most men would kill to have a boy so handsome. If you doubt it, offer him up at market and see how rich you'll be."

"I'm not going to sell my son!" Xerxes growled.

"Then you admit he's yours?"

Xerxes snorted at his brother's trickery. Estes had always been able to outmaneuver him. It was what made his brother such a brilliant military commander. He could always think nine steps ahead of anyone else and he knew how to manipulate people to get them to do exactly what he wanted.

Even so, Xerxes couldn't get past the feeling in his gut that told him Styxx had a father other than him. That Styxx was more Acheron's brother than Xerxes's son.

Estes rubbed at his beard. "Brother, have you seen the scars Styxx carries?"

Xerxes scowled. "What scars?"

"He's your son. How have you missed them? They cover the poor child. Down his back, across his groin and ribs ... Not to mention his own mother tried to kill him and his older sister berates him every time he speaks and many times when he doesn't, and all the while you laugh at her attacks and think her disrespect is cute. Given all that, I should think he's entitled to being a little strange from time to time. He's been through more tragedies and challenges in his short life than most men experience in a lifetime."

That might be part of what he sensed.

But there were times when he felt absolute hatred for him radiating from the boy. Times when he felt like Styxx was plotting and conniving against him. "He keeps things from me."

"Should I remind you of the secrets we hid from Father? Starting with that red-haired slave girl we shared when we were at our Uncle Arel's?"

He laughed at the memory of two of the best weeks of his life. "She was a sweet treat."

"Indeed."

Maybe Estes was right, after all ... "I suppose I am overreacting. I just worry about him and our kingdom."

"That is what kings and fathers do."

Xerxes laughed. "Then I am great at both."

"Of course you are."

Xerxes smiled at the brother he loved more than anything. "I miss you so when you're gone. I hate that I only get to see you once a year, and always too short a stay."

"Perhaps I could remain longer on my next visit. Maybe take

Styxx hunting for a week without you? He might confide in me if he's away from here and his responsibilities. Then I could observe him and see if he's normal or not, and report back to you what I find."

"Wonderful idea. And I think he'd like that. He's been rather sad and withdrawn for quite some time now."

Estes smiled. "I shall look forward to my time alone with Styxx. His hair should be back to its normal length by then, and his body more developed."

"What has that to do with anything?"

"He should have more confidence in himself. Feel more like a man and less like a frightened boy."

Xerxes scoffed. "I doubt he could have any less. 'Tis another matter that irritates me where he's concerned. He skulks about like a terrified peasant and not a prince." And that, too, made him doubt Styxx's paternity. Surely, *he* wouldn't father such a scared little mouse.

Estes crossed the room and clapped him on the shoulder. "Put it out of your mind, brother. I will take care of my nephew and his needs. I promise you. One week with me and he will be an entirely different person. Trust me. I know just how to make a man of him."

MAY 9, 9533 BC

Styxx sat alone in the dining room, drinking wine as he sought to silence the screaming gods in his head. He didn't know why on this day and his birthday they were so much worse than normal, but they were. It was as if they sought to drive him to true madness.

Leave me alone!

Still, they raged.

He added another round of wine and water to his cup and wondered how much more he'd have to consume before he passed out from it. Surely he was almost there. He'd been at this for hours now and had downed almost three full jugs.

As he sat back in his chair, he felt a presence in the room with him. At this hour of the night, no one should be awake except for the soldiers patrolling outside. Even his personal guard was now snoozing out in the hallway.

I need to replace them with two who don't snore so loudly.

Turning his head, he found one of his sister's maids standing in the doorway, watching him.

"What do you want?" he growled.

"I saw the candle burning and thought it'd been left alight by accident."

Sure she did. 'Cause candles were always being left unattended like that . . .

Liar. Just once, he'd like to find a woman who honestly admitted that she spied on him because she wanted to fuck him. Instead, they played their games as if he was too stupid to know the truth.

"As you can see now, it isn't." He took a deep quaff of his wine.

Instead of leaving, the pretty blond came closer. Licking her lips suggestively, she leaned against the table next to him. "Would you care for some company, Highness?"

"Not particularly."

"Truly?" She dragged her hand over her right breast, causing the nipple to harden and protrude through the thin white linen.

Fascinated, he couldn't take his eyes off it as his mouth watered for something sweeter than wine.

She slid closer so that she could straddle his knees. His own body hardened at the sight of her like that. The sides of her peplos parted, showing him the entire length of her luscious flesh. "Have you ever touched a woman's breast, my lord?"

Too drunk to think straight, he couldn't speak.

So she reached up and removed the fibula from her peplos. The material fell to her waist, exposing her upper body to his hungry gaze. His throat went dry. Though her alabaster breasts weren't very large, they were nicely formed and would easily fill his palm.

Licking her lips, she slid her hips on top of the table in front of him then lifted the hem of her gown up to her thighs and flashed him an image of the curly blond hair at the juncture of her thighs. "Would you like to touch me?"

The cup fell from his numbed fingers as an incessant need to be inside her consumed him. She leaned back onto the table and bent her knees so that he had a perfect view of her. Then she reached between her legs and ran her fingers down her wet cleft. He watched in silent awe as she gently opened herself for him.

"Well?" she asked, her voice thick with needful hunger as she pressed her fingers deep inside her body and slowly masturbated for him. Moaning, she thrust her hips against her hand, and rode her fingers until they were slick and dewy.

His breathing labored, he arched a brow at her actions. *Well, you don't look like you need me . . .*

"What is going on?"

The maid let out a small squeak as she jumped from the table and covered herself.

Styxx sighed as he saw Ryssa's angry form in the doorway, glaring daggers at him . . . thank the gods she didn't have one in her hand or it'd probably be buried in his chest by now. "Nothing, sweet sister."

She curled her lips in disgust as she faced her wayward maid. "You were supposed to be fetching me something to drink, Eirene."

"Forgive me, my lady."

Now the maid was meek and bashful? Really?

"Get upstairs!"

"Yes, my lady." She went down on the floor to retrieve her brooch, giving him a prime view of her shapely ass as she did so.

With one last regal snarl, Ryssa turned and left them. The instant his sister was gone, Eirene looked up from the floor and smiled at him.

"Should you need me, Your Highness, I'm not far away." Rising up, she pressed her fingers to his lips playfully so that he could smell and taste her.

Completely disinterested in the stench of a whore, Styxx wiped it away as she left him. People, and especially women, never ceased to amaze him.

You should have taken her up on her offer.

But he had no interest in a communal quim that welcomed any handy cock. His father had probably even tupped her. And that thought immediately softened him. He had no desire to tie himself to a spiteful, crazy bitch like his mother or Ryssa because he was hard for her charms.

He'd sooner take care of his own needs.

Or fuck a goat.

Shaking his head to clear it, he retrieved his cup from the floor and set it on the table. Then he headed for bed. Alone.

As he reached the top of the stairs, he found Ryssa waiting there for him.

"You are to stay away from my maids, do you hear me?"

"Then you should tell your maids to stay away from your brother."

She slapped him. "They're servants. They can't say no to you and you know it. It's sickening to have you prey on them the minute my back's turned."

Styxx wiped at the blood on his lips as his buzz gave way to anger. "What do you want from me, Ryssa?"

I want you dead.

Her unspoken response slapped him harder than her hand had. Her palm had only made his lips bleed. Those furious words cut his heart to the quick and he hated her for making him care about the fact his own sister despised him.

"I want you to stay away from me and my maids. They are good and decent women. Not your own private harem."

Why can't you be like Acheron? He would never *prey on someone else.*

He clenched his teeth. What would she say if she knew how

many lovers her precious Acheron had taken while Styxx was still as virgin as the day he'd entered this world? And that was even with a god chasing after his virginity, along with every female unrelated to him.

She wouldn't believe it. For whatever reason, she wanted to hate him and went out of her way to find reasons to fuel her resentment and fury.

All I ever did was try to please you and Mother. But those days were over. There were some people who couldn't be pleased no matter how hard he tried and there was nothing he could do about it. He was tired of banging his head against that wall.

His head hurt badly enough. He didn't need a concussion to go with it.

"Good night, sweet sister. May Morpheus cradle you kindly to his bosom." Turning, he walked to his room and locked the door lest another of her maids get lost on her way to the kitchen.

His head throbbing, he went to his bed and threw himself across it.

Was there anything more treacherous in this world than a woman, especially when the bitch was conniving?

MAY 10, 9533 BC

Pacing the floor of his personal temple, Archon cursed as another anniversary passed without their having located his wife Apollymi's missing brat.

Time was growing critically short . . .

If they didn't find Apostolos and kill him, his "beloved" wife was going to free the little bastard's powers and the two of them would join together to destroy every single member of his pantheon.

Starting with *him*.

He glared at his sister, Epithymia. The Atlantean goddess of desire had promised him that Apostolos would die. She had been there at his birth and touched him so that anyone who saw him would covet his body. The humans were supposed to have ripped the child apart.

And yet another year had passed and he still lived.

"You have to tell us where he is," Archon snarled at her.

"It won't matter. He's not there."

"What do you mean?"

"After a few years, I went back and the brat was gone."

Archon cursed. "How can he hide from all of our collective powers?"

She gave him a droll stare. "You had to marry a primal god . . . Remember? None of us can touch Apollymi's powers. The bitch is potent, which is why *you're* so afraid of her."

And once her son came into his majority, it would be the end of everything.

"Your best bet is to keep hammering him with voices and pain. Sooner or later, it's bound to drive him to suicide."

"And if he doesn't?" Archon asked.

"I suggest you learn to swim." She flashed out of his study.

Archon cursed. They would have to step up their plans. There was no choice. Even if he had to tear the human world apart, he needed that boy's head on a platter. Sooner rather than later.

AUGUST 18, 9533 BC

Styxx stood by his father's side with his spine ramrod stiff as he did his best to ignore the voices that fought each other for time inside his skull. The loudest was the strident shrew tone he knew best.

Ryssa.

You're such a spoiled little brat. You repulse me. Standing there like you're already king. You're nothing but a worthless bully. I'm surprised you haven't ordered someone else to take your place to welcome Uncle for his visits.

He slid his gaze to her. She gave him a cold, mocking smile. Whatever. He'd never forgiven her for her reaction to him years ago, anyway.

Against his will, her nasty words replayed in his mind. *"You're the reason they took my brother from me. Just because you look like him, it doesn't make you what he is. You could never be Acheron. You're just a poor copy of him. Get out of my sight. You sicken me."*

Love you, too.

Since that day, he'd done his best to comply with her wishes. He only interacted with her when he absolutely had to. But what baffled him most was how she could hate him so when she knew nothing about him. And yet she felt completely entitled to her animosity. To the point she wrapped herself in it like a warm, familiar cloak.

You're glad Acheron is gone. I know you are. I know you made Father send him away so that you wouldn't have any competition. You're such a selfish, ugly beast. Her most current rant against him.

And there she was definitely wrong. He missed his brother more than words could convey. Unfortunately, given the things he'd felt these years past, he had a bad feeling that the Acheron who existed today was nothing like the memory he held of his beloved brother.

No more than he was the same Styxx he'd been as a boy.

Time changes all things. And seldom did they change for the better.

Smiling, his father clapped him on the back. "Here he comes."

With a sick lump in his stomach, Styxx followed his father down the steps to wait while Estes and his unexpected entourage dismounted and moved toward them. Why were so many noblemen with his uncle? In the past, Estes had always come alone with his escort.

Today, he rode with five others as companions . . .

After closing the distance between them, Estes pulled Styxx into a tight hug. "Look at you, my precious nephew." Then he whispered in his ear. "You've become even more handsome than your brother." He squeezed Styxx's biceps. "Beefier, too."

Strange how, unlike his vain, vacuous sister, Styxx didn't feel attractive at all. Whenever someone came on to him, he assumed it had much more to do with his title than his person. An instinct usually fully corroborated by their thoughts.

Even the Olympian who wanted him always called him by his title. Seldom his name.

"Thank you, Uncle. How is my brother?" Styxx whispered, knowing that if his father overheard the question, he'd be furious at him. Any time he asked after Acheron or begged his father to allow his brother to come for a visit, his father beat or insulted him for it.

Estes glanced over to make sure his father was still out of hearing range before he answered. "Extremely well. You should consider coming for a visit. I'd love to have you."

"Father would never allow me to leave." At least not for a trip Styxx might actually enjoy. But let it be a trip to Tartarus . . . the old man couldn't throw him out fast enough.

"What's that?" his father asked as he rejoined them. "You're not trying to steal my heir, are you?"

"I'd take him in a heartbeat if you'd let me."

"He has too many obligations here at home."

Like cleaning stables and decorating temples he hated, listening to mewling, petty complaints, and observing his father's "benevolent" wisdom—which meant oooing and ahhing everything his father did as if the bastard didn't have enough sycophants already.

"Pity." Estes turned to Ryssa and scooped her up in his arms.

Styxx frowned as he caught the men with Estes giving him peculiar looks. But then if they'd met Acheron at his uncle's home in Atlantis, they were probably wondering, as all people did, if Styxx had any godhood in him, too.

The only thing he didn't miss about having his brother with him was the way people wanted to line them up and inspect them like they were freaks of nature because they matched so perfectly.

Except for their eyes.

And now their external scars, and voices—Styxx's had never lost the hoarseness from his time spent in the Dionysion. As Ryssa was so quick to point out, he perpetually sounded as if he had a cold.

Uh, don't speak, and for the sake of the gods, don't try to sing. Your voice is repellent. You sound like you need to clear your throat.

Releasing Ryssa, Estes stepped back and gestured toward his friends. "Since I'm here to take Styxx for a week . . ."

Styxx's scowl deepened as he looked to his father for confirmation. No one had told him this.

His father wouldn't meet his gaze at all.

" . . . I thought he'd enjoy a party for it," Estes continued. "Allow me to present my friends." He pulled the man closest to him up the stairs for Styxx and his father to greet. "Lord Kastor, whose father is a philosopher in Ithaca. Kastor was sent to Atlantis as a tutor for several prominent sons." No older than his mid-twenties, Kastor had dark hair and a thin beard with a thick nose.

They exchanged pleasantries.

Estes gestured to the three who stood together. "Also from Greek kingdoms, Lords Noe of Athens . . ." He appeared to be closer to his father's age, but extremely unattractive with heavyset jowls and a thick, unkempt black beard. "Leon of Macedonia . . ." On the unremarkable side, he was tall, red-haired, and very thin, and most likely in his mid-thirties. "Nestor, also an Athenian . . ." His brown hair curled around a bony face that held an exotic kind of beauty.

Descending the stairs, Estes went to the last man in their group. "And an Atlantean prince who is second cousin to the current queen . . . Xan." Perfect in form and face, Xan had the kind of physique Styxx would give anything to possess. He kept working out for it, but so far . . .

He had a long way to go. His muscles were highly defined, but very lean.

The group bowed before his father and then to him, except for Xan, who met them as equals. He shook hands with his father then turned a friendly smile to Styxx. "I've been looking forward to this since Estes invited me. I hear you're quite the man to ride with, Prince Styxx."

The unexpected praise made him decidedly uncomfortable. "I don't know about that, but it's a pleasure to meet you, Your Highness."

This should be an enjoyable week with my favorite pastime, and a handsome prince to boot.

Estes was right. He matches Acheron in every way, except Styxx has perfect, beautiful eyes. Fascinating.

I am so glad I changed my mind about coming . . .

Styxx shook his head as their silent comments assailed him and then tripped over each other so fast that he could no longer distinguish their individual words, which were a mixture of Greek and Atlantean.

"Gentlemen," his father said with the full diplomacy of his crown, "please come inside and rest for a bit. I have plenty of libations for your welcome."

Ryssa led them in.

Styxx pulled his father aside. "Why didn't you tell me of this?"

Why are you complaining? I wish I could spend a week with my brother and have no responsibilities.

"I didn't know he was bringing a retinue with him. But I don't see a problem with it. We both thought you'd enjoy a hunting retreat with your uncle away from the stress of the palace." His father left him on the stairs as he followed after the others.

Grinding his teeth, Styxx wanted to curse them all. Did no one in his family know the most basic thing about him? How could he share a home every single day with people who knew so little about his personality?

He couldn't stand being around strangers. At all. Nor did he care for hunting.

How do I get out of this?

Maybe Galen could break my arm again . . .

But the worst part? He had a bad feeling in his stomach that something awful was going to happen. He just didn't know what.

AUGUST 19, 9533 BC

Styxx couldn't remember the last time he'd been so happy. As much as he hated to admit it, he was glad his father and uncle had done this for him. It was wonderful to be off without his father nagging him and Ryssa's constant bitching. No tutors telling him how stupid he was. No glancing down hallways to make sure his mother wasn't there before he walked them. No wanton maids or women grabbing for his cock.

Even with his head throbbing, it was great.

I could definitely live like this for a while.

"Here." Estes gave him a handful of dried meat as they hid near a brook, waiting for deer to sniff out the bait they'd left for them.

Styxx quickly ate it. "That's delicious. What's in it?"

"A special herb that's only grown in Atlantis. We have nothing like it here in Greece."

"You should import it. You could make a fortune."

Estes smiled. "So they tell me." He handed Styxx a wineskin.

Styxx took a quick drink then lowered it as he heard leaves rustling where they'd dropped bait. Pulling his bow up, he nocked his arrow then leaned to sight it.

Estes moved to stand behind him, so close that he could feel his uncle's breath falling on the back of his neck. "Steady. Hold the shot."

His head cocked, Styxx waited.

"Lift your elbow," Estes whispered in his ear. He gently pushed it up to show Styxx how to stand properly. "Hips straight." His uncle dropped his hands to Styxx's hips and twisted them slightly. As he did so, Estes's groin pressed up against his buttocks, letting him know his uncle was *fully* erect.

Styxx's eyes widened in shock.

"Release!"

Completely unaware of the arrow's trajectory, Styxx let it fly and quickly stepped out of his uncle's embrace so that there was some distance between them.

But Estes acted as if nothing had happened.

Had he imagined it?

Estes smiled. "You got him, little squirrel! Congratulations."

His thoughts still on the disturbing intimate contact, and whether or not it was intentional, Styxx blinked, not understanding what Estes had said.

Xan clapped him on the shoulder as he joined them. "Great shot, Styxx."

Only then did Styxx realize he'd made the kill. The other men were already at the deer, inspecting it. Noe had a small cup he was using to capture some of the deer's blood.

"What are you doing?" Styxx asked him.

"It's your first kill. You always drink the blood of your first." Noe held the cup up for him to take.

Grimacing in distaste, Styxx hesitated.

"It's all right," Estes said from behind him. He pulled out the wineskin and more of the dried meat. "I have this ready to banish the taste. But it is a rite of passage we all take."

Xan took Styxx's bow and smiled at Estes.

Not sure about this, Styxx lifted the cup of blood. Closing his eyes, he drank it then shivered in revulsion as the salty, metallic taste assaulted his taste buds.

Gah . . . how could a god stomach drinking human blood?

"Here." Estes swapped the meat for the cup.

Styxx quickly shoved it in his mouth and chewed it then drank the wine. His uncle was right again. It thankfully killed the taste immediately.

"We'll all dine well tonight." Leon grinned at his friends.

Kastor winked at Leon. "Good thing, too, for I am long famished for the hindquarters of an unsullied buck. Even if it means sharing him with the lot of you."

They all laughed.

Frowning, Styxx didn't understand what was so funny about his comment.

"So who gets to clean our meal?" Nestor asked.

Estes tossed his dagger to land at Nestor's feet. "It's your turn to skin and cook the venison. And the five of you can draw straws for dessert." His uncle put his hands on Styxx's shoulders to guide him away from the others. "Come, Styxx. Let's get that blood off you."

"What blood?"

"On your chiton."

Looking down, Styxx cringed as he realized he'd spilled some of the deer's blood on his clothes. *I am completely incompetent.*

What else was new?

Estes grabbed his saddlebag and led him to where the brook widened to a stream. He handed soap and towel to Styxx. "You might as well bathe the day's sweat off, too."

While Styxx went to clean himself, Estes started a small fire. By the time he returned for his clothes, his uncle was sitting on a blanket, mixing herbs into a small clay pot.

"What are you doing?"

Estes motioned him closer. "Have you ever heard of Eycharistisi?"

Styxx shook his head. "What is it?"

"Another special plant they grow in Atlantis. Truly, it is a place of wonder and marvel. They have the most advanced medicine you've ever seen." Estes set fire to the herbs then blew the flames down to low embers. "Would you like to try some?"

Styxx hesitated. They didn't look particularly appetizing, but then neither did the meat, and it was exceptionally tasty. Kneeling beside his uncle, he reached out to take the herbs with his fingers.

Pulling the pot back, Estes laughed. "You don't eat them, dear boy. You inhale their fragrance." He held up a small cup that was attached to the pot. "Put this over your nose and mouth and breathe in deeply."

"Is it safe?"

"Very. You know I'd never hurt you. I love you too much for that."

You are definitely going to enjoy this, little squirrel . . .

Styxx scowled at his uncle's thought. "What does it do?"

"It'll ease your headache and the soreness you had from the ride out here."

He'd do anything short of cutting his head off to get the throbbing pain to lessen. Between his uncle, Estes's five friends, and the four guards who rode with them, his head had been nothing but a cacophonous mess of their thoughts. They were so overwhelming, he couldn't even understand more than a random word or two at a time.

If this worked to silence the noise, he'd buy bushels of it.

Pulling the cup to his face, Styxx did as Estes had instructed. It smelled like some exotic fruit and it made his head reel. But the best part was that it completely shut out the voices of the gods and people in his head.

For that silence alone, he was grateful beyond measure.

"Here. Have more wine."

Styxx took the skin and drank deeply of it. But this was different from what he'd had earlier. Spicier. It hit his stomach then fanned out through his veins with a warm thickness he could feel. The calmest peace he'd ever known settled over him, like he was sleeping while awake.

Then out of nowhere, his body felt as if it was engulfed in flames. He blew cold air across his skin.

Estes took the wine from his hand and set it aside. "It's all right, Styxx. Don't fight it."

Don't fight what? It burned and ached. He rubbed at his neck, trying to cool down his flesh. "I'm so hot . . . "

"It'll pass in a minute."

Styxx licked his suddenly dry lips as the fire in his body went lower . . . straight to his groin. The instant it did, it gave him an erection unlike any he'd ever had before. Every part of his body ached with a ferocious need to be touched. Eyes wide, he stared at Estes, who smiled.

Estes moved to sit behind him. Rising onto his knees, he brushed the hair back from Styxx's face and leaned forward to whisper in his ear. "Are you virgin still?"

"Yes."

Suddenly afraid, Styxx tried to get up, but Estes held him fast. Before he could escape, his uncle pinned him facedown on the ground with his arm twisted behind his back. Panic filled him as he realized what his uncle had planned for him.

Praying he was wrong, he cringed as Estes buried his hand in Styxx's hair and used his knees to wedge Styxx's thighs apart. "What are you doing, Uncle?"

Estes tossed his chiton down beside them and pressed his naked body to Styxx's. "You've no idea how hard it's been for me to wait until you were old enough for this. I was forced to sell Acheron's virginity to recoup the loan I had to make for his training. But yours, little squirrel, I intend to savor taking for hours to come."

AUGUST 28, 9533 BC

"We have to sober him up."

"Do we really have to?"

"One more day, Estes. We can take him back on the morrow."

"If we keep him any longer, my brother will send out a search party. He is the royal heir, after all, and we are deep in his father's kingdom."

"Yes, but I want to be buried deep in Styxx's kingdom one last time."

They laughed.

"Come on, Estes. I just want one more ride on the royal stallion."

His head spinning, Styxx tried his best to focus as they talked over him, but he couldn't. Someone poured something warm down his throat. Bitter, it caused him to sputter and choke.

Then it made him heave violently.

Estes rolled him over as his stomach unloaded itself. Repeatedly. It went on for so long that Styxx didn't think he'd ever stop regurgitating.

But finally his stomach settled and his vision began to clear. Completely weak, naked, and sore, with bruises all over his body, he lay on top of a stained blanket.

"Come on, boy," Estes said, his voice distorted and slow to Styxx's drug-numbed mind. "We need to get you washed and cleaned."

It wasn't until Styxx was waist-deep in the stream that he began to recall the last week he'd been with his uncle . . .

You know, Estes, you should bring him to Atlantis. I'd pay you a fortune for a go at him and his brother at the same time.

No, better yet, to watch the two of them have a go at each other.

Styxx covered his ears, trying to blot out things he didn't want to remember hearing. Things he didn't want to remember doing . . .

Absolute horror consumed him. He started to bolt, but Estes caught him and held him tight against his naked body.

"Shh. Calm yourself."

"You . . . you . . ." Styxx couldn't bring himself to say that his uncle and friends had gang-raped him.

Repeatedly.

Their laughter while they swapped turns with him echoed in his ears. Tears gathered in his eyes as shame filled every inch of his bloodied heart. How could the uncle he'd loved so much have done this to him?

Gods, his father trusted this man. He'd brought him into their home . . .

Estes tightened his hold on him. "You wanted to be a man, like Acheron. Now you are."

No, his uncle had used him like he was a chamber pot set there to service his needs, with no regards to his feelings or humanity. Worse than that, the bastard had whored him for his friends.

Styxx's legs buckled as he remembered Estes laughing after he'd finished with him the first time. *I've cracked his tight little ass for you. Now who wants to break it in good?*

Oh gods . . . Now he understood some of the phantom pains he'd felt on the most private places of his body. And he knew exactly what Estes had done with his brother.

"Acheron's your whore."

Estes smiled proudly. "You're not as well trained as he is yet, but one day you'll be as good a fuck, I promise."

Styxx shoved at him and tried to run, but he slipped on the rocks and fell into the water.

Estes grabbed him again. "Don't be like that, little stallion. Acheron enjoys it. He even begs for my cock. As his twin, you will, too."

Shame, horror, and agony shredded his soul. "You're disgusting! Pervert! I'm going to tell my father what you've done!"

The humor fled his uncle's face at that threat. Seizing Styxx's arms in a brutal grip, he glared at him with fury. "And who do you think Xerxes will believe? His beloved younger brother who has stood at his back and protected *his* secrets, or the son of a drunken, demented whore who's already been treated for mental instability? You breathe one word of this to him and I'll not only ensure you never inherit the throne, I'll make you a permanent Dionysion resident. And once your father abandons you there, I'll bribe the priests and take you to Atlantis where you can join your brother as a high-priced piece of ass I rent out to anyone with enough coin."

"You wouldn't dare."

"Try me." Estes ran his tongue down Styxx's throat then laughed. "Fucking you, little squirrel, almost makes being away from Acheron tolerable. Now be a good boy and wash yourself or I shall do it for you." He dropped his hand to illustrate his offer.

Styxx vomited again.

Estes shoved him away. "Clean yourself and be quick about it or I'll give Nestor his additional day with you."

Abashed and shaken, Styxx sank down in the water, wishing himself dead. He felt so unclean. So filthy and fouled. And as he washed himself, he remembered their hands on him as they violated every part of his body.

In that moment a deep-seated rage seized him and he wanted to lash out and kill them all. Why had his powers failed to warn him when he needed them most? Why?

Because there had been too many of them with Estes. Their thoughts had trampled over each other's and the gods' and his own to the point he hadn't been able to discern any of them singularly. It was part of what gave him such bad headaches.

"Damn you!" he screamed. But the words were directed more at himself than anyone else.

Why did I ever trust Estes?

He knew better. No one could ever be trusted. How could he have forgotten that one vital lesson?

Because Estes had shown him kindness when no one else had. He was family and family wasn't supposed to be like this. They were supposed to love each other. Protect each other.

Says who?

Styxx laughed bitterly at his thought. *That* was the truth. Ryssa would be thrilled beyond measure to see him used like this and reduced to the level of a common whore.

I hope you get what you deserve. How many times had she said that to him? *Someone needs to take you down a notch.*

Estes had taken him down a lot more than that.

Tears filled his eyes and spilled over his cheeks. He didn't feel like this was his just deserts, but maybe it was. He'd ruined his mother. And if he was the real godspawn and Acheron wasn't, he'd ruined his innocent brother, too.

Out of everything Styxx had screwed up in his life, that was the one real regret he had. He should have spoken up and told his father the truth. That he had the god powers while Acheron only had divine eyes. Then they would have been hated equally.

Together.

What do I do now?

I just want to go home.

It was wretched there, but it was the only place he had. *You should run away and leave it all behind.*

And do what? He had no practical skills. He was a prince who knew diplomacy and languages. Useless in the real world. Besides, if this was how his family treated him, how much worse would strangers be?

"Wherever you are, Acheron . . . I hope you don't feel the way I do right now."

But he knew better. There was no way Acheron could be used like this and not feel the same.

Worthless. Powerless. Despised.

Yet the worst was the self-hatred.

You are a prince! his mind shouted at him. *Heir to the Didymos throne. Get your ass up! Now! Who are you to complain about your fate?*

"I'm a used whore," he breathed as pain racked him again. How could he ever hold his head up after this, knowing what they'd done to him for a solid week? It'd been bad enough when the priests had held him down and tortured him as they tried to drive out the demons that didn't exist. And the unknown Olympian had made lecherous offers he'd baited with the promise of freedom.

This was so much worse.

I should have let the god have me. At least that would have seen him released from the Dionysion faster. Had he only known then what his fate was, he'd have embraced it. Then the god would have protected him from them . . .

Maybe.

Sick to his soul, Styxx left the water and dressed so that he could put this behind him as quickly as possible.

If he could just get home, Estes and the others would leave. No one would ever know what had happened to him here. He could keep the secret. He was good at that.

I just have to get home.

Styxx didn't speak a single word the whole way back. While they rode, his gaze kept going to the guards who had been sent along to protect him. Guards his uncle had bribed . . .

Not with coin, but with Styxx.

Even now, he could hear their mocking laughter. They thought what had been done to him was funny, and they had watched and participated with a glee that was nauseating.

Spoiled son of a king . . . Here's for all the times I've had to lower my eyes to you and your father. Let the royal prick take a prick in the ass for all the pains I've had to suffer . . .

Next time I avert my gaze from you, Highness, know that it's banging your sweet ass I'll be thinking of.

Styxx didn't know if he'd ever be able to leave his room again, knowing they were in his father's service. How could he face anyone ever again?

And when his father met them at the palace steps with a wide smile, shame and humiliation slapped him even harder. How would his father look at him if he knew how he'd been used?

Styxx's gaze fell to the scar on his arm that his father had given him. And he knew the truth.

His father would hate and blame *him* for it.

"How did it go?" his father asked with a delight that sickened Styxx even more.

Estes laughed. "We rode mostly. I tell you, brother, there's nothing better than feeling your favorite royal stallion under you."

Bile rose in Styxx's throat.

"Styxx took his first buck and we made a man of him. It's been a great week, brother. One we'll all remember for the rest of our lives, is that not right, Styxx?"

117

Styxx cringed at the double entendres he now fully understood.

His father frowned at him. "Are you all right, boy?"

He wanted to tell him the truth, but one glance at Estes and he
knew his uncle was right. His father thought the world of his
brother and was suspicious of a son he wasn't really sure belonged
to him. It was why he favored Ryssa so. With her birth, there was
no doubt.

Styxx would never hold his father's full confidence or love.

"Prince Styxx was stuffed with too many rich figs this past week
for his taste, I'm afraid."

Styxx winced at Nestor's bold reference to their rape that went
right over his father's head. It was meant to shame him, and that
arrow hit its target dead on.

Estes ruffled Styxx's hair. "Nestor's right. He partook too much
of our potent nectar, brother, and is still sick from it. Forgive me
for corrupting your heir and opening him to more manly activi-
ties than he was ready for. Still, the event has stretched him quite
a bit and taught him things he won't soon forget."

Every single word cut him like jagged glass across his heart. All
of them openly mocked his pain and degradation at their hands.
Worse, they reveled in it.

Styxx ground his teeth to keep from showing any emotion
whatsoever. Estes was testing him and he knew it. Throwing what
they'd done in his face to see if he'd break and betray them while
Estes was here with his friends to lie against Styxx should he say
one single word about what they'd done.

That was why Estes had brought them along. Who would ever
believe one mad boy against two princes, one of whom was a decorated war hero, and four noblemen? They would stand united to
call him a liar so that Estes could have him returned to the temple.
And from there . . .

He felt his stomach cramp with utter misery.

His father pulled him into his arms and clapped him on the
back. "My poor Styxx. The first hangover is the worst of all. But

you have to learn to work past it. Or never get another." Kissing his forehead, he released him and went to greet his brother.

Styxx glared at his uncle as his father embraced Estes, resenting the affection his father had for him. Over his father's shoulder, Estes raked him from head to toe with a lecherous, taunting grin. Averting his gaze, Styxx caught the smug smiles of his uncle's friends. And when Nestor winked at him and dropped his gaze to Styxx's groin as he licked his lips, he all but ran up the stairs and into the palace.

Ryssa met him just inside the door and swept his body with a sneer of her own. "You must think you're something truly special now. Having gone off with Uncle and his friends like you're their noble equal. But you're not a man, Styxx. You're still a pathetic, spoiled child."

He'd never wanted to punch her more than he did right then. How could she look into his eyes and not see the horror inside his heart? Not see how shaken and upset he was? It took everything he had not to put her through the wall behind her. "And you're a stupid bitch."

She gasped as he stormed past her. Shrieking, she ran to tell on him.

Honestly, he didn't care. There was nothing worse his father could do to him now. No beating that could possibly hurt more than this did.

He started past the upstairs larder then paused and opened it to grab two jugs of wine. With them in hand, he retreated to his room and bolted himself in. He had no intention of leaving the safety of these four walls until long after Estes and the others were gone.

Pulling the pillow from his bed, he placed it on the floor to cushion his sore body and guzzled down the undiluted wine, wanting it to take away his shame. But all it could do was create a very temporary shelter and he knew it.

Over and over, against his will, his mind kept replaying the utter misery he'd just survived. No matter what he did, he heard their voices and felt their hands on his flesh.

Please, gods, talk to me and drown it out.

But all he heard was Estes and the others laughing and mocking him. How ironic that the only thing he'd found to fully silence the sounds in his head were memories he'd sell his soul to banish ...

AUGUST 30, 9533 BC

For two full days, Styxx stayed barricaded in his room until he heard the horses gathered in the drive for his uncle's departure. Making sure to stay out of sight, he opened his window only enough to look down and verify the sounds.

Thank you, gods, they're leaving ...

"Where's the prince?" his father demanded on the steps below.

Ryssa made a derisive face. "No one's seen him, Father. Most likely he's off impregnating a servant. After all, he went a whole week without one. Gods forbid."

Styxx despised her for that.

Estes shrugged Styxx's "rudeness" off. "Don't worry about it, Xerxes. I'm not offended. I'm sure he feels like he's had enough of me this past week. Give him my regards when you see him and tell him that I can't wait until my next visit. I look forward to being his riding partner in the future."

Styxx's stomach shrank at those hated words and the veiled threat beneath them.

"You are far too kind, Uncle." Ryssa kissed him lightly on the cheek. "May the gods speed you home."

"May the gods overturn your chariot and spill your guts, far and wide," Styxx snarled. "Or better yet, send your boat to the bottom of the sea."

"Gods speed you, brother."

Styxx didn't feel like he could breathe again until he saw his uncle and his entourage ride out the gates. Only then did he lean back and relax. He expelled a long breath.

His nightmare was finally over. The bastard was gone and couldn't touch him anymore.

He was safe again . . .

But his relief was short-lived as guards pounded on his door. At first he wasn't going to answer it at all, but when he heard them calling for a battering ram, he knew if he didn't come out, his father would never be placated with a simple apology.

Forcing himself to stand strong, he opened the door to find four burly guards waiting to escort him down to his father's study.

Styxx braced himself for his father's fury and lecture.

They marched with him all the way inside his father's study and didn't pull back until he neared his father's desk where the king sat with Ryssa standing behind him. His father glared at him with a venom Styxx wished was lethal.

"What have you to say for yourself, boy?"

"I don't feel well, Father. Please forgive me. I think I caught something." And hopefully it wouldn't be some venereal disease.

"Do you think I care how badly you feel?"

No. Of course he didn't. He never cared when Styxx was ill.

"Is this to be your answer when you're king? To crawl into your bed anytime you don't feel well and let the kingdom rot while you rest?"

It was all Styxx could do not to mock those words in time with his father's recitation of a lecture perpetually branded in his mind.

His father rose to his feet and stormed his way to stand before Styxx. "And what is this I hear about your calling your sister a bitch?"

He cut a murderous glare to Ryssa who smirked at him. "She misunderstood me."

His father backhanded him. "Don't you lie to me! And is that alcohol I smell on you? Is it?"

No, the alcohol wasn't the pungent smell. Rather it was the aphrodisiac Estes had forced down his throat for nine days straight then forced him to vomit up. No matter how hard he tried, he couldn't get rid of the rancid odor. "It's some medicine Estes gave me."

His father shook his head. "You disgrace the name of Didymos and our noble Ariclean ancestors. I give you every luxury and consideration a man can give his son, and how do you repay me? You lie in bed like some wastrel. I won't have it, Styxx. I won't!" He shoved him back into the arms of the largest guard. "Take him to the scold and see that he's given fifty strikes. More if he cries."

Styxx winced at the severity of his punishment.

"How many more, Majesty?"

"As many as it takes to make him stop."

Styxx met the smug expression on Ryssa's face.

"I think he should have more, Father, for what he said to me. It was completely uncalled for."

"Fifty is sufficient, kitten. Besides, he always cries like a woman." He sneered at Styxx. "I should put a dress on you."

Why not? It was the only degradation Estes had spared him.

"Get him out of my sight."

Styxx didn't bother following the guards. He led the way. After all, he was intimately acquainted with the path to the scold.

The instant he entered the guard's room, the scold looked up with an arched brow at his sudden appearance.

"Fifty," Styxx growled. "More should I weep."

He scowled. "How many more?"

"Until I stop, and yes, you're pardoned. Now just get it over with." Styxx went into the room and tried to blot out the guards' voices in his head as they waited outside for the scold to beat him. They were relishing his punishment even more than his sister did.

He took the leather piece from the scold and placed it in his mouth then assumed the position he knew so well. A slow smile curled the scold's lips as he secured Styxx's hands to the post.

Don't worry, I'm not going to wet myself. He'd long passed that point.

Brushing Styxx's hair back from his eyes, the scold lowered his face until their gazes met. "I am fully pardoned, Highness, for my actions against you?"

Styxx frowned. "Yes," he said around the leather. Was the man daft? Why did he need him to repeat it?

The scold picked the largest cane then moved around so that he could expose Styxx's scarred and sore buttocks.

Placing his cheek against the cold stone, Styxx held his breath and waited for the cane to be rubbed against his skin as a signal that the whipping would begin. Instead, he felt the scold's calloused hands pushing his legs apart so that he could run his hand down Styxx's inner thigh over the scars the priests had given him.

"My brother said you had the sweetest little ass he'd ever ridden. I've never had a nobleman's ass before, never mind such a pretty royal one. But I have to say that I have dreamed of doing this to you for years."

Screaming in terror, Styxx tried to break free, but the ropes were knotted too well.

"Shh, Highness. You cooperate and I'm sure we can come to a sweet compromise regarding your punishments from now on."

An hour later, Styxx stood in the corner of his punishment room, trying to find even a tiny shred of dignity. But he had none left. Worse, he couldn't stop his tears no matter how hard he tried.

I am a woman.

He'd been used like one.

The door opened behind him. His stomach shrank as he feared the scold returning for more. Surely to the gods, the bastard was well sated by now . . .

"Why are you still here?"

Great. It was his adoring father. Just what he needed.

"Answer me, boy."

"I don't feel well."

His father curled his lip in disgust. "I am so sick of that excuse. Can you not think up a better lie? And those tears . . . you're weak

123

and pathetic!" The king slammed his hand down on the table where the scold had . . .

Styxx vomited at the memory.

Jumping back, his father screwed his face up. "I guess you are ill."

His breathing ragged, Styxx wiped a trembling hand over his mouth and did his best to control his raging and raw emotions.

For the first time, his father's features softened as if the bastard finally had some tender feeling for him. He pulled him into his arms. Styxx had to force himself not to recoil.

Or cry harder.

"Come, child. Let me help you to your bed and have a bath prepared. Do you wish to have a maid help bathe you?"

"No." The last thing he wanted was another pair of hands on his body, especially since he could still feel the evidence of the guard's intrusion sliding out of him. If anyone else bathed him, they'd know what had happened.

"All right. I shouldn't have been so harsh to you. Had I known you were really ill, I wouldn't have been."

Maybe you should listen when I try to tell you something, old man.

But he never did.

"Father!" Ryssa snapped as she saw them on the stairs. "How is he to learn any lesson while you coddle him so?"

"Enough, kitten. Your brother is severely ill. I can feel his fever radiating through his clothes and mine. You should have pity for him."

"What I pity is this empire when he sits on your throne."

Styxx glared at her.

"Father, he's threatening me again."

His father paused beside her. "How so?"

"The way he looked at me just now. Like he could go through me."

"You would do well to remember that one day, he will be your king, kitten. And he conducted himself with honor today. He walked to the scold without aid and gave no complaint." Looking down, he tightened his arms around him. "I'm proud of you, Styxx."

Great. After all I've done to please you, it's my rape that makes you proud.

Bloody figures.

Styxx couldn't meet his father's gaze. Not when he could still feel the scold's groping hands. He tried to pull away, but his father tightened his grip. It took every ounce of will not to break at the memories that stirred.

"Please, Father, I need to lie down for a while." He choked on another spasm.

His father finally quickened the pace and got him to his room just in time for him to reach the chamber pot.

"Should I send for a physician?"

"No . . . I'll be fine. I just need to be alone." Styxx started to sit then thought better of it. Between the beating and other matters, he wasn't sure if he'd ever be able to sit again.

"Let me know if you need anything." Finally his father retreated.

Styxx crawled onto his bed and slowly lowered himself down. Closing his eyes, he tried to imagine another life. One where he was welcomed with a loving hand that never turned violent on him. One where no one hated him without cause . . .

In his mind, he saw the image of a woman. She would be as sweet as the morning sun, with the voice of a songbird. And she would smile whenever he approached her. A real smile that said she enjoyed his company . . .

Not his title.

But he knew that dream would never come to him. Commoners married for love. Princes married for alliances. His marriage would be negotiated and he'd be lucky if she tolerated him long enough to conceive his heir. The only real friend he'd ever known in his entire life was locked away in Atlantis, suffering endless days like this one.

How do I get us out of this?

There was only one answer. If he could heal enough to ride by the morning, he would be able to get to Atlantis before Estes did. Hopefully his uncle and his friends would take their time returning home.

He could free Acheron and then they'd ... do something. It didn't matter what. The goal was to get them both out of this torment and find a place where the world would just leave them in peace.

But even as he had the thought, he couldn't help wondering if such a place existed.

SEPTEMBER 8, 9533 BC

Damn it, Estes, how many rooms are in your home?

The number seemed to be infinite. His uncle's villa was even larger than their primary palace in Didymos. Worse, Estes had a full staff of servants and guards Styxx had to avoid. Since it was well after midnight, no one should be awake. Yet there were a number of maids and men walking about.

But what sickened him was the reason for all the rooms. The majority of the ones he'd searched had been set up as sex playrooms with different themes and props. And every time he opened one, his heart broke more at what had been done to Acheron.

I hate you, Father.

No human being should be reduced to this. Especially not his brother.

Styxx snuck to another door and pressed his ear against it to listen. He didn't hear anyone inside it, either. Looking right and left, he slowly, carefully pushed it open. When he didn't see anyone, he slid inside to double-check. Like the others, it was set up with sexual holding racks and a large bed near an oversized fireplace.

He approached the bed then froze. There in the center of it lay Acheron, peacefully sleeping on his stomach. That sight slammed him back to their childhood when he'd sneak into Acheron's room at night to talk, play, or sleep. Whenever he was alone in his bed, Acheron slept in that position. But he'd never slept like that when they were together.

An overwhelming urge to curl up at his brother's back and press his feet to Acheron's went through him. And in its wake was a brutal pain for what they'd both lost these past years.

Innocent brotherly love.

Friendship.

Two things he didn't know if they'd still have or not. But the one thing he couldn't deny was how much his brother meant to him. How much he loved Acheron.

Forever and always.

Yet the man on that bed right now was a complete stranger to him. The changes in Acheron's body slapped him with a harsh dose of cold, disturbing reality. Funny how, even though he was well aware of the changes in his own body over the years, he'd come here expecting to see the same young brother who'd been taken.

But that wasn't what he found.

They were both grown men now and neither bore much resemblance to the twins who'd been separated. Just like him, Acheron was taller than most Greek men, with lean, well-defined muscles that were still in the process of filling out. Acheron's skin was slightly paler than Styxx's, yet both possessed the same exact wavy blond hair. Styxx kept his cut to just past his ears while Acheron's fell to his shoulders.

His brother was completely naked except for gold bands on his ankles, wrists, biceps, and neck. A thin gold chain linked his wristband to the one on his biceps. Styxx winced at them and what they signified. Those tsoulus chains were put on young men and women who were essentially kept as pets for the sexual perversions of the ruling class. While his father had never owned one, Styxx

127

knew plenty of noblemen, princes, and kings who were not so kind. Men who bragged about their property and how they loved to debase their slaves who had no choice except to take it.

But what made him angriest of all were the small loops on the wrist and ankle bands. Those were to tie his brother into different positions so that his owner would have full access to his body to do anything he wanted while Acheron would be powerless to stop it. The fact that they were cast in gold and left on Acheron's limbs even while he slept said it all.

His uncle used his brother well and often.

Styxx wanted to kill Estes for what he'd done. *You worthless bastard . . .*

Moving closer, he dropped his gaze to Acheron's open hand where Estes had burned a slave's mark into his palm. That sight repulsed him even more as he realized that had been the pain he'd felt on the day he'd come home from the Dionysion.

Though his uncle had told him what he'd been doing with Acheron, he'd held out hope that Estes was lying or exaggerating the abuse.

But there was no denying this.

His brother really was a well-used whore.

Yet what screwed with his head most was the fact that while he knew it was Acheron on that bed, he saw himself there. They were identical in every way, except for their eyes and physical scars. But for one small birth defect that could have been his as easily as it was Acheron's, he would be the one being bought and sold every day of his life.

He ground his teeth at the injustice of fickle random luck. It was so unfair.

This stops now!

No matter what it took, he was getting Acheron out of this nightmare. Styxx knelt on the floor and reached to touch his brother. The pungent smell of fruit hit him hard. It was the same scent of that damned aphrodisiac his uncle had forced him to take. *Please be more coherent than I was.*

"Acheron?" he whispered, shaking his brother's shoulder.

Moaning low, Acheron turned his face into Styxx's hand and licked his palm.

Styxx jerked his hand back, stunned and disturbed by Acheron's actions. "Brother?" he tried again.

Acheron moved closer to him. "*Idikos,*" he breathed.

The Atlantean word hit him like a fist to his groin. It was one a slave used for his master.

"Acheron!" he said more sharply, shaking him. "Wake up!"

His brother pushed himself up by his arms immediately, but was so groggy that he couldn't focus. Of course, he was drugged. How else would Estes be able to keep him here?

"What would you have of me, *Idikos*?" Acheron asked in Atlantean. He was so out of it that he had no idea to whom he was speaking. Even his thoughts were incoherent jumbled words that were a mixture of Greek and Atlantean. Worse, he kept his gaze on the ground as all slaves were forced to do.

Styxx cupped Acheron's face in his hands and tilted his chin until Acheron met his gaze. "Look at me, brother. Do you remember me?"

Styxx? The hopeless agony of Acheron's thought wrenched his stomach hard.

"Yes, *adelphos*. I've come to take you from here."

That succeeded in breaking through Acheron's drugged stupor. His swirling silver eyes flared wide as terror consumed him. He tore himself from Styxx's hands and scooted back on the bed to cower in a corner.

Styxx shot across the bed after him. "We have to hurry. Where are your clothes?"

"I can't leave," Acheron said in a low, vicious whisper.

"Yes, you can."

Acheron met his gaze and shook his head hard. A tic worked in his jaw. "I can*not* leave."

"Are you insane that you would stay here?" Styxx glanced around at all the sex toys and the tag on Acheron's collar that marked him as property and not a human. All slaves were viewed as nothing more than tools with feet. "I will protect you."

"You can't."

Gods, what had they done to him that he'd be so frightened he shivered at the mere thought of having freedom?

Styxx tried to make sense of Acheron's rushing thoughts, but he wasn't thinking in a single language. Rather in about nine of them, only four of which Styxx was truly fluent with. He also used words Styxx wasn't sure about, but he had an inkling they had to do with sex.

"Listen to me!" he said, cupping Acheron's face again. His brother refused to look at him. "Estes isn't here. I've ridden day and night, only stopping to change out horses, to make sure I'd beat him back so that I could help you. I didn't know what he was doing to you, little brother. But now that I do, I swear to you that I will keep you safe."

"You can't."

"Why won't you believe me?"

This time Acheron did meet his gaze, and the abject shame, misery, and pain in his brother's eyes stole his breath. "Because you *are* me and I couldn't stop them."

"You were a baby."

Acheron shook his head. "You don't know ... you don't know."

"Know what?"

A moment later, Styxx sucked his breath in sharply as Acheron's thoughts spun even faster and with so much emotion they pierced his skull with pain. What in the name of Hades? "Acheron, calm yourself. Where are your clothes?"

"I have none."

Of course he didn't. Why would he? A tsoulus wouldn't need any for his duties.

Styxx removed his cloak and wrapped it around Acheron. Once they were away, he'd buy something for Acheron to wear. The important thing right now was to get him out of here before a guard or servant heard them.

He pulled his brother from the bed, but it was hard to get him across the floor. Acheron fought him every step of the way to the point Styxx was ready to hit him for it.

He's afraid.

And I'm not?

If they were caught . . . he didn't want to think about the consequences. Frustrated and angry, Styxx slammed his brother against the wall. "Damn it all, Acheron. Stop this! I'm taking you from here. Stop fighting me."

Acheron glared at him with so much hatred it cut through him. "You think you can control things because you're a prince. But you don't control shit!"

"What I think is I'm putting my ass on the line for you, brother, and you're being *stupid*. I'm well aware of what's at stake . . . for both of us. But we can't live like this. Not me and definitely not you."

"Acheron!"

Both of them froze at Estes's loud bellow.

Crap! How had the bastard returned so fast?

Because it'd taken two days for Styxx to recover enough to ride. He should have factored that in. More than that, his uncle must have rushed to get back to Acheron.

His brother started to go to Estes.

Styxx grabbed his shoulders and stopped him. "We have to leave. Now! Is there another way out of here?" It was only then that he realized there were no windows for this room.

Before Styxx could move, Acheron shouted. "In here, *Idikos!*"

"Why would you do that to your own brother?"

Acheron gave him a cold, hard stare. "I have no brother. My brother sold me to this."

I protect myself . . .

Wanting to beat Acheron for his selfish thought that came through loud and clear, Styxx covered Acheron's mouth with his hand, and grabbed him. With no clear-cut plan, he pulled him toward the only other door in the room. It led to a bathing chamber. Styxx tried to pick Acheron up to carry him, but his brother dropped his weight, making it impossible.

Even so, couldn't leave him here and save his own ass. He couldn't.

Styxx was still trying to make it to the door on the opposite side of the room when Estes entered from the bedroom they'd just left.

He went cold as Estes's jaw dropped.

After a few seconds, a slow smile curved his uncle's lips. "Well, well . . . what gifts the gods do give us who are faithful."

Styxx released Acheron and ran for the opposite door, but Estes caught him before he could open it. He slammed him back against the wall with enough force to knock the air from his lungs.

"My little squirrel . . . If you wanted to stay with me, all you had to do was ask."

"I hate you! Let go of me!"

In spite of his struggles, Estes pulled something from his purse while holding him against the wall.

"Acheron!" Styxx held his hand out to him. "Help me, brother!"

Shaking his head adamantly, Acheron stepped back and sank to the floor in abject submission.

Furious at him, Styxx shoved at Estes with everything he had. It loosened Estes's hold enough that he was able to break free. But he didn't make it far before Estes had him again. This time, he covered Styxx's face with a rag.

Styxx bellowed and fought, but before he could do much his vision dulled and the room swam. An instant later, everything went black.

Styxx came awake slowly to find himself tied to a chair. It took him a few seconds to clear his vision enough to see that he was in his uncle's study. Estes sat behind a large table in a padded chair similar to his father's throne. But what really pissed him off was that Acheron knelt on the cold stone floor at the right side of his uncle. Completely naked, Acheron had his gaze on the ground. He sat back on his haunches with his hands resting on his parted thighs, within easy reach of Estes.

You fucking idiot!

If Acheron had only run with him, they wouldn't have been caught.

"So you're finally awake."

Styxx lifted his gaze to his uncle. "You can't keep me here."

"No? You rode out alone. And I'm quite certain you didn't tell your father where you were going. I know you damn sure didn't tell him what you intended to do once you got here. Even if he did know where you were, all I'd have to say is that you left and that I have no idea what happened to you. You're a prince. Any of your father's rivals or enemies would love to lay hands on you. For ransom. Torture . . . and other things. You have no idea how much money a prince is worth on the market." He smiled as if the thought warmed him through and through. "Especially one so young, pretty, and fair. Blue-eyed blonds are the most valued of all, even when they're scarred and used."

Estes reached for a sugared fig that was in a small dish on his desk. He cradled it in his palm then held it out for Acheron. Cupping his uncle's hand, Acheron took it into his mouth, and gently laved Estes's palm and suckled his fingers.

The sight disgusted Styxx.

"Because of your arrogance and actions, you leave me with a bit of a dilemma." Estes pressed his thumb into Acheron's mouth so that his brother could suck on it in a manner that let Styxx know fast his brother was extremely skilled with using his tongue to please others. "Tell me, Styxx, do you know what *erotiki sfairi* are?"

Sex balls? That would be the closest translation. One that made him fearful of answering.

"I'm going to wager that you don't." He pulled his hand back. "Acheron, open your mouth and let your brother see yours."

When Acheron obeyed, Styxx feared he might vomit. Down the entire center of Acheron's tongue was a solid line of small silver balls that had been pierced into it.

133

So that was the pain that had caused him to be "treated" in the temple.

"Do you know what they're used for?"

Styxx glared at him. "I think I can guess."

Estes gave him a cruel, taunting smile as he pulled the hem of his chiton up until he was completely exposed to Styxx's gaze from the waist down.

Styxx quickly looked away as bile rose high in his throat.

"Acheron? Let us show the prince what you can do with your jewelry."

Styxx slammed his eyes shut as Acheron rose up on his knees and leaned over his uncle's chair. He didn't want to see this. But he couldn't close his ears while his brother pleasured his uncle.

"Stop!" Styxx roared as he fought against the ropes that held him tight.

But neither took mercy on him, nor did they stop until Estes was fully sated.

His uncle drew a ragged breath then laughed as he stroked Acheron's hair like the fur of a beloved pet. "How I've missed that sweet mouth of yours, Acheron. I'll raise the price on you come the morrow. While you're well used for your tender age, you are also far more talented than any I know. Now go . . . prepare yourself for your next patron."

Without a single word or any protest, Acheron rose and obeyed.

Horrified, Styxx tried his best to blot all of this out. Why had he even tried to save Acheron from this? His brother seemed so content and receptive. How, he had no idea. He'd rather be dead than submit to such an animal as Estes or live such a life.

Getting up, Estes moved to stand by his side. He grabbed Styxx's jaw in a fierce grip. "Look at me, boy!"

He opened his eyes.

"I know what you're thinking. You would *never* stand to be treated thus. You'd fight until you died. After all, you defeated me when we fought in the arena. You could defeat me again. But I think I shall teach you a few things just so you know exactly how powerful you really aren't." He tightened his grip so that his fingers bit into Styxx's jaw. "First, when you won against me, it was in a fair fight with rules of combat. In real life and war, there's no such thing and I *never* fight fair. But I will give you a chance. You make it from here to the front door and I will free both of you. I'll even do better than that. I'll give the two of you an escort with fanfare home to your father's loving arms. All you have to do is make it to the front door." He cut the ropes holding Styxx.

Knowing it was a trick, but with no idea how, Styxx bolted for the door. The damned thing was locked. He fumbled with the latch. Before he could free it, Estes grabbed him.

Styxx elbowed him in the stomach.

Estes lifted him from the waist and threw him on the ground. Rolling, Styxx shot to his feet and tried to reach the sword that was on Estes's wall. Estes caught him at the waist again and wrapped his entire body around Styxx's. They fell to the floor. Styxx did his best to break the hold, but it was impossible.

Worse, in this position, he could feel Estes's hard erection against his hipbone.

His uncle pressed his hand to Styxx's neck, just under his jaw. He choked as his breathing was cut off. His ears buzzed.

And as he passed out, he felt his uncle lick his throat. "You think you were fucked before, little squirrel? You're about to learn lesson two."

OCTOBER 22, 9533 BC

His head reeling and his body aching as if he'd been run over by stampeding horses, Styxx came awake to find himself facedown on a bed with black sheets. There was a huge fire roaring just across from him along with four braziers. He started to move then realized his arms and legs were secured to the bedposts by the same kind of gold rings Acheron had worn.

He now had an identical set of bands on his wrists, ankles, biceps, and neck.

Furious, he snatched as hard as he could.

"Stop before you hurt yourself."

He glared at Estes as his uncle neared the bed with a small tray. Setting it down beside Styxx's hips, he slid onto the mattress.

Styxx tried to insult him, but he had a gag in his mouth that prevented it.

Estes poured a thick milky liquid onto his fingertips. Once they were well coated, he slid them into Styxx's rectum.

Styxx screamed out in protest.

"Stop!" Estes snapped again. "I'm trying to teach you how to tend yourself on your way home. Believe me, you're going to want the numbing gel, especially since you'll be riding a horse for the next week, and probably a few other things, too."

Styxx ground his teeth as tears of frustration and shame welled in his eyes. As much as he hated to admit it, the cool, soothing gel did feel good, and it went a long way to making that part of his body not burn and throb anymore.

"That's it, my royal stallion. Relax." Estes pulled his hand away then added more gel before he reapplied it to Styxx. "You want to make sure you coat yourself well."

Next, Estes reached for the red clay pot. He pulled out a small rod and met Styxx's angry glare. "This is called a suppository. It's for the pain you're in."

Styxx screamed again as his uncle pressed it deep into his body.

"Shh. Stop clenching. It needs to go in far enough that your body keeps it or it won't do you any good."

Styxx growled as more humiliation stabbed him.

After a minute, Estes pulled back and wiped his hands off on a small, damp towel. There was an evil, smug glint in his icy eyes. "Now as you lie there in your fury, I want you to note that the last thing you remember is being in my study right after Acheron left.

I don't know if you remember our fight or not, but that was over six weeks ago."

Styxx's breath left him as if he'd been punched. Six weeks? No. The bastard was lying. He had to be ...

Six weeks?

"Atlantis has a lot of wondrous innovations. And they excel at medicines and knowledge of herbs and their effect on humans and their emotions and memory. Which is why your pain should be fading right about now."

He was right. Not even his head hurt.

"The first thing I learned when I was sent here was how to manipulate their herbs and medicines. Just as you have no memory of the last six weeks, Acheron has no memory of your being here at all. Even though you've been with him off and on these weeks past, and even though you tried to free him. The last memory he has of his brother is the day we rode away from your palace."

Styxx was stunned.

"*That* is your second lesson. I *can* take you from your father at any time and own you. You won't even know that I've done it. Nor will you know what's been or is being done to you. But you will be a willing participant. In fact, I learned a few fascinating things myself that I shan't soon forget. Such as I can make you suck a cock in less than a day, and in less than two, I can have you begging to be fucked in the ass until you bleed."

Styxx felt his stomach heave at those words. He was lying.

He had to be.

"I know you don't believe me. But I promise you, having you and your brother together is one of my fondest memories. And you've no idea how much money I've made off the two of you these weeks past ... Oh, and just so you know, your most uttered phrase while you've been here? 'Hand, ass, or mouth? Where do you want to come on me, my lord?'"

While Styxx gagged, Estes sighed as if savoring the memory. "Letting you go home is the hardest thing I think I've ever done. For that, you have your father to thank. So I suggest you treat him with all due respect." He ran his hand over Styxx's buttocks. "As much as I love this hot little ass of yours, I know how much you mean to my brother. And I do love my brother. I'd never cause him harm."

You're mad! Did he not know how much grief this would cause his father if he ever learned what Estes had done?

"That's why I know you're not going to tell him anything about our time together. Because if I have to kill him over *you,* there will be no one to stop me from owning and fucking you forever. Nothing to keep me from selling you to anyone I choose."

Estes ran his hand up Styxx's back. "While I've kept you, I've been writing to Xerxes and letting him know that you were staying here. He thinks that you wanted to talk to me privately and had tried to catch me before I left Didymos, and that I convinced you to come stay with me here for a few weeks so that we could bond. I've told him that I continued your studies while you were with me . . . and that I have. When next you fuck someone and you realize you have knowledge and skills that leave them begging you to stay with them, you'll know whom to thank. Were I you, I wouldn't tell him that, though. I'd say that you were practicing your conversational, economic, and political skills with Atlantean noblemen and princes. Which is true. You have been quite the diplomat as I whored you, and you've learned a whole new Atlantean vocabulary."

Estes leaned forward and bit Styxx's thigh so hard, Styxx cried out in pain. "You will also tell Ryssa that Acheron is well and happy. And that you had a great time with your brother and with me . . . which you did. And when next I come to visit you in Didymos, you will receive me and be happy to do so. From now on, like Acheron, you will do anything I ask you to."

Bullshit!

Estes smiled. "I see that fury, little nephew. But let me show you something." He left the bed to fetch a hand mirror. He brought it over and lifted Styxx's hips to show him that all of his pubic hair had been removed. And as disturbing as that was, it paled to what he saw branded way too close to his cock. The words "tsoulus whore" in both Atlantean and Greek. If that wasn't bad enough, below the words was a smaller version of the slave stamp that Acheron had branded into his hand.

"Once your hair grows back, no one will know it exists except me, you, the guard I paid this morning to brand it there ... and whatever lover you allow to suck your cock. In theory, if it disturbs you overmuch, you can have someone brand over it. Of course, they'll know what it is. And even if you do distort the brand, it will be obvious what you've done and why you did it."

Estes pulled the mirror away. "Now, all I have to do is report you as a missing slave anywhere outside of Didymos and you will either be returned to me or sold at market. And keep in mind, my little squirrel, I didn't just brand you as a slave. I've marked you as a trained tsoulus. If you want to know what happens to any tsoulus who is caught without their *idikos,* talk to Acheron. One time was all it took for him to learn not to leave this palace without me and a substantial escort."

So that was why his brother had refused to go with him ...

Great.

"Lastly, in case you're thinking you can bribe one of my servants to tell your father that I kept you here against your will ... none of them except two members of my personal guard ever knew you were here. *None* of them. And while you were fucked numerous times by twenty-two different men, not counting me, they will never breathe a word of it for many reasons."

Estes returned the mirror to the bedside table. "As I said, I'm letting you go this one and only time with a warning because I love Xerxes, and while he is uncertain about your origins, he does love you, and your loss would completely devastate him. But should you *ever* come near Acheron or Atlantis again, I will own you, body and soul. So rather than worry about your brother, you should be worried more about your own lusciously fuckable ass."

He lifted Styxx's right ankle up, freeing it from the hook that had held it. Next, he removed the gold cuff. Then he moved to the other.

"Oh . . . I almost forgot." He went back to Styxx's head and pulled out his gag. "Open your mouth."

"Fuck you!"

Estes laughed. "Little stallion, you already have. Many times and in many ways, and you will do so again many more. Now open your mouth."

Styxx refused.

"Suit yourself. But do be careful. Should the *erotiki sfaira* in your tongue strike your teeth, it will break them."

No . . .

Styxx rubbed his tongue against the roof of his mouth and then froze in horror. It was true. He did have one.

Estes winked at him. "You're not quite as accomplished at using it as Acheron, since he's had a lot more experience, but you came a long way fast . . . Now, would you like me to remove it?"

Styxx opened his mouth immediately.

Laughing, Estes took it out then held it up with a smile. "I shall keep this as a memento of our sweet time together, and in hopes that one day you will be stupid enough to return here." He released Styxx's right arm. "Now ready yourself to leave while I try to find an escort that will take you home without riding you every step of the way. And don't worry if they do—I'll send some herbs with you that will help with any pain they cause." Then he was gone.

Stunned to the core of his being, Styxx lay there, trying to absorb everything Estes had said. To come to terms with what had been done to him without his consent or knowledge.

Things he had no recollection of at all . . .

After a few minutes, he got up and went to bathe. The fact that he knew instinctively where to go added validity to everything Estes had told him.

In the bathing room, which had mirrors lining all four walls, he froze at the sight of himself. His hair was longer and he had a light dusting of whiskers on his chin and cheeks. Yet what filled him with complete consternation were the marks all over his body. Not just the brand that was still raw and bleeding, but dozens of bruises, scratches, and bite marks. He could see where someone had suckled different parts of him, and in some places, such as his thighs and arms, there were complete handprints.

And he had no memory of any of it. Not a single glimmer.

Part of him was grateful for that. Yet at the same time it was the most disconcerting thing imaginable. To know that you had been violated and used and to know nothing of the people who had done it to you.

Not entirely true. He knew Estes . . .

Covering his face with his hands, he wanted to scream from the horror of it.

At least Acheron doesn't remember. Unlike Styxx, his brother would never know what had happened to them. What they'd been forced to do.

It's all my fault. All of it. Had he just stayed home, like Estes had said, it wouldn't have happened. He should have worried about his own ass more than Acheron's.

I won't ever make this mistake again. He'd come to help his brother and Acheron had handed him over to their uncle. It was a lesson he wouldn't forget. Ever.

He would never forgive Acheron for that. How could he? Given how twisted Estes was, it was the worst sort of betrayal.

Styxx looked down at the words branded on his groin and rage filled him anew. While Acheron was marked with a general slave symbol, he didn't have "whore" written on his body.

In two languages.

If anyone ever saw it, it'd be worse than having them ask about the scars the priests had given him. They would know Styxx had been whored . . .

No. Trained and then whored.

Consumed with hate and fury, Styxx picked up the stool next to him and slammed it up against the glass, shattering it. Bellowing with the weight of his humiliation, he pounded the wall until he was spent and too tired to continue.

Surrounded by broken glass, he sank to his knees and raked his hands through his hair. How could he ever face his father? Or anyone else knowing what'd been done to him?

Acheron was right . . .

For all his title and worldly position, Styxx *was* powerless.

OCTOBER 28, 9533 BC

Styxx's hands shook as they rode through the gates of his father's palace grounds. He found no joy at his homecoming. Just an awful sense of dread and desolation. But at least now he'd be free of his uncle's men, who'd proven to be every bit as depraved as the bastard they served.

As they neared the palace, he looked up to see his father, Ryssa, and their servants gathered to welcome him back. The musicians started their fanfare.

It took every ounce of his will not to jerk his horse around and spur it into a dead run to get as far away from here as he could. He couldn't imagine what punishment his father would give him for leaving without notice. He could already hear the rant in his head.

Is that your answer to your problems, boy? To run away like a coward? To abandon your kingdom because you didn't feel well, et cetera, et cetera.

He'd be lucky if he didn't get slapped on the stairs in front of everyone.

Dismounting, Styxx took a deep breath and forced himself to climb the steps to where his father waited. He'd only taken two of them before his father came rushing down them to grab him into a fierce embrace. He cradled the back of Styxx's head in his great paw of a hand and held him as if he were a small child.

"I have missed you, boy," he breathed before pulling back to place a kiss to each of Styxx's cheeks. "No, not boy." He put his hands on Styxx's shoulders and smiled at him. "You're a man and I mustn't forget that."

Who are you and what in the name of Hades have you done with my father?

Terrified, Styxx glanced around, but no one else seemed to think this odd.

His father pulled him back into his arms and held him there for a full minute before he kissed his head and released him. "How was your trip?"

I'd have rather journeyed through Tartarus with scorpions strapped to my groin.

"Fine."

"You look as if you've grown again. I swear you're taller every day. Let me know if your armor doesn't fit and I'll have more made immediately."

You're fucking with me, aren't you, old man? We're going to go inside the palace and then you'll slap the shit out of me.

Taking his arm, his father led him to Ryssa, who greeted him with her usual snotty aloofness.

At least someone hasn't been partaking of lotos.

She lightly kissed each of his cheeks. "I want you to know that you almost killed your father with worry. Until he received Uncle's letter, he thought you kidnapped or worse."

"Ryssa!" his father snapped. "Mind your place, woman."

"I am minding my place, Father. He should know what he put you through with his thoughtless selfishness. It's time he learned to think of someone other than himself."

"Bah, pay her no heed. She's a woman. She doesn't understand the needs of men. Come, Styxx, I have the wine warmed and fresh bread and cheeses for you. I'm anxious to hear how things are with Estes and Atlantis."

Styxx felt his sister's glare on him the whole way up. And he also noticed the one person who wasn't there. "How's Mother?"

His father sighed heavily. "Ever the same. Lost in her cups."

And hating them all with every sip she took. Except for Ryssa, who could never do wrong.

As they entered the dining room, his father released him so that he could take a seat while the servants brought them refreshments.

This messed with his mind even more than what Estes had done to him. "Father? May I ask something?"

"Absolutely."

Styxx indicated the mini banquet that was set out. "What is all this? I was expecting your anger and censor." *The back of your hand across my mouth . . .*

"To be honest, I am angry. Furious, point of fact. But when your uncle wrote to me, he reminded me of a few things."

His stomach drew tight with dread. "Such as?"

"That at your age, I was married and expecting my first child."

Both his father's wife and child had died during the birth. He'd married Styxx's mother a year later.

"And that I was only a handful of months older than you when I ascended to the throne. He was right. I do still see you as an infant and I have too long treated you as one. I should never have had you whipped on your return. You're too old for that. It's time I trusted myself and your tutors to have given you the foundation you need to be the man I know you can be. Far too long, I have allowed my fears and doubts to color my sight where you're concerned." He tapped his fingertip against the table. "From this day forward, that changes."

Leaning back, his father rang for his servants. "Fetch the prince's gifts."

Completely floored, Styxx didn't move until they brought in a kopis, xiphos and hoplon and placed them on the table before him. They were supposed to have been given to him months back, but his father had refused.

You're not fit for them . . .

144

Rising, his father handed him the sword. "Galen assures me that this will please you."

Amazed by its beauty, Styxx stood and unsheathed it. Similar to Galen's, this one was marked with a laurel crown and the words "to be rather than to seem." Then he looked at his red hoplon that held a black phoenix with the same crown above it. The crest was topped with the words "I defend." Even though he'd been informed of their creation, this was the first time he'd actually seen them.

"Thank you, Father."

His father inclined his head to him. "You are now the champion of this kingdom, and you have earned the honor."

Strange, he felt more like a fraud. He wasn't a man. In truth, he wanted to go hide until his shame and pain were gone.

How would you look at me, Father, if you ever learned what was done to me? That he was so weak and ineffectual that he'd been held down and used against his will, and that the only thing he'd been able to do was cry while they violated him.

Even their scold . . .

His father gave him a quick embrace. "I know you're tired from your journey. Go and rest. We can speak later."

Yes, he was tired. But more than that, he was confused and he had no one to turn to with it. No one to confide in. The bitter reality of that slapped him hard. He was alone in his hell and maybe that was the way it should be.

'Cause the gods knew he never wanted anyone to know the horrors he'd been through.

As he turned to leave, his father stopped him. "By the way, your room's been moved."

"Pardon?"

"It was a boy's room."

Frowning, he followed his father up the stairs to the opposite wing, where his father's chambers were. While his father's room was at the end of the hall, Styxx's was just off the stairs now.

His father opened the door then stood back for Styxx to enter.

The moment he did, his eyes went wide. Massive compared to his old room, this one was finally the size of his sister's. Made up of four rooms that opened into each other, it had its own dining room, bedchambers, receiving area, and bathing room.

"Does it please you?"

"Yes, Majesty."

His father started to leave then grabbed him into another massive embrace. "Your sister was right," he whispered in Styxx's ear. "I thought I'd lost you forever. I pray to the gods that you never know the sorrow and fear I felt in my heart when I found you gone with no explanation, and I pray that I never know it again. I love you, Styxx. To the depth of my soul."

The incongruity of that statement with the things his father had said and done to him in the past . . .

It ranked with his mother's semi-sober declarations of maternal love and affection she'd occasionally given. And they all left him baffled.

If you really loved me, how could you banish my twin as if he was nothing?

How could his father have walked out on him when he'd been broken and bleeding in the Dionysion?

No matter what his father said, did, or gave, nothing would ever undo either of those actions. How could it?

Clapping him on the shoulder, his father turned and left.

Styxx set his swords and shield on the dining table and tried to come to terms with everything that had happened to him in such a short amount of time. Nothing felt real right now. It was as if he walked in a dream, detached from his body and from the world.

And while he had no memory of what Estes had done to him these weeks past, he had full knowledge of the hunting party, the scold and the journey home.

I will never be the same . . .

Styxx opened his purse and pulled out the herbs his uncle had sent home with him. Wanting to get away from everything, he went to his bed. But not even that was comforting.

His father had placed all of his linens and pillows in here, not knowing that the smallest pillow on that bed had belonged to Acheron.

Styxx ground his teeth as a wave of pain so severe it left his heart bleeding ravaged him. They had been so close as boys. Best friends. He'd shared everything with Acheron.

And now . . .

Acheron hated him as much as Ryssa did. His brother had no use for him whatsoever.

He winced as he remembered Estes's confessed perversions about his time in Atlantis. He still didn't know if it was true or not. *I hope to the gods that I never know.* Because he wasn't sure he could handle it if it was the truth.

Dropping his cloak, he looked down at the bruises that verified his use. Why wouldn't the damn things heal already? Not that it would matter. Even once they were gone, he'd still be branded as a whore.

That mark would be with him forever.

Unable to deal with it, he dropped a handful of herbs into the kylix near his bed and poured wine over them. The sooner he could drug or drink himself into oblivion, the happier he'd be. He gulped it all down in one shot and then glared at the pillow that reminded him of the childhood he'd lost. The love and friendship he'd never have again.

The innocence.

Most of all, it reminded him of the fact that when he'd risked his life to save Acheron, Acheron had called out for Estes and caused Styxx to be taken. While he'd tried to free Acheron, Acheron had trapped him.

"You fucking bastard!" he snarled, grabbing the pillow. His rage spurring him, he threw it into the fire and let the flames burn it to embers.

Then he sank to his knees on the floor and tried his best to blot out everything. But it was useless. The new memories tortured him even more than his old ones had.

I am damned.

And there was no escape from his mind that flogged him a thousand times worse than any scold ever could.

OCTOBER 30, 9533 BC

"Did you say or do something to your sister?"

It took Styxx a moment to make sense of those words from his father. He'd only seen her once since his return. She'd asked him about Acheron and he'd refused to speak a word of anything to do with Atlantis. She'd called him selfish, slapped him, and left.

Blinking, he looked up from his breakfast and shook his head. "No, Father. Why?"

"She's gone to visit my sister in Athens. I know she gets her whims and travels, but this one seems more sudden than normal."

Styxx rubbed at his brow as his head spun. While the herbs Estes had given him made his thinking fuzzy, they removed the pain and voices. It was worth the delayed reaction time to have that small peace.

"Ryssa doesn't talk to me about such things. Perhaps you should ask Mother."

"She flies into a rage if I go near her."

But she never tried to stab you in the heart.

"Then I'm at a loss, Father. I've never understood Ryssa's mind."

"I wonder if it has anything to do with her maid . . ."

"Her maid?"

"The one you impregnated. Ryssa's been in a foul mood since the chit confessed it. She dismissed her immediately."

148

"I didn't—"

His father held his hand up to silence him. "I took care of the matter. Don't let it concern you."

If he were sober, he probably would, but as it was . . . whatever.

His father left him.

"I still didn't sleep with her," he mumbled, reaching for his kylix of wine. He'd never touched a woman and now he doubted if he ever would.

Even his wife.

The last thing he wanted was to risk anyone seeing the word on his groin. And with a woman, if she did, she'd run and tell everyone about it because that was what they all did. He had yet to meet one capable of a maintaining a secret unless it protected *her*.

As for men?

He'd rather die than *ever* do that again. So here he was, a well-trained tsoulus who was celibate. He would laugh if the entire matter didn't sicken him so.

Estes had taken much more than his virginity and innocence . . . more than his little brother, he'd stolen part of Styxx's soul and all of his future.

How could he ever trust anyone now?

All of his dreams of finding a woman who could love him . . . gone as fast as Estes had drugged him that first time.

He would hate his uncle if he had any room left for it. But he hated himself too much to hate anyone else.

Fuck it, he snarled silently as he reached for his pouch and pulled out more of the herbs. He was getting low on them. Later, he'd go into town and see if he could find someone who peddled them.

For now.

He sucked his breath in sharply as a sudden pain went through him, and placed his hand to his groin where the brand still hurt at times. The moment his fingers accidentally brushed against his cock, he jerked his hand away.

I can't even masturbate now. Because every time he touched himself, even to bathe or piss, he remembered Estes holding him with their hands entwined . . .

Grimacing in distaste and horror, Styxx grabbed the rest of the herbs and dumped them in his cup. "I just want to forget everything."

He downed the entire contents of the cup and cursed out loud. Why, when Estes had the ability to remove it, had his uncle left him with the memory of the nine days he'd spent with them in the woods?

Because he's a fucking sadistic whoreson.

And Styxx was his well-used whore.

NOVEMBER 4, 9533 BC

Styxx clenched his hand before his father saw it shaking uncontrollably. They were holding open court sessions for the nobles and citizens, and he knew well how his father reacted whenever he tried to excuse himself. He ground his teeth to keep them from chattering.

What is wrong with me?

He felt ill and disoriented, and for once, he hadn't drugged himself. Theoretically, he was sober. But it sure didn't seem that way.

"Majesty? Is His Highness all right?"

Styxx cringed at the senator who'd asked the question. Why did someone always have to pull him into a fire?

His father glanced over at him then gaped. "Styxx? Are you ill?"

He wiped at the sweat in his eyes. "I'm fine, Father."

To his shock, his father came over to him. "Look at me."

He obeyed as his father placed his hand to his brow.

"Fetch a physician!" His father stepped back. "Teris? Carry the prince to his bed and be quick about it."

He must be near death for his father to be *this* concerned. "I'm fine, Father. We can continue."

His father shook his head as Teris, his father's personal guard, moved to pick Styxx up. "Have the rest of the sessions canceled with my apologies. Tell them we'll resume in the morning."

When Teris reached to touch him, Styxx bolted from his throne. "I can walk." But it wasn't easy. He was so dizzy.

"At least let Teris help you."

Styxx shook his head. He *never* wanted to feel another pair of male hands on his body again. They could all rot in Tartarus.

Suddenly, out of nowhere, Galen appeared by his side. "Give me your arm, Highness."

Styxx relaxed at the presence of the one and only person he trusted, and did as Galen ordered. At least when Galen knocked him around, he was open about it.

And Styxx always had a weapon in his hand.

Galen draped his arm around his shoulders and walked him to his room. Without a word, he put Styxx to bed then withdrew as the king came forward to stand next to Styxx.

"Galen?" Styxx called.

The old man turned at the door. "Yes, Highness?"

"Thank you."

He saluted him. "Any time you need me, good prince. I am ever at your service."

His father touched Styxx's brow again. "I don't understand why it is you sweat, but your skin is so frigid."

He didn't know either. For the last couple of days, he'd broken into a sweat and shook for no apparent reason. It never lasted that long and, thankfully, he'd been able to hide it.

Until today.

He wasn't sure what made this different. All of a sudden, he sneezed and his nose poured blood. He cursed, pinching his nostrils together as he sat up in spite of the spinning room. The whole side of his face burned. In that instant, he knew what was happening.

Acheron. Someone had struck his brother's face. Hard. So much so that Styxx had several loosened teeth from it.

But he couldn't let his father know that.

"Here." His father gave him a towel. "I thought your nosebleeds had stopped."

"No, Sire." He'd just gotten better at hiding them from his father over the years.

Styxx wiped at his face. His eyes flew wide as he felt a new pain in the last place he wanted to feel one. It took every bit of strength he had not to cry out as something impaled him. What was Estes doing to his brother?

He was desperate to get to the drawer where he kept the numbing gel, but he didn't dare use it while his father hovered so close. Nor could he allow his father to see his discomfort. And it was merciless. Like he was being cleaved in half.

"Finally," his father said as the physician joined them.

The physician bowed low to his king. "Your Majesty. I was told the prince is unwell?"

"He is." His father stepped away so the physician could examine Styxx's body.

Styxx cringed every time the man touched him.

"Where did these bruises come from, Highness?"

"Training," he lied.

His father scowled. "I didn't think you'd been training since your return."

"Master Galen wasn't there. I trained on my own."

Frowning, the physician pulled back. "Then how did you bruise yourself?"

"It was with the staff and spear," Styxx quickly added.

The physician sighed before he spoke to the king. "I think to be safe, we should bleed him."

"No!" Styxx roared as raw, pure fury burned through his veins.

After what the priests had done to him, he couldn't bear the thought of being bled again. Never mind the matter of his having suckled a god on his blood.

"Styxx!" his father snapped.

"Beat me. Kill me. I do not care. I will *not* be bled. Ever!"

The physician shrank away from the bed as if terrified. "Is he possessed again, Majesty?"

Styxx's fury gave way to panic. "No. Father, I am fine. I swear to all the gods."

The doubt in his father's eyes set his heart to pounding.

"Please, Father. I beg you." *Don't send me back there. Please, I can't . . .*

Time hung still until his father shook his head. "If you need to be bled—"

"My nose bleeds. Surely there's enough on the bed already."

"Sire—"

His father held his hand up, cutting the man off. "I will defer to the prince. But if he's not well by morning, we will proceed with your remedy, physician. Now leave us."

With a curt bow, he departed.

Scowling, his father moved to stand next to the bed. "What is wrong with you?"

"I was bled to the brink of death by the priests, Father."

"And they healed you."

You stupid bastard. "No, Father. It weakened me in ways I can't explain. Suffice it to say, I've had enough of a cure I know for a fact doesn't work. This will pass on its own, please trust me."

"And if you're possessed?"

He could almost laugh at that. How could he be possessed by the gods that had abandoned him? "Father, please. I've had nose-bleeds the whole of my life. As for the other . . . a stomach ailment. I've felt unwell since this morning and didn't want to bother you with the complaint. It's nothing."

His father inclined his head. "I shall defer to you then. And I'll send a servant to tend you."

153

"I'd rather be alone."

He scowled. "You're—"

"Father, please . . . I don't want someone in here, disturbing me in any way. I shall be fine on my own."

"I will leave someone posted at your door. Call if you need anything."

"Thank you."

As soon as his father was gone, Styxx rolled out of bed to the chest where he'd hidden his small purse. His hands shaking, he seized one of the suppositories and quickly administered it, along with the numbing gel.

His breathing ragged, he returned to bed and sighed even though he could still feel the very thing that was causing both him and his brother pain. Closing his eyes, he wished he was still ignorant of what it was. Because now that he knew exactly what was being done to Acheron, he understood the true horror of what his brother lived with.

And there was nothing he could do about it. He'd tried to free his brother and Acheron had refused.

Damn him for it.

Styxx gasped as another pain stabbed him and then he laughed bitterly. His brother wasn't the only one damned. It was both of them. Two lives tied together in complete and utter misery.

NOVEMBER 15, 9533 BC

Styxx raked his hand through his hair as his head reeled. He was so high right now that he'd give his mother a good run. The herbs he'd bought in town had been even stronger than Estes's mixture. The merchant hadn't been kidding when he'd told him it would ease whatever ailments plagued him.

But honestly, he didn't want to feel like this. He just wanted to be normal again.

What do you know of normal?

Nothing. He'd never been normal. Not like other people. And all because of his brother. If Acheron had just been born with human eyes, no one would have ever known. Neither of them would have been tortured . . .

A knock sounded on his door.

"Yes?" He lifted his head to see a small pretty maid there.

She bowed low. "His Majesty requests you join him in the outer courtyard, Highness."

Requests . . . He loved whenever his father used such words. As if Styxx had a choice in the matter. If he didn't go, his father would be furious.

He shook his head to clear it then pushed himself to his feet.

The maid didn't budge as he neared her. Instead of moving out of his way, she planted herself so that he'd have to brush up against her lush body to leave.

Biting her lip, she gave him a hot, needful look. "Would you like for me to prep your room while you're away, Highness? I could easily be here on your return." *I'd make the best mistress you've ever seen. I could and would gladly suck your nectar until you're blind from it* . . .

She was beautiful and tempting. But right now, his mark was still plainly obvious. He'd been lucky the physician hadn't seen it. The last thing he wanted was her gossiping to the rest of the servants about their whore prince.

"No, thank you."

She poked her lip out into a seductive pout. "Perhaps later, Highness?" *If I could carry a royal bastard, I'd never have to work again.*

That quelled his erection better than an icy bath. Unlike his progenitor, he didn't believe in abandoning the children he fathered. The world and people were far too cruel for that. "No. Thank you."

He left her and headed to where his father was waiting out in the bright sunshine that split his head with pain. Holding his hand up to shield his bloodshot eyes, he stopped next to the cushioned chair his father reclined on. "You summoned me, Majesty?"

His father snorted. "I'd hoped it would take you longer to answer."

"How so?"

"You were supposed to be enjoying the charms of the little minx I sent you. I'd hoped she would please you. She's extremely talented. One of the best we have."

Great. Just what he wanted. One of his father's cast-off whores.

"Forgive me, Father. In the past, whenever I dawdled after a summons, you didn't take it well."

His father laughed. "That is true. In the future, when I send a man or old woman for you, come swiftly. Should it be a winsome maid ... take your time." He gestured to the seat beside him. "Come and sit with me for a while. I have some things I wish to discuss with you."

His head still messed up quite a bit, Styxx moved to the chaise and did his best to keep his father from detecting his condition.

A servant came forward to pour his wine then returned to a distance out of hearing range.

"We may be going to war soon."

Styxx arched a brow at that. "With whom?"

"The Arcadians. They're encroaching on Corinth, and as you know, the Corinthians have long been allies of ours. King Clietus has requested a commitment of forces from me so that he can repel the Arcadians."

"Why are you conferring with me?"

"I'd like to know what you would do if you were king."

"Meet with my advisors and not my inexperienced son."

His father actually laughed at that. "I have met with my advisors, and I've made my decision, but I wanted to know what *you* would do in my place."

Ah, that explained this futile lesson. "You're testing me."

"I am, indeed."

"And if I fail?"

"I'd rather you fail as prince than as a king."

Styxx took a small sip of wine and laid his head back while his thoughts whirled about. "What did your advisors say?"

"That we owe it to the Corinthians to help them. They have been vital allies for a long time. They don't believe we should make a new enemy when we don't have to ... So tell me, boy, what would *you* do?"

Make the decision when I'm not high.

But he couldn't tell his father that. So he answered to the best of his fogged mind with the lessons Galen had taught him. "The decision to go to war isn't just about thinking what will happen *if* you win. It's mostly thinking about what will happen should you fail, and weighing the benefits of winning against the consequences of losing. What I wouldn't do is send good Didymosian men out to die for a king too weak to hold his throne on his own. If the Arcadians are set on Corinth, they won't stop. They never do, and like the Dorians, their soldiers are fiercely trained professionals who are ruthless to their bitter cores." Meanwhile the bulk of the Corinthian and Didymosian soldiers were ordinary citizens who only trained a few days each month, or two weeks a year. "The Arcadians hold much more territory and have four times the army of the Corinthians. Even if we send all we have trained, it won't be enough to stop them, and the Corinthians will fall. Then, angry at us for our alliance and aid, the Arcadians will turn their sights to Didymos, knowing we're now weakened from war, and unable to repel their greater army. Rather, I'd send an emissary, and tribute, to the Arcadian king to start an alliance with *them*. Especially since the Arcadians border the Dorians, who are our biggest threat. Should the Dorians ever turn their eyes on our wealth and lands, it would benefit us to have an alliance with the kingdom that borders them on the north and east while we have them on the south. Even with their greatly trained forces, the Dorians can't win a war on three fronts against a united enemy with mutual disdain for them."

"Why should the Arcadians trust us after we've just broken an alliance with the Corinthians?"

"What fool truly trusts an ally? The Arcadian king's smarter than that, and he will understand and respect that you are too intelligent to be pulled into a losing war. Besides, he knows that an alliance with us could help him should the Dorians ever come after *his* holdings. If that's not enough of a reason, the Arcadian king is recently widowed. Your virgin daughter is one of the most beautiful of all women in Greece. Offer her hand to sweeten the tie."

I should have thought of that.

Styxx pretended not to have heard his father's mental comment. "So what did you do, Father?"

"I went with my advisors' suggestion." *I wonder if we can call back the emissary . . .* He lifted his cup in salute to Styxx. "Perhaps it's time I appoint you as one of my advisors."

Styxx scoffed. "Your advisors would be highly offended to have me in their ranks, given my age and war experience. They'd take it as a personal affront and think you're mocking them with my presence."

His father frowned. "When did you become so good at diplomacy?"

Birth. He'd been forced to navigate both his mother's and his father's capricious moods all his life. But his father had never asked his opinions before, and in the past, he'd been too sober to give them.

His father narrowed his eyes at him. "Here's my next question. Would you have the same answer if the Corinthians were led by a beautiful queen instead?"

Styxx laughed at the thought.

His laughter died an instant later as he looked up to see his sister approaching. By the pinched look on her face, he wondered if she hadn't heard his suggestion to marry her off. She was in a fierce pique and didn't care who knew it.

That brought out the little brother in him and he couldn't resist rankling her more. "Hey, it's lamb-head. Where have you been, sweet sister?"

"Away," she snapped angrily with a glare that should have left him in bloody pieces on the ground. Rudely, she dismissed him and turned to address her king. "Father, might I have a word alone with you?"

His father glanced at him before he answered. "Anything you have to say to me can be said in front of your brother. One day Styxx will be your king, too, and you will be answerable to him."

The expression on her face said that she couldn't think of anything worse. If only she knew what true hell and misery were. But then no one had ever beaten her for any offense. And they'd never held her down and . . .

Styxx winced at the vicious memories and lashed out at the one bitch who had slapped him every time she drew near. If not physically, verbally.

He should be whipped, Father . . . He's nothing but a spoiled, selfish bully.

Any time she could, she'd worsened his punishments. No doubt had she been on the hunting trip, she'd have encouraged them to be even rougher with him. Crueler.

Had he been sober, he'd have probably said nothing to her. But today . . .

"That's right," he said snidely, taking another drink of his wine. "That means you have to kiss my feet just like everyone else."

As if anyone ever had . . .

His father laughed at him. "You're such a scamp."

Ryssa bit her lip and pinned him with a glare that told him plainly she wished he were dead and burned. That she begrudged him every breath he took.

"So why are you here, kitten?" their father asked. "Do you wish a new trinket or clothes?"

"No. I want to bring Acheron home."

Styxx averted his gaze as those words went through him and

made his heart skip a beat. Did she somehow know what Estes had done to them?

His father sputtered indignantly. "Now see here, what has gotten into your foolish head? I've told you repeatedly how I feel. That monster doesn't belong here."

Panicked terror spread through Styxx as he brushed his hand against the words Estes had branded into his groin. If his father sent for Acheron now, Estes might expose both of them just for vindictive meanness.

And how could Styxx deny what was clearly branded onto his body?

In fact, there was no telling what Estes would do, or Acheron, for that matter. His brother had gone crazy when Styxx had tried to free him. Acheron was completely docile and submissive to Estes's every whim.

What if Acheron said that Styxx had been a willing participant? That he'd begged them to whore him . . .

Styxx curled his lip and spoke out loud before he could stop himself. "Why would you want him here? He's a danger to all of us."

"A danger how?"

In ways you can't even begin to fathom, little girl.

The king glared at her. "You don't know what a demigod is capable of. He could kill your brother while he sleeps, kill me, kill all of us."

Acheron could tell the entire kingdom that I'm a whore he helped to train . . . No doubt, she'd enjoy seeing his humiliation made public. To know how he'd been degraded and abused.

For Acheron, she'd weep. For him, she'd only laugh.

I hope you get what you deserve . . .

Ryssa stamped her foot. "Why do you not fear for Estes?"

"Estes keeps him under control."

Styxx ground his teeth as those words echoed in his head. So his father knew that Estes drugged his brother. For that matter, he might even know that Estes beat Acheron into submission. And why should he care? The gods had borne witness that his father had very seldom spared *him* a beating.

For all he knew, his father had sent Estes the whips he used on Acheron. That thought sickened him to the point he almost vomited.

What else did his father know?

"Acheron belongs here, with us," Ryssa said, her voice cracking with her emotion.

Their father came to his feet. "You are a woman, Ryssa, and a young one at that. Your mind is best occupied with fashion and decorating. Planning your dress for a party. Acheron doesn't belong in this family. He never will. Now go find your mother and gossip. Styxx and I have important matters to discuss."

She glared at them both. "Matters more important than your own son?"

"He is not my son!"

Those words slashed at Styxx's heart. Every time his father said them, a part of him died. Because he knew the truth.

There was no way to legitimately deny one twin and embrace the other. The scar on his arm testified to the king's doubt where Styxx was concerned.

Just like Acheron . . .

Ryssa shook her head. "So that whole story you told me about protecting Acheron was wrong?"

Their father scowled. "What are you talking about?"

Her lips quivered before she answered. "You told me when they took Acheron away that you were doing it to protect him. You said that two heirs shouldn't be raised together, as it would be an added target to enemies. You said you would bring Acheron home when he was old enough. You never intended to return him here, did you?"

"Leave us!"

She spun on her heel and stormed off.

Stunned, Styxx replayed her last bit through his head. "Did you really tell her that, Father?"

161

He sat down in a huff. "Who knows? Who cares? I told her what I had to, to keep her from nagging at me. Take my word, Styxx, there is nothing more annoying than a woman wanting her way."

Ignoring that last bit, Styxx braced himself for the question he needed answered. "Why *did* you send Acheron to Atlantis? The truth, Father."

Because whenever I see his wretched eyes I hate you. His father's thought splintered his heart.

"What does it matter?" his father snapped angrily. "Acheron was *not* a member of this family. He didn't belong here."

"And the fact that he shares my face?"

"A trick of the gods."

But I'm the one with the powers. Acheron only has the eyes.

And his father would hate and deny him, too, if he *ever* learned that truth.

I really am nothing . . .

Worse, he had nothing.

DECEMBER 9, 9533 BC

Styxx was sound asleep when someone grabbed him and dragged him from his bed in the middle of the night.

"Where is he?"

His attacker slammed him against the wall so hard, his breath left his body.

"Damn it, boy! Answer me, or so help me, I'll gut you!"

Styxx finally recognized Estes's voice in the darkness. But for his life, he didn't understand why his uncle was so angry. "He's gone to Arcadia."

Estes backhanded him. "Not *my* brother, you stupid whore. Yours! What did you do with Acheron?"

What?

Styxx stared at him blankly. "He's with you."

Estes punched him in the stomach then began raining blows on him so fast and furiously that Styxx couldn't even put his arms up to defend himself. He was too dazed by the herbs, his sleep, and now the beating. Falling to the ground, he tried to crawl away, but Estes followed, kicking him as hard as he could with every step.

After a few minutes, he grabbed Styxx then jerked him over onto his back and pinned him to the floor. He pressed his forearm against Styxx's throat, cutting off his breathing.

Panting and in absolute misery, Styxx glared at Estes. Moonlight cut across his uncle's face, showing him the extent of Estes's fury . . . not that the beating hadn't clued him in.

"Where did you put your brother?"

"I haven't seen him since I left Atlantis."

Estes choked him so hard, Styxx's ears buzzed. His vision dimmed. "Don't lie to me."

"I'm not."

Evil glinted in his uncle's merciless eyes. "Let's see, shall we?" He pulled something from his purse and forced it into Styxx's mouth.

Styxx tried to spit it out, but Estes wouldn't let him. He sat on his chest and held him there with his hand over Styxx's mouth and nose until he was forced to swallow.

"If you're lying to me, boy . . . if you've taken Acheron from me, everyone in your entire empire *and* Greece will learn just what a whore you really are. They will all know how much you've begged to have a cock shoved in your mouth and ass. You hear me?"

Growling in fury, Styxx tried his best to fight his uncle off, but it was no use. Estes was too much stronger and larger.

And he wouldn't budge.

He held Styxx's hands by his face until the drug he'd given him took effect.

Styxx's breath left him in one gasp as the room swam and he lost complete control of his body and mind.

His uncle finally let go of his hands. "Can you hear me?"

163

He answered against his will. It was as if he had no ability to control his oral responses. "I hear you."

"Where is Acheron?"

"I don't know."

"When did you last see him?"

Styxx blinked slowly as the memory returned. "When he held my ankles while I was branded a whore by your guard. You had him blow across the burn and then you ordered him out."

"You haven't seen him since?"

"No."

Estes stroked Styxx's hair back from his face. "What else do you remember about Atlantis, little Styxx?"

A single tear slid from the corner of his eye as horrid memories assailed him. "Everything."

His uncle smiled in his face. "Everything? Let's put that to the test, shall we?"

DECEMBER 12, 9533 BC

Styxx came awake covered in blood and bruises, and aching all over. His head pounded and his throat was so raw, he wondered if it was bleeding, too.

"Here."

Something hit him in the head then landed on the mattress by his side.

Confused, he opened his eyes to see Estes in the room, not too far away. In that moment, the last two days slammed into him. "You fucking bastard!"

"But I'm not the one who's branded as a whore."

Styxx glared at him.

"Take the medicine. I know you're raw and in pain. But I

wanted to make a point. As bad as it is, it would have been a lot worse had you helped him . . . and if I can't find your brother, I will be back for you."

"What about my father?"

"He's in Arcadia, isn't he? Pity you didn't go with him. But he left you behind to attend to anything that might come *up* here at home."

Styxx's teeth chattered as more pain racked him. Estes had beat and raped him well. But at least he hadn't passed him around to anyone else.

This time.

"What are you waiting for, Highness? Do you want me to help you administer it?"

"No!" Styxx snarled. "I don't ever want your hands on me again."

"Well, that's not going to happen." Estes jerked his chin toward a small chest next to the bed. "I've left you a gift. Now I'm off to search more for your brother. I will find him, and if I learn that you've helped him in any way, you will regret it."

His hand shaking, Styxx pulled the suppository out of the pouch his uncle had thrown at him and inserted it while Estes watched.

Estes rolled him over, onto his back. He cupped Styxx's chin in his hand. "Don't worry, all of the bruising will heal before your father returns. As for your servants . . . I told them you've been sick with your nosebleeds and that I've been caring for you." He slapped him lightly on the cheek twice. "You might want to keep the lie going for a few more days."

He slid off the bed and raked a hungry smirk over Styxx's naked body. "Until next time, dear nephew."

Styxx felt his unshed tears prick his eyes as he stared at the ceiling. *May the gods damn you, Acheron!* If he was going to run, why couldn't he have gone *with* Styxx?

Why?

Because it would have saved you these past two days of abuse . . .

Deep inside, he hated his brother. But another part of him was happy that Acheron was free. That he'd managed to get out from under Estes's hostile fist.

Even if it meant hell for him later, he hoped Acheron was never found. Then at least one of them might have some peace and happiness.

FEBRUARY 20, 9532 BC

It was an unseasonably warm day as Styxx sat in the common seats of the gymnasium, watching the play below. His father had given him the morning off while he conferred with his advisors about war. There was a chance that his father might have to travel again, and he wanted Styxx to stay behind.

Something that terrified him.

Neither of them had heard from Estes. Styxx didn't know if that was a good thing or a bad one. Had Estes found his brother or was Acheron still free?

He hoped for the latter, but since Estes had left him alone, he feared his brother had been found.

Sighing, he glanced to the right and froze as he made eye contact with a man he'd never seen before. It was a licentious interest Styxx was acquainted with more times than he'd wanted to be.

Styxx pulled his cowl lower, making sure that none of his face was showing.

As soon as the play was over, he got up to leave. But he didn't get far before the man who'd been staring at him took his arm and pulled him to a stop.

At first Styxx thought he might have recognized him, yet if he knew who Styxx was, he'd know better than to touch him.

"Are you free-born?" the man asked. *Gods, I hope not. I'd love to be able to have you without issue.*

"Excuse me?"

He raked a hungry gaze over Styxx's body. "I wanted to talk to you for a bit."

Styxx turned and put as much distance between them as he could. But the man followed and caught up to him just outside the gymnasium.

This time, his grip was fierce. "Don't turn your back on me, boy."

"What do you think you're doing?" a deep male voice growled. "Have you any idea who you're addressing?"

Styxx turned his head to see Dorus, the youngest son of his father's head advisor. Though they'd only spoken in passing, they'd known each other for years.

But the last thing he wanted was to be outed like this. He glared a warning at Dorus.

"Who is he?" the man demanded.

"My servant," Dorus said quickly, catching on to the ruse. "Unhand him, right now. Or I'll have you arrested for trying to abscond with my property."

The man let go. "He belongs to you?" A speculative light darkened his gaze. "Do you ever rent him out?"

"No."

"Would you like to start?"

Dorus stiffened in anger. "Again, I say no. Now, if you'll excuse us." He snapped his fingers at Styxx, who fell in right behind him. After they rounded a building, Dorus stopped and looked back. "Ah, thank the gods, he's gone."

Styxx let out a relieved breath until Dorus arched a curious brow at him.

"I don't mean to be rude, Highness, but what are you doing dressed as a commoner?"

"I went to a play."

"And?"

Styxx shrugged. "I didn't want to sit in the royal box. No one leaves me alone there." Someone was forever trying to serve him or join him. It was a constant interruption to the point he couldn't hear the actors.

And everyone outside the box stared their hatred at him.

"So you went in common clothes and sat in the common area without your guards ... fascinating."

Styxx froze as he realized he wasn't hearing Dorus's thoughts. How rare and wonderful. It didn't happen often, and he loved the mental silence. "Thank you for your aid. I won't forget it."

Dorus bowed to him. "Ever at your service, Highness. And should you ever desire to go again, let me know and I'll get you the worst seats in the house."

Styxx almost laughed at his unexpected humor. He started to leave then stopped himself. There was nothing at the palace to do. But the man beside him seemed a decent enough companion. At least for a few hours. "Dorus? Would you like to dine with me?"

"It would be my honor, Highness."

Styxx lowered his cowl as they walked toward a small kentro where they could eat in relative peace.

The owner came up immediately and bowed low before Styxx. "Highness, it's so good to see you again. Come, I have a private table for you." He led them through the small building, to a table and chaises in a back corner that had a curtain drawn up to shield it from the rest of the occupants. "Would you like your usual fare?"

"Please, Cosmos. Thank you."

He ran to gather it.

Styxx sat with his back to the wall while Dorus took the chaise across from him.

"It's good to be king, eh?" Dorus teased.

If the bastard only knew the truth ... "Prince, and yes. Some days it is."

"But not all days?"

Styxx swallowed hard. It was very rare he enjoyed the privileges of his rank. But he wasn't about to confide in someone he didn't know that well. Someone who would think him petty for complaining. "Were you at the play?"

"No, Highness. I was returning home from the market when I just happened to catch a glimpse of you. At first, I wasn't sure if I was correct. But once I was ..."

Cosmos returned with kylixes of wine, while his servants brought food. Styxx and Dorus poured a small bit of wine on the floor as tribute to the gods before they took their own drink.

Styxx spent several hours with Dorus, talking about nothing and everything. By the time they parted company, he had a friend. At least that's what he assumed they were. Since he'd never had one before, he wasn't sure.

He's probably only talking to you because you're prince. Maybe. But he'd seemed sincere in his interest. And since Styxx couldn't hear his thoughts, why not? Even if Dorus had ulterior motives, it had been nice to laugh and converse with someone for once, while not knowing that the person thought him a complete and utter spoiled ass.

"Where have you been?"

He paused inside the palace at his father's demanding tone. "In town." He frowned as he saw the king's stern glower. "Is something the matter?"

"I have received disturbing news from your uncle."

Styxx went cold as dread washed over him. "What does he say?"

"Acheron has run away. He wrote to ask if I'd seen him. Have you?"

Styxx forced himself to betray no emotion whatsoever. "No, Father. Did Uncle say anything else?"

Like how he whored me to others ...

"Not really. He asked after you and sent you a gift."

His stomach cramped with dread. "What gift?"

"I didn't open it. It's in your room. Why don't you freshen up? Dinner will be served in about an hour."

He gave his father a curt bow before he went to his room on shaking legs. What would Estes send to him?

This can't be good.

Closing the door to his room, he saw the box waiting on the table. His heart pounded as he crossed the room then lifted the lid and cursed out loud. Inside was the *erotiki sfaira* his uncle had removed from his tongue and the small gold tag that had been around his neck. The tag of a tsoulus.

Styxx opened the note.

If I don't have my property back in my home by your birthday, you will take his place. Were I you, I'd do everything I can to help my father find him.

Styxx slammed the box shut and started to throw it into the fire. But he caught himself.

What if it was found only partially burned?

So he hid it deep in his chest near the window. He'd take it and throw it in the sea on the morrow.

The note, however, he burned, making sure not a trace of it was left behind.

What am I going to do?

He refused to help Estes find Acheron. He'd never be able to live with himself if he returned his own brother to that existence.

Are you willing to be a whore in his stead? After what he did to you?

Acheron betrayed you and held you down and laughed while Estes branded you a tsoulus . . .

"*Welcome to my world, brother. I want you to think of me every time you see 'whore' next to your cock . . .*"

He was furious about that and Acheron's harsh words. He wanted his brother's blood for it.

But wanting blood and actually condemning someone to something so horrific . . .

I can't do it. He wasn't his father.

Besides, he was already a whore himself. And as Estes had shown him, he could be attacked even in the safety of his own bed. A bed he hadn't slept in since. He couldn't bear it. Every night, he dragged his blankets into the receiving room to sleep on the floor and every morning, he returned them to his bed so no one knew.

Yet if Estes had his way, everyone would learn what he was. And how he'd been used.

JUNE 21, 9532 BC

"I do not understand women."

Styxx didn't say anything as his father continued to rail against Ryssa as they journeyed to the summer palace. His father had summoned her home and she'd refused to return.

So here they were, fetching her back.

"What gets into their minds?"

Styxx shrugged. "Mites?"

His father laughed. "Only you could lighten my mood this day." Sighing, his father dismounted at the steps.

Styxx slid to the ground as the guards with them dismounted. The palace looked empty. But then it always did when they weren't in residence.

Normally, they'd have moved in a month ago, but with the war looming, his father had decided to stay closer to the mainland and in the palace that was easier to fortify and more centrally located.

His father waited for the guards to open the door before he entered to find the palace as empty inside as it appeared outside. But as they searched through it, it was obvious that someone was in residence. The furniture was uncovered in several of the smaller rooms, and Ryssa's bedchambers were fresh with flowers.

The king shook his head as he glanced around. "She must be out back."

Styxx followed his father through the doors and into the garden.

"She's always favored the orchard," he reminded his father. Though she'd had a fit any time Styxx had tried to join her there. The last time they'd stayed here, she'd even hit him in the head with an apple when he'd gone down to tell her she had a letter from their aunt. Then she'd had the nerve to tell their father that he'd spied on her.

He'd been given a dozen lashes for that. *A woman needs her privacy, boy. You don't ever spy on your sister.*

And he'd never told his father about the apple he'd taken to his head. Because *that* his father would have viewed as being a crybaby on *his* part, which would have resulted in another beating.

As they entered the orchard, Styxx slowed at the sound of two voices.

Ryssa's and Acheron's.

He wanted to grab his father and pull him away from here, but it was too late. His father had already seen them and he was furious over it.

Ryssa pushed herself up from where she'd been sitting on the ground beside Acheron. "Father. Why are you here?"

"Where have you been?" he demanded as he moved forward. "It's already the middle of the year and no one has seen you."

"I told you, I wanted time—"

"Father?" Acheron's excited voice interrupted Ryssa and it turned their father's attention toward him.

Damn it, Acheron. Why can't you learn when to run?

Then again, Acheron did run. Just not in the right direction. His face alight with joy, he rushed to embrace their father.

Styxx winced as his father shoved Acheron away ruthlessly and raked his twin brother with a repugnant grimace that cut through him like a dagger. *How can you be like that with him and claim to love me?*

They were absolutely identical.

Except for the whore brand on Styxx's groin . . .

Acheron frowned in confusion as he looked to Ryssa for an explanation.

I'm sorry, Acheron. I didn't want you to know. Ryssa's thoughts were loud and clear. She'd been lying to Acheron all this time. Telling him that their father loved him and would welcome him home.

Stupid bitch. Why would she be so cruel?

But that answer he knew . . . *No woman can ever be trusted. They are all treacherous beasts.* His mother had schooled him well on that knowledge.

"What is *he* doing here?" their father demanded.

Styxx wasn't paying much attention to them as Acheron locked gazes with him. His brother looked so happy to see him . . . It definitely wasn't the same reception Acheron had given him in Atlantis when Styxx had tried to set him free.

In many ways, this wasn't the same Acheron at all. The man in front of him was much more akin to the brother he'd once known. The brother Styxx had risked his life for.

And the thought that their father would send Acheron back to Atlantis horrified him.

Why didn't you run farther than this, brother?

Why hadn't his stupid sister taken Acheron someplace really safe?

"Guards!" his father shouted.

Styxx winced, wishing he could grab his brother and run. But they would catch them and there was no telling what their father might do to them.

What Estes would do or say over it.

Ryssa gaped. "What are you doing?" she shrieked at her king and father.

There was no mercy in their father's eyes. "I'm sending him back where he belongs."

Acheron's jaw went slack as he turned toward Ryssa with terrified eyes.

She shook her head. "You can't do that."

Their father turned on her with a glare so hateful it made her take a step back in fear. "Have you lost your mind, woman? Why would you coddle such a monster?"

"Father, please," Acheron begged, falling down on his knees before him. He wrapped his arms around the king's leg. "Please don't send me back. I'll do anything you ask. I swear it. I'll be good. I won't look at anyone. I won't hurt anyone." Acheron kissed the king's feet reverently.

Styxx thought he'd vomit at the sight that reminded him of when he'd been tortured in the Dionysion. He'd made the same pleas, and his father had walked out on him with no compassion or regard.

Just as he did Acheron.

"I am not your father, maggot." He kicked Acheron away then glared at his most beloved Ryssa with venom. "I told you, he doesn't belong with this family. Why would you defy me so?"

"He's your son," she sobbed. "How can you deny him? It's your face he has. Styxx's face. How can you love one and not the other?"

Because he doesn't love me, bitch. Not really.

Their father reached down and gripped Acheron's jaw tightly in his hand. He pulled him roughly to his feet so that Acheron faced Ryssa. "Those are not my eyes. Those are not the eyes of a human!"

Ryssa turned to him then, weeping. "Styxx ... He's your brother. Look at him."

He glanced to his father in panic, unsure of what his father would do if he stood up for Acheron right now. In the mood his father was in, he was as likely to turn on Styxx as he was Acheron.

Better to let the old man calm down than to anger him further.

Sorry, brother. Last time I put my ass on the line for you, you handed me over without a second thought or ounce of remorse.

No ... worse, you helped whore me and branded me as one.

His gut knotting, Styxx shook his head and repeated Acheron's vicious words that he'd said to Estes in a very similar situation. "I have no brother."

His father shoved Acheron back.

Acheron stood there quietly, his eyes dazed by the harsh reality of how their father felt about him. It was something Styxx coped with every single day of his life.

But what hurt was that he knew the exact thoughts in his

brother's mind. They were the same ones that haunted him constantly. Acheron was reliving every perversion of Estes's. Every disgusting, humiliating touch . . .

His brother dropped his head and wrapped his arms around himself.

"Take him back to Atlantis!" the king ordered the guards.

Styxx cringed at his father's harsh sentence. A sentence the stupid bastard didn't even comprehend. But Styxx knew.

And so did Acheron.

Without a word of protest or fight, Acheron followed them to the front of the palace.

He was again the petrified slave who'd caused Styxx to be captured . . .

Ryssa glared at their father with hatred burning deep in her eyes. "Estes abuses him, Father. Constantly. He sells Acheron to—"

Their father slapped her.

"That is my brother you speak of. How dare you!"

Stunned, Styxx went bug-eyed. *Never* had his father laid a hand to her. That alone testified to what Estes had told him. His father would defend Estes to the bitter end.

Even against his own children.

"And that is my brother you cast off. How dare *you!*" Ryssa snarled before she stormed after Acheron.

"Lying whore! Just like her drunken mother!"

Styxx couldn't breathe as those harsh words slammed into him. His father had *never* spoken of his beloved kitten like that. If he would turn on his treasured daughter, Styxx didn't have a single hope. "What if she isn't lying, Father?"

The expression on his father's face made him take a step back. "Are you to defame my brother, too?"

Not with that look on your face, old man. I'm not that stupid or drunk. "Forgive me, Father."

Wanting to put distance between them, Styxx hurried after Ryssa.

He found her in the front entranceway of the palace. Acheron held his head even lower than before. His grip on his arms was so tight that his knuckles were white.

"Acheron?" Ryssa breathed.

He refused to look at her while Styxx hovered in the doorway behind them.

She brushed the hair back from Acheron's face with a tenderness she'd never shown Styxx. "Acheron, please. I didn't know they'd come today. I thought we were safe."

"You lied to me," he said simply as he stared blankly at the floor. "You told me my father loved me. That no one was ever going to make me leave here. You swore that to me."

Styxx shook his head as his own anger and pain ripped through him. How could she lie to Acheron like that? Surely she'd asked for Acheron's return as much as he had and had been given the same hate-filled *no* from their father, who would never acknowledge his other son.

"I know, Acheron," she sobbed.

Acheron turned to her then to glare at her with a hatred that was searing. "You made me trust you."

"I'm so sorry."

Styxx had to bite back bitter laughter. *Sorry, Ryssa?* Really? The pathetic moron had no idea what Estes was going to do to Acheron on his return. But Styxx knew. His uncle had already shown him.

Acheron was going to wish himself as dead as Styxx did.

His brother shook his head. "I was never to step foot out of my chambers without escort. Never was I to leave the household. *Idikos* will punish me for leaving. He'll . . . " Horror filled his eyes as he tightened his grip on himself even more.

Styxx's stomach heaved. He took a step forward then caught himself. If he tried to help Acheron now, they would both pay. Dearly.

The horses were brought forward.

His brother looked at Ryssa. "I wish you'd left me as I was."

She should have. Because this was going to be so much worse

on him. The Acheron who'd fought him months ago in Atlantis had been relegated to his fate. The one in front of him now had tasted life without Estes and his perversions.

To send him back to that now . . .

His sister was the worst of all. Estes would tighten his grip on Acheron even more. His brother would never know another moment of peace or freedom. Not so long as Estes and their father lived.

Styxx forced himself to stay and say nothing as the guards hauled Acheron into a chariot. His brother never looked back as they drove him away.

"Acheron!" Maia, the cook's young daughter, screamed as she came tearing out of the doorway.

Only then did Acheron look back. His face stoic, tears glistened in his swirling silver eyes.

Styxx panted, knowing better than to let his father see his emotions. The king was too volatile. And the last thing Styxx needed was a beating. Not if he was to do what he planned.

Ryssa fell to her knees and pulled the little girl into her arms. The two of them wailed until his ears rang with it.

"Get up!" his father snarled as he finally joined them. "I will not have you cry for something like him."

"I hate you!" she screamed.

Styxx snatched her back before their father slapped her again or did something worse to her. "Go to your room, Ryssa. Now."

She raked Styxx with the ugliest sneer imaginable. "I wish it was *you* I'd found tied to that bed! *You* I would have left there to be used like the worthless whore you are. It's what *you* deserve the way you use people and discard them!"

For a full minute, Styxx couldn't catch his breath as those brutal words slapped him harder than any blow. In his mind, he saw himself on that bed again being used like he was nothing.

Knowing if he stayed, he'd beat her himself, Styxx left her to their father.

Breathe. Calm down. She doesn't know.

Still, it didn't take the pain away. She truly meant what she'd said. He heard it in her thoughts. She held no love or regard for him whatsoever, and she would gladly condemn him to Estes's custody to be a whore in Acheron's stead.

Her hatred of him was as unreasoning and unfounded as his father's for Acheron.

Styxx pressed his hand to his stomach as grief, shame, and horror racked him. But beneath all that was the bitter agony of Ryssa's rejection of him. Why did she hate him so much? Never in his life had he done anything to her.

"Styxx?"

He flinched at his father's call. Blinking, he took a deep breath and forced his emotions into restraint. Gods help him if his father saw him like this.

Styxx couldn't stand being hurt anymore. He just wanted a modicum of peace for a few minutes.

"Majesty?" he said as he returned to his father's side.

"We'll stay the night and leave at dawn."

"Yes, Sire." Styxx hesitated. "Father? Would you mind if I took a few hours to myself tonight?"

A slow smile curled his lips. "There's a brothel in town that's one of the best in all Greece. Have fun."

Disgusted with what his father's mind had defaulted to, Styxx waited until his father was gone before he made his way to the stable. As quickly as he could, he saddled two fresh horses and took off after his brother.

For the love of the gods, Acheron. Don't get me caught again.

Styxx hung back until he was sure the guards were asleep. Taking care to make no sound whatsoever, he made his way over to Acheron, who'd been tied to a stake in the ground.

"Acheron?" he whispered, touching his brother on the shoulder.

Acheron came awake with a start. He grimaced as he saw Styxx in the fading firelight. "What are you doing here?"

"I'm freeing you." When Styxx went to cut the rope, Acheron stopped him. "What are you doing?" he asked Acheron in a shocked whisper.

"You already told me I was no brother of yours. Why are you really here?"

Styxx glared at him. "You denied *me* first."

With a fierce scowl, Acheron scoffed. "I have *never* once in my life denied you! You and your father are the ones who threw *me* out."

Styxx ground his teeth. Acheron truly had no memory of his being in Atlantis. At all. And unfortunately, this was not the time to argue about it. "We have to go."

"Go where?"

"Anywhere. I can't leave you to this. Not again."

Acheron caught his hand then shoved him back before he could cut the tie. "Are you fucking stupid? Do you know what happens to boys our age on their own?"

Yes, but they weren't drugged out of their minds now. While one of them alone was weak, the two of them could protect each other. "I can work as a mercenary. They make good money."

"And I'm what? The camp whore?" Acheron asked incredulously. "What do you think they'd do to me while you're out playing hero and warrior? Really?" He raked a brutal glare over Styxx's body. "And don't fool yourself, *Highness*." He sneered the title. "You have the same unnatural lure I do that makes everyone who sees you want to fuck you, too. The only reason you're left alone is because you're a known prince. If you think you're any better than me, I defy you to walk into a town where they don't know you and watch how fast you're thrown on the ground and butt-fucked until you can't walk straight."

Those words tore through him, especially the part that was truest. But still . . .

"You really want me to leave you here?"

Acheron's glower sliced through him. "I want *all* of you to leave me alone. Forever. I'm done with you."

He well understood that feeling and declaration.

Even so, Styxx couldn't leave his brother defenseless. He pulled the dagger from his belt and buried it in the ground between them. "Do us both a favor. When you get back, drive that straight through Estes's dead heart."

Acheron raked him with another sneer. "You're the soldier. Why don't *you*?"

Wanting to soothe his brother and make him see reason, Styxx reached for him. "Acheron—"

He knocked his hand away. "You're dead to me. You've been dead to me since the day you let them take me from my home."

Styxx was aghast that he'd throw *that* in his face. "I was seven."

"*So was I.*"

Rage darkened Styxx's gaze. For *this* selfish asshole, who held something against him he couldn't have even begun to fight, he'd been whored? Beaten?

Branded?

"Fuck you, Acheron!"

"Why not? You're the only one who hasn't."

Styxx scoffed. "Not according to Estes."

"What's that supposed to mean?"

Unable to even contemplate *that* nightmare, Styxx held his hands up in surrender. "You have a weapon. Use it, if you're man enough. I'm done with you, *brother*. I will never again jeopardize my ass for yours. *Ever*."

Rising, Styxx glared down at his twin then he turned and walked away.

You can't save those who don't want to be saved.

Like Ryssa, Acheron made no sense to him. If he were Acheron and he had any chance to stay away from Atlantis, he'd take it.

But what the Hades . . .

His deadline was almost up. Now Estes would have his pet back. Styxx wouldn't have to go to Atlantis in his brother's stead. He should be happy.

Yet he wasn't. How could he be happy that his brother was so terrified and beaten down that he wouldn't even try to fight anymore?

In this, no one won. Least of all Acheron.

Styxx swung himself up on his horse and took the reins of the one he'd brought for his brother. Against his will, he looked back to see Acheron lying down on the ground by the campfire as if he was completely content to go back to Estes's home.

Part of him still wanted to charge into camp and force his brother to leave. But Acheron and Estes had already shown him what that would get him in the end.

Fucked.

When someone is drowning and you try to save them, they're more likely to drown you before you pull them out.

Acheron had done enough damage to him. He would not allow him to do any more, no matter how much pity Styxx held for him in his heart.

"Good luck, brother. May you find peace someday."

JUNE 23, 9532 BC

"Happy birthday, you little prick!"

His head throbbing in agony, Styxx barely had time to duck before Ryssa lobbed her gift at him. It struck the wall beside his face. "What is your problem?"

"You! Every day I have to look at you, knowing what Acheron is going through, is one I hate you more."

Styxx bent over and fished his "gift" from the floor. He held it up for her to see. "Thank you, dearest sister. I shall treasure it always, and especially the manner in which it was received."

Twisting her face up, she silently mocked his words. "You think you're so clever. You're nothing but a fatuous, spoiled brat."

"One wrapped so tight in familial love that it suffocates me," he said sarcastically.

"You absolutely disgust me. How can you stand here in your comfort while your twin suffers so?"

It wasn't easy, but Acheron had given him no choice whatsoever. Styxx curled his lips at her. "What do you know of it?"

"I know that Estes sells him!"

Styxx froze as he saw his father nearing them. If he heard one word of this . . .

There was no telling what the king might do to her.

He dropped his tone so that only Ryssa could hear him. "And you'd best listen to me, dear sister. For your own good. Estes would never do such a thing. It's another of your lies designed to make us free Acheron. Do you understand?"

She slapped him so hard his ears rang from the blow. "You're a selfish, worthless coward! I burn for the day when I stand over your corpse. Better yet, I would gladly pay any cost to see you whored one day the way Acheron is."

Styxx glared at her as those words pricked memories he tried to keep buried. "And you should be grateful I'm not king yet. I'd have you whipped for such treachery." Wiping the blood from his lips, he left her and headed for his room.

"Styxx?"

He hesitated at his father's call from downstairs. Given how badly his face burned, he knew his sister's handprint would be plainly evident.

Shit . . .

"Yes, Father," he said without moving.

"Could you come here, please?"

Double shit.

Sighing, Styxx turned and closed the distance between them.

His father's eyes widened as he saw the mark. "What happened to you?"

Styxx rubbed his hand over his stinging cheek. "Said something to a woman I shouldn't have."

"What woman? Name her and I'll have her whipped for the audacity."

Sure you would . . . But honestly, he didn't want to chance it. "It's fine, Father. Some might say I deserved it."

That didn't placate the king at all. "You are the prince and must be respected as such!"

Did that include his uncle molesting him, or his twin? He had to bite back that hostility before it got him a lot worse than a bitch-slap. "Did you need something, Father?"

"I wanted to go over the banquet tonight with you."

Styxx glanced up to see Ryssa standing beside his mother on the stair ledge. Both were staring a hole through him. He was so tired of it all. The lies, the deceit.

The shame.

But worse was the knowledge that if the truth ever came out, Ryssa would gloat. His mother, too. The two of them would probably pay Estes for a front row seat to watch his uncle plow him open.

Unaware that Styxx was distracted, the king continued on. "Would you mind seeing Senator Nileas about the proposal he said he'd have to me yesterday? He should be in the forum this time of day."

"I shall see it done, Father." Ignoring his mother and sister, Styxx left the palace then headed for the forum in the center of town.

His face had finally stopped burning by the time he reached the building where many of the noblemen gathered to drink and philosophize away from their wives. Since he could hear their thoughts and knew the majority of them despised him with a venom that made Ryssa look like a devoted fan, he tended to avoid this place whenever he could.

Ironically, the thing they criticized and held against him most was the fact that he'd refused to pick one of them as his "mentor." Rather he'd designated Galen instead of a nobleman because he knew Galen wouldn't expect him to bend over when they were alone together. Nor would Galen expect political favors from him later.

And the old war dog held at least a modicum of regard for him. While his choice was extremely unconventional, it gave him one less nightmare to endure.

"Where's Nileas?" Styxx asked the first senator he found in the complex.

"In the back, Highness. With Patrokles."

Styxx paused to turn toward the two guards who trailed him. The nobles didn't like "commoners" spying on them while they spoke freely. "Stay here. I'll be right back."

Reluctantly, they obeyed.

Styxx made his way through the building until he heard two voices that locked his legs.

"I'm telling you right now, it's true. I had both the prince and a boy who looks just like him, except for his eyes, in Atlantis, in my bed at the same time."

"You're lying!"

"Ask Melus if you doubt me. He was there, too, and took a turn with both of them."

"When?"

"Last fall."

"You're such a liar."

"Liar, am I? Next time you're around Styxx, drop something and look up his chiton. His entire left side and buttocks are horribly scarred. He even has a brand mark on his ass and left nipple."

Styxx couldn't breathe as those details racked him and verified the truth of the boast. When Estes had told him he'd sold him, Styxx had assumed all the men had been Atlantean.

Not . . .

"You've no idea how distracting it is to see him now when all I can think about is how much I'd love to have him on his knees in front of me again. You can't tell it by looking at him, but he has the most amazing tongue. I don't know who trained the prince, but kudos to a most apt pupil."

Unable to deal with it or face the men who were talking about him like that, Styxx spun about and left. By the time he returned to the palace, it was all he could do not to scream in horror. Panic took full possession of him.

What do I do?

That bullshit would eventually reach his father. And there was no telling what he'd do to Styxx for it. The only thing he knew for certain was that his father would find some reason to blame him for the whole ordeal.

Everyone would know he was a whore. That he was a branded tsoulus . . .

How many other Greeks and Didymosians had bought him?

Had Estes lied about the number?

They know I'm a whore . . .

My father will brutally execute me for this.

Terrified, he walked furious circles in his room as he tried to decide what to do.

And he had a banquet tonight where they'd all be in attendance . . . laughing and reminiscing. Possibly dropping things to verify his scars.

I'll be able to hear their thoughts.

If he got around anyone who'd slept with him, he'd know it. Their thoughts would override his.

I can't do this.

Even if his father beat him. He could not go to that banquet. How could he walk out there with his head held high while "whore" was branded on his body and there were men in the crowd who'd bought and screwed him?

His hands shaking, Styxx grabbed the wine from his table and drank it.

No, he needed his herbs.

He went to the chest and pulled out the last batch his uncle had brought him. After taking out three times the normal amount, he used his finger to stir it into the wine then he downed it in two gulps.

Please, gods, please let me die . . .

He laid down on the floor and closed his eyes, hoping and praying he never opened them again.

JUNE 24, 9532 BC

"You disgust me!"

Why am I not dead? Styxx groaned as his father continued to shout at him through the pounding agony of his head.

"I've never been more embarrassed in my entire life!"

Then you should try waking up naked, chained to a bed by your uncle who sold you to men you're forced to see repeatedly.

"How could you do this to me?" his father continued to rail.

Oh yeah, I really screwed *you, old man . . . I'm not the one who sent you into the woods to be raped, and then laughed with your rapists for two days.*

The one who left you to be tortured for your own good by your beloved priests.

He'd laugh if it wasn't so damn pathetic. Licking his dry lips, Styxx cracked his eyes open to see his father standing over him. "What did I do?"

"You laid up here drunk while we held a banquet in *your* honor. Do you know how that looks?"

Like I'm the spoiled, happy prince everyone stupidly thinks I am?

"It was so disrespectful to me and to the senators and their families. Is this the kind of king you want to be? Is it?"

I don't want to be king at all, especially not to senators who paid my uncle to screw me.

"Get up!" His father kicked him.

Styxx grimaced before he sat up. His eyes widened instantly as his stomach heaved. Scrambling, he barely made it to the chamber pot before his stomach lost all its contents.

"Look at you. You're pathetic. I have never in my life seen a sorrier sight."

You should get out more. He vomited again.

His father raked him with a merciless glower. "As soon as you finish with your self-absorbed, self-inflicted illness, you're to be caned for it."

Styxx wiped at his mouth. "You said I was too old for that."

"You're too old to act like a petulant, out-of-control child. If you're going to behave as one, I'm going to treat you as one."

He started to protest then his stomach churned again.

"And I intend to watch every stroke you're given."

Styxx closed his eyes, grateful beyond measure for that mercy even if it meant more strokes for him. Thank the gods. He could almost smile at the relief he felt.

Drawing a ragged breath, he propped himself against the wall and stared up at his father. "I think I shall need help walking down for it."

"You think this is funny?"

Hilarious, really. In a pathetic horror story kind of way. Why not laugh at this point? Tears certainly had gotten him nothing but mockery. Why not try a different approach?

"What do you want me to say, Father? I'm sorry? Fine. I'm sorry. Please, find the gentle benevolent mercy in your heart to forgive me for the dishonor and disservice I've done you with my neglect."

"You dare mock me? No, you're not sorry at all. But you will be." He kicked at Styxx's feet. "Guards!"

They entered immediately.

Styxx swept them with a hooded glance, wondering if one of them had fucked him, too.

His father stepped back so that they could seize him in rough grips that enjoyed giving him as much misery as possible. "Take His Highness to the scold."

Styxx winced as they jerked him to his feet and all but dragged him down to it. Their unspoken insults rang in his head alongside the ones his father hurled at him.

As if I care anymore.

187

They threw open the door to the guards' room and hauled him inside. The scold's eyes lit up with greedy, lust-filled delight when he saw him there.

Styxx gave him a cold smile. "Bad luck, old man. My father intends to watch."

That took the joy out of him, but the look that replaced it promised Styxx dire retribution.

Oh yeah, this was going to hurt. Badly.

So be it.

"Seventy lashes."

Even the scold sucked his breath in on the severity of his father's order.

Styxx met his father's gaze without flinching and laughed. "Why stop there, Father? Why not go for one hundred?"

"You continue this insolence and I will."

Before he could say another thing, the scold shoved the leather into his mouth. "For the sake of the gods, Highness, shut up," he breathed in Styxx's ear.

The scold met his father's gaze. "Am I pardoned, Majesty?"

"Yes."

"Highness?"

Did it matter what he thought? Who was the bastard who came up with this twisted formality?

Glaring at his father, Styxx nodded curtly.

The scold took him into his "beautiful" room and tied him to the bench he knew so well. Styxx watched in silence as the scold selected the cane then went behind him to lift his chiton and expose his buttocks for the beating.

"Wait!" his father said before it began.

Styxx ground his teeth in fear as a new horror seized his heart. Had Estes branded "whore" there, too?

Gods, what does he see?

"Remove his gag."

"Yes, Your Majesty." The scold pulled the leather out then stepped back and averted his gaze.

"Where did the scars on your thighs and buttocks come from, boy?"

Styxx gaped at the stupidity of that single question. "They burned and bled the demons out of me, Father. Don't you remember?"

"With hot brands?"

No . . . cold ones.

Was the old man senile? What did he think they'd use? Rose petals?

"You saw my wounds when Estes brought you in."

His father tugged at Styxx's chiton until he'd exposed Styxx's left side and the vicious, puckered scars that marked him from armpit to thigh. For several seconds, his father said nothing as his gaze flitted over them, and then down to the scar on Styxx's forearm where the bastard had cut him, and finally to the scars his mother's tender loving hand had dealt him.

Thankfully, Styxx was bent so that the most horrifying scar that marked him as a whore was hidden from his father's gaze.

"You're excused," the king finally said to the scold.

Bowing, he left them.

His father swallowed hard. "I never really saw your body when you were at the Dionysion. I barely looked at your face."

Funny, it hadn't seemed that way to him. He would have sworn his father glared at his wounds with sick satisfaction.

His father covered Styxx's side with his chiton so he wouldn't have to see the scars anymore. "How many months were you there again?"

That question slapped him hard. "You don't remember?"

His father shook his head. "But you do, don't you?"

How could he ever forget? "Every heartbeat I spent there under the priests' *tender* care is *branded* into my memory, Father."

His father winced then untied his hands. *You've been through enough, boy.*

Styxx pushed himself up as his father left without another word.

His head pounding, Styxx made his way back to his room. He knew how bad the scars on the front of him were. How much worse were the ones on his back that his father had been so revolted by them?

I should ask the senators who've screwed me since they've seen them.

He pressed his hand to his skull, wishing he could squeeze his head until he drove it all out forever.

I can't take this anymore. He was too young to have this much horror. Too young to hurt like this when there was no end for it in sight. No way out ...

Damn you, Acheron.

Ever since his brother had thrown it in his face, he'd noticed how true Acheron's words were. The hungry stares from everyone who saw him. Looks and actions he'd assumed were from his being prince. But Acheron was right. People coveted his body even when they didn't know he had a title. And they were a lot more aggressive when they didn't know.

Even if he ran away, they would treat him just as his uncle had. Like a piece of savory meat on a banquet table. He'd become his brother ...

A well-paid, overused whore.

Not that he wasn't already.

I just want one single moment of peace where my memories don't shred my soul. One day without pain.

With no better thought, he washed himself and changed his clothes then snuck past his guards to get his horse.

There was only one thought on his mind as he rode from the stable, toward the high shoreline.

To end this stygian nightmare once and for all.

Styxx cursed as he reined his horse and slid from the saddle so that he was on solid, nonmoving ground. "Ah, gods ... " Why today of all days did he have to have one of his more vicious headaches?

It hurt so badly he couldn't even breathe. And then it started ...

That damned nosebleed.

Unable to stand it, he sank to his knees and didn't bother trying to stop his nose. Pressing his hand to his eye, he stared out at the sea far below. The waves crashed against jagged rocks. It looked so soothing and pleasant.

He remembered when he'd been a small child and his father would take him to the ships to meet with their captains and owners, and he'd watch fishermen's children playing and laughing in the surf. He'd wanted to join them, but his father had refused.

It's common entertainment for common people. You are a prince. It's time you acted like one.

As the prince, according to his father, he wasn't to mix with *them*. The familiarity would cause them to see him as a lesser being. *You must always hold yourself to a higher standard and conduct yourself with dignity. A king can only lead when others respect him.*

And who could respect a king who'd been tied facedown over a punishment bench and violated? One who'd been bartered and sold, and . . .

Branded.

Styxx cried out in anger. *I'm done with this world. I've had enough.*

That was what he'd come here to do. End it. He watched the surf below with a hungry gaze. One step. Then both he and Acheron would be free of this horror. Free to play in the waves and laugh like other people did . . .

You're stronger than this!

Was he? He didn't feel strong. Not today. Today, he felt like the incompetent wretch they accused him of being. He felt used and powerless.

Shamed to the core of his blackened and burned-out soul.

One step . . .

No more headaches or nosebleeds to suffer. No more gleeful humiliation shoved down his throat. No more hatred glaring at him from his mother's and sister's eyes. From the eyes of everyone who thought him a spoiled, beloved prince who had no care in the entire world.

I just want peace.

Determined to see it through, Styxx pushed himself to his feet. His horse, Troian, sniffed at his shoulder. Styxx sank his hand into the long, soft black mane then gently patted him. Troian had been his only real friend.

He hugged his horse tight. "It's all right, boy." He pulled the bridle off, knowing his horse would return to the stable without it, and this way he wouldn't have to fear Troian snagging it on something and getting hurt or trapped.

After nuzzling the horse's neck one last time, he stepped away. His heart pounded in a rhythm that matched his head as he watched the waves roll in. It would hurt when he hit the rocks, but hopefully it wouldn't last long.

With luck, he'd be dead before he hit them.

He dropped the bridle to the ground and turned around so that he could see the countryside he'd been raised and groomed to rule. It would survive without him. His people would probably be better off. At least they'd have a king now who was worthy of his crown.

One who hadn't been mocked and sold.

Swallowing the pain that never ceased, Styxx stepped back and fell into nothing.

Winds rushed over his falling body, whipping his hair and clothes. It seemed to take forever before he hit the water. He slammed into it so hard, he swore every bone in his body shattered. The waves rushed over him, dragging him down to the frigid depths of the vibrant blue sea. He swallowed and choked on the water as it violently invaded his body then sputtered and coughed.

Everything went black.

But after a brief period of nothing, he was still alive.

Even underwater . . .

How? It couldn't be possible. It couldn't. Yet, the surf carried him to shore and threw him roughly against it.

Battered and bruised, he lay on the sand, aching and freezing.

And dismally alive.

I can't even die right. How pathetic am I?

As he lay there in more pain than he'd ever known, a raw, hateful truth slapped him in the face. The gods had no intention of sparing him even one heartbeat of the misery they'd damned him to. They wouldn't even allow him death as a way to escape it.

You sick bastards!

He would cry at the despair he felt, but there were no more tears in his eyes. Why bother? All tears had ever done was cause him to be beaten more.

Disgusted, he dragged himself out of the water and staggered up the shoreline. One ankle felt badly sprained. Maybe his arm, too. Not that it mattered.

Nothing mattered now that he knew his real place in the world. Not to be king or prince.

Not even to be human . . .

I am damned and cursed. Forever.

With a ragged sigh, he crawled up to the road and paused as he saw how far he'd have to go to get home. Had he been whole, it would have been too damned far.

As he was right now . . .

"I'll never make it." Not like this.

Maybe some bandits will . . .

What?

Kill him?

He laughed at their imagined stunned dismay when they learned he was immortal then winced as pain tore through his entire body. There was no use in lying here. It wouldn't do any good.

Pushing himself up, he stumbled along the road as best he could.

After a while, he saw a small break in the trees on his right that led to a peaceful, bubbling stream. Needing to rest for a few minutes, he headed for it.

He was so focused on getting a simple drink of water, that he didn't notice the tiny girl with a fishing pole until she shot to her feet with a cry of alarm. She brandished a small knife in front of her with enough skill to say she was well proficient at its use.

For a full minute, he couldn't breathe at the sight of her. She was beauty incarnate. Yet not the same as Ryssa's perfect fragile beauty. With bright tawny skin and thick black hair, she had eyes the color of light, precious greenish-gold. Her red and white gown draped over her lean body and highlighted the fact that she was very nicely proportioned. Lusciously so ... She was also a lot taller than his sister. But she was still tiny in comparison to him.

He'd never in his life seen anything more inviting ... More beautiful or pure.

"Who are you?" she demanded, gripping her knife even tighter. "You touch me and I'll stab you, I swear it."

Styxx frowned as he realized by the way she moved her head and arm that she was completely blind, and he felt like a total shit for terrifying her.

"Please," he said, struggling to breathe through his pain. "Calm yourself. I'm sorry I scared you, and I mean you no harm. Even if I did, I'm in no shape to do anything more than bleed on you in my current condition. I promise you, girl, I have much more to fear from you than you do from me."

She straightened up and finally lowered the knife. "How old are you?"

"Ten-and-six. Now please, I just need to sit for a moment to catch my breath and then I'll leave you to your ... whatever it is you're doing." He sank to his knees and groaned out loud.

She returned her knife to the sheath on her wrist. "Are you all right?"

"Yes ... " He hissed as more pain lacerated his middle. "No. Not really. I ... "

What was he going to say? He jumped off a cliff, trying to die, only to find out he was immortal?

Not a wise confession by any means.

"My horse threw me."

She tsked in sympathy for him. "You poor thing. Do I need to get you help?"

He caught himself before he laughed at her offer. Really, there was no help for him.

Still, it was one of the kindest things anyone had ever offered where he was concerned. "Thanks, but that's all right. I just need a moment to sit and try to remember how to breathe." Styxx leaned over the water to splash his face and wash some of the blood and sweat away. His hand shook as his stomach heaved from the agony of it all.

In one heartbeat, against his best efforts, he collapsed into the water. It took several seconds before he was able to push himself back to the bank. *Great . . . now I'm covered with mud, too.* Leave it to him to look like a complete, incompetent ass in front of the most beautiful girl he'd ever met.

One who wasn't trying to molest him.

She crawled toward him, patting gently against the ground until she located his leg. Slowly, she made her way up his hip and back to his shoulder and then head. She pulled back the moment she touched his cheek. "You're bleeding."

"Sorry . . . here . . . " He ripped a part of his chiton off and used it to clean her hand for her.

She frowned at his actions. "Why are you cleaning my hand when you're the one bleeding?"

"I didn't want you to soil your gown."

"But *you're* bleeding." She was incredulous.

"It's all right. Really. I do that a lot."

She took his makeshift cloth from his hand to the water and dampened it then returned to gently bathe his injured cheek.

Lying on his back, Styxx closed his eyes at the tenderness of her graceful hand on his skin. She smelled like lilies and eucalyptus. Of warmth and sunshine. And a part of him wondered if her glowing, flawless skin would taste as sweet as it appeared. "What's your name?"

"Bethany."

He repeated it silently, savoring the beautiful syllables of a name he'd never heard before.

"And you are?"

He caught himself before he automatically answered. Like hers, his name was unusual, especially for a man. If she heard it, she'd know immediately who he was, and he didn't want her to hate him the way everyone else did. To her, he wasn't the spoiled, idiot prince. He was just . . .

An incompetent, idiot commoner.

"Hector."

She smiled at him. "Hector, do you know where your horse is?"

"I fear he went in search of a more competent rider who wouldn't embarrass him in the future."

She laughed out loud. A light, sweet sound that made his heart skip a beat. She pressed her lips together. "How can you joke when you're in so much pain?"

"To hear you laugh, my lady, I'd gladly throw myself off a hundred cliffs."

Cocking her head, she frowned. "Are you flirting with me, Hector?"

Was he?

"I . . . I don't know."

She widened her hazel-gold eyes. "You don't know?"

"I'm not exactly experienced with women, my lady. I don't normally converse with them. So I'm not sure if this would be considered flirting or not."

She pulled back to rinse out the cloth. "What do you do that you're not around women?"

Ah . . . damn. What did normal people do? Did men interact with women in a regular life? He had no way of knowing.

"I . . . um . . . I work with my father. The only girl I'm around is my sister and we don't really talk. And I definitely don't flirt with her."

"I should hope not." Smiling again, she moved her hand down his neck, feeling for more injuries. In spite of the excruciating pain he was in, her touch set fire to his blood. He couldn't explain it, but there was something familiar and comforting about her. As if he'd known her forever.

"Why are you here alone, Bethany? Is there no one watching over you?"

She pulled back.

He caught her hand in his and held it gently. "I–I didn't mean it that way. I merely worry that you're here with no protector."

"I have my knife."

"And I admire that about you, but ..."

"I come here often to sit and fish. Usually no one disturbs me."

No doubt the last thing she wanted was a cursed, bleeding whore to ruin the rest of her morning. "Forgive me, my lady." Styxx rolled to his side to leave.

"Hector? What are you doing?"

"I'll leave you to your peace. I know what it's like to need time alone and not have it. Forgive my intrusion on yours."

She placed a gentle hand on his shoulder and nudged him back down. "You're not intruding. Now lie still and let me make sure nothing's broken. If it is, I shall go get help and be back."

"I'm really quite fine, my lady. I've already limped and crawled a good distance. I just need a moment to rest before I continue on my way." Sucking his breath in, he placed his hand to his eye.

"What is it?"

"Nothing, my lady. I have headaches that plague me often, and as my luck would ever have it, I have one trying to cleave my skull in half right now. 'Cause I'm just not in enough pain to suit the gods."

She tsked. "Poor Hector. Here ..." Ignoring the fact he was dripping wet, she lifted his head and placed it in her lap. "I've been told that I have a healing touch when it comes to such things."

He started to deny it, but the moment she sank her hands into his damp hair and began to rub his scalp, it lessened the agony immediately. The voices that ever tormented him grew so faint, he could barely hear them. Even *her* thoughts were hidden from him. It was so wonderful to hear nothing ...

Sighing in blissful peace, he closed his eyes and savored her sweet scent and her precious, soothing touch. For the first time in his life, even though he was wet, bleeding, and injured, he was warm and content.

He took a deep breath of her sweet smell and smiled.

Bethany paused as she realized Hector had fallen asleep in her lap while she played in his soft curls. *Should I be offended?* But then he was hurt badly. Even though he'd denied it, she had felt his numerous injuries and the blood that stained his clothes and skin. She could smell it.

As a goddess, she had the power to heal him, but refrained. It would make him suspicious, and even though he was nothing more than a mere human, she'd enjoyed their peculiar brief exchange. No one had ever been so preciously sweet with her. So considerate. Not unless they wanted something, and she despised such false people.

She preferred to be liked for herself, not for her powers or favors.

But that was the way it worked. People groveled, gods bartered, and she never had a moment's peace from their machinations and schemes. It was why she came here whenever she could to be alone with her thoughts and pretend for a while that she was normal . . .

Whatever normal was.

Closing her eyes, she tried to picture what her mysterious Hector looked like. If she went into her goddess form, she'd be able to see him. But then she might be terribly disappointed. He was human after all, and she was used to the extraordinary beauty of the gods.

No. Better to use her imagination than risk finding out he was a hideous toad. Besides, if she appeared as a god in Greece, the Olympians would throw down a tantrum. Gods didn't handle other gods invading their territories without an express invitation well. And they had enough trouble with Greece. They didn't need a war to break out over some peasant boy and her curiosity.

She carefully brushed her hands over him. His face was finely boned and perfectly proportioned. He had a long aquiline nose and hair as soft as a bird's wing. It curled around her fingers and the manly stubble along his jaw teased her flesh. His lips were full and soft, unlike his body that was rock hard and toned. By the length of his arms and size of his hands, she could tell he was as tall as a god, or an Atlantean. But his accent had been decidedly Greek. His voice deep, husky, and pleasant.

Given that he was Greek, she shouldn't even be talking to him. While they were no longer at war with the Greeks, their truce was a very fragile thing and she didn't trust the Greeks not to break it.

Any day now, they could be back at war.

But her Hector wasn't a politician and he wasn't a god. No god would ever be stranded in the poor shape he was in.

He would need his horse to get home.

Using as little of her powers as she could, she searched the ether until she found it and then she called it to her. It took a few minutes, but finally the horse came and nudged her shoulder.

"You were wicked to throw your master," she said gently to the horse. "Try not to hurt him in the future."

The horse whinnied then went off to graze. Bethany hummed and sang while Hector slumbered peacefully in her lap. She didn't know why, but his presence soothed her even though he was unconscious. There had been something so sweetly sincere about him. So innocent and honest. Humble.

Things she was not used to.

While she'd taken a handful of lovers through the centuries, none had ever made her feel like this . . .

Protective of them.

How very strange.

He's like a pet. That was what her mother would call him. Yet that didn't describe it either. She brushed her hand along his cheek where his whiskers teased her fingers. She wanted to run her tongue along it, yet she didn't want to scare or offend him.

I don't know what it is about you, Hector . . .

But she wanted to kiss his firm, parted lips. Instead, she brushed a kiss to his forehead and let the warm, masculine scent of his skin wash over her.

"Sleep well, my sweet." She'd much rather play in his soft hair than fish anyway.

Styxx came awake to the most amazing sound in the world. It was a low, gentle contralto. And someone was stroking his cheek . . .

Afraid it was his uncle molesting him, he shot up with a curse to find the alarmed face of beauty incarnate.

"Hector?" That sweet gasp made him feel like a complete ass that he'd startled her again.

"Bethany, I'm sorry. I forgot where I was. Did I fall asleep?"

She nodded. "For several hours now."

He looked up at the sky that confirmed what she told him. The sun was well past noon. "Forgive me. I didn't mean to keep you. I hope you're not in trouble."

Reaching out to touch his face, she smiled. "I am not in trouble at all. I was beginning to worry about you, though. I'm glad you're finally awake."

Reluctantly, Styxx pulled back from her tender touch, amazed that his head no longer hurt at all. And still the voices were silent. It was so strange to be with someone and have no idea whatsoever what they thought of him.

"And look . . . " She held her hand out toward the water. "Your horse has returned."

He smiled at the fact that Troian was on the opposite side of where she gestured. "So he has. Apparently, he likes to be embarrassed, after all."

"I'm sure you didn't embarrass him."

Styxx got up slowly. While his body wasn't completely healed, it was much better now than it'd been when he passed out in her lap. "I've taken up enough of your day, my lady. I won't bother you anymore."

"You were hardly a bother."

She was far too gentle and sweet.

"I don't know about that. I bled on your beautiful dress and used you for a pillow. I can't see how I'm anything but a nuisance."

"My dress will wash and it wasn't a hardship to sit with you while you slept."

"Thank you, my lady. You're very kind. Would you like for me to help you to your feet?"

"That's very gallant of you." She held her hand out in a dainty, feminine gesture.

Styxx clasped her hand in both of his and helped her rise. She was as tiny as he'd suspected. She barely reached his shoulders. Her soft hair fell against the flesh of his arm in a light caress that quickened his heartbeat. He felt a sudden desire to bury his face in those dark tresses and inhale the scent of her skin until he was drunk with it. A scent that now clung to him and his clothes, making him so hard that it was impossible to think straight with her near him.

"Would you like me to take you home?" he asked.

"It's unnecessary." She wiggled her fingers inside his hand. "And I'm on my feet now. You can let go."

Heat exploded over his cheeks as he released her hand even though he didn't want to. "Is there any way I can thank you for your kindness today?"

She frowned. "You don't have to pay me for being kind, Hector."

"You're very different from the people I've known. They all expect some form of recompense for any charitable act."

She rose up on her tiptoes to whisper to his shoulder as opposed to his ear. "I am not one of those people. But there is one thing I think I should like."

He smiled at the sweetness of her actions. "Anything."

"So long as the sun shines, I am here at the beginning and end of every week. Should your horse ever throw you again on one of those days, I wouldn't be opposed to seeing you here as you rest on your way home."

His heart pounded at those words. "Really?"

She nodded. "I'll be here tomorrow, too."

"Then I shall be here, and I promise I won't soil your gown." He took her hand one last time and placed a chaste kiss over her knuckles. "Safe journey home, my lady."

She curtsied to him. "And to you, my lord."

His heart lighter than he could ever remember it being, Styxx swung himself up on his horse and took a moment to watch her gracefully gather together her items.

She paused. "Are you watching me, Hector?"

Her abilities amazed him. "I couldn't help myself, gentle Bethany. You are too beautiful for words and I don't just mean your face. You move with such grace and assuredness that it takes my breath."

"For a blind woman, you mean?"

"For any woman. And I meant no disrespect to you, in any way."

She smiled. "None taken."

Styxx clenched his teeth as he looked about their small clearing. "I feel terrible leaving you here alone. Are you certain you don't wish for me to take you home?"

"My father would not approve. He would want to interrogate you and I don't think you're up to that today."

And if her father saw him, he might recognize him. That could be disastrous. "Very well then. I am gone now. Until the morrow."

"Until the morrow, good Hector."

Styxx sank his hands into the mane of his horse and used his hands to guide Troian home. And with every step that put distance between them, his thoughts stayed with the most beautiful, gentle creature he'd ever met. One who was as pure and innocent as he wished he was.

You barely know her.

True, yet he wanted to know her better. No one had ever made him feel like she did. Funny and welcome. Heroic and noble, even though all he'd done was bleed all over her and sleep in her lap. How stupid was that?

202

Somehow she'd eased the pain in his heart and made everything better. Made him smile even when he wanted to cry. How could he leave such a miracle?

May the gods have mercy on him, he wanted her with everything he had.

What can you offer a woman so fine? You're a scarred, worthless whore. She would be horrified to know what she'd held today.

Would she have been so kind if she knew the truth of him? Or would she curl her lip and run? But she didn't know who or what he was. To her, he was just a normal man.

And to him, she was perfection.

Counting down the seconds until he could see her again, Styxx dismounted in the drive then slowly climbed the palace stairs.

Damn, it hurt.

Did they really need so many?

The guards opened the door to the palace. Styxx had just reached the stairs that led to his room when his father's voice stopped him.

"What happened to you?"

He paused at his father's approach and let out a tired breath. His father would be furious at his unkempt state. "I slipped from my horse."

"Your tutors said that you didn't attend your lessons, nor your training."

No, shit. Really? The man truly couldn't see his pain. He was filthy, covered with bruises and cuts, and blood and mud and dirt . . . Still his father berated him.

"I fell, Father. I had meant to return much earlier, but had to find my horse. Please forgive me for my inconsideration to all of *you.*"

As I bled my way home . . .

His father's gaze sharpened in warning. "Careful of your tone, boy. Now, should I call the physician for you?"

Styxx shook his head. "I shall live," he said bitterly. For now he knew the truth of what the wise woman had proclaimed at his birth. He could only die if Acheron died first. So long as his brother lived, he lived, too. Or perhaps they were both immortal. Either way, he had no need to fear death now.

Thanatos would never come for him.

Maybe if I were beheaded . . .

Then again, did he want to test that theory? It could be rather grotesque to walk around carrying his head in his hands . . . Given the perversity of the gods, anything was possible.

Yet as he thought of Bethany, he no longer minded living in this stygian nightmare. Not if he could spend another day with her like this one.

Only, more preferably, he'd be awake for it.

His father's brow drew tight as he finally realized that Styxx wasn't bleeding for no reason. "Are you sure you're all right?"

"Fine, Father." Styxx took a step then paused. "Majesty? May I ask a favor of you?"

His frown deepened. "Yes. Of course."

Styxx doubted his father would be so accommodating once he heard it. But he had to try even if it meant more humiliation for himself. "Might we please bring Acheron home?"

Rage darkened his father's eyes. "You know how I feel about that. He was sent away for your protection. Why would you have him return?"

Because he's my brother . . .

And he couldn't stand the thoughts of what was being done to him. Regardless of what Acheron said or thought, he didn't want to leave him in Atlantis. Not with Estes.

"Doesn't it concern you that he could be harmed while away from us and thereby cause me harm?"

"Estes keeps him guarded. There's no danger to him there."

To be so highly intelligent, you're so stupid.

Why was his father so blind to Estes's vices and no one else's? Styxx couldn't even imagine having someone love him like that. Someone who would never judge or hate him, no matter his committed atrocities.

And none of that mattered right now . . .

"Please, Father. I've never, in my entire life, asked you for anything else."

"And it is the one thing I will *never* give you. Understood? Now get yourself cleaned up. Your filth and stench offend me. You smell like a woman."

Yes, he did. He had to bite back a smile at the memory Bethany's scent awoke. If he could, he'd carry the smell of her on him forever.

Styxx started past his father only to have him grab his arm in a tight grip. He narrowed his gaze as he gave Styxx a hard, fierce stare.

"I know you keep secrets from me, boy. You always have."

Because whenever I tried to tell them to you when I was a child, you slapped me for them.

Now those secrets would only give his father a real reason to hate and resent him.

"And I don't believe you about today. I think there's more to where you were."

Styxx kept his features blank, his eyes hooded. "As you can plainly see, *Father,* I fell and was badly injured." The only thing he'd lied about was his intention to return home.

"Get out of my sight." He pushed him away.

Gladly. Styxx headed upstairs as best he could.

As he turned toward his room, he slowed down at the approach of his sister and mother in the upper hallway. Their laughter died the moment they saw him.

He inclined his head to them respectfully. "Mother. Ryssa."

A deep frown creased his mother's brow. "What happened to you?"

For a moment, he thought he might detect a note of maternal concern. But the additional curling of her lip that derided him said it was either nonexistent or fleeting.

"I was thrown."

"From what?" His mother laughed bitterly. "A whore's bed?

205

You reek of her stench. You must have been wallowing in her for hours."

"She's not a whore," he snarled before he could stop himself.

"Men," his mother sneered to Ryssa. "They are ever fickle with their affections. Pray, daughter, that you never give your heart over to one. They couldn't care less about it so long as you welcome them to your body." She turned her hate-filled eyes back at him. "In the future, I suggest you put yourself in order before you return home. You are a prince of this realm. I don't think it's too much to expect a modicum of decorum and dress from you when you leave your whores behind."

Styxx felt his jaw tic. "I know, Mother. I offend my entire family. If not my manner or speech then my dress, and above all, it's my penis that offends you and Ryssa most."

They sucked their breaths in sharply.

"Xerxes!" his mother shouted.

"Have me whipped. It won't change anything. You speak to Ryssa about men when you know nothing of us. You've never bothered to learn. We're simple creatures, really. You just have to be nice to us." He cocked his head at the sound of his father's approach.

"You called?" his father asked.

Styxx answered for her. "She's going to tell you how I've offended her and Ryssa with the truth, Father. How I've used inappropriate language before ladies. Do you wish me to bathe before or after I'm beaten?"

His father scowled. "You're not the same as before. What has changed you?"

Styxx swallowed the pain that choked him. He'd been raped, whored, beaten, and threatened for it, seen his father turn his twin out into the cold. He'd had his brother curse him for trying to help him, and then had discovered he couldn't die. How could all that not change him?

"Life has changed me, Majesty. I live only to serve you and my people. I have no other purpose."

His father stiffened. "Are you being smart with me?"

206

"No, Sire. Tell me how to please you and I will do so."

"His insolence should be punished, Father. He mocks you and insults us."

"Look me in the eye, boy. Are you mocking me?"

Styxx met his gaze without flinching. "Nay, Sire. Why would I?"

"And what did you say to your mother and sister?"

"I merely remarked on the irony of Matisera teaching Ryssa about men when she knows nothing of us. And how the part of me that truly offends them most is my penis."

His mother gestured angrily at him. "You see how he treats us."

For once, his father laughed. "He speaks the truth. I shan't punish him for that."

His mother's eyes flared before she stepped forward and slapped Styxx where his face was already bruised.

Styxx tasted blood from his lips as the cuts there were reopened.

"I weep over the day I birthed *you*." She raked his father with a sneer before she stormed off with Ryssa trailing behind her.

"Ignore them, boy. Women only have two uses. In the bed and as bargaining tools. Other than that, you'd do well to avoid them. And speaking of, I paid off another of your whores earlier while you were out."

"Excuse me?"

"One of the serving wenches came to me with a daughter she claims is yours. Have no fear, I've set them up for you and they won't be back to plague you."

Styxx ground his teeth. "It's not mine."

His father laughed. "Of course it is. Don't worry. I'm not angry. It happens. I can't even begin to catalogue all the bastards I have. The trick is to send them far enough away so that neither you nor your sons accidentally tup one of your bastard daughters."

Styxx shook his head in disbelief of his father's nonchalance over something he found highly offensive. And the fact that his father had paid off some unknown woman while he was virgin still . . .

Well, not technically after Estes and the animals he traveled with. Yet even with the servants and others throwing themselves at him for the last few years, he had yet to sleep with a woman. Any woman. He hadn't even kissed one. He'd been too afraid of embarrassing himself with his inexperience.

And now ... he had no desire to be with one who might uncover his brand.

Not to mention, after having been abused himself, he wasn't about to bed with someone who had no authority to turn him down. The last thing he wanted was to have sex with someone who didn't want to be with him.

His father clapped him lightly on the shoulder. "Go clean yourself and rest in peace. I'll see you at dinner."

Styxx bowed slightly before he went to his room and shut the door. He didn't know what hurt most. The fact that his own mother despised him for things he hadn't done or the fact that the only thing his father took pride in was something he hadn't done.

Hissing in pain, he quickly sat on his bed as his feet began to burn. Acheron was being caned there. He knew it. While his own feet had never been struck, he'd taken a cane across his buttocks enough to recognize the sensation.

Damn you, Estes.

At least this time he was alone so that he could deal with the pain and not have to pretend he felt nothing. Sitting down, he pressed his feet flush to the floor. As he moved, he caught the scent of lilies and eucalyptus.

Bethany.

He closed his eyes and summoned an image of her beautiful face and gentle touch. The sound of her voice as she sang to him. For the first time in his life, he knew exactly what he wanted.

And his perfect woman had the most beautiful of names.

"What are you doing?"

Bethany paused at the sound of Archon's voice behind her. Shedding her human skin, she turned to glare at the king of the Atlantean gods. Just over seven feet in height, he thought every member of his pantheon should bow down before him.

But it wasn't in Bethany to cow before anyone. Even a gorgeous golden god-king. "I suggest a new tone for you, Archon, when you address me . . . One with less bass."

"You're supposed to be looking for Apostolos!"

The missing Atlantean god-child Archon had foolishly fathered with his queen, Apollymi—the great destroyer of all worlds.

Bethany had to give Apollymi credit. The fact that the god-queen could hide her child and keep him safe from all of their combined powers was extremely impressive. No one else could have gotten away with it.

"I *was* looking for him, Archon. In Greece, as *you* suggested."

"And?"

"And what? Apollymi is still imprisoned and I'm here alone. Obviously, Lord High King God, I don't have your son nor did I kill him while I was out."

Archon's eyes flared with fury. "You're the one who needs to watch her tone."

Bethany scoffed at his rage. "Don't threaten me. Need I remind you what happened the last time you crossed a goddess of this pantheon? It didn't work out so well for you, did it? The last thing you want now is for me to join ranks with your wife against you."

A tic worked fiercely in his jaw. "We barely have five years before she releases his powers and the two of them attack us. Something that won't go well for you either . . . I can feel him out there. I know he's alive and well."

"Then *you*," she pressed her fingertip against his massive chest, "find him. As his father, it should be easy for you."

He growled at her before he stormed off.

Rolling her eyes, she pulled the small bit of Hector's chiton from her pocket and smiled at the softness of the cloth. She lifted it to her nose so that his scent could warm her again.

How foolish of her to be so smitten over a mere boy, especially since she'd always mocked the gods who took human lovers. She'd never understood the appeal of them. They were frail and pathetic, whiny creatures.

But not Hector. Even while he'd bled all over her, he'd been funny and sweet. Kind. Considerate.

Precious.

"Bet'anya? Are you all right?"

She met Chara's gaze as the Atlantean goddess of joy joined her in the foyer of their main hall in Katateros—the Atlantean paradise realm where the gods made their homes. With flame-red hair and skin the color of alabaster, she was absolutely stunning. Tall and voluptuous, Chara was forever smiling and laughing.

Bethany returned the cloth to her pocket before the other goddess saw it. "I'm fine. Why do you ask?"

"You're smiling. It scares me."

Bethany laughed at that, which then caused Chara to take a step back from her.

"Now I *am* terrified. When the goddess of wrath and misery is happy . . . it cannot bode well for others."

True, but then Bethany couldn't help it. She was born of Darkness, Chaos, Death, and Tears. It was hard to be lighthearted with that kind of conception and upbringing.

But just the thought of Hector made her heart light.

How ridiculous am I?

"Have you ever . . . " Bethany hesitated, unsure if she wanted to let anyone else know what was on her mind.

"Have I ever what?"

Bethany glanced around the huge, white marble room to make sure no one else could hear them. "Been with a human?" she whispered.

Chara flashed a bright grin. "Many, many times. They can be very entertaining."

"So it seems."

That made one of her red brows shoot straight up her forehead. "I take it you found one in particular who pleases you?"

Bethany shrugged with a nonchalance she definitely didn't feel. "It's stupid, isn't it? He'll be old and dead in no time . . . "

"He doesn't have to be. *You* could spare him that."

"Why would I? Infatuation never lasts more than a breath or two. I'm sure I'll be bored with him the next time we meet. *If* we meet again."

"Don't let Agapa hear you say that. You'd hurt her feelings."

Bethany snorted. "The goddess of love can take her seeds and put them in a most uncomfortable place. I don't want her poison taking root in me. Ever."

Laughing, Chara wrinkled her nose. "Now that is the Bet'anya I know and love. Ever a pessimist."

"Ever a realist. You should try it sometime."

"No, thank you." Chara rocked up onto her tiptoes. "I prefer to dream and see the beauty in the world and all its possibilities."

"It shrivels and it dies. All things do."

"But not us," Chara reminded her. "We are eternal."

"Only with limitations."

Chara held her hands up. "I concede this fight. It's nice to see Her Holy Crabbiness back. I've missed you so."

Bethany was crabby and cantankerous. She'd always been that way. But for one brief afternoon, she had been lighthearted. And she'd laughed . . .

"I must be getting sick."

And she had better things to do than waste time with some mortal nothing. She had a missing god to find before the goddess of destruction was unleashed and destroyed them all. That and that alone was what she needed to be focused on.

JUNE 25, 9532 BC

Styxx held his breath as he made his way back to the small clearing where Bethany had said she'd be. It'd taken him hours to get away from his father and tutors. After yesterday, his father had taken to watching him much more closely and he'd been forced to sneak away.

Had he taken too long? Was she gone already?

Emotionally wrecked at the thought, he broke through the trees and winced as he saw no trace of her. Damn it! He'd missed her because of *them*.

Suddenly, he heard the faint steps of something moving away in the trees.

"Bethany?" he called.

The noise stopped instantly. "Hector?"

Relief flooded him so fast and furiously, he almost lost his balance. He rushed toward her voice and found her just a few feet away, in the dense woods. Dressed in a light green gown, with her hair pulled up into a beautiful cascade of falling curls, she had a basket on one arm and her pole in her other hand.

"I'm here." He let go of his horse to touch her shoulder so that she could locate his whereabouts.

She smiled instantly. "I thought you'd changed your mind."

"No. Never. I'm so sorry. I just couldn't get away any earlier."

Bethany shivered as he took her hand into his and kissed it. The warm, masculine smell of him filled her head and made her heart pound. A scary, unexpected urge to hug him went through her and she had to force herself to refrain. "I brought you some lamb and cheese with wine."

"I love cheese. It's one of my favorites." After taking the pole from her, he pressed something into her hand. "I brought you flowers."

She brushed her fingers over the small bouquet. Her smile widened at the softness of the petals. "Poppies?"

"They are, indeed."

"Thank you." Rising up, she placed a chaste kiss on his cheek.

Styxx closed his eyes and savored the sensation of her lips on his skin. He ached to sink his hand into her hair and hold her there, against him until time itself stopped moving. "I'm sorry I was so late. If you need to leave . . . "

"I don't. Not really." She started back toward the stream.

"Here, let me carry that for you." Styxx took the basket from her arm.

As they walked, she pulled a blanket from the basket in his hand. Once they reached her spot, she spread it out on the ground. It amazed him how she moved with such ease and grace when she couldn't see anything. How she remembered the exact place she'd been in when they'd met.

"May I ask you something personal?"

She paused. "It depends. How personal are we talking?"

He leaned the pole against a tree. "It's . . . never mind. I shouldn't have mentioned it."

She arched a brow at him. "Now you have my curiosity fully tweaked. What is it?"

"I . . . um . . . " He scratched nervously at his cheek, hoping to the gods he didn't offend her with his stupidity. "Were you born blind?"

She laughed lightly as she set out her items from the basket. "You and I have completely different definitions for the word 'personal.' No, I wasn't born blind. I had my sight at birth."

"Is that why you move so easily?"

"No. I move easily because I'm not old."

It was his turn to laugh. "That's not what I meant."

"I know what you meant and no, it's because I have over-developed senses that allow me to know where things are, and it's why I tend to hum or make noises as I go. Whenever I get near something, sound will echo back from it, letting me know it's in my way."

"Really?"

She nodded as she sank down on the blanket. "What about you? Were you born with your eyesight?"

He laughed again. "I was indeed. Though I have no memory of it. And sometimes it doesn't work as well as it should." He set the basket down beside her then took a seat on the opposite side of the blanket so that he could admire the way the light cut across

213

her skin that reminded him of warm, dark honey. "You changed your hair."

"I curled it."

"I like it . . . though it was nice straight, too," he quickly added.

Her sweet, beautiful smile hardened him instantly. "My poor Hector. You're really not very comfortable around women, are you?"

"Not even a little, but I have to say that you're a lot easier to talk to than most."

"How so?"

You don't deride me, for one thing . . . "I think it has to do with the fact that I met you at the height of my ineptitude. I have nowhere else to go in your estimation except up." Cringing over those words, Styxx cleared his throat. He'd said too much about his stupidity and clumsiness. No need in reminding her of it when he didn't have to. "Nice weather, isn't it?"

She tsked at him. "You're changing the subject. It makes me wonder why."

He sighed wearily before he answered her original question. "Women tend to want to use or judge me."

"Use you how?"

He plucked a blade of grass and ran it through his fingertips. "They see me as a hefty purse."

"Are you?"

"No. I'm quite certain I'm human. Most days anyway. Mornings not always withstanding. Instead of a purse, I'm much more of a bear in the early hours of the day."

Her laughter washed over him like the sweetest wine and had the same intoxicating effect on him. "But do you have money?"

That succeeded in sobering him. Was she like the others, after all? "Why are you asking?"

"Because I don't like people who are wealthy. They tend to be arrogant and hold the belief that any problem can be solved by applying more funds toward it."

While that would be true of both his father and uncle, it wasn't

214

his philosophy. "Honestly, my lady. I have no personal wealth at all." As his father was so quick to remind him ... Everything belonged to his father. Even the horse he rode. "I'm quite worthless."

"You are definitely not worthless."

"And to that, I would remind you that you're blind." Styxx cringed again as those words left his lips. Oh gods, how could he have been so stupid and insensitive? "Bethany, I didn't mean—"

"Shh." She pressed her fingers to his lips. "The truth doesn't offend me, Hector. I am blind. I can't deny that. But because of it I see much more clearly than those who have working eyes."

She picked up the bread and tore a small piece from it that she held out to him. "Here, sweet. Perhaps this will remove the taste of foot from your mouth?"

Smiling, he started to take it from her then before he could stop himself, he leaned forward and ate it from her hand.

Bethany shivered at the sensation of his lips against her fingers as he took the bread in his teeth. She heard him pour and mix the wine into the two goblets she'd packed. With the tenderest of touches, he took her hand and placed it against the cup. Sweeping her finger over the edge, she had to bite back a smile. He'd barely filled it halfway.

"You're definitely not trying to get me drunk."

"I don't believe in taking advantage of others."

"Then you are a rare man."

"Just an honest one."

His sweet humility warmed her. "As I said, you are very rare."

"Do you really believe that?" he asked in that richly deep voice of his. She could listen to the manly resonance of it all day long ...

"Experience has tutored me well that most will lie or cheat to get the better hand. It's why I prefer solitude to social interaction."

He took a sip then set his cup aside. "And I hate to be alone, yet it seems to be forever forced upon me."

She frowned at the pain she heard in his tone. "Why do you hate being alone?"

215

"It's lonely."

"You can be surrounded by people and still be alone."

"And that is a lesson I've learned well. Still, it's better to be distracted by the crowd than to be left with memories that serve no purpose other than to torture the conscience and flog the heart."

His wisdom surprised her. He seemed a lot older than his years.

"You aren't old enough to have such regrets."

"Pain doesn't respect age, my lady. Sometimes I think the Algea rather enjoy going after younger victims just for spite." Styxx hesitated as a stricken look went across her brow. "Forgive me, my lady. I didn't mean to be so maudlin. I've tainted your beautiful smile, and that was definitely not my intent. As I said, I spend far too much time alone. It leaves me lacking in all social graces."

She shook her head. "I find your sincere conversation and heartfelt comments refreshing. I have no patience for guile and even less for artful wordsmiths who mask their claws behind double entendres and cleverly practiced lines. So give me your honesty, Hector. That is why I waited for you today when I never wait for anyone."

How did she do it? She made him feel so ...

Human. Worthy. And it was so effortless for her. While others degraded him, she made him feel like he could fly.

"You are not like anyone I've ever met before, Bethany."

She tucked her chin in, in the cutest manner he'd ever seen. "I should hope not. I pride myself on being unique in this world."

He hardened even more and wished he had the courage to steal a kiss from her. "And well you should."

She swallowed her bit of bread. "What about you?"

"What about me, what?"

She leaned forward and wrinkled her nose. "On what do you pride yourself?"

Stupidity. It was what he seemed to possess an abundance of, but he had no wish to out himself so soon to her. "Nothing."

"I'm serious, Hector."

He glanced away from her. "As am I."

She scooted closer to him until her scent made his head reel again. "There's nothing you excel at? Honestly?"

Before he could stop himself, the truth poured out. "Angering my father, and definitely my sister. I can turn her from a smiling beauty to a vengeful shrew by merely walking into a room. My powers in that regard are truly awe-inspiring. But I take no pride in either. And as you've seen firsthand, my skill with horses is even more lacking than my social graces."

"There has to be something you're good at. Surely you can name me one thing besides angering your family."

"The only other thing I'm accomplished at is hiding pain behind the guise of stoicism."

Bethany froze as she heard the torment inside him. Her heart breaking for him, she reached to touch his hand, but couldn't find it.

"I'm sorry, my lady. I didn't mean to ... I should be going." He was moving away, she could hear his retreat.

"Hector? Please, don't go. Stay with me."

Styxx savored words no one had ever said to him before. Never once. Rather, people were forever sending him away. Before he could stop himself, he headed back to her side.

She held her hands up to feel for him. "Are you still here?"

He placed his hand into hers and allowed her to pull him down next to her. The urge to cup her hand to his cheek was so strong, he wasn't sure how he kept from complying. "I am here."

The smile on her face slammed into him. "Should we just speak of the weather?"

"Whatever topic pleases you."

She reached up to finger his jaw and lips. "The one thing that is hard without sight is judging moods at times. Since I can't see your expression, I can't tell yours right now. You *are* good at hiding it."

217

"My mood is that I am happy and content just to sit with you, Bethany." He brushed a stray piece of hair back from her cheek. "You don't even have to speak to me at all."

"But I would like to know you."

Those words tore through him. "There's nothing really to know. I work. I study and I sometimes sleep."

"What do you do for pleasure?"

Not a damn thing. Except for one . . .

"I ride to this stream where there is an amazing girl who plies me with beautiful smiles and wine and bread so that I can remove the taste of foot from my mouth."

She shook her head at him. "And before me?"

"There was no before you, Bethany. I had no pleasure whatso-ever."

Bethany hesitated at those words. She heard the sincerity in his voice. But was he serious? "None?"

He placed her hand to his face so that she could feel his earnest expression. "None."

Before she could stop herself, she pulled him into her arms and held him close. His strong arms surrounded her with warmth as she breathed his scent in. He held her as if she was unspeakably precious. As if he loved her . . .

But she knew better. In fact, he could be lying about everything. Most men, in her experience, did.

She felt his jaw tensing as he tightened his arms around her and cupped her head in his hand. He took a deep breath in her hair then released her.

"I can't believe no man has married you."

"Who says I want to marry?"

"Don't you?"

She shook her head. "I refuse to answer to anyone for anything. My life is my own, as is my body. No one is ever going to command me. Have I offended you yet?"

"Not even a little. I cherish your spirit and I hope you always have it."

She frowned. "Why do you say that?"

Styxx fell silent as his past churned inside him. He might have held her conviction at some point in his life, but he couldn't remember a time when he hadn't felt like a tired, whipped dog. "Life has a way of breaking even the strongest among us."

Bethany's breath caught as she heard his underlying agony. "The strongest of metals is forged under the most violent of conditions, my lord. It is buried deep in the hottest coals and then beat and pounded until it is bent into shape. Then it becomes the strongest, most lethal of weapons. A thing of absolute beauty and force."

But only when it's wielded by the right hand. Galen's words whispered to him and he finally understood what the old man had meant about the reasons to fight.

For this woman's safety, alone, he would battle.

"You have the most amazing outlook, my lady."

"And you don't?"

"Mine is much bleaker. It is one of responsibility and expectation. But I would much rather see this world through your eyes than mine."

"But my eyes are blind."

"And yet, as you said, they see so much more than others . . . My beautiful Bethany. I feel like I've known you a lot longer than one day, and I don't know why."

Bethany fell silent. She felt the same and it made no sense whatsoever. Why did he call out to her when others never had?

What floored her most was that he wasn't grabbing at her or even trying to kiss her. He was so respectful of her space and her body.

Her Hector was unlike any man she'd ever known.

He sighed. "It's getting late and I don't want you out alone in the dark. I need to let you go."

She had a feeling he wasn't just talking about this meeting. "Will you visit me again?"

"Would it please you?"

219

"It would."

"Then I shall come." He stood up then helped her to her feet.

When she bent over to pack her basket, she bumped heads with him. "Ow!" they said simultaneously.

Laughing, Styxx righted himself and realized that once again, all the voices in his head were quiet. He never heard them when he was with her.

Why?

"I hope I didn't concuss you, my lady."

She rubbed her head. "Not yet, but I fear you might be trying." Rising up on her toes, she pressed her cheek to his. "Until next we meet."

He closed his eyes and savored the sensation of her body next to his and her breath falling against his neck. "I will be counting down the heartbeats."

Styxx handed her the basket and pole and watched as she vanished into the forest. He didn't move until she was completely gone from his sight.

There was nothing he wanted more than to stay with her forever. But it was an impossible dream. He'd be more likely to convince his father to return Acheron to the line of succession.

And yet . . .

She is just another trick of the gods sent to torture you with something you know you'll never be worthy to have.

It was true. Why else would she be here?

JULY 26, 9532 BC

"Styxx! Come in here, there's a matter of great importance I need to speak to you about."

Resisting the urge to let out a frustrated breath, Styxx turned on the stairs and headed for his father's study.

Just what I was looking forward to. Another lecture on how I've disappointed you.

He entered the room and shut the door behind him. "Yes, Father?"

"Have a seat."

What did I do now?

Styxx complied as his father sat back in his own chair to stare at him with an unsettling intensity. Yes, this was going to go badly for him.

His father stroked his beard as if seeking the right words. "A troubling matter has come to me."

The blood left his face. *He knows I'm a whore . . .*

Don't overreact. Calm yourself.

"And that is, Father?"

"You haven't sired any bastards."

A relieved breath left him so suddenly that he was slightly dizzy from it. How was that a bad thing?

"I learned that the last whore I paid off wasn't yours and so I went and investigated the others only to learn that none of them had slept with you either."

If his father had only listened to him, he'd have known it a lot sooner. "How did you find out, Father?"

"None of them had knowledge of your scars."

That would do it. Not like any of them could be hidden from a lover.

Styxx sighed. His poor father. The only thing he'd been proud of was bastard children Styxx didn't have. "I don't see how this is a problem."

"It disturbs me that I can find no woman you've ever touched."

His anger exploding with that comment, Styxx rose to his feet. "This is not a discussion I want to have."

"Sit!"

He debated the wisest course of action. Well, not necessarily the wisest, but the one that would leave him with the most dignity. Unfortunately, it was the last action he wanted to take.

He sank back into his chair.

His father moved to stand beside him. Cupping his chin, he forced Styxx to meet his gaze. "Are you Ganymede?"

Styxx screwed his face up at the accusation. Not just because he wasn't, but because his uncle and others had used him as if he were. "No!"

"It's all right if you are. While I prefer a woman's soft sheath, I have been known to spear a worthy ass or two in my day."

Styxx cringed at a thought that made him want to vomit. There were things no one wanted to know about their parents and this was definitely at the top of his list.

But his father took no mercy on him as he continued. "Really, Styxx, it's nothing to be ashamed of. Estes has always had a preference for men, and it's never bothered me."

Styxx sat in stunned silence as hatred flowed thick through his veins. *You knew how he was and you turned me loose with him?* What kind of father would do such a thing?

His jaw went slack.

"But my brother has taken women on occasion. When he told me he'd seen to your training in Atlantis, I'd assumed they were female whores he used."

Oh, this just got better and better. "What all did he tell you about my time in Atlantis?"

"Don't be angry at Estes. I merely voiced my concern that you haven't been acting as most men your age . . . that you passed on the women I've sent to you for your pleasure. And that I worried the priests might have damaged you."

Styxx rubbed at his face, wanting to punch his father. Yes, they had damaged him, but not in the way he meant. Gods . . . how much more of this shit would he have to suffer?

"Estes told me that when you were first with a lover you were quite bashful because of your scars, but that once you got started, you forgot about them. He said I shouldn't be worried about your ability to perform. That he'd seen you erect himself. However . . . when I learned that the maids had lied about your using them . . . I am worried. How can you be king with no heirs?"

How could he sit here with his father talking to him in this manner and not die of abject horror, shame, and humiliation?

The wonders of the world never ceased to amaze him, either.

"So I've taken it upon myself to set you up with a mistress."

Styxx gaped at him. "I don't want a mistress, Father."

"Then a tsoulus. Male or female. Your choice."

"I damn sure don't want that!" he growled as more pain slammed into him.

That ignited his father's fury as he glared down at him. "Then explain to me what is going on with you? Why is my son as chaste as my daughter? It's deplorable."

Deplorable.

Maybe you should have thought of that before you left me to be manhandled by your priests and gods. Or better yet . . .

Your perverted brother.

Styxx rose slowly to his feet and forced his anger down before he made his father do something neither of them would forget or forgive. "I don't need your help getting laid, Father. Really."

When he opened his mouth to speak, Styxx held his arm up to his father's face so that he could smell his skin. "I have a woman. Not that it's any of your business."

His father smiled in relief as he caught Bethany's unique feminine scent of lilies and eucalyptus. "You're in love?"

Styxx nodded. "It's where I disappear to when you can't find me."

"Thank the gods of Olympus!" His father drew him into a hug. "Is she noble?"

"No."

"Then why haven't you set her—"

"It's my concern, Father. I'd appreciate your staying out of it and away from her . . . please. She's a good, decent woman and I would never shame her in any way."

"How can being a prince's mistress shame anyone?"

How indeed?

There were times when he truly hated the man who'd sired him.

"I want her left alone. I mean it, Father."

His father held his hands up in surrender. "Fine. I will stay out of your affair, except to say this ... you will have to marry a princess at some point and breed an heir with her."

"I know. But I'm not king yet."

"No. You're not." His father clapped him on the arm. "Very good, then. I shall see you at dinner."

Styxx inclined his head to him then headed for his room. His father would really shit if he ever learned that he had yet to kiss the woman he loved. That all they'd done to date was sit and occasionally hug.

But that was more than enough for a man who'd been given so few that he remembered every one he'd ever received.

AUGUST 18, 9532 BC

Bethany smiled as Hector read his philosophy lesson to her while she reclined in the quiet circle of his warm, muscular arms. She had her hands curled around his forearm, which lay against her stomach while his chin rested on top of her head. His body was so hard and ripped, yet at the same time extremely comfortable. She loved spending afternoons with him like this. He'd read his assignments out loud and then they'd discuss the ideas for days. In all her life, she'd never met anyone more intelligent or thoughtful. Anyone more kind and humble.

Even now, his erection pressed against her back, but he didn't say a word about it. He never did. Nor did he press her for anything more than the pleasure of her company.

He was content just to hold her and talk about absolutely nothing for hours on end. She'd never known a man like him. Reaching up, she laid her fingers against his jaw so that she could feel the hard muscles there work while he spoke in that deep husky voice that soothed her better than nectar.

As she swept her hand against his lips, his erection jerked in response. Still, he read to her between gentle, playful nips to her fingers.

After a few minutes, he paused and placed his scroll to the side. He leaned back against the tree behind them and cupped her cheek in his large hand.

"Bethany?"

"Yes?"

He bit his bottom lip as he hesitated. She felt his heartbeat quicken against her shoulder blade. If she didn't know better, she'd think he was afraid of something. But her Hector was always fearless and forthright.

Hector took a deep breath before he spoke again. "Would you mind terribly if I kissed you?"

Her smile widened. "No, my sweet. I've been wanting you to for weeks now."

Still, he hesitated.

"What's wrong?"

He swallowed hard. "I've never kissed a woman before. So please, don't be offended or think badly of me if I screw it up with my ineptitude."

Her poor sweet Hector. He was so bashful at times ... but always so preciously sincere and honest. Wanting to please him, too, she pulled his lips down to hers.

Styxx growled in pleasure as her tongue swept playfully against his. Never in his life had he tasted anything better. With the most dulcet of laughs, she nipped at his lips then gave him a kiss so scorching it left him dizzy and breathless.

Bethany sank her hands into his soft curls as she explored the sweetest mouth she'd ever tasted. For a man who claimed he'd never kissed, he was exceptional at it. She could breathe him in all day.

And when he finally pulled back, he placed his thumb to her bottom lip as if savoring the feel of it.

"That was so much better than I'd imagined. Thank you." He kissed the tip of her nose then her forehead.

Closing her eyes, she snuggled back into his arms and let him hold her again. "Why are you so reserved with me, Hector?"

"What do you mean?"

"Most men wouldn't be so content with a mere kiss. Nor would they have waited so long for it. Why are you different?"

"It is not your kisses I come for, my lady. It's your tender company that means so much to me ... though now that I've had a kiss from you ... " He placed a chaste one on her lips.

She laughed then gave him a much deeper kiss. Mmm ... the taste of him and the length of his long, hard body ... He was so insanely delectable. Never in her life had she wanted any man as much as she wanted this one.

Human or not.

Wanting to please him as much as he pleased her, she took his hand into hers and led it to her breast.

Styxx sucked his breath in sharply as he felt her through the soft linen and his body hardened to the point of pain. Slowly, he ran his hand over the contours of her breast then swept his thumb over the taut nipple. His body on fire, he wanted to sink himself deep inside her so badly that he could already taste it.

But he would never dishonor her like that. Never make someone cry because he'd touched them. Especially not his Bethany.

He involuntarily flinched as he remembered how he'd felt when Estes had purged the drugs from his body and he'd first realized how badly and rudely they'd used him.

Like he was nothing.

Bethany pulled back with a frown. "What's wrong, Hector?"

"What do you mean?"

226

"You jerked just now like something bad went through your mind. What plagues you, my lord?"

Sighing, he laid his head against hers. "I'm terribly scarred, Bethany."

"I've never felt any on you, except the one on your forearm."

Not wanting to think about the cut his father had given him, he took her hand and led it to the skin he always kept covered with his chiton and chlamys.

Bethany hesitated as she felt the puckered flesh that covered his ribs. His scars were truly deep and numerous. "What happened?"

"I was burned."

"Oh, Hector . . ."

"And there are more. In more private places."

Turning in his arms, she knelt between his legs. "You know I don't care."

"But I do."

She kissed his hand and offered him a bittersweet smile. "Then I will patiently wait until you trust me more. But know that I would never, ever hurt you in any way."

Styxx stared at her in awe. She was the only person in his life to say that to him, but did he dare trust her? Everyone in his life, including his twin, had betrayed him. Trust always meant profound pain . . .

And Bethany's would sting most of all.

Even so, he couldn't help the way he felt about her. How much she meant to him. In all the world, she was the only thing that mattered. Cupping her face in his hands, he kissed her. "I love you, Bethany."

"And I love you."

"Then run away with me."

She pulled back with a frown. "What?"

"Now. Today. Let's leave this place and—"

"Hector, I can't do that. I have things I have to do here. And so do you. What would your father say?"

"I don't care."

"Yes, you do. I know you better than that. You are a man of responsibility. It's part of what I love about you. You always put the needs of others before your own."

Yes, but this one time he wanted to be completely selfish. In all his life, he'd never wanted anything the way he did this woman. For her, he'd give up everything he had and more.

"I would walk away from it all for you, Beth."

She pressed her cheek to his. "But in time you could change your mind."

"No, I won't."

"I know you mean that today. But time and circumstance have a way of mocking our best intentions, and I'm not willing to take that chance."

Sighing, he laid his head against her breasts and let her cradle him there. Her heart beat slowly against his ear while her breath fell against his skin. The scent of her warmed him more than the sun. Honestly, he never wanted to leave the circle of her arms. It was the only place he'd ever felt as if he was welcome.

Loved.

Bethany smiled down at him. Her Hector never failed to surprise her.

She tightened her arms around him, wishing she could leave everything behind and be with him. How wonderful would it be?

But the other gods would come for her and they would kill him for distracting her from her duties.

After a few seconds, he lifted his hand to brush it against the breast he faced. To her complete shock, he hooked his thumb into the material of her peplos and pulled it aside so that he could blow a stream of cool air over her bared nipple until it puckered tight.

It was so unlike him . . .

She frowned. "Hector? What are you doing?"

"Hopefully, not offending you. Since you haven't slapped me or yanked my hair, I'm assuming I'm allowed?"

She smiled down at him. "You're allowed."

Styxx's heart pounded at the sight of her lush perfect naked breast. His mouth watering, he moved his head so that he could sample the taut peak. He groaned at the incredible taste of it as he rolled his tongue around the areola then suckled her gently.

Bethany cradled his head as he moved to taste her other breast. Her body was so hot and needful that it was all she could do not to betray herself as a goddess. She wanted him inside her so badly that it was absolutely painful.

Leaning back, she pulled him with her and released the pins that held her gown up so that he had complete access to her breasts. Then she brushed her hand against his hard erection.

Styxx froze as a fleeting bad memory went through him . . .

"Hector?"

He allowed her sweet voice to keep him grounded in the present and not on what Estes had done to him. "I'm right here, love." He placed a kiss on her stomach, before he pushed her gown down, over her hips until she was completely naked to his gaze.

His throat went dry at her unadorned, flawless beauty. Unlike him, there wasn't a scar on her body anywhere.

Frowning, she reached to cover herself. "Hector?"

He shook himself mentally as he realized he was sitting back from her. "I'm right here, precious." He took her hand and led it to his face as he laid his body over hers. "I was just temporarily stunned by how beautiful you are."

"Then you're forgiven for scaring me. I thought you'd run off and abandoned me naked in the woods."

"I would never do that to you." He made sure to keep his skin against hers so that she could feel him with her.

As she reached to remove his chiton, he caught her hand.

"Is something wrong?"

Even if she felt the brand on his groin, she'd have no way of knowing it said "whore."

But still it was there. Mocking him with the cruelty of his past. And because of the scars from that and the priests, he had sparse

229

pubic hair. So little that the brand was easily seen and not really covered at all.

He leaned his head down and ground his teeth. "Before we go any further . . . " He led her hand to the scars on his thighs and buttocks.

Bethany sucked her breath in sharply as she felt what had been done to him. When she'd touched his side, she'd assumed it had been caused by a fire. But these . . . she could feel the outline of a poker. It'd left deep welts down the inside of his thighs, all the way to his scrotum. There were places where he had little to no hair from the scarring. But what wrung her heart was the sheer number of them. He'd been tortured over and over again.

"Why would someone do this to you?"

"They thought I was possessed by the god Dionysus. And the priests sought to burn the evil daemons out of me."

Heartbroken over what they'd done, she placed her hand to his cheek. "My poor baby. I'm so sorry they hurt you like this."

"Please don't ever tell anyone."

"I would never be so cruel."

He kissed her then. So slow and tender that it made her breath catch. When she reached to remove his chiton, he jerked back.

"Sorry," he whispered. "I don't like being seen."

"I can't see you, Hector."

"That's not true. You're the only one in my life who does." This time he remained perfectly still while she undressed him.

"Are you all right?" she asked.

He placed her hand to his cheek and nodded then he nibbled her fingers and palm. Bethany sighed in pure pleasure. No one had ever made love to her like this. There was no rush at all. Rather they were truly exploring and sharing not just their bodies, but a part of their souls.

"You're so beautiful," he whispered against her throat as his hand skimmed over her hip and thigh.

She parted her legs for him.

Styxx hesitated as he realized that she was a bit more experienced at this than he was ... and a lot less bashful. "Beth? You've been with other men, haven't you?"

She went rigid under him. "I have, but I'm not a whore."

He cupped her face, wishing she could see his sincerity. "I would *never* call you that. It's not what I was implying at all. I just ... I don't want to accidentally hurt you with my inexperience. Or disappoint you."

Bethany felt tears prick the backs of her eyes. He was always so concerned about letting her down. Though he seldom mentioned his family, that ever present worry let her know just how harsh they must be toward him.

About everything.

"You could never disappoint me, Hector." She took his hand into hers and led it to the center of her body.

Styxx couldn't breathe as he felt how wet and warm she was. But his hand in hers ...

He cringed at the memory of Estes.

"What's wrong, *akribos*?"

Unable to answer, Styxx had no choice except to pull away. He couldn't deal with the painful memories that slammed into him and left him impotent and shaking.

Damn you, you bastards! Why couldn't he forget what they'd done to him for even one heartbeat? Why?

I am worthless.

Bethany frowned at his actions until she put everything together. His reluctance to kiss or touch her. His fear of harming her ...

The scars that lay in extremely private parts of his body. All the way to his scrotum.

He'd suffered something a lot worse than being burned. Someone had raped and tortured him.

In that moment, she felt her god powers surge. She was the goddess of fury and vengeance. It was her job to avenge those who'd been so wronged.

He's Greek.

It didn't matter. She wanted the heart of whoever had done this to such a gentle and caring man.

Clearing his throat, he reached over her to retrieve his chiton. "I'm sorry. This was a mistake. I shouldn't have . . . "

Bethany placed her hand to his lips to stop him. "Let me replace your evil demons with happy ones."

"I don't know if you can."

"Will you let me try?"

Styxx pulled her against him and held her close as self-loathing and hatred shredded his soul. "I'm sorry, Beth. You deserve a man, not—"

"You are a man," she said, interrupting him. "More so than any I've known. It's not manly to hurt others or belittle them. Respect and kindness require more courage because people take advantage of those. I don't know what horrors haunt you, but I know that you haven't allowed them to destroy the most beautiful part of yourself. You have the heart of a lion. Fearless. Tell me what is manlier than that?"

Styxx savored the sensation of her hand on his cheek. In spite of her impassioned, wonderful words, he felt so weak and pathetic. *I can't even make love to the woman I gave my heart to.*

For all intents and purposes, they *had* gelded him.

She nibbled at his chin. "Forget the animals who've hurt you. Think only of the woman who loves you with every bit of her heart, and that, Hector, is a part of me no man has ever touched before. Not even close. You're the only one who has held it. The only one who ever will."

He sucked his breath in sharply as she kissed her way down his chest and ran her sweet tongue over his scarred nipple. She pulled back to smile at him then nudged him to lie back on the ground. He obliged. She straddled him and took his hands into hers then led them to her breasts. Large and well shaped, they overflowed his hands. Leaning forward ever so slightly, she slid down his stomach to rest against his hips.

The moment she did, his body erupted and he was even harder

than before. Smiling wider, she began to sing to him. Between the sound of her sweet contralto and sight of her naked in his arms, he forgot about everything else. There was no past to hurt him. No future to worry over.

Just Bethany.

She lifted herself up onto her arms and slid her legs between his in one sensuous wave that left him breathless. Still singing, she kissed her way down his abdomen to the scars he hated so much. But as she laved them, he no longer saw them either. She brushed her hands through the hair at the juncture of his thighs then played gently with him.

He sucked his breath in sharply as pleasure speared him to the ground. With a wicked grin, she took him completely into her mouth. For the merest heartbeat, he flashed to a memory he didn't want. But he refused to stay there. Rather he watched as she toyed with him while she continued to hum.

His hand shaking, he reached down to stroke her cheek and lay the back of his fingers against skin so soft it wrung his heart.

Bethany savored the salty taste of him while he gently sank his hand into her hair. She knew he was struggling to forget. He would tense and then relax. Yet he bravely stayed with her. In that moment, she wished she could see the face of the man who was so haunted and still so giving.

But his looks didn't matter to her. At this point, she wouldn't care if he were a three-headed toad. He held her heart and it was as blind as her eyes in human form.

Wanting only to soothe him, she gave one last lick then crawled up the long length of him to lie against his body.

Styxx sighed at how good her soft curves felt flush to his skin. Cupping her head, he kissed her deeply then rolled over with her. She opened her legs so that his body lay between her thighs while they kissed.

She didn't know it, but she'd saved his life. In the darkest moment when he'd wanted nothing more than death, she'd appeared and given him a reason to get up each morning. Now, he lived

233

solely for the time they shared. It made everything else bearable. Just knowing he'd be able to see her sweet smile. Hear her precious voice . . .

He kissed her lips then carefully slid himself inside her. They moaned simultaneously. For a full minute, he couldn't breathe as the warmth of her body cradling his overwhelmed him. It felt so good it made him shiver. This was the first perfect moment of true happiness he'd ever known.

She had no idea how much she meant to him. Words would never be able to convey the depth to which his heart beat solely for her.

Styxx brushed the hair back from her face as he stared down into her hazel-gold eyes, wishing she could see how happy she made him. "I love you, Bethany."

She smiled at him. "And I, you."

Nipping her chin, he slowly began to rock himself against her hips.

Bethany arched her back, drawing him in deeper. She groaned at his thick fullness inside her. He was absolutely huge and yet so very gentle. She ran her hands over his muscular back and down to his waist then to the scars that made her want to hunt down whoever had dared to mar his perfection and make them pay for their cruelty. But she didn't want to think about them right now.

She only wanted to feel Hector and the love she had for him. Lifting her head, she kissed him lightly on the lips. "What color is your hair?"

He paused then gave a light laugh. "A strange time to ask, my lady."

"I know. But I'm curious about the man inside me."

"I'm blond," he whispered in her ear as he deepened his strokes.

"And your eyes?"

"Blue."

She sank her hands into his hair and imagined the beautiful blond curls that teased her skin. Then she traced his brows above his blue eyes, and his sharp cheekbones and jaw. Her Hector *was* handsome. She knew it.

Styxx bit his lip as she met him stroke for stroke. Every part of him felt like it was on fire and yet strangely calm. Bethany swept her hands from his face down his chest and then even lower.

He gasped as she placed her hand to where they were joined and touched him as he slid in and out of her. The pleasure was so intense that he growled with it. He'd always loved how she used her graceful hands to see, but never more than he did right now. Most of all, he loved that she wasn't timid or reserved. She gave every part of herself to him.

Arching her back, she cried out as she clutched him to her and shook in his arms. He took his cue from her and moved faster and harder. She sang louder and laughed.

Relieved that he'd pleased her and not embarrassed himself, he felt his body starting to tip. But he forced it down until he was sure she was completely satisfied. Only then did he bury himself deep inside her and growl as his own release came. His senses reeled with exquisite pleasure.

For a full minute, he couldn't breathe or think as every part of him shouted in joy. Then ever so slowly, it faded.

Spent and sated, and breathing raggedly, he lowered himself and savored the way she cradled him with her body. His heart pounded so fiercely, he was surprised it stayed inside his chest. A fine sheen of sweat covered both of them.

No wonder men killed over their women. He fully understood that possessiveness now. The need to keep her safe from all threat or harm. There was nothing he could think of that would ever compete with the complete peace and quiet he felt right then in her arms. He never wanted to leave her.

"That was amazing," he breathed in her ear.

"Yes, you were." Her smile made his breath catch as she lifted his hand so that she could nibble his fingers and send even more chills over him.

Styxx tilted his head as he saw the necklace that never left her.

It was her sole piece of jewelry. He tugged gently at the thin leather cord until the small silver, oddly-shaped disk was untangled from her black hair. It held the impression of a bow and arrow, and appeared as if it were half of a larger amulet. "What is this you always wear?"

She reached down to cover his hand with hers and touched it then smiled. "My father gave it to me when I was a little girl so that I could feel loved wherever I went."

No wonder she treasured it. Almost every gift he'd received had eventually been taken from him or destroyed as punishment. It was why he didn't like to be given anything at all.

"What does the symbol mean?"

"It's my personal emblem for the goddess of the hunt."

Styxx ran his thumb over it as he remembered the bracelet he'd given his mother before she stabbed him. The goddess of the hunt, Artemis was said to be the protector of women and children ... She must have been favoring his mother over him that day.

He placed the disk between her breasts where it normally fell. "I hope she always protects you, Beth."

"She will."

Not wanting to think about the gods who hated him as much as he hated them, he ran his index finger along her bottom lip, wishing he could stay with her forever. It was so hard to contemplate going back to a place where no one wanted him while he lay cradled by her warm body.

But unfortunately, it was getting late and she didn't need to be walking home in the dark. If anything were to ever happen to her ...

He would be driven insane by it. The mere thought of any harm coming to her filled him with rage.

"As much as I hate to withdraw from you, it'll be dark soon." Rising, he swept her up in his arms.

Bethany's eyes widened as he carried her to the stream as if she weighed nothing at all. Because of her height, she was used to towering over most men, not having them make her feel petite in comparison. And no one had carried her since she'd been a child.

In truth, she loved the feeling of it.

He set her down in the water so that she could wash.

"Beth?"

She paused. "Yes?"

"I will do my best to see you at week's end, but I might not be able to. My father usually has an annual banquet he throws for my uncle then, and if I don't attend, he'll be furious."

Straightening, she put her hands on her hips and glared in what she hoped was the correct direction. "So that's it, eh? You sleep with me and then you abandon me." She tsked at him.

"Never!" The intensity of his denial shocked her.

She reached for him to comfort the pain she'd heard. "I'm teasing you, *akribos*. It's fine. I'll see you the next time."

He pulled her against him and held her as if he couldn't bear to let her go. "I would kill or die for you, Beth. *Only* you."

She held him tight. "I know, sweet. I love you, too."

He kissed her then went to dress while she continued her bath.

By the time she finished, he had everything packed up for her. She smiled at his thoughtfulness. "You really can't wait to get away from me, huh?"

This time he took it as she meant it. "What can I say, my lady? You're such an onerous burden. The sooner I'm away, the better."

Laughing, she took her basket and pole from him.

He cupped her face in both of his hands and kissed her lightly on the lips. "Be safe, my heart."

"You, too." Bethany waited for a few more seconds before she laughed. "Hector? I can't leave if you don't let me go."

"Sorry." He forced himself to release her. "I will see you later, my lady. But never soon enough to suit me."

"Good night, my fair prince. Until I feel you again."

Her parting words made him suck his breath in. She had no idea how close to the truth she was.

Still, Styxx didn't move until he watched her vanish into the woods. Only then did he swing himself up to the back of his horse and turn toward home.

What he didn't want to scare her with was the fact that he knew war was coming soon. His father and advisors had been preparing for it for weeks now. All their allies were rallying for the march to the south.

And when it came, he could have to go fight it.

While he wasn't afraid, he didn't look forward to the days of not seeing his Bethany.

Would she wait for him, or would he be forgotten as soon as he left?

AUGUST 19, 9532 BC

Shocked and confused, Bethany paused outside her temple in Katateros as she saw Archon with Apollo.

A Greek god in their sacred lands?

It was forbidden. Of course it'd been forbidden by Archon, but still . . .

Why would a Greek god be here? It was as shocking as one of them going to Mount Olympus for tea. Normally whenever they had business with Apollo, it was conducted in one of their temples in Atlantis.

Curious, she walked closer to them to see what was going on. Like her, Apollo was said to be born of more than one pantheon. There were several contradictory stories about the identity of his mother, and the Greek god had never owned up to any of them. He enjoyed the mystique of it all.

One of the stories would make him her cousin through her father's family. But she didn't think he really had Egyptian blood in him. If he did, she should be able to perceive it. All she'd ever sensed from the Greek was a vicious streak of cruelty that made her wonder how his people ever thought him benevolent.

Obviously, he didn't let the Greek humans see him often, or they'd know better.

"You are well aware of my feelings on this," Apollo said to Archon. "If you want to attack Greece, you have my full backing."

Archon held his hand up to keep Apollo from saying anything more. "Who goes there?"

She stepped out of the shadows.

Both of the gods breathed in relief, which made her all the more curious. Why would they welcome her presence when it was obvious they were conspiring something?

Bethany moved to stand beside Archon. "What are you two talking about?"

Archon glanced to Apollo before he answered. "War."

That was always one of her favorite topics. People were never more honest than when they were fighting for their lives. Cowards were exposed and heroes sprang from the unlikeliest of places.

Apollo crossed his arms over his chest. "I was just telling your uncle, that as always, I would fully back Atlantis in the coming conflict with Greece. I haven't forgotten how your people welcomed mine in when Zeus ordered my Apollites killed. It's a debt I will always be loyal to and respect."

The Apollites were the race Apollo had created after a disagreement with his father over mankind. Taller and stronger than humans, and possessing advanced psychic abilities, the Apollites had quickly decided to subjugate their Greek brethren. Something Zeus had taken offense to. He'd ordered Apollo to kill his "children" and Apollo had adamantly refused.

Feeling sorry for them, the Atlanteans had opened their doors to the Apollites, who had become "model" citizens for Atlantis. As a result, the relations between Greece and Atlantis had been strained ever since. And it'd left Apollo with loyalties to both pantheons and nations.

So far, he'd always sided with them over the Greeks, but

Bethany still didn't trust him. She suspected his only real loyalty was to Apollo and no one else . . .

There was just something about him that had always made her skin crawl. An innate distaste.

"Just tell me what you need and I will do my best to make it happen," Apollo assured him. "Now I'd best return before I'm missed and the other Olympians wonder where I've gone." He vanished.

Bethany narrowed her gaze at her uncle. "We've barely had a truce with Greece. I thought you wanted it maintained."

"That was before Apollymi hid a baby in their ranks. He should be old enough to fight now. I'm hoping he'll be among the Greek soldiers we kill, especially if we attack the whole of Greece. Our primary targets will be their royals and noblemen. No one will think it odd if they all die in battle, or as a result of conquest."

Insidious . . .

Frowning, Bethany tried to make sense of the emotions she felt from him. "Apostolos is your son, Archon, can't you—"

"He's not my son. *That's* the problem."

She froze at those growled words. "What do you mean?"

He lowered his voice. "After the debacle of Apollymi's firstborn, we all decided that I was to marry her and keep her happy. As you know, I am not barren, and neither is she. I've purposefully kept her from conceiving. And the fact that I don't know who the father of her bastard is . . . "

Oh crap. She stared incredulously. "You honestly have no idea who fathered him?"

"No. Most likely it would be one of her Charontes or another god." The Charontes were Apollymi's army of demons. Morally ambiguous, they were absolute killing machines with the powers of gods. To mix one of those with Apollymi's powers and with her army to back him . . .

Yes, that would be a *very* bad thing.

"Why haven't you told the others?"

Archon's nostrils flared. "No one can ever know that he's not mine. Can you imagine what they might do out of fear?"

He had a point. Even gods were known to panic. And this situation was highly panic-worthy.

An unknown rogue god with no known loyalty and an army of morally ambiguous demons to command . . . Scary stuff, that.

Archon's eyes darkened to red. "I don't care if we have to slaughter every Greek prince of his generation, her son has to die before his powers are unleashed."

As much as she hated to admit it, he was right. "Then I will back this war with you."

"Thank you. And I can trust in your discretion?"

"Of course."

Inclining his head to her, Archon returned to his temple.

Bethany swept her gaze over the breathtaking landscape of Katateros, which had been the home of the Atlantean gods since before the dawn of human time.

Counted among the oldest of gods, Apollymi was a mighty force that only one other had ever been able to fight with success—a goddess that had long ago vanished.

And after all these centuries, Bethany finally understood Apollymi's temperament and motivation. First, for the husband she'd once loved who had betrayed her with other lovers. Second, for the loss of two sons. It wasn't until Hector that Bethany had any real knowledge of love. If he were to touch another woman . . .

She would gut him where he stood.

That being said, she could think of no sweeter gift than to have a baby with him. Strange how she'd never wanted one before. She'd always found children whiny and gross. Odious. Little tyrants who needed to be locked up until they became human.

But now . . .

She would love to have a little blond baby to hold and love. One with its father's quick witticisms and soft curls. And if she were ever so lucky as to have one, she would annihilate anyone who threatened it.

241

Just like Apollymi.

Honestly, the thought of killing the goddess's son didn't sit well with her. It never had. But sometimes the one had to be sacrificed for the many.

Or did it?

Maybe, just maybe there was another way out for all of them.

AUGUST 20, 9532 BC

Styxx stood behind his father as his uncle rode through the palace gates with his friends. His blood ran cold at the sight of his uncle's entourage and what it meant for him.

Panic, cold and brutal, gripped him and it took everything he had not to run and bolt himself into his room. Only the knowledge that his father would batter down the door and beat him for it kept him where he was.

Estes dismounted and rushed to embrace his father. "Xerxes! It's so good to see you again."

"And you, my brother. A pleasure as always."

Estes walked up the three steps to pull Styxx into his arms. "How's my favorite stallion?" he whispered in his ear. "Are you ready to ride?"

Styxx would have shoved him away, but Estes held him too tightly.

Kissing him on his cheeks, Estes stepped back so that he could return to his father's side.

Styxx refused to look at the men who'd traveled with his uncle. He had no wish to see their faces or the hunger he was sure darkened their gazes. Nor did he pay attention when his uncle introduced them.

His father threw his arm over his uncle's shoulders. "I can't tell you how glad I am that you're here. Even more so than normal."

"How so?"

"I have to journey to Thessaly in the morning and I didn't want to leave Styxx alone for so long."

Styxx stumbled at that.

His father scowled at him. "Are you all right?"

Fuck no. Literally.

Styxx glared at his father. "Why didn't you tell me about this?"

"I only found out two days ago and didn't want to worry you." Against his will, Styxx glanced to his uncle. The lascivious light in Estes's eyes nauseated him. "I'll be more than happy to stay as long as you need me to, brother."

Of course you would, you sick bastard.

As his father led them inside, Styxx hung back, his head reeling with panic. Why had he not gone to the summer palace with Ryssa and his mother last week?

Because they hated him and would have made his trip and stay with them miserable. Not to mention, he wouldn't have been able to see Bethany until his return.

But this . . .

He felt suddenly queasy. His stomach cramped in dread. No one would be here to keep Estes from him. *No one.*

Day or night . . .

His heart pounding, he waited until his father was alone to speak to him.

"Father?"

Sighing, he turned to Styxx with high agitation showing on his face. "What?"

"May I please go with you to Thessaly?"

His father scowled. "Are you insane? Didymos needs someone in the capital to make decisions, especially now that war's looming."

"Estes is here. He can do it without me. Please, Father."

Still his father glared at him. "He's not the heir. *You* are. We're

243

on the brink of war. Our people need to know they have strong leadership should I have to be away for any reason."

Styxx couldn't breathe as true fear gripped him. He couldn't stay here with Estes. Alone . . .

"Please, Father."

"What is wrong with you?"

Estes's threats rang in his head and he had no doubt his uncle would carry out any and all of them. He wouldn't hesitate to drag Styxx off to Atlantis and use him for his perverted games and personal profit.

Styxx couldn't breathe a word of his fears to his father. If he did . . .

Somehow, like Ryssa, his father would blame him for causing it. He'd be thrown out like Acheron and then forced to whore for a living.

I have no one . . .

With no choice, he backed down. "Nothing, Majesty."

"Then leave me in peace to make preparations."

Styxx bowed then headed to his room, intending to bolt himself inside until his father returned.

He fastened the door and turned around only to realize he wasn't alone. *Shit.*

Estes was seated in his receiving room. "Greetings, fair nephew."

"What are you doing here?"

Estes dropped his hungry gaze to Styxx's groin. "I'm sure you know what I want."

Styxx started for the door, but Estes cut him off faster than he'd have thought a man could move.

Estes leaned back against the door with a taunting grin. "Should we call for your father?"

His breathing labored, Styxx glared at him. "Why did you sell me to Didymosians?"

That knocked some of the cockiness out of the bastard. "What?"

"Contrary to what you told me, I heard them talking. Two of

my father's senators. How many more of our citizens know what you've done to me?"

That evil, lewd light returned to his uncle's eyes. "I don't really think you want that answered. For the sake of your mind. But don't worry. They won't tell your father. He'd kill them for it." Estes jerked him into his arms. "Now give me a proper welcome, nephew." He moved to kiss him.

Styxx shoved him away. "Get off me." He tried to run to his bedroom, but Estes tripped him, knocking him to the ground.

Before he could regain his feet, Estes had him pinned with his arm twisted painfully against his spine and his wrist between his shoulders. "Shh, little squirrel." He bit Styxx's earlobe then breathed into his ear. "While I adore your brother, there are some things that you do excel at over him." He shoved something into Styxx's mouth and held his jaw shut. "Swallow."

Styxx did his best to spit it out, but it was useless. Against his will, Estes forced it down his throat.

Laughing, Estes kissed his neck. "That's it, my little stallion. We're going to have a lot of fun in the coming weeks while we wait for your father's return. But don't worry. I shall be kind and you won't remember any of it."

The room began to spin out of control.

Styxx closed his eyes as he thought about Bethany. If he didn't show up for weeks would she still be there for him?

Or would his lengthy absence make her hate him, too?

SEPTEMBER 17, 9532 BC

Styxx felt a single tear slide from the corner of his eye as his uncle finished with him and "dismounted." As their latest twisted game, they'd tied him facedown on a table with his arms spread and his ankles secured to the table legs. But the worst was the mock bridle Estes used to gag him with. A bridle they'd utilized while "riding" him.

Laughing and congratulating him on his "skills," his uncle's friends applauded Estes and handed him a kylix of wine. Estes took a drink then grabbed a handful of olives before he returned to kneel down beside the table so that he met Styxx's shame-filled gaze.

He tsked. "Sorry, little Phallas. I hadn't realized you were lucid, and here I'd promised you I wouldn't do that to you, didn't I?" He brushed the hair back from Styxx's face.

Bellowing in rage and horror, Styxx tried to break free. He wanted his uncle's throat so badly, he could taste it.

Estes laughed then stepped back.

Before Styxx could stop it, his gaze swept the room to see that there were more than just six men in it. He slammed his eyes shut as complete humiliation racked him. He was the center entertainment for a party of Didymosian noblemen . . .

Damn you, Estes!

And damn me.

Estes pressed Styxx's head against the table then kissed his brow. "Shh, squirrel. Calm down before you hurt yourself." He opened the small chest that was near Styxx's head and rummaged through it. "This should make you quiet and compliant again."

Styxx winced. He was so tired of being drugged, especially against his will.

Estes moved out of his line of sight so that he could insert the drug in the rudest manner possible while the others bid for the next ride on him. As his uncle held it inside him to make sure it took effect, Xan stepped forward to speak alone with Estes. "I heard the princess returns next week."

"She does, indeed."

"How much for a night with her?"

Estes tsked. "I can't do that. She has to go to the marriage bed pure. Or else my brother would have both our lives."

"A woman has more than one hole in her body. Put a chastity belt on her and name your price. I want her, Estes."

"It will be as dear and costly as my sweet niece is."

"I knew it would be. You'll do it?"

"I'll make it so."

Styxx tried to fight as those words slammed into him, but there was nothing he could do as his head and the room began to spin. Closing his eyes, he expelled a breath and let the drug take him far away from their cruelty.

Styxx came to as someone cut his hands loose from the table. Groaning, he winced as the bridle was rudely yanked from his mouth and he saw his uncle in front of him.

Estes freed his legs. "Get up."

Styxx tried, but his arms and legs were numb from having been tied for so long. His entire body was stiff and aching. He wasn't sure how many hours or days had passed. With Estes and his herbs, there was never any telling.

His uncle pulled an Atlantean formesta around him. "Your sister and mother have returned early." He backhanded Styxx. "I need you lucid enough to greet them."

Styxx licked the blood away from the corner of his lips as he tried to focus.

Growling, Estes seized him and dragged him into the bathing room. He threw him down beside the pool then dunked Styxx's head into the water to revive him.

Styxx sputtered and coughed as his thoughts finally cleared enough for him to think for himself again.

"Your mother and sister just docked a few minutes ago. They're on their way home. Wash and dress, and meet me downstairs. Hurry." Estes dunked his head one more time then got up and left.

His breathing labored, Styxx coughed the water out of his lungs then crawled into the pool to bathe the stench of Estes and the others off him. And as he did so, he remembered Xan's proposal for Ryssa.

Estes's acceptance.

Dear gods, they were going to do this to Ryssa. That sobered him instantly. While Ryssa hated his guts, he couldn't allow them to rape his sister. The shame alone would kill her. She wasn't strong enough to survive something so foul.

Or worse, she'd tell their father and he would throw her out for it. A ravaged princess would be worthless to the king, and she was just stupid enough to think her father wouldn't do that to her.

Styxx pulled himself out of the pool and quickly dressed. When he reached for his razor, he froze at the sight of his reflection. His eyes were sunken and swollen. Red and bloodshot from the drugs. He barely recognized himself. He'd lost weight and was extremely pallid. His wrists were bruised and cut from where he'd fought to free himself and there were small cuts around his mouth from the bridle. Even his lips were chapped and bleeding.

Gripping his razor, he quickly groomed himself so that neither his mother nor Ryssa would berate his disrespectfulness in meeting them unkempt. As soon as he could, he went downstairs to find Estes and the staff waiting to greet the royal envoy.

Estes smiled at the sight of him. "I forget how handsome you are when you're fresh and upright."

Styxx seized him and shoved him back into the wall. "You touch my sister, you bastard, and I will bathe in your entrails."

His uncle laughed. "Ryssa holds no interest for me. She never has. It's only beautiful men I covet."

"You sell her and—"

Estes grabbed his throat in a grip that instantly immobilized him. "Keep your impotent threats to yourself. I'm not one of your servants to be cowed by a royal frown, boy. I'm a veteran of more battles than you'll ever see. And I've made meals off bigger and tougher men than you. So don't think for one moment you can sober up and intimidate me. You *ever* threaten me again and you will pray to the gods to return you to these days where I actually care what happens to you. Do you understand?" He tightened his grip to the point that Styxx almost lost consciousness.

Then he shoved him back and released him.

Panting as the blood returned to his head and pierced his skull with a pain so foul Styxx saw stars, he glared at the bastard. *I have to stop this.* It was bad enough that Estes abused him and Acheron.

"She's your sister, boy. You protect her, no matter what." His father's words rang in his head.

It was the only thing he'd never failed to do. And it was the one thing his father would find unforgivable.

The musicians began playing outside. Estes nodded to have the doors opened and went out to greet them. His throat still burning from Estes's hold, Styxx followed then descended the steps so that he could help his mother and sister down from their chariot.

The moment she saw him, his mother curled her lip. "You look appalling. I don't know what whore you withdrew from on my arrival, but you could have at least washed before you approached your mother." She refused to take his hand. Instead, she brushed rudely past him, letting everyone know that the queen had no use for her son.

But then he was used to that.

He held his hand out to Ryssa.

Like her mother, she refused to touch him. She stepped down and raked him with her disdain. "What have you done? Drank and whored every day Father's been gone? Your condition is execrable."

I should let you be gang-raped, bitch, and throw it in your face. See then how you'd take being bridled and ridden like a horse.

Ryssa headed for the stairs.

Styxx pulled her to a stop. "We need to talk."

She jerked her arm out of his grasp. "In spite of what you think, you're not king yet. You do *not* command me."

"Ryssa—"

"Go back to your whore and wine, brother. Or better yet, for the sake of the gods, get some sleep and sober up before your father sees you and learns what a pathetic waste stands to inherit his throne."

Unlike their mother, Ryssa ignored Estes and continued on into the palace.

Laughing, Estes moved to clap Styxx on the back. "That was certainly rude of them, wasn't it?" He leaned in to whisper to Styxx. "So tell me, nephew. Are you ready to pay me to watch your sister be violated and put in her place?"

A part of him wanted to see it so badly that it frightened him. He was so tired of Ryssa's and his mother's criticisms when he'd done nothing to deserve them.

It would serve Ryssa right to taste the degradation he knew so intimately. But as his gaze fell to Xan and he saw the giant size of the Atlantean, he knew that bastard would tear his sister apart. Just as he'd done Styxx.

No matter how much he hated her, he couldn't allow that to happen. He had to stop this.

But how?

SEPTEMBER 19, 9532 BC

Since the queen's return, Estes hadn't dared to keep Styxx as drugged as before. It was both a curse and a blessing. And right now, Styxx didn't want to remember any of the past few horrific hours he'd spent while he occasionally heard his mother and Ryssa laughing together as he'd been kept against his will in Estes's rooms, next to his sister's.

With any luck, he'd never have to be so debased again.

Styxx finally got the rope free from his bruised, bleeding wrist. It'd taken him hours to work it through.

His hand burned from the strain of contorting it so that he

could tug at the rough, thick strands. As quickly as he could, he untied his other one. Normally Estes chained him or tied his hands apart from each other. Tonight, for reasons he didn't want to think about, Estes had tied them together and stretched them over Styxx's head to secure him to the bed.

Then the bastard had passed out before he had a chance to part them.

Grimacing, Styxx snatched the gag from his mouth while Estes slept soundly by his side. With a deep sigh, Estes rolled over and threw his thigh over Styxx's. His hand quested a part of Styxx's body that revolted him. Careful, lest he wake his uncle, he disentangled himself enough so that he could free his ankles and slide off the bed.

His heart pounded as he considered his options. There was no way to get word to his father in time. Even if he did, he fully believed that Estes would be able to twist it so that his father would never believe him. His mother would be worthless. Ryssa was stupid to a supreme level.

If he tried to arrest Estes, everything would come out. And he had no doubt that his uncle would have him committed again and then taken to Atlantis to be bought and sold.

The only real option he had left him sick to his stomach.

But it was the only way to make all of this stop. The only way to protect his brother and sister.

Himself.

You're a pathetic coward. His own disdain rose up to silence the voices of the gods in his head. *A real man would have already done it.*

Yet it wasn't that easy. He'd never hurt anyone before. Not intentionally.

I have to do this. His uncle had left him with no choice. If he didn't, Ryssa would be raped, too.

If I let that happen, how would I ever be able to live with myself?

The same way he'd been living with his conscience and the humiliation Estes and the others had given him.

One heartbeat at a time.

But no matter what, he couldn't let Ryssa be harmed. Not when he could stop it.

And Acheron would never leave Atlantis. Not so long as Estes lived . . .

With a trembling hand and abject horror in his heart, Styxx pulled his pillow across the bed. He held it to his chest, staring at his uncle's naked body.

Gods forgive me for what I'm about to do.

Before he could change his mind or run, Styxx forced himself to slam the pillow down over Estes's face. Estes let out a muffled bellow as he grabbed Styxx and tried to fight him off. Styxx wrapped his body around Estes's as he used every trick Galen had taught him to hold on and make sure that he didn't loosen his grip until Estes went limp in his arms.

Even then, he waited, afraid it was a trick. If his uncle had even a single breath left, he'd kill Styxx for this.

His hands were colder than ice when he finally reached to feel for a pulse.

Nothing.

He's dead.

I killed him.

Tears filled his eyes as bile rose in his throat. He'd taken a life. And not just any life. His uncle's.

His father's beloved younger brother.

Styxx pulled the pillow back to reveal Estes's glazed, open eyes. Ironically, Styxx didn't see the sadistic bastard who'd spent the last year molesting him . . . he saw the uncle who'd been kind to him when he was a boy. The one who'd brought him presents and who had tried to help him.

Unable to cope with what he'd done and what had happened to him, Styxx ran to the chamber pot and unloaded his stomach.

My father will kill me if he ever finds out.

He'd committed murder. Cold-blooded. Brutal. A capital offense.

You had no choice.

But it didn't seem like that now. Not with this kind of finality. *I killed my own uncle. My flesh and blood.*

Horrified, Styxx fell against the wall and tried to fathom why his eyes were dry. He glanced back to the bed and gasped as he saw the ropes he'd untied. They would let others know that Estes hadn't been alone in his bed.

Panicking even more, he got up and quickly gathered them and any evidence that betrayed his presence here tonight. The second kylix. His gag. The "toys" his uncle had used on him. Then he closed Estes's eyes and put the bed in order.

Terrified and queasy, he snuck from his uncle's room and went to his, where he burned all the things he'd gathered until there was nothing left to betray him.

He set the kylix on his table and forced himself to lie in a bed that made his skin crawl. Guilt and fear, shame and horror mixed inside him, overriding any grief he might have known. And all he could do was wait for someone to discover Estes's body.

And accuse him of a crime that would surely cost him his head.

It was midmorning before one of Estes's entourage found him in his bed. Listening to the commotion outside, Styxx clung to his pillow as fear wrapped him tight and threatened to suffocate him the way he'd killed his uncle.

"Styxx!" his mother shouted as she threw his door wide. "Come! Your uncle's dead."

For a full minute, he couldn't move as he tried to think of how to react. What would be acceptable.

And what wouldn't get him convicted.

Before he could decide, his mother snatched the covers and pillow off him. "Did you hear me?"

Feigning sleep even though he had yet to close his eyes, he frowned at her. "What?"

"Estes is dead. He appears to have died in his sleep. Get up and dress, you worthless dog! We need you."

He drew a ragged breath and got up to bathe and dress.

By the time he joined his family, his mother was kneeling on the floor next to Estes's side, wailing with a grief he knew she didn't feel. His gaze went to Ryssa, who knelt beside their mother. She had tears in her eyes, but he knew they weren't for Estes. It was Acheron on her mind.

Xan narrowed a suspicious glare at him that told him the Atlantean prince knew what he'd done, but didn't dare make the allegation without proof.

"Where have you been?" Phanes, his father's oldest advisor, demanded.

Before Styxx could answer, he felt the air leave the room as all eyes went to the door behind him.

Turning, Styxx saw his father there with a stern glower as he took in the sight of everyone standing over his brother's cold, naked body. Without a word, his father rushed to the bed and touched Estes's shoulder. He winced in pain.

"Leave us!" his father roared.

Ryssa helped their mother to her feet and they made a hasty retreat.

As Styxx moved to follow them, his father stopped him.

"Not you, boy. I want you to stay."

Fear pierced his heart as he closed the door behind the others then returned to his father's side.

"What happened?"

"I don't know, Father. I just found out about it myself."

Tears flowed down the king's face as he reached for Styxx and jerked him into his arms to hold him. Violent sobs shook his father's entire body. Stunned, Styxx couldn't move while his father wept against his chest. Never in his life had his father shown so much emotion over anything.

But what cut deepest were his father's thoughts of the childhood he'd shared with his beloved brother. How much he'd loved the man the son he held had killed.

Styxx stiffened. Anger welled up inside him, demanding he

shove his father away and tell him what his brother was really like. What Estes had done to him and to Acheron, and what he'd planned to do to Ryssa. But he knew his father would never believe him. Just as Ryssa would never believe Styxx was capable of any good deed, his father would never believe Estes was capable of a bad one.

And he would *never* forgive Styxx for killing him.

After a few minutes, his father pulled himself together and straightened. He wiped his tears and cleared his throat. "We shall give him a state funeral. Then we'll have to see to his affairs in Atlantis."

Styxx inclined his head to him. "What of the pending war?"

His father glanced back at his uncle and hung his head. "You're right, boy. We'll need to hurry this. We'll have Estes buried tonight in our crypt and leave for Atlantis first thing. Have your sister and mother oversee the body preparations."

Styxx hesitated before he complied. "I'm sorry, Father."

The king pulled Styxx's head down and kissed his brow. "Pack lightly."

"Excuse me?"

"I don't want to travel alone to Atlantis. I need you to go with me to do this. You will be my strength."

His fear and remorse turned to cold rage. For his father's benefit, Didymos could be left without a king on her throne.

But when *he'd* needed to go with his father . . .

There had been no way in Hades it could happen.

Had you once considered my needs, you bastard, your brother would still be alive. Styxx glanced to the bed where he'd been tied and wanted to tell his father the truth. He wanted to see his father's face when he learned his own brother had turned both of his sons into whores.

Don't. The truth would not go well for him. His father had never loved him the way he loved Estes, and he never would.

Styxx glanced down at the scar on his forearm and accepted a reality he couldn't change. Bowing, he left his father and went to tell the others about the burial, and then to pack.

When he reached his rooms, Xan was inside, waiting for him.

The giant Atlantean stood with his legs wide and arms folded across his chest. Anger bled from every cell of his body. "You killed him, didn't you?"

With all the training he'd received since birth, Styxx arched a regal brow. "What are you talking about?"

A good seven inches taller, Xan moved to tower over Styxx and did his best to intimidate him with his massive size. "I fucked your tight little ass with Estes last night. When I left, you were out of it and tied to the bed." Xan snatched Styxx's hand and held his bruised, scabbed wrist for Styxx to see. "Estes wouldn't have freed you until he got up this morning and yet you weren't there when I went in to fuck you again."

"I awoke in the middle of the night and found him dead by my side. I panicked."

"I don't believe you."

"Should we take the matter to my father and let him decide the truth? But you'll have to confess to him how it is you know for a fact that I couldn't get free."

Xan curled his lip. "You think you've gotten away with this. But the gods know what you've done. You killed him in cold blood. I've heard the Furies in your pantheon have a special wrath they visit on the heads of those who murder their own family."

"Then I welcome them with open arms." Styxx glared at him. "And I'm not the one who killed my uncle. You did the moment you decided to hunger for my sister."

Xan slammed him back against the wall so hard, it knocked the breath from him. "I shall miss Estes. He was a good friend. But most of all, I shall miss watching you and your brother suck my cock until I come in your pretty little mouths, and seeing you swallow every last drop of me."

Styxx moved to attack, but the bastard kneed him in the groin and left him to his misery. Both physical and mental.

*

Bethany sighed as she packed up her basket. Again. It'd been over a solid month since she'd last seen Hector. Faithless bastard that he was, she seethed mentally. *Give men what they want and they can't leave fast enough.*

How she hated them all.

Trying not to think about how she'd let a mere mortal hurt her, she was just about to teleport home when she heard a rustling nearby.

"Beth?"

At first she thought it might be wishful thinking on her part.

Until she heard him call out again. "Hector?"

All of a sudden, he was by her side, pulling her gently against him. He held her so tight that she could barely breathe as he buried his face into the crook of her neck. His entire body was shaking so much that it frightened her.

"Is something wrong?"

"Not now that I'm finally with you again." He tightened his arms around her. "I'm so sorry I haven't been here. Believe me, I tried to come. I've thought of absolutely nothing else except being with you. Night and day."

Those words and the truth in his desperate tone brought tears to her eyes. "I thought you'd forgotten all about me."

"How could I forget the air I breathe? You alone sustain me."

He was a great deal leaner than he'd been and there were cuts and swelling on his body she didn't understand.

"Have you been ill?"

"You've no idea how much I cherish the concern in your sweet voice." He held her hand against his cheek and kissed her palm. "How have you been?"

"Missing you and mad at myself for it."

"Really?"

She cocked her brow at him. "You delight at the fact that I've been angry at myself?"

"No. Never. You should never be cross with yourself. Did you really miss me?"

257

"Of course."

He kissed her hand again. "A pittance compared to how much I've ached for you, I promise."

"Doubtful."

"Truth."

And still he was shaking uncontrollably. "Why do you tremble so?"

"Your beauty. It always leaves me quaking in its mighty presence."

She scoffed, even though his flattery warmed her. "You are ever a silver-tongued master."

"No. I am helpless before you, my lady. Always." He knelt in front of her and placed his head to her stomach.

Even more concerned than before, Bethany held him there. "I am worried about you. I know something dreadful has happened."

"And it was terrible, indeed. I was kept from seeing you, my precious lady."

She rolled her eyes at his silliness. "You awful, wretched, thoughtless beast. You make me forgive you when I want to be angry at your neglect." Smiling down at him, she brushed her hand through his soft hair.

"I will take your anger so long as it doesn't turn to hatred. I could never live if I thought you hated me."

"See, there it all goes. No trace of anger inside me now. Damn you, Hector. You stink!"

He pressed her hand to his face so that she could feel his smile. "How I've missed you cursing me."

"And how I've missed loving you, you aggravating man." She lifted his hand to her heart so that he could feel it beating for him. "Against everything I've tried to do to prevent it, you have crawled into a part of me where only you can do me harm. Do you understand, Hector? And I am a vengeful woman whose wrath is unimaginable. Do not make me turn that against you. For both our sakes."

"So long as there is breath inside me, I will never do anything to intentionally harm you, Beth." He rose to his feet and gave her the sweetest kiss she'd ever known. "I unfortunately have to travel for the next few weeks. But I will be back here as soon as I return. I swear it."

"You better."

He pulled her into his arms and breathed her in. "One day, I shall tell you what happened. But for now . . . " He kissed her. "I will be counting down the heartbeats until I see you again."

Bethany held him to her and let the innocence of his kiss breathe life into her. "I miss you already."

"Not as much as I miss you."

Styxx forced himself to let her go and turn back toward his horse. He took a moment to watch her pick up her basket and pole, and wondered if she'd still love him if she knew what he'd done. How ruthless he'd been to his own uncle.

She deserved so much better than him. He couldn't fathom why she loved him when no one else did.

Please don't ever hate me, Bethany.

There would truly be no worse torturous hell.

SEPTEMBER 26, 9532 BC

Styxx hung back as his father and Ryssa approached his uncle's Atlantean home. Unwanted memories brutalized him as he remembered what had happened to him the last time he was here. And still the most agonizing were the memories he didn't have. He'd never know exactly everything that had been done to him.

I wish we could burn it to the ground . . .

Nothing about the abysmal place had changed. It was just as Styxx remembered it. Right down to every horrid stone.

Lenas, his uncle's manservant, opened the door to stare at them.

His father stiffened at the servant's insolence. "I've come to collect Acheron. Show me to him."

Lenas opened the door wider to admit them. He raked a heated stare over Styxx's body.

They do look alike . . . amazing. I wonder if he's as good in bed.

Styxx cringed. Estes hadn't just shared Acheron with his friends and patrons, but also his staff. As they headed down the hallway, strange images flashed in his mind.

Were they memories?

They came and went so fast that he couldn't be sure what his mind wanted him to see or know.

Trying to push those thoughts aside, Styxx slowed as they neared a room where the sounds were all too familiar. Lenas gave him a knowing stare before he opened the door of the bedroom where Acheron was working with two patrons.

"What in the name of Hades is this?" his father roared.

Eyes wide with horror, Ryssa covered her mouth and turned away.

Styxx couldn't breathe at the sight that greeted them. Completely naked, Acheron was buried between a woman's legs while a man took full advantage of Acheron's squatting position for his own pleasure.

The man pulled back from Acheron with a feral curse. "What is the meaning of this?" he demanded with an equally imperious air. "How dare you interrupt us!"

There was a tone his father wasn't going to appreciate, and Styxx was extremely glad he wasn't the fool who'd used it.

Acheron gave one last playful lick to the woman's body before he rolled over onto his back. He lay unabashedly naked on the bed, smirking.

"Prince Ydorus," Acheron said to the angry man addressing their father. "Meet King Xerxes of Didymos."

That took some of the bluster out of the prince, but not much.

"Leave us," their father demanded.

Offended, the prince gathered his clothes and companion and did as the king commanded.

Wise move, buddy.

With a sickly gray cast to his skin that Styxx was all too familiar with, Acheron wiped his mouth on the sheet. His features gaunt, he wore those damned gold bands on his neck, arms, wrists, and ankles.

Licking his lips suggestively, Acheron intentionally flashed the *erotiki sfairi* that lined his tongue. Styxx gave his brother credit for that stupidity. Especially when Acheron lay back on his bent elbows and spread his legs wide to their father to ram home what he was.

"So what brings you here, Majesty?" Acheron asked, his tone mocking and cold. "Do you wish to spend time with me, too?"

Styxx flinched at an angry, defiant offer he knew went through his father like a sword. Acheron had no idea what he was setting into motion, but Styxx did. He just didn't know how to stop it.

Worse, were the memories of the times he'd been where Acheron was. All too well he understood that hatred and rage that wanted to lash out and throw into his father's face what Estes had made them do. To make the king deal with the reality that had been forced onto them against their wills. Acheron's volatile emotions set his own on edge and left him raw and emotionally bleeding.

"Get up," their father snarled. "Cover yourself."

One corner of Acheron's mouth quirked into a mocking expression. He bent his knees and assumed a sexually inviting position Styxx was glad Ryssa couldn't see. "Why? People pay five hundred gold pieces an hour to see me naked. You should be honored you get to look for free."

Brother, stop!

But Styxx couldn't get the words out as forgotten details slammed into him. Suddenly, he remembered being in this room.

With Acheron and without.

"Four thousand solas for the first crack at them! Who wants to taste Greek divinity and royalty?"

"How do you like that, Highness? Tell me how much you crave my cock . . . Beg me for it like the little bitch you are."

Styxx flinched as he tried to force it all away and focus. But it was impossible. He wanted to do something other than stand here and relive a horror that never should have happened to either of them.

Their father grabbed Acheron roughly by his arm and pulled him from the bed.

Acheron covered his hand with his own and tsked at him. "It's a thousand gold pieces an hour if you want to bruise me."

Fifteen hundred to make him bleed . . . Styxx flinched as he called Estes's price list.

The king backhanded Acheron so hard, he fell to the floor and sprawled naked onto his back.

Styxx gasped as pain exploded in his own skull. It was so harsh a blow that for a few seconds, he couldn't see straight.

Laughing, Acheron licked the blood from his lips before he wiped it away on the back of his branded hand. "It's fifteen hundred to make me bleed."

Styxx backed away as Acheron validated his earlier memory.

His father curled his lips. "You're disgusting."

Styxx's stomach heaved. That was what his father would think of him, too, if he ever learned that he'd worn the same bracelets as Acheron. He saw himself bleeding on the floor, not his brother. This was exactly what would happen to him if his father ever found out he'd been sold.

If he ever saw the brand Styxx carried next to his cock.

And if he ever learned Styxx had murdered his uncle . . .

His father would gut him himself. Just as his mother had done him.

With a wry grin, Acheron rolled to his side and pushed himself up from the floor. "Careful, Father, you might actually hurt my feelings." He walked around their father like a proud, stalking lion,

262

looking him up and down. "Oh wait, I forgot. Whores don't have feelings. We have no dignity for you to offend."

"I am not your father."

Styxx winced at the severity of his father's condemnation against his twin brother and he remembered how tortured and conflicted his father had been when he cut Styxx's arm open.

"Yes, I know the story well. It was beaten into me years ago. You're not my father and Estes isn't my uncle. It saves his reputation if everyone thinks I'm some poor waif he found on the streets and gave shelter to. It's fine to sell a homeless beggar, a worthless bastard. But the aristocracy frowns on those who sell their blood relatives."

How Styxx wished that was true.

Their father backhanded him again.

Styxx wiped away the blood on his face before anyone saw it. But his father and Ryssa were too intent on Acheron to pay his condition any heed. Thank the gods for that one small mercy.

Acheron laughed, unfazed by the fact that his nose was now bleeding, along with his lips. "If you really want to hurt me, I'll ring for the whips. But if you continue to strike my face, you'll make Estes unbelievably angry. He doesn't like for anyone to mar my beauty."

"Estes is dead!" their father roared.

Styxx cringed at the unadulterated rage in those words.

Acheron froze in place then blinked as if he couldn't believe what he'd heard. "Estes is dead?" he repeated hollowly.

The king sneered at him. "Yes. Were that it were you in his place."

Acheron took a deep breath and the relief in his eyes was tangible. His thoughts rang in Styxx's head. *It's over. It's finally over. The twisted bastard's dead and I'm free . . .*

For the first time, Acheron met his gaze. Styxx saw his own shame, self-loathing, and absolute relief mirrored in those swirling silver eyes that were set in an identical face.

And while they were free of Estes's future acts, nothing would ever erase those done to them in the past.

I know, brother. And I'm so sorry.

Acheron's relief made their father furious.

"How dare you have no tears for him. He sheltered and protected you."

Scoffing, Acheron turned his dry gaze toward the king. "Believe me, I've paid him well for his shelter and concern. Every night when he took me to his bed. Every day when he sold me to whomever paid his price."

"You lie!"

Those words slashed across Styxx and stole his breath, and left him gaping in disbelief. *You fucking piece of shit! How could you deny what is right in front of you?* How could he call Acheron a liar when he bore witness to it?

In that moment, for the first time, Styxx was truly glad he'd killed Estes. His only regret was that it hadn't been more violent and painful an end.

Acheron glared at the king. "I'm a whore, Father, not a liar."

With a bellow born of grief, fury, and hatred, the king attacked his brother. He beat and kicked furiously at Acheron, who didn't bother to fight back or protect himself in any way.

Styxx struggled to breathe under the ferocity of his father's assault as his own body reacted to every blow. It was all he could do to remain standing. If he didn't do something fast, they were all going to learn the truth of the twins.

Gods help them both if that happened.

Racked in agony, he pulled his father away from his brother. "Please, Father," he said between gritted teeth as he struggled not to show his own pain. "Calm down. The last thing you need is to tax your heart. I don't want to see you die as Estes did."

As expected, the reminder that Estes had been younger and had died of a supposed seizure in his sleep calmed his father and gave Styxx a chance to suppress the damage his father had done to him. He wiped the blood from his face again while his father glared down at his twin.

Ryssa had gone to Acheron's side.

"Don't," Acheron said, pushing her away. He spat the blood from his mouth to the floor where it landed in a stark red splatter.

"Get out," their father snarled at him. "I don't ever want to see you again."

Those words hit Styxx even harder than his fists had.

Acheron laughed at that and met Styxx's gaze without flinching. "Rather difficult, isn't it?"

The king started for him, but Styxx put himself between them. He had to get them apart and sort through this.

Somehow.

"Guards," he called, wanting them to pull his brother to safety until their father calmed.

They appeared instantly.

Acheron glared at Styxx with a hatred that was palpable. *I know you hear me inside your head, brother. Just like you always did when we were children, and I want you to see how much your precious father really loves you that he could throw us out so easily.*

Tell me truthfully, Styxx, do you suck and lick Father's cock and balls at night? You must choke on his testicles and suck him hard and dry for him to be able to love you so and deny me.

Rage, dark and deadly, blinded him as Acheron's vicious thoughts hit him hard. How dare Acheron throw that in his face when Acheron knew exactly how much it hurt! It was beyond cruel. Even harsher was the memory he had of Acheron oiling Styxx's body and prepping him for the men Estes sold him to.

Welcome to my world, brother . . .

There had been no remorse in Acheron over what had been done to Styxx, not even when Acheron had seen Styxx's horrendous scars left by the priests. His brother had mocked those, too.

Next time you should let the brands cool before you masturbate with them.

In that moment, Styxx wanted to kill his own brother. Twin or not.

Instead, Styxx jerked his chin toward Acheron. "Put this trash on the street where it belongs."

Acheron pushed himself to his feet. "I don't need their help. I can walk out the door on my own."

Styxx glared at him with the same hatred Acheron had for him. *And you better while you're still able.*

Ryssa shook her head. "You need clothes and money."

Their father curled his lip. "He deserves nothing. Nothing but our scorn."

Acheron's battered face was completely stoic. "Then I am rich indeed from the abundance of that which you've shown me." In all his naked glory, he sauntered to the door then paused to smirk one last time. "You know, it took me a long time to realize why you hate me so much, Majesty." Acheron locked gazes with Styxx. "But then it's not me you really hate, is it? What you truly hate is how badly you want to fuck your own son."

Their father bellowed in anger as the brutality of his words tore across Styxx's heart. In that moment, Styxx knew the full depth of his uncle's depravity. He had driven a permanent wedge between him and Acheron.

One that nothing would heal after this. Styxx would never forget this slap in the face.

And neither would Acheron.

With his head held high, Acheron left the room.

Ryssa raked them both with the full weight of her condemnation. "How could you? I told you what Estes was doing with him and you denied it. How can you blame him for this?"

Their father shook his head. "Estes didn't do this. Acheron did it himself. Estes told me the way he parades himself and flaunts his body. The way he tempts everyone. He's a destroyer just as they said at his birth. He will not rest until he ruins every person he's around."

"He's just a confused boy, Father. He needs a family."

Her words cut straight through Styxx. *And what am I, dear sister?* She was every bit as blind and self-absorbed as their father. How could she see Acheron so clearly and him not at all?

But then given the harsh brutality of his brother's parting

comments, he knew his brother was as far from innocent in thought as he was in action.

In that one moment, Styxx hated all of them. His father. His mother. Ryssa and Acheron.

But most of all, he hated himself.

SEPTEMBER 27, 9532 BC

"You repulse me, Styxx! What kind of man, and I use that term loosely, could just sit here and let his own twin brother be cast into the world alone? Without coin or clothing? Acheron's not the monster, *you* are! I wish you'd been the one Uncle sold. It should have been you all these years who was forced to be a whore handed over to anyone with enough coin! But no, you sit here in selfish comfort while your brother is cast adrift and say nothing! Nothing! I hate you, Styxx. I hope one day you suffer for all you've done!"

Styxx ignored Ryssa's shrill tone as she railed against him and called down the wrath of every god on Olympus to punish him. She'd been doing it steadily since she returned from seeing Acheron off.

Even without her insults, his own emotions were in turmoil. There was no longer any doubt how his father would react should he ever learn that his heir had been whored, too.

He's a repulsive catamite. He knew Estes's preference and he used it to his advantage. Think you, I don't know how that sick monster's mind works? None of this was Estes's fault. He was victimized by Acheron. I'll bet the bastard crawled into his bed and begged him for it.

Like Ryssa was doing right now against Styxx, their father had ranted throughout the night against Acheron. Styxx had no peace from either of them. And neither had a clue that every time they spoke, a part of him died more.

Really, he just wanted to run away from it all.

But one look at the strangers who eyed him hungrily until they learned of his regal title kept him close to his father's side. And while he knew Acheron was hungry, he knew his brother wasn't being molested or beaten.

At least not yet.

Why couldn't you have gone away with me when I tried to free you, Acheron?

Just once?

But then he wouldn't have met his Bethany and . . .

"Shit!" Styxx cursed as Ryssa kicked him hard in the shin. "You're not even listening to me, are you, you little pig!"

"I hear every precious word that falls from your dainty lips, sweet sister."

She kicked him again.

Hissing, he glared at her and moved his legs so that she couldn't reach them. Thank the gods she wasn't any taller.

"Why am I stuck with *you* as my brother?"

Styxx didn't respond as they reached the docks and he descended from the wheeled litter. He reached up to help her down. She spat in his face and ignored his hand.

Grinding his teeth, he wiped his cheek.

As they neared the ramp, she turned on him with a vicious sneer. "I wish they'd drag you belowdecks and rape you the whole way home like they did poor Acheron when I tried to help him."

That explained those pains . . .

"And had you not been so stupid, Ryssa, *that* wouldn't have happened. What kind of moron attempts to take a marked slave onto a passenger ship? You're far too old to be so puerile."

She slapped him before turning in a huff and leaving him to trail in her wake.

His father clapped him on the back as he reached him. "I know she plagues you, boy, but you have to admire and respect her spirit."

Ah . . . Ryssa's disrespect was cute and spirited, while Styxx's was never to be tolerated.

Scowling in distaste, Styxx stopped as his father continued on. He'd never understand his father's complicated and arbitrary double standards. And honestly, he was tired of trying.

At the top of the deck, Styxx stopped and looked back at Atlantis. In spite of it all, he wished his brother well and he hoped Acheron made it to Greece before the pending war broke out.

But regardless . . .

"May the gods grant you peace somewhere, little brother."

Glancing over to Ryssa, who eyed him like he was filth, he sighed knowing the gods had no intention of granting any to him.

OCTOBER 6, 9532 BC

Styxx reined Troian to a stop as he caught sight of Bethany at their spot. In spite of the day's warmth, she was covered from neck to ankle in a peculiar white garment that obscured every part of her. Yet as she moved, he heard light jingling bells. She'd placed flowers on the blanket along with a small drum. Her sandals were left to the side of it, near a jug of wine and a small platter of cheese and crisp, flat bread.

Baffled and curious, he slid from his mount and left his horse to graze. "Beth?"

A beautiful, welcoming smile curved her lips as she turned in his direction. "Hector?"

"I'm right here, love." He dropped his saddlebag next to the blanket and touched her lightly on the shoulder.

Rising up on her tiptoes, she placed a chaste kiss to his lips. Her scent hit him and made his body instantly hard as his senses reeled from her gentle ways, and warm reception.

"Where's your pole?" he asked. She normally kept it near the pond.

A teasing light made her eyes sparkle as she reached down to stroke his hard cock. "Right here, it seems."

He arched a brow at that. As always whenever she touched him, he couldn't quite think straight.

She stepped back. "I thought today we'd do something a little different."

"Whatever my lady wishes."

She bit her lip seductively. "Can you play any instruments?"

"Sadly, no. My father thinks they're a complete waste of time and boorish. Why?"

She sank down to the blanket and pulled him to sit beside her. "The why is a surprise." She reached for the drum then placed it in his lap. Taking his hands into hers, she showed him how to keep a basic rhythm.

He felt odd and self-conscious with the small round drum as he waited for her to criticize his efforts. As a boy, he'd tried to play a flute, lyre, and drum, and had seen each burned in turn by his father, sister, or mother, who quickly told him he was inept and stupid for even attempting that which the gods had given him absolutely no talent for.

But Bethany didn't say a word. She merely smiled and kissed him then rose to her feet.

"Don't stop," she said when he slowed his pace.

Styxx returned to what she'd taught him. Frowning, he watched as she pulled finger cymbals from her basket and slid them onto her hand. Next, she pulled out a sistrum. Before he could ask what she intended, she loosened the ribbon at her neck and dropped her outer garment to the ground.

His throat suddenly dry, Styxx froze at the sight of her in a *very* sheer white outfit the likes of which he'd never seen. The small top was heavily beaded with pearls and shiny silver disks. It cupped her full breasts and lifted them high, and left the swell of them exposed for his hungry gaze. The top stopped just below her breasts and left her abdomen completely bare. Not that it mattered. The material was so sheer that he could easily see the full outline of her breasts and puckered nipples that made him hunger for a quick taste. Three rows of pearls fell from the middle of the top to brush against the perfection of her belly where she'd painted Egyptian symbols for the goddess Hathor.

Silver armbands encircled her biceps. Two rows of tiny bells secured to them and the hem of her skirt were what made the jingling sound he'd heard on his arrival. She wore additional bells as anklets.

Her wide, full skirt had slits at each side that went all the way up to the thick beaded silver belt that had numerous white veils fastened to it. Like the top, it was sheer enough that he could see the full outline of her body and the dark hair at the juncture of her thighs.

"You stopped playing, my lord."

He wanted to say something witty in response, but his brain seemed to have stopped completely. His jaw worked, yet no sound came out as her beauty left him completely senseless. Thank the gods she couldn't see what an idiot he was. Otherwise, she'd be running as far from him as she could. He wasn't all that sure he hadn't drooled on himself.

"Hector? Are you still with me?"

"I'm here, my lady. Just completely overwhelmed by the magnitude of your grace. Your beauty has rendered me quite useless for the moment."

She smiled at him. "Keep playing, my love. I have a treat for you."

"I can't imagine anything sweeter than what I'm already savoring."

"Keep playing."

He wasn't sure how he managed it, but he obeyed. And as he did so, she began what had to be the most erotic dance he'd ever seen in his life. With every graceful move of her arm or swaying of her hips, her bells, cymbals, and sistrum rang and his body sizzled. He'd never seen anything like it. If this was how the Egyptians trained their daughters, he wondered how any of them managed

271

to leave their bedchambers. No wonder they had such large families . . .

As she danced, she freed her veils. Her hips and shoulders moving in perfect synchronicity, she sank down by his side and continued to undulate in time to the music they made. He was completely captivated.

Until she tied one end of her scarf to his wrist and lightly tugged on it.

Reacting on pure instinct, Styxx shot to his feet, leaving the drum to roll away. He tore the frail scarf off him until it was shredded.

Bethany froze as she heard Hector's ragged breathing and felt his panicked anger. "Hector?" It took her a moment to find him. He was pacing near a tree and shaking uncontrollably. "Are you all right?"

He didn't speak. He walked about in a feral panic as if waiting to be attacked.

"Hector? Precious . . . Speak to me. Tell me what's happening?"

Styxx tried to calm down, he did. But it was so hard as horrifying memories assailed him. "I don't like to be tied to anything. Honestly, I don't even like to have walls or doors around me." He laughed bitterly. "I even keep a window open on the coldest nights just so that I know I have a way out should I need it."

Bethany felt the tears prick her eyes as she realized the true terror of his past. They would have tied him down to torture him, and probably when they raped him, too. "I'm so sorry, Hector. I didn't think."

He pulled her against him and held her close. "Don't apologize, Beth. You went to a lot of effort for me . . . to make this day special, and I ruined it. I'm the one who's sorry."

She sank her hand into his soft hair and pressed her cheek against his. "Never apologize to me for your pain. What was done to you was wrong and it wasn't your fault. You have the most amazing heart of anyone I've ever met. In spite of what the world has done to you, you still carry on with quiet dignity and humor.

It's what I love about you. You are a true warrior, brave to the core of your soul."

Styxx swallowed the lump of pain in his throat that choked him. Funny, he didn't feel brave. He felt more like a frightened mouse, cowering in the corner. He would never understand how a woman as wonderful as Bethany could stand to be with him.

His hand trembling, he picked the torn veil up from the ground and returned it to her. He would buy her a new one the next time he was at the market. "I will try not to overreact."

She squeezed his fingers. "I respect your pain, my lord. I won't do it again. I promise. There are plenty of other things we can do."

He arched a brow at that. "Such as?"

She loosened her belt and sent her skirt straight to her feet. Completely bare from the waist down, she smiled as she knelt in front of him and lifted the hem of his chiton until he was as exposed to her as she was to him. To his complete shock and utter pleasure, she slowly drew him into her mouth.

A single tear slid down his cheek as he truly felt her love for him. Only Bethany had never judged him or caused him harm. In all the world, she alone made him feel human and manly. Normal. She didn't see a prince to be hated or a boy to be scorned. She didn't insert ideas and words into his actions that he never intended.

Bethany accepted him as he was. Scars and all. She didn't use his past against him. She didn't throw his words in his face. All she did was love him with her heart and rare goodness.

"I love you, Beth," he whispered.

She pulled back to lick him then smiled up at his face. "I love you, too."

In that moment, he almost told her the truth of who he was. But the fear in his heart locked his lips together. Being a prince had never served him well. The only happiness and acceptance he had in his miserable existence was found in these afternoons with her. If he were to ever lose them . . .

He'd rather be confined in the Dionysion again.

Don't ever leave me, Beth.

Because if she did, he feared what he'd become. But in his heart, he knew this couldn't last. Nothing ever did.

Not the bad ...

And especially not the good.

OCTOBER 14, 9532 BC

"I know something's on your mind, sweetest. What is it?"

Styxx sighed as he held Bethany's naked body against his. He was so grateful for these preciously few moments with her. She lay facedown with her head resting on his chest while he leaned against an ancient tree where they sometimes left things for each other. The bark bit into his back, but he was so content with her on top of him that he didn't care or protest.

His thoughts sought a way to break his news to her as he toyed with the tiny shell-shaped bells on the silver armbands she wore whenever she danced for him. Just thinking about the sensual Egyptian dances she performed made him hard again.

Closing his eyes, he decided there was no easy way to break it to her. "I have to leave tomorrow, my lady. And I don't know when I'll be back."

Gasping, she shot up instantly and almost kneed his groin as she tried to feel his facial expression.

He placed her palm against his cheek and mouth so that she would know how serious it was.

"Why?"

"Atlantis has attacked a kingdom in the south. King Xerxes is assembling a contingency to render aid and march against them."

"But you're a merchant's son!"

"He's demanding any free man my age and above to go." A partial lie he hoped she didn't call him on. The law stipulated that their army consist of any free man above the age of eight-and-ten, and single noblemen over the age of one-and-twenty. It was unheard of for someone his age to be sent. But, in spite of Galen's defiant protests, his father had insisted Styxx go to fight.

"Not another word, Galen, or I'll have you whipped ... He is going. Perhaps this will finally make a man of him!" Styxx ground his teeth in memory of his father's hate-filled words from the night before.

She shook her head. "No. I won't let you."

"I have no choice."

"Have you any training whatsoever, Hector?"

"Some." Actually, he had a great deal more than many of their men. Most only trained two weeks out of the year. The rest alternated days in the public barracks, and trained with Galen's hand picked instructors a few days each month.

Tears filled her eyes. "War is brutal. It's ... you can't go. You can't! I quite forbid it."

Those words lightened his heart and made it ache simultaneously. "I don't want to leave you, *akribos*. Believe me. But it's treason for any man to refuse a hoplon and xiphos when he's called. I'd be locked away if I didn't go."

And he hated that. Bethany knew from their time together there was nothing he despised more. He didn't even like for her to playfully tie his hands. Her Hector couldn't stand any kind of bondage game. Not even a frail scarf around his wrist.

To be confined for real would kill him.

Terrified for her human, she reached up and removed the necklace that had never been off her since the day her father had placed it there. She closed her eyes and imbued it with protective power. Taking his hand, she wound the leather cord around his wrist and secured it, knowing his vambrace would cover it and it wouldn't accidentally fall off in battle. "Then you take this and don't remove it for anything."

"Why?"

"It will protect you as it has always protected me."

"Beth—"

"I promise you, Hector. So long as you wear it, no blade or arrow will be able to cut you. Not even one forged by the gods. Please, don't take it off for anything."

He kissed her cheek. "All right. I will keep it where you put it until I return to you."

Her bells jingling, she laid herself back over him.

Styxx felt her hot tears on his skin. For a full minute, he couldn't breathe. No one had ever shed a single tear for him before. Not even his own twin. He touched the moisture, amazed by it.

"Don't cry, Beth. I'm not worth this."

"You are to me, and I will make sure the gods end this quickly so that you return to me. You are taking my heart with you ... Please, please be careful."

"I will, and I will be counting down the heartbeats until my return."

And for the first time in his life, he wanted to live to come home. He finally had a reason to.

OCTOBER 15, 9532 BC

Dressed in his black and bronze armor, Styxx walked down the stairs toward the front door with his helm cradled beneath his arm. Concealed by his vambrace, Bethany's necklace was still wrapped around his left wrist where she'd placed it.

His father, mother, and sister were gathered to see him off ... In theory anyway.

Drunk, his mother raked a glare over him. "May the Atlanteans gut you on your first day so fast you feel no pain from it."

The servants close enough to hear her sucked their breaths in sharply.

Styxx didn't react at all. "Thank you, Matisera. From you, I could wish no sweeter parting words."

Ryssa's expression was just as cold. "I know you won't die. I'm sure you'll cower behind the others as you always do, or stack them in front of you so you can use them for a shield."

"May the gods continue to bless you with your kind disposition in my absence, sweet sister."

She sneered at him. "I hope your horse throws you in the midst of battle right into the heart of our enemies."

"Ignore them." His father drew him into a light embrace. "Return with honor, boy."

Styxx had to fight not to roll his eyes. His father had drilled that into him the night before. *"Whatever you do, boy, don't you dare embarrass me with the other kings and generals. I will not stand for it."*

Ἦ Τάν Ἦ Επί Τάς—*either with your shield or upon it.*

And with that in mind, Styxx slid his signet ring from his finger and handed it to his father, who scowled at his actions.

"They can't ransom me if they don't know who I am and if they have no proof they hold me."

"Styxx—"

He held his hand up to silence his king. "Keep it, Father. I don't want it." The house of Aricles was cursed and he didn't desire anything with him that reminded him of people who begrudged him every breath he took. If he was riding to his death then he only wanted Bethany's token with him. Let him die with her face and memory in his heart, not theirs.

Without looking back, Styxx left his "family" and headed down the steps to where Galen waited with Troian. By Galen's grim expression, Styxx could tell his mentor was as thrilled by their generous farewells as he was.

"Are you all right, Highness?"

Styxx slammed his helm down on his head then swung up on the back of his stallion, who was as black as his mood. He took his hoplon from his old trainer's hand and slid it to his back for the ride. "Fine, Galen. Thank you for asking."

Frowning, Galen glanced up at the royal family while Styxx spurred his horse forward without bothering to look back at them. He knew where all of them stood on his well-being.

Gods willing, they'd all get their wish to not see him again.

OCTOBER 25, 9532 BC

Styxx let out an elongated breath. Tomorrow, they would be in battle. For the last few hours, he'd worked with Galen on the speech he was supposed to deliver to their men to rally, unite, and inspire them for war.

As he rode to the front to give it, the hostile thoughts of the Didymosian army assailed him like rapid-fire arrows.

We have to follow that worthless quim into battle? Seriously?

The king insults us to send a boy in when we need a man at our helm.

When did Didymos become such a joke? The other Greeks mock us, and why shouldn't they? We're led by a beardless child who should still be suckling at his mother's tit.

But what truly hurt was that their thoughts mirrored his own. At least the ones that weren't sexual in nature.

Damn, Estes could have made a fortune here selling him to all the soldiers who wanted to grudge-fuck him. It was extremely disconcerting to know they'd be at his back tomorrow . . .

Heavily armed.

Styxx reined Troian in so that he could address them with Galen on a horse by his side. His stomach shrank as he faced their outright and obvious contempt and disdain. Though he was used to it, for some reason it stung more today.

Because you're about to ask them to die for you and they hate you for it.

He looked down at the scroll in his shaking hands and the words they'd so carefully penned. *I can't read this.* To them, it would sound disingenuous. They were pissed enough. His luck, they'd think he was mocking them and attack.

Better to address their real concerns.

Look at the royal quim. He's too scared to speak. How's that frightened little girl supposed to lead us into battle?

That's to be our future king? Gods help us.

Is it too late to defect to the Thracian army?

Lifting his chin, Styxx forced himself to face them. He cleared his throat then wadded up the parchment in his hand. *Please don't let my voice tremble.*

"I know what all of you are thinking . . ."

What a pathetic quim leads us?

Those were bad, but Styxx ground his teeth at the one thought that rang in his head louder than the others—*We come to fight for a king who sends his worthless child to hang back and watch us die . . . Least you could do is share that sweet little ass of yours with us before you ask us to die for it.*

The animosity and criticisms mounted until Styxx couldn't speak. They were right. He had no business being here. Maybe that was his father's plan. To have him killed by his own people.

"Enough!" Galen roared.

It was only then Styxx realized they'd not only been thinking their hostilities, many had been shouting them, too.

The old veteran they did respect glared at them. "All of you should be ashamed of yourselves. The prince, himself, came here to personally thank you for your service, even while the lot of you sneered and jeered at him. You humiliate a warrior who has more courage than the entire Greek cavalry. Any other *strategos* would have you beaten for this impudence. And I will not see him so debased and insulted when you know nothing of his fierce skills or true noble character. I swore after our war with Phthia that I would *never* again bleed in battle for any king or cause. Nor would I fight for any banner. Yet here I am this day. Why?"

Galen placed his hand on Styxx's shoulder. "Because I have seen, in spite of his young age, the wisdom and courage of our *strategos*. And it is an honor for me to fight under his banner. How many men who are the age of our prince would come to battle with his army without a single word of protest? Prince Styxx could be at home, right now, with a wench in his lap and wine in his hand. Instead, he has laid aside his own comforts and safety to be with all of you as you fight for his father. He does not deserve your scorn, but rather your respect."

"Doesn't matter. He'll be dead in battle tomorrow anyway."

"Or fucked in the ass by an Atlantean hero while he chokes on the testicles of another."

Their army burst into laughter as they started taking wagers on who'd be the first to screw their prince.

Galen started for the soldiers.

Styxx held him by his side. "We don't need to fight each other while we have enemies on our shores."

With a tic thumping furiously in his jaw, Galen saluted him and kneed his horse back.

Styxx looked at his men and started to speak then realized there was nothing he could say that they wouldn't twist into an insult or take offense to. They had set their minds to hating him, and as with his mother and sister, there was no way to win them over. The one thing he'd learned from his blessed family was when to let it go and not try for a lost cause.

Sighing, he clapped Galen on the shoulder then reined his horse about so that he could return to his tent.

"That's right . . . go back to your cradle, boy, and let the men do their jobs!"

Holding his head high, Styxx ignored their laughter. *At least it's not as bad as the strategi meeting.*

While his soldiers were harsh, the noble-born commanders, who had been insulted by his mere presence and who had dared him to speak a single word, had flogged him harder with their tongues than all the scolds in his father's service. His hide was still raw and bleeding from their vicious insults yesterday. They'd all but run him out of the meeting on a rail.

So be it.

If he was lucky, they'd all be right and someone would cut his head off in battle tomorrow.

OCTOBER 26, 9532 BC

"Look at the pathetic bastards," Misos, the Atlantean god of war, sneered to Bethany as they joined the Atlantean army that was preparing to attack the Greek colony of Halicarnassus, one of the richest Greek cities. The Atlanteans wanted to make a point and show their lesser human brethren why they needed to leave off Atlantean shores.

But more than that, they were here to slaughter every Greek prince dumb enough to fight.

Bethany reined her white winged horse beside her great-grandfather. Her mother, Symfora, the goddess of sorrow, was already walking the battlefield in expectation of the men who would die here today. "Have you chosen your champion, Tattas?" she asked Misos.

The god of war smiled down at her. "Zerilus." The leader of the Atlantean army. Almost eight feet tall, he was so massive that it was said one swing of his mighty axe could fell a stout tree. "What of you, precious? Who is your chosen?"

Hector. But she could never allow her family to know that her heart lay among the enemy camp and with a lowly foot soldier.

So she picked the Atlantean least likely to cause harm to him. "Xan."

"The Atlantean prince . . . a fine choice, indeed."

"Now, if you'll excuse me, Tattas, I shall go through the Greek ranks and do my job."

He laughed. "Make sure you call out to us should one of the Greek gods see you. The sooner we start this fight, the better."

Saluting him with her sword, Bethany swung her winged horse, Herita, away from them and flew into the Greek camp. Not really to stir up her usual misery and discontent in their hearts, but rather to find a merchant's son who bore her medallion around his wrist.

Where are you, Hector?

Honestly, she was impressed by their numbers. The Greeks had amassed a large army in a very short amount of time. She pulled her gold helm off so that she could better see the faces of the men who were preparing for the coming fight.

To her right was the Didymos banner. She headed straight for their encampment. As she started to the back of it to look through their foot soldiers, a flash of bright red distracted her.

Athena . . .

She could feel that bitch's presence here. Theirs was a grudge match that was legendary throughout the Mediterranean. One that had started centuries ago when Bethany had speared Athena's chosen through the heart, during battle.

So who is your favorite I will kill today?

Bethany set her horse on the ground then slid from the saddle. She touched random Greek soldiers as she passed them, making them immediately clench with painful fear and mental anguish. They were not her Hector. They weren't tall enough. So she didn't care if they fell or not.

She came around a tent and froze as she caught sight of the infamous Didymosian prince, Styxx. While she'd heard his name countless times, she'd never seen him before.

Arrogant snot. That was her first thought as she saw him swathed in his expensive black armor with a bright red chlamys, and rigidly perched on the back of an exceptional black stallion. His regal pride bled from every pore of his body. Still, he cut a gorgeous picture as the light breeze ruffled his unruly blond curls that gave him an unorthodox, boyish appearance. Dark brown brows slashed above intelligent eyes so blue they matched the Aegean Sea for clarity and vibrance.

His stern expression made his cheekbones sharp and well sculpted. Too young for a full beard, he held the lightest bit of dark brown dusting around his chin and upper lip.

He was truly a thing of great beauty.

"Your aspis, young prince."

Bethany's gaze narrowed as she saw Athena, in the guise of a foot soldier, holding the red shield up to her champion who had no idea the Greek goddess intended to ride with him into battle.

So this is your choice? Really? An arrogant prince with no battle experience?

She'd laugh if it weren't so pathetic.

The prince inclined his head to Athena and took the shield that held a black phoenix topped by a Greek crown of laurels and the words "I defend." The weight of the hoplon caused the muscles in his arm to protrude and define themselves even more. He said something to the goddess that made her smile.

Athena handed him his black helm.

With one hand, the prince slid it down over his head then reached for his xiphos. What a pity she'd have to kill him. Beauty such as his was all too rare in the human world.

If only Athena had chosen another to favor . . .

Sighing at the waste, Bethany manifested her bow and nocked an arrow. She took aim for the prince's heart.

Just as she released her arrow, he kicked his horse forward.

Damn it! The arrow flew past the stallion's flanks and hit a tent post.

The moment it did, Athena turned to glare at her.

Bethany made a rude gesture at the Greek goddess. Summoning her horse, she flipped onto Herita's back and flew away before the Greek goddess could return her fire.

The battle was starting.

Her heart heavy, Bethany glanced over the Greeks, hoping her Hector was safe.

"Well?" Diafonia asked as Bethany returned to their side of the field. "Did you stir them up?"

"Not as much as normal. I caught Athena's champion and almost had him. But the bitch saw me."

The goddess of discord patted her on the shoulder. "Have no fear, sweet cousin. The day is young. We will drink well on the blood of the fallen Greeks tonight." Diafonia spread her wings and dove for the soldiers with her brother Pali at her side. She and her brother Strife always ran among their enemies to incite their wrath and create confusion.

Times like this, Bethany truly missed Apollymi. The goddess of destruction had always been her best ally in battle.

Oh well. They had a war to fight and she had a Didymosian prince to slay. "Get ready, Hades. I'm about to send Athena's newest pet knocking on your door."

She flew to Xan's side and kept his arm strong throughout the day as he slaughtered Greek after Greek.

Until she finally sighted the young prince of Didymos again.

He'd dismounted at some point during battle, and was fighting on foot beside his men, with Athena nowhere to be found.

Bethany paused as she watched the grace and beauty of his brutal art. Someone had trained the prince well. Even at his young age, he fought like a seasoned veteran. Fearless. There was no hesitation in his attacks or blocks. He met every enemy without flinching or tiring. Indeed, he looked to be gaining strength with each opponent.

Incredible. Blood soaked him, dripping from his armor and skin, and still he fought on in a graceful dance of the absolute macabre.

"Styxx!" Xan's unexpected bellow startled her. She'd had no idea that her prince knew Athena's champion. And judging by the rage of that tone, they were not friendly.

Xan ran at the prince, slashing his way through the men who came between them.

With the sound of screams, cries and clashing metal echoing in his ears, Styxx drove his sword into the middle of the man he was fighting and had barely recovered when a mighty shadow fell across his line of vision. He looked up just as an axe was coming for his head. Lifting his bowl-shaped shield, he gasped at the ferocious blow that numbed his entire arm and forced him to his knees. It sent a piece of the wood flying out of his aspis to the ground.

After yanking the axe back for another strike, his newest attacker shrieked in frustration. The giant jerked Styxx's shield, throwing him sideways. Somehow, Styxx managed to keep his grip on the hoplon, but the action felt like it'd torn his arm out of his shoulder.

Styxx rolled with attack, and landed on his feet to face Xan. For a moment, he couldn't breathe as he felt the memory of the bastard's hands on his body while he laughed in Styxx's ear and taunted him.

Xan narrowed his eyes. "I owe you a debt, little quim. Your life for Estes's."

As Galen had taught him, Styxx clenched his jaw shut to keep from responding to the insult. *"Never let the enemy in your head, boy. Your emotions will get you killed."*

This was not about rage, ego, or fear. It was war. Cold. Brutal. Final.

One mistake and he could lose a limb.

Or his head.

Focus and skill were the only things that would keep him alive and in one piece. And while he knew he couldn't die, he didn't want to live with severed body parts.

Xan swung his axe down again. Knowing the power of those blows and the fact that he couldn't stand long against them, Styxx dropped his hoplon and launched himself at the much larger man, driving his shoulder into Xan's stomach and forcing the giant to stumble back as the axe slipped from his hands and landed harmlessly on the ground behind Styxx.

The Atlantean prince grabbed him as Xan fell, pulling Styxx down on top of him. "If you wanted to suck my cock, boy, all you had to do was ask."

Styxx scrambled to get off him, but Xan wrapped his massive limbs around his body and held him tight. Panicked memories assailed him as he struggled not to scream out.

"I think I shall capture you instead of killing you, little prince, and then you can be my personal tsoulus until I wear your tight ass out and sell you to a dung dealer for his amusement."

To Styxx's horror, Xan slid his hand down to cup and grope him through his armor.

"Leave it to the flaccid Greeks to send their pretty little whores into battle."

Rage clouded Styxx's sight. Something deep inside him shattered and released. With a battle cry born of a lifetime of shame, Styxx twisted in Xan's arms and drove his kopis into the giant's side.

Releasing him, Xan cried out.

But Styxx gave him no reprieve as he stabbed him again and again, until he was no longer moving. His heart pounding and limbs shaking, he climbed off the bastard and saw Xan's pale skin and glazed eyes.

"For Acheron," he breathed.

And for himself.

Turning from the Greek she'd just killed, Bethany froze at the sight of her chosen Atlantean dead on the ground. Shocked to the core of her being, she gaped as she watched the Greek prince retrieve his shield and move on to his next opponent.

What had just happened? Her champion had never been defeated before. Ever. It was why she'd turned away for a few minutes to fight others.

"Tough break, old girl," Athena said to Bethany as she appeared beside her. "Now you know why I chose a soldier so young. He's fearless and bold. Indefatigable."

Bethany turned to punch the goddess, but Athena was already gone.

Fine, bitch . . . I'll show you power.

She wasn't just the goddess of misery and wrath. She was the Atlantean goddess of the hunt.

Bethany manifested her bow and took off after Styxx. Before this battle was done, she was going to bathe in his blood. She aimed at his head and let fly her arrow.

Just as it would have cleaved his skull, he lifted his shield as if he knew it was coming at him and blocked it.

No . . .

How was that possible?

She tried again. This time, he dodged the arrow, and the next one he cut in half with his sword.

Someone a lot more powerful than Athena guarded this one. It was an old power . . .

Chthonian?

If she didn't know better, she'd say it was primal in source. But there was no way a primal power would waste itself on a young human prince. Not even one so pretty.

Summoning her horse, she joined ranks with her great-grandfather to go after Styxx and end his putrid existence.

Misos's glowing green eyes widened in surprise of her sudden appearance. "What are you doing?"

She pointed to Styxx. "I want that one dead."

"He must be Athena's."

"Get him, Tattas!"

He smiled at her. "Anything for you, my precious."

Prince Zerilus bellowed as he saw his cousin Xan lying dead and Styxx moving away from his body. Intent on vengeance, the giant Atlantean made straight for the Didymosian prince.

Styxx knew something bad was about to happen as the men around him shrank back, including the Atlantean he'd been fighting. He practically ran away from Styxx.

This cannot be good.

287

He turned to find a mountain of a man charging him like a stampeding house.

Aw shit . . .

Suddenly, he felt like he was ten-and-two again and Galen was hammering him with blows while he lay helpless on the ground, unable to counter them.

The giant threw a spear. Styxx turned out of the way, but it passed so close to his body that it scraped his bicep. He'd barely lifted his hoplon before the mountain brought a sword down on him with enough force that he thought he'd broken his arm. No, not broken . . .

Shattered.

Hissing, Styxx rolled away then checked to make sure his arm still worked.

It did, but it wasn't happy about it.

The giant lunged. Styxx stepped aside then brought his xiphos down across his opponent's extended arm. His opponent rolled and met the stroke with his own sword.

Turning, Styxx stepped back. The giant was breathing hard, labored. That was his key to surviving this. While the man was insanely huge, he was a lot older, and he was tiring. If Styxx could just stay out of range and wear his opponent out a bit more, he should be able to take him.

But he'd only have one shot. If he missed . . .

He'd be testing that immortal claim again.

Lowering his head, Styxx charged in then darted back, making the man overextend and step quickly after him. As he did so, he realized that all the men around the two of them had stopped fighting so that they could watch them.

Great. An audience for my humiliation and probable death. Just what I craved . . .

Whatever you do, old man, don't throw me down on the ground in front of everyone and feel me up before you kill me.

His worst fear, other than losing his head, was that someone might have seen Xan groping him.

Styxx arched his back as the giant made a swing that narrowly missed him. Then he brought his xiphos up. The giant stepped back and slammed his smaller round shield into Styxx's bruised side. More pain exploded and his sight dimmed.

His ears buzzed so that he couldn't hear anything other than his heart pounding in his chest.

Laughing, the giant stabbed straight at his chest. Instead of trying to deflect the blow, Styxx lifted his arm and allowed the sword to pass between his elbow and side. He clamped his arm down on the soldier's forearm to hold the giant in place and dropped his own xiphos to the ground. With one swift move, Styxx yanked his kopis from his waist and drove it into the giant's side, between the laces of his bronze cuirass.

With a ferocious hiss, the giant stumbled, bringing his head within Styxx's striking range. Before the beast could shove him back, Styxx drove the kopis into his neck.

The giant fell like an oak, dragging Styxx with him. For several seconds, no one moved. Not until Styxx caught his breath and rolled from the giant's body.

A loud, fierce cheer went up among the Greek troops. Gaping and confused, the Atlanteans remained frozen.

Still shaken by the closeness of that fight, Styxx retrieved his xiphos and hoplon, and waited for his next attacker. But no one seemed eager to take him on now. Rather, the Atlanteans shrank away as if terrified of him.

All of a sudden, voices rang out. "The Atlanteans are retreating!"

Stunned, Styxx looked up as the cry rushed through their ranks, and the Greek charioteers and cavalry rushed past the hoplites and archers to give chase. The Atlantean troops were running for their ships and pulling back. He couldn't believe it. To his knowledge, no Atlantean army had ever withdrawn from battle.

He started to run after them, but he was too tired and sore to try. Really, all he wanted was to sleep for a month or more.

Galen laughed as he joined him and clapped him on the back

so hard, Styxx stumbled from the blow. "You survived, boy. And in one piece, no less. Good for you! Good. For. You."

"Um . . . thanks. Way to boost my confidence, old man." Styxx snorted at Galen then grimaced at how bad his head hurt. The gods' voices had been merciless during the battle and one in particular had been after him.

"Galen? Have you ever heard of Bet'anya Agriosa?"

"The Atlantean goddess of misery and wrath? Oh yeah, young prince. She's not one you want to invoke for anything. Once she's set on a course, she's relentless. Why?"

"I heard her name mentioned by some of the soldiers and was curious."

"Take the advice of an old war dog, son. Don't even say her name in passing."

Nodding, Styxx headed toward their portion of the encampment and did his best to ignore the horrendous sights, sounds and smells around him. In all directions, men were dead or dying. Their cries and moans were even worse than the voices in his head. The ground was saturated with blood and other things he didn't want to contemplate.

For that matter, there was so much blood on him that it literally dripped from every part of his armor and even his nose. Though that might have been his. He honestly couldn't tell.

As he crossed the field on foot, he realized that not all the loud voices he heard were in his throbbing head. The men around them were chanting his name.

Shocked to the core of his soul, he slowed down in apprehension. *Why are they calling me like that?*

Had he done something wrong?

From his left, a messenger came running up to him. He bowed low. "Prince Styxx? His Majesty, King Kreon, wants to see you immediately . . . without hesitation."

But he was filthy. Covered in blood, sweat, and dirt.

His father would have him or any soldier whipped if he dared appear like this in his presence.

He glanced to Galen, who winked at him then took his shield, swords, and helm. "You've been summoned, my lord. Obviously, the king needs to see you right away."

Unsure of what to expect and extremely apprehensive, Styxx wiped his face and arms as best he could on his chlamys while he followed the messenger to the largest encampment where King Kreon of Halicarnassus waited inside his lush tent that was packed with noblemen and the elite commanders of each unit and city-state.

Wonderful. A full audience for whatever new humiliation awaited him. Shit . . . Over and over, he heard their insults from their previous meeting in his head again.

Xerxes sends his brat for us to watch when we have a battle to fight? What's he thinking?

Where's your nurse and tit, boy?

Should we burp him after he drinks his wine?

Wine? You mean milk. Those honeyed cheeks are too smooth for anything stronger.

Poor Galen. Yesterday, he led the strongest army in all of Greece. Now he's stuck changing the pana for Xerxes's infant.

One of the bastards had even flicked at his ear. *"Just as I thought . . . you can still see the placenta on him!"*

Holding his head high in spite of his rising panic, Styxx walked down the center past the bastards who'd belittled him until he reached the king's throne. He fell to one knee and saluted him. "Majesty."

"Rise, Prince Styxx."

He returned to his feet. Assuming a soldier's stance, he folded his hands behind his back and waited for the king's leisure. *Please tell me you didn't see Xan grab my cock before I killed the bastard . . .*

Or was it something even worse than that?

"I have been told by my spotters and generals that we owe this day's victory to your sword arm and to the inspiration your courage provided to all who saw you fighting without flagging."

Huh?

Nonplused and even more nervous than before, Styxx glanced around at the men who were gathered in the tent. Men who had mocked and insulted him just hours before battle, never mind their harshness the day before when they'd openly spat at and on him.

And not to wish him luck.

Their current thoughts overwhelmed him to the point he couldn't pick out any single one. Several averted their eyes, unwilling to meet his gaze even in passing. "It was a battle won by all, Majesty. I fought no harder than anyone else."

The king stepped down from his throne and approached him. "Yes, but you're the one who single-handedly brought down the two highest commanders and greatest heroes of the Atlantean army. You're the sole reason they retreated."

Even more confused, Styxx lowered his gaze, waiting to hear how he'd screwed something up and embarrassed them all.

Kreon stopped in front of him with a stern frown. "Your father is counted among the most arrogant and bullish men I know. When I first learned that you would be leading your father's army in today's battle, I had a few choice things to say about it and none of them were complimentary to either of you. Honestly, I thought your father was mocking me, as is his wont. But it seems the gods have sought to humble my own arrogance. And I cannot tell you how grateful I am that you and Didymos came to our aid this day, young prince. I will be sending you home with gifts for both you and your father. Now come. I offer you my own private bath and the services of my most favored slave girl."

For a full minute, Styxx was so stunned he couldn't respond. Finally, he found his voice. "Thank you, Majesty. I am truly humbled by your generosity, and while I am more than happy to partake of your bath, I most respectfully decline your slave. While I'm sure she's all you say and more, I have a lady who waits for me in Didymos and I would never do anything to dishonor her faith in me . . . I hope you understand."

The king smiled and nodded. "I envy your father the heir he has raised. And it is an honor to know you, Prince Styxx. Now enjoy your victory this evening and the festivities to come."

Bethany hungered for blood as they were forced to withdraw from the Greek island. She still wanted the throat of Prince Styxx, but she couldn't be in another pantheon's territory with her goddess powers. Not unless they were fighting.

Damn it!

"How could we be defeated?" Misos snarled. "We've *never* been defeated!"

Pali shrugged in disgust. "Did you see the Greek champion? Styxx of Didymos? Has anyone heard of this bastard before?"

"He was young," Bethany said. "I saw him right before the battle began. And I almost had him . . . Ugh!" It pained her that she'd missed.

Repeatedly.

Bloody Greek dog!

Misos threw his shield down. "Is he a demigod? Or Chthonian?"

Bethany shook her head. "He was human with standard human equipment. How could he tear down our brethren? They have psychic powers . . . they should have cut through the Greeks like vegetables in a garden."

Diafonia raked her hands through her dark hair. "How did he fight like an immortal?"

"Maybe he was trained by one?" Pali suggested.

Bethany ground her teeth. "Athena fought beside him."

Misos scoffed. "That hasn't stopped us in the past."

No, it hadn't. Bethany sighed as she saw their newfound champion in her mind. "It's just one battle. He was lucky."

Misos narrowed his gaze on all of them. "Then let's see to it that the young prince's luck runs out."

As they started to disperse to watch over their troops' withdrawal, Apollo joined them. "What in the name of Hades just happened?"

Pali gave him a droll stare. "We got our asses kicked. What were you doing? Napping through it?"

Apollo glared at them. "How are we going to take Greece if we get driven from their shores like spanked little girls?"

"We?" Misos raked a sneer over Apollo's golden fair form. "*We* doesn't include *you*, Greek."

"It does as long as *my* people are fighting and dying. Especially my grandson! Which of them killed Xan?"

"Prince Styxx," they shouted in unison.

Pali snorted. "Are you deaf, too? How did you miss your people chanting the little bastard's name?"

Apollo's eyes blazed with sudden recognition. "That little prick was the Didymosian prince and heir?"

"Where have you been?" Diafonia asked. "Obviously you weren't here for the battle."

"Of course not. I couldn't let Zeus or Athena see me siding with our enemies. I only came after I heard you were retreating. And I have to say the news shocked me."

Misos folded his arms over his chest. "Well, if you'd like some vengeance, by all means, remove your prince from our future battle plans."

Apollo smiled wickedly. "Don't worry, old man. I *will* take care of him."

OCTOBER 26, 9532 BC

Styxx sighed as he returned to his tent to try and sleep. But honestly, his head hurt so much he wasn't sure if he'd be able to manage a single nod. Outside, his men and the rest of their Greek armies were celebrating fiercely. Styxx considered joining them, but he didn't want to risk being mocked or rejected again. He'd had enough of being judged for things he could neither help nor change.

After Styxx's bath, Kreon had gifted him with the fine silk stola and wool chlamys he wore and enough treasure to please even Styxx's volatile father.

For himself, Styxx had only taken one thing. A small gold ring he wanted to give to Bethany when he saw her again. He wore it on his pinkie so that he wouldn't accidentally lose it.

While she didn't normally wear anything more than the necklace she'd given him and occasional bracelets or armbands, he wasn't sure if it was because she didn't like other pieces of jewelry or couldn't afford them. But he hoped she smiled over the ring.

Just don't stab me for the gift.

He poured himself a kylix of wine. Out of the corner of his eye, he saw something flash. He jerked his head to find a beautiful golden man inside his tent. There was a glow to his skin that Styxx had only seen on two others . . .

His blood ran cold.

"Are you a god?"

The man smirked. "Are you asking me . . . or do you remember me?"

Styxx's stomach clenched with dread. No . . . it couldn't be.

Surely not after all this time.

The wine cup slipped from his hand as the god's teeth elongated. Styxx tried to run, but somehow the god held him immobile.

"Strange how swiftly time moves forward when you're immortal. I had no idea that my little prince had grown into such a fierce, handsome warrior that he could take down a psychic army and kill two of their strongest heroes . . . one of whom was a demigod."

In a completely different form than the one he'd had at the Dionysion, the god closed the distance between them and gave Styxx a cold, evil smile. "And you're so much more beautiful and delectable with hair and ripped muscles."

He grabbed Styxx's head and jerked him against his side. "You have killed a member of my family this day, little prince. That is something I cannot and will not let pass. This time, there will be no bargaining. And I will show you no mercy."

The Olympian dragged Styxx over to the table and threw him against it so that Styxx was facing a mirror where he could see himself and the god who held him down by the scruff of his neck. A tic worked in the Olympian's jaw as he glared at him with potent fury. He ruthlessly pulled the stola up until Styxx was bared to him.

In the reflection of the mirror, he locked gazes with Styxx. "As you ravaged my army today, I'm going to ravish every part of you. And every time you feel me violently take you, prince, I want you to remember which of us is the god and which is nothing but a pathetic piece of human waste."

OCTOBER 27, 9532 BC

"Highness, the men are wanting—" Galen's voice broke off at the sight of Styxx lying on the floor of his tent.

Styxx couldn't move. He could barely breathe. Every part of him felt as if it'd been pulverized. He could only imagine how he must appear. Completely naked, he stared at his arm, which was covered with bruises and blood. No doubt he looked like that all over.

Except for his face. The god had taken great care to leave his face undamaged . . .

"Styxx?" Galen breathed as he carefully rolled him to his back.

His breathing labored, he met his old tutor's gaze. "Don't tell . . . please."

Tears filled Galen's eyes as the old man pulled him gently into his lap, covered him with his cloak, and held him like no one had done since the night his father had cut open his arm.

I must look like total shit. He hadn't even known Galen possessed any kind of tender emotion.

Galen cradled Styxx's head to his chest and rocked him like a child. "I would never betray you, my prince."

Only then did Styxx relax. As long as no one knew, he could find a way to live with this as he lived with everything else that had been done to him.

"I should never have left you unprotected. I assumed you would stay with the others and celebrate your victory, but I should have known you better." Galen placed a fatherly kiss to his brow. "I heard from the men that you felled the grandson of a god and I've seen their retribution before. I should have warned you, my lord. I am so sorry."

Styxx patted his arm. "It's all right . . . I can be taught."

Galen gave him a bitter smile. "You are the best pupil I've ever had." *And I love you like a son, boy . . .*

Styxx's lips quivered as he heard Galen's thoughts. "I know we need to leave. I'm sure they're ready to pack the tent."

"You can't ride in your condition, Highness."

"I just need some water to bathe with. I'll manage the ride."

"Styxx—"

"Galen . . . I won't keep them or you here. Let's go home." But home wasn't what he really craved returning to.

Then again, the only thing he craved right now was one single, unimpeded breath.

NOVEMBER 3, 9532 BC

"Bethany?"

Her heart quickened as she finally heard the deep, husky voice she'd been longing to hear. "Hector?"

He sat down beside her on her blanket and laid his head on her shoulder then he wrapped his arms around her.

By the way he breathed, she knew he was in a great deal of pain. "Were you wounded?"

He placed her hand on his wrist so that she could feel her necklace there. "Not cut, but bruised to the point I can barely draw breath. Of course, it didn't help that I rode ahead of all the others and snuck back here to see you as soon as I could."

She cradled him against her. "Did you really?"

He nodded. "Night and day. I wasn't tired at all, until now."

She kissed his brow and savored the scent of his skin. "Does your head hurt?"

"Like I've been kicked by my horse."

"Then lie down in my lap and let me see if I can help."

"You already have."

She smiled at him as he complied, but her smile died at the sound of his pain and the way his breathing intensified. He hurt so much, he was absolutely shaking. "I heard you won," she said, trying to distract him from it.

"We did."

Brushing her hand through his hair, she felt several large bumps on his head. Careful not to touch them, she massaged his temples and scalp as best she could. "Were you scared?"

His breathing came easier now. "Petrified. But I would only admit that to you."

She paused as she touched a cut on the back of his head where it felt like he must have fallen against something. "I heard Prince Styxx was the battle's hero. Did you see him?"

He was quiet for several seconds. "I did."

"And?"

"Should I be jealous that you're so interested in the prince? I thought money didn't matter to you."

"It doesn't. I just wanted to know about this man who dared to pull my sweet Hector from my arms."

"Mmm . . . I was too busy fighting to pay attention to him."

"Is it really true that he took no tribute, but rather had it divided between his men?"

He made a light sound that let her know he was slipping fast into sleep.

Leaning down, she rubbed her nose against his and savored the sensation of his breath on her skin. Even though it galled her that they'd been defeated, she was grateful her Hector was back and whole. It went a long way in soothing her ravaged ego. Still . . .

She had a grudge to settle and she wasn't going to forget it. One way or another, Styxx was going to pay for what he'd done to them on the battlefield. And hers would be the hand that dealt the final blow to that arrogant little prick.

NOVEMBER 10, 9532 BC

Bethany laughed as Hector nibbled a scorching trail down her stomach until he took her into his mouth. Lifting her hips, she buried her hand in his soft hair while his tongue danced over her until she was breathless and weak. In just a matter of minutes, her body exploded into pure bliss. She cried out in ecstasy and still his tongue flitted over her until she was drunk from his masterful touch.

No one had a tongue like his . . .

Body either.

Slowly, methodically, he kissed his way over her, taking time to savor her breasts before he claimed her lips. She felt the tip of his erection pressing against her, begging for entry.

Desperate to have him inside her body again, she wiggled her hips. He deepened his kiss, and laced his fingers with hers then he took mercy on her and slid himself inside. Sighing in delight, she ran her free hand down to where they were joined so that she could feel his cock as he thrust against her hips.

Styxx sucked his breath in at the sensation of her hand on him. His sweet Bethany took him away from all the nightmares he didn't want to remember. From the horror of Apollo's attack. "I love it when you do that."

Smiling, she kissed him.

He should have gone home days ago, but he'd been holed up with Bethany in a small hostel on the outskirts of town where no one knew who he was. In truth, he had no desire to leave here.

To leave her.

She lifted her hips so that he went all the deeper inside her body. "I can't believe how hungry you still are."

"I'm never satiated where you're concerned, *akribos*." He nipped her fingers as she danced them over his lips.

She moaned deep in her throat.

Styxx buried his face against her neck as he quickened his strokes. He knew from experience that when she made that sound and tightened her arms around him, she was on the brink of orgasm.

A moment later, her dulcet cry filled his ears. He rolled his hips against hers, driving her climax on until she laughed and kissed him passionately.

Her lips were all he needed to tip him over into ecstasy. Growling in his throat, he buried himself deep and held her close. Strange how he only found peace with her. The rest of the world could burn and he wouldn't care. Not so long as he could feel her hand on his cheek.

It felt as if he'd always known her. As if he'd been born solely to love her with every part of himself.

She sighed contentedly. "Oh, what you do to me, my sweet prince."

His heart lurched at the endearment. "I wish you wouldn't call me that."

She frowned. "Why?"

Too many people had used the title to mock him. And now . . . he heard Apollo's repugnant voice saying it in his ear. It made his skin crawl.

He was so grateful that Bethany couldn't see the "wonderful" souvenir that bastard had left him with. A sun symbol between his shoulder blades so that everyone who saw it would know the sun god had violated him. Every time he thought about it, he wanted to scream and run his sword through that bastard's gut.

"I'm not a prince, Beth. I'm just a man."

"But you are so much more than that to me."

Closing his eyes, he savored those words and reveled in the sensation of her hands gliding over his sweaty back. "Your father is most likely going to kill you for your absence."

"I'm sure yours won't be pleased either."

"No . . . he won't." He teased her earlobe with his teeth. "I still wish you'd run away with me, Beth. I would give you anything you ask."

"But you can't run away from your responsibilities or problems. They always follow."

"They don't have to."

"Please, Hector, don't ruin this week by asking for something I can't give you."

He ground his teeth at the pain in his chest whenever he thought about leaving her and returning to a life he hated with every beat of his heart. "All right. I won't trouble you again with it."

Someone pounded on their door. "The prince returns!" They ran down the hall, banging on all the doors to announce it.

Styxx scowled then growled as he realized it meant their army had returned home.

Not him.

Bethany traced the line of his brow. "You should be marching in with them to receive your honors."

Yes, he should. His father would be furious when he learned

Styxx wasn't with the others. "I would have to leave you in order to do that. Is that really what you want?"

She bit her lip playfully. "No. I rather like you where you currently are."

"As do I."

But there would be rancid Tartarus to pay whenever he left her . . .

NOVEMBER 11, 9532 BC

It was just after midnight when Styxx entered the palace through the front door. He thought he was home free until he topped the stairs and met his father there.

The expression on his father's face was anything but welcoming. His father backhanded him so hard, it knocked his teeth loose.

"You are ever determined to publicly embarrass and humiliate me, aren't you?"

His lips already swelling, Styxx wiped the blood on the back of his hand. "How so, Father?"

"You turned down a king's offer, you disseminated royal treasure to commoners without permission, and then you deprived the city of welcoming you home and insulted the noblemen and their wives by not attending the celebratory banquet held in *your* dubious honor."

That was quite a list of offenses his father had made.

"What have you to say for yourself, boy?"

Styxx licked at his still bleeding lips. "I thought King Kreon had been more than generous with his gifts to you, Father. So much so that you wouldn't miss what little he gave to me personally for my services to his army. I thought those were better served going to the men who'd left their families and risked their lives for us than into the treasury to pay for Mother's drink and Ryssa's gowns. Forgive me for my selfishness. As for the noblemen and their wives, I doubt they missed me once you opened the reserves. And honestly, I didn't want the humiliation of returning home and having my mother and sister snub me on the palace steps or see the anger in your eyes over the fact that I squandered my portion of the tribute I earned. So again, please forgive me for insulting you while I sought to save myself from more public embarrassment."

"I should have you whipped for your insolence."

"Fine. Would you like to wake the scold or should I?" Styxx started past him, but his father caught his arm and pulled him to a stop.

A tic beating furiously in his jaw, he met his father's baffled expression.

"I don't understand you, boy. I have given you everything a prince could have or want, and it's not enough for you. You're petulant. Thoughtless . . . Perhaps I should have kept Acheron and let Estes whore you in his stead."

Those words slammed into him like one of Apollo's fists. "You knew?"

"Not . . . in so many details. But I had suspicions."

Styxx couldn't breathe as the cold, harsh brutality racked him hard. "How could you suspect and do nothing?"

"I did it to protect you and control him."

Styxx snorted. "Protect *me*?"

"Your life hinges on his."

So . . . ? "And what about now? You don't know where . . . " Styxx's voice trailed off as a brutal realization slapped him in the face. "You *do* know Acheron's whereabouts."

"Of course I do. You don't really think for one moment I'd let him loose when his life is tied to yours, do you?"

Styxx glanced away from him before he gave in to the urge to beat the old bastard. "I don't know what to think anymore, *Father*."

The king reached for him.

Styxx stepped back, out of his reach. "Don't touch me. How could you allow my twin to be bought and sold?"

The lack of remorse on his father's face appalled him completely. "It was a perfect revenge. The gods whored my queen. It's only right that I whore their by-blow."

How was Styxx supposed to take that? It was okay for Acheron, his identical twin, to live in utter misery and to be used every single day?

Was that why *he* was now being tortured by Apollo? The gods were exacting their own retribution over what the king had done to one of them? And Styxx was their tool?

"And what of me?"

His father scowled. "What about you?"

By his father's thoughts, Styxx knew the king had no idea Estes had used him, and he definitely didn't know about Apollo's attacks. "Did Estes tell you he molested Acheron?"

His father grabbed him by the throat and shoved him back. "My brother never did such a thing. It's a lie that bastard told. I know better."

No, he didn't. Styxx knocked his hand away. "Where's my brother?"

"In a place where he can't hurt us."

Right then, Styxx could have killed his father easier than he'd killed his uncle. "Where?" he asked through clenched teeth.

"A stew."

"I want the name of it."

"Why?" His father narrowed his gaze on him. "You want to fuck him, too?"

Styxx went cold. No ... surely not. "Too?"

His father slapped him again. "I never touched that filth. But why else would you want to know where he is?"

Because I might actually care and love my brother.

Yet he knew better than to say that out loud. So, he gave his father the only answer the heartless bastard could comprehend. "I certainly don't want to chance going to it and being mistaken for my brother, now do I?"

As expected, it placated the wretched beast. "Catera's."

"Thank you." Styxx headed for the stairs.

"Where are you going?"

"Ultimately to Tartarus, I'm sure. For now . . . out."

"Styxx!"

He ignored his father's shout as he left the palace and headed for the center of the city. At this point, he really didn't care what his father did to him. What difference would it make?

"If it's a whore you want—"

Styxx cut the man off with a fierce growl. "I told you, I want to see Catera. *Now!*"

"She doesn't see clients."

Styxx shoved the small man back into the shadows and lowered his hood. "I am not a client and unless it is your wish to have this brothel burned to the ground and everyone in it arrested and then executed, I suggest you get the owner to me immediately and tell no one who I am."

He ran to comply.

Styxx covered his head again, making sure to keep his identity completely hidden. His blood ran cold as he listened to the bargains being cut all around. Worse were the fleeting memories of people bargaining for him . . .

"Can I help you?"

He glanced over his shoulder to see a tiny older woman with henna red hair. "Catera?"

"Yes?"

"I need to speak with you alone."

She shook her head in denial. "I don't do that anymore."

"I don't want to tup you, woman," Styxx snarled. "I'm here to give you the terms under which this brothel will be allowed to continue operating."

She made a subtle gesture for a burly man to join them.

Styxx scoffed at that. As if he'd be intimidated after everything he'd been through. "If you value his life and yours, you will see me privately, right now."

She held her hand up to stop the man's approach. For several seconds she debated then nodded. "Follow me." She led the way to a small room in the back part of the brothel.

The moment the door was shut, Styxx lowered his hood.

All the color drained from her face as she sank to her knees in front of him. "Your Highness, please forgive—"

"It's all right," he said, cutting her off. "Now get up."

She stood immediately. "What can I do for you, Highness?"

"It's my understanding that you have a ... an employee here who looks like me."

"Acheron."

He wasn't sure if he should be relieved or appalled. "It's true then?"

"It is." Fear and worry lined her brow.

"Relax, woman. I only want to make sure he's cared for."

She scowled. "I don't understand."

For the first time in his life, Styxx took full advantage of his rank and position. "It's not your place to understand. Only to obey." He pulled his purse out and opened it. "I don't want you to overwork him. He's to have half the week off to do as he pleases, and you're to make sure he has the best of everything you can provide him, including care when he's sick." He set his purse on her desk. "So long as you abide by that, I'll have money delivered to you every month. If any word of his abuse reaches me, I will see you personally held responsible, and the repercussions will be neither pretty nor enjoyable."

Her eyes glittered with greed. "Yes, Highness. Is there anything else?"

He shook his head. "Just take care of him."

She opened his purse and her eyes widened then she smiled. "Most gladly." She hesitated before she closed it and slid it into her desk. "May I speak frankly, Highness?"

"If you must."

She ran her gaze over the length of his body. "At first, it is quite startling how much you favor. But you two are nothing alike."

If only that was the truth. They were a lot more similar than anyone would guess. However, there was one important matter they differed on.

"Believe me, I know, madam. I'm the one who's a lethal bastard when crossed." And with that, he lifted his hood and left.

DECEMBER 10, 9532 BC

It was war. Open and full-scale. His father had received the notice just an hour ago and Didymos, along with all Greek city-states, was rallying troops. They had to leave immediately.

Styxx sighed as he found no sign of Bethany at their spot. "Beth?" he called, hoping she was wandering about, as she did sometimes when she didn't know he was coming.

There was no answer.

Damn it.

He'd be gone by dawn. All he'd wanted was to see her one last time, and tell her what was happening. But then, she'd know. Everyone was well aware that the Atlanteans were stepping up their attacks and determined to conquer all of Greece. They planned to slaughter every royal family they could find.

But it wasn't his family he cared about.

"I will fight for you, my Bethany." And he would make sure that Greece stayed free from Atlantean control to keep her, alone, safe. The rest of them could go straight to Tartarus for all he cared.

He looked down at the ring he'd brought for her. A ring he

should have given her on his return from Halicarnassus, but it'd been tainted by Apollo and he'd wanted to wait and give it to her when he didn't have something so brutal to tarnish the joy of watching her receive it.

Unsure if she'd ever find it, he tucked it into the base of the tree where they met and hoped that she'd understand why he couldn't wait for her.

His heart broken that he wouldn't see her again for who knew how long, he mounted his horse and left.

Bethany wanted to scream. She'd been waiting here for hours, hoping Hector would come. Given the vicious attack Apollo had led against his own people and blamed the Atlanteans for, she knew they'd be sending Hector to war again and she wanted to see him before he left.

This time, she was going to mark him so that she'd know which soldier he was.

Frustrated, she lay down and flung her hand over her head. She grimaced as it slammed into the tree behind her. Then it brushed against something with a sharp edge. Frowning, she turned over and patted the small knothole in the tree where Hector would occasionally leave something for her.

No ...

Tears filled her eyes as she realized he'd come here and she'd missed him. Aching, she pulled the small box into her hands and opened it to find a ring inside.

Desperate to know for certain if it was from him, she took it to her temple on Katateros. Biting her lip, she pulled it from the box to see a beautiful gold ring that was impressed with a winged horse—something she'd told him she fancied without telling him she actually owned one. And on the inside of the band was stamped the words ΔΙΚΟΣ ΣΑΣ. *Faithfully yours.*

He had been there and she'd missed him. Pain shredded her as she realized she might never see him again. *Please remember to carry my necklace with you. Please.*

What if he didn't?

No, she wouldn't think about that. She couldn't. If anything happened to him . . .

She would rain Kalosis itself down on every Greek. Archon would never again have to fear Apollymi's child. *She* would be the one to tear this world apart.

But how would she find him?

Because it was open war, the Greek troops would be combined and split. Some of the Didymosian regiments could be in the southern part. Some in the north. Or if enough men were lost in Hector's regiment, he could be assigned to one from another city-state. There was no way for her to know which regiment he'd be assigned to.

"I *will* find you, Hector."

She had no idea how, but she wouldn't rest until she was sure he was safe and whole.

Most of all, protected.

MAY 23, 9531 BC

Hephaestion, the Atlantean messenger god, shoved open the doors of the gods' main hall on Katateros. "The Stygian Omada is on our beaches!"

Bethany looked up from the precious letter Hector had paid a messenger to hide in the tree at their meeting spot while the gods around her scrambled to action. She grabbed Hephaestion's arm as he started past her to notify the gods who weren't in attendance, and pulled him to a stop. "What has happened?"

"They just landed on the beach at Ena. If we don't stop them now and turn them back to Greece, they could make it to the mainland and take the city."

309

She saw red at the mere thought of a Greek in her beloved country. How dare they! "Who leads their forces?"

"Styxx of Didymos."

Oh, it figured ...

Athena's dog they'd named the Στύγιος ομάδα—Stygian Omada—after. Fury blinding her, Bethany manifested her armor and summoned her horse and bow. This time, she was going to teach that bastard a lesson. In Greece, her powers were limited even when she rode with the Atlantean army, but here in her own lands ...

Prince Styxx would feel her full bite this day and wish to the gods he worshiped that he'd stayed home.

Exhausted from battle, Styxx wiped the blood from his face as he watched his army move inward from the beach where they'd landed. Though it'd been a fierce fight, they'd overtaken the Atlantean guard who'd been charged with the safety of their outermost island. Most of the Atlantean guard lay slaughtered on the beach. But a small contingency had escaped inland to warn their people.

"Fortify!" he called to his commanders. They'd need to be ready when the next onslaught came. There was no way the Atlanteans would leave them to advance without a staunch, brutal fight every step of the way.

Styxx winced as his side started bleeding again. Damn it ... Bethany's token only protected him from weapons. Not from broken wood poles and blatant stupidity. During the fighting yesterday, he'd stumbled against one. Somehow, it'd gone between the laces of his cuirass to slice and stab him across his ribs.

And it burned like Greek fire.

Trying to ignore the pain, he went to retrieve his horse then paused as he saw fires off to the north, not that far away, in one of the villages. At first, he thought the people there might be signaling the mainland. Until he saw the Greek banners that had been placed in the sand in front of it.

Shit . . .

Against orders, his men were raiding.

"Galen!" he shouted to his second-in-command. "I need my *dekarmatoli*. Fast." The *dekarmatoli* were the ten men his former tutor had hand-selected and charged with making sure Styxx was safe at all times. After what had happened at Halicarnassus with Apollo, Galen had guarded him like a psychotic mother hen.

But right now, Styxx was going to need loyal men to quell this rebellion before it started.

He swung up onto Troian's back and spurred his horse to the site as fast as he could.

Bethany was furious as she flashed into the small Enean village where their followers had been desperately imploring the Atlantean gods for rescue. While the rest of the gods had gone to render aid to the bulk of their forces, she'd agreed to come and check on the inhabitants here.

The village had taken in wounded Atlantean soldiers . . . wounded men who had been slaughtered by Greeks at the foot of her great-grandfather's statue in the center of their small hamlet.

She raised her hand to blast them all straight to their beloved Hades.

"Halt!"

That deep, fierce, commanding tone froze them all. Even her.

Curious, she frowned at the sight of the Didymosian prince as he leapt from the back of his ebony horse and strode angrily through the fallen bodies and looting Greeks without any backup whatsoever.

Was he insane?

The Greeks here weren't from Didymos. And they would have no love or respect for the young prince. Something evidenced by the derision on their faces.

His blue eyes full of angry verve, Styxx headed straight for two soldiers who had hauled a beautiful young girl from her home and into the street. It was obvious by her torn gown what they intended.

"Release her!" Styxx demanded.

Instead of following orders, the large, burly soldier wrapped his arm around the girl's waist. "She's spoils, *Highness*." He sneered the title.

"She's a girl, not property. Now release her or you will regret it."

"What? You'll have your men whip me?" He laughed. "I'm a Thracian. We don't bow down to a Didymosian crown and we hold no fear of your men."

The Thracians with him cheered in support.

Undaunted, the prince approached him like a fierce predator who was aware of every sword around him and yet feared none of them. "Then it's time you learn to fear me."

They all laughed at Styxx's bold words.

Wanting a closer view, and to make sure the terrified girl wasn't harmed in any way, Bethany flashed herself into the girl's body. Her arms burned from the soldier's brutal grip.

He buried his face in her neck. "She smells sweet for an Atlantean whore. I'm sure we can find one for you, prince. Now go back to your own men and leave this to those of us old enough for pubic hair."

Styxx's celestial gaze didn't waver as he slung his arm out. An instant later, the soldier released her and fell back, dead, with a small throwing knife planted between his eyes.

Bethany's jaw went slack at the sight.

Styxx had killed one of his own men?

To protect her people?

Drawing his sword, the prince put himself between her and the men who'd come here with him. "Get to your mother, girl. Fast."

Stunned at his flawless Atlantean, she obeyed then watched in absolute fascination as he stood alone to defend his enemies from his own army.

The Greeks attacked him.

He downed six of their soldiers before his reinforcements arrived to stand with him against the rest of the angry Thracians. His men quickly subdued them, and drove them back.

Styxx grabbed the one who had stood beside the first man he'd killed. "Send word to your Thracians that we are not here to rape wives, sisters, and daughters. Our fight is with the Atlantean queen, her soldiers, and their gods, not their women or children. Any Greek who defies my orders will be castrated and offered as a sacrifice to the Atlantean god Dikastis for their crimes against his people."

"Do you think they'd be so kind to our women?"

Styxx shoved him away. "That is why we're on Atlantean soil, fighting them before they reach our homelands. We're here to protect our families from Atlantean slavery, and I will not shame our innocents by slaughtering and debasing theirs. Now go and warn your men."

The prince returned to Bethany and the small hut where the girl had been hiding with her mother and sisters.

To her complete stupefaction, the prince retrieved a fallen doll just outside the hut then came to kneel in the doorway, on the ground by the girl's little sister who was probably no older than ten.

He held the doll out to her as she clung to her mother's skirt. "It's all right, little one," he said again in flawless Atlantean. "We are not here to harm you or your family. You have my word."

She looked up at her mother for confirmation.

Her eyes wide, the mother snatched the doll from his hand then stepped back to protect her daughters.

Styxx bowed to them before he stood. "Tell your villagers to gather together here in the square and I will personally see all of you taken to your city walls to be protected. If anyone is unable to walk or travel, let us know and we will carry them."

She eyed him suspiciously. "Is this a Greek trick?"

"I swear on my life that it's not. Please, good mother, for the sakes of your daughters, hurry. I don't know how long my army can hold the other Greeks back should they choose to fight my orders. We must get you to safety."

He went to relay his intentions to his own men who acted as if the orders were typical and expected from him. It wasn't until he stumbled and caught himself against his horse that Bethany realized he was badly wounded. Blood trickled down his left leg.

Yet he let no one know it as he quickly wiped it away and mounted.

True to his word, he helped round up her people and escort them to safety. Never in her life had she seen anything like this. A Greek who killed his own men to protect his enemy's women and children . . .

It was unheard of, especially from a prince who'd shown no mercy to his enemies over the last few months as he fought them. The one thing everyone knew about Styxx was that he'd been ruthless on the battlefield. His army alone, remained undefeated by the Atlanteans. Utilizing new tactics that were radically different from the rest of the Greek forces, Styxx had waged a malicious and successful campaign against her people.

And while he was showing mercy to the people right now, she knew once they were gone he'd order the abandoned homes searched for supplies and then burned to the ground. It was another thing he was known for.

Even more curious about him than before, she paused by the side of his horse. Still in the guise of the girl he'd saved, she looked up to watch the prince as he oversaw the removal of her people.

He held himself with the same rigid arrogant stance that had irritated her the first time she'd seen him in Halicarnassus.

Or was it arrogance? Now that she was closer, she saw the torment and pain inside those blue eyes. The wary resignation and exhaustion that made him seem much older. And more vulnerable.

"Highness?"

His emotions evaporated into an expression of stoicism as he looked down at her. "Yes?"

She placed her hand to his black and bronze greave and noted where exactly in his side he was wounded. "Thank you for your aid."

He inclined his head respectfully to her.

Boldly, she lifted her hand to brush the hard calf muscle that bulged between the laces of his greave. "For your kindness, I'd like to offer you my services."

He nudged his horse away from her. "While I appreciate your offer and am truly flattered, I must decline."

Confused, she started away.

"Elea?" he called out.

Amazed that he remembered the girl's name from when her mother had used it almost an hour ago, she paused to look back at him. "Highness?"

"Don't let anyone, especially yourself, barter your body for any purpose. The temporary and immediate benefits are not worth the eternal cost to your soul." Leaning forward, he gently tossed an expensive brooch at her.

She caught it in her hand and saw that it bore the same phoenix emblem as his shield. It was the badge of his Stygian Omada.

Without another word, he wheeled his horse about so that he could personally carry an infirmed woman and her small grand-daughter to the walled city, farther inland.

Stunned by his unexpected wisdom and kind charity, she went to join them in their trek to safety. A part of her still waited for it to be a trick of some sort.

As they walked, she scanned his men, looking for her Hector. But these were all cavalry. There wasn't a foot soldier among them. Another unexpected honor to her people that he used noblemen and his best-trained soldiers—not peasants—to protect them.

And as she watched him, something about the prince reminded her of her love, but Hector wouldn't be wounded. Not if he wore her charm, and he'd had it on the last time she saw him. There was no reason to think he'd remove it. Plus, the prince appeared a bit older than Hector. Definitely more stern and sure of himself. Hector was bashful and reserved. He would never rush into a fight so recklessly.

No, Styxx was not the man who set her on fire.

But now she finally understood why Athena had chosen this prince as her pet. He was honorable when others weren't. And he treated everyone around him with respect . . . as if they mattered.

Even his enemies.

Still, this good deed changed nothing. They were at war and she would eventually destroy him for daring to come to her shores and kill her soldiers. His compassion today had won him a small reprieve while she saw to their followers.

Tomorrow, however, she would be after him with everything she had.

Entering the city walls, she watched as Styxx gently carried the old woman into Agapa's temple, which had been set up to receive those left homeless by these invaders. He turned her care over to a young priest, but not before he said something that made the old woman smile and kindly lifted her granddaughter up to sit next to her.

Honestly, it surprised her that none of the Atlanteans attacked his soldiers. It would be an easy way to end the war now.

But her people weren't as treacherous as the Greeks. They never had been. Instead, they honored Styxx and his men's decent intentions and allowed them to deposit the villagers then leave without incident.

Come morning, though, they would be at war again.

With that thought foremost in her mind, she left the girl's body and went to find her great-grandfather at his temple just down the street from here.

The Atlanteans were invoking his name and making sacrifices. Not that they needed to. Misos would have been with them regardless.

Unseen by their people, her great-grandfather arched his brow at her approach. "What news do you have?"

"The Greek prince is wounded in his left side, three ribs down. He will barely be able to hold his hoplon with that arm."

"Good work. We will see him dead on the morrow, and send his putrid Greeks home with their tails tucked between their legs."

MAY 24, 9531 BC

It was just after midnight and, as usual, Styxx couldn't sleep. As a boy, the voices in his head had kept him from rest. Now it was his conscience and recent memories that beat him so brutally. He hated everything war forced him to do to protect his men and his people.

Everything.

He cradled his aching head in his hands, wishing he were with his Bethany. The thought of her sweet touch and scent brought a rare smile to his lips as he wondered how she fared. If she'd found the letter he'd had delivered to their meeting spot. And if she was being cradled by Morpheus in her dreams tonight.

"Highness?"

He opened his eyes to see Galen entering his tent. "Yes?"

"I just received word that the Thracians are angry, but complying for now."

Styxx sighed heavily. "Tell me the truth. What rankles them most, Master Galen? The fact they can't rape any woman they find, or the fact that a child calls their orders?"

Galen snorted. "I see no child in our veteran ranks."

Styxx saluted him sarcastically with his kylix. "Both of us know I have no business leading men into battle. The Thracians were right today. I don't have enough experience for this."

Scoffing, Galen sat down in the chair beside Styxx, and retook the wine he'd been drinking earlier. "No other commander could have gotten us this far with as few casualties as we've had. Look at your history, my lord. Name me the only man who has ever made it to Atlantean soil with an invading army from *any* foreign land?" Galen paused. "There's only one. Styxx of the House of Aricles. Prince of Didymos."

Maybe, but he was tired of the blood and sickened by watching men, young and old, hacked to pieces, and for what? Power? Money? Glory?

What good was it when you only needed a single obolos to pay Charon for the final crossing?

Every decision he made, good or bad, ended with someone being slaughtered. With someone calling out for a mother, wife, or one of the gods . . . With them burning someone's home and possessions until nothing but ashes remained. A lifetime of memories and savings to build, a few minutes of war to destroy.

Styxx raked a hand over his eyes, trying to banish the images that wouldn't leave him in peace any more than the voices would. He would give anything to have a handful of minutes with Bethany so that she could kiss away his nightmares, and give him something beautiful to look at.

Something beautiful to hold on to.

Galen leaned forward. "How's your side, my lord?"

"Like my head. Throbbing."

The old man's gaze fell to Styxx's hand on his cup. "You're still not wearing a signet ring?"

Styxx glanced down at his bare fingers and shrugged. "To what purpose? If I fall, I'm not worth the price of a ransom. Why should I go home when the other soldiers fighting under my banner would be put to sword or market by our enemies? Better I should join them in death or slavery than live on in peace, knowing I failed to keep them safe." He poured more wine for himself and then handed the pitcher over to Galen, who declined drinking any more of it.

Sighing, Styxx toyed with Galen's flute the old man had been playing earlier. "Tell me, Galen, how do you sleep at night? I've seen nothing compared to the battles I know you've fought and led. Please tell me how to make peace with my conscience."

The old man's breath left him in a ragged rush. "It's hard, my lord. I won't lie. And I walked away from this way too late."

"How so?"

318

Galen reached for the dish of olives on Styxx's desk and took a handful. "My father was a simple farmer with a tiny farm. I hated working it in ways you can't imagine. Every day, I swore I was going to get away from the pig shit and plow no matter what I had to do, or who I had to kill. And then one day, I saw an army coming through our back field. The sun glinted off their armor and they looked like proud gods. Before I could stop myself, I ran to them and joined their ranks. But nothing, not even our fall slaughters or a butcher's hall, had prepared me for the true horrors and cold brutality of a soldier's life."

He swallowed. "Still, to me, it was far preferable to that little farm I'd despised. The fame and glory, and in particular, the riches and women, kept me distracted for a long time. And then one day, as my army was traveling through another backwoods field, I saw the most beautiful woman the gods had ever created. Her winsome smile dazzled me even more than that armor had when I was a boy, and so I stopped, right then and there, to talk to her."

Galen paused to savor his wife's memory. "She gave me two fine sons and two beautiful daughters. And while I was at war, she buried our youngest daughter who was stricken with a fever, and our son who fell from a tree and broke his neck. I still, and always will, hate myself for leaving her alone to deal with that in my absence." Unshed tears glistened in his old gray eyes. "My oldest son followed me into war and I was so proud." His voice cracked with the weight of his paternal love. "My Philip was a lion on the field. Tall, strong, respectful, and glorious. I would look at him and thank the gods for their benevolence in giving me such a magnificent child. Who was I to deserve such given how many sons I'd taken from their fathers?"

Swallowing hard, he swiped at his eyes and cleared his throat. "And then the day all fathers fear came. I can still see him as I slipped and fell in battle. I lay there thinking it was my time to have my thread cut by mighty Atropos's shears. Crying out, Philip ran toward me to save my life. And just as he reached me, his head was sent flying by the single stroke of an enemy's axe." His eyes burning

319

with rage, he wiped his hand across his mouth. "I pray to the gods, young prince, that you never know the horror of picking through bodies, trying to find a part of the only thing in this world you truly took pride in. There is no greater nightmare and it's one that continues to stalk me even when I'm awake."

With an unfathomable strength, Galen took a deep breath and calmed his emotions. "After my Philip was gone from a battle we shouldn't have been in, I broke my xiphos in half and swore I'd never bend to the call of Ares again. I was done with him and Athena both. So I retired to that farm I'd hated so much as a boy and spent the best years of my life with my sweet Thia. I watched our last child grow into the most beautiful of women and wished I had more to give to my precious Antigone and her children. Then one day, another soldier came to my door and told me that the king wanted me to tutor his brat for war. I laughed in his face. But not at the mighty coin he offered."

Lifting his cup in salute, Galen grinned. "How could I pass on that? Plus, it gave me the opportunity to knock around the spoiled son of the man who had ordered me into the unnecessary battle that had taken my boy's life."

Styxx snorted as he drank his wine. "I commend you on your prowess, Master Tutor. Whenever the weather turns cold, I can still feel some of your finer lessons in my bones, and in particular, my wrist."

Galen pinned a malevolent glare on him. "The moment I first laid eyes on you, Highness, I hated you passionately. There you stood, barely reaching my waist, in child-sized armor far finer than any I'd ever worn to battle for the sake of your father or that my Philip had worn when he was slaughtered in service to a king who couldn't care less about his life or death. You held your head high with a commanding arrogance that offended me to the core of my soul. And I wanted to put my fist through your pretty, pampered face."

"As I recall, you did. And then you kicked me in the ass and sent me sprawling, pampered face first, into a pile of horseshit."

Galen chuckled at the memory. "And you said not a word about it to anyone. You got up, took your training sword, and faced me as if you'd landed in a bed of poppies. All the while, shit dripped off you."

"I stupidly thought you liked me and feared what you'd do if you didn't."

Galen shook his head. "I know you better than that, boy. But it took me awhile before I could let go my hatred and see that what I'd mistaken for disdainful arrogance was afflicted defiance that was trying to stand strong against all those determined to watch you burn and to do the right thing for others, even when it cost you dearly. It was that boy, who even then had the heart of a man, who taught me to respect a crown I'd grown to despise. A crown I'd sworn to never again defend. Forgive me for the treason, young prince, but I still hate your father and I always will. He cares nothing and thinks nothing of those who fight for him. But you ... it is and will always be my honor to stand with you against any foe. In battle, you don't hang back and order others to die for you. You lead us in, and I've seen you, time and again, throw yourself against much larger and stronger opponents to protect your men. I've seen you carry wounded soldiers, low and high, to safety with no regard for your own well-being, even today when you're badly wounded yourself."

"And I see the faces of all those I couldn't save. The faces of those who stared into my eyes as they died by my hand. Who am I to stand as their executioner?"

"You are Styxx of the House of the most famed Aricles, the prince and heir of Didymos. And one day, you will be king. Who better to rule the kingdom than a man who realizes he isn't a god and who knows the value and sacrifice of those who serve him and protect his people?"

"I don't feel like a prince, Galen." He felt like a tired whore.

"And that, Highness, is what makes you the worthiest to wear your father's crown."

Styxx laughed bitterly. "I wish I saw myself through your eyes." His saw only his flaws and shortcomings.

To his shock, Galen pulled him forward until their cheeks touched and held him in a fatherly embrace. Then Galen kissed his head and released him. He set his wine down on Styxx's desk and retrieved his flute. "You should try and sleep, Highness. The morning light will bring more battle to our swords."

And more ghostly shades to haunt and plague his conscience ...

MAY 24, 9531 BC

Invisible to the humans around her, Bethany picked her way through the Greek camp, looking for Hector. She kept hearing his name, but every time, it was another soldier they called. Apparently, it was an extremely popular name among the Greeks.

Frustrated and angry, she paused as she found herself outside Prince Styxx's tent that was guarded by four men.

Really? The Greeks hated him *that* much?

Disgusted, she glanced around at the men who slept in the open and fought for him while he used them to bring comforts from home at their expense and effort. And one of those packhorses was probably her beloved Hector. Her anger rising at his pompousness, she entered the tent, and froze.

This was not the lush environment she'd envisioned for a young prince. The tent was empty except for a strategy desk, maps, a handful of folding chairs, a small washing basin, his arms mannequin, and a plain soldier's pallet on the ground.

He didn't even have a pillow ...

Already dressed in his black armor, Styxx was lacing on his greaves. Alone.

Where were his servants?

His hair was much shorter than it'd been months ago when

she'd first seen him fighting with Athena. He'd cropped it so short that it held no hint of his thick blond curls. And he was no longer clean-shaven. Because of the helmet he'd worn yesterday, she hadn't seen that his sculpted cheeks, upper lip, and chin were covered with dark whiskers. He smelled of oil, blood, sweat, leather, and horse. A far cry from Hector's pleasant masculine scent.

As he armed himself, there was no fear in this prince. Only a quiet torment that tugged at the edges of her heart. His eyes were shadowed with an inner turmoil and a raw intelligence that few mortals held. He looked far wiser than his young years.

As he straightened up, he grimaced and placed his hand to his injured side. He took several quick, ragged breaths before he expelled an elongated one and subdued his misery. He reached for his swords and buckled them on. His heavily defined biceps and shoulders rippled with every move he made.

Why do you fascinate me so? She couldn't understand it, especially since her heart was already claimed by an innocent, sweet boy. It made no sense. Perhaps because the prince and Hector were about the same height. And their voices were similar . . .

Both were blonds with lean, ripped bodies.

Bethany sucked in her breath as the comparison slapped her again. *Are* you *my Hector?*

Could it be?

No. It wasn't possible. Why would the prince pretend to be a merchant's son to spend time with a blind fisherwoman? A man of Styxx's station would be quick to let her know he was wellborn. And he would *never* deign to beg a commoner to run away with him. Why would he when he owned the world in which he lived?

Everyone knew how much the king of Didymos loved and cherished his heir. The exceptional quality of his armor and horse said as much.

No priest would hazard to mar this man's body or his beauty with red-hot brands.

Not to mention this powerful, fierce beast would never be

clumsy enough to fall from his horse and stumble alone through the woods to find her fishing spot. Her Hector was hesitant and sweet. Bashful and unsure. There was no uncertainty in the prince's movements. This was a man who was confident in his role and place.

Ferocious.

No one would have ever dared to rape *him*.

And Styxx would never deign to ask to kiss a lowly peasant girl. He'd take it if he wanted it, and dare anyone to punish him for his actions. And while he'd declined her offer yesterday when she'd been disguised as a young Atlantean woman, he held such powerful sexual magnetism and prowess that it was obvious he was well tutored in the physical side of Agapa's domain. Most likely, the girl hadn't been pretty enough for his tastes.

Or, more probable, too far beneath his station for him to touch.

Unaware of her presence, Styxx tugged at the laces of his vambraces to make sure they were tight. Rolling his shoulders, he reached for his helm and shield then left the tent.

"What are you doing here?"

Bethany looked over her shoulder to find Athena watching her. "Checking out my next victim."

Athena laughed. "You won't defeat my champion. His is a core of steel the likes of which you can't fathom. He has the heart of a Titan and the mind of a philosopher."

"All mortals fall eventually."

"As do some immortals."

Bethany glared at her. "You have brought your army onto our shores. Do you really think we'll let you come any closer?"

The mocking smile on Athena's face made her want to yank out the bitch's hair by its roots. "You didn't *let* us come this far. I do believe we've done it with you battling us every step of the way. And we will continue onward. The Greeks love my chosen prince. They will follow him anywhere."

"Then let them all follow him to your Elysian Fields."

JULY 27, 9531 BC

Styxx paused in the garden of the Agriosan—the sacred temple of Bet'anya Agriosa, the Atlantean goddess of misery, wrath, and the hunt. She was said to be the right hand of Dikastis, their god of justice. And she was the goddess the Atlanteans prayed to whenever they'd been wronged. The one who meted out justice and retribution. Testament to their belief in her were the numerous *katadesmoi*—curse stones and tablets and lead sheets—that littered her altar and gardens. Each *katadesmos* held the specific action the invoker wanted the goddess to take against the person they felt had done harm to them.

The harsh curses outlined in Atlantean in extremely vivid detail made him wonder how many *katadesmoi* Ryssa had inscribed for him at home in Didymos.

Unwilling to speculate on so great a number, he frowned at Bet'anya's statue at the end of a large outdoor atrium pool that reminded him of Athena's in Didymos. The Atlantean goddess was tall and slender, dressed in a sheer peplos that showed the outline of a perfect body while running. She held a shield decorated with a winged horse in one hand, and a spear in the other, angled over her shoulder as if she was about to throw it. A mop of unruly curls spilled out from beneath an Atlantean helm that had been pushed up on her head to expose her beautiful features. At the opposite end of the pool was the statue of a fierce male soldier who faced the goddess.

Dressed only in a chlamys that fell from his left shoulder, he stood proud and defiant in a helm very similar to the one Styxx wore. His long hair spilled just past his right shoulder. He held a xiphos in his right hand while his left held a quiver of arrows.

"Is there something I can do for you, Highness?" a priestess asked nervously.

Styxx turned slightly to see the tiny woman who barely reached mid-chest on him. He offered her a slight bow. "Forgive me, priestess, I meant no disrespect to your goddess or you. The temple door was open and I was curious about the city's patron."

His army had defeated the Atlantean city of Bettias two days ago and were awaiting reinforcements to hold it before they continued onward to the mainland. Since their occupation began, they'd been bringing wounded Atlantean soldiers to the temple next door that belonged to the Atlantean god of healing. Styxx had overseen the last of their wounded deposited into the priests' care just a short while ago, and as he'd started back for their camp, he'd spied this temple.

For some unknown reason, he'd been drawn to it.

"Are you familiar with our gods?" she asked.

"I have limited knowledge, but no real understanding. Such as the two statues here. I assume she's the goddess the city's named for, but I have no idea who the soldier is."

"It's a wise man who admits what he does not know and who doesn't pretend to know something he's ignorant of." The priest-ess smiled. "Theirs is a tale of supreme heartbreak, Highness. And it's why Bet'anya's the goddess of wrath and retribution. Before Dikastis was consecrated to our pantheon, Bathymaas was the ori-ginal goddess of justice and order. The daughter of Chaos, she was born from the light powers to balance out her father and to keep him on the side of good. During the first war of the Chthonians, Bathymaas assembled a team of seven warriors called the Ēperon."

"As in υπερασπίζω?" he asked. Ēperaspizo was the Greek word for "vindicate" or "defend."

She nodded. "The Ēperon was made up of two humans, two Apollites, two Atlanteans, and a demon who trained and led them. Theirs was a sacred band charged with protecting the intelligent species of the earth from all threats. Hand-selected by Bathymaas, each one was the epitome of courage, strength, integrity, and decency. The best of their species. And during the Chthonian war, they fought in defense of the innocent."

Styxx studied the male statue. "Was he the demon who led them?"

The priestess shook her head. "He was the greatest hero of the war. Indomitable and intrepid. It was said no army could defeat him and no hero could kill him. Not even the collective Mavromino—the darkest of all powers. And in honor to the goddess he served, he took a vow of virginity. His heart and soul belonged to Bathymaas alone."

Frowning, Styxx was confused by her story. "I don't see where the heartbreak comes in."

The priestess pulled a handful of herbs from her pouch and dropped them into the flames at the goddess's feet. "Our virgin goddess fell in love with her hero, even though it was forbidden, and that it'd been foretold that should she ever know a man carnally she would be punished severely . . . All she could think about was how much he meant to her. They kept their relationship secret until one day, an enemy discovered it. Jealous and angry, their enemy spread word to all of what the two lovers had done. To protect his lady's honor, our hero challenged their betrayer to combat. But before he had the chance to battle and restore the goddess's good name, a jealous god who'd wanted Bathymaas for himself tricked her into shooting an arrow of lead into her beloved's heart. He died in the arms of his goddess, swearing to her that if it took him ten thousand lifetimes, he'd return to her and that he'd never love anyone save his precious Bathymaas."

Styxx flinched in sympathetic pain. He well understood that sentiment and would do the same for his own lady.

"When he died," the priestess continued, "he took her heart with him to his grave. She, who had been a goddess born of light, embraced the darkness with everything she had, and she went after the god who'd taken her hero from her. That was the moment when ruthless retribution was first born. Yet she couldn't kill the god—not without destroying the world. And even though the other gods warned her of this, she didn't care. She refused to stop until justice had been served and she bathed in the blood of the god she hated."

"I take it, since the world is still here, that they stopped her."

She nodded. "With no choice, the other gods banded together to kill her. They chased her deep into the desert where they cornered her, but before they could take her life, her father, who was a primal god, stopped them. He removed one half of her broken heart—the part that had belonged to her hero—and had her reborn as Bet'anya, which means House of Misery. It is said that she will be a goddess of darkness until the day her Aricles is reborn and makes her heart whole again."

Styxx frowned at the familiar and unexpected name. "Aricles?"

The priestess inclined her head to him. "He was the brother of the prince who founded your royal lineage. After he died, his younger brother took his name to honor him."

That baffled him even more. "And so you honor a Greek hero in the temple of your Atlantean goddess?"

Her eyes flared with indignation. "Atlantis has *never* honored any Greek."

But if that was true ... "Are you telling me I'm Atlantean?"

"Didymos was our outermost island at one time."

Strange ... he'd never heard that before and he wasn't sure if he should believe it.

"If you doubt me, Highness, there are maps still in existence in the city's capital building that show it."

Fascinating. "When did we become Greek?"

"Twelve hundred years ago, the king married a Greek princess. His heir was just a babe when he died and the queen invited her brother to rule until the child was old enough for the throne. Her brother immediately began converting the Atlantean temples to your gods, and the child grew up with them and their ways, thinking himself Greek. His mother never told him differently. Didymos has belonged to Greece ever since."

Styxx started to deny it, but the more he thought about it, the more sense it made. Didymos was physically closer to Atlantis than

Greece—which was why it was so important to hold it strategically. It would also explain why the Didymosian temples had more in common with Atlantean temples than Greek. "Am I part Apollite, then?"

"No. Your lineage was pure Atlantean. From one of our oldest houses. But sadly, your blood is polluted now. There is very little Atlantean left inside you."

Still not sure he should believe that, Styxx returned the conversation to the previous topic. "So does the goddess now sit and wait for her Aricles?"

"Sadly, she has no cognizance of him at all. To keep her from mourning him, her father removed the memory of Aricles with her heart. She holds no knowledge of her previous existence and role."

"How is that possible?"

"Her father had her reborn from Sorrow and she was told that she is a descendent of Bathymaas and that they share some powers. But until her hero returns, she will never know the truth. The world can't afford for her to."

Styxx scowled at the story. "How is it you know something your goddess doesn't?"

"Because I was there when it happened and I was one of the creatures who helped bind her."

Styxx stepped back as the priestess transformed into a tall, robust demon.

"How dare you defile the temple of Agriosa, Greek pig! You may have been born of the House of Aricles, but you are not he! You are nothing but a human dog, unfit to breathe Atlantean air." The demon shoved him back. "And our goddess has a fierce bounty on your head that I intend to collect."

Styxx barely had time to draw his sword before the demon attacked. The beast spit acid at him. Ducking, he stabbed the demon and twisted away.

It grabbed the back of his armor. Styxx felt his Apollo mark heat up before something blasted the demon against the garden wall.

The demon fell into a heap on the ground. Laughing, it wiped at the blood on its face. "Careful of the gods who protect you, dog. One day, they will all turn on you and show you what vermin you truly are." It vanished into a foul-smelling cloud.

Styxx scanned the garden, looking for other attackers as he backed his way out of the temple and returned to the street.

So, Agriosa had a bounty on him. Perfect, just perfect.

As for Apollo . . . Styxx was grateful the mark had protected him from the demon, but honestly, he'd have rather been gutted than go through the horrors of that one night. He still had panic attacks and flashbacks from it. And he had no doubt that Apollo would eventually turn on him. The god had turned on every lover he'd ever taken.

Just don't let me die here. Alone. Not in this godforsaken country that had never housed anything but utter misery for him and his brother.

If he had to die, he wanted to be like his esteemed ancestor and die in the arms of the woman he loved, with her beautiful hazel-gold eyes being what he carried with him into eternity.

But deep in his gut was the fear that it would be Apollo who killed him and that bastard's cold gaze that was forever implanted in his mind.

AUGUST 8, 9530 BC

One year later

Styxx looked up from his map table as he heard a loud fanfare outside. What the . . . ?

He knew his father wouldn't deign to visit a war camp, especially not one on foreign soil. And definitely not after all this time.

Curious, he went outside to investigate the ruckus then froze at the unexpected sight of his men gathered around his tent.

Were they revolting?

Other than their collective smell, which was highly offensive . . .

For that matter, he would rival the back end of his horse, too. There was no way to stay clean and fight a war.

Another cheer rose up from them.

"Happy Birthday, Prince Styxx!" they shouted in unison, and then cheered again.

His scowl deepened. "Thank you, but it's not my birthday."

"We know," Gaius, a hipparchus who led one of his cavalry units, said as he stepped forward. "But we learned that it was weeks ago and you said nothing about it."

Styxx swept his gaze over the men in his camp. "I'm not the only one here who has had an unremarked birthday come and go while we've been fighting."

His men went down on one knee before him.

Completely nonplussed, he wasn't sure how to react to their sudden genuflecting. In truth, it made him nervous.

Gaius rose and brought a folded, bright red cloak to him and placed it in his hands. "It's not very much, Highness, but it's all we could acquire without breaching your laws of conduct. We went in together to purchase it from the town we passed by yesterday."

Aghast at their thoughtfulness, Styxx held it tenderly. "Thank you. All of you. It's truly the noblest gift I've ever received and I shall treasure it as such."

Gaius saluted him. "We know the sacrifices you have made on our behalf, Highness, as well as the fact that you pay us extra from your own officer's salary and take almost nothing for yourself. Even though you've tried to hide it, we've seen you sell personal items to buy medicines and supplies for us when we needed them, and turn them down for yourself when they are in short supply so that the rest of us wouldn't have to do without. Everything you do for us has been most duly noted and deeply appreciated. There is no prince or king who would have remained by our side throughout these last two years without heading home for a few days of comfort. It is why we respect and follow you."

"That and the glory of the victories we've had," one of the men shouted from the crowd.

Laughter rang out.

Overwhelmed by their kindness, Styxx swallowed. "May the gods continue to bless us with victory."

"Gods bless us," they repeated then they began chanting his name.

One by one, they came up to bow before him.

Humbled to the depth of his being, Styxx patiently stood and spoke with each member of his army.

Galen was the last to approach him. "Are you all right?"

"My shoulder is killing me," he said under his breath while smiling at his departing men. "I could really use a chair."

Laughing, Galen held the tent flap open for him. "Come and sit, Highness."

Styxx obeyed and carefully placed his cloak on his desk. Stifling a groan, he sat down and sighed. Earlier in the day's fighting he'd been kicked back into a broken wooden lance that had stabbed him through the armhole of his armor.

Next time Bethany gave him a token for protection, he'd make sure she included wooden objects.

And clumsiness.

"You told them my birthday had passed?" Styxx asked.

Galen shrugged. "I mentioned it in passing to Gaius three days ago. I had no idea they'd do this."

Styxx felt tears prick his eyes over the unexpected gift that meant so much to him. But he wasn't about to let Galen see him weeping like an old woman. "I hope you didn't tell him my age."

"I'm not a fool, Highness. While they know you are young, there's no need in their learning just how green their esteemed victorious leader really is. It might send them screaming for home."

332

It might indeed.

Ten-and-eight. Barely. And yet he felt ancient.

Changing the subject, Styxx took a drink of wine. "Have you heard from your Antigone?" They'd received a messenger earlier in the day, and it was rare for one not to have at least one missive or gift for Galen from his daughter.

Galen pulled a shell necklace out from under his cuirass then took a seat next to Styxx so that he could hand it to him. "She and my granddaughter sent this. They are all well and can't wait to see my grizzled face again. What of your family?"

"All well," Styxx guessed. Yet honestly, he didn't know for sure. No one, not even his father, had contacted him. He assumed if Didymos had been invaded or something had befallen them, his family would have sent word.

But day after day, when messages came for him they were from other military commanders and kings, and had to do with the war, not with wishes for his health. Though to be honest, he liked to think that Bethany, in spite of her blindness, would have sent things to him had she known his real name. For all he knew, she'd tried numerous times.

At least that was he hoped and pretended.

Not wanting to contemplate his fear that she'd found another man in his absence, Styxx jerked his chin toward the table where his maps were spread out. "I was reviewing our progress. We should hit the mainland shore of Atlantis in four days."

"I heard from the messenger earlier that the boats are being prepped. Our men are eager to dance in Apollymi's hall on capital hill."

Over the last months, they had conquered six of the outlying islands and held them until more Greek forces had been sent to occupy them while Styxx marched toward the Atlantean capital. He was the only one who'd had any kind of success against their stronger enemy. From what they heard through messengers, the rest of the Greek forces were being obliterated by their enemies at home.

But if Styxx and his army could make the Atlantean capital and breach the palace there, they would win this war in spite of the losses the other armies had taken. He couldn't wait for it.

"Have you ever been to the Atlantean capital, Highness?"

Styxx tried not to think about the last time he'd seen his brother and the hurtful things they had both said to each other. "I have."

"Is it as advanced as they say?"

Another thing he'd rather not have diverting his attention. "It is."

Galen met his gaze over the map. "Do you really think we can win this, Highness?"

"Yes, I do." And Styxx fully intended to ram his retribution down a number of aristocratic Atlantean throats.

Both for him and for Acheron.

AUGUST 10, 9530 BC

Bethany pulled back to watch the Stygian Omada break through another line of Atlantean defenses in spite of her people's superlative abilities. While her brethren were winning the fight on Greek soil and annihilating their royal houses, Styxx was kicking the crap out of them at home.

How was it even possible? It was as if he could read their minds. Every tactic they used, he headed off with a skill that went far beyond his age. Over and over, he used maneuvers the likes of which none of them had seen before. Somehow he'd shorn up every weakness of Greek warfare her people had always relied on to ensure victory.

The bastard was invincible.

And over the last few battles, as she'd watched him overcome incredible odds and emerge victorious when he should have been put in his grave, she'd had a realization about his true identity.

It was the only thing that made sense.

How ironic really. The very child Archon had torn their kingdom apart to find had come marching home with a Greek army in his wake . . .

Styxx of Didymos was Apollymi's hidden son. She'd stake her life on it.

Wheeling her horse about, Bethany flew away from the battle where Styxx was busy driving the Atlanteans back, and went into the realm that her great-grandfather had ruled until the other gods had joined forces to make it Apollymi's prison.

At least until Apostolos was dead.

Dark and dismal, Kalosis was not anyone's idea of a vacation destination. Unless they were truly into terrifying death motifs. Ironically, this was where Bethany had spent most of her childhood, and one of her favorite places.

Which said much about her personality.

Bethany ignored the Charonte demons who watched her suspiciously as she made her way to the dark palace in the center of the hell realm. Barely dressed, the Charonte were a dangerous demonic race whose skin was made up of swirling colors—usually only two, but occasionally more. They had wings that matched the color of their horns and their eyes were always creepy.

"Where is Apollymi?" she asked the blue male demon closest to her.

"In the back courtyard," he said in their unique singsongy accent.

She headed down the dark, reflecting hallway with curtains that billowed from a sourceless wind.

Bethany pushed open the large glass doors that let out onto a courtyard with high black marble walls.

Apollymi sat in front of the fountain that ran backwards up the wall. Dressed in a flowing black gown, the goddess of destruction was as breathtaking as she was lethal. Her long, white hair was braided down her back and her swirling silver eyes saw much more than others.

Archon was right to fear her. She was without mercy or compassion.

"Why are you here?" Apollymi snarled.

"I have learned the most coveted secret of all time and wanted your help in dealing with it."

Apollymi smirked. "What is this secret you've found?"

"Your son is leading an army into our capital."

Apollymi's smirk turned into an arched brow and an innocent expression. "My son?"

"Prince Styxx of Didymos. He's Apostolos, isn't he?"

Apollymi laughed out loud then turned back to her pond. "Nice try. Wrong, but I give you points for creativity."

Bethany didn't believe her for a second. "I know it's him."

"Then why haven't you betrayed me to the others?"

"Because lately I've come to understand . . . your sacrifice."

This time, Apollymi's laughter was cruel. "Are you seriously telling me that the goddess of misery and wrath is in love? You really expect me to believe that of you?"

"Why not? If the goddess of utter destruction can love . . . why not me?"

"Oh, Bet . . . you are naive and foolish. And if you were truly in love, we would all know it." Apollymi ran her hand through the black water. "My son will return home soon, but he won't need a foreign army to destroy this pantheon. Now go and leave me before I remember how much I hate all of you."

"Fine, I'll go. But I wanted you to know that the gods have gathered together, and they will kill Styxx the moment he steps foot on the main shore. In unison."

"Doesn't concern me in the least."

Bethany wasn't so sure about that. While Apollymi seemed to be telling the truth, there had been a slight flare in her eyes when Bethany had first mentioned Styxx's name.

The prince did mean *something* to the goddess. But if he wasn't her son, what was he to her?

AUGUST 11, 9530 BC

The Atlantean gods sat together in their white marble hall as they discussed the advancing Greek army that none of their people had been able to quell or turn back.

"How?" Archon growled at the gods standing in front of his dais. "We are better armed. Higher tech. Our soldiers have psychic abilities, and yet this puny, putrid human and his army are able to outmaneuver us and kick our collective asses. For the love of *us,* can someone tell me how?"

They exchanged nervous and disgusted looks.

"A god protects him," Bethany said, pushing her way through the crowd until she stood in front of Archon. "I don't know who, but it's a powerful one. Whenever I try to shoot him, it's deflected as if he can see it . . . which we all know is impossible."

"Apollymi?" Archon asked, going straight to her initial assumption.

Dikastis, their god of justice, shook his head. "Can't be. There's no way her son would be in Atlantis, leading an army, without our knowing it. He *is* using powers, but they're not ours. We would all feel it if it were."

"Maybe he's just that much better trained and more intelligent than our armies."

They all turned to glare at the sea god, Ydor. Tall and dark-haired, he stood apart from the rest of the group.

"What?" he asked innocently. "Tell me none of the rest of you have had that thought. Have you seen this kid? He's a beast on the battlefield. There's a burning fury inside him he unleashes the

337

minute he takes a sword into his hand. I've never seen a mortal so fearless. It's as if he's daring us to kill him and wants to die . . . He's definitely not a god with that mind set."

Archon returned his attention to Bethany. "You said he was Athena's champion?"

She nodded. "But it's not Athena protecting him in battle. It's an older god. Surely the rest of you have felt it, too."

Misos agreed with her. "She's right, brother. I tried to strike him down with my own hand, and he broke my axe."

His face turning red, Archon roared furiously. "Then how do we stop this little bugger prince?"

"Apollo." Moving forward to speak, Epithymia swept her gaze around the gathered gods. "As much as it galls me to say this, that Greek bastard is our only hope."

Archon snorted in derision of her proposal. "He wants this throne." He punctuated the word with a slap to the armrest. "Why would he stop his best commander to help us?"

"Because if the Greeks take Atlantis, he'd have to share our domain. He'd be as he is now . . . just another god in the Olympian pantheon, ruling here, under Zeus." Epithymia addressed the entire group. "As you said, his ambitions are bigger than that. He wants to sit on your throne, and we all know it. He doesn't want the Greek pantheon here any more than we do. He wants us to conquer *them,* which is why we're winning in Greece."

Sitting back on his throne, Archon stroked his beard while he considered her words. "It makes sense, and you're right about his ambitions. But we can't tell him the truth about why we need his help to deal with that . . . *human.* He'd mock us. So how do we sway him to our cause?"

Epithymia gave him a droll stare. "Use his lust against him. For a god of moderation, Apollo's licentiousness is well known and documented. He will nail anything. Animal, vegetable, mineral."

Archon nodded thoughtfully. "It's said the princess of Didymos

338

is the most beautiful of all the Greek women. We can use the prince's sister against him. If we tie her to Apollo, King Xerxes will recall his son and his army for the ceremony ... Let them think Apollo is switching sides to be with the woman."

Epithymia smiled. "We tell Apollo we intend to use the truce to solidify our position for a larger attack on Greece in the future. But that we need time for it."

"He's dumb enough to buy that," Misos said with a laugh.

"Bet'anya?" Archon pinned her with a stare. "You negotiate with the Greek."

Was he serious?

Gaping, she was incredulous. "Do I look like Hermes or"—she gestured to the beautiful god standing on Archon's right—"Hephaestion? I'm not a messenger god."

"No, but you are more powerful against Apollo than we are. You have two pantheons you can call on. And while he disregards us, he fears your father ... and you."

Oh, right, throw *that* in her face. Like she could help it? But she knew arguing was futile. Archon was a prick that way.

Bethany held her hands up in surrender. "Fine. What do you want me to say exactly?"

"That if he helps us with this, we will tear down the gods of Olympus, and leave the entirety of Greece to him and his Apollites."

And that would definitely appeal to the god and his massive ego.

Bethany sighed. "All right. I'll go meet with him. But for my service, there is one thing I want."

Archon arched his brow. "And that is?"

Bethany hesitated. However, at this point, she no longer cared if they mocked her for her love. In spite of her best efforts, she'd been unable to locate the one person whose life mattered to her. And she was not about to do this and put him in danger. "A Greek soldier named Hector from Didymos. He is not to be harmed in the fighting by anyone, god or otherwise."

He inclined his head to her. "Agreed. Now go and let's get this Greek bastard off our backs and out of our lands."

Bethany paced outside of Apollo's Delphian temple. While she could appreciate the architecture and beauty of the island, she hated this place and the god who claimed it as home base.

"My father will be with you shortly."

She paused to study Strykerius. Like Apollo, he was tall and golden with vivid blue eyes to rival Styxx's. The two princes were probably about the same age, too. Though to be honest, Styxx seemed much older and more worldly. "You're part Atlantean?" She could smell it on him. Unlike the Olympian god, Apollo's son held a lot of their powers.

"From my mother, the queen."

Bethany scowled as she remembered Archon and the others slaying the infant Strykerius claimed to be. "I thought her son died at birth?"

"Strykerius!" Apollo barked, making the boy jump in response. "Go inside and leave us."

There was something extremely strange about all of this, but she didn't have time to worry about it. She had an idiot god to win over.

"What can I do for you, little cousin?"

She cringed at Apollo's play on the rumors that the Egyptian goddess Isis had birthed him. But Bethany wasn't fooled. Her aunt had much better taste than to get knocked up by Zeus. There wasn't enough nectar or wine in the universe for that union.

"I have been sent to negotiate terms."

Apollo smirked. "Tired of having your asses handed to you by a Greek prince?"

She glared at him. "Fine. I don't need this. I can go home to Egypt and live quite happily while you take second throne to Zeus as you always do." She started to leave.

"Wait!"

Bethany turned back to face him. "Yes?"

"What exactly are you asking me?"

"They want you to tup a Greek princess as distraction for your people and pantheon while we fortify our army and position to renew this war at a later time. We take Greece and overthrow your lovely family, and then hand it over to you to enjoy."

"Why would you do that?"

"Because Atlanteans, unlike Greeks, have never craved war. We'd rather live in peace. If Greece has a single god, he—or in this case, you—will be too busy to turn your eyes to our shores. So Greeks can be owned by your Apollites, your son will have a throne, you will rule Olympus, and we can be left alone."

"And which princess do you want me to tup?"

"The one at Didymos."

A full-fledged smile spread across his face. "Didymos? Really? I'd much rather have their prince than their princess."

Bethany shrugged nonchalantly. "You can have them both for all I care. But I wouldn't use the prince to negotiate over. Even Greeks tend to frown at offering up their sons as whores to their male gods."

Apollo laughed. "You are wise, Bet'anya. And you are right . . . By the way, tell Archon thanks for this leverage. I appreciate it and will remember it."

She inclined her head to him. "Have fun with your prince. Just get that bastard off our shores."

"Don't worry. I will gladly do both."

AUGUST 15, 9530 BC

With Galen by his side, Styxx watched in grim determination as their men boarded the ships that would take them to the shores of the Atlantis mainland.

Within hours, they'd set sail. By nightfall, they'd make shore, and come the morrow, they'd own Atlantis and every Atlantean would bow down to his Stygian Omada . . .

"Prince Styxx!"

He turned at the sharp cry as a messenger came into camp at a dead run. The boy reined his horse, and jumped from it. He rushed to Styxx and knelt down then extended a rolled scroll toward him.

This shit can't be good . . .

Not given the boy's expression or his hurry. Dread riding him harder than the messenger had his horse, Styxx took the scroll and saw six royal seals on it from the largest city-states who were their allies. Those seals included his father's. Never in the last twenty-one months had his father sent anything to him. And nothing this official.

Styxx could sense in his soul that his day was about to be ruined.

He tore the scroll open and read it. And with every word, his jaw dropped more. No . . . Not after they'd come so far and gotten so very close.

You stupid sons of whores.

"Did something happen, my lord?" Gaius asked.

Styxx snapped his jaw closed. "We're being recalled to Greece." He enunciated each word with great irritation.

"What?" Galen roared.

Styxx handed him the scroll. "It's unanimous from all the kings. They want us back in Greece. Effective immediately. We are to abandon all future campaigns. Should we continue on, they will charge us with treason."

Galen stayed behind and sputtered indignantly while Styxx went to relay their new orders to his commanders.

He still couldn't believe it, but since all the Greek kings were in on the decision for a cease-fire, he had no choice. If he continued on, they would see his entire army slaughtered.

And his men weren't any happier about the news than either he or Galen.

Their one resounding complaint was as unanimous as the kings' decision to stop ... *It's not fair that we're being penalized because the rest of the Greek forces are incompetent losers.*

Styxx agreed with his men, but he couldn't say that out loud. "We are soldiers and we obey our orders."

Even when they stank to the highest point of Mount Olympus.

"But at least you'll all go home to your families now," Styxx offered as consolation.

That sent a cheer through their morose ranks. And in truth, Styxx couldn't wait to get back to Bethany. It'd been almost two years since he had last felt her hand on his face. Seen her sweet golden-green eyes as she welcomed him to her side.

Hopefully, she hadn't found another to love during his long absence.

As he returned to his tent, he felt the sun mark on his back heat up until it burned. Styxx froze.

Was Apollo here? Or another demon, perhaps? Why else would the mark do that? Glancing about, he pushed aside his fear. They were going home. Why attack them now?

But then why did the gods do anything they did?

"I hate you bastards," he snarled under his breath to the gods. "All you've ever done is screw up my life. I wish every one of you was gone."

And Styxx hoped that he never had to see another god in the flesh as long as he lived.

AUGUST 31, 9530 BC

Galen reined his horse and smiled. "Smell that delicious olive-scented air, my lord ... we're back in Greece."

Styxx snorted at Galen's uncharacteristic enthusiasm. "I think battle might have addled your brains. It smells no different to me."

"Of course it does!"

Styxx scoffed, "I could be wrong, but I really don't think the wind stops at our borders."

Galen tsked at him. "Such patriotism from an esteemed war hero. You should be ashamed."

Shaking his head, Styxx swept his gaze over the soldiers who'd fought well and brought honor to all of them and their various city-states. But even so, there was a darkness inside him that hadn't been there before. Battle had changed him. As bad as Estes had been, and the atrocities his twisted uncle had committed, Styxx had seen a far worse side of humanity that made him wonder why he fought at all. What was there about mankind worth saving?

You don't fight for them. You fight for Beth and her life, alone.

"Highness?"

He glanced over as Gaius rode up on his opposite side. "Yes?"

"There's a hostel not far from here. We were wondering if we could make camp near it tonight?"

"We?" Styxx glanced back at his army.

Gaius gave him a lecherous grin. "There are women there, Highness, and it's been a while for some of us."

Styxx exchanged an amused stare with Galen. "If it's what all of you wish. Who am I to deny you?"

Gaius shouted in happiness before he went to tell the others.

Galen sighed. "To be that young again."

"You're not *that* old."

"Old enough ..." Galen nudged his horse forward. "So, Highness, are we dicing in your tent tonight while the others frolic with their women?"

Styxx lifted his brow at the presumptuous question. "How do you know I won't be joining the men?"

Galen snorted at his challenge. "Because I know the look of a man who wants to go home to a particular woman, and no other will do. Not even when it's been the better part of two years for him."

Styxx suppressed a smile over the fact that Galen knew him better than anyone. A part of him hated being so transparent, but another was glad to know that at least one person saw him for who he was and not for what they assumed him to be. "Dice it is then."

Galen laughed. "I look forward to finally beating you at something again."

Hours later, Styxx sat in his tent thinking of his beautiful Bethany while his men were divided between camp and the town where the hostel was located. The sounds of revelry were loud and cacophonous. They mixed with the voices in his head until he could barely think straight. There were just too many of them.

Alone, he rolled the dice on his desk, waiting for Galen to join him. He'd taken Bethany's necklace off and left it within hand's reach. Smiling, he picked it up and rubbed his thumb over the bow-and-arrow mark that was stamped into a small silver disk. Many women her age were devotees of the goddess Artemis who was said to be a fierce protector of women and children. And he prayed that the goddess would always protect his beloved from all harm.

Bethany was the sole reason he wanted to go home and she was all he looked forward to. "Soon, my love. And this time, I will hold on to you forever." Closing his eyes, he conjured the sight of her beautiful face. His body hardened instantly as he imagined her dancing for him again.

Of her holding him close while he made love to her with all the need he'd kept under fierce restraint for the last two years.

There was a sudden knock.

Wishing he could stay in his dreams with her for awhile longer, Styxx laid her necklace down and reached for his wine. "Enter."

An Athenian soldier he'd never seen before came inside, leading a small group of similarly dressed men. "Prince Styxx?"

"Yes?"

"We heard you were arriving any day now, and wanted to welcome your army home."

"Thank you." Styxx cocked his head as he realized that the sounds outside had grown much quieter.

A bad feeling went through him as he glanced over to his weapons and armor on the other side of the tent, near his pallet. In that instant, it dawned on him that one of his *dekarmatoli* should have escorted these men into his tent and hadn't.

Styxx narrowed his gaze on them. "So what can I do for you?"

"In short, Highness . . . you can die." The leader leapt forward.

Styxx rolled from the chair. He punched the first soldier hard in the solar plexus, knocking him back. As he twisted past the second one, the third one slid a dagger into his side before he could outmaneuver him. Styxx hissed in pain then kicked him back. But it was too late. The first one had recovered and stabbed him in the back.

His ears buzzed from their hatred and his pain. Styxx sank to the ground while they rained stabs down on him. Warm blood rushed over his skin until it coated him.

Their leader kicked him over onto his back and raked his bloody body with a contemptuous sneer. "A homecoming present, prince, from the commanders who weren't victorious in the war." The soldier used his dagger to pin Styxx's sword hand to the ground.

Laughing, they left him there to die.

His breathing labored, Styxx stared at the Thracian dagger buried in his palm and choked on his own blood. After everything he and his men had been through, after all the attacks and battles they'd survived against enemies, it was their own allies who annihilated them on their home shores.

And not for glory or for family.

For petty fucking jealousy.

SEPTEMBER 3, 9530 BC

"Careful, Highness, drink slowly."

Styxx groaned as someone lifted his head and gently poured water into his mouth. Then that person laid his head back so that he could see Galen's concerned, grizzled face. Of course Galen was the one tending him. Who else would bother?

His old tutor had a deep cut down his left cheek, but otherwise appeared whole.

Styxx squinted against the pain and brightness of the light coming in through heavy drapes. "The men?"

"About half survived."

Half?

Half . . .

He winced at the mental pain of their loss. That news cut him far worse than the daggers the cowards had used on him. "Did you get the ones responsible?"

"Not enough of them. I did manage to capture one of the men who attacked you. I bled him dry and got *some* information from his traitorous tongue."

"And?"

"They were mercenaries. The coins used to pay them were from all the Greek city-states, including Didymos. You were their primary target. Our men were only a bonus." Galen pressed something into his uninjured hand then withdrew.

"Continue," Galen shouted.

Styxx's bed was lifted and moved forward. Galen had placed him inside a litter to be carried home. Grimacing in pain, he opened his hand to find Bethany's necklace in his palm. Thank the gods, Galen had saved it. Leave it to his mentor to know it would be important to him.

He held it to his heart and closed his eyes then thought of his men who'd been ambushed and killed. Anger consumed him that he'd let his guard lax. Why had he not been more vigilant? Armed? Why had he given them freedom to wench?

Because they'd finally made it home where they were supposed to be safe. These were the people they'd all fought and bled to protect.

Grief and agony shoved his anger aside. No one could be trusted. His uncle and father should have taught him that.

His own mother.

Would Bethany one day turn on him, too? The thought kicked him hard, but he refused to let these beasts destroy his faith in the only woman he'd ever loved.

Styxx rapped on the frame of his litter. After a few seconds, the men outside set it down.

In spite of the pain, he sat up. As he started to rise, Galen appeared by his side.

Galen scowled at him. "What are you doing?"

"I don't deserve to be carried."

"Highness—"

"I lapsed my guard and my men died for it. I will not lie here and be coddled when I should have died with them."

"Styxx!" Galen snapped, but Styxx refused to listen as he pushed himself to his feet and did his best not to stumble as he left the litter.

"My horse!" Styxx shouted.

Galen pulled him into his arms and held him close. "I know the pain you carry, αγαπημενος μου γιός," he whispered in Styxx's ear. *My beloved son . . .*

That single endearment choked Styxx and brought tears to his eyes. It was the first time in his life anyone had referred to him as such.

"I've carried it myself," Galen continued, "but dying now will not bring them back."

I'm not going to die. He knew that with bitter certainty. And he would not be carried on the backs of men who were injured and grieving themselves.

A young shield-bearer brought Troian to him and held the horse by his side.

Styxx embraced Galen like a father then withdrew. "My men deserve better." After thanking the boy who'd brought him his horse, he ignored the shocked looks on the faces of his litter-bearers and soldiers as he slowly pulled himself up into the saddle unassisted.

Ignoring the pain, he kicked his horse and rode to the front of his troops then wheeled around to face them. One by one, he swept his gaze over the grim expressions of men who should have been returning in high spirits. And as he scanned them, he noted that Gaius wasn't among the survivors.

His gut clenched tight.

He wanted to say something, but words failed him just as he'd failed to keep his people safe.

All of a sudden, his men began chanting his name and cheering for him then as a single unit, they went down on one knee.

Styxx couldn't understand it. He definitely didn't deserve this honor after they'd been slaughtered on home soil.

"Good men," he said, his throat tight. "I vowed to all of you when we left Didymos that I would *never* forget the sacrifice I was asking each of you to make. That I would never be capricious or careless with your safety, and I failed all of you. For that, I beg your forgiveness."

Tersus, one of his advisors, kicked his horse forward. "Highness, you didn't fail us. We were drunk on victory when we were attacked. You were the only sober man among us. It was our duty to protect our future king. Your father will have us whipped for our dereliction that almost got you killed."

"No one will be punished for what happened," Styxx assured him. "You have my word on that. All of you have suffered enough." He bowed to his men. "Now let's go home to our families and pray we never have to raise our swords again."

SEPTEMBER 3, 9530 BC

Exhausted and aching, Styxx lay on his pallet in his tent. The physician had just finished checking his bandages and left him to rest for the night. But he couldn't relax or sleep. Over and over, images of being attacked, of battle, and a thousand other things he didn't want to remember tortured him.

He couldn't breathe. A part of him wanted to run like a madman, screaming out into the night. But how would that look to the men who'd trusted him with their lives?

Shaking and scrambled, he pushed himself up and stumbled toward his desk. He poured wine into his cup and downed it all in one gulp then reached for more.

Outside, he heard his men's anger. They blamed the kings for this attack. Had they not been called back so soon, they would be celebrating a victory in Atlantis tonight, not suffering defeat at home.

From their own people.

And still none of them knew why they'd been summoned back . . .

Unless it was to be slaughtered.

Surely not. But as Galen would say, wars were nothing more than old men bragging about their own withered prowess while sending their sons out to die in their stead. And while there were many political ideas worth killing for, none were worth dying over.

Although Styxx no longer agreed with the latter.

Pissed and disgusted, he glared at his injured sword hand as the images of the men he'd killed in battle tore through him.

No, he definitely didn't agree with Galen. There were political causes he would die for, but never again would he kill for one.

Nor would he ask anyone else to do so. Life was too precious for that.

He would only raise a sword to protect Bethany and Galen. No one else. And definitely nothing else.

"Why so sad, young prince? You're heading home. You should be thrilled."

Styxx went cold at the voice he hated most of all. His breathing intensified even more as he looked up to find Apollo on the other side of his desk. "What are you doing here?"

"I've come to welcome home the victorious Didymosian prince. Is that not what I'm supposed to do?"

Styxx hissed as the mark on his back heated up and burned his skin. He shot to his feet only to have Apollo materialize right in front of him. The god reached to touch his face.

He stepped back, out of reach.

"Don't be like that, prince."

For a moment, Styxx considered calling out for his guards, but there was no telling what Apollo might do to them. Two of the ten had already been slaughtered on home soil. The rest had barely survived.

He wouldn't sacrifice another of his men.

"I want you to leave me alone."

Apollo laughed. "That's not going to happen. See ... you're headed home now because your father and the other Greek kings intend to offer up your sister as a virgin sacrifice to me."

Granted, his head was swimming from pain and drink, but surely he'd misunderstood what Apollo just said. "What?"

Smirking, the god nodded. "It's true. They want the war with Atlantis to stop and to have their lands left alone. To keep me happy and to assure my continued benevolence for Greece over Atlantis, Ryssa is to be my sanctified mistress."

Great. He'd laugh if it wasn't so damned horrifying. He'd killed his uncle to save his sister from rape, only to have his father whore her to the one creature he hated most.

Why did I bother?

Apollo vanished then reappeared right behind Styxx. Wrapping his arms around his waist, he pulled Styxx back against him and leaned down to inhale the scent of Styxx's hair.

Cringing with repugnance, Styxx tried to pull free, but Apollo held him fast. "Just so you know, Ryssa's not the one I *really* want." His teeth elongated as he nuzzled Styxx's neck. "I hunger for someone much more robust and filling."

"Release me!"

Apollo dragged his fangs over Styxx's jugular and applied just enough pressure to hurt, but not break the skin. "You will give me what I want, prince," he whispered. "I've seen how much your men mean to you, especially that old one who coddles you. So be honest with me and yourself. What do you value more? Your own precious ass or theirs?"

In spite of the horrendous pain it caused, Styxx struggled even harder against him. "I will not whore for you! I've heard too many tales about what happens to your cast-offs."

Apollo laughed as he ran his hand over the place on Styxx's back where he'd burned his mark into Styxx's skin and to the wound where one of his attackers had buried a dagger in the center of that hated sun symbol. "That's nothing compared to what happens to the ones who deny me. Remember what I told you when you were in the Dionysion? Sooner or later, all people will whore for something. If you don't accept me, I will see the rest of your army destroyed by your enemies who still trail you, seeking to finish the job they started . . . your precious kingdom broken into dust, that old man you love slaughtered, and your sister trained and sold as a tsoulus at market."

The Olympian dropped his hand down to where Styxx was branded as a tsoulus and pressed his fingers against the mark, letting Styxx know that he'd seen the brand the last time they were together.

"And once I have destroyed all their lives, I will take you to Olympus and make you serve us all alongside Prince Ganymede. So your basic choice is you whore for me alone, anytime and anyplace I desire you, and no one knows about us, or you bend over for every god on Olympus and spend eternity listening to Greek scribes regale your fate as a cautionary tale for others for thousands of years to come."

Styxx clenched his teeth at his options. "What's my third choice?"

"There's not one, and if you try to kill yourself . . . let's just say, don't." Apollo kissed the back of his head and cupped him. "So what's your decision, little prince? And don't forget, either way, *I* win."

SEPTEMBER 9, 9530 BC

Unlike his men, Styxx felt no joy whatsoever as he rode through the palace gates and neared the steps where his "family" waited to welcome him home. Honestly, he hadn't missed anything about this place.

How sad, he'd rather be in battle than face his father, mother, and sister.

Reining his horse, he braced himself for the pain to come then dismounted slowly. While most of his wounds had healed, some of the deeper ones remained, and all caused him misery as he made his way up the stairs to greet his king.

His father embraced him. "Welcome home."

Styxx inclined his head before he saw Ryssa standing behind their father.

"Brother." She curtsied to him.

Amazed he didn't have frostbite from her tone and glare, he gave her a curt bow. "Sister."

His father clapped him on the back right where he'd been stabbed then headed for the palace doors.

Unable to catch his breath, Styxx froze as sheer agony tore through him. For a full minute, it stung so badly he saw stars from it. Worse, he could feel fresh, warm blood seeping down his spine.

Unaware he'd reopened a wound, his father didn't know Styxx wasn't with him until he reached the doors. He turned back with a deep scowl.

His breathing labored, Styxx forced himself to continue onward. Sweat broke out on his forehead as his gaze dimmed and he feared he'd pass out on the stairs.

His father ran his gaze over the dispersing army. "Your returning numbers aren't as great as I'd hoped."

Styxx cut a glower at his father, but said nothing as he entered the palace. "Where's Mother?"

"I exiled her, and she killed herself last spring."

Gaping at the emotionless disclosure, Styxx turned to his father. "And you didn't send word to me?"

"To what purpose? She was dead. There was nothing you could do."

He didn't know why, but grief racked him hard. Harder than he would have thought possible given their tumultuous relationship. Still, Aara had been his mother, and it saddened him that she was gone. He met Ryssa's aloof stare, but he knew that was a front. She and their mother had been close and the death had to sting her deeply.

"My deepest condolences, Ryssa."

"Don't spit on her memory with your insincerity. It's not becoming of the great war hero who got half his army slaughtered on his return."

"Ryssa!"

She blinked innocently at their father. "What? Your own advisors are the ones who've been calling him incompetent and saying that you should never have trusted your army to him."

And his men had actually feared his father would whip them for allowing him to be attacked . . .

Styxx let out a bitter laugh. "It warms the cockles of my heart to be cradled against the loving bosom of my adoring family. Thank the gods I survived to return to such affection." He headed for the stairs.

"Where are you going?" his father snapped. "I have a welcome party full of noblemen for you in the banquet hall."

Styxx glanced to where he'd been standing a second ago. His blood had made a small red puddle on the floor, marking the spot. He wiped at the sweat on his brow as his vision dimmed more. "Please forgive me for my insult to you and to them, Majesty. But I would rather bleed alone and not listen to how I failed Didymos and disappointed my king when I was the only Greek commander who won any *fucking* battles against the Atlanteans whatsoever . . . and I did it on their home soil without Greek resources or reinforcements for battle."

Ryssa gasped. "If I spoke to you like that, Father, you'd have me whipped."

Styxx laughed bitterly as he continued up the stairs, leaving a trail of bloody footprints in his wake. "Please, sweet sister, name me one time in your entire spoiled bitch life that anyone laid a hand to you?"

"You have!"

"Years and years ago, when I was half your size. And I paid for it dearly." He turned at the top of the stairs to face them. "Now excuse me, beloved family, but I need to lie down before I pass out, and mourn a mother whose contempt of me is only surpassed by her bitch daughter's."

What has happened to you, boy?

He snorted derisively at his father's shocked thought. How pathetic that his father didn't know and didn't really care to learn.

Aching inside and out, Styxx went to his room and pulled a pillow from the bed. He'd been sleeping on the ground for so long that he wasn't sure what a bed would feel like anymore.

Without bothering to remove his armor, he sank to the floor and stretched out to rest.

Ah, beautiful home. How much he loathed it.

SEPTEMBER 13, 9530 BC

Bethany toyed with the ring on her finger as she waited, yet another day, for a visit she was certain would never come again. Her Hector was dead. She knew it.

If not from their war then from his homecoming slaughter that had all but destroyed Prince Styxx's Stygian Omada. While her family had laughed and rejoiced over the treachery of the Greek dogs, the news had struck her like a blow.

Hector had to be dead or he'd have come to her by now.

Sick to her stomach and saddened more than she'd ever been, she started to rise then felt a sudden presence near her. "Who goes there?"

For several heartbeats, she heard nothing.

Then a deep, low whisper answered her. "A weary soldier who is fearful that he's been forgotten or replaced."

Tears filled her eyes and choked her. "My Hector has not been forgotten and he could *never* be replaced."

Only then did he kneel by her side and pull her against him. He was much leaner than he'd been, but also much more ripped. His muscles were even larger and harder than before. She cradled his head in her hands as he rocked her in his arms. While his hair was shorter than it'd been when he left her, he now had a full beard.

"I lived only for the chance that I could come back and hold you again."

Hot tears flowed down her cheeks. "I hate you for the pain you've caused me in your absence. You beast! The fear that you were dead and burned . . . "

He sucked his breath in sharply as she touched his back.

"Hector?"

"I've returned, but not in one whole piece." He pulled away and carefully sat down on the ground by her side.

"What happened? Why did you remove my amulet?"

"Once we reached Greece, I foolishly took it off to toy with it. I had no idea we were about to be attacked by our own allies. But have no fear . . . " He placed her hand over his wrist to show her that it was back in place.

"You were hurt?"

"I certainly didn't stab my own back. Though, given my superior incompetence, I'm surprised I haven't found a way to do so."

She kissed his cheek. "Is it just your back?"

"Sadly, no. I took twenty-and-four stabs to my back, hand, side, and front, and one to my left cheek, just to make sure I was good and humiliated."

She touched his face.

"Not that cheek, my sweet. That one wouldn't have bothered me so."

In spite of the seriousness, she laughed. That explained the peculiar way he was sitting, but . . . "You are not funny . . . Can I do anything to comfort you?"

He pulled her hand to his lips and inhaled her skin before he nibbled her fingers then he stretched out on his side . . . with his left cheek up. "You comforted me the moment I saw you here. I swear you've grown even more beautiful in my absence."

She lay down, facing him. "I'm scared to touch you for fear of causing you pain."

He placed her hand over his heart and held it there so that she could feel the rapid beat through his chiton. "Even if you hurt me, I'll enjoy it."

"You're so masochistic."

"I am indeed." Sighing, he laid his head down on his arm next to her head then moved her hand to his bearded cheek so that she could feel the expressions on his face. "What pains me most is that after all these long, arduous months, I can't make love to you like I've dreamed of doing every single night."

She moved her hand to toy with his curls that wrapped around

357

her fingers. His hair was shorter than when he'd left, but it was still long enough to tease her. "Has anyone ever told you that your voice is very similar to Prince Styxx's?"

"And when did you hear his voice, my lady?"

"Several times when he's been in public. But you're nothing like him."

"How are we so different?"

She kissed his nose. "You are sweet and precious. And there isn't an arrogant bone in all of your body."

"Perhaps the prince isn't as bad as you assume."

She arched a brow at that. "You defend him?"

"I've suffered and bled for him these many months past. I'd have to be a royal bastard to not defend him now."

She made a face at him. "Let's not bicker over my opinion of your worthless prince. You're the only man I want to think about right now." She kissed him lightly on the lips. "I've missed you so."

Styxx closed his eyes as she licked and teased his neck. This alone had been worth coming back for.

But even as that thought brought a smile to his lips, fear made his stomach ache. He'd heard the same contempt in her voice when she spoke of the prince as his family had for him. How would she react if she learned who he really was?

Never mind the fact that for almost three years now, he'd lied to her.

She would hate you as much as everyone else. Worse, she'd never forgive him. She'd think that he'd mocked her and, like Ryssa, accuse him of horrible things he'd never thought or done or intended. And if she ever learned of the wretched, degrading bargain Apollo had forced on him ...

He wanted to vomit as fear and hatred mingled inside his heart.

Why can't I find someone who can accept all of me? The only one who did was Galen. Only he saw Styxx's heart and understood his real intentions and actions.

"Why are you so sad? Did I say something wrong?"

"No." It was both a lie and the truth. He didn't want her to censor her words around him. Not even when they kicked him in the crotch and left him bleeding. "I'm not quite the boy who left you, Beth. I fear war has changed me."

"How so?"

"In ways that are hard to define. I spent almost two years ankle-deep in blood and body parts. I've held the hands of old men and young boys as they took their last breaths. I've seen boys who were far too young, who weren't even old enough to shave yet, cut down and taken by illnesses we couldn't treat. We burned our dead, day and night, until the stench of it is permanently lodged in my throat and nose. There were days when the fighting was so thick that enemy arrows and spears blocked out the sun from us."

Bethany's heart clenched at the pain she heard in his voice. She knew each of the battles he spoke of, and the horrors. But this was the first time she'd seen them through the eyes of the men who actually fought them. Men who didn't know if they'd live through it or lose a part of their body.

Never before had she understood the fear of the families left behind and how hard it was to wait for a loved one they might never see again. Tears welled in her eyes as she wished she could take those memories from him. "How did you stand it?"

"I would think of you. Knowing you were here, depending on me to come back . . . that you would cry if I didn't . . . I'm not sure I would have made it through some of the battles had you not been in my heart." He rubbed her hand against the line of his jaw. "I definitely wouldn't have ridden home so fast."

She smiled at his humor then kissed him. "I don't ever want to be without you again."

"Hopefully you won't. I've heard that the city-states have joined together for another truce that should last."

Bethany's stomach shrank at his words. She knew just how temporary the truce would be. "Promise me, if something happens and we have to go to war again, you won't fight."

"I can't do that, Beth."

"Why not?"

Styxx clenched his teeth as he sought a reason he could give her that wouldn't reveal his true identity. "How can I stay at home knowing that men who have fought by my side and protected me, men I have bled to protect, are going to die? As hard as it is to live with the memories of war, I would never be able to face myself as a coward."

She didn't take his words well, but neither did she speak against them.

Leaning forward, Styxx nibbled her lips, reveling in the taste he'd missed more than any other. "I'm tired of speaking and thinking about war. Tell me how you've been. Is your uncle still annoying you? Has your mother finally killed your Aunt Epi? How's your mother? Did your grandfather ever get his sword back from his brother?"

Bethany was stunned by his words. "I can't believe you remember all of that."

"There is nothing about you I forget."

Bethany rolled onto her back and pulled him down to lie against her. He tensed as his pain increased, but after a few minutes he relaxed while she told him partial stories about her extensive family. For a few minutes he was so still that she thought he'd fallen asleep. Until she realized he was slowly working his way through the side of her peplos.

"What are you doing?"

He shifted his weight ever so slightly then skimmed his hand across the skin of her thigh. "What I have dreamed of doing every night since I last saw you."

Chills spread over her at the warmth of his hand questing for the part of her that was instantly throbbing for his touch. Bending her knees, she parted her thighs.

Styxx sucked his breath in sharply at how wet she was already. Even though his body protested, he pushed her peplos aside and opened her for his hungry gaze.

She moaned as he toyed with her. He sank his thumb deep into her body. Biting her lip, she rode his fingers for several minutes while he nibbled her hand and watched the pleasure playing out on her face.

"I've missed you, Beth," he breathed then he dipped his head to taste her.

Bethany cried out as his tongue replaced his fingers. Reaching down between her legs, she sank her hand into his hair and savored the way he licked and teased her. He used his whiskers to heighten her pleasure as he dragged them down her cleft, sending chills all over her.

"Come for me, Bethany. I need to taste your pleasure."

Those words sent her over the edge. Throwing her head back, she screamed out as her release tore through her. Still, he didn't stop. He licked and teased and suckled every last tiny bit of pleasure out of her body.

Panting and weak, she laid her fingers over his cheek. "I think you killed me, Hector."

"I can think of much worse ways to go."

She laughed at that then sat up and patted the ground until she found him.

Styxx frowned as she slid down his body. "What are you doing?"

"Returning the favor, my lord."

He arched his brow as she lifted the hem of his chiton and exposed his hard cock to her warm, soft hand. Thanks to Estes and Apollo, he didn't like to be fondled or cupped as a rule.

But the sight of her hand on his body . . . He kept his eyes open to watch as she bent her head and swallowed him whole.

Sucking his breath in, he shivered at the sensation of her tongue swirling and teasing him with pure bliss. In his heart, he wanted this to last, but it'd been too long since he'd been with her.

Way too soon, he growled and released himself.

Great . . .

He'd done better as a virgin. Total embarrassment filled him. "Sorry, love."

She licked him clean then smiled. "Why are you apologizing for something that means the world to me?"

"How so?"

"Given how much pain you're in and how quickly you came just now . . . I know you haven't been near another woman while you were gone."

"That I definitely haven't." He cupped her face in his palm. "Did you find the ring I left for you?"

She held her hand up for him to see it in place.

He smiled in happiness. "Did anyone read the inscription to you?"

"Faithfully yours."

Styxx traced the line of her lips with his thumb. "I don't promise anything lightly, Beth. And I would die before I willingly did something that hurt you. You are the only woman I will be with. Ever. On my honor."

She smiled at his words then stood up. To his shock and pleasure, she removed her peplos and, completely naked, laid back down by his side. Taking his uninjured hand, she kissed his palm then placed it over her heart, between her bare breasts. "I love you."

Touched to the core of his soul, he leaned down to nuzzle her breast then her cheek. "I love you, too. I always will. And I pray to the very gods I despise that they never separate us again."

"Gods you despise?"

He had to stamp down his anger so as not to offend her with his blasphemy. Unlike him, she was a devout follower. "I know you love them, Beth. But I don't. They've been too cruel to me for far too long."

"Sometimes—"

He covered her lips with his. "Please don't defend them. You can't. But . . . if they will just keep you with me, I might one day forgive them and be at peace with them again."

"I will teach you how to love them."

Tears filled his eyes at her words. He didn't doubt her abilities.

If anyone could convert him, it was she. After all, he wouldn't have known any kind of love had she not tamed him with her gentle heart and touch.

For that, he was willing to forgive the bastards who'd cursed him.

Just don't take her from me . . .

That would begin an even greater war than the one he was returning from.

OCTOBER 31, 9530 BC

Styxx froze as he came face-to-face with Acheron as they both left the open, public gymnasium. His brother wore a dark gray chiton and blue cloak—something that would have Acheron beaten if seen. All prostitutes were required to wear a specific red chiton whenever they were in public.

But Styxx would never tell.

He was glad Acheron looked a good deal healthier than he'd appeared the last time they'd met. And the irony that both of them were here this day, pretending to be someone they weren't while doing the same exact thing, wasn't lost on him.

They were twins, after all.

For a moment, he thought Acheron would speak to him.

He didn't. Instead, he pulled his cowl down lower over his face and made his way out of the amphitheater.

A part of Styxx wanted to chase after him, but what was the use? Really? Time and bitterness divided them.

They had both said and done things to each other that were unforgivable.

And yet . . .

He missed his brother. Dearly. Those stolen moments of friendship when they'd played together and laughed. He would give anything if he could go back to that time when the world hadn't been quite so cold and harsh. Back to when he hadn't been what he was now.

Although, anymore, he wasn't quite sure what he was.

Other than lost.

His soldiers treated him like some mythical hero. His father and the senate like some overindulged brat who should be spanked. His sister like he was a demon sent to torment her. And in his heart, he knew he was a killer . . .

And a whore.

Like his brother.

Only Bethany made him feel noble and cherished. But that would change instantly if she ever learned the truth of his identity or what Apollo had forced on him against his will. Then she would hate him forever for the lie he'd told her to protect himself.

Galen alone treated him like a son. But he hadn't seen his old mentor since their return. Before Galen had even dismounted, Styxx had sent him on to be with his family—had ordered him to take at least three months with them before he even considered returning to town.

Honestly, Styxx envied Galen's daughter and grandchildren. He hoped they knew what a rare gift it was to be cherished by Galen the way they were, and that they never took the old man's love for granted.

"Highness?"

Styxx paused as he heard a familiar voice. Frowning, he turned to see Dorus in the crowd.

The nobleman headed straight for him and gave a curt bow. Dorus glanced around as if seeking Styxx's ever-present guards, but said nothing when he didn't find them at their usual post. Having grown tired of his every belch being reported to his father while their thoughts insulted everything about him, Styxx had slipped out of the palace to be alone for awhile.

"I haven't seen you since your return, Highness. Welcome home."

"Thank you, Dorus."

"I've heard great things of your victories. My father said that you were headed for the Atlantean mainland when you were recalled."

"We were."

"It must have been incredible to fight so many victorious battles. Exciting."

More like bloody and terrifying. Haunting. Grueling. A thousand adjectives came to his mind, none of them good.

But Dorus didn't want to hear the truth any more than Styxx wanted to remember it. "I heard they elected you to the senate. Congratulations."

"They did. At one-and-twenty, I'm one of the youngest members."

Styxx felt so disconnected from Dorus and the other noblemen his age. Unlike the king, their fathers wouldn't send them to war for at least two more years. For that matter, all his experiences were so radically different from theirs and from what they believed his to be that it was hard to converse with any of them.

But at least Dorus tried. Best of all, Styxx never heard his thoughts. And for that, he was eternally grateful.

Dorus, Galen, and Bethany were the only ones who didn't bombard him whenever they were around. Every once in a while, he might overhear something, but overall, their thoughts were blissfully hidden and silent.

"Did you know there's a new brothel that opened near Catera's? They have some of the most exotic beauties they've imported . . . "

Forcing himself not to grimace at something he found utterly revolting, Styxx held his hand up. "I'm not interested."

Dorus laughed. "I understand. A prince never has to pay for sex. I imagine any woman is yours for the taking."

Yeah . . .

If only I lived the life everyone thought I did . . . He might actually be happy.

Unable to stomach any more of this conversation, Styxx

inclined his head. "Pardon me, Dorus, I have an appointment to keep. I hope you don't mind."

As Styxx started past him, he felt a strange sensation over his skin.

One he'd only felt on the battlefield . . . like something powerful was watching him. Slowing down, he glanced around for the source of it. But nothing was there.

Putting it out of his mind, he headed back to the palace.

"What are you doing with Styxx?"

Apollo glanced up from the lyre he was tuning to see Athena in his temple, heading straight for him with more venom than a cobra nest. "I haven't seen the irritable bitch, why?"

"Not the goddess, you moron. The prince of Didymos."

Apollo strummed a note. "Ever wonder what his father was thinking when he allowed you to name his son for the River of Hatred? For a Titan bitch so cruel that none of us will even consider crossing her?"

"What has this to do with anything?"

He shrugged. "I thought we were talking about things that don't matter."

With her hands on her hips, Athena stopped in front of him. "I'm serious, Apollo. He is my champion. Why are you—"

"Fucking him?"

Athena snatched the lyre from his hands and had to grip it hard to keep from bashing him against the head with it. "Don't push me, brother. I'm not that fond of you, and unlike your twin sister, I don't fear you."

"What I do or don't do with the prince is no concern of yours. Why do you care anyway?"

Because I can't stand what was done to an innocent boy who should have been coddled and loved. Not cast into the harsh existence he has because you and your Atlantean conspirators screwed with his life.

Unfortunately, she couldn't say that. "There are plenty of mortals for you to pick from. Leave mine alone."

"Jealous?"

"He is a loyal follower of mine and you are single-handedly turning him against all of us."

Apollo leaned back against his chaise. "I have him well in hand."

She winced at his cruel double entendre.

"No need in you concerning yourself with our relationship, dear sister."

Athena ground her teeth in anger. "I don't understand why you can't leave him alone when it's obvious he can't stand you."

"Cast off your virgin robes," Apollo said with a sadistic twist to his lips, "and you'll understand it fast. He is a very sweet piece of ass."

She curled her lip. "You sicken me."

He mocked her words. "And you bore me. Now hand me my instrument and begone."

Athena wanted to shove it where the "sun" didn't shine. But it wouldn't do any good. Apollo was a prick. "For a god of prophecy, you're a complete and utter idiot. Can you not see what you're about to do to him if you don't let him be?"

"You wanted him strong."

She growled at her idiot brother. "Not like this, I didn't. And you are to leave him alone, Apollo. I mean it!" Glaring at him one last time, she turned and stormed from his temple.

Apollo shook his head and laughed. "Had you not threatened me, I might have turned my eyes to another. But . . . sweet Athena, no one threatens me. And they damn sure don't do it over a piece of human trash."

JANUARY 18, 9529 BC

Styxx rubbed at his aching head as he and his father went to meet with the senators and emissaries to discuss the Atlantean truce. That alone would be reason enough to make his brain hurt, but

Ryssa trailed them, whining over the fact that her beloved father was offering her up as a sacrificial goat. The selfish shrew had no concept of what real humiliation felt like.

"Father, please . . . "

Damn, if they could harness the sound of her noxious whine, they'd have one hell of a battle weapon to unleash against their enemies.

"Enough, Ryssa." Finally, the old bastard cut her off. "The decision is made. You are to be offered to Apollo. We need him on our side if we're to ever win this war against the Atlanteans. So long as he continues to favor and aid them, we will never stand a chance. If you are his lover, he will look more kindly toward our people and might be swayed to our cause."

"It's not fair!"

Because life was ever about fairness.

Oh, to be as naive as his sister.

Just as they approached the atrium, their conversation was interrupted by the voices of the senators who were waiting for them on the other side of the wall.

"He looks just like Styxx."

Styxx froze instantly as his stomach knotted. Obviously, some of the senators had discovered Acheron at Catera's brothel.

This can't be good.

The one who'd spoken, Senator Barax, had been a longtime friend to his father and one of his top advisors.

His father paused by his side as Ryssa smirked at Styxx. She was absolutely gloating.

"What say you?" Krontes asked. He, too, was a friend and advisor to the king.

Barax laughed deep in his throat. "It's true. They couldn't look more alike had they been born twins. The only difference is their eye color."

Even though Acheron had been gone for a decade, how could they not remember his brother? That thought angered him even more than their topic.

"His eyes are eerie," Senator Peles, his father's oldest friend, joined in. "You can tell he's the son of some god, but he won't say which one."

"And he's in a stew, you say?" Krontes asked.

"Yes," Peles said. "I'm telling you, Krontes, you have to visit him. Pretending he's Styxx has helped me immensely in dealing with the royal prick. Spend an hour with Acheron on his knees and the next time you see Styxx, you'll have a whole new perspective."

They laughed.

"You should have been at our banquet last night," Barax continued. "We dressed him in royal robes and passed him around like a bitch in heat."

Styxx's stomach heaved as fear, rage, and hatred rose to choke him. While the three of them must not have bought him from Estes, Styxx knew there were members of the senate who had.

Members he was sure had passed around the same stories about having ridden the royal stallion.

Styxx wanted to die where he stood.

Snarling in rage, his father charged around the wall to have them arrested for defaming his heir. What would he say if he knew Styxx had been as debased by members of his senate as Acheron had?

Ryssa raked him with a sneer. "It should have been *you* they used instead of Acheron. You deserve it."

He glared at her. "I hope you think of that curse when Apollo violates your precious loins, sister."

She slapped him then stormed away.

Closing his eyes, Styxx leaned against the wall and struggled with the agony inside his heart. Not just for himself, but for Acheron who was still being bought and sold.

He felt his father's presence and opened his eyes to find him standing by his side. "This. Ends."

Ends how?

Other than badly for all of them.

"What do you intend to do, Father?"

"What I should have done to begin with." He turned to leave.

Styxx stopped him. "Father? What are you planning?"

"To have that bastard arrested and put in a place where he can't shame me."

Prison.

Styxx shook his head at the thought of Acheron suffering like that. But his father would reject any plea based on compassion. So he used something he knew his father would care about.

The king's ego.

"You can't. Instead of having senators bragging about tupping your heir, you'll have commoners doing it. Is that what you want?"

His father glowered at him.

"Bring Acheron home, Father. It's time."

"You sound like a *methusai.*"

I'd rather be an old woman than a heartless bastard.

Styxx wanted to argue, but he knew that expression. His father had made his mind up about the matter and no amount of logic would be heard at this point.

As always, he'd have to find some way to deal with the aftermath of his father's lunatic hatred and try his best to modify whatever actions the king took, while trying to keep his own ass out of the line of fire.

JANUARY 20, 9529 BC

Styxx reined his horse to a stop as he held Bethany in his lap. Leaning down to bury his face against the nape of her neck, he inhaled the sweet eucalyptus scent of her lotion and smiled. Her scent made him rock hard and caused his head to spin even more than the drugs Estes had once used on him.

She placed her hand to his cheek. "Are we here?"

He squeezed her gently. "We are, love. I'd tell you to close your eyes, but ... "

She leaned back against his shoulder and kissed his clean-shaven cheek. Since she didn't care for his beard as it interfered with her ability to feel his expressions, he'd bid it adieu. "You're not funny."

"And yet you tell me you love my humor. What is wrong with you, woman?"

"The very fact I'm in love with *you*. It rather says it all."

He laughed at her gentle teasing then dismounted. Placing his hands at her waist, he pulled her down to stand beside him. A large dog started barking ferociously.

She frowned at the sound. "Where are we?"

"Were you not paying attention to my directions from the stream?"

"I was, and I know where we are, but not *where* we are. Or why we're here."

He left his horse to graze and took her hand to lead her. "We are someplace very special."

"And that would be?"

He placed her hand against the wooden door of the small stone cottage.

Her scowl deepened as the dog barked even louder. "What is this?"

"Shush, *skylos!*" he said to the dog then he gentled his tone to speak to Bethany. "I bought this for you. It's a place for you to escape to whenever the weather is bad."

She went rigid. "Hector—"

"Beth, there are no strings attached to it at all." He put both her hands on his face so that she could feel how sincere he was. "It's yours, plain and simple. You can keep your things here and not have to tote them anymore. It has a large lake that's just down the hill, fully stocked with fish. I made sure before I bought it."

"I don't understand ... "

He kissed her palms as terror rode him with spurs. Since he'd

371

come home, he'd been tortured with images of someone hurting her. Of another man stumbling upon her spot and not being wounded as he'd been when he first found her there. Or worse, Apollo harming her to get back at him. "I know you have your knife, but I worry about you when I'm not with you. Constantly. I'd feel better if you had a safer place to be alone."

Bethany smiled as tears welled in her eyes at his thoughtful kindness. Even so, she couldn't help teasing him. "I believe you were thinking of yourself more than me. You won't have to worry about grass burns on your knees or random, randy limbs in your back-side."

He laughed. "You know me so well. But I must admit that I'll be missing those intimate moments with the tree. I think after my last encounter with its branches we might be married ... at the very least betrothed."

She groaned at his twisted sense of humor as he opened the door. The moment he did, a huge dog mauled her.

"Down!" Hector snapped, pulling him away. "Beth, meet ... *skylos*. He hasn't been named yet. But he's the size of a horse and is here to also keep you safe. I have a woman who'll come to feed him every morning for you. Or you can take him with you when you go home ... which I'd prefer. I'd rather you have a protector at all times."

She heard the fear underlying his tone. He really was afraid for her. Leaning down, she stroked the dog's ears as he licked her face. "What color is he?"

"Black."

"Hey there, boy." She kissed his furry head. "I think I shall call you ... Dynatos."

"Dynatos it is," Hector agreed then he took her inside and gently led her around so that she could find where everything was placed and not get hurt.

The front door opened into a room with a table, two chairs, and a place to cook and prepare food. There was a room off to the right with a bed, chest, and two more chairs set before a fire.

Though tiny, it was very cozy.

Still ... "I can't take this from you, Hector. It's too much."

"Yes, you can. I want you to have it."

"Hector—"

"Beth ... " He pulled her back against his front and nuzzled her neck. "Please take it and give me some peace of mind about your safety."

He so often broke her heart. Whatever had happened to him at war had really damaged a part of him. While her safety had always concerned him before, he was now obsessed with it. He was forever teaching her new ways to disarm an attacker—not that she needed his tricks, but she couldn't tell him that. Whenever he fell asleep, he had ferocious nightmares that caused him to wake up frantic and angry.

Even now, he trembled in her arms.

Offering him a grateful smile, she kissed his cheek. "All right, Hector. Thank you."

Styxx closed his eyes as he held her and just let the scent of her skin soothe him. There was nothing in this world he valued above her. Nothing he wouldn't do to make her happy or keep her safe.

"So," he whispered in her ear. "What should we test first? The lake or the bed?"

She snorted playfully. "I knew you had an ulterior motive."

"Hey, I gave you the choice of the lake first."

"Umm-hmmm ... but I know you didn't mean it."

"I've been a perfect gentleman."

"That's not what the part of you poking me says." She turned his arms and kissed him. "I suppose I should take mercy on you." She nipped his chin, making him all the harder, before she dropped her hand to stroke his erection. "But no. I'd rather fish." Laughing, she ran past him.

Styxx groaned out loud as Dynatos chased after her. "You're so cold, my lady! Cruel. Heartless!" He caught up to her at the front door.

Expecting her to open it, he was surprised when she spun about and fell back against the wood. She buried her hands into his chiton and pulled him into her arms for a kiss so hot, it made his head reel.

Then she sank down on her knees in front of him and lifted the hem of his chiton.

Styxx couldn't breathe as she ran her hand over him, and when she took him into her mouth, it was all he could do to remain upright. "I love you, Bethany," he breathed as he sank his hand into her soft hair.

She licked the underside of him. "I love you, too."

His legs trembling, Styxx was completely distracted by her when Dynatos came up behind him unexpectedly and slammed into his back. He barely caught himself against the door before he knocked Bethany over. "Damn it, dog!"

Laughing, she pulled away. "Are you having trouble with your gift, sweetie?"

Styxx tried to push the mountainous beast back. "Not at all."

Bethany laughed harder as she heard Hector grunting in his attempts to move the dog out of his way. "Are you sure it's a dog and not a bear?"

"I'm thinking horse, given its weight."

She could hear the dog jumping and licking. "He doesn't seem ferocious."

"He can be when he's not yours." The door opened and then closed.

Suddenly, Hector scooped her up in his arms and ran with her to the bedroom, where he laid her on the bed. "Now, where were we?"

Dynatos barked at the door then rammed it.

"Distracted, I believe."

Hector placed his head down on the center of her chest and sighed. "I swear I'm cursed."

Laughing again, she led his lips to hers. "I can ignore him if you can."

374

He lifted the hem of her gown until she was exposed to his questing hand. "I can definitely ignore him ... And a house fire ... " He teased her breast with his lips. "End of the world ... "

She spread her legs farther apart and whispered in his ear as she guided his hand to the juncture of her thighs. "Then come inside, my lord, and play to your heart's content."

JANUARY 22, 9529 BC

"Where was Acheron taken?" Styxx demanded as he entered his father's study.

The king looked up with a scowl. "You dare use that tone with me, boy?"

Penalty for striking the king is death.

Moments like this, he really didn't care. Especially since his back, wrists, face, and side burned in such a way as to let him know his brother had been viciously beaten. But angering the old bastard wouldn't get him what he wanted.

Even though it galled him, he modulated his tone. "Where is he, Father?"

"Downstairs. You said you wanted him home. So he is."

In the dungeon? It was the only "downstairs" they had from here.

"That's not what I meant and you know it." Styxx spun about, intending to free Acheron immediately.

"Boy?"

A fierce tic started in his jaw as he turned back toward his father. Aside from setting his brother free, the only other thing he really wanted to do at present was tutor his father well on the fact that there was no boy left inside the man who'd taken hundreds of lives in battle for this kingdom. "Majesty?"

"Before you consider putting your will over mine. Or think for one instant that because my army believes you're some great war hero they want to follow, you have leverage . . . think again. I know all about your little blind Egyptian whore and where the two of you meet. I even know you bought her a place to live. I suggest, for her continued health and well-being, that you learn to curb your temper."

Styxx went cold at his threat against Bethany. "You wouldn't dare."

His father arched his brow. "I am king. You would do well to remember that. And I will do as I please, and *you* will do what pleases me or I will show you the exact extent of my power. While I would hate to be without an heir, I am still of an age that I could father another. Now . . . where were you going?"

Don't. Kill. Him.

"Riding."

"Good choice. Give your beautiful mistress my best."

It took everything Styxx possessed to not murder his own father. But what good would it do him to spend eternity in prison? Or to be beheaded . . .

Sooner or later, the bastard would die on his own. Just not soon enough.

Styxx paused outside the room to eye his father's guards. They were with the king everywhere he went. Even to piss. They stood over his bed at night, even when he screwed. The only place they weren't was in the king's study, but there was no way in or out of that room except the doors where they stood. Should he kill his father, they would know it.

Damn them all.

While he couldn't care less what happened to him, he would never risk Bethany's life or happiness. Not for anything.

"They're being put to death."

His thoughts were so focused on Bethany, it took him several heartbeats to realize Ryssa had spoken to him. "Pardon?"

"The senators who insulted you? Father's putting his friends to death over it to make a point that no one is to defame his precious heir. In case you didn't know, I thought you should."

No one had mentioned it to him. "I should think it would thrill you."

"To have you so regaled? Hardly."

His mood darkened in the wake of her ridicule. "But they screwed your beloved Acheron. I'm surprised you're not the one calling for their deaths."

She glared at him. "They abused him because of *you*. Had they not hated you so, they would never have touched him."

What have I ever done to you, Ryssa? Really?

"And what do you think I did to warrant such hatred from them?"

"You're a selfish bully. You look at everyone like they're beneath you and you speak to them as if they're nothing."

Was she as insane as their mother? "I rarely speak at all. To anyone. Dear sister."

She shook her head in denial. "I don't understand you, Styxx. You're the only one Father listens to. You could help us and yet you refuse."

"And you know this how?"

"By your own admission. You say nothing. You haven't spoken up about Acheron, ever. Just as you refused to talk to Father about offering me to Apollo."

Offering *her* to Apollo . . . she'd die to learn the truth of that.

Or worse.

She'd gloat and laugh.

Still, he knew she wasn't as selfless as she claimed. "Tell me. What bothers you most, sweet sister? Acheron's status or your own—"

She slapped him.

Styxx narrowed his gaze on her. "I'm getting tired of your blows, Ryssa."

"Then stop being such an ass."

Stop being a bitch and I might.

He wiped the blood from his lips. "Just so you know, your father doesn't listen to me any more than he listens to you."

"You're such a liar. I know better. Anything you want, he gives."

Right . . .

"You have the two of us confused, sweet sister. You're the one he dotes on."

"No. I don't. I saw the way you sat complacent when he and the others told me I was to be sacrificed. You could have spoken up and I know for a fact you didn't. Not once!"

"You're right. I didn't."

"Why not?"

Honestly, it wouldn't have mattered. Apollo was the one leading this and if Styxx tried to stop it, Bethany would pay for his interference. Styxx had already killed one man to protect Ryssa. He wasn't about to cause harm to the one and only person who held his heart in her hands for a bitch who begrudged him every breath he took.

But Ryssa wouldn't care about Bethany. At all. So he used the one thing she might actually listen to. One of the main reasons he'd submitted to Apollo even though it sickened him to the core of his being.

"Because of the faces of the men I have watched the Atlanteans hack into pieces. If we can save one soldier's life by tying you to Apollo, I'm all for it."

"So it doesn't bother you at all that I, your sister, am to be used as a whore?"

Yes, it did. But her precious virginity was nothing compared to the horrors he'd seen. The horrors he and Acheron had survived. Sooner or later, she'd be given to someone. And while she wouldn't be a wife to Apollo, they weren't selling her off to a dung dealer.

Besides, her fate with Apollo was much kinder than his. At least she was a woman. Every time the Olympian came near him, he wanted to vomit and curse. To fight with every part of his abilities.

But he couldn't. For the sake of his men, country, family, and Galen and Bethany, he had to submit to Apollo's whims regardless of how he felt about it.

Their collective asses or his alone . . .

"Say something, you selfish bastard! Oh wait, I know, you don't speak, do you? Not for anyone." She curled her lip. "You're the one who should be tied down and raped until you beg for mercy."

His temper snapped at a wish he was sick of hearing and experiencing. "Instead of whining like an infant, dear sister, I suggest you do what the rest of us have had to do. Remove your clothes, get on your knees, and take his cock wherever he sees fit to shove it."

She shrieked and headed for their father.

Styxx rolled his eyes as he made his way to the stables.

Bethany hummed lightly as she felt a slight tug at her pole. Before she could pull in her catch, she heard a horse approaching at a furious run. Hector wasn't supposed to be here. He normally forewarned her of his visits so as not to startle her when he arrived.

Pulling her feet under her in case she had to rise and run, she reached for her knife as Dynatos stood up and growled low.

"Beth, it's me." Hector had come, after all.

She expelled a relieved breath and patted Dynatos's huge head as he lay back down next to her. "You said you wouldn't have any free time today."

"I don't . . . but I needed to make sure you were all right."

She frowned. "What's wrong?"

"Nothing."

"I know better. I hear it in your voice. What has you troubled?"

Hector sat down behind her and stretched his long legs out on each side of her body. Wrapping his arms about her waist, he held her close and leaned his head against hers. "I know I promised I'd never ask again, but please, run with me."

"Honey, I can't."

He tightened his arms around her. "I would die if anything ever happened to you."

"Nothing is going to happen. Why do you worry so?"

"Because I have seen the worst of humanity. What men will do when they find a beautiful woman alone. And while I would kill anyone who hurt you, I don't want you hurt. Period. No matter how hard you try, you can never take those moments back or undo the lingering damage you're left with that shreds every part of your soul for all eternity." He kissed her cheek. "In all my life, I've only had one thing that mattered to me, and she sits in my arms. I can't stand the thought of not protecting you . . . of you needing me and my not being there for you."

Bethany's heart ached at the pain she heard in his voice. Leaning back, she cradled his head. How she wished she could run with him. But she'd have to give up her godhood to do so.

And her eyesight. Forever.

No, not forever. For an extremely finite human life. One where she'd be as helpless as he feared her. That she couldn't do. Not for a mortal man, even one she loved as much as this one.

"I love you, too, Hector. And I have *never* said that to a man I wasn't blood-related to. But I can't leave with you."

"Then promise me one thing?"

"What?"

He removed her necklace from his wrist and put it back around her neck. "You won't take this off, and if anyone ever tries to hurt you, you will kill them."

"I would rather you have my necklace."

"And I can't take it while you have nothing to protect you."

"Hector—"

"I won't give on this, Beth. Don't even try to argue."

Styxx tightened his arms around her. There was something evil coming. He could feel it with every instinct he possessed. But he didn't know what it was.

For himself, he couldn't care less about it. Fear for his own safety had abandoned him a long time ago. His fears now consisted of one woman only.

Too many people had made threats against her lately. If she wouldn't leave then he had no choice. He had to protect her.

No matter what it took.

JANUARY 23, 9529 BC

Styxx winced as he stood outside the cell where Acheron had been placed. Worse, he heard the fear and anguish in his brother's thoughts. The anger that justifiably cursed their entire family.

Most of all, he heard the unwarranted hatred and hostility Acheron bore for him personally when all he'd ever done was try to help him.

Fuck it . . .

Knowing his hands were tied where his brother was concerned and guilty over the fact that he treasured Bethany's safety more, Styxx opened the tiny hole at the base of the fortified door and slid in the basket he'd brought. Bread, wine, cheese, and the sugared figs Acheron had loved when they were boys. He didn't try to speak to him. There was no need. Rather he let Acheron think it was Ryssa who brought the food.

After all, what could he say to his twin?

Sorry, brother. I can't help you?

While I love you, I love someone else more?

That wouldn't go over well, and he understood. If he were Acheron, he'd hate him, too.

Heartsick, he placed his hand on the door and ground his teeth in impotent frustration. But what hurt the most was the knowledge that it could have just as easily been him in that room as Acheron.

And maybe it should be.

The only thing that had saved him from Acheron's fate was his eyes. It was so ridiculous, he'd laugh if it didn't hurt so much.

One day, Acheron, when I'm king, I will set you free. Then no one will hurt you ever again. I swear it with every part of me. I will make this up to you.

Unfortunately for his brother, today wasn't that day.

OCTOBER 22, 9529 BC

Styxx woke up to an awful queasy feeling. Again. He hadn't felt well in days and he knew why. Acheron had stopped eating. Even though he'd been making drops of food to the cell, his brother had chosen a slow suicide.

Over the last week as the symptoms had worsened, Styxx had considered telling his father then reconsidered it.

He wouldn't take this from Acheron. His brother wanted an end to his suffering. The least he could do was allow it. Even if it hurt like hell.

So he hadn't breathed a word of it to anyone. Not even Bethany. Instead, he'd spent most of yesterday with her, knowing it wouldn't be long before Acheron killed them.

He shook his head, trying to clear the hazy fog. It was useless.

Styxx reached for his wine, ignoring the food. It wouldn't matter how much *he* ate, he'd still be hungry and his stomach would continue to gnaw viciously ... As it always did whenever Acheron starved.

"Styxx? Are you listening?"

Blinking, he met his father's cold stare. "Majesty?"

Ryssa twisted her lips into an ugly face. "He didn't hear a word, Father. He's ignoring us as always."

"I asked what you thought of putting your sister in yellow and gold to offer her to Apollo."

"Sure." The wine slipped from his hand.

"Styxx?"

He heard his father, but he couldn't respond. His knees buckled. He hit the ground hard.

His father and the priest ran to him. They were speaking to him, but he couldn't understand them or respond. He was too weak to even move his own hand.

All the color drained from his father's face as he lifted him up and carried him to his bed. For a moment, Styxx could almost pretend his father loved him. But he knew better. No one could do the things his father had done and care about their child. It wasn't possible.

The bastard never even called him "son," not unless he was speaking to someone else about him. His father had never once used any kind of endearment for him at all. Unlike Ryssa, his precious kitten . . .

Styxx blinked slowly as bitter memories churned inside his head.

Ryssa came forward to sit on his bed and hold his hand. With the exception of slapping him, she hadn't deigned to touch him since . . .

Ever.

I am definitely dying.

Thoughts and voices mingled in his head, but he shoved them aside so that he could conjure an image of Bethany yesterday when he'd given her a gold necklace he'd bought for her. Her face had lit up his world like the sun after a long rain.

And then, singing with her beautiful voice and playing her drum, she'd danced for him with her bells jingling lightly with every graceful movement of her hips and arms. There truly was nothing more beautiful.

How he wished he were in her arms right now, listening to her hum in that sweet, dulcet contralto. But he would never see her face again, never feel her gentle touch on his skin.

Aching at the thought that she was lost to him, he closed his eyes and surrendered himself to the gods he hated.

OCTOBER 29, 9529 BC

Styxx came awake with a start. Grimacing, he struggled to breathe as he glanced around his room to find himself alone except for Galen who dozed in a nearby chair.

Gods, he was so thirsty.

He reached for the clay cup on the table beside his bed, but accidentally knocked it over.

Galen woke up instantly. "Highness?"

Styxx sucked his breath in sharply as more pain racked him.

Galen shot to the bed to make sure he was all right. "Don't move. You've been extremely ill."

Styxx tried to understand what was going on. "W-why are you here?"

"Why do you think? I heard you were dying."

And Galen had left his daughter to be with him . . .

Styxx coughed before he spoke through his dry, hoarse throat. "I'm sorry I interrupted your time with Antigone."

"Sorry? I'm rather sure you didn't do this on purpose." Galen helped him sit up then poured him some wine. He held the cup to Styxx's lips so that he could sip at it.

"How do you feel?"

Styxx swallowed before he answered. "Like you ran over me in your chariot."

His gray eyes irritated, the old man sighed. "You are never going to let me forget that, are you?"

Styxx smiled then grimaced. "How long have I been ill?"

"A week."

A week? He frowned at Galen's unkempt state. "When did you get here?"

"Five days ago."

That explained the way Galen appeared. He'd come immediately and had ridden hard.

Styxx took Galen's hand and squeezed it. "Thank you."

Galen inclined his head respectfully. "Your men have all gathered as well and are awaiting news of your health. I think the sight of their loyalty and love of you has frightened your father."

Beautiful. Just what he wanted to deal with.

"May I ask a favor, Galen?"

"Anything."

Styxx cringed as more pain hit him. "There's a small cottage on the edge of town . . . part of a small farm."

"Your woman?"

He nodded. "Her name is Bethany. Please let her know that I'm ill, but thinking of her. And that I'll see her as soon as I'm able to travel."

"Do you want me to bring her to you?"

"No!" He licked his chapped lips then lowered his voice so that no one could overhear him. "She doesn't know, Galen."

"Know what?"

"That I'm prince. I . . . um . . . I kind of lied to her. She thinks me a merchant's son and that I'm your foot soldier. Please, don't tell her otherwise."

Galen gaped at his words. "How can she not know?"

"She's blind."

"And you've never told her the truth?"

He shook his head. "She thinks my name is Hector."

Galen laughed and clapped him gently on his shoulder. "You're the only prince I know who wouldn't have forced her to your palace to be your slave or mistress."

"She's happy where she is."

Galen glanced around Styxx's ornate chambers. "Don't you think she'd be happier in a palace, draped in jewels?"

Styxx scoffed. "You know better than that. Money means nothing to her, and honestly, I'd rather be in her cottage with her than here."

Galen smiled at him. "We pig farmers must stick together, eh?"

"Indeed."

"You rest, Highness, and I will see the matter done for you."

Bethany stood as she heard the approach of a horse. By the sound of it, she knew it wasn't Hector's. Dynatos came to his feet to growl and bark.

Her hand on her knife, she cocked her head, waiting to see if her visitor was friend or foe. Until she knew for certain, she held on to Dynatos's collar.

Someone with a very heavy footfall approached her hesitantly. "Are you Bethany?"

"You are?"

"Galen. I'm the top *strategos* to Prince Styxx."

Why would the leader of the Didymosian army be here? Unless . . .

"Hector?" She stumbled from the pain of his death. Dynatos circled her, trying to calm her down.

"Shh, my lady." Ignoring her dog, Galen pulled her up against his hard, muscled body. "Your Hector lives, but he's very ill. He asked me to get word to you."

Closing her eyes, she breathed in relief, and patted his hand. "Thank you, Master Galen."

"You're trembling," he said as he released her.

"You scared me. I thought I'd lost my Hector."

"So you do love him?"

Her breathing ragged, she nodded. "More than my own life."

"Good, because he is completely devoted to you, my lady. In all our travels and battles, I saw him turn away countless women by saying he had a lady at home whose trust and heart he would never willingly break."

Those words brought a smile to her lips. "Really?"

"Aye. While other men, married and betrothed, wenched and drank, he kept himself sober and loyal. And I can see why. He spoke of your great beauty, but even his eloquent words failed to do you justice."

She smiled. "Again, thank you."

"He also wanted me to let you know that he'd come to you as soon as he was able."

Tears filled her eyes at Hector's consideration. Even sick, he thought of her. "Please send him my best and tell him that I won't breathe again until I see him ... " She swallowed then used Hector's words he spoke whenever they were parted for very long. "That I will be counting down the beats of my heart until his return."

"I will do so. Before I go, do I need to get you someone or—"

"Now that I know he's all right, I'll be fine, Master Galen. Thank you."

He patted her hand. "Should you need anything in the meantime, please don't hesitate to come to me. I live in the palace barracks."

"I appreciate it, but I'll be fine."

"Very well. I bid you good day, my lady."

Bethany didn't move until he was gone. But as he rode away, she frowned. Why would such a high-ranking member of the prince's army run an errand for a lowly foot soldier?

OCTOBER 31, 9529 BC

Still weak and in pain, Styxx paused in the doorway of Ryssa's room. His father and sister were downstairs with the priests and advisors making plans for her coming union with Apollo.

Except for Galen and the occasional servant who brought food and drink, Styxx had been left alone to recover. Though during the first days of his return to consciousness his men had formed a steady line of well-wishers through his room, finally, both he and Galen had convinced them to go home to their families. Their time was much better spent there than in the barracks.

Today was the first time he'd been strong enough to leave his bed unassisted. And he'd come straight to see his brother.

Ryssa had ordered Acheron brought to her rooms and placed in her bed so that she could personally oversee his care and tend him. While Styxx was grateful for her concern for his brother, a part of him was extremely jealous. She'd see him whipped and burned as dead before she ever cared for him like this. In fact, once it was determined Acheron was in danger and not Styxx, Styxx hadn't seen her since. She'd spent every waking second she could with Acheron, and not so much as a single inquiry had been made about Styxx's recovery.

Of course, she'd been like that when Styxx had come home from war, too. She hadn't once asked about his health or wounds. Not even when they'd openly bled in front of her.

It is what it is.

His sister would never love him. He'd long ago accepted that reality.

Styxx cursed silently as he saw his brother. Under their father's "kind" orders, Acheron was tied spread-eagle to Ryssa's bed. Styxx hated to see anyone treated like that . . . tied the way Estes had once done him.

He could only imagine the nightmares it gave his brother.

And Acheron looked every bit as wan and weak as Styxx felt.

Breathing slow and easy so as not to pass out, Styxx made his way across the floor until he stood next to his brother's side.

Acheron cut a sullen glance to him, but said nothing.

Styxx couldn't blame him. Words failed him, too. What did brothers say to each other after all that had happened to divide them? After all the nightmares they'd experienced together and apart?

But the one thing that struck him was how unscarred Acheron's skin was. Except for the slave brand on his palm, his body, unlike Styxx's, was pristine. There was no trace of the abuse he knew his brother had been through. And he'd felt every lash himself.

"Why are you staring at me?" Acheron finally growled. "You want to fuck me, too?"

He winced as Estes's cruelty tore through him. "You have no memory of my going to Atlantis, do you?"

"You led your conquering army to their shores. Bully for you, *hero*."

Styxx ignored the venomous snarl. "No . . . before that."

"You mean when you came, beat the shit out of me, and threw me into the street to whore again? Yes, *brother,* I recall it vividly."

No, Acheron remembered none of Styxx's six weeks with him. Good, and yet . . .

He wanted Acheron to know what he'd tried to do for him. To know that Styxx had loved him enough to put his own life and freedom at risk to save his brother. But why bother? His brother wanted to hate him and perhaps Acheron needed that focus. Perhaps his ignorance was kinder than knowing Styxx had tried to save him and failed. It kept Acheron's mind off his own pain.

Hatred was a lot easier to deal with than guilt or remorse. And memories that couldn't be changed. Styxx knew that better than anyone.

Acheron's swirling silver gaze burned into him. "I hate you, you fucking brat."

"I know," Styxx breathed, glancing away.

"Why didn't you let me die?"

Styxx laughed bitterly at his accusation. "I tried. Believe me, I did nothing to save either of us."

"Liar!"

It's not fair that you get to live in comfort while I live in Tartarus! Why you? What makes you better than me? A pair of eyes I want to rip out.

Acheron's thoughts flogged his conscience and his heart.

"My life hasn't been easy, either, you know."

"Oh forgive me, *Highness*. Did the cook burn your toast this morning? Or was your bathwater too cold? Did your valet forget to leave out the right garment?"

Styxx stiffened as his own hatred ignited while his brother trivialized his life and what he *thought* Styxx's problems were. Acheron was just like everyone else. Making assumptions based on nothing but stupidity. "How dare you mock my pain. But for *you,* my father—" He caught himself right before he admitted a truth that cut him to the depth of his soul.

"Your father what?"

Would have loved me.

Instead, because of Acheron, the king had always been suspicious and cold. Never quite certain Styxx was his. While their father doted entirely on Ryssa, there had always been a hint of reservation in his eyes when he looked at Styxx.

And always reservation in his heart whenever they were alone. It was why his father never called him son.

"You're the one who betrayed us, Acheron. Not me."

"And I think I've paid well for it. After all, I'm the one tied naked to a bed and you're the one wrapped in a gold-trimmed chlamys. You're the one everyone bows before and seeks to please your every whim."

Yes, that was so his life . . .

Never.

Styxx sighed wearily. No, they'd both paid for it. Dearly. But Acheron would never believe the truth, any more than Ryssa did, and Ryssa had borne witness to some of it. Still, she had it in her mind that *he* was the one their father favored.

People make their own reality. That was what Praxis had taught him years ago. A hundred people can witness the same exact event, and give two hundred and three different accountings of it.

"Everything is filtered through our emotions that change over time, young prince. As king, your job will be to listen to both sides of every matter and try to find the truth that lies somewhere between the opposing accounts."

He'd seen the veracity of that time and again as he sat with his father and listened to testimony from the nobles and citizens as they brought trial against each other. The subtlest gesture that was misread . . .

Tone of voice.

All of it could lead to war.

Even between brothers.

No, *especially* between brothers.

Styxx looked away as tears choked him. He wanted his twin brother again. The one who'd held his hand and stood with him against the horrors and hatred of their world. The brother who would sneak into his room and lie at his back with his feet pressed against his. The Acheron who'd rolled apples to him through the small hole in the wall that divided their rooms . . .

But that brother was gone forever. There was no trace of the Acheron he'd once known. And maybe there was no young Styxx left in him either. War and life had changed him completely. Perhaps Acheron was right to forget how they'd once been. *There's no grief over its loss if you don't remember it.*

Acheron raked him with a sneer. "So when am I to be dragged back to my shit-hole, *Highness*?"

"How would I know? I never leave mine."

Styxx was amazed the scathing glare Acheron gave him didn't raise a blister on his skin.

"Now who mocks whose pain?"

"I have never mocked your pain, Acheron. Only your self-pity."

"And what of yours?"

"I suppose we're both selfish bastards. Two pieces of one whole."

"I'm not a part of *you*. I have no brother and I have no family."

A tic started in Styxx's jaw as those words shredded him worse than any others. "Think well, Acheron, before you draw that battle line."

"I'm not the one who drew it. You did when you allowed me to go back to Atlantis."

You bastard! Acheron would dare throw *that* in his face?

"I tried to save you," Styxx snarled. "I offered you an escape and you refused to leave with me."

"No. You wanted to play hero. Rescue me like I was some bitch who would be forever grateful to the noble prince for his good deed. Had you really wanted to help me, you would have stood up to your father and not allowed them to take me back to Estes."

Of course. Because his father listened to him so well. Acheron was as bad as Ryssa with his delusions. "Had I stood up for you then, I assure you, I'd have met the same fate you did."

"You should have, you coward."

That ignited his fury as Styxx looked at his brother's pristine, unscarred body. A body that hadn't been ravaged for months by priests trying to drive out demons he didn't have, while his father carried on as if he'd never been born. One that didn't have "whore" branded into it in two languages and hadn't been marked by a god who coveted it and hated him for it . . .

A body that had never seen the horrors of heads, brains, guts, and limbs flying past it as he fought for his life. Or held the hands of boys who should have been at home with their mothers as they died from dysentery and ferocious battle wounds.

From starvation.

Yes, it sucked to be whored . . .

Styxx knew that as well as Acheron did. But the atrocities Styxx had suffered went far beyond Acheron's. His brother had never seen the horrors that lived inside his mind and heart. The nightmares that never failed to haunt him . . . even with his eyes wide open.

He seized Acheron's jaw and ignored the pain he caused himself. "I know your nightmares, *brother*. You should be grateful to the gods that you don't know mine."

Acheron's scornful gaze turned icy. "I would pay anything, just once, to see you held down and get fucked in your sanctimonious throat."

Those words and the brutal memories they conjured from where Styxx tried to keep them buried tore him apart. He wanted to kill

Acheron. If he'd had a weapon on him, he probably would have sliced him open. Instead, he lashed out with what he did have.

His words.

"And I would pay to see you butt-fucked until blood runs down your legs and you can't walk."

Acheron laughed at him. "Too bad you weren't there when it happened."

Styxx punched him in the ribs with everything he had and cursed as the blow stole the breath from his own lungs. "I wish to the gods they'd have let you die."

Acheron spat on him.

Wiping the spittle from his cheek, Styxx lifted his head and turned to leave.

As he reached the door, Acheron's last act of cruelty slapped him harder than any blow. "And as they butt-fucked *me,* Styxx, it was *your* ass they pretended to pound on until it bled ... *Your* name they called out and insulted the entire time they were inside me or whenever I sucked their cocks until they came in my mouth ... *Including Estes.* If you think I hate you, Styxx, you have no idea how much others begrudge your every breath!"

NOVEMBER 9, 9529 BC

Exhausted and weak, Styxx lay down on the cottage bed. *I just need a moment to rest before I head back ...* He'd come to find Bethany, but she wasn't here today. Disappointment stabbed his heart and filled him with pain. All he'd wanted was to feel the warm hand on his skin of someone who cared about him.

Funny how all these years he'd stupidly thought having his brother at home with him would make everything better. Instead, it was so much worse.

Ryssa used it to fuel her hatred of him. As did the servants and nobles.

And his father . . .

The king could barely meet his gaze, and when he did, the disdain there scorched his soul. His father no longer saw Styxx as anything other than the bastard of some god who'd tricked him.

I should have kept Galen with me. But he'd sent the old man home to his daughter.

Utterly alone, Styxx had been drinking for days, trying to forget them all and their sneers and condemnation. Trying to forget Acheron's words and his brother's "good" wishes for him. But it was no use. He had no escape whatsoever.

The cottage door opened.

Styxx grabbed his dagger and started to rise when he heard a beautiful voice that brought tears to his eyes.

"Hector?"

"In here, *akribos.*"

Dynatos came running and barking into the bedroom. Styxx grunted as the dog launched itself onto him and jumped around the bed then to the floor and back again. Patting the huge dog's head, he fell against the mattress.

Bethany pushed open the bedroom door more. Dressed in a gray peplos that made her skin glow in spite of its drabness, she stole his breath. "Where are you?"

"In bed."

She arched a censoring brow as Dynatos returned to her side. "Rather presumptuous of you, isn't it?"

It felt so good to smile again. To be around someone who didn't hate him. "Indeed, but I was hoping some stray maid would happen by and ravish me."

She sat down next to him and gave . . . the wall an arch look. "*Some* stray maid?"

"Mmm." He took her hand and kissed her palm. "Would you happen to know one who's available?"

Her playfulness gone, she scowled at him and quickly lifted her hand from his lips to his brow. Then she gasped. "You're burning with fever."

"No wonder I feel so awful."

She cupped his cheeks in her hands. "Hector . . . it's *very* high. Why aren't you in bed?"

"I am in bed."

"No . . . *your* bed. You shouldn't have come here while you were still so ill."

"I wanted to see you."

Even so, she was livid.

Styxx ground his teeth as her reaction slapped him like a blow. No matter how hard he tried, he couldn't please anyone. "I thought you'd be happy to see me."

"Yes, were you healthy. But damn, Hector. Damn!"

A part of him shriveled with every expletive. He shouldn't have come here and bothered her when it was obvious she'd rather do something else. If he knew anything in life, it was that people didn't like to tend others when they were sick.

He'd been wrong to burden her. "Sorry. I'll leave." He rolled to get up.

She shoved him back onto the bed. "Don't you dare move." She growled at him. "How could you do this?"

"Do what?"

"Risk my life!"

Maybe it was the fever, but he was completely confused now. "I'm not risking your life, Beth. I'm not contagious."

"Yes, you are killing me. Do you not understand that every breath you draw is tied to mine? Now take your clothes off."

He bit back a smile. "That's my girl."

"No. Not for *that*. I need to get your skin cooled down."

"Fine . . . but would you please stop yelling at me. I've rather had my fill of it for a while." He pulled his chiton off, and started shivering immediately.

Bethany covered him with the blanket then coaxed the dog to

lie down by his side and keep him warm. "Who's been yelling at you?"

"Everyone. It's to the point I'm beginning to think my name has been changed to 'Damn It' or 'Asshole.'"

Tears glistened in her eyes. "I'm not yelling at you, Hector. I'm scared for you. There's a big difference."

"All right. But from inside my head, it's hard to hear that difference."

Bethany kissed his brow then went to fetch water and a cloth so that she could bathe him to lower his body temperature.

His head throbbing, Styxx shivered even more while he idly stroked the dog's head.

Returning, she placed her bowl on the small table by the bed and wet her cloth. As she sponged his cheek, she fingered the whiskers there and along his jaw and chin. "You haven't shaved in a while."

His gut clenched at the unintended insult he'd given her. "I didn't mean to offend you with it. I—"

"I'm not offended, sweet. Just surprised and concerned. It's not like you, and it tells me exactly how sick you really are. I can't believe you came here when you're so ill. Someone should have kept you at home and tended you better than this. I could beat them senseless over your lack of care."

Styxx held her hand against his lips and savored the softness of her skin and the precious scent of it. Then he kissed her palm. Gods, it felt so good to be with someone who wasn't hating him.

"By the way, I was surprised by your messenger."

"Galen?"

She nodded.

"How so?"

Bethany ran the cloth over his chest, raising chills in her wake. "It struck me as odd that such a high-ranking officer would bother ng an errand for a foot soldier."

cringed as he realized Galen would have given rank out amn . . .

"It is odd," he admitted. "For reasons that mystify me, too, the old buzzard took a liking to me. When I became ill, he actually returned from leave to check on me, and he was the only one I trusted to get word to you. I'm very lucky he agreed." There, all of it was honest truth.

She wrung out the cloth. "I don't find it odd that other people see the greatness in you that I do."

"You and Galen are rare. Most people have little use for me."

"That's their loss." She paused in bathing him as her wrist brushed against his hard cock. Her right brow shot north.

"I know your intent was to cool me down, *akribos*, but your tender touch has the opposite effect on my body."

She shook her head. "You're not well enough for *that*."

"I know, and it's not really why I came here today. I just needed to be with someone who cared about me for a little while."

Bethany's stomach lurched at the sincerity in his voice. "Your family loves you."

"No, they don't. I sometimes pretend they do, but I know better. You and Galen are all I have in this world. And you're the only one who has never hurt me."

Tears pricked her eyes at the raw pain he unknowingly revealed. "I would never hurt you."

"And that's why I came even though I'm fevered. For two weeks I've been with people tending me because they had to. It's very different than being with someone who tends you because you matter to them."

"Hector—"

He placed a finger to her lips to silence her. "I don't want your pity, Beth. I want the fire in you that warms me. I live for your insults and taunts."

"I don't mean them."

"I know. Believe me, I can tell the difference between your good-spirited teasing and the barbs that are meant to bleed me." He pulled her against him. "Just let me hold you for a little while and then I'll leave you in peace."

397

She set her cloth aside and closed her eyes, savoring the warmth of his fevered body against hers. Her Hector broke her heart and yet he held so much quiet strength that he never ceased to amaze her. She didn't understand the bits of his life he shared. How could his family be so reckless with their care of him?

His heart was so gentle and sweet. He tried so hard to please and take care of others. Why would anyone be unkind to him? But the scars on his body and the inner ones his words betrayed told her exactly how careless and heartless the people around him were.

And she hated them for that.

The mere fact he'd come to her when it was obvious he wasn't fit to travel, and no one had stopped him, said it all. How could they have left him alone in this condition? For even a heartbeat?

She ran her hand over the muscled ripples on his stomach. The heat from his skin was searing. "Have you eaten?"

"Mmm."

She frowned and smiled at his noncommittal answer. "Are you awake?"

"I'm awake," he mumbled.

Bethany toyed with the trail of hair that ran from his navel to his groin.

"If you keep doing that, I'm not going to rest."

She ran her hand down the length of him. He sucked his breath in sharply. "Sorry," she whispered.

"It's all good. Right now, you could set me on fire and I wouldn't complain."

Knowing she should be out looking for Apostolos, she placed a kiss to his hard abdomen. It was so strange how calm he made her. Whenever she was with him, nothing else mattered.

She remembered asking her mother once when she'd been a small child why her mother had chosen an Egyptian god to be her father.

"Gods are boring creatures, Bet. Most are nothing more than spoiled children with powers they never hesitate to use against those weaker. And while your father can be juvenile at times, there is a danger to him. He

understands his power and he's fierce with it. More than that, he doesn't prey on those weaker, he only attacks those who are stronger. That was what drew me to him and why I agreed to be the mother of his daughter. His strength, and the fact that never once did he use it against me. Your father is like having a lion for a pet. You know that it's a creature of utter and supreme violence whose mere nature and only talent is murder, and yet it lies down at your side and purrs for your touch alone. There's nothing more titillating.

"But more than that was how your father made me feel. He awoke something inside me that had never lived before. He breathed life into my soul, and I was a better person for having known him. It was why I wanted to have you as a piece of him that I could keep and love even though we weren't allowed to be together. And it's a decision I've never once regretted. Not even when your father almost destroyed our pantheon because Archon refused to allow him access to you. Your father doesn't give his devotion lightly or carelessly. When you are given a piece of someone like that, someone who doesn't naturally trust others, it's more special than when it comes from those who are capricious with their love. As with all things, the rarity makes it all the more precious."

Hector trusted no one. Not even his own family. And he'd never given his heart, body, or his love to any other woman.

Only her.

And while he was young in human years, he held a maturity and understanding far beyond that of any ancient.

Most of all, whenever she was with him, she felt beautiful and powerful. Things that were a given as a goddess and yet . . .

She'd never really felt them until he'd stumbled into her world and made her laugh.

That was why she loved him and why she risked the anger of Archon and the others to be with him.

He was worth it.

But in the back of her mind was the fear of how he'd react should he ever learn that she'd lied to him about her identity. He hated the gods and their interference in human lives.

Would he one day learn to hate her, too?

NOVEMBER 15, 9529 BC

Styxx couldn't breathe as Acheron was savagely beaten in the courtyard below. Writhing on his bed, he had a portion of his chlamys in his mouth to keep from crying out from the pain. He fisted his hands in his blanket and arched his back as more blows struck him.

It always hurt when Acheron was beaten, but now ...

Their close physical proximity made it hurt all the more. He'd forgotten that one small fact.

He couldn't imagine what his brother had done to deserve this.

Sure you know ...

His father had been embarrassed somehow. It was the only time they would be beaten like this. And for this long.

Damn it, Acheron.

It'd taken Styxx years to figure out how to stay out of the line of fire. Just as he'd finally learned how to avoid his father's wrath, enter his idiot brother.

At last, it stopped.

Panting and weak, Styxx lay on the bed, aching all over. But it was his back that really burned. Thank the gods he hadn't been in public when it started or he'd be on his way to the temple again to have demons driven out.

He'd barely stopped his hands from shaking when his father threw his door open. Styxx tried to sit up, but the pain was still too much for that.

"Are you ill?"

"Bad stomach," he lied, hoping that would explain the sweat on his brow and pallor of his skin. "Did you need something, Father?"

"I found the bastard out in the square this afternoon. Apparently, he screwed his guards for his freedom. They're to be executed in the morning for their treason, and he's been beaten. Should you see him outside of his room, I want you to have him arrested immediately."

Styxx sighed at the ridiculous fury his father held against Acheron. "Why bother, Father? Just give him his freedom."

"Is that really what *you* want?"

"Yes. Why not?"

"He bears *your* face. Anything he does, reflects on you."

"I'm not that concerned about it."

Styxx realized too late that that was the wrong thing to say. His father stormed across the floor and grabbed him up in an angry fist.

"You want them to mock you as a whore? What kind of king would you be? No one would respect you. They damn sure wouldn't listen to you."

And yet some of them had already paid to fuck him . . .

"You better learn to care, boy. In the minds of the people, that whore down the hall is you."

Don't do it . . . don't say it . . .

But he couldn't stop himself.

"Maybe you should have thought of that before you had your brother train him and sell him as a whore."

His father backhanded him so hard, it knocked him from the bed.

Gasping, Styxx hit the floor and tried to clear his rattled senses. Before he could, his father kicked him hard in the ribs several times.

"How dare you! I should have you whipped for such impudent defamation!"

Styxx rolled over and looked up at his father. But for once, he didn't taunt him.

"If you want to be known as a whore, maybe I should have put both of you in a stew. Is that what you want?"

Not really.

His father kicked him again. *You disgust me. You're not my son. You can't be.*

"Get up off that floor. You're a future king, not some groveling peasant."

His body screaming out in protest, Styxx pulled himself to his feet and faced his father.

The king raked him with a look of scorn. "I can't believe I was saddled with *you* as an heir."

"Then perhaps you should see about acquiring that new queen and fathering more sons."

"Why? So they can grow up and be as big a disappointment to me as you are?"

"What can I say? I always strive to be the best I can at everything I do."

"Then you succeed. For you are truly the greatest mistake of my life. I should have bashed your head in when you were born and saved myself the misery and cost of raising you."

Styxx didn't say another word as his father stormed from his room. Really, what was there to say after that?

Other than he wished his father had bashed his head in, too.

NOVEMBER 20, 9529 BC

Styxx felt the venom of his sister's glare like a sword slicing down his spine. Glancing away from Galen as they trained, he saw Ryssa in the stands with their father, who'd come in earlier to watch them spar and make complaints about the fact that Styxx wasn't training hard enough.

"How can you be a war hero against Atlantis? What? Did they send only their young daughters out to fight you? I swear, I've seen peasants fighting in the street who showed more energy and vigor than you do.

"If you're going to hit like a woman, we should put a peplos on you. At least then, your pretty face and body might stop them from killing

you . . . Or perhaps we should have you join the Sacred Band of Boeotia and have them assign you a boyfriend who'll be willing to protect your effeminate ass in battle.

"I'm embarrassed I sent you to war after seeing this pathetic display. I should have your armor dismantled or given over to someone who actually knows how to use it and not cause it shame!"

His complaints had been so fierce and foul, Galen had finally gone over to remind his father that barely three weeks ago Styxx had almost died, and that he'd only been out of his bed for a handful of days. The purpose of the exercise was to keep him from losing flexibility and rebuild his damaged muscles. Not prepare for war.

Only then had his father stopped insulting him and allowed them to train in peace.

Styxx frowned as he watched Ryssa screaming. He couldn't hear their rapid-fire conversation, but given the angry way she gestured toward him, he was sure it was about him and Acheron.

Galen lowered his sword as he realized Styxx was distracted. "For once, I'm glad I'm not king."

Styxx laughed. "You've no idea. I've been on the receiving end of her tongue-lashings enough to know it's highly unpleasant. I think he's the one who could use armor."

"Are you the cause of her vexation?"

"Who knows. Could be the wrong material was delivered to her for a dress."

Galen chuckled then jerked his chin back toward them. "Your father must have placated her. She seems pleased enough now."

"It won't last. It never does." He took the wineskin from Galen's hand and slaked his thirst.

"Styxx!"

He winced at his father's bellow. What had the bitch blamed him for now? Returning the wineskin to Galen, he headed over.

"Father?"

"Take my advice . . . should you ever have a daughter, marry her off the day she's born."

"I take it Ryssa's visit wasn't pleasant."

"The bastard's being freed and moved to his own room. Just thought you'd want to know."

The bastard. Acheron. Every time his father referred to his brother like that, it was a slap in his face, too, and betrayed what his father truly thought of them both.

Styxx was glad that Ryssa had succeeded where he'd failed, but he knew better than to let his father know his real thoughts.

"I don't see how that affects me."

"It shouldn't, but I wanted you to know about it." And with that, his father left him.

At least his brother would finally have his place again in their home. There was a time when he would have rejoiced over that news.

Now . . .

All Styxx felt was sadness. Not because Acheron would have his own room, but because he no longer had a brother. He just had another person in the palace who wished him dead and burned.

No, he thought bitterly. Acheron wished him raped first.

DECEMBER 5, 9529 BC

Bethany smiled at the sensation of Hector curled against her back as he slept with his arms wrapped around her body. Her head rested on his hard biceps, while his face was buried so deep in her hair that she could feel his breath against her neck. He'd made love to her for so many hours that she still wasn't sure if she'd be able to move later.

Not that she ever wanted to leave this bed, or him again.

In all her life, nothing had made her happier than her mortal. And while the war with the Greeks had ended before they'd been able to spear Prince Styxx's head to the wall, she honestly didn't mind. She wouldn't take anything, even the prince's throat, in exchange for the last few months of having Hector with her in peace.

Nothing compared to these lazy afternoons of being cocooned by his long, hard body. Of tasting his lips that drove away all thoughts except how much she adored him. How much she wanted to have his child . . .

Don't go there.

She couldn't help it. The more she was with Hector, the more she wanted to have him permanently in her life. Worse, she'd even started dreaming of a future with just the three of them as a family.

How stupid was that? She was a goddess, not some farmer's daughter.

And still those dreams tortured her.

Dynatos started whining and scratching at the door. He'd been so quiet for the last few hours that she'd forgotten he was in the room with them.

The instant she moved to tend him, Hector came awake with a start.

"Beth?" He breathed her name like a beloved prayer.

"Dyna wants out."

He made a disagreeable noise in her hair before he pulled back. "I'll put him outside. You stay in the bed where it's warm."

She smiled at his consideration. "You sure?"

He grumbled under his breath as he rolled away from her. "Yes."

Laughing at his subdued irritation, she pulled the covers up higher. "You don't sound it."

"Keep my place warm and I promise I won't murder your dog for disturbing us."

She listened as he let the dog out then stoked the fire before he returned to bed. He piled the pillows up and reclined against them. "I'm sorry I fell asleep. I hate to squander even one heartbeat of my precious time with you."

She draped herself over his chest so that she could rub her hand against the sharp ridges of his abdomen. The scent of his skin made her crave him inside her again as she dipped her hand lower to stroke him. "I don't mind." Honestly, she adored the fact that he trusted her so completely. She knew how rarely he slept.

He brushed his hand through her hair as he sighed contentedly. "It's late. Well past dark . . . can you stay the night with me?"

Bethany hesitated. They rarely spent nights together. Although here lately, they'd done so a lot more often as their days were so much shorter.

Still, she was supposed to be searching for Apostolos. "How late?"

"I'm not sure, but the moon was rather high."

"Will you not be in trouble with you father?"

He didn't hesitate with his answer. "I would brave a thousand angry fathers for more time with you, my Beth."

"Then I shall stay."

Styxx smiled in relief. He never liked for her to travel late on her own. Not even with Dynatos as her guardian. He didn't trust the world to leave his Beth unharmed.

Fingering her cheek, he savored the sensation of her breath falling against his skin. This was what he'd craved most while he'd been at war. What he'd tried his best to hold onto. Not just the ability to make love to her, but the closeness he felt whenever her limbs were tangled with his. The feeling that they, together, formed a single, whole heart. It was the emotional intimacy that meant as much, if not more, than the physical. The fact that he could talk to her about anything and not have her judge him.

That she, alone, loved him and welcomed him to her life.

She pulled back from him and unhooked the necklace her father had given to her.

"What are you doing?"

She coiled it around his wrist again. "I want you to wear this."

"Beth—"

She stopped his protest with a kiss. "I have a bad feeling, Hector.

And I don't know why. I have Dynatos to protect me. I don't want to leave you with nothing. So, please . . . Take it. Let it protect you when I'm not around."

"Only to make you happy, my lady, and because it reminds me of you when you're not with me." Not to mention, he couldn't count how many times he'd started to stroke it out of habit, and had felt crushed that it was gone. During his time at war, it'd been the only thing that had comforted him. No matter how bad things had been, he'd look at her necklace and feel better instantly. It'd been in his life so long that it had become a part of him.

Like her.

She smiled. "I do love you."

"And I, you." He kissed her gently and inhaled the sweet scent of her skin. "Marry me, Beth," he breathed before he could stop himself.

She pulled back with a sharp frown. "Hector—"

"I won't stifle you. I swear it. But I need you, Bethany. When you're not with me, I exist as a shade. A mere shadow of a human."

"You know I can't, Hector."

Styxx ground his teeth. Like her, he had a bad feeling he couldn't shake, and it wasn't just because his sister was about to be tied to a god who refused to leave him in peace. It was a sense that Bethany wouldn't be with him much longer. That something was going to divide them.

He just didn't know what.

"I wish you didn't have to leave," he whispered. She'd told him earlier that she'd be traveling with her father for the next few weeks. "I shall miss you terribly."

"Not nearly as much as I'll miss you. But I will be back as soon as I can."

Styxx sighed as she dropped her hand to cup him gently in her palm. As bad as he hated whenever he had to leave her, it was so much more painful for her to leave him. At least, when he left, he knew he'd be back, no matter what.

With her . . .

He could only hope that she'd return. "I will count the heart-beats until I see you again."

"And I will make your count as brief as possible. I promise."

Closing his eyes, he savored her fingers stroking him as much as he did those precious words. At least he had her tonight. He wouldn't think about the morrow. It would come.

His only hope was that it would treat him much better than the past had.

And that Bethany kept her promise to return to him.

DECEMBER 9, 9529 BC

Styxx stood to his father's right-hand side as they waited for another royal entourage that had been sighted heading for the palace. Just what Styxx had been dying for, more witnesses to Ryssa's desecration in two days.

During the last week dignitaries had been arriving from all over Greece, and as prince, Styxx was expected to meet every one. And he looked forward to these wonderful moments as much as he did Apollo's midnight visits to his bed.

Meanwhile, his father's private words and insults rang in his ears, making these moments all the "sweeter." The more his father saw Acheron, the more he detested Styxx. And there was nothing he could do nowadays to placate the man. His father was absolutely determined to hate him.

Truthfully, he no longer cared. He merely treated these days as he'd done the endless months of war. He buried his emotions deep and just got through them as mechanically as possible, on the promise that he'd soon be with Bethany, and she would be able to erase the misery and replace it with emotions worth feeling.

But as Styxx saw the banners of their latest guests, he couldn't help feeling a little better.

King Kreon of Halicarnassus. Styxx hadn't seen him since he'd fought to repel the Atlanteans from Kreon's kingdom. The man had been kind to him and his soldiers, and he'd appreciated it.

As soon as the retinue stopped, the king of Halicarnassus and his court left their chariots and walked up the palace steps.

Kreon gave a curt nod to his father then turned to Styxx and smiled wide before he pulled him into a fatherly embrace. "It's so good to see you again, Highness. And I swear by Zeus, I think you've grown even taller. You're looking very fit, indeed."

Styxx smiled. "And you, Majesty. You had a safe journey, I trust?"

"Could have been better. Could have been worse. Remind me in a bit, I have brought gifts for you, young prince."

Styxx glanced to his father who wasn't pleased in the least. "I appreciate it, Sire. Thank you."

Kreon clapped him on the back. Then he turned toward his father. "Your son is the only thing of yours I envy, Xerxes. I hope to the gods you appreciate the gift you've been given."

You don't have to live with the little prick and his mouth. Or put up with his lazy sullenness.

Styxx stiffened at his father's silent insults.

As the kings ascended the stairs, he followed them in, but hung back. The palace was far too crowded now. The voices were more than he could bear and he had no way to blot them out.

Intent on his room, he didn't pay attention to anyone until he ran into his sister.

Literally.

Ryssa glared her hatred. *You did that on purpose, didn't you, you giant oaf!*

Styxx grimaced at the pain her angry thoughts added to his pounding head. "It was an accident, sweet sister. Forgive me."

"Acheron's right. You are an asshole."

He sighed. "It does my heart good to know the fond discussions my siblings hold of me in my absence."

"You think this is funny, don't you?"

"There are very few things in life I find amusing, Ryssa. And I can assure you, none of the few have anything to do with my family."

She raked him with a lethal sneer. "You should be afraid, Styxx."

Oh, this had to be good. "Of?"

"If I please Apollo, I will have much more power than you do. And since he's the god of plagues, I could make your life miserable. I will have the ability to hurt you in places you won't forget."

Styxx laughed bitterly at her empty threat. He should be so lucky, but Apollo wasn't about to break his current toy. The gods knew, Styxx had been trying to repel the god for months now.

But that wasn't what really bothered him about her words. It was Ryssa's blind stupidity that offended him most. "Dearest sister, you've held that power over me all my life and have never once hesitated to use it."

DECEMBER 11, 9529 BC

His stomach churning, Styxx left Apollo's temple while his sister was being offered to the god. In spite of what Ryssa thought, he couldn't bear to see it. Not that the bitch didn't deserve this fate and more.

But what truly sickened him were the smirks and amused glances Apollo kept passing to him during the ceremony. The god thought it was funny that everyone made such a big deal of tying Ryssa to him when it wasn't the princess the Olympian really craved.

Styxx flinched as he saw Apollo in his mind, grabbing him right before it'd started and shoving him back against the temple wall in the secluded private area.

"I may be with your sister tonight, prince, but it's your lips I'll be thinking of when I kiss her. *Your* hard, muscled body I'll be hungering for . . . "

The only thing that had saved Styxx from having a worse memory had been his father's impeccable timing. He could still see his father's bemused stare as he'd stumbled upon them and dragged his gaze from Apollo, who had both his hands fisted in Styxx's gold-trimmed, white chiton as he held him pinned to the wall with his leg between Styxx's thighs and his head bent low to whisper in Styxx's ear. Styxx, who'd been cringing at Apollo's close proximity, had his head turned away from the god and his hands splayed on the wall beside him.

With a low, private laugh in Styxx's ear, Apollo had covertly rubbed himself against Styxx's hip so that he could feel how hard the god was for him. Then he released Styxx and walked off as if nothing had happened.

Pushing himself away from the wall, Styxx had met his father's angry glare.

"Did you offend Apollo, boy?"

No, the bastard offends me.

"Nay, Father." The steadiness of his voice had surprised him.

His eyes darkening with rage, the king had closed the distance between them so he could snarl privately at Styxx. "You do anything to screw this up for me, and I swear I will see you disowned and on the street with your whore brother. You think you know what tragedy is, boy . . . you can't imagine. And don't you believe for one minute that Kreon or any of the other kings would welcome you to their kingdoms. If I threw you out, none of them would dare speak to you. Ever."

His father's jealousy had stunned him. Not that it mattered. He really couldn't care less at this point. "I promise you, Father, Apollo isn't angry at me."

Then the part of him that wanted to lash out at his father and hurt him couldn't resist adding, "He was embracing me. *That's* what you saw. He was merely telling me how much he looked forward to spending more time with me in the future."

"Good. See to it, it stays that way."

Tears had pricked the backs of his eyes as his father had stormed off. But what hurt most wasn't that his father was selling his son and daughter to Apollo for the benefit of his people or for peace.

He was doing it for bragging rights with the other kings so that he could claim Didymos was the city-state most favored by the gods.

Unable to deal with it anymore, Styxx headed for the small corner apothecary that specialized in herbs and medicines from Atlantis. Even though he hated what the herbs did to him and had sworn he wouldn't touch them again, he needed something to get everything out of his head. Just for a little while.

I can't believe I killed my uncle for this shit.

But then maybe that was why the gods had done this to him. It was recompense for his actions. All the things he'd killed Estes to prevent had happened anyway, only now they were so much worse. Ryssa was still being whored, and instead of Styxx being held and raped for one week out of the year, he was now at Apollo's mercy anytime the god had a hard-on.

Only Acheron's situation had improved.

His head throbbing, Styxx walked through the marketplace, toward the shop.

Right now, all he really wanted was to be with Bethany. She would ease the pain in his heart and make him forget for a few minutes how much he hated every part of royal life. But she wouldn't be back for a week. Her family was traveling and she'd left him bereft without the brightness of her smile. Honestly, he couldn't stand not being with her.

But at least she took Dynatos with her everywhere she went. She kept the massive dog close to her so that Styxx could breathe, knowing Dynatos would always protect her.

"Please, sir . . . can I not buy half the loaf?"

Styxx paused at a girl's voice as he passed the baker's stand.

"Get on with you! I don't want a beggar here. Coin or nothing. I don't sell half loaves."

"But I don't have enough. Please. It's for my mother. She's sick and starving . . ."

The lecherous look on the man's face as he swept the young teen's body made Styxx's stomach turn. "If you want to pay with something other than coin, we might have a deal, girl."

Horrified, she stumbled away and started to turn then she closed her eyes.

Rage darkened Styxx's gaze as he saw what she was about to do to feed her family.

As she stepped back toward the stand, Styxx cut her off. He knelt on one knee in front of her so that she could look him in the eyes. "Get what you need and I will pay for it."

The suspicion in those young, brown eyes shredded his heart. "And what do you want me to pay *you* with, my lord?"

Those words and what she was really asking thoroughly pissed him off at the Fates who would do this to a child so young. "Nothing. I swear." He handed her a basket. "Get whatever you need to feed your family."

When she started away, Styxx caught a flash of gold around her neck. Stopping her, he pulled a tattered string to find a large gold ring tied at the end of it.

A soldier's ring.

"Please don't take that," she whispered. "It's all I have left of my father."

Recognition slammed into his gut like a fist as he saw the markings he knew as well as his own. They had adorned a shield that had stood at his side and back in many a battle. "Gaius? Son of Philoctes? Was he your father?"

"Did you know him, my lord?"

Anger and grief almost brought tears to his eyes as he remembered Gaius and his kindness with the cloak. "You must be Helen."

A bright smile finally made her appear to be the young girl she was. "You did know my father!"

Styxx returned her smile. "Yes, I did. He told me much of you and your brothers, and baby sister, and mother, and how much he loved all of you." He placed the ring in her hand. "And he was a great friend to me. Now gather your items, Helen. Whatever you need or want. Have no fear of the cost. Now or later."

Tears filled her eyes. "Thank you, my lord."

He kissed her on the brow then stood while she quickly shopped.

The baker scoffed as he watched her fill her basket. "She's not that pretty, my lord."

Lowering his cowl to expose the gold laurel crown he seldom wore, Styxx arched a regal brow at the man.

The baker fell to his knees. "Highness . . . forgive me. I didn't recognize you without your guard."

Helen froze then, eyes wide, gaped. "You're Prince Styxx?"

"I am."

She bowed then curtsied then bowed again.

Styxx laughed. "You don't have to bow to me, Helen. As I said, your father was a good friend to me, and I consider you and yours family."

That only confused her more.

Closing the distance between them, he brushed the dark hair back from her cheek. "Think of me like your cousin."

"I don't like my cousin very much. He smells, and insults me."

"Then think of me as the cousin who doesn't smell or insult you."

Nodding, she quickly finished her shopping.

Styxx passed an irritated look at the baker. "Have her bill sent to my scribe at the palace, and in the future, anything she or her mother needs or wants is to be billed to me. Understood?"

"Yes, Your Highness."

Taking the basket from her, Styxx held his hand out for her. She bit her lip and hesitated. Then she wiped it off on her himation, and placed it into his.

As she led him to her home, he noticed the way she slowed down as they passed a fruit stand.

"Would you like some apples or figs?"

414

She bit her lip again. "May I?"

Styxx released her hand. "Absolutely."

Letting out a cry of joy, she quickly grabbed a single apple and cradled it with a smile. "Thank you, Highness."

He cupped her precious, innocent head to his side. She didn't even think to ask for more. He bought a sack of them for her then they continued on their way.

As soon as they neared her small, dilapidated home, her brothers, who'd been playing in the street, came running up.

"Did you get some bread?" the younger brother asked.

The older one eyed Styxx suspiciously. "Why are you here with my sister, my lord?"

"He's the prince," Helen whispered loudly. "Show him respect, Iason."

Styxx went down on one knee so that he was closer to Iason's height. At nine, the boy showed promise of equaling his father's massive size one day. "Don't take your brother to task for seeking to protect you, Helen. It's his job and your father would be proud to see it." He held an apple out to Iason. "Gaius was a friend and I'm here to see how your mother does."

"She's very sick, Highness." Philoctes eyed the bread with a hunger that reminded Styxx of Acheron when they'd been boys.

He handed a loaf to him.

At seven, he was half the size of Iason. "Thank you!" He ran off with it.

Helen opened the door to their meager home. Styxx followed her inside with Iason right behind him. Though sparse, the interior was bright and clean. But there was no food and only a handful of spices strung up on one wall to keep.

Styxx set the basket and apples on the table in the center of the room. Helen took one loaf and led him to the room where her mother lay on a small bed with a toddler by her side.

Pale and sweating, Danae was trying to play with the little girl next to her, but it was obvious she should be resting and not tending children. "Did you get . . . " Her hoarse voice trailed off as she took in Styxx's ornate festival clothes. She tried to push herself up.

"Please don't," he said gently. "I'm not here to cause you any stress, good Danae. I happened upon Helen in the market and wanted to see how Gaius's family fared."

She coughed for several minutes.

Styxx helped her up and held her until the spell passed. Her fever radiated from her small, frail body. "Have you seen the physician?"

"No, my lord." Her breathing was so labored that it wrung his heart. "We have no coin for such."

"I'm confused. Is Gaius's pension not enough?"

Danae frowned. "His pension was suspended, my lord. Our money comes from what Helen and I earn."

"Suspended? I don't understand. He died at war."

Her eyes filled with tears. "He died in a brothel. Murdered in the arms of a whore. The king's man announced it to everyone when I went to apply for his pension. As such, we don't qualify."

The cruelty of those words and actions burned him with fury. "I was there when it happened, my lady. Your husband was one of my finest soldiers and he was not with a whore." Probably not true, but his widow didn't need to know anything other than the one fact that was undeniable. "Gaius loved you and your children to distraction. It's how I know all your names and ages . . . even little Elpis here who is named for your mother. Gaius died at my back and after fighting many battles for me and Didymos. Your husband was a great hero, and I will personally see his pension reinstated and make sure you receive every bonus due him and you."

"Who are you, my lord?"

"He's Prince Styxx, Mama," Helen whispered.

Her eyes widened. "Highness . . . " She tried to get up, but Styxx held her back against the bed.

"Shh . . . don't stress yourself." He glanced to Helen. "Do you have anyone who can help you until your mother is better?"

"I help her, Highness."

"And you've done an admirable job. But you're just a girl and you should be playing, not having so much placed on your young shoulders." He cupped Danae's head and offered her a smile. "I will not see Gaius's family treated this way." Rising, he scooped her up into his arms.

"Highness?" she gasped.

He cradled her against his chest. "Helen, can you carry your sister and fetch your brothers?"

"Yes, Highness."

"Good. Follow me."

He's going to see us punished . . .

Her fearful thoughts struck him like a blow. "Danae, please believe me. On my honor and crown, I will not harm you, and I will allow no one else to do so either."

She relaxed, but still suspicion haunted her dark eyes. She made no other protest as he carried her through town and to the military barracks.

"Highness?" Galen froze in the hallway as he saw them entering the building.

"It's Danae, Gaius's wife, and their children. I'm bringing them to Gaius's quarters to be looked after until she heals."

Galen stepped to and took Elpis from her sister's arms to carry her. "What do you need me to do?"

"Send for my personal physician to tend her. I'll have a retinue of ladies sent to help care for her and the children."

Danae gaped at them as Styxx laid her down on the bed and she noted the size and splendor of Gaius's military quarters. He took the toddler while Galen set about starting a fire for her and fetching water.

Eyes even wider than before, Danae opened and closed her mouth as her emotions overwhelmed her.

The boys ran around, yelling and celebrating while distressing their poor mother. Until they found their father's spear.

Styxx caught it right as they pulled it off the wall. He gently took it from Iason's hands. "Let's wait until you're both older to bring out the weaponry." As he started to put it away, something warm spread across his side. Frowning, he looked down at the toddler he held in one arm. She smiled up at him and slapped a wet hand to his cheek. "Um, Galen . . . This one is leaking."

Galen laughed.

Danae cried out in horror. "I am so sorry, Highness! I—"

"Bah," Galen scoffed, interrupting her. "Not the worst thing that boy's had on him, is it, young prince?"

"Definitely not. But . . . " He passed Elpis back to Galen. "I fear I have no experience with this realm of domesticity. I've never even seen a pana, never mind tried to apply one to such a small person."

The girl squealed as she buried her hands in Galen's beard and kicked her legs happily.

Galen's grin widened. "I, on the other hand, have more than my share of experience with applying them, and will take care of it for you."

Styxx returned the spear to the wall and saw that poor Danae was near dead with horror over her children's actions. "Madam, really. It's fine. I was a boy, too, and while my parents and nurses tried, I fear I failed at home-training and manners with honors."

Tears filled her eyes. "Thank you, Highness, but I doubt you were ever so ill-behaved."

"Believe me, I was. I still have the thrash marks to prove it." Styxx turned to the boys. He needed to get them outside so their mother could rest. "Guess what we have here for you two?"

"What?" they asked in unison.

"A giant arena for you to run around and play in." He took them outside while Helen helped her mother.

The instant they saw the size of it, the boys took off and started a game of chase. Styxx paused as he watched them play and wrestle with wild abandon. But it wasn't two dark-haired brothers he saw. It was him and Acheron.

Even now, he could remember the sound of their matching

laughter as they dodged and ran about with careless abandon. See Acheron tackling him to the ground.

I'll pin you first!

Hah! You hit like Ryssa . . .

Brothers . . . Forever and always.

Grief tightened his throat. He'd give anything if Acheron would just look at him with something other than contempt and hatred. But who could blame him?

He hated Acheron, too.

Nothing would ever reunite them. What had been severed by their own harsh words and the actions of others couldn't be mended. It was too late for that. Sighing with regret, he returned to find Danae asleep and Helen on the floor, playing tickles with Elpis. He went to Galen, whose eyes showed he was thinking of his own daughter and grandchildren. "I put the boys in the yard."

"Wise choice, my lord."

"I thought so." He pulled Galen out into the hallway. "Did you know they'd denied pensions to those killed during the ambush?"

Galen's jaw dropped. "What?"

Styxx nodded. "It's why I brought them here. They have no money."

"I had no idea, my lord. You know I didn't."

Styxx ground his teeth. "Neither did I . . . I should have checked on it. But I assumed—"

"You can't blame yourself."

Yet, he did. He'd been their commander. It was his job to see to it that his men and their families were cared for. "Will you do the accounting? I want to make sure everyone gets what is owed them."

"Absolutely, Highness. I'll see to it, personally."

"Thank you." Styxx started to head back toward the palace, but Galen pulled him to a stop. The old man's gaze dropped to where Elpis had soiled Styxx's chiton. Before he realized what Galen intended, the old man pulled him into his arms and held him tight.

After a moment, Galen stepped back and kissed each of Styxx's cheeks. He cupped Styxx's face in his rough, calloused palms and gave him a hard stare. Then he patted Styxx's cheek with enough force that it almost felt like a slap.

But he knew better.

"I love you, too, Galen."

"Love? Bah! You sound like an old woman. Get out of here, boy, before I take offense to you . . . and my sword."

Styxx laughed at him. "Yes, sir."

I do love you, son. More than you'll ever know.

Styxx smiled at Galen's thoughts that warmed his heart and then left him to watch over the women until he could send help down from the palace.

As he started past the larder, Styxx backtracked and headed inside to pull together a platter of fruit. He carried it out to the arena where the two boys were still trying to kill each other in the unique way loving brothers did.

"Hey, boys?"

They turned toward him. He held the platter up for them to see then set it down on a small wooden bench. Whooping, they came running.

Laughing at the way they descended like starving locusts, Styxx grabbed an apple for himself and left them to their snack. He bit into it and held it with his teeth before he pulled his cowl up to conceal his identity as he normally did whenever he went about on his own.

He took the apple in his hand and chewed his bite, but his smile faded as he left the barracks and headed "home."

Bethany scowled as she followed the prince up the hill, toward the Didymosian palace. Archon had sent her here today to oversee Apollo's cooperation with their plans. But from the moment the Greek god had thrown the prince against the temple wall and she'd seen the abject shame and turmoil in those tormented blue eyes, she'd been haunted by them.

Worse was the guilt she felt for having told Apollo he could have a man who obviously wanted nothing to do with him. Guilt that had tripled when she'd heard the king's cold words to his son, and Styxx's stoic acceptance of the fact his father was a selfish asshole who held little regard for him.

She would never forget the sympathetic misery on his face as he watched his sister being offered to the god. Misery so potent that she'd feared he would be ill when he finally snuck out the back so as not to witness any more of it.

That degree of compassion had surprised her.

Yet what had truly thrown her were his actions toward the family of his dead soldier. What prince would deign to carry a sick commoner through town?

And every time she thought about the little girl wetting him, she smiled. Not because it'd been humiliating for the prince, but because of his kindness.

No, not kindness.

His humanity.

Not to mention Galen's informality and laxness toward Styxx that had spoken volumes about the prince's true nature. As did Styxx's concern for the fact that his men, both those living and dead, hadn't been treated justly. And among those men he worried over was the one who held her heart.

I have so misjudged you . . .

But the most painful of all was the fact that she'd unknowingly wronged Styxx. That she'd offered him up to Apollo with no regard of how it would affect him.

I am such a bitch . . .

Wanting to make amends, she followed him and noted the way his mood darkened with every step that took him closer to home. By the time he walked through the palace doors, the bitter agony in those pale eyes was so thick it made her breath catch.

Inside the palace walls, he closed his eyes and she watched as his entire demeanor changed. He buried his emotions and held his head high. He lowered the cowl and the raw, masculine beauty of him struck her even more than it had earlier.

Gone was the gentle, sweet man who'd taken a platter of fruit to two boys while they played, and the one who'd said nothing unkind as a toddler soiled his expensive clothes. Now, he was again the arrogant prince with a ramrod-stiff spine and a guarded gaze.

This was the man she'd seen at war.

His features were absolutely perfect. Flawless. Cold and unfeeling. The cowl had tousled his blond waves around his gold crown and face, and given him an adorable boyish appearance to a presence that was overwhelmingly fierce warrior and regal prince.

And that body . . .

Even though Hector owned her heart, she had to give the prince credit. He was a fine manly specimen as he went down a back hallway and knocked on a door.

A young maid opened it. Her face lightened expectantly as if she was used to the prince seeking her out. "Yes, Highness? Can I do something for you?" But her expression said she'd rather be doing something *to* him.

He stepped back as if the woman's interest made him uncomfortable. "I need you to assign three women to the barracks. There's an ill woman there with her children and she needs help until she's recovered."

The girl screwed her face up in distaste. "Princess Ryssa will not approve of us doing such and she's the only one with authority to reassign our duties."

Her refusal caught Bethany off guard.

But apparently the prince was used to it. "Is there not one decent woman among your company who will help a hero's widow?"

Hestia boldly stepped forward and placed her hand on his chest. "Depends on the recompense, Your Highness."

His expression turned ice-cold. Without a word, he spun about and headed down another hallway. Then he paused as if thinking better of his errand.

He pulled his cowl up and left the palace to head back into town.

Even more curious now, Bethany followed him to a small house not far from the market. He knocked on the door and after a few minutes, a large burly man answered.

"Darian," Styxx said in a friendly tone as he extended his hand to the peasant.

Smiling, Darian shook the prince's arm. "Your Highness . . . are we being summoned to war again?"

"No. With luck, all that's behind us. But . . . I have a favor to ask."

"For you, my lord, anything. You know that." He opened his door wider. "Would you like to come in?"

She expected Styxx to decline, instead he nodded.

"I'd be honored to meet your family."

Keeping herself invisible, she followed the men into the tiny, yet cozy home that was filled with women and children.

"Gia! Meet Prince Styxx, the man who thrice saved me from an enemy sword."

Styxx bristled at his compliment. "I'm not sure about that, but it's a pleasure to meet you, Gia. Darian told me often how beautiful you were, and I can see that he didn't exaggerate in the least."

She was completely speechless and flustered before her prince.

"Children!" Darian called. "Come and meet the man who carried your father and placed me on his regal horse to ride to safety while he held back an entire army to save me."

Styxx held his hands up. "I definitely did *not* do that."

"He might not have held back an entire army, but he did carry me to safety and put me on his horse while he stayed behind to fight."

"I might have done that." Styxx grinned sheepishly. "But only because I knew how much he wanted to return to all of you."

Darian clapped him on the back. "So Highness, to what do we owe this honor?"

"Gaius's family is in need."

The humor fled Darian's face. "How so?"

423

"His widow is very ill. I took her and his children to Galen and I remembered that you mentioned you had a number of sisters who were always looking for work as companions and nurses."

"I'll send them over immediately."

"Thank you." Styxx pulled out his purse.

"Nay, no money is necessary. We take care of our own."

Styxx pressed the purse into his hand. "Yes, we do, Darian. Please take it for their services."

Darian hesitated before he nodded. "Thank you, Highness."

"Thank you, brother." Styxx embraced him. "They're at the barracks, in Gaius's quarters. And I would love to stay, but I'd best be getting back for my sister's banquet so as not to insult her or my father with my absence."

"Give our best to the princess and king."

"I will, and if you need anything at all, let me or Galen know immediately."

Darian started to salute then pulled Styxx into a brotherly embrace.

Styxx returned it before he made his way through the door. As he started to leave, Darian's youngest daughter, who appeared around the age of six, came running up to Styxx. "Highness?"

Styxx knelt down by her side. "Yes, Eleni?"

Bethany was as shocked that he knew her name as she'd been when he'd greeted Gaius's children by name.

"Thank you for bringing my daddy home." She fell against him and hugged him tightly.

Styxx returned the hug and kissed her lightly on the head. "My pleasure, *akribos*."

A chill went down Bethany's spine at the way he said that. She knew that tender tone of voice.

Those words.

No . . .

It's not possible.

Her heart pounding in fear, she followed him after he left and went to buy herbs she was more than familiar with. Why would

424

a prince want Nyx Root and Onero? Either was strong ... together they could be lethal.

Styxx didn't speak to anyone else as he returned to the palace, where servants were now rushing about in expectation of guests. None of them paid any attention to the prince as he made his way up the stairs and to his room.

He put the herbs in a small chest by his bed then pulled off his crown and placed it on top of them. He unpinned his chlamys and moved to get a fresh chiton.

Bethany didn't think anything about it until he took off the one he was wearing and confirmed her worst suspicions.

Styxx *was* Hector.

Stunned, she covered her mouth as her gaze took in the sight of his naked body. A body she knew every contour to. Every single horrifying scar that marred what should have been a flawless royal physique.

Her breathing ragged, she couldn't avert her gaze. Later, she would be angry over the lies he'd told her, but right now, she wanted to cry as she saw exactly how much damage they'd done to him. It was one thing to feel those scars. Another to see them and to know how badly he'd been abused and hurt by others.

And when he took off his gold cuff and exposed her cheap-looking charm that was still wound about his wrist from the last time she'd seen him, tears welled in her eyes. Not just because it was right where she'd put it, but because he lifted it to his lips and placed a tender kiss to her emblem.

His eyes sad and aching, he caressed her necklace with loving fingers. "I miss you, Beth," he whispered. "Please come back to me soon."

She started to materialize in his room then caught herself. *What are you doing?*

He'd be furious to find out that she'd ...

Lied?

He'd lied to her, too. There was no way he could hold *that* against her.

She moved to confront him then paused as he turned around and she saw Apollo's mark on his back. Not just on it . . . *across* its entirety.

Her stomach pitched over.

Gods didn't lightly or arbitrarily mark humans. For them to place their symbol on a human body was a sign of fierce ownership. For one god to touch a human who'd been marked by another was an act of war.

And Apollo had quite visibly claimed Styxx.

The Atlantean gods would kill her if she breached this temporary alliance or threatened their pact with Apollo. The Olympian would have every right to call down all of his fellow Greek gods to attack her and Styxx both.

And Styxx would be the one who suffered most for allowing another god to touch him after he'd been claimed by Apollo. The others wouldn't care that he hadn't known her true identity. It was a breach of faith . . .

What have I done?

But then she knew. She'd callously played with a human life without taking into account what it would mean for the pawn. All the while not knowing, or even considering for one moment, that the pawn she used was her heart.

She winced as memories burned through her. How many times had she taken aim for Styxx's head in battle? No wonder she hadn't been able to kill him. Her own amulet had deflected her blows. Those primal powers she'd felt had been her father's . . . the very powers she'd called on to keep Styxx/Hector safe.

He froze and cocked his head. "Bethany?"

The familiar sound of her name on his lips tore through her.

Styxx raked his hand through his hair. "I swear I'm going insane. I feel her even when I know she's not with me."

I'm here, love.

She held her hand out to touch his shoulder, but the sight of Apollo's sun emblem slapped her hard.

War.

426

Over a meager human ...

How could she do that to her people for a human male who would be dead in a few short years? One life wasn't worth thousands of others.

Not even his.

She'd known when she started this game that it couldn't last. That eventually she'd have to walk away and leave him to his mortal life.

Now was the time to end it. Before either of them went further into a relationship that was doomed and damned.

Besides, their time for finding Apollymi's son was drawing critically short. She had to focus on that and help the others while Apollo prepared to replace the Greek pantheon.

Her eyes teared as she took her last look at him. This time, she would leave and not look back.

"Farewell, Hector," she breathed then she returned to Katateros where she belonged.

DECEMBER 13, 9529 BC

Styxx sat on the throne beside his father, wanting to beat the man senseless. For the last two days his back had throbbed unmercifully and all because Acheron had dared walk Ryssa to Apollo's temple at her behest for her binding ceremony. She was always so concerned about her precious Acheron, and yet she continually put the fool in harm's way.

And she dared to call *him* selfish.

Stupid *kuna*. She was the one who didn't care about anyone except herself.

Grinding his teeth, Styxx grimaced as more pain cut through him and he wiped at the clammy sweat on his forehead. He was just about to piss his father off by asking to be excused when the doors opened, and guards dragged Acheron into the room with them.

Styxx bit back a curse as they forced Acheron to his knees in front of their father's throne.

What have you done now?

Got caught picking your nose?

"As per your instructions, he hasn't left his room, Sire," the guard on the left of Acheron said firmly. "We've made sure of it."

Acheron cast a murderous glare at Styxx as if he was to blame for his sudden appearance here.

Don't cut those silver eyes at me. Brother, I'd set you free in a heartbeat if I could.

The king curled his lip at Acheron. "You weren't in the square earlier, *teritos*?"

Styxx's jaw ticced at the insult that meant "slug."

To his brother's credit, Acheron gave his father a fearless, malevolent glare. It was a look he knew well as one he'd been known to give their father whenever he felt particularly suicidal.

No wonder Father backhands me.

It took everything he had not to applaud Acheron.

"Why would I have been in the square, Father?" Acheron asked boldly.

Styxx cringed at what he knew would follow such a comment. It was the same sentence he always received for his own verbal stupidity.

"Thirty-six lashes for his insolence then return him to his room."

Khalash! The king was nothing if not consistent.

Acheron closed his eyes as the guards grabbed him by the hair and hauled him through a set of double doors that opened out into a small courtyard.

Thanks, brother. Styxx almost gasped out loud as the first lash went down Acheron's back. More sweat beaded on his forehead and he forced himself to hold still and not react.

Think of Bethany. Think of . . .

Another vicious lash tore through him.

Styxx gripped the arms of his throne until his knuckles protruded. His stomach heaved.

"Are you all right, Highness?"

He glared at the advisor who'd spoken. *Damn you, Xoran, for noticing.* He inclined his head to him. "It's a war wound acting up."

For once, his father actually looked concerned. "Do you need a moment?"

I need you to stop beating the hell out of my twin, you idiot.

Styxx's breathing came in short gasps as he struggled for composure. Last thing he needed was any more pain added to what he already had. "I would deeply appreciate one. But it's not necessary."

His father lifted his hand to signal for the next case then paused. "Let's continue this after lunch."

Thank the gods.

Wiping at his forehead, Styxx narrowed his gaze on his father. So the bastard *could* have mercy. That was a first.

"Thank you, Father." Styxx didn't move until the king and his advisors and guards had vacated the room.

Biting back another groan, he could hear them beating his brother from outside. He buried his head in his hands, wishing he knew something he could do to help them both.

Kill your father.

He winced as that unbidden thought cut him. How could he? The guilt of killing Estes, who had truly deserved his death and more, still plagued him. While his father was a complete and utter bastard, he mostly did what he thought was best. Right or wrong. And Styxx knew that for a fact since he could hear the moron's thoughts.

No, as angry as the man made him, he could never kill him.

There had to be some other way to stop this shit and he needed to find it.

Fast.

DECEMBER 26, 9529 BC

"Beth?" Styxx called out as he searched the cottage property. She should have returned by now. But there was no sign of her.

The welcome back necklace he'd bought for her was still in its case on the table. Untouched. As was her pole and everything else.

Heartbroken, he wheeled Troian around and went to the stream, where they'd first started meeting.

She wasn't there either. There was nothing waiting for him in the tree. It was as if she'd never existed.

Where could she be?

"Bethany!" he shouted even louder as tears choked him. Why hadn't he insisted she name her father?

You wouldn't approve of him, Hector.

Because he'd been so reluctant to tell her more about his family, he had honored her privacy. And now . . .

He had no way of finding her.

Where are you? Could something have happened? Was she ill? Did she need him?

Agonized grief overwhelmed him as tears flowed down his cheeks. She'd promised to meet him today and she never broke her word. Not to him. Not ever.

Maybe she was delayed. Maybe he was panicking for no reason. It was only early afternoon . . .

She could still show.

Forcing himself to calm down, he went back to the cottage to make a fire and wait. She would be here. She would.

And yet as the hours passed and the sky darkened, more fear filled him. Even though he knew it was useless, he spent the night in their cottage, waiting for her. But by midday when there was still no sign of her, he knew something was wrong.

He just didn't know what.

DECEMBER 28, 9529 BC

Sick to his stomach and heartbroken, Styxx entered the palace and ignored his father's look of disdain as the king saw his unkempt state. He hadn't eaten or shaved in two days. Not while he'd waited for Bethany to come to their cottage.

"Are you ill?"

Yes, but his father would never understand. "I'm fine, Father."

"You look shameful."

Styxx didn't even react. He didn't care. The only thing he loved was gone and he had no way of finding her.

Tears pricked the back of his eyes as he pushed open his bedroom door and saw Apollo in his receiving room. Ah, beautiful. Could his day be any better?

Apollo raked him with a sneer. "Where have you been?"

Styxx sighed. "I didn't know you were looking for me."

The god materialized at his back and grabbed his jaw in one powerful fist. He snatched Styxx's head back until he could see Apollo's angry glare. "Are you breaching our agreement?"

Hopeless despair filled him. What difference did anything make now? He felt as if his entire life force had been ripped out of his body. He was nothing more than an empty shell. "No."

Apollo nuzzled his neck, scraping his skin with his fangs. Then he punched Styxx in the back with his fist, knocking him forward. "Bathe yourself and return to me. I've had my fill of your mewling sister and her whiny voice. And don't be long. If I have to come get you, you won't be happy about it."

As if any of this made him happy?

Styxx resisted the urge to pass an obscene gesture at the god. The last thing he wanted to do was have the bastard think it was an invitation.

Without a word, he went to bathe and tried his best not to think about what would happen once he finished.

Styxx paused in his bathing pool as he heard Acheron and Ryssa laughing together in her room. The two of them had always done that. When he'd been a boy, he used to try and join them, but Ryssa had never allowed it.

You have other people to play with. Leave us alone, you little brat.

But his tutors had never allowed him to play and other children had been too afraid. So he'd wander off to make up friends.

He dunked his head under the water and tried his best to ignore his siblings. Yet their laughter and conversation continued to stab his heart. He understood his father doubting his blood relationship, but Ryssa knew he was as related to her as Acheron was.

And with Acheron . . .

They were full-blooded brothers.

And still they ignored him at best, rebuffed him at worst. All he'd ever wanted in his life was to feel like he belonged somewhere.

That he belonged to someone.

No one would have him. Except for the brief time when he'd found happiness with Bethany. Tears filled his eyes as he looked down at her necklace on his wrist. *Please don't leave me here alone, Beth. I can't survive this without you.*

What if she really was gone from him?

Forever?

"Styxx!" Apollo's snarl cut through his thoughts as he made the mark on Styxx's back burn.

With a ragged breath, Styxx wiped away the tears with the heels of his hands and left the water to do what he did best.

Endure hell.

JANUARY 27, 9528 BC

"What is wrong with you?" Styxx snarled as he found Acheron drunk and naked on the floor of Acheron's room.

Sneering at him, Acheron grabbed the wineskin he'd been cradling under his body and drank from it. "Go away, you quim! I hate you! I wish we were dead ... " His voice broke off into sobs.

Acheron's pain reached out to him, making him feel bad that he'd yelled at him.

Styxx knelt beside his twin and took the wineskin away. "Acheron ... listen to me. I know you haven't eaten in at least two days." Their shared hunger pangs attested to it. He took the bread that Hestia had left earlier for his brother and held it out to Acheron. "You have to take some. Do you understand?"

"Fuck you ... you worthless whore!"

Flinching at the insult that cut to his bones, Styxx tried to put a piece of bread in Acheron's mouth, but he bit him so hard, he bled.

Styxx cursed and snatched his hand away. He glared at his twin, wanting to kill him. "Father is going to have you beaten or restrained and force-fed again. Is that what you want?"

Tears welled in Acheron's swirling silver eyes. "No. My want has abandoned me. Slapped me." He glared at Styxx. "Beat me. Because I'm not *you*! If I were a prince and not a whore ... But you're both. You are. I know you are. You aren't that, but you are. I saw it. They saw ... you. It ... "

Acheron was so drunk, he was incoherent. Even his thoughts made no sense whatsoever.

Styxx pressed the heel of his hand to his eye as he tried to sort through Acheron's mad ramblings. They were so fast and nonsensical, they set his brain to aching.

Sobbing hard, Acheron curled into a ball on the floor.

Styxx's throat tightened at the sight of his brother's agony, and at his own need to join him there. Like him, his brother was in absolute misery over something that had happened. But what?

He knew he was the last person Acheron wanted to confide in. He'd go get Ryssa for him, but she was with Apollo.

I'm all he has.

Gods help us both.

"*Adelphos,*" he whispered, placing his hand on Acheron's arm. "Please, I'm trying to help you."

Acheron punched at him. "Get off me!"

Break the whore in for the rest of us . . .

Pass him this way . . .

Styxx cringed as those phrases shouted at him from Acheron's scrambled mind. No wonder his brother was so upset. He had the same flashbacks and nightmares that haunted him, too. Worse, Acheron's memories were similar to what Xan had said to Estes after they'd raped Styxx the first time. No matter what he did, the jeers of those who'd violated him and then laughed and gloated about it would return to torture him.

He laid his head down on Acheron's shoulder and tried to comfort him. "Shh, brother. I know your pain."

"You know nothing of my pain! When has anyone ever spurned you, *Highness*?"

You and Ryssa both have. Constantly.

As had their father and mother.

And now his precious Bethany.

But this wasn't about his pain. He could drink himself stupid later, as he'd been doing for days. Right now, his brother needed him.

"Acheron—"

Faster than even Styxx could react, his brother spun on him and caught his throat in a fist so tight it was crushing. Acheron rolled with him and pinned him to the ground with a strength that was startling and unimaginable.

"Acheron," he coughed and wheezed, trying to dislodge his

brother's iron grip from his throat that reminded him of how Apollo often did him.

And as he stared up at his brother, Acheron's eyes turned to a bright, burning bloodred. His hair darkened as his skin became a marbled blue. His lips turned black.

"You say you know my pain," Acheron snarled, showing a set of fangs that caused Styxx's anger to mount as he involuntarily felt Apollo biting him in places that made his stomach heave. "You know nothing of my pain. No one has ever defiled you, prince. Never held you down and made you beg for a cock you'd rather be dead than taste or feel."

Rage and pain darkened Styxx's sight at those words. Worse, he heard what Acheron had said to him in Atlantis.

"Tell me how it feels to have your royal hole stuffed tight, Highness. Just wait till they flip you over, it gets even better.

"Welcome to my pain, brother . . . "

Acheron's mocking laughter as others raped him rang in his head.

Roaring, Styxx punched Acheron's blue arm as hard as he could, breaking his hold. Styxx cried out as his own arm hurt. But he didn't care. Too many memories of his own were mixing with his brother's.

And they were all brutal.

He kicked Acheron's demonic form back and rolled to his feet. Terror filled him as he saw Acheron return to a human appearance. His brother lay on his side now, panting and weak.

"What are we?" Styxx breathed.

Acheron's eyes were still red. "Damned." Then he started laughing hysterically.

Shaken and terrified by all that had happened, Styxx left him there and headed for his own room. He looked down at his hands and turned them over. Would his skin become blue, too? Would his eyes and lips do that?

Did Ryssa know about Acheron's alternate form? Was that why she was so protective of him?

And as he leaned against his bedroom door to block it, he could just imagine what their father would do if he ever saw *that*.

They would both be confined to the Dionysion.

Forever.

Raking his hands through his hair, Styxx felt some of his sanity slip at the mere thought of returning to that nightmare.

And this time there would be no Estes to intervene.

Because I killed him.

JANUARY 28, 9528 BC

Completely drunk and high on Atlantean herbs, Styxx sat in the banquet hall with his father, Apollo, and his sister as the night wore on interminably. He feigned laughter, even though he wasn't really sure what Apollo had said. Not that it mattered. Apollo wasn't here for conversation, he merely wanted them to fawn over him, and since Styxx was used to being ignored, he followed his father's cues.

And drank heavily.

So much so, that he'd passed extremely drunk probably a good day ago. How he was still conscious, he wasn't sure. At this point, he couldn't even remember the last time he'd been sober.

Which was good. Because whenever he sobered, his mind went to places he wanted to avoid. And focused on the fact that Bethany, like everyone else in his life, had abandoned him.

His head spinning, Styxx held his red clay kylix out for a servant to refill. He sat on Apollo's left while Ryssa sat on the right and his father on the other side of his sister, which was how Apollo had wanted it.

This way, the god could lean across Ryssa to speak to the king while he covertly fondled Styxx out of their sight. Although Styxx had finally found a way to deal with it. Every time Apollo groped him, he drank another cupful.

It was becoming quite a game and making him all the drunker, all the faster.

"Is that not right, Styxx?"

Frowning, he blinked at Apollo. "What?"

Apollo laughed then picked up a slice of cheese. "I fear we're boring your heir, Xerxes." He took a bite of it.

"Styxx? Where's your head, boy? Pay attention! You're with a god! Give him his due."

Styxx lifted his cup to hide the snarl of his lips over his father's comment.

Smirking in satisfaction that he had the king's blessing for their twisted relationship, Apollo held the cheese out to Styxx for him to finish off.

He hated this game. If they were alone, he'd knock Apollo's hand aside, but the god knew he didn't dare do that in front of his father. Cringing, Styxx opened his mouth and let Apollo place the cheese on his tongue.

Apollo caressed Styxx's chin. "My compliments to you, Xerxes. You made two beautiful children."

Styxx jerked as Apollo's hand drifted a little too far south on his body while Apollo kissed Ryssa's cheek.

"Excuse me," Ryssa said. "I'll be right back."

Styxx watched as she went to meet Hestia off in a corner. While his father was distracted by her actions, Apollo took Styxx's hand and led it to his hard cock.

Grimacing, Styxx snatched his hand back to his own chair and glared at the Olympian who laughed as he gave Styxx a lecherous smile that promised him retribution later tonight when the god came for him.

"I know not, Your Highness." Hestia's loud whisper made Apollo arch his brow. "I haven't seen him in days. I leave food and when I return it's untouched. No one's slept in his bed."

"What?" His father's roar made all of them jump. "Guards! Follow

437

me." He stormed out and headed in the direction of Ryssa's rooms.

Shrieking in protest, Ryssa ran after him.

Styxx groaned as he realized his father was about to go beat the shit out of his brother. Needing to head it off, he went after them with Apollo following him while trying to shove his hand into parts of Styxx's body he didn't want touched.

Was Apollo trying to get caught?

But then what did Apollo care? Not like his father would hate *him* for it. Styxx, on the other hand, wouldn't be so lucky. Either his father would beat him down over their twisted relationship, or box him up like a gift for the Olympian.

Either way, Styxx would be screwed.

In more ways than one.

"What's going on?" Apollo asked in his ear, pressing his groin against Styxx's hip.

Making a sound of disgust deep in the hollow of his throat, he moved away from Apollo. "It's Acheron," he said before his drunk mind could think better of it.

Apollo arched a curious brow with a speculative light in his eyes Styxx knew all too well. *There's another prince?* Apollo's thought almost sobered him. In that one heartbeat, Styxx saw his future and it was nauseating.

You know, Estes, you should bring him to Atlantis. I'd pay you a fortune for a go at him and his brother at the same time.

No, better yet, to watch the two of them have a go at each other.

Yeah, Apollo with his greed would want the full matched set . . .

And his father was just sick and greedy enough to agree to it. Styxx almost threw up at the mere thought. But how could he stop it from happening?

The god's ego.

It was the fact that Styxx was a renowned prince and Apollo had power over him that appealed to the bastard. The only way to keep Acheron out of their repugnant relationship was to make his twin appalling to the Olympian . . .

Make Acheron beneath Apollo's desire.

438

"He's a worthless slave who used to be a tsoulus." Styxx cringed as Apollo appeared intrigued and he remembered that *he* bore the brand that Acheron didn't. A brand Apollo had already seen and bitten on many occasions.

"Um, unfortunately his life is tied to mine so we have to keep him healthy. Although I feel fine so I'm sure he's only doing this for attention. May the gods forbid we ever be allowed to forget his presence here for one single day." Styxx clamped his mouth shut as Apollo frowned at him as if he'd lost his mind.

Fuck, what did I just say?

Did any of that even make sense?

Whether it did or not, it succeeded in causing Ryssa to give Styxx a vicious sneer.

I'll pay for that later. But so long as he paid for it alone, it was fine by him. He just didn't want a ménage à trois with his brother and Apollo. His ménage à deux was miserable enough.

His father threw open the doors to Acheron's room and stormed inside with Ryssa right behind him, while Apollo returned to grabbing at Styxx.

His temper snapping, he glared at Apollo. "Stop!" he said in a fierce whisper.

Apollo flashed his fangs at him then licked his lips. "You know you're going to pay for this later," he whispered.

"Fine," Styxx said under his breath.

"I told you he couldn't be trusted." Furious, his father turned on Ryssa, who ignored him as she ran to the balcony.

The Olympian finally left Styxx alone as he went to investigate what had everyone so distraught.

Unsure of what was about to explode all over him and Acheron, Styxx edged closer to the commotion.

Lightning flashed as rain poured down outside. Acheron sat on the balcony with his knees bent and his arms folded over them. Completely naked, he stared into space as if unaware of the rain and frigid cold. His hair was plastered to his head and at least two days' growth of beard dusted his cheeks.

Ryssa approached him slowly while taking care to remain under the awning that shielded her from the rain. "Acheron?"

He didn't respond. At least not verbally. But mentally, he was as far gone as Styxx was.

Styxx scowled as he tried to understand what thoughts were his and which were Acheron's. Ironically, they overlapped, and if he didn't know better, he'd swear his brother was heartbroken, too. That a woman had left Acheron the way Bethany had abandoned him. But that couldn't be. Acheron didn't have a woman.

Those are my thoughts.

Aren't they?

Damn, I'm seriously fucked up tonight . . .

Worse, Styxx's shredded emotions were tangling with Acheron's to a dangerous level.

Ryssa knelt beside Acheron. "Little brother?" The tenderness in her voice enraged Styxx and it made him more volatile as it brought home the fact that without Bethany, no one loved him.

Not like that.

No one ever cared when he was hurting and in pain. If he were the one on the balcony, there wasn't one person here who would get wet to help him. No one who would ever check to see if he was all right.

Acheron turned a hate-filled glare toward her. "Leave me," he growled.

You ungrateful kopros . . .

His father had the same reaction. "Don't you dare speak to her that way!"

Acheron met Styxx's gaze. He raked him with a sneer. "Fuck you, you bastard."

Something inside Styxx snapped at that. The whole family had come to check on Acheron and who had bothered to come to him these last few days while he'd been pawed and chewed on by Apollo?

No one . . .

Not a soul gave a single shit about him and Styxx was their "beloved" heir.

Growling low in his throat, he rushed Acheron. His brother came to his feet and ran at Styxx with the same fury.

Styxx caught him by the waist and slammed him back on the floor. Ignoring the pain it caused him, he went after Acheron with everything he had.

"I hate you!" Acheron snarled in his ear as he rolled and punched him in the jaw.

Styxx flipped him over his head and rose to his feet. He kicked Acheron in the ribs and gasped as the pain hit him, too. "You're pathetic."

Rolling away from him, Acheron pushed himself up. Rain dripped off both of them as they faced off with mutual disdain and hatred. As Acheron went for him again, Styxx knocked him back.

Rain ran down his face, mixing with the blood that poured from his eye, nose, and mouth. And still Acheron came at him, over and over again.

"Guards, take him," the king ordered.

They started for Styxx, but his father cut them off and pointed to Acheron.

His brother tried to fight them, but he was too weakened by their fight. They hauled him back into his room.

Styxx wiped the blood from his own face as their father buried his hand in Acheron's wet hair and snatched his head so that Acheron could see the full contempt of the king's expression. "Beat him until there's no skin left on his back. If he passes out, wake him and beat him again."

Styxx winced at an all too familiar order. He had those same scars courtesy of his own stupidity.

Acheron laughed coldly. "I love you too, Father."

The bastard backhanded him. "Take him out of here."

"Father?" Apollo asked with an arch stare.

The king scoffed. "He calls me that, but he's no son of mine. My former queen whored herself and begat that abomination."

Tears fell down Ryssa's face. "He's just a boy, Father."

441

The king laughed at something Styxx didn't find particularly amusing.

Infuriated, Ryssa ran after the guards and Acheron.

Well aware of the fact that he didn't have long before Acheron's beating would render him screaming in pain, Styxx headed for his rooms.

The moment he entered them, Apollo appeared in front of him.

The Olympian screwed his face up at the sight of Styxx's damaged features. "You found a way to ruin my fun tonight, didn't you?"

"Sorry."

"No, you're not. But you will be." Apollo left as quickly as he'd come.

Before he could take more than three steps, Styxx cried out as his back exploded with pain. It was so fierce that it cut through the herbs and alcohol in his system and dropped him to the floor.

Writhing in absolute agony, he couldn't move as lash after lash tore through him. He shook all over from the cold of his wet clothes and the pain of Acheron's punishment.

By the time it stopped, Styxx was shaking uncontrollably. His breathing labored, he crawled to his bed, but hurt too much to even attempt to rise and get into it. Instead, he reached up from the floor and pulled the blanket off then wrapped himself in it.

Tears streamed down his face as he remembered being a boy and cocooning like this whenever he was hurt and aching. Only then, he used to pretend the blanket was his mother and that she was hugging and consoling him.

As he lay there, he heard Ryssa's muffled voice through the wall as she tended his brother. "Don't worry, Acheron. I'll take care of you."

Closing his eyes, Styxx pretended that he was Acheron and that Ryssa was in here with him. But just like when he'd pretended the blanket was hugging him and all the times he'd made up friends to play with, he knew the bitter truth.

Without Bethany, he was completely alone.

And no one cared about the prince.

Not even him.

JANUARY 29, 9528 BC

While his brother and sister laughed through the walls, Styxx stared at his gaunt and bruised features as he shaved in the mirror. He looked like utter Hades. For all his cowering, Acheron could hit. Styxx's right eye was completely red and his brow cut.

But what did it matter? There was no one to look at him. No Bethany to run her gentle hands over his face now and sympathize with his pain.

And as Styxx pulled the razor over his chin, he tried not to remember anything about her. Tried not to think at all.

But still those memories surged . . . He could see her so clearly in his mind the day she'd fingered the center of his chin and scowled at what she found there.

"What is this?"

"A goatee."

She'd made an adorable face at him. "The goat part is right. Why would you intentionally do that to yourself?"

"I thought you'd think it manly and sexy."

She'd scoffed until he'd shown her what he could do to her with those whiskers. Then she'd been all behind his keeping it.

Tears filled his eyes, but he blinked them away. He missed so many things about her. Yet it was the loss of having someone to laugh with that burned most.

Unable to deal with it anymore, he lowered his hand and pulled the razor across his forearm, careful to pick an area he knew he could cover with his ornamental gold cuffs so no one would see it.

He hissed in pain, allowing the physical to overshadow the mental anguish as he made several long cuts there. It'd been awhile since he'd done this.

Not since he met his Bethany. With her, he hadn't needed the painful distraction.

Styxx glanced at the scars on his thighs and arms where he'd cut himself repeatedly when he'd been younger . . . anything to divert his emotions and thoughts from what really hurt. Most of the scars were so faint and fine, they were only visible whenever his skin darkened from the summer sun.

A sudden knock sounded. "Highness?"

He set the razor aside and went to answer his door. It was one of his father's scribes.

"Sorry to disturb you, Your Highness. His Majesty requests you join him downstairs in his study immediately."

"I'll be there in a moment." Styxx shut the door and finished dressing, making sure to cover the cuts he'd made in his forearm with the thick gold cuffs he wore for decoration then went to see what his father wanted.

The instant he entered the room, a feeling of dread consumed him.

This won't please you, boy. His father gestured toward the chair in front of him.

Shit.

Styxx sat down while everyone withdrew to leave them alone. Double shit.

Worse than the haste with which the room was vacated was the expression on the king's face. One of controlled fury that had never boded well for Styxx in the past. "Father?"

"What is this I hear about your interference with the soldiers' pensions?"

Interference? He'd merely seen to it that they'd been paid properly. "They weren't getting what was owed them."

"Pensions are only awarded to those who are killed in battle."

"I know."

"Then why did you authorize payment to be given to those killed in a whorehouse?"

"They—"

"You do not speak!" his father roared. "You listen!"

I thought you wanted me to answer . . .

"Have you any idea the drain you've put on our resources?"

Styxx kept his gaze on the floor.

"Have you?"

"You told me not to speak."

His father backhanded him. "I should have you whipped for going behind my back as you've done and draining my finances with such frivolity. How dare you!" He growled furiously then kicked at Styxx's chair. "Get up!"

Careful to keep his expression blank, Styxx stood.

"Since you think it's funny to spend my money so recklessly, I'm selling your farm and your horse."

The farm he'd bought with his own coin from the blood of his own brow and back . . . for Bethany.

Styxx ground his teeth as pain racked him. But he didn't dare let it show. He knew better.

"You are being stripped of your military rank. And your armor, hoplon, and swords were sold and melted down this morning. Furthermore, you are cut off financially. Since I can't trust you to spend wisely, I'll treat you as I do Ryssa. You will have to come begging to me for every obolos, and then only if I deem your need worthy will you get one. I'm increasing your daily obligations for work and you will pay back every single bit you authorized paid for such rampant stupidity. Now what have you to say for yourself?"

Don't do it . . .

Stay silent.

But he couldn't. He was too raw and angry. Glaring at his father, he pulled the gold cuffs off and slammed them down on his father's desk. Next he removed his fibula and chlamys then his shoes.

The king curled his lip. "What are you doing?"

"This is about punishing me, is it not? You're stripping me of everything I own to pay for *your* soldiers. Fine. Take it. Sell it all. I don't want it, anyway." Styxx dropped his silk chiton to the floor. With his gaze locked on his father's, he jerked his signet ring off and slammed it down next to the cuffs.

Completely naked and with what little pride he possessed, he turned and walked out of the room. Ignoring everyone who turned to gape at his horrifically scarred and marked body and speculate over it, Styxx headed out the main doors and descended the steps.

With no place else to go and too sick to walk very far today, he went to the barracks. Thankfully, they were empty of Didymosian soldiers.

Galen rose to his feet as soon as he saw him nearing his head-quarters. "Oh dear gods, son ... " Pulling his cloak off, he wrapped it around Styxx. "What happened?"

"Nothing."

Galen frowned, but didn't question him further as he guided Styxx into a chair. "Your eye should have had stitches."

"I know. But there was no one there for it."

Galen poured a cup of wine and handed it to him. Then he went to fetch him clothes.

Styxx didn't say a word as he dressed. Unfortunately, Galen's shoes were too small for freakishly large feet. "Would it be all right if I bunked with you for the night?"

"Of course, son. You know you're always welcome wherever I am."

"Thank you, Master Galen."

"Highness—"

Styxx held his hand up to stop him. "I've been disowned, Galen."

His old mentor gaped. "What?" he asked incredulously. "When they came for your armor and equipment this morning, I thought it was for you to be dressed in it."

He shook his head. "I've been decommissioned. The king has sold off my armor."

"This is outrageous! Why?"

Styxx refused to tell him the reason. Galen would feel guilty for his part in it and Galen was not at fault at all. "It doesn't matter."

"You should go to your Bethany."

"She's gone, Galen. She left me . . . a while ago." Styxx bit back a sob at the loss of the only thing that really mattered to him.

That and his horse. He was really going to miss Troian. Bethany more, but he'd been through a lot with that horse.

"What can I get for you?"

"I'm fine, Master Galen."

"You're not fine, Styxx. I'm old, not stupid."

"And I'm stupid and not old."

Galen laughed at him. "You look like you've been swallowed by Charybdis and spat back out. Come with me and lie down and rest for awhile."

Styxx started to argue, but he had a bad fever and vicious sore throat from being chilled last night after his fight with Acheron. Coughing, he followed Galen to his quarters.

Styxx lay down on the bed and Galen pulled the covers up around him and tucked them close to his body. Strange, it was the only time in his life someone had done this for him.

"Sleep if you can. I'll be back to check on you soon."

"Thank you, Galen." Closing his eyes, Styxx tried to sleep, but it was useless. Too many voices and too many bad memories tormented him. And the worst were the memories of a gentle hand in his hair that he'd never know again.

JANUARY 31, 9528 BC

"Get up!"

Styxx flinched as someone slapped at his head. His fever was so high that at first he couldn't focus on what was happening. Finally, his vision cleared enough that he saw his father standing over him.

"I said, get up, you worthless dog!"

When Styxx didn't move fast enough to suit him, his father jerked him to his feet.

"You ever pull another stunt like this and I will have you killed while you sleep. You understand?"

No. He didn't. Scowling, he looked from his father to Galen. "What are you talking about?"

"He doesn't know, Majesty. He's been burning with a fever for two days and hasn't left the bed except to piss."

Styxx was stunned that Galen would speak to his father like that. "What's going on?"

His father curled his lip. "Get him cleaned up and returned to the palace."

"Yes, Your Majesty."

His father stormed off.

The instant he was gone, Galen helped Styxx back to bed. "Rest, boy. Don't worry about anything."

"But my father said—"

"He's only angry because he learned a frightening lesson over the last two days."

"Galen, I'm too ill to follow. Please don't riddle me."

Laughing, Galen took a cloth from the basin by the bed and ran it over Styxx's forehead. "How are you feeling?"

"Very confused . . . has it really been two days?"

"It has. About three hours after you fell asleep here, the armorer took your equipment back to your father and refused to melt it."

"What? Why?"

Galen poured wine for Styxx. "His youngest nephew is Darian and his son was Sandros." Sandros was one of the men who'd died on their return. As with Gaius's family, his widow and children had been denied his pension and Styxx had paid it. "He was the same man we bought the armor from originally, and he remembered how thrilled you were when he laced you into it the first time. And how you didn't have the money yet for the helm or greaves, but humbly asked him if he would save them and allow you to make payments." When the armorer had refused, Galen had stepped forward to loan him the money until Styxx had paid them off. "He told your father that he would never dishonor you by destroying something you'd worked so hard for and paid for with your own coin. That it wouldn't be right to melt down a hero's armor or sell it to another. And when your father had it taken to another armorer, he also refused once he learned it belonged to you."

"Why?"

"He was at Halicarnassus with us . . . and said that having seen your bravery and skill firsthand, he would never dishonor you by dismantling your armor."

"I still have it?"

Galen nodded. "The third armorer brought it to me and said that he'd pay the king the value of it out of his own pocket to make sure it was returned to you intact. And then, while you slept, word from the armorers went round to the soldiers and veterans that you'd been stripped of everything because of what you'd done for us and for the families of our fallen. That your father had taken your rank, your armor, your horse and titles, and left you unclothed to wander the streets. One by one, every single member of the Stygian Omada came and threw down his weapons and stripped naked in front of the palace in protest of what had been done to you. More to the point, they vowed that they would see Didymos fall before they picked up another weapon to follow any man save Prince Styxx into battle."

Styxx was stunned that they would dare his father's wrath for him. "And I slept through all of that?"

"You did, indeed."

Honestly, Styxx didn't fully believe him until an hour later when he got up and dressed not in Galen's clothes, but his own that had been left for him and headed outside. There in the arena, his army had gathered, and as they saw him, they struck their shields with their swords and chanted his name.

Amazed and awed by their actions, he turned around, looking at them in disbelief. Every shield there had been repainted with his personal emblem on it. A black phoenix rising. It was an act of complete solidarity. The ultimate show of their support and respect.

For the first time in his life, Styxx felt worth something. Not much . . .

But worth something more than the dirt under his father's feet.

"We have a serious problem."

Apollo arched a brow at Zeus's dire tone. "And that would be?"

"Have you been to Didymos lately?"

"Of course."

"Did you see the uprising?"

Apollo snorted. "You mean the army stripping naked? Yes. It was rather amusing."

"Yes, well, what isn't amusing is that little bugger of yours who doesn't respect us, leading an army of men who are willing to overthrow their king for him. Can you imagine what they'd do if he wanted our temples burned?"

Apollo rolled his eyes at Zeus's unwarranted fear. "I've got him in hand."

"I don't think you do. Nor do I think you appreciate how dangerous he could prove to be. Didymos is one of our richest city-states and she was hard won from Atlantis. The last thing we need is to lose her to them again."

"You're not going to lose Didymos." But hopefully soon, Zeus and the rest would lose all of Greece.

Provided Apollo's pact with the Atlanteans held.

Apollo knew just what to do to make sure that everyone was kept in their rightful place.

And that Styxx learned a lesson of respect that he'd never forget.

450

FEBRUARY 1, 9528 BC

Styxx was still extremely ill from his fight with Acheron. The last thing he'd wanted was for his father to call him down to his study, especially given what had happened the last time he'd been here.

His head aching, he paused in front of the king's desk. "You summoned me, Majesty?"

His father handed the scroll he'd just signed over to the scribe on his left. He unrolled another and responded without looking up. "I wanted to let you know that I've negotiated a marriage contract for you."

Stunned, Styxx was frozen for several heartbeats as that unexpected news slapped him hard. "May I ask to whom?"

"An Egyptian princess . . . what's her name . . . Ned . . . Nef . . . Nera . . . " He searched about his desk. "Ah. Here it is. Nefertari. She and a royal envoy will arrive in about two weeks so that you can meet her. If you're acceptable to her, the marriage will proceed." His father pierced him with a malevolent glare. "You *will* be acceptable to her, understood?"

Don't worry, old man. I promise I won't piss on her.

"Is there anything else, Majesty?"

"No. I'm done with you."

He didn't miss the anger underlying his father's words or the next thought . . .

Get out of my sight, before I do order you whipped. Ironically, his father wasn't as mad at Styxx as he was at Acheron. The king had never intended for Apollo to find out about his brother. But now that the Olympian knew, his father was holding Styxx responsible for it.

Whatever. Styxx turned around and left then grimaced as his nose started bleeding. Knowing better than to let his father see it, he returned to his room and grabbed a cloth to hold against it while he waited for it to stop.

But what hurt worse than the remains of the beating was the shattered remnants of his heart. He didn't want to marry a princess.

He wanted Bethany back.

Unable to stand it, he went to search for her again. Still, the chest that held her necklace was where he'd left it and there was no sign of her anywhere. For whatever reason, she'd never returned to him.

Even their original spot was completely undisturbed. Nothing had been left in his tree. No trace of her whatsoever.

Bereft, he returned to the cottage and opened the chest that contained her necklace. The moment he saw the contents, his world truly came undone.

On top of the necklace was the ring he'd given her that he'd accepted from Kreon. The one she'd been wearing the last time he'd seen her that he'd playfully twisted round her finger.

She *had* been here.

And this was her way of saying good-bye.

Tears fell down his cheeks as he roared in anger and overturned the table. He sent the chest with the ring and necklace flying.

At least she'd finally let him know that she was all right. That nothing had happened to her.

She'd gone on with her life, and left him to his.

Fine. There was no need in searching for her anymore. It was over . . .

Like everyone else in his life, she didn't want him. He wasn't worthy of her heart or her love.

I am nothing.

Furious and hurt to an unbelievable level, he considered burning the cottage to the ground. But he couldn't bring himself to do it. Maybe someone would happen upon it who needed a place to stay. Maybe they could find happiness here in his stead.

Heartbroken, he glanced around then left without bothering to close the door.

He swung up onto Troian and turned the horse toward the city.

Without looking back, he dug his heels in and rode away from the only place he'd ever been happy.

What is so wrong with me that no one can love me? That no one will keep me?

Stop it! You're a prince. Who are you to feel sorry for yourself?

But in his heart, he knew the truth. He wasn't a prince. He was a just a tired whore, and the only one who wanted anything to do with him was a god he couldn't stomach. Not because Apollo loved him, but because Apollo craved the sense of power he had whenever he made a royal Greek hero beg and suffer. Their relationship was all about dominance and force.

Pain.

Styxx's abject humiliation and subjugation to Apollo's higher power. He was nothing more to Apollo than a toy was to a toddler. Something to be used and discarded, or bashed against furniture whenever its owner was displeased about something.

I have no real value to anyone . . .

There was no use in fighting it or crying. It was merely a fact. Even worse, he couldn't change it.

FEBRUARY 13, 9528 BC

"You're being remarkably accepting of your marriage. Should I be worried?"

You might be if I was sober, old man.

Styxx shrugged at his father's question as they walked toward the throne room. "This is my duty, is it not? To marry and breed for you and Didymos. It's what you've trained me for."

"I'm still shocked over your complacency."

Styxx slowed down as he felt the mark on his back heat up to the point it stung.

453

"Apollo," his father greeted happily as the god appeared in front of them. "Glad to have you join us for the betrothal ceremonies."

"Betrothal?"

"Styxx is to marry an Egyptian princess."

Apollo gave Styxx an arch stare and there was no missing the light of jealousy in his eyes. "Really? I hadn't heard."

Styxx knew better than to say a single word on the matter since it would only succeed in pissing off either his father or the Olympian.

"Indeed," his father continued. "She arrived earlier and is about to be received in the throne room. Would you like to join us?"

"Absolutely."

As the king resumed his walk, Apollo cut Styxx off. The expression on his face said he was as pleased by the news as Styxx was.

"How long have you known about this?"

"Two weeks, roughly."

Apollo caught his wrist and pulled him into a small alcove where he shoved Styxx against the wall and held him there by his throat. "Have you forgotten who owns you?"

Styxx kept his gaze on the floor. "You'll have to take the matter up with my father since he believes he's the one who holds my leash."

Apollo tightened his grip on Styxx's throat. "Don't get smart with me, prince. I still haven't forgotten about the last time I saw you, and the promise I made."

How could he forget? Apollo had promised him his full wrath. But it changed nothing. "What do you want from me?"

Apollo's gaze turned hungry. "You know what I want."

I'd rather be dead.

Sighing, Styxx tried to leave, but Apollo slammed him back against the wall again, hard enough to bruise his back.

"You have not learned your place, have you?"

"Right now, my place is at my father's side. Unless you wish to have me beaten, and then I won't be so pretty for you later."

Apollo laughed. "You are spirited. But be careful. Even the best stallion has to be broken."

Styxx's temper ignited as bitter memories of being a royal stallion tore through him. "They've also been known to throw and kill their riders."

"Are you threatening me?"

"I thought we were talking about horses."

Apollo grabbed Styxx's jaw and held him against the wall in a crushing, iron grip. "Do not *ever* think you can threaten me, human."

"Styxx? Where are you, boy?"

Apollo glanced over his shoulder at the sound of the king's voice. "Enjoy the next few hours, prince. Because I assure you, they'll be the last ones you have to yourself for quite a while."

"I look forward to it."

"Styxx?"

Apollo slung him away from him.

Straightening his clothes, Styxx went to his father, who glared angrily. "Where were you?"

"Forgive me, Father. I had something I had to attend to."

The expression on his father's face said he wanted to backhand him, but didn't dare since that would leave his face damaged for the princess. Though to be honest, he was surprised Apollo's handprint wasn't embedded on his neck.

He followed his father into the throne room and moved to stand in front of his chair while his father took his seat. Styxx sat down and scanned the room for Apollo. But the god was nowhere to be seen.

A fanfare began as the doors were opened and the procession began. A troupe of dancing girls led in three sets of slaves carrying chests of treasure for the king. One by one, they brought the chests forward and opened them for his father to see their contents. But that wasn't what held Styxx's attention. In the doorway, two large Nubian males held poles that had transparent linen strung between them to show the outline of the princess's body.

She possessed the carriage of a queen as she followed them into the room.

Once they reached the thrones, the men lowered the screen to show an exquisitely beautiful woman who was a few years older than Styxx. Her dark skin was flawless. She wore a black wig laden with turquoise and gold, and her eyes were thickly lined with kohl, very similar to how Bethany often painted hers. Gold snake bracelets coiled around her arms and her thin linen sheath showed the outline of a perfect body.

But she was no Bethany.

And his body didn't react to her at all. Not the way it did whenever he thought of the woman who had carelessly thrown his heart away.

Styxx forced himself to smile and rise to his feet. Heartsick and aching, he descended the dais to take her hand and kiss it.

A slow, seductive smile curled her lips. *Thank the gods you're handsome. I definitely wouldn't mind taking a bite out of those arms ...*

The relief in her tone almost made him laugh.

"Welcome, princess."

And thank the gods you have a deep, manly voice to match the rest of you. Holding his hand, she gave him a slight curtsy. "Your Highness."

Her parents came forward and were introduced to his father, who then excused Styxx and Nefertari so that they could walk, with a heavy Egyptian guard, out to the gardens.

Styxx folded his hands behind his back as she led the way.

"I hear you're a war hero, Prince Styxx."

"Really just a soldier."

"Oh." There was no missing the disappointment in that one single word.

Awkward silence stretched out between them as they walked. Styxx couldn't think of anything to say. Strange how he'd never had that problem with Bethany. They had been able to talk forever about absolutely nothing.

"Did you have a pleasant journey to Greece?" he asked her.

She walked down to the garden that had once been his mother's favorite. "Yes."

More awkward silence.

Nefertari stopped and faced him. "You don't speak much, do you?"

"No."

"That's not necessarily a negative . . . Still, I propose we get one thing out of the way."

"And that is?"

She reached up and pulled his lips down to hers so that she could kiss him. Closing his eyes, Styxx followed her lead, but his heart wasn't in it. Yes, his body reacted to her. Still, it wasn't the same as when he held his Bethany. There was no overwhelming need to breathe in her scent. To lay himself against her and stay with her for eternity.

She was just there.

Nefertari pulled back with a satisfied smile. "You are acceptable to me."

"My father will be pleased."

"Are you not pleased, Prince Styxx?"

No. But he didn't want to hurt her feelings. "Of course, princess. You're exquisitely beautiful."

She narrowed her eyes on him. "Does it bother you that I'm Egyptian?"

"Not at all. Does it bother you that I'm Greek?"

"I thought it would. But no . . . and you speak Egyptian incredibly well. I find your accent and voice exceptionally pleasant."

Nice to know he wasn't totally repellent. "Do you speak Greek at all?"

"A little, but not well. Would you help me learn?"

"Of course." That would at least give them something to talk about besides the weather.

She sighed. "So . . . Styxx. What qualities do you expect from your wife and queen?"

"Nothing specific."

That stunned her so much, she actually gaped. "Nothing?"

"I would appreciate it if she liked me, but other than that, no. Do you have a list?"

"Absolutely. I expect courtesy and preference to be given to me and my children at all times. While I accept that you'll have mistresses and possibly other wives, they are not to be kept in our home. You may visit them in town or wherever you wish to place them. But as your first wife, I will not have them in my direct line of sight or near any children I birth. I want my children educated in Egyptian as well as Greek and they are to worship my gods. I expect an altar to be built for my gods in my end of the palace and for my personal priests to be given their own rooms with full, unrestricted access to mine."

Now it was Styxx's turn to gape.

"While I am not opposed to Greek servants," she continued, oblivious to his incredulity, "I will require that I have Egyptians kept, too. I expect you to give me notice in the morning if you'll be spending the night with me. I will not bed with you whenever you are drunk and you are to bathe before you come to me. I have a scent that I've brought from home that you will need to wear for those occasions. You are not to raise your voice to me or make demands of my private time. I require at least two hours a day for my own personal use. I prefer them in the morning, but they can be moved if necessary."

"Thought about this a lot, have you?"

She glared at him. "Are you mocking me?"

"No. I was joking."

"I don't like jokes. I find humor offensive."

Great. No laughter.

Maybe he could bribe Acheron into committing suicide so that they could both be put out of their mutual misery . . .

"Duly noted. What else, princess?"

"I expect a separate residence and rooms to be kept for me at all times. I will reserve the right to deny you access to my rooms should you displease me in any way or for any reason. And you are not to force yourself upon me. Likewise, I will not receive you if you are ill or infirmed or when I have my monthly flow. While I understand you may wish to strike me at times, you can use nothing other than your hand. And you are not to touch me at all during any pregnancy. Once I've given birth, I will require a six-month respite from your bed. I will expect lands as a gift for any sons and jewelry for daughters. You are to hold feasts on my birthday and declare them sacred holidays."

"Should I summon a scribe to take notes?"

"I told you I don't like jokes."

"I was quite serious. I'd hate to forget one of your dictates, princess."

"Fear not. I've already had them noted for you, and translated into Greek." She paused to look up at him. "Do you wish to negotiate any of my terms?"

Why bother? It was obvious they were far more important to her than they were to him. "Not really."

"Then you accept them?"

"Sure."

Good . . . I wanted a weak husband I could control. I'm glad to know you're flaccid. She offered him a smile then started forward.

A fierce tic started in his jaw at the way she dismissed him as if he were nothing. "By the way, Nefertari, contrary to your opinion of me, I'm not a pussy. The reason I'm not negotiating is not because I'm weak. But rather I don't honestly give a shit, and your puerile terms aren't worth arguing over. And I do have one requirement of you. Whatever children we have, you are to be a loving mother to them, regardless of your feelings for me. You will never threaten or raise a hand to one of them. If you do, I will see you dead for it . . . by my hands."

She gaped at him as he turned around and headed back into the palace. Without a word to anyone, he returned to his rooms to be alone.

He poured himself a cup of wine and opened a packet of herbs for it. His heart heavy, he looked down at his arm to see the scar his father had given him when he'd been a boy, and then his gaze went to Bethany's necklace on his wrist. He should cut it off and toss it in the fire, but he couldn't make himself cast her away as easily as she'd done him.

But then that seemed ever his destiny . . . to only love women who couldn't stand him.

Except Nefertari. There would never be any love lost between them. Only royal duty and obligation.

And endless days of humorless misery.

Hours later, Styxx tried to breathe as his head pounded from the crowd of people who'd come, in theory, to wish him and Ryssa well. In reality, they were here to see the god Apollo, and to drink his father's wines and eat the elaborate banquet foods being carried in by waves of servants.

Nefertari stood beside him, but he could freeze ocean water with the glances she directed at him. Still, he gave her credit. She was as adept at hiding her feelings as he was. Together, they were able to allow their parents and the guests to think them a happy couple.

An illusion that would be helped if he didn't hear her thoughts.

His father stood up. Forcing himself to smile, Styxx stood and helped Nefertari to her feet while Apollo did the same with Ryssa on the other side of his father.

The king lifted his kylix to their guests. "Thank you all for coming to celebrate with me. It's not every day that a king is so blessed. Let us all raise our cups in honor of my only daughter, the human consort for the god Apollo, who is now expecting his child, and to my only son, who will be marrying the Egyptian princess Nefertari. May the gods bless them both and may our lands forever flourish."

As Styxx took a drink, he felt a malevolence so strong, it actually drowned out all the other voices tormenting him.

Acheron. He glanced up to see his twin in the shadows, glaring at them.

Brother, Styxx thought silently, *you can have every bit of this with my blessings and gratitude.*

Acheron's anger grew as the king leaned over and kissed Ryssa and then Styxx. "To my beloved children," he said to the crowd once more. "Long may they live."

A deafening shout rose up from the crowd. Styxx kept his gaze on his brother. He knew exactly how Acheron felt. It was the same pain he had whenever he heard Acheron and Ryssa laughing through the walls of his room.

It cut and it bled. But the difference was that with Ryssa, the affection wasn't for show.

It was sincere.

FEBRUARY 14, 9528 BC

Styxx smiled as he came awake to a gentle hand playing in his hair. "Bethany?"

"Not quite."

He jerked away at the sound of Apollo's deep voice in his ear. "What are you doing here?" He shoved at Apollo. "Ew . . . you reek of my sister."

Apollo buried his hand in Styxx's hair and snatched his head back. "You seem to have forgotten the bargain you made. Or do you no longer care what happens to the people you love?"

"Our bargain didn't include your mauling me in front of my family."

"Your family isn't here now."

Styxx cringed as Apollo wrapped his arms around him and pulled him flush against the Olympian's chest.

"You still haven't learned obedience."

Styxx tried to move away from him. "I'm not a dog."

Apollo laughed in his ear. "No, but I'll bet I can teach you to beg."

461

"I'd rather not learn."

"Then roll over and kiss me."

Styxx ground his teeth as he did everything he could to force himself to obey Apollo's order. *It'll be easier if you just do it.*

But he couldn't. He was too tired of living like this. Tired of being threatened and tormented. By everyone. At this point, he didn't care anymore. Bethany was gone and there was really nothing else that mattered to him. "Why can't you leave me in peace?"

"Peace?" Apollo snarled as he pinned Styxx to the bed by his throat, facing him. "Do you not comprehend the honor I'm doing you? I have marked you!"

Staring at the wall, Styxx kept his head turned away from his tormentor. This was an honor he would gladly do without.

Apollo slapped him. "Look at me."

His lips bleeding, Styxx met his livid glare with one of his own.

Apollo backhanded him again. "I've had it with your insolence. You think you know what pain is, human? You don't. But you're about to learn. And this time, I won't have mercy on you, prince. I will take absolutely everything from you, and I do mean *everything*. There will be nothing left of you when I'm through, and I promise you, you will go down on your knees to beg me for my mercy."

Sick of everything and everyone, Styxx laughed at his threat. "Fine. Do your worst to me and I will relish it."

JANUARY 11, 9527 BC

Almost a year later

"Bet'anya ... we need you to settle a bet for us."

Bethany paused as she entered the grand hall on Katateros where statues of the main gods lined the massive round foyer. The white marble floor glistened brightly and held the sun symbol of Apollymi in the center. She'd been on her way to report to Archon that she had yet to find a trace of Apostolos.

But before she could make it to the doors that led to his throne room, her cousins Teros and Phanen, gods of fear and panic, stopped her. "Settle what?"

"Is this your emblem or Artemis's?"

Her heart clenched as they handed her the necklace she'd given to Styxx so long ago. At first, she thought it belonged to another, but there was no mistaking the spell she'd put on it. While it was extremely weakened for some reason, she could still feel some of her father's protection powers remaining. "Where did you get this?"

Teros crossed his arms over his chest. "You answer us first."

She moved into his personal space and glared at them in turn. "Where did you get this!" Not a question. It was a demand.

His dark eyes widening, Phanen took a step back from her. "Calm down, cuz. It's a souvenir we took."

"From?"

"A prisoner of war," Teros answered for him.

"Prisoner, my ass." Phanen snorted at his brother's explanation. "He was a gift from Apollo to Atlantis. A tribute, as it were."

She grabbed Teros by the throat and held him in a grip that let him know exactly how serious and angry she was. "Start at the beginning and tell me about the man you took this from."

"Why—"

She cut him off with a lethal stare. "The next words off your tongue better answer my question or they will be your last. And we both know I have the powers to do it."

He swallowed hard before he finally answered without hedging. "Styxx of Didymos. As an act of good faith on his part to all of us, Apollo handed him over to Archon about a year ago."

Her head swam with his news. It couldn't be . . .

She knew better. If Styxx was in their realm here or in Atlantis, she'd know it.

Wouldn't she?

"Styxx is in Didymos," she insisted.

"No ... one of Apollo's servant spirits is in Didymos, masquerading as the prince. The real Styxx was brought here last year when you were in Egypt with your father and aunt. There was a huge celebration over it. He was trussed like a festival goose and dropped butt-ass naked into the center of the hall, at Archon's feet."

Bethany stepped back from them as horror and pain for Styxx invaded every part of her. *Please be lying ... please.* She looked back at the gloating brothers who were now on her last nerve as they laughed about something she didn't find amusing at all. "How did you get my necklace?"

Teros slapped Phanen on the chest. "Told you it was hers."

Phanen ignored him. "We took it from Styxx two nights ago right before they led him down to the arena for another exhibition match. He struggled like a demon to keep it though. Damn near had to take his arm off to get it. You could say thank you to us for returning it, you know." He jerked his chin toward her amulet. "How'd he get it, anyway? Steal it from one of our troops during the war?"

She ignored his question as she tried to make sense of what he was saying. "Arena?"

Teros scowled. "Is that all she got out of that?"

Bethany grabbed him by his formesta and jerked him closer. "What fucking arena!"

The brothers exchanged a gape over her language before Teros spoke again. "Atlantean main amphitheater. Three times a week they trot him out for public games and fights. Sometimes they just torture him for sport."

Sick to her stomach, Bethany flashed herself from Katateros to the main arena in the capital city. She took a moment to disguise herself as an Apollite servant before she entered the holding area below the main arena stage. Animals and props for shows were kept here. As were prisoners who were held for public executions or games where they could sometimes win their freedom.

"So did you get your pound of flesh?"

She paused at the sight of two huge fighters heading toward her.

"No, but I got to pound his little Greek ass. I can't believe that piece of shit ever led an army."

"As I recall, he led that army right over yours and burned it to the ground."

"Shut up."

Bethany's stomach churned over their cruelty as she headed down the hallway they'd come from. She knew who they'd been talking about and it sliced her like a thousand knives. *How could I have left him to this?*

Alone and unprotected.

All around her prisoners cried and begged for mercy or food as a guard ladled water into misshapen or broken bowls and then shoved them through small cutouts at the bottom of the locked doors.

"Where's Styxx of Didymos?"

The guard quirked a brow at her. He spat on the ground by his feet then wiped his mouth with the back of his hand as he gave her a speculative glare. "There's a fee for that information, and the fee depends on what it is you want to do to him."

"Talk to him."

He laughed. "No one *talks* to him, girl. I'm not stupid. And I can't let you bleed him. He has a fight today and I have money bet on it."

She rose up in her god form to tower over the little weasel. "Where is he?" she snarled.

He shrank back in fear. "Forgive me, goddess. I didn't realize it was one of you wanting him again. He's there." He gestured to a door on the right.

Grabbing the water bucket from him, she went to the door and opened it. But what she found inside froze her to the spot as it drove horror straight into her heart.

Completely naked and filthy to an inhuman level, Styxx was

chained like an animal. He had a thick iron collar around his neck that had a huge chain connected to it. A chain that ran to iron cuffs on his wrists and ankles. The chains went from him to a system of pulleys by the door that determined how much freedom he was allowed in the room. She winced as she remembered how badly he hated to be bound by anything.

Even a frail, light scarf.

Blood, dirt, cuts, and bruises covered his entire body. Tears choked her. His beautiful blond hair was greasy and filthy and matted with blood and dirt.

Styxx wrapped his hand in the chains that held him as he saw his latest "visitor" entering his dark cell. Still raw and bleeding from the last two, he only wanted a few minutes to lie in the darkness and try to forget what they'd done to him.

But the greedy bastards wouldn't allow him even a moment's peace.

At least this one was a petite blond woman who appeared unarmed. Because Atlantean women lacked the strength and stamina of their men, he much preferred their torture. Usually they were content to slap or scratch, or spit on him. They were only really dangerous when they were armed.

As the door closed behind her, he sprang into a feral crouch so that he could watch her and see what foul game she wanted to play. His head spun from pain and hunger. Shaking his head, he forced himself to stay focused and sharp.

He had to.

Bethany wanted to weep as those beautiful blue eyes locked with hers. For a moment, she thought she'd vomit as she saw the insanity inside him. They had reduced him to a rabid animal. And worse was the knowledge that Epithymia had kissed him, and as such, had given him a truly unearthly allure now. Even filthy, he made her heart quicken and desire tear through her. Not that she wouldn't have felt it anyway. But she knew her cousin's sick touch.

"Styxx?"

He growled at her, backing away, deeper into the shadows.

Moving slow and easy, she held the water bucket out toward him. Still, he retreated from her.

Bethany placed it within his reach and then stepped to the door.

Only then did he approach it ... on all fours like a beaten dog. He was so wary and skittish, it broke her heart. He kept his gaze on her as if waiting for her to hurt him as he inched his way to the bucket. He sniffed it carefully then dipped his fingers into the water so that he could taste a few drops. Satisfied it was untainted, he expelled an elongated breath. Those blue eyes didn't waver from her as he cupped his hand and took a drink as if he hadn't had any water for days. There was no refinement to him at all as he drank fast and furiously.

Someone coughed in the hallway.

He shot away from the bucket, back into the cell's corner, where he crouched, ready to fight.

Bethany manifested a loaf of bread. Holding it out for him, she approached him slowly. This time she got close enough to see the ragged scratches and cuts on his face. The blood and dirt matted in his beard. The deep and ugly healing wounds from weapons, fangs and claws on his arms, legs, chest, abdomen and back.

As badly as his body had been scarred before, it was nothing compared to what she saw now. Did they not allow him any armor in the arena?

From the look of his body, he must fight against his opponents completely naked ...

"I won't hurt you," she said gently. She tore a piece of bread for him. "Here."

The suspicion in his gaze shredded her conscience. Even though she heard his stomach rumbling from hunger, he refused to take her bread.

When she was almost close enough to touch him and he'd reached the limit of his chains, his eyes flared with anger.

"It's all right." She got rid of the bread and held her necklace up for him to see it. "Do you want it back?"

The moment his gaze focused on it, a single tear slid down his filthy, swollen cheek.

And that succeeded in wringing a sob from her. "Give me your arm and I'll return it to you."

Styxx hesitated before he obeyed and scooted close enough for her to reach only his wrist. He held out his scarred right hand that he still couldn't open all the way from when the Thracians had attacked him and pinned it to the ground with a dagger.

Ignoring the scars, scabs, and bruises on his forearm, she wound it about his wrist and secured it.

He crawled back to his corner and sat in a tight ball, clutching his good hand over her necklace as if it was a priceless treasure.

This time when she approached him, he didn't move. He sat rigid, his breathing ragged as he continued to rub her necklace with his ravaged fingers.

"What have they done to you?" she breathed, reaching to brush his hair back from his battered face. Given his condition, the more appropriate question was probably what had they *not* done to him.

He closed his eyes and held his arms over his head as if he expected her to slap or claw him. And he kept his good hand locked over her necklace to protect it.

And that broke her heart even more. Wanting to comfort him, she traced the line of his jaw.

"Don't." His ragged whisper surprised her.

"Don't what?"

His eyes filled with tears, but none fell as he glanced away.

Her fury mounted. She wasn't about to leave him here to be treated like this. Rising to her feet, she blasted away the chains that held him. Instead of being relieved, he scrambled away to try and find something to protect himself with. His eyes wild, he searched the room with his gaze.

That only made her madder. As bad as Apollo had behaved, her own pantheon had traumatized him worse than anything imaginable.

Damn them all!

She held her hand out toward Styxx. "I won't hurt you. Bethany sent me."

For a moment he calmed then he shook his head as agony refilled his gaze. "You're lying."

"I swear, I'm not. Take my hand and I'll get you out of here."

Styxx knew better. He was only allowed outside for deplorable things. Better to be tortured and raped in private than out in the arena for everyone to see and cheer. Nothing good ever happened outside of this place. 'Course nothing good ever happened *inside* either.

But at least in here, he was sometimes left alone.

She reached for him.

He recoiled and glanced to the door he knew was locked. Or worse, it wasn't, and if he went into the hall they'd throw him down and cage him then haul him into the arena to fight until they beat him down and punished him again.

"Take my hand. I promise I'll take you away from this."

But he wasn't stupid or naive—they'd beat that out of him a long time ago. "And go where?"

"Where I can heal you before I send you home."

Bullshit. He was never going home again, and at this point, he no longer wanted to. If his father ever found out about this . . .

No. He just wanted them to kill him. Yet even that was asking for a mercy no god was willing to extend.

Bethany's eyes teared up at the suspicion in those celestial blue eyes. *How could I have allowed them to do this to you? How could I say I loved you and not have bothered to check on you, at all?*

Guilt tore through her. "You can trust me."

He scoffed at her words as if they were bitter to him. But with no real choice, he finally placed his hand in hers.

Bethany took him to her temple on Katateros. Summoning a formesta, she wrapped it around his battered and bruised body.

Styxx held his breath as the goddess gently urged him to follow her to an indoor atrium that had a huge pool in the center of it.

"Would you like me to help you bathe?"

He shook his head. He didn't want anyone to touch him.

"Very well. I'll be right back with food."

His stomach knotted with dread and hunger, he glanced around, waiting for it to be another trick. Somehow it had to be . . .

But that steaming water looked so inviting. He couldn't remember the last time he'd had a real bath and not buckets of ice-cold water dumped on top of him. He started away from it, but the temptation to get some of the filth off his body was too great.

Either way, they're going to fuck me. At least let him have a little comfort before the next violent round began. Slowly and with great trepidation, he made his way to the stairs that led down into the warm, steamy salt water.

He tested the step, expecting it to give way or for something to come out of the water and attack him. But nothing happened. Taking a deep breath, he dropped the formesta and tentatively entered the pool.

He'd barely begun to relax when the woman returned.

Styxx made his way to the far end of the pool, and backed up so that he could keep her in his line of sight and his spine and hand against the tile. Just in case.

Bethany blinked away tears as she saw the way he continued to watch her as if expecting an attack. She set the tray of food down not far from him then she went to get bathing implements.

When she returned with them, she noticed that the only thing he'd taken to eat was an apple. One he scrubbed and inspected very carefully. He put it in his teeth to hold it while he kept one hand on the edge of the pool and the other free.

She uncovered the canisters to show him the soaps, oils, and lotions. Then she picked up the razor and mirror and left them for him. She backed away to sit on her white chaise.

Only then did he continue to eat his apple. All the while his gaze would only leave her so that he could randomly search the shadows from time to time.

When he finished with his single apple, he placed the core on the tray and took the razor.

Fascinated, she watched him shave without using a mirror. She'd never seen a man do that before. But as he cleaned himself, he uncovered evidence of what had been done to him. Fresh scars and bruises and injuries in places that made her want to hunt down those who'd hurt him and make them pay for it.

She conjured him a towel and fresh clothes.

When she started for him, he shot to the opposite side of the pool.

"It's just a towel, pants, and a formesta." She set them down and backed away again.

Only then did he leave the pool.

While he dressed, Bethany averted her gaze from his back, which was a bleeding, bruised mess of injuries and fresh scars. Those bastards. How could they have tortured him like this?

When she returned her gaze to him, he had a deep frown on his face as he studied her emblem on the back of the formesta. "What's wrong?"

"Is this you?" he asked through clenched teeth.

"Yes."

Anger and panic darkened his eyes as he dropped the formesta and looked for an escape.

"It's all right."

His breathing intensified. "You hate me. You've tried to kill me repeatedly. You set a bounty for my head."

"No ... I mean, I did. But I don't."

That only confused him more.

"It's the same emblem on your necklace that Bethany gave you. Look at it."

He did and his scowl returned.

"I'm her patron goddess. I didn't know you were her Hector. Had I known, I would never have tried to hurt you. I swear it to you, Styxx."

Tears filled his eyes as he caressed her necklace. "Do you know how she fares? Is she well?"

"She is."

Swallowing hard, he let go of the necklace and picked up the formesta. His movements were so slow and pain-filled that it wrung her heart. This wasn't the graceful warrior and lover she'd known. This was someone who'd been beaten to the brink of death and kept as an animal for far too long.

"Would you like something else to eat?"

His hungry gaze made her own stomach cramp in sympathetic pain. But he shook his head.

Then she realized why. "It's not drugged." Getting up, she went and took a bite of the food herself. Next she poured the wine and tasted it for him.

Even so, he didn't take it.

"What's wrong?" she asked.

"I've already fallen for that trick. You'll have to think of a new one." It was only then she realized he still had the razor tucked into his hand as he watched her warily as if waiting for her to turn on him. "Are you going to rape me, too?"

She winced at his question. "No."

His eyes accused her of treachery and lies. But the worst was the agony and exhaustion she saw in the depths of his crystal gaze as he continued to search out every shadow. "I'm not stupid. I know you didn't bring me here and clean me up to be nice. Where are the others?"

"There are no others."

"Don't lie to me," he snarled. "You only clean me up when you're going to pass me around. I'd rather you get on with it than pretend to be kind." His gaze returned to the shadows. "Is Archon or Asteros watching? Ydor?"

She winced at the confirmation that her family was every bit as depraved as the Greeks. "There's no trickery or treachery, Styxx. I swear."

But he wasn't about to believe her, and honestly, she couldn't blame him. He'd been abandoned by his family. His gods.

And her.

Right now he needed to rest. Yet she knew he wouldn't relax after what they'd done to him. How could he? They had put him through horrors that no one should suffer.

And she couldn't send him home until she found out what Apollo was doing in Didymos. How he was keeping Styxx's imprisonment a secret from his ever-neglectful family.

So she used her powers to lull him until he *was* drugged.

"Put the razor down, Styxx."

He hesitated before he obeyed.

"Take my hand."

Again, he tried to fight it, but couldn't. In the end, he placed his hand into hers and she pulled him to her bedroom. Even though he couldn't resist or fight her wishes, she felt his panic as he feared her intent. She pulled the formesta off his shoulders and tucked him into her bed.

She leaned over him and kissed his bruised cheek. "Sleep in peace, prince. No one is going to harm you."

His breathing ragged, he fought it, but in the end, his eyes fluttered closed and he finally relaxed. While he slept, she heard his stomach rumbling in hunger.

Silent tears fell as she ran her hand over the new scars on his chest and arms. Over handprints, cuts, and bruises, both fresh and healing, that attested to the nightmare he'd been through.

Alone.

For Apollo to hand him over to his enemies, who wanted vengeance not only against him, but against his people . . .

What had made the rotten bastard do something so cold?

In the end, she blamed herself for all of this. She'd walked away from him and gone on with her life.

That wasn't entirely true. She'd missed him every minute of every day, which was why she hadn't checked on him. She'd been too afraid to see him again. Because in her heart, she'd known that if she saw him, she wouldn't be able to leave him alone.

And she'd been right.

This had been the hardest year of her life. Every day she'd gotten up thinking it would be easier and instead, it'd been harder. Knowing he was out there and she couldn't go to him . . .

It'd been pure hell.

Against her common sense, she tucked herself into bed and snuggled up to the only man she'd ever loved. And with every glimpse of his injuries, she hated herself for allowing this to happen to him.

He would never have willingly left her to such a fate. Never willingly have walked out of her life for any reason . . .

She was a goddess. She'd known how alone he was, and what had she done?

Left him unprotected in a world that hated him.

"I am so sorry, Styxx." But that changed nothing about the horrors he'd endured and survived because of her heartless neglect. "I will make this right for you. Whatever it takes." She had no idea how, though. Apollo would be furious when he found out that she'd taken possession of Styxx. Technically, he still owned him.

And knowing that her own pantheon had participated in Styxx's abuse . . .

That they had allowed him to be held here and tortured for entertainment.

It was enough to make her side with Apollymi. *Damn you all for this!* How could they be so incredibly callous?

One thing was certain, she had no intention of helping them hunt down Apostolos. They could all burn for what she cared.

They deserved it for what they'd done to a decent man whose only crime had been fighting for his own people in a war hers had started.

Bethany wrapped her arms around him, wishing she could erase everything from his memory. But she didn't have those powers.

And for the first time in a year, she was finally happy again as his spicy, masculine scent and the warmth of his long, hard body lulled her. All she wanted was to hear him say what he used to say whenever they had a long separation, *"I missed you with every beat of my heart."*

Most likely, he would never say that to her again. And who could blame him? She'd betrayed him in the worst sort of way.

Would you be able to forgive this?

No, she wouldn't. Not for anything.

It was unconscionable and cruel. Closing her eyes, she cradled his head and laid her hand over the horrible bruise on his cheek. "No one will ever hurt you again, *akribos*. I won't let them."

Styxx took a deep breath and sighed. *I must be dreaming.* Even though he was starving, he was too warm and comfortable. More than that, he felt soft curves against his body and smelled the sweet eucalyptus and lily scent that he'd craved more than anything.

Unshed tears tightened his throat as he waited for it all to dissipate, and leave him back in his filthy hole, chained to the wall.

That was his thought until the body next to his rolled over and threw a knee into his crotch.

Hissing in pain, he opened his eyes to see a golden green gaze that mirrored his own shock. For a full minute, he couldn't move as he waited for her to vanish.

"Beth?"

Bethany was frozen by the anguished longing that seared her. She must have fallen asleep next to Styxx ... which would have returned her to her real appearance.

And since they were in her temple, she had her eyesight.

I should leave. But she couldn't. Those blue eyes held her immobile.

"Hi," she breathed.

He stared at her as if she were the last delicacy on the planet and he hadn't eaten in a year or more. Before she could move, he slowly lowered his lips to hers.

Bethany groaned at how good he tasted. He rolled her to her back as he deepened the kiss and made her head swim. He'd always been a phenomenal kisser, but this one . . .

It made all his previous kisses seem chaste.

Styxx closed his eyes as her tongue danced with his and her scent filled his head until he was drunk from it. *You know this isn't real. It's a trick . . .*

But he knew her taste. Her smell. The way she held him. How could this be a trick? He buried his face in the crook of her neck and let the horror of the last year fade away. She felt so good in his arms. And when she cupped him, he trembled.

"I've missed you," she breathed in his ear.

"With every beat of my heart," he whispered back to her.

Bethany choked on a sob as he slid his long body against hers. He dipped his head down to suckle her breast. Cupping his head, she sank her hands into his soft golden hair.

"Please be real." His ragged plea tore through her.

Guilt stabbed her so hard, she couldn't breathe. "I'm real."

He laid his head down on her stomach and gathered her into his arms. His hot, silent tears scorched her as they fell against her skin. He held on to her as if she was his lifeline. As if she was unspeakably precious.

Then he reached out and took her hand into his and pressed it against his cheek. The expression on his face as he savored her touch made her heart break for him.

Until he tore himself away from her and backed away. "Just kill me . . . please."

"Styxx—"

"You're not my Beth," he growled ferociously.

Another tear fell down his cheek. Throwing his head back, he roared out in pain. "You wanted me broken, you fucking bastard! Fine! I yield!" he shouted then he lowered his voice to a whisper.

"I yield." The pain on his face as he looked at her tore her apart. "Please, don't do this to me. I'd rather you beat or rape me than use my Beth against me." He reached for her then balled his hand into a fist.

Leaving the bed, he sank to the floor and curled into a ball. He covered his head with his arms.

She knelt down beside him and brushed her hand through his hair. "Styxx . . . it's me."

He refused to look at her. "No. My Beth doesn't call me Styxx . . . she doesn't hate me." He cupped his hand around her necklace and sobbed like his heart was as splintered as hers. "Please don't taint the only good thing I've ever known. I'll do anything you ask. Just don't taint her memory. It's all I have left."

"Okay." She kissed his head then withdrew from him. "You rest and I'll return later."

He slinked back on the floor, into the corner like a whipped dog.

Bethany got up slowly as her fury tripled. In her mind, she saw him as he'd been. Proud. Fierce. Defiant.

Protective.

And now he was completely shattered.

It's my fault. All of this. She'd known how isolated he was. How willing he was to give up everything he had, even a throne, to be with her as a poor blind peasant.

Yet for *her* family's sake, for the sake of her people, she'd let him go. She'd put all of them before him and how had they repaid her?

They'd violated and destroyed the only thing she'd ever loved. They had torn him apart and laughed while they did it.

Rage darkened her sight as she went to Archon. He was alone in his own temple, using a sfora as he tried to find the child she hoped would kill him.

Forcing herself to appear calm, she approached him slowly. "Did you know Prince Styxx was in Aeryn?"

"Huh?" He wasn't really paying attention to her. "What did you say?"

"I asked if you were aware that Prince Styxx was being held by the Atlantean queen."

Archon snorted derisively. "Have you been under a rock? He's been the main attraction for months now."

"Not under a rock. Searching for Apollymi's son." Actually, she'd done everything she could to stay away from Atlantis and to not think of all the times she'd tried to kill Styxx as he invaded her homeland. Thank her father's powers for keeping her from making the biggest mistake of her life.

Archon finally looked up with his full attention. "Unfortunately, he's not nearly as feisty as he was when he was first brought here, but if you want to take a turn with him, he's still good for a few laughs."

Her stomach cramped at those harsh words. "What all has been done to him?"

Archon sat back as he thought about it. "Apollo had been passing him around on Olympus until Athena found out and stopped it. Then he brought him here for our amusement."

Those words hit her like a blow. "What type of amusement?"

"What do you think we did to him? He led an army into our nation and slaughtered our citizens and mortal family members. We couldn't let that go unpunished. Once we got bored with him, we threw him to the queen as Apollo's gift and she had him put in the arena for fights and other highly creative events so that her people and soldiers could take out their own grievances against him and the other Greeks."

"And no one in Didymos has noticed his absence?"

"No. Apollo took care of it."

Did she even want to know more than what Frick and Frack had already told her? "Care of it. How?"

Archon shrugged. "Don't know. Don't care. So why the interrogation over him?"

"I didn't know he was here until today."

"Ah. Well, if you get a chance, you might want to attend the fight this afternoon. Even as wrecked as he is, he manages to hold off his attackers until they spring a trap on him, or unleash the dogs or cats to bring him down. It's much more entertaining to watch when you know he can't win no matter what he does. Still he tries to win. It's so strange, really. The humans and Apollites also take wagers to see how long he'll last. Then at the end, they let the crowd determine the punishment for his crimes."

"Punish him how?"

"He's either sentenced to be beaten or ceremonially raped for the crowd's entertainment."

Her breath left her lungs. Hard. It took everything she had not to attack Archon. "And you find this acceptable for the man who refused to harm our innocent people? One who used his own troops to make sure Atlanteans weren't raped while the Greeks fought here?"

He shrugged nonchalantly. "Our people are the ones who decide his punishments. Not me. I'm not about to interfere with their entertainment after the terror he put them through."

"And how long do you think this punishment should last?"

"Talk to his owner. Again, I'm not interfering for a piece of Greek shit that doesn't matter to me."

But he matters to me . . .

Bethany counted to ten and forced herself to leave before she gave in to the urge to blast Archon where he sat.

Instead, she went to Didymos next to see what had happened during her year of extreme stupidity. How was it possible that Styxx could be gone from home for a year and no one would notice?

Yes, she was violating all kinds of pacts, treaties, and bylaws, but she didn't care at this point. She wanted too much blood . . .

Bethany started for the palace then stopped herself. Galen would be the one who would have missed him. Surely if anyone knew Styxx was gone, it would be his sole friend and mentor. So she went to the barracks where she found the old man in his quarters.

Assuming the guise of a Didymosian soldier, she entered. "Where's Prince Styxx?"

Galen sighed wearily. "I don't know. I haven't seen him in a *very* long time."

She used her powers to compel him to speak what was on his mind. "Are you all right, Master Galen?"

"Not really, but it's not me I'm worried about. The prince hasn't been right since his woman left him."

"How so?"

Galen sighed heavily. "I know war often changes people, and losing someone you love ... but he's just not the same boy I trained. It's almost like he's possessed by something. Like a demon has control of his body. But don't breathe a word of that. I don't want to see him returned to the Dionysion. Not after what they did to him the last time."

In that moment, she knew exactly what Apollo had done. She just didn't know why. Her anger mounting, she left Galen and went to the palace where she found "Styxx" laughing with a member of the senate. "He" felt her foreign god powers immediately and turned all attention toward her.

Bethany crooked a finger.

The "prince" excused himself to join her in the hallway. As soon as they were out of sight of the others, Bethany turned on Poena—the Greek spirit of retribution—and slammed the Olympian daemone against the wall. "Why are you masquerading as the prince?"

Poena shrugged. "Apollo told me to while the prince is being punished."

"For?"

"Hubris."

Hubris? Really? To the Greek gods, that was the greatest sin any mortal could commit, and she couldn't imagine Styxx, as humble as he was, ever thinking himself a god or above one. "Against?"

"My assumption would be Apollo since he's the one who called me in for it."

With every spoken word, Bethany's rage tripled. "And where would Apollo be?"

Poena shrugged.

Bethany grabbed her by the throat and shoved her into the wall again. "Fetch him to me. I'll be in his temple here in town. And if you value your existence, you will not pretend to be Styxx another day."

"Excuse me?"

"Oh bitch, please, give me one. Right now, I'm ready to call down every Olympian and Titan, and open a major can of Atgyptian whoop-ass on the whole lot of you. Or better yet, how do you think the Greek people would react if I told them how their gods blithely allowed one of their beloved heroes to be wrongfully punished for a full year by their enemies? How many converts do you think I'd get to our pantheon?"

"You wouldn't dare."

"Really, don't push me right now. Fetch your master to me and be quick about it." Bethany flashed herself straight into Apollo's temple . . . which could be construed as an act of war.

A war she was aching to start, even if she had to fight it single-handedly.

Disgusted, she walked around the open area and sneered at the altar where people had made offerings to Apollo for a benevolence the worthless prick totally lacked.

"What are you doing here?"

Bethany turned around to face him. "I am so glad you didn't keep me waiting."

Apollo glared at her. "You should have met me in Atlantis. Not here."

"If I were sorry, I'd apologize. As it is, this is merely a courtesy visit to let you know that I've freed Styxx from your hellhole."

Apollo shook his head. "You can't do that. He's not yours."

"My understanding is that you gave him away."

"I didn't give him to *you*."

"You cast him to my brethren to torment," she reminded him. "I am allowed to take him after that."

"Not unless you want a war."

"Really?" She raked Apollo with a sneer. "You'd start a war over a mere mortal?"

"Why not? I've started them for a lot less. Besides, he hasn't learned his lesson."

"And what lesson is that?"

Apollo's eyes flared with anger. "To bow down before his gods and to show proper respect to us."

She laughed bitterly. "Are you insane? You've damn near killed him. He's barely human after everything you've put him through."

There was no remorse in Apollo at all. "So?"

"He's a prince, Apollo. An heir. One of your own."

"And both he and his brother have committed hubris against us."

She frowned at something Styxx had never mentioned to her. Ever. "Brother?"

"Yes. The little whore sleeping with *my* sister."

"And you're sleeping with theirs. What's the problem?"

Apollo sent a burst of power through the room. One so violent, it blew her hair back. "Problem," he roared. "They're trained whores!"

"Then take your anger out on his brother," she said between gritted teeth.

"Oh believe me, *I have*. But I'm still not done with him. Not for the crimes Acheron's committed against me."

"While you amuse yourself with vengeance against his brother, let Styxx go."

Apollo curled his lip at her. "This doesn't concern you. Why are you even here? You told me when we made this bargain that you didn't care what I did with Styxx."

And those words sliced through her like broken glass. She'd been stupid and thoughtless.

Unfortunately, she couldn't tell Apollo the truth or he'd use Styxx against *her*. Something that would bode a lot worse for Styxx.

So she settled on a lesser reason. "That's before you brought him to our shores. Now it *is* my business. I am the goddess of retribution and I know when someone deserves to be punished. He conducted himself honorably toward my people. I will not have him debased on Atlantean soil."

"Fine, send him home. I'll debase him here."

Oh yeah, that was what she was after . . .

Not even a little.

Bethany wanted to curse at the trap she'd stumbled into. But she couldn't allow Styxx to be hurt anymore. Not after this. "I want him left alone."

"What I do in Greece is none of *your* business."

"And what I do to your Apollites in Atlantis is none of yours . . . oh, and that list includes those Apollites who are in Greece . . . such as your son, Strykerius, and his children."

The color faded from his cheeks. "You wouldn't dare."

"Please, try me."

Apollo growled at her. "I still own Styxx."

"And I want you to release him."

"No."

"No?" she asked incredulously.

"He has thrice defied me. Blatantly and without remorse. I will not have a human do that any more than you'd tolerate it. I told him when I started this that I wouldn't stop until he begged me to. Which he hasn't. Just three days ago, he laughed in my face and refused to heel. He told me he was enjoying himself immensely and had no intention of begging me for shit, and so let him have his bellyful of fun, I say." Apollo glared at her as if she was the one who'd laughed at him. "I will not stop until he begs me like a putrid human should!"

Bethany growled at both their obstinacy. Begging wasn't in Styxx's nature, and it shouldn't be. He was a prince and a hero.

"Have you not punished him enough?"

"He told me to do my worst to him. I'm only giving him what he asked for."

At that moment, she wanted to choke Styxx herself for being

so very stubborn. But his defiance and strength were part of what she loved most about him.

Just not today. Today she wanted to murder both Apollo and Styxx.

She glared at the Greek god who really pissed her off. "You are such an asshole."

"And you're not? Tell me, Bet'anya, when have you ever taken pity on someone your pantheon sent you out to punish?"

"For your information, I have. I don't blindly follow anyone's dictates."

"Bully for you, and it changes nothing. I have marked him and he stays marked."

"Fine. Now consider your son and grandsons marked . . . *By me.*" She turned to go home.

"What!" Apollo roared.

She smiled back at him. "When you're ready to trade, let me know."

"Careful what you're setting into motion, girl."

"You're the one who needs to tread carefully, *boy.*" She closed the distance between them so that he could clearly see just how serious she was on this matter. "And remember who my father is. You claim Isis as your mother. I know better. Set *is* my father, uncontested, and unlike your weenie pantheon, he *has* killed and mutilated gods. I not only inherited his powers, but I happen to be the baby girl he adores. His *only* child. When I was born and Archon refused to allow him access to me, he singlehandedly went to war with the Atlanteans and beat the shit out of them until Archon himself agreed to allow my father full visitation rights to me anytime he wanted them. And while I don't make it a habit of running to my daddy with my problems, I will for this. Are you ready for *that,* Greek?"

The light in Apollo's eyes said he wanted to put her through a wall. "Fine, you want him free? Get him on his knees and have him beg me for it. Only then will I grant it."

"Swear to me."

"I swear by the River Styx that if he gets on his knees and begs me for forgiveness, I will renounce my ownership to him."

She inclined her head to him then left to return to the barracks where Galen had gone to sharpen his sword. This time, she wore the guise of Athena.

He immediately genuflected to her. "My lady."

Hating her deception, Bethany took his hand and pulled him to his feet. "There is someone we both love who needs us, Galen."

"Styxx?"

She nodded. "The man you've seen here for the last year wasn't him. But rather an imposter sent by the gods to play havoc with his life."

"I knew it ... I knew my prince wouldn't be so rude and harsh." His nostrils flared. "Apollo, you bastard."

"You know?"

"I suspected. He has plagued the prince since the day Styxx killed his grandson in battle."

"And he has exacted a very nasty vengeance upon him. Since Styxx hasn't been home and no one other than the three of us know it, I don't want to put him right back into the palace. He needs to be someplace with someone I can trust to help him adjust to being free again. And he needs time to physically heal from what has been done to him."

"I would do anything for my prince."

Grateful to the old man, she inclined her head to him. "I will bring him to you tomorrow, but be warned, he is much changed."

"Thank you, my goddess."

Patting his arm, she left to return to her temple.

As she started into her bedroom, she caught her true reflection in the black marble of her walls. Styxx hadn't handled seeing her as Bethany very well and the last thing she wanted to do was hurt him more. Swallowing, she changed forms again to a blond Apollite then she opened the door.

At first she didn't see him. It wasn't until she realized her balcony door was open that she knew where he'd gone.

She pushed the door farther ajar to see him sitting in a corner with his legs drawn up to his chest and his arms wrapped around them. Appearing more vulnerable than she'd ever seen him, he stared out across the valley and was so still he looked more like a statue than a fierce warrior prince.

"Styxx?"

He said nothing, but he glanced over to her. She walked slowly toward him.

Unmoving, he watched her warily.

"On your behalf, I've made a deal with Apollo for your release." She knelt by his side. "He wants you to beg him for it. On your knees. Can you do that?"

He scoffed bitterly as if he didn't believe her at all. "Sure. Why not? What does it matter now?"

She reached to brush his hair back.

He caught her hand in his and stopped her from touching him. The self-loathing and shame in his eyes burned her soul deep. "What fee do I owe you for your services, goddess? You want to fuck me, too? Publicly or privately? Or would you rather I pay you in blood? I would offer you my soul, but it's already damned."

None of that was what she wanted. What she missed. "What of your heart?"

He glanced down to the necklace wrapped around his wrist and winced. "I gave it away a long time ago and it was crushed and broken. I have nothing else to offer you."

"Would you give me your friendship?"

Styxx blinked slowly before he looked away. "I have no understanding of that word."

"None?"

He shook his head.

"Tell me of this woman who has your heart. Could you ever forgive her for hurting you?"

"It doesn't matter."

That was so not true. It mattered greatly to her. "Why?"

He withdrew back into himself.

486

Bethany wanted to touch him, but she knew he wouldn't welcome it. Not the way they'd all used him. "Will you not answer me?"

"What do you want me to say, *akra*?"

She flinched at the Atlantean term that meant "lady and master." It was a slave's term they used for their owners.

"I'm just a whore and a dog. I matter to no one and I have no feelings." His emotionless tone ripped out her heart.

You matter to me . . .

Her gaze fell to the scars that crisscrossed his entire body. To the brand marks that lined his left side from armpit to thigh. Then she glanced to the jagged one above his heart that she used to always make a point of kissing. The stab wound his mother had given him when he'd taken his gift to her.

How many times had she told him that she'd never hurt him and yet she had done as much damage or more than they had. She'd walked away and abandoned him when she knew he had no one else to love and comfort him.

I have no right to ask for your forgiveness.

She'd been too careless with a most precious gift. His heart.

A tear fell down her cheek as she remembered the first time he'd told her that he loved her.

Sitting by her stream, she'd been leaning against him in the circle of his arms. He'd taken her hand in his and drawn an Egyptian heart shape over the center of his chest.

"Hector, what are you doing?"

"I'm giving you my heart, my lady, but please be gentle with it. It's brand new and unused."

"You're so silly . . . Precious, but silly."

"As long as I make you smile, I will always be a fool for the woman I love."

"You love me?"

"Like the full moon loves the night. I might always be around, but I only shine in your presence. And no matter where you go, I will follow you, even if I'm a million miles away." He'd held her hand to his chest for her to feel his heart beating. "And this part of me will never belong to anyone else. I don't give gifts lightly and I never take them back."

That day seemed like a century ago to her and she could only imagine how much worse it was for him.

"Is there anything I can get for you, Highness?"

He frowned as if he didn't understand the question.

"If I brought you food, would you eat it?"

Again no response. So she conjured him a bowl of apples and set them beside him. Bittersweet memories tugged at her heart as she remembered how often he'd bring apples when they met. He'd use his dagger to cut them into slices then gallantly feed them to her.

"Why do you like apples so?"

At first she didn't think he'd answer then he whispered, "Easy to carry."

"Is that the only reason?"

He swallowed, but still didn't meet her gaze. "When I was a child, my father would send me to bed without dinner whenever I disappointed him. Which was a lot. So my brother would sneak apples to me before he went to sleep. They remind me what it's like to have someone who loves me."

Those words wrung a sob from her. "But you never talk about your brother."

He laughed bitterly. "There's no need to. He hates me now."

"Why?"

"Acheron thinks that just because he has it bad, I have it good."

"Does your brother not see the truth?"

"People make their own reality, goddess. We hate and we love for reasons that are known only to us."

And this was what she'd missed most about him. His heart and his intelligence. They'd spent countless hours talking about ideas and human nature. Philosophy. He could speak to her in numerous languages and whenever there was a Greek word she struggled with, she could use the Egyptian or Atlantean and he'd translate it for her.

"You still haven't told me your price, goddess."

She conjured him a platter of meat, fruit, and bread with a kylix of wine. "Eat for me."

Even though she could hear how hungry he was, he hesitated. Dear gods, what had they done to his food that he was so afraid to take any?

A sad shadow of resignation darkened his eyes. He picked up a slice of venison and ate it. Once he was sure it was safe, he forgot all manners and dug in to the rest of the food. She winced at the sight of her refined, dignified prince eating like a rabid animal.

And he cleared the whole platter. There wasn't even a crumb left.

"Would you like more?"

He shook his head then licked his fingers.

"Are you sure?"

Suddenly aware of his lack of decorum, he reached for the napkin and wiped his hands and mouth. He looked so tired and defeated. She ached to hold him and soothe his pain.

When he yawned a second later, she frowned as she caught a strange light of something ... "What's that?"

He returned her scowl. "What?"

"Open your mouth again."

He did and her heart wrenched. Someone had pierced a row of small silver balls down the center of his tongue. Her vision turned dark at the sight. It was a common practice in Atlantis to do that to sex slaves.

"Who did that to you?"

The shame in his eyes made her own tear up. "Apollo when he took me to Olympus."

She'd felt them earlier when they kissed and he'd licked her breast, but hadn't realized at the time what it was. Now that she knew, she wanted blood. "Would you like me to remove them?"

"Your will is my will, *akra.*"

Bethany touched his lips with her fingers and used her powers to dissolve them.

Styxx took her hand in his and held her wrist to his nose. "You smell so much like my Beth."

"I am your Bethany."

He shook his head and released her.

Sighing, she stood up and held her hand out to him. "Come, Highness. You look like you're about to pass out."

He rose without touching her and followed her back to bed. She tucked him in and started humming.

Styxx pressed his hand to his ear. "Why do you mock me?"

"Mock you? How?"

"Please put me back in the arena. I don't want to be here anymore."

She was flabbergasted. "You'd rather be chained like an animal than rest in my bed?"

He nodded.

"Why?"

"I don't want to be reminded of what's forever lost to me. It hurts enough without your making it worse." The ragged tears in his voice made her ache as she realized that anything she did that reminded him of her cut him more.

"Very well. I won't sing. I'll leave you to sleep in peace." But that was something much easier said than done. Because he didn't sleep peacefully. Rather, he tossed and turned as nightmares tortured him. They were even worse now than they'd been whenever he'd napped in their cottage.

And as bad as it hurt for her to see that pain, it was the number of times he called for her in his sleep that sliced deepest. Unable to stand it, she sat on the bed beside him while he fitfully slept and mumbled a heartrending "Bethany."

"Shh," she breathed in his ear, trying to soothe him. Using her powers, she awakened him so that he could see it was her in his arms, but not so much that he'd be lucid enough to shove her away.

"Bethany?" He spoke her name like a prayer.

She laid her hand against his sculpted cheek. "I've missed my Hector."

Closing his eyes, he buried his face in her hair and breathed her in. He hardened immediately. Her eyes widened as she felt his cock on her thigh. She'd forgotten how big he was.

"I think you've missed me, too."

He answered her with a kiss so hot, it left her breathless and weak. Desperate to please him, she nibbled her way over his bare flesh. It was so strange to finally see the body she knew as intimately as her own.

Or so she thought.

Frowning, she brushed her hand through the sparse, short hairs of his groin to see a brand that infuriated her to an unbelievable level. Her hand shaking, she laid her fingers over the slave's mark and ground her teeth. It was bad enough he'd been used as a whore, but to mark him as one . . .

It was unbelievably cruel.

Why didn't I leave with him all those years ago when he asked me to?

It would have saved him so much pain and degradation. So much misery. Right now, they could have been in a little cottage somewhere with a baby . . .

Just the three of them.

Instead, she'd chosen duty and obligation, and left him in the hands of people who weren't fit to watch a doormat.

How can I ever make this up to you?

Could she ever make it up to him? She didn't know, but she was determined to try.

Styxx growled as Bethany took him into her mouth. His head spun. It'd been so long since he'd last known her precious caress. So long since a loving hand had touched him at all. Was this real? It felt like it, yet it seemed more like a dream.

But he needed it to be real. Just for one moment. One heartbeat.

Don't leave me again.

Even though Bethany had abandoned him, he wanted her back so badly that when they'd taken her necklace from him, it'd felt like someone had ripped off a limb. Nothing had hurt him more.

And as she touched him, memories surged. Some so painful they threatened to rip him to the core of his soul. But somehow her touch grounded him in the present and made them recede.

For one moment, he forgot everything except those precious afternoons where he hadn't been Prince Styxx. Where there had only been him and a beautiful woman who'd given him laughter in the midst of utter Tartarus. Someone who had taught him to smile and look forward to something.

Someone who had taught him hope and love.

His jaw quivered as pleasure shot through him. And as good as her mouth felt on him, that wasn't what he wanted.

"Hold me, Bethany," he breathed.

She kissed her way up his body and then laid herself against him. Styxx expelled his breath in a rush before he cupped her head in his hands and kissed her.

Rolling over, he pinned her beneath him as she spread her legs in invitation. He took her hand into his and kissed her palm as he slid into her.

Bethany moaned at how good he felt. It seemed like an eternity since she'd last held him. Over the past year, she hadn't allowed herself to remember this. It'd been too painful.

But as she looked up at him and felt him inside her while he held on to her as if she was the most important thing in the universe, she tried to remember how she could have been dumb enough to walk away.

How could she have ever chosen anything over someone who loved her like this?

I don't deserve you.

She hissed in ecstasy as he thrust against her. "I love you," she whispered in his ear.

He lifted himself up to look down at her and cupped her face in his hand. He had no idea that she could see what she'd never seen before when they made love.

The tenderness in those blue eyes for her. The love and pain. It seared her. He buried himself deep inside her body. "Never once in my life did I feel sunshine on my skin until the day you touched me," he breathed in her ear. "And without my Bethany, I dwell in total darkness."

Her throat tightened. "I've missed my poet so." No one had ever talked to her the way he did. He could be so bashful and clumsy and at the same time so eloquent and graceful. It was what she loved most about him.

He was always unexpected.

In that moment, her body erupted with pleasure. Arching her back, she cried out as he thrust harder and deeper, giving her more pleasure until he finally joined her there. His breathing ragged, he shook in her arms. "I love you with all my heart, Beth," he whispered gently as he kissed his way to her stomach.

Sighing, he lay down between her thighs with his head on her belly. His breath tickled her skin along with his eyelashes and whiskers.

After a few heartbeats, she realized he was sound asleep. Laughing, she brushed her hand through his hair and thought about the day they'd first met when he'd fallen asleep in her lap.

But then he always fell asleep with her. She knew from their chats that he didn't sleep well on his own. Yet any time they were together, he'd doze off for a bit. It'd always warmed her that he trusted her when he never trusted anyone else.

Her smile fled as she looked down at the mark of Apollo on his back, and all the other wounds and scars there. Styxx would hate her if he ever learned that she was a goddess who had abandoned him to Apollo's cruelty. That she belonged to the pantheon that had gone out of its way to humiliate and punish him.

And who could blame him for that? She should have fought for him instead of walking away. He would have fought for her with

493

everything he had. Styxx would never have abandoned her. Not for any reason.

Don't think about it.

She couldn't change what she'd done. But she could make sure that no one ever hurt him again. And she would. Even if she had to defy every god on Olympus and Katateros. No one would ever lay another hand to her prince.

Please forgive me, Styxx.

Yet even then, she didn't know how to reenter his life after all this time. What would be crueler? To stay away or to return to him and remind him of how she'd left him when he needed her most?

How could he ever trust her again?

For that matter, would he ever be normal? She glanced down to watch him sleep. Even unconscious, he held on to her desperately. There had been no accusation or reservation while he made love to her. That gave her hope.

Of course, he hadn't been fully conscious either. Still, it boded well that he might welcome her back.

Or curse her to the level she knew in her heart that she deserved.

JANUARY 12, 9527 BC

Coughing and weak, Styxx came awake to bright sunlight pouring through a white marbled room. At first he had no idea where he was, until he remembered the goddess who'd freed him from his cell. He pushed himself up from the ornately carved and gilded bed with bloodred curtains.

"Careful."

His head spun as the blond goddess helped him to sit. "Why am I so dizzy?" He glared at her. "Did you drug me?"

"No, I swear it. You have a fever."

That explained why he was so chilled and hot.

She wrapped a formesta around him and drew it tight to his neck. "Let's get you bathed and dressed, and then I'll take you home."

Pain slammed into him at the thought of returning to the arena. But he held it in. Whatever fun she'd wanted from him she must have had. And in spite of what she said, he was sure she'd drugged and used him. They all did.

Except for when he fought. For that and what came after, he was always sober. Because it would be too kind for them to let him forget *that*.

Weary and disgusted, he followed her back to the pool and quickly bathed. There was no need to stay here any longer than necessary. At this point, kindness was the cruelest torture of all, because it made him feel human. Made him long for things the gods refused him.

Warmth. Friendship. Happiness.

Dignity.

She put a gray chiton on him then took his hand. Dreading his return to Tartarus, Styxx ground his teeth as they left her temple and materialized in a barracks area. An instant later, recognition hit him.

This was Didymos?

"Highness?"

Styxx couldn't breathe at the sound of that familiar gruff voice. "Galen?" His knees buckled.

The goddess kept him from falling.

Galen took his other arm and slung it over his massive shoulders. "What did they do to you, boy?"

Words failed him as his emotions surged and Styxx realized that he really was home again. It wasn't a dream or hallucination. It was real. He held on to Galen and wept in utter relief and gratitude.

Galen walked him to his quarters and helped Styxx into bed. He pulled covers over him. "I'll get the physician."

"You can't."

Galen turned to scowl at the goddess. "He's extremely ill."

"I know. But they think that he's been here the whole time. How are you going to explain all the marks on his body that tell a different story?"

Galen clenched his teeth as he saw the old and new cuts and bruises. "What did they do to him?" he repeated.

Bethany wanted to cry as she remembered the way she'd found Styxx in his cell. "You don't want me to answer that question and I know Styxx doesn't. Suffice it to say, he's been in the hands of people who hate him for a long time."

Styxx ignored them both as his breaths came in labored gasps while he stared at the whitewashed wall with disbelief.

"Thank you for bringing him back."

She inclined her head to Galen. "Please remind him once he's able to walk unassisted that he has to . . . " She curled her lip in anger at what the Olympian bastard required for his freedom. "Make reparations with Apollo."

"I will."

And with that, she was gone.

Styxx looked around the room, waiting for it to vanish. "Am I really here, Galen?"

"You are."

Still unable to believe it wasn't a dream, Styxx licked his chapped lips. "How long have I been gone?"

"I'm not sure. What was the last thing you remember?"

How could he forget? "The betrothal feast. Father announced Ryssa was pregnant."

Galen went pale as he sucked his breath in sharply.

That didn't bode well. Styxx frowned at the old man. "What?"

"Her son is almost five months old."

Styxx gasped as he realized it'd been almost a full year. And there was one terrifying event he wouldn't have been here for that would have come and gone in his absence. "I'm married?"

"No. You sent the Egyptian princess home after Acheron tried to rape her."

Deepening his scowl, Styxx tried to make sense of what Galen was saying. "I'm no longer betrothed?"

"No, Highness. Not for months now." Galen swallowed as fear shadowed his gray eyes. "Where have you been all this time?"

Styxx winced at the memories that tore him apart. "Atlantis." He didn't elaborate beyond that. There was no need to tell Galen he'd been kept caged, beaten and used as a tsoulus and worse. Not that it wasn't obvious given his physical condition. There were bite marks and handprints all over him and in places that said exactly how badly used he'd been.

Sighing, he tried to come to terms with everything. The last time he'd been gone this long, his mother had died. This time, he'd missed a birth. "Her son's really five months old? What's his name?"

"Apollodorus."

Gift of Apollo. It was enough to make him sick. How could he ever call his nephew by the name of his bitterest enemy? Especially knowing that enemy was the child's father?

But he wasn't going to be like his parents. He'd never hold the child's father against him. Of all men, he knew what that felt like. No matter what, he would love and protect the innocent boy.

Closing his eyes, he continued to sift through the events he'd missed. Until he remembered something else Galen had said. "Wait . . . *I* sent Nefertari home?"

Galen nodded. "I knew something was wrong. You haven't been acting like yourself, but I thought it was premarital jitters and battle fatigue. I should have known the minute I saw the imposter pick up your shield and fight that it wasn't you. He held it like it repulsed him."

Styxx laughed bitterly. "Don't be surprised if I have that aversion now, too." Because every time he'd touched one over this last year, win, lose, or draw, the outcome had always been the same.

Abject and public humiliation at the end of the fight.

"Yes, but I was able to knock *him* on his arse."

That would definitely not happen. Especially not after battling

497

the larger Atlantean fighters they'd thrown into the ring with him. His skills had never been more honed.

Or lethal.

And still they hadn't been enough to protect him.

"What else have I done?" He dreaded the answer.

Galen ground his teeth. "Honestly? You've been a royal asshole. Well ... not you. The other Styxx. And you ... or rather *he,* pissed off a lot of your men."

"How so?"

"He repealed the pensions and upped their yearly service quotas with no extra pay. He insulted all of us and has been behaving like an out-of-control brat to everyone. Even your father has had enough of you."

Styxx would give Apollo credit. He'd warned him that he was going to ruin him and he had. Not that Styxx had all that much to lose in terms of his reputation. But he hated that his men had suffered for it. That wasn't something he'd foreseen.

First thing he'd do was take care of them.

And Galen.

He tried to get up and start on it, but the moment he moved, he groaned in absolute agony and fell back onto the bed. Grimacing, he glanced to his mentor. "How bad do I look?"

Galen held up Styxx's arm that was riddled with bruises and cuts. "This is the least damaged part of you. You look like you fought Echidna and all her children. And I'm pretty sure the hydra swallowed you whole and shit you out her back end."

Styxx let out an exhausted breath. "Nice to know I look like I feel."

Galen laughed. "Now that's the prince I remember. Welcome home, son. I've missed you."

But I'm going to bet no one else has.

"Is the imposter still here?" Styxx asked.

"I don't know. I'll go to the palace and check then report back." After rising, Galen hesitated. He went to his chest and pulled out a mirror.

Styxx took it from him and gasped. One side of his face was bruised and swollen. His left eye was completely red and purple, and his nose and lips were crusted with blood. Even with his heightened ability to heal, it would be days before he could be seen. Unless ... "We could say I had an accident."

Galen pulled the top of Styxx's chiton down to show him the perfect handprint around his throat. "I guess someone attempted to save you by strangling you?"

"My father would probably believe that."

Galen snorted. "The goddess was right. If you go home right now, your father will summon a physician, and I'm rather sure you have other injuries you don't want him to see."

"Fine." Styxx relented. "What month is this?"

"Gamelion."

"Oof ... " The month of marriage and Apollo's festival. Bad fucking timing all the way around for him. "Has the festival passed?"

"Finished two days ago."

Thank the gods for that small mercy. Except for the fact that his double would have been here for it. "Did I attend?"

"Like a drunken camp whore."

Styxx could have done without that analogy. But at least the festival gave him an easy excuse for not being home. "Tell my father I was abducted by a lucius nymph and pulled to her lair."

"For the record, I resent being called a lucius nymph."

His mentor's humor caused a tear to slide from the corner of his eye as his homesickness and gratitude slapped him hard.

Galen frowned.

Styxx cleared his throat as he forced his emotions into restraint. "Sorry, Galen. It's just good to be home ... and safe. Even if it means looking at your grizzled face."

Galen took his hand and held it. "It's good to have you back and I will tell your father, but I'm sure your so-called laziness will not endear you to him."

"Let him beat me for it. At least he won't fuck me first." Styxx sucked his breath in as he realized the slip he'd made.

But there was no judgment in Galen's eyes. "Rest easy, Highness, and I'll return as soon as I can."

Styxx watched until Galen left. He still couldn't believe he was here. He'd never thought to see home again.

Let's show His Highness *how we treat puny Greek whores in Atlantis!*

He flinched at the memory as hostile voices assailed his thoughts. Images of him being brought down by packs of dogs and leopards, and shoved into traps, tore through him. But as bad as they were, they were infinitely better than the other memories he had. And nothing was ever going to drown out the sound of the crowds cheering as he was brutalized for public entertainment.

Growling out loud, he wished to the gods he could go back in time. Regardless of his orders or the repercussions, he'd have marched his army straight up the Atlantean queen's ass and planted his phoenix banner through her forehead.

JANUARY 17, 9527 BC

"You ready?"

Styxx nodded. "No."

Galen laughed. "For a moment, I almost thought you were."

Taking a deep breath, Styxx left the barracks. He was still extremely sore and cut in places he was able to cover. But worse was the fear in his heart. He had no way of knowing what he was about to walk into.

How much damage had Apollo done to him and his family relationships? While Galen had filled him in on what he could, there were still giant gaps in his information.

As they neared the palace, Galen pulled him to a stop. "We can always go back and let you rest for a few more days."

Don't tempt me.

"My father is already going to be pissed beyond endurance. No need in making it worse." Grinding his teeth, he started up the stairs and cursed the architect for every one of them.

By the time he reached the top, he was trembling in pain.

Galen stood at his back. "Take a moment if you need it."

Styxx wiped the sweat from his forehead then walked in. It was even stranger to be here now than it'd been when he'd come back from war.

The most disconcerting part was that no one knew he hadn't been home. *I am totally irrelevant.*

While he'd always had the suspicion, facing the reality was a lot harder.

"Where in the name of Hades have you been?"

Styxx exchanged an I-told-you-so glance with Galen. "In bed, Father."

The king's glare intensified until he burst out laughing. "At least you're honest. I trust you rode her well, then?"

Styxx was too startled to answer as his father approached him with humor in his blue eyes. *Who are you and what have you done with my father?*

Was this another imposter?

Styxx looked back at Galen. "She didn't complain."

Galen arched a brow.

Much, Styxx amended silently.

Frowning, his father took Styxx's chin in his hand and turned his face so that he could study Styxx's neck.

Cold panic gripped him. Was the handprint not gone?

"She must have been a biter. I can still see her teeth marks."

A shiver of revulsion went down him at the memory of Apollo and his violent feedings. Styxx lifted his chlamys to cover that side of his neck.

His father clapped him on the arm. "Rest easy today. Since I didn't know you'd be returning, I have nothing scheduled. You can resume your normal routine tomorrow."

Still baffled by his father's complacency at his absence, Styxx led Galen to the stairs. "What was that?"

Galen shrugged.

When they reached the hallway, Styxx paused and turned to the opposite direction of his room.

"Highness?"

"I want to meet my nephew."

"Are you sure you're up to it?"

He nodded as he made his way to Ryssa's room. Just as he reached it, a servant opened the door to show him where they'd put the nursery.

Unsure of what to expect, he tentatively entered the room the servant had just left.

The nurse looked up and grimaced at his presence as if the mere sight of him sickened her. Styxx ignored her as he saw the boy lying on his back on top of a white fluffy sheepskin blanket. Someone had strung stuffed and wooden toys over him so that he could slap at them.

A smile curved his lips as he watched the most adorable baby he'd ever seen. Styxx sank down on the floor next to him. "Hey, sprout. Where's your hair?"

Apollodorus's blue eyes sparkled as he laughed and reached toward him.

Amazed and instantly in love with the tiny creature, Styxx held his hand out and smiled wider as his nephew grabbed on to his finger and squeezed. "You've got an impressive grip there, sprout. One day, you'll be a fierce soldier ... or at least good at holding your reins." He wanted desperately to pick him up and hold him, but was scared to try. Apollodorus was way too small. But he was absolutely perfect and precious.

The door opened behind him. "What are you doing in here?"

He cringed at Ryssa's shrill, angry voice. "I wanted to see my nephew."

Shoving Styxx aside, she scooped Apollodorus up and stepped

away from the brother she loathed. "You're not welcome in here. I told you that. I want my son to grow up to be a man, and not a putrid bully like *you*. You are to stay away from him before you corrupt him."

Styxx bowed to her. "I'm sorry I upset you, sister. Forgive me. I won't disturb you again."

The look on Galen's face said that he wanted to say something to her, but Styxx shook his head. There was no need.

Styxx opened the door to find Acheron on his way in. His brother's eyes flared with anger.

He stepped back to let him enter.

Acheron slammed his shoulder and elbow into him as he passed by. "Fucking bastard," he growled under his breath.

Styxx laughed bitterly. "At least I've graduated up in rank from a generic asshole."

Acheron turned on him.

Ryssa grabbed Acheron's arm before he could attack. "Let it go, little brother. He's not worth your being harmed again. He's not worth anything." She placed Apollodorus in Acheron's arms then slammed the door in Styxx's face.

Styxx took a deep, sarcastic breath. "Ah, blessed family. How I've missed them all."

He saw his own grief and pain mirrored in Galen's eyes. "That was wrong."

Styxx tried not to think about it. "A wise man once told me that life, like war, is neither right nor wrong. It just is. And rather than worry over a philosophy you can't change, you should just try to live through it as best you can."

"You should have kicked that old bastard in his balls."

"Yes, but you kick back, and hit like a stampeding horse."

Galen pulled him into a fatherly embrace and kissed his head. "Let's get you settled into bed so that you can finish healing."

Styxx lifted his cloak to show him the blood that was seeping through his bandages and soaking his side. "My brother also hits hard."

JANUARY 20, 9527 BC

"This was not our agreement," Bethany breathed as she glared at Apollo and his dictate for Styxx's absolution. The Olympian sat on his throne, smirking. Her fist itched to knock the smugness off his face.

You unbelievable bastard!

Tears choked her as she watched Styxx walk naked down the center aisle of Apollo's temple in Didymos on the Apollodorian . . . the day when all freeborn members of the city were required to make offerings to their patron god. The temple was packed with citizens who were mortified and stunned by the condition of their prince's body, which still bore telltale traces of what had been done to him in Atlantis.

He was cut, bruised, and scarred all over.

So much for trying to keep it from his father. The king stood to Apollo's side with furious eyes that condemned his son. Meanwhile, Ryssa simpered next to Apollo, blatantly amused by her brother's public humiliation.

"You have something to say to me, Prince Styxx?" Apollo asked loudly, making sure everyone in the temple knew exactly who he was.

With a dignity that astounded her, Styxx sank down to his knees on the cold stone floor in front of Apollo's throne. "I am here to beg your forgiveness, my lord, for any offense I may have caused you."

Apollo scoffed rudely. "You don't sound particularly contrite. I think you need to repeat that, louder this time. And try to make it sound like you mean it."

The people around them whispered and conjectured on the handprints, injuries, scars, and bruises that marred their prince's body. Especially the huge sun symbol Apollo had burned into the center of Styxx's back. Some laughed about it, thinking that was what caused Apollo's outrage.

Their open mockery disgusted her.

Then she saw it . . . Styxx flinched at their ridicule and laughter, and his jaw quivered as if he was reliving the horrors he'd suffered in Atlantis. Somehow, he managed to get a hold of himself and repeat his apology. "I have come here to beg your forgiveness, my lord, for any offense I may have caused you."

Apollo sighed. "I'm still not hearing the appropriate tone from you. Indeed, there's more insolence than apology."

"My lord," the king said, stepping forward. "May I ask what offense he committed against you?"

"Hubris."

The king glared at Styxx as if he wanted to personally slaughter him.

Without a shred of compassion or care in her eyes, Ryssa sneered at her brother. "Surely such a high offense deserves a public beating, Father. Not even a prince is above a god. Let Styxx stand as an example to others to show what happens when they offend true divinity."

Styxx's breathing turned ragged, but he said nothing in defense of himself. He couldn't. One word, and this treaty would be breached and Apollo would continue to own him.

The king nodded to the guards. They moved forward to take Styxx into custody while Apollo smiled in smug satisfaction.

His father curled his lip. "One hundred lashes. If he passes out, revive him."

Her vision turned dark at the severity of that heartless and undeserved punishment. *You want a war, pig, you've got one . . .*

Bethany took on the guise of Athena and moved forward to stop the guards from taking possession of Styxx. As soon as she was seen, there was a collective gasp among the crowd.

She glared at Apollo. "Hubris you say, brother? Please, tell us the nature of the prince's actions against you. Let everyone know exactly how Prince Styxx offended you."

That definitely got the smirk off his face. "He has held himself up as a god. His arrogance and pride are an affront to us all."

She arched her brow at him. "Held himself up as a god? Pray tell, when was this?"

Apollo's look turned deadly.

"Ah, yes, I remember . . . " Bethany continued for him. "It was when he dared to slay your *Atlantean* grandson during battle. Is that not right, brother? I'm sure, like me, you remember that day well. The Atlanteans, led to our shores by your own blood kin, were slaughtering hundreds of Greeks until the beach sands turned red from good Greek blood. The onslaught was so fierce that entire veteran regiments fled from the Atlanteans and cowered. Even the brave, noble Dorians pulled back in fear. But not Prince Styxx. He rode in like a lion and jumped from his horse to save the life of a young shield-bearer who was about to be killed by one of the Atlantean giants."

Bethany swept her gaze around the people there, who were completely silent now. "And with reckless disregard for his own life and limb, this prince picked the boy up and put him on the back of his royal steed and told him to ride to safety. He spent the rest of the day fighting on foot. Not as a prince or a god, but as a mere, heroic Greek soldier."

She turned back to Apollo. "His actions so enraged the Atlantean gods that they turned all of their animosity toward him. And still Prince Styxx fought on for his people, wounded, bloody, and tired. He never backed off or backed down. Not even when your own grandson almost buried his axe through the prince's skull. He hit Styxx's hoplon so hard, it splintered a portion of it off. And as Xan held the prince down, the prince, who was barely more than a child, managed to stab him through the ribs. But now that I think about it, you don't remember that day, do you, Apollo? You weren't even there when it was fought, but later that very night—"

"Enough!" Apollo roared. His face turned bright red from his fury. Bellowing, he kicked Styxx back. "Get him out of my sight."

Bethany went to Styxx. She pulled her cloak off and wrapped it around his shoulders then she faced Apollo. "You never did answer the question, brother. Is Prince Styxx forgiven for saving the lives of thousands of Greeks and driving the Atlanteans from our shores, or do you intend to keep punishing him for such awful hubris against you? Do you, finally, release him from your slavery?"

"He's released. Now get him out of my sight!"

She helped Styxx to his feet.

"Thank you, my lady," Styxx breathed as unshed tears glittered in his eyes.

Nodding, she let Galen take him from her hands and walk him out of the temple.

And as they moved through the crowd, the people of Didymos went down on their knees to bow before their prince.

Bethany's smile died as she looked back at Apollo and the wrath on his face. He was not going to forgive this. The only problem was he didn't know it was Bet'anya who'd embarrassed him.

Crap . . .

Athena's going to kill me for this ruse.

She'd deal with that later. Narrowing her eyes at the bastard, she turned to leave. When she reached the temple door, an old man caught her eye. She started to ignore him until recognition kicked her.

Athena.

Quadruple crap . . .

The Olympian goddess followed her outside.

Bracing herself for the fight, Bethany turned to face her.

Athena held her hand up and smiled. "You have no idea how many times in my life I've wanted to publicly bitch-slap my brother. Thank you for the amusement."

Bethany laughed and took her hand. "I thought you were going to choke me for it."

"Not for this. But don't think for even one heartbeat that we're friends."

"I know. But I am a goddess of justice, and while I have no

507

problem tearing open someone who deserves it, I cannot stand to see anyone, even a Greek, wrongfully tortured."

Athena nodded. "Now can I have my body back? No offense, but I don't wear old man well."

Bethany resumed her true form. "I know now why you chose Styxx as your champion, Athena. You did well."

"You did better, I think."

"How so?"

Athena transformed into her goddess body. "He might fight under my badge, Bet'anya, but you're the only one he would die for."

"Leave us."

Galen hesitated at the king's furious order.

"It's all right," Styxx assured him, but he held the same doubt about that as Galen.

Inclining his head respectfully, Galen left him alone with his father.

His entire being throbbing and aching in protest, Styxx pulled himself up in the bed as his father approached him.

The king yanked the blanket from him, exposing his full naked body. "This isn't from a whore. What happened to you?"

Before he could think up a lie, his father hissed as his gaze fell to the cruelest mark he bore. His father rudely grabbed him so that he could examine it. Fury blazed in his father's eyes and for a moment Styxx was stupid enough to think it was indignation on his behalf.

"You think this is funny or cute?" his father roared in his face. "You're a prince, for the gods' sakes!" He backhanded him. "I don't know what kind of perverse games you play, boy, but if you *ever* publicly embarrass me as you did today, I don't care what army backs you, I will see you sold as the tsoulus whose mark you proudly wear. Do you understand me?"

Styxx couldn't answer as memories ripped through him. He heard the roar of voices that called out for his humiliation and punishment.

Fucking Greek whore! He's even branded one!

Prince, my ass. You're a worthless dog. Not even worth the brand you carry.

Are all Greek heroes pathetic quims like you?

And the whole time he'd been so cruelly held and tortured by the Atlanteans, he'd only wanted to come home.

For this . . .

His father backhanded him again then painfully grabbed his hair to force him to meet his angry stare. "Do you understand me?" he repeated.

Styxx nodded.

Curling his lip, his father wrenched his hair so hard, he was amazed he didn't yank a handful out. "I don't know what you did to upset Apollo, but you better make it right even if it means licking his ass and sucking him off for the rest of your putrid life. Whatever he asks of you, I expect you to bend over or go down on your knees and do it with a smile while thanking him for the honor." His father spat in his face then stormed out of the room.

Cold and shaking, Styxx wiped away the spittle then curled into a ball as the horrors of the last year replayed through his mind. But what hurt most was the knowledge that his father was fine with whoring him to Apollo.

So long as the Olympian god was pleased and happy what did it matter how his own son felt about it?

"Styxx?"

He couldn't respond to Galen. He just wanted to go someplace safe and warm. Someplace where no one hated him.

Most of all, he wanted his Bethany back. Only she had ever been able to make him forget the hatred he lived with.

"Highness? Are you all right?"

No. He'd never been right. That's why no one wanted him. Why Bethany had left him to this nightmare. Alone.

He felt Galen wipe away the blood on his face then cover him with the blanket.

Styxx ignored everything and crawled into the dark place inside himself that he'd discovered in Atlantis where the voices in his head screamed and he found a sick kind of comfort in the pain of it all.

Galen brushed his hair back from his forehead. How weird that the only tenderness he received came from a scarred warrior renowned for his ferocity in battle.

He stared at the xiphos strapped to Galen's hip . . . a sword Galen hated to wield. "You should go back to your Antigone."

Galen frowned at him. "What?"

Styxx blinked slowly. "Families should be together," he whispered. "Always. Nothing should keep them apart. And you shouldn't waste time with me when she's so much more important to you."

"You're my family, too, son. And you're every bit as important to me. More than that, you're the one who needs me right now. Tig understands and she sends her love to you."

Galen's kindness succeeded in breaking him out of his numb cocoon. Styxx sobbed as all the pain stabbed him and he fell apart from it.

The old man gathered him in his arms and held him while he cried until he was completely spent.

Exhausted, he pulled back from Galen. "I'm sorry."

"Don't you dare apologize for being human, Styxx. I never fought a war that I didn't go home to my Thia and cry for all the horrors I'd seen and committed. And after she was gone, I cried to my cups." He wiped the tears from Styxx's face. "You're a strong man. You've been put through Tartarus. And there's not a person I've ever met who could have done what you did today and not fall apart. It was harsh and it was wrong and you didn't deserve it."

"Maybe I did. Surely I had to commit some heinous act to chafe the gods' asses as much as I do."

"Bah," Galen scoffed. "You're just a pain in my old ass, and if I can tolerate you, I know they can." He pressed a fatherly kiss to his forehead. "Rest and I'll get you something to eat before you waste away to nothing. You're so skinny right now, one blast from Aiolos and you'd blow away." Patting him on the arm, Galen rose and left him.

The smile on Styxx's face died the moment he saw Apollo in the corner of his room. "What do you want?"

Apollo screwed his face up. "There's that tone again . . . You still, after all this time, have yet to learn your lesson about humility before a god."

That was because Styxx had no respect for the rancid dog. "You don't own me anymore. You released me."

Apollo laughed then flashed himself into bed with Styxx. He grabbed him by the hair and used it to yank him into his arms. "You're right. I no longer own you. But no one said I couldn't still fuck you or fuck with you. In fact, your father told me to let him know should you ever fail to please me again."

FEBRUARY 16, 9527 BC

Trying not to think about anything at all, Styxx paid for the hand-carved reed flute he was buying for Galen's birthday. He'd never really understood the old man's fascination with the instrument, but Galen loved to play, and while staying with Galen in the barracks, he'd learned that his mentor had accidentally left his flute at Antigone's. The old man missed it so much that his fingers twitched anytime he was around any object that remotely resembled one.

And at least Galen wouldn't stab or insult him for the gift. He might even appreciate it.

As Styxx took the flute and turned, he heard a dog barking not that far away. He ignored it until a huge black half-horse mongrel almost knocked him over. The giant dog jumped up on him and assaulted him with happy licks.

Recognition slammed into him. "Dynatos?"

The dog gave another happy bark.

It couldn't be. Styxx looked around for the dog's owner.

"Dyna? Here, boy!"

He couldn't breathe at the sound of a voice he'd never thought to hear again.

What do I do?

She'd made it abundantly clear that she didn't want to be with him . . .

Ever.

Suddenly, he saw her graceful form in the crowd, feeling her way toward him. He couldn't move at all as agony shredded every part of his heart and soul. Dressed in a long white Doric chiton and a red Egyptian drape, she was stunning. As was evidenced by his inability to move or breathe. Her long black hair was pulled up to the crown of her head and left to fall in thick, fat curls. Her hazel-gold almond-shaped eyes were ringed with kohl and pointed to look like a cat's. The gold bracelets he'd bought her were coiled around her forearms from wrist to elbow.

All he wanted to do was touch her, but she didn't want him at all. And he was tired of being rebuffed and thrown aside.

"Dynatos?" she called again. The dog ran back to her then he charged Styxx.

"Highness? You forgot your change."

Bethany froze instantly.

Shit. He was caught. If he spoke, she'd know instantly who he was. So he took the change and started to leave without saying a word.

But as he drew even with her, she spoke to him. "Styxx?"

He ignored the stares of the people around them who watched with fascination. Deepening his voice to disguise it, he braced himself for her public outrage. "Yes?"

Tears filled her eyes as she reached out for him.

Damn it . . . he couldn't stop himself. He took her hand into his and led it to his cheek, where he savored the warm softness of her skin, and the gentle scent of lilies and eucalyptus that he'd missed so much. A scent that hardened him so fiercely and quickly he was sure every person staring at them saw his erection.

She let out a happy sob then jerked him into her arms and kissed him with a passion that left him senseless.

Styxx fisted his hands in her red drape and held her close as Dynatos circled them and barked—as if they weren't enough of a spectacle without the dog calling attention to them.

Breathless, she pulled back and ran her hands over his face. "I've missed you so much."

Styxx arched a brow. "You kiss every stray man you meet in the market?"

She actually popped him on the biceps hard enough to hurt. "As a matter of fact I do. What was your name again?" She started to turn toward the merchant and reach for him.

Styxx took her arm and gently kept her by his side. He cupped her face in his hand and kissed her cheek. "I thought you were gone forever."

"We need to talk and I have a bad feeling that people are staring at us."

He laughed as he kept his face buried in her hair so that he could breathe her in. "They are, indeed." Reluctantly, he pulled away and tucked her hand into the crook of his elbow so that he could lead her through the curious crowd.

"Tell me when we're alone."

Styxx hesitated. "Why does the tone of your voice make my sphincter clench?"

"Don't be crude."

"You told me to always be honest with you, and so there you have it."

Anger darkened her brow. "But you weren't honest with me, were you . . . *prince*?"

"We're still in public."

She drummed her fingers against his arm, letting him know she was in a fierce pique. "Are we alone yet?"

"No."

"I don't hear anyone."

"That's because they're all gaping as we walk by. It's like a temple, precious. Statues everywhere, and they're listening intently to every word we speak."

An old woman frowned at them as they passed her. "I thought he sent the Egyptian princess home?" she asked her companion.

"Case in point," he whispered to Bethany.

"At least they think I'm a princess."

"You've always been a goddess to me."

Bethany stumbled at a comment that struck a little too close to home.

Styxx stopped immediately. "Am I walking too fast?"

"No. The dog bumped into me."

He continued walking . . . on and on.

"Where are you taking me? Asia?" she asked when it seemed like he had no intention of stopping.

"Away from people . . . Didymos has a dense population that I never considered the density of until right this moment. Damn, there's a lot of people here. And they're all really curious about us. Probably because they've never seen me in public with a woman not my sister, and since you're not spitting on me, slapping me, or calling me names, they know you're not Ryssa."

"Nor am I blond or Didymosian."

"Very valid points. How do you know Ryssa's blond?"

"Same way I know you are."

"I didn't tell you Ryssa's blond."

"Other people did."

"Ah . . . Galen!" he called out, startling her and letting her know they'd entered the military barracks. "May I borrow your quarters?"

"Sure. Good day, Lady Bethany."

"Greetings, Master Galen." She tried to find him to converse longer, but Styxx didn't pause as he continued leading her away.

"Cover her ears, boy," Galen said then added, "Make sure you change my sheets before you leave!"

"Na-ha-ha," Styxx feigned laughter. "You're so funny. I'm going to kill you later."

Finally, Styxx pulled her into a room and slammed a door shut. But since Dynatos was on the other side of it, he immediately started barking and scratching for entrance.

Styxx growled low in his throat before he opened the door and let him in. Then he closed and locked it. "All right. We're alone . . . except for the dog."

"All alone?"

"Except for the dog," he repeated.

"Good." She punched him hard in the stomach.

"Ow! You didn't warn me to arm myself."

"You might want to take a moment and grab a hoplon."

"Why?"

"Why do you think? *Prince* Styxx."

He expelled an irritated breath. "I shouldn't have lied to you about that. But I didn't want to scare you the day we met. Had I told you who I was, you wouldn't have talked to me."

"How do you know?" she asked defensively.

"Because no one ever does."

The pain of his whispered reply sliced through her, but while the truth saddened her, his opinion of her pissed her off. "You don't give me a lot of credit, do you?"

"Really?" he growled. "I'm wrong? Look me in the eyes and tell . . . "

She glared in his direction.

"Sorry."

Bethany reached up and pulled him into her arms. "I hate you."

"Most people do."

"I don't."

"You just told me you did."

"That's because I do."

He sighed in her ear. "Should we make tablets or lead sheets for you to flash your mood at me? I don't want to fall behind as you change it."

She kissed him then pulled back and popped his buttocks.

"Ow!" Styxx barked, moving away from her. "I'm very confused."

"So am I. I want to hate you so much, and yet you break my heart."

"I'm not the one who left." The tremor in his voice made her choke on tears.

"I didn't know what to do, Styxx. I found out who you were and I panicked."

"You could have talked to me. Preferably without the hitting."

"You deserve the hitting."

"I promise you, I've been adequately beaten in your absence."

Bethany flinched as she remembered the sight of his bloodied and bruised body when she'd found him in his cell.

Even though she couldn't see him right now, she covered her eyes with her hands as frustration, anger, confusion, and love mixed inside her. "I've run this meeting over a million times in my mind. I've seen me falling into your arms and kissing you then taking a sword to you for not telling me who you really were. And now my emotions are all over the place. I don't know what to think, and I should, but I don't, and I hate that I don't. But I don't hate you, Styxx. I could *never* hate you."

Styxx pulled her against him and kissed her forehead as all of his own volatile emotions warred inside him. But the one that was most overwhelming and the only one he couldn't suppress was how much he loved her.

How much he'd die for her.

Just how damn grateful he was to see her again.

"And I want to be mad at you, Beth. In ways you cannot conceive. You are the only thing in my entire life that I have ever loved. The only thing I have ever looked forward to. And you abandoned me without a single reason why. One day, you were just gone. And when you left, you banished me to the darkest pit of Tartarus and I didn't know what I'd done to you to deserve it."

He ground his teeth as agony tore through him. "Your parents love you, Beth. Yes, your mother irritates you, and your cousins annoy you, but your father lives and breathes for your smile. Your mother would kill anyone who threatened you. And I have *no* concept of what any of that feels like. I never have."

Styxx laughed bitterly at the reality of his existence. "Dear gods,

I never get a hot meal because I have to have someone taste my food for me before I eat it then wait to see if they die or are sickened from it. My bed has to be checked every night for poisoned sheets or lethal animals. My own family is as likely to poison me as a stranger. I went to give my mother a present and she stabbed me, multiple times. My father burst into my room and sliced my arm open in the middle of the night. My own brother and sister glare daggers through me anytime I happen into their presence. And my uncle ... "

"What?"

"It doesn't matter." He lived in a world fraught with nightmares and torture. One he had no right to ask her to share. In fact, he'd gotten used to being alone in it. He didn't need another thing to worry about or the added hell of thinking she would run off and abandon him again for no reason.

He'd had enough. All he wanted now was peace. Solitude from those who wanted to hurt him.

"You know what ... go back to your family, Beth. I can't let myself be hurt any more. I'm done with it. I'm tired of reaching out to people and being slapped for it. Except for not telling you I was a prince, I was brutally honest with you. I let you into places in my heart and soul that no one has ever had access to. And you carved my heart out and shoved it down my throat. The one thing that I learned most this past year was exactly how unimportant I am. To everyone ... Even me."

Styxx turned to let himself out the door, but the stupid latch was stuck. Growling, he kicked it.

"Styxx ... " Bethany wrapped her arms around his waist and leaned against him. "I never meant to hurt you."

"Oh, Beth ... " he breathed in a tortured whisper, "you didn't hurt me. You *gutted* me ... in my darkest hour, when I needed you most."

"I know, *akribos*. And I have no right to ask for your forgiveness. I'm not sure I could forgive me in your place. But I have missed you and I do want you back. I need you in my life."

Tears filled his eyes as he felt his resolve weakening. "I told you in the beginning to be gentle with my inexperienced heart. And that I would always be a fool for you."

"So you do forgive me?"

Taking her hand from his waist, he pressed it against his lips. "I don't know. I'm so messed up right now. It's even worse than when I came home from war. I can't eat. I can't sleep. I keep having nightmares that are so real I don't know if I'm awake or hallucinating. I'm paranoid of everyone around me. I've gotten to where I not only lock my door at night, I block it and I still don't feel safe."

Bethany flinched over the damage that had been done to him. *And it's all my fault.*

"If you will forgive me, Styxx, I promise I will never, *ever* do anything to hurt you again. Please. I beg you for one more chance." She started to kneel.

"No . . ." He turned around to face her and pulled her against his chest. "Don't you dare! I don't want to hear your pleas. I want your fire, Beth. It's what warms me."

"And I will keep you warm and safe from now on."

He tensed an instant before he kissed her.

Bethany melted the moment she tasted his lips. Then she squealed as he lifted the hem of her dress and ran his hands over her flesh. "What are you doing?"

"Galen gave us permission . . . I might be a prince, but I do know how to change bedsheets."

Laughing, she didn't say a word as he carried her to the bed and laid her back against it. But her laughter died the minute he opened her and tasted her with a passion that was absolutely raw. She arched her back and widened her legs, giving him full access. Biting her lip, she reached down to sink her hand into his soft hair only to realize he'd cut it so short he was practically as bald as Galen. It was even shorter than it'd been when he was at war.

She would have asked him about it, but his tongue was doing the most wicked things to her. Things she had missed terribly.

Styxx growled at how good she tasted. While he'd known he was starving for her, he had no idea how much until now. He just wanted to wrap himself up in her and never leave. If he could, he'd spend the rest of his life with her like this.

And when she came a moment later, he smiled as he continued to lick and tease her until she begged him for mercy. Only then did he climb up her body and slide himself into her.

She kissed him fiercely then frowned. "You're still dressed."

"I couldn't wait to be inside you."

Laughing, she stripped his chlamys and chiton off.

"We both have our shoes . . ." His words ended in a sharp gasp as she lifted her hips so that she could remove hers and it drove him in even deeper into her body. "You've been hiding talents from me."

She nibbled his ear. "I can't reach yours, though."

"Do you really want me to stop and remove them?"

"No."

Styxx lifted himself up to stare down at her while he thrust against her hips. She ran her hands over his body, raising chills in her wake.

Biting his lip, he rolled with her, making sure to stay inside until she straddled him. He reached up and removed the pins from her dress then pulled it from her. His mouth watering, he cupped her breasts in his hands, but as she rode him, unbidden nightmares overwhelmed his pleasure.

Suddenly, he couldn't breathe. Total panic swarmed him.

"Styxx?" Bethany frowned as he slid out from under her and rolled to his side. "Honey, what's wrong?"

He was absolutely trembling.

She brushed her hand against his arm.

"Don't touch me," he snarled, putting more distance between them.

Tears filled her eyes as she realized what had happened. He'd never liked the feeling of being physically restricted or tied down in any way. There were only a few positions that he could tolerate while having sex without them dredging up painful memories for him.

Her heart breaking, she cradled his head against her. "What happened to your hair, baby?"

He swallowed hard before he answered. "I grew tired of people using it to control and hurt me." Closing his eyes, Styxx allowed her to pull him to her so that she could hold him tight against her naked body. "I'm sorry, Beth. I told you I'm not the same as I was."

She kissed his cheek. "It's fine. You're always perfect to me."

Those words ravaged his heart. "I'm so broken, Beth. I don't know if I'll ever be whole again."

"You're not broken. You're wounded, and wounds can heal." She caressed his cheek before she laid a gentle kiss there. "The most beautiful heart of all is the one that can still love even while it bleeds, and especially after it's been shattered into thousands of pieces. You are the most courageous man I've ever known."

In that moment, he was glad that she'd run from him. Had she stayed, the imposter would have been with her. That would have been a blow he'd have never survived. Knowing someone else was lying with her like this . . .

Perhaps the gods had given him a very small mercy, after all. And as the agony and humility of the last year washed over him, he felt the hot, silent tears slide from the corners of his eyes.

She brushed them away with her lips.

"I'm so sorry."

"Don't be, Styxx. You're stronger than anyone I know."

But he didn't feel strong. He felt battered and beaten. A shell of what he'd been. Something that wasn't helped when she brushed her hand down the scars on his side. And yet her touch made it somehow all right.

No one loved him like his Beth did. She didn't look at him as if he was lacking. She teased instead of mocked.

And as he lay with her, she kissed her way down his body until she reached his feet. A smile tugged at the edges of his lips as she removed his sandals and said nothing about it.

Then she crawled up his body to lie against him so that she could place her hand to his cheek. "I have missed you so much."

He pulled her hand to his lips and nibbled her fingers. "I'm sorry I didn't tell you my real name. I just get tired of everyone hating me for who I am."

"I know nothing of that. Only that I love you because of who you are."

Closing his eyes, he breathed her in and let her touch erase the part of him that was still jagged and bleeding. And when she cupped him, he almost felt whole again. Within a few heartbeats, she had him even harder than before. He savored the sensation of her fingers teasing him while her breath fell against his skin.

She rolled to her back and guided him inside her. Styxx gladly followed, and this time when he began to thrust against her, there was no past haunting him. It was just the two of them. He stared down into her precious face and let her touch soothe his ragged emotions.

"I love you, *akribos,*" she breathed.

Those words, along with the softness of her touch, sent him over the edge. He buried himself deep inside her and growled as his body released itself. He lay on top of her, panting and weak, but happy for the first time in over a year.

Bethany cradled him with her body and ran the bottoms of her feet over the short hairs on his legs. As she went to nip his chin, she realized he was sound asleep on top of her. She rocked her forehead against his cheek and sighed. "I should be highly offended." If it were anyone else, she would be. But in his case, this was the ultimate of compliments.

Kissing him, she grimaced at how short he'd cropped his hair. But her anger wasn't at him for it. It was at all the bastards who'd used it to brutalize him to the point he'd wanted his beautiful locks gone.

Aching for him, she wrapped her arms around his body and held him close against her. "I promise you, Styxx. I will make this up to you."

And a promise made by her bound her eternally. If she failed this time, it would mean her life.

FEBRUARY 18, 9527 BC

Styxx held his cloak to his nose and breathed in Bethany's scent. He still couldn't believe she was back. He kept waiting to wake up and find it all a dream. For once, he didn't even mind coming home. He was still smiling as he reached the palace door and the guards didn't open it.

Instead, they seized him and dragged him to his father's study then forced him to his knees in front of their furious king.

"Fath—"

He backhanded Styxx so hard, his face exploded with pain. "Don't you dare speak to me, traitor!"

Frowning up at his father, Styxx wiped the blood from his lips.

"I know what you did last night. Damn you for it!"

Baffled, Styxx tried to think what about *that* would have his father so enraged. He'd spent the entire night with Bethany in their cottage.

Just the two of them.

"The next words out of your mouth had better be the names of your coconspirators."

I'm missing something here . . .

"What—"

His father backhanded him again. "Their names! Now!"

"Whose?" Styxx held both hands up as his father went to hit him again. "Please, Father. I don't know what you're asking about. What do you think I've done?"

Tears glistened in the king's eyes. "You betrayed me!"

"How?"

"You were seen! Last night. Overheard plotting *my* death with your friends!"

Styxx was aghast. While the thought of killing the old bastard had occurred to him on multiple occasions, he'd *never* be stupid enough to mention it out loud. Was his father insane?

Never mind the fact that his list of friends was only two.

Galen and Bethany.

"And you believe that?"

This time when his father went to hit him, Styxx dropped him to the floor and pinned him there.

The guards moved in to attack. With the skills he'd honed this past year while battling Atlanteans in the arena, Styxx grabbed the first one to reach him and disarmed him before knocking him out then he kicked the second one into the wall. He pulled the dagger off the guard's belt, twirled with it, and buried it in the stones less than an inch from his father's shocked face.

Not even breathing heavily, Styxx rose to his feet and glared down at his father. "If I wanted you dead, *Majesty* ... you would be dead already. By *my* hand. While I know you don't think much of me, I *am* your *protostratelates*. And I am the sole Greek commander who led an army into Atlantis and would have had them on their fucking knees in tribute to you and Greece had *you* not recalled me. *I* did that, Father. Alone. Pray to the gods you adore and that I spit on that you *never* face my full skill set when it comes to taking a life. Believe me, I don't need help killing you. But I don't want your fucking useless crown. If I did, I'd have taken it the day I rode home leading *my* army through the gates of Didymos."

Styxx stepped back and held his arms out to the sides of his body while his father pushed himself to his feet. "But I'm not going to argue this. I'm done begging for your love or anything else from you. If you truly think me guilty, execute me. I'll gladly walk to the block and lay down my head for the executioner's axe. Right now."

His breathing labored, his father looked from the dagger in the floor to Styxx and back again. "How did you ...? That's stone."

Styxx laughed bitterly. "I've cracked skulls through iron and bronze helms, struck off limbs with a single blow, and shattered shields a lot stronger than that."

"But in the practice ring—"

"I was sparring against an old veteran I love and adore. A man I would *never* harm." Styxx gestured to the dagger then to the humongous guard who was just now rousing himself. "And now you know why King Kreon and the others are so generous to you. It's not that they're afraid of *you*, Father. They're terrified of facing *me* on the battlefield because I don't fear death and I damn sure don't fear you. *That's* the hubris Apollo punishes me for. And I am done being hit and threatened by you or anyone else. Kill me or release me. Decide now and be done with it."

Incredulous, his father shook his head. "Who *are* you?"

"Fuck if I know most days." Styxx took a deep breath. "As for last night, I was with my lady, Bethany, from midday two days ago until I rode home and was dragged in here this morning, and I will not have her awakened to be questioned by you or anyone else. You either believe *me* or you don't. If you can't accept my word then be done with me forever." He glanced around at the guards who were gaping as they rubbed the bruises he'd given them. "So what's it to be, Majesty? Am I heading to bed or to death?"

"You were *seen*."

Styxx snorted. "And I'm not the only one with my face, am I?"

No sooner were the words out than Styxx cringed.

Aw shit . . . Why did I say that?

His father roared with anger as he ordered six guards to fetch Acheron to the throne room and stormed out the doors.

What have I done? Too tired to think straight, he hadn't even considered how his father would react to Acheron's possible guilt.

Please be guilty. Please be guilty . . .

The litany ran through his head as he followed after his father. His fury tangible, the king took his throne to wait for the arrival of the son he *really* couldn't stand.

Sick to his stomach, Styxx sat down as guilt tore him apart. What were the odds that Acheron was actually conspiring against the king?

He could be. He had a much bigger reason to hate their father than even Styxx did.

But the moment he saw Acheron's panicked face and heard his brother's confused thoughts, he knew better.

Fuck me . . .

He'd just thrown an innocent man into the fire. Acheron had been shackled. The guards forced him down on his knees in front of their father's throne while Ryssa came tearing into the room with her face flushed bright red to defend the only brother she loved.

Ever defiant, Acheron glared at them. "Why am I here?"

Their father came off his throne with a bellow of rage. "You do not ask questions of me, traitor!"

Styxx ground his teeth in anger.

Stunned, Acheron couldn't even blink for a full minute.

"Father!" Ryssa snapped. "Have you lost your reason?"

His answer was to backhand Acheron. "Where were you last night?"

Styxx forced himself not to react to a blow that exploded through his cheek and eye.

Acheron panted in pain. *I was with Artemis . . .*

Styxx froze as he heard his brother's thoughts. *Triple shit.* Acheron and Artemis? No wonder Apollo had such a hard-on for his brother. Now Styxx fully understood the god's fury and Apollo's incoherent rants that had preceded some of his more vicious attacks against Styxx in the past.

That, more than Styxx's defiance, was what had set Apollo off on his lunacy.

Acheron, you dumb shit. You're screwing Apollo's "virgin" sister? Really? Was Acheron out of his mind?

And it explained *the* groin pain that had hurt so badly there were times Styxx still ached from it.

525

Styxx had been in Atlantean custody, in the ring, when it'd felt like someone had gelded him. Literally. He would have sworn someone had cut him open and torn him apart.

Either Apollo or one of the others must have gelded Acheron. *How could you be so stupid, brother?*

Acheron locked gazes with Styxx and the accusation there scorched him. "I was in my room."

His father struck Acheron again. "Liar. I have witnesses who saw you in a stew, plotting my murder."

Terrified of anyone discovering that he felt Acheron's blows, Styxx covered his face with his hand to shield the blood on his lips.

"I've done no such thing." Acheron's voice trembled with his fear.

His father hit him again before he turned to the guards. "Torture him until he decides to tell us the truth."

Acheron cried out loud the same internal denial Styxx shouted in his head. His brother fought the guards holding him.

"Father, no!" Ryssa moved forward.

The king turned on her with a feral snarl. "You're not going to save him this time. He's committed treason and I will not allow *that* to go unanswered."

Styxx growled silently in his throat as utter agony filled him. *Why didn't I keep my mouth shut?*

Because he'd been tired and hadn't thought it through.

When will I learn?

His breathing ragged, Acheron, who was being restrained by the guards, met and held Styxx's gaze. *How could you plot the death of a man who worships the ground you walk on? I would sell my worthless soul to have just a portion of the love you spurn.*

Damn you, Styxx. Damn you!

Styxx winced at Acheron's thoughts. If he only knew the truth . . .

But Acheron would never believe it. Like everyone else, he thought Styxx had the beautiful, perfect life. But no one lived that.

No one. No life was spared grief or agony. The gods weren't

that kind to anyone. Ever. Everything looked so beautiful from the outside. But the interior view was never the same. Just like all the times as a small child Styxx had envied Acheron for living with Estes in Atlantis.

Yeah . . .

Acheron was hauled out of the throne room and taken to the prison below.

What have you done, Styxx?

He flinched at Ryssa's silent condemnation in his head. Like Acheron, she believed he was the traitor and that he'd framed his brother for it.

I'm as innocent as Acheron. Not that she'd ever believe him, any more than their father would believe his brother. What a messed up family they had.

But that wasn't the biggest concern. If neither he nor Acheron had done it, someone had lied to his father. Someone who wanted them all dead. Raw anger filled him as he looked about the room. It *had* to be one of the senators who stood back in silence. No one else would have a reason to come after him and lie like this.

Except Apollo. Was this what the bastard had meant when he said that he intended to screw with him?

Styxx almost came off his throne when he felt the first lash cut across Acheron's chest. Thankfully his father was preoccupied with Ryssa's tantrum.

She stormed to Styxx and glared at him. "I will call down the wrath of every god on Olympus for you, *brother.* And I intend to laugh when they chain you to a rock and have your traitorous heart cut out."

"Love you, too, lamb-head."

If looks were lethal, he'd be as dead as she wished him.

His body ached as more blows were given to Acheron. He glanced to his father who looked older than he ever had before. And that right there was why Styxx didn't covet his father's crown. Even now, his father wasn't sure if Styxx was lying or not.

The king would always be suspicious.

And there was nothing he could do to alleviate it.

Tired and aching, Styxx bit back a groan as another lash was given. "Father? May I have time to wash and change?"

The king nodded.

Styxx flinched as more pain hit him. Determined not to show it, he went over to his father before he left the room. "Who is our accuser?"

"I'll tell you once I get to the bottom of this."

Styxx ground his teeth in anger. *You don't trust us, your own children, but you trust a liar.*

Why was he even surprised?

Because he expected better from his father. He always had. But his father had never ceased to disappoint him.

Fine. There was nothing he could do about it. Disgusted, Styxx went to his room, and with every foul pain, he cursed himself more. How could he have been so stupid as to incriminate Acheron? But then he'd been caught off guard with no sleep.

How do I get you out of this, brother?

Determined to try, Styxx went to his bedroom door to leave so that he could find the one who'd accused them.

It was locked.

What the . . . ?

He pounded on it as hard as he could.

No one answered. Worse, he was suddenly so sleepy that he couldn't stand. Yawning, he tried to focus his fuzzy gaze. But it was useless. One minute he was standing, the next, he was lying on the floor.

Sitting in his Olympian temple, Apollo nodded to Poena and Eris, who had pleased him well with their wonderful cruelty against Styxx and his siblings. But then that was what they excelled at.

Tearing families apart.

"Good work . . ." Apollo said with a smile. "Now finish it."

They took off immediately.

528

Dionysus waited until they were alone. "Question, brother. Why do you hate the Didymosian princes so badly?"

Apollo ground his teeth. "Styxx has been a thorn in my ass since the day you introduced us. What mortal dares to turn away the affections of a god?"

"Not a bright one, that's for sure. And the other one you torture?"

Apollo hesitated. While he mostly trusted his brother, he wasn't about to tell anyone about Artemis's "pet." As much as he wanted to hurt Styxx for spurning him, he wanted Acheron's heart in his fist for daring to touch Artemis and contaminate her with his filth. But unfortunately, he couldn't kill one twin without killing the other and starting a war with his sister he wasn't ready to fight. Unfortunately, he needed that bitch to live . . . So he settled on a lesser explanation. "Collateral damage."

Dionysus arched a brow at that. "You gelded the boy for collateral damage? Damn, remind me not to piss you off."

Apollo gave him a droll stare. "I wasn't about to geld the one I'm sleeping with. I enjoy him too much for that."

Dionysus shook his head. "Harsh, brother. *Very* harsh."

"This from the one who sends madness out as punishment? *I* haven't made them slaughter their own children or eat their own body parts."

"As you would say, it is our moral obligation to keep the humans in line."

Yes, it was. And he wasn't through with the Didymosian twins . . . not yet. Not until Acheron learned to leave his sister alone and Styxx learned to bend to Apollo's whims and presence with a smile.

Ryssa was terrified as she returned to her room and handed her crying son over to his nurse. What was she going to do?

Unlike her father, she knew who the real traitor was. If witnesses saw someone tall, blond, and looking like Acheron, it was Styxx. It had to be. Acheron would have nothing to gain by killing the king, other than vengeance, and he wasn't the kind of person to go after vengeance for anything.

Not to mention Acheron would *never* have been in public uncovered, especially not a stew. Had he done so, he'd still be there, facedown, beating people off him.

"What have you done, Styxx?" she whispered through the tight lump in her throat.

Why would he plot against his own father? But then she knew. The history of mankind was written by sons and brothers wanting more, and willing to do anything to get it.

Even kill their own fathers.

"I have to find Artemis." There was no one else who could save Acheron from this madness.

Ryssa headed for her door to leave, but before she took three steps, the doors opened to admit the same guards who'd arrested Acheron.

"Your Highness, you're to be taken for questioning."

Her heart chilled at those words. "Questioning? This can't be."

But it was. Surrounding her with their muscle and terrifying visages, they took her to her father's study where he waited with Styxx. Never had she hated her brother more.

She gave them both the coldest look she could muster. "What is this, Father?"

He appeared so worn and exhausted that she felt awful for him. This was the worst sort of treachery. His handsome features were drawn tight with sadness. "Why would you betray me, daughter?"

She scowled at his question. "I've never done anything to betray you, Father . . . Ever."

He shook his head. "I have a witness who just came forward and said that you were with Acheron last night as he plotted my death."

She leveled a killing glare at Styxx. He had to be the one who'd named them. There was no one else. "Then they are lying as they lied about Acheron. I was with Apollo last night. Summon him and see."

Styxx's face went white.

530

So, he'd thought to rid himself of her, too. She couldn't believe her father's stupidity where Styxx was concerned. How could he be so blind to such a selfish villain?

Relief etched itself across her father's brow as he approached her. "I'm glad they're mistaken, kitten." He laid a gentle hand to her face. "The thought of my beloved daughter turning on me . . . "

What of his beloved son?

She looked past her father to see Styxx staring at the floor. "Acheron is innocent."

"No, child. Not this time. I have too many witnesses who saw him there."

Why couldn't she make him see the truth? "Acheron would never be in a stew, Father."

"Of course he would. He worked in one. Where else would he go?"

Anywhere *but* there. Her brother had hated every minute of being trapped in those places and being forced to sell himself for food and shelter. "Please, Father. You've done enough to Acheron. Leave him be."

He shook his head. "There is a nest of vipers coiled around me, and until I uncover the name of everyone he spoke to, I won't stop."

Tears filled her eyes as she considered the nightmare they were going to put Acheron through. Again. Needlessly. Why could her father not see the truth? "The priests say that Hades reserves a special corner of Tartarus for betrayers. I'm sure the name of your real traitor is being carved there even as we speak."

Styxx refused to meet her gaze.

So she looked back at her father. "In all these years, Acheron has sought nothing but love from you, Father. One moment of your looking at him with something other than hatred burning in your eyes. Nothing more than a kind word, and at every turn you've denied him and hurt him. You have shattered the son who only wanted to love you. Let him go before you do irreparable harm, I beg you."

Still, her father refused. "He's betrayed me for the last time."

"Betrayed *you*?" she asked, aghast at his reasoning. "Father, you can't believe that. All he's tried to do is stay out of your sight. Away from your notice. He cringes any time your name is brought up, or Styxx's for that matter. If you'd stop being so blind for one minute, you'd see that he has *never* willingly mixed with people and he has *never* betrayed you."

"He was a prostitute!" he roared in her face.

"He was a boy who had to eat, Father. Thrown away by his own family. Betrayed by the ones who should have protected him from harm. I was there when he was born, and I remember how all of you turned away from him. Do you? Do you even recall when you broke his arm? He was only two years old and could barely speak. He reached for you to hug you, and you knocked him away so forcefully that you broke his arm like a twig. When he cried out, you slapped him for it, and walked away."

"And that's why he plots your murder, Father," Styxx spoke up finally in a whiny, nasal tone. "Don't let a woman sway you from what needs to be done. Women are our greatest weakness. They prey on our guilt and our love of them. How many times have you told me that? You can't listen to them. They think with their hearts and not their minds."

Her father's face turned to stone. "I will not let him get away with it this time."

Tears flowed freely down her face at her father's blindness for the one true son he had. "This time? When have you ever allowed Acheron get away with anything?"

She blinked away the tears in her eyes as she tried to make him see reason. "Beware the viper in your closet. Isn't that another thing you're always saying, Father?" She cut a meaningful glare at Styxx. "Ambition and jealousy are at the heart of all betrayals. Acheron's only ambition is to stay out of your sight, and were he to have jealousy, it wouldn't be directed at you. But I do know of another who would gain immensely in his life were you gone."

Her father backhanded her. "How dare you implicate your brother."

"I told you, Father. She hates me. I wouldn't be surprised if she hasn't bedded the whore, too."

Ryssa wiped the blood from her lips. "The only person in this family that I know of who sleeps with whores is you, Styxx. I wonder if Acheron was supposedly seen in your favorite stew . . ." And with that she turned and headed out of the room and to the street to find Artemis and stop this before it was too late and Acheron was dead.

"Leave us!"

Acheron barely recognized the sound of his father's voice through the vicious, throbbing pains that racked his body. No part of him had been left unviolated or free of abuse. It even hurt to blink.

Once the room was empty, his father approached him where he lay on a cold, stone slab.

To his complete shock, his father brought him a ladle of water. Acheron cringed, expecting the king to hurt him worse with it.

He didn't. His father actually lifted his head and helped him to drink. But for the fact it would kill the king's beloved Styxx should he die, Acheron would think it poisoned.

"Where were you last night?"

Acheron felt a single tear slide from the corner of his eye at the question that had been asked over and over again. The salt from it stung the open wounds on his cheek as he drew a ragged, agonized breath. "Just tell me what to say, *akri*. Tell me what will keep me from being hurt any more."

His father roared with rage as he slammed the ladle down on the stone by Acheron's face. "I want the names of the men you met with."

And he didn't know the names of the senators. They'd seldom offered any before they'd screwed him.

And Artemis would *never* speak up in his defense. If he breathed a single word of their relationship to anyone, she would make this torture session appear desirous.

Acheron shook his head. "I met with no one."

His father buried his hand in Acheron's hair and forced him to look at him. "Give me the truth. Damn you!"

Lost to the pain, Acheron struggled to think of some lie that his father would believe, but as with the interrogator, he came back to the one single truth. "I didn't do it. I wasn't there."

"Then where were you? Have you a single witness to your whereabouts?"

Yes, but she'd never come forward. If he were Styxx and a prince, the goddess wouldn't be ashamed of their relationship. But Artemis would never stand up for a worthless whore. "I have only my word."

His father roared in anger. He reached for him, but before he could make contact, he froze in place.

Acheron held his breath as he tried to understand what was happening. An instant later, Artemis appeared beside him.

Stunned, he couldn't do anything other than stare at her.

"Your sister told me what they'd accused you of. Don't worry, your father will have no memory of this. Nor will your brother."

Acheron swallowed as he tried to understand what she was saying. "You're protecting me?"

She nodded. An instant later, he was returned to his room and healed. Acheron lay back on his bed, more grateful than words could express. But even so it didn't erase the pain of what he'd been through. Any more than it concealed the fact that Styxx was planning to overthrow his own father. The father who loved him more than the air he breathed.

How selfish could Styxx be? Their father doted on him . . . gave him anything he wanted, and still it wasn't enough.

Styxx wanted . . . no, he *demanded* everything.

What am I going to do?

Artemis materialized beside him. Her expression was sorrowful as she brushed the hair back from his face.

"Will Ryssa remember us?" he asked her.

"No. From this moment forward she won't even remember that you and I know each other."

That was for the best.

Acheron stared at Artemis, amazed at what she'd done. No, she hadn't stood up for him, but she *had* saved him. It was a major breakthrough from the last time she'd left him to their "tender" care and he'd been gelded. "Thank you for coming for me."

Artemis laid her hand to his cheek. "I wish I could take you away from here."

She was the only person who could do it. But her fear of being caught with a worthless whore was too great. And maybe she was right. What good would it do for her to be ruined over him?

He wasn't worth it.

Acheron kissed her on the lips even though he was still cold inside. He had nowhere to go and he was sick and tired of being here with people who hated him.

I want out. But every time he'd tried to kill himself, he'd been stopped.

Because of his idiot brother.

Acheron froze at the thought.

Styxx . . .

In the blink of an eye the simplest answer to his predicament came to him. Why had he never thought of it before? It wasn't himself he needed to kill.

Pulling back from Artemis, he held her hand. "You should go before someone stumbles in here."

"I'll see you tomorrow."

Not if he had his way. "Tomorrow."

Acheron watched as she faded, and the second she was gone, he immediately made plans for what was to come.

His father refused to let him die so long as his life was tied to Styxx's, and Styxx was plotting the death of his father.

The answer was so simple.

If he killed Styxx, his father would be safe and Acheron would be free.

Peace. He would finally have peace from this stygian existence.

535

FEBRUARY 19, 9527 BC

Styxx scowled as he readied himself for bed. Something had been off all day. He remembered leaving Bethany and then . . .

There was a significant gap in his memory. The kind he only experienced whenever his uncle had drugged him or one of the gods had done something with him they didn't want him to remember—and that was what concerned him most. Why had someone tampered with his memory?

Who had tampered with it?

Most importantly, what had happened during those missing hours?

His jaw was sore as if it'd been punched, but he had nothing else to answer his questions. Frowning, he kept trying to piece the day together. How had he gotten from the palace steps to falling asleep in fresh clothes on the floor of his room? Had a servant not come to wake him for dinner, he might still be asleep there.

It didn't make sense. No one else seemed to have noticed anything being off or odd. And because of his past, he couldn't stand not knowing what had happened during those missing hours of his life.

There's nothing you can do.

Still, it bothered him. Finishing off his wine, he went to bed, hoping that he slept through the night for once.

But he knew better.

The only time he had any kind of peaceful sleep was with Bethany.

He crawled into bed and sighed. Four more days until her return. Closing his eyes, he focused on her and did his best to shut out everything else.

*

Styxx woke up to a fierce, stinging pain. Gasping, he opened his eyes to see a shadow staggering away from his bed as something warm gushed from his chest.

Blood. Someone had stabbed him while he slept ... Rage consumed him. Fucking coward! *No one kills me and lives!*

Determined to mark his killer, Styxx jerked the dagger from his chest and shot across the bed after him. But the pain was so severe, he could barely breathe for it. Blood poured over him as he staggered from the bed. He went to throw the dagger, but his legs buckled.

He hit the floor hard. Over and over, he relived that moment when the Stygian Omada had returned from Atlantis, and had been ambushed by Thracians ...

I'm dying. He knew it. Which meant Acheron must be dying, too.

The wound had gone straight through his heart and ruptured an artery. It was the only explanation for this amount of rapid blood loss. Tears filled his eyes as he thought of his Bethany.

How cruel to lose her now.

He fought Thanatos as hard as he could. But in the end, against all effort, he expelled one final breath and everything went dark.

Styxx came awake with a sharp, painful groan. Completely disoriented, he scowled at the amount of blood on the floor and on his body. Grimacing, he touched the wound that was directly over his heart. Blood still seeped out, but it was light compared to earlier.

His assassin was going to be shocked when he learned he'd failed. The coward must have checked his pulse, since he was now on his back and he'd fallen on his stomach.

At least he knew Acheron wasn't dead.

Unsure of how much time had passed since his attack, Styxx feared for the rest of his family. The attacker could have gone after his father, sister, or Apollodorus. He had to make sure they were protected.

Ignoring the pain in his chest, he pushed himself up and

grabbed the red cloak Gaius and his men had given him. He took his sword then headed for his father's bedroom.

He bypassed the snoozing guards in the hallway and threw open the doors. "Father?"

Groggy, the king pushed himself away from the naked young slave woman in his bed and glared at him. "What is the meaning of this?"

Styxx pulled the cloak aside to show him the blood. "Someone tried to kill me while I was sleeping. I wanted to make sure they hadn't come for you."

His father paled at the sight. "You live?"

Obviously.

Somehow he managed to bite back that sarcasm before he responded. "Yes."

Styxx stepped away from the bed and turned on the guards who'd finally awakened and joined him in the king's bedchambers. "You," he said to the one on the right, "stand fast and protect your king. You, rouse the others for a search. Lock down the palace until we've looked everywhere for my attacker."

As they went to follow his commands, Styxx headed straight for Ryssa's rooms.

He checked Apollodorus first. The babe was asleep with his nurse. Styxx left two guards with them as an alarm was sounded for the others then he entered Ryssa's bedroom. She lay so still and pale that panic gripped him. Was she dead?

Gently, he touched her arm.

She came awake with a fierce screech.

Styxx breathed in relief, until she slapped him twice for waking her so rudely.

"What are you doing here at this hour? How dare you barge into my room uninvited! Who do you think you are? Are you trying to scare me to death?"

He ground his teeth as his cheek stung. "No, sweet sister. I wasn't trying to kill you. I was stabbed in my sleep and wanted to verify that you weren't attacked, too."

Her eyes widened as she saw the blood on him.

"Acheron!" She bolted from the bed and grabbed a red wrap. She was so worried about Acheron that she didn't even bother to close the door.

"Follow the princess," Styxx ordered the guard nearest him. "Don't let her out of your sight."

She didn't even ask if I was all right.

Even though he was covered in blood. Nor did she apologize for slapping him when all he'd done was come to ensure her safety . . .

The pain of that stung deep as he quickly searched her room to make sure it was clear. He left a guard posted in it then moved to check his brother. He was rather certain Acheron was unharmed, since Styxx felt no pain and lived.

"What do you mean?"

Styxx paused as he heard Acheron's question. He glanced at his two siblings, and the concern on Ryssa's face for his brother while his own cheeks stung from her slaps cut him deeply. There was no telling how red they were. Not that she cared. She'd never given him a single kind thought.

Acheron met his gaze over the top of Ryssa's head. The panic in those silver eyes felt like a kick to his groin. *He probably fears that I'll blame him for this.* But Styxx wasn't Ryssa. Having been on the receiving end of many false allegations, he tried not to jump to conclusions without hard evidence.

But as the defender of Didymos, it was his responsibility to keep his family safe.

"Find my attacker," he ordered the new group of guards, rushing toward them. "I want him now. Do you hear me? Search every corner until we have him."

"Have you seen anyone?" Ryssa asked Acheron.

He shook his head. "I was in my room."

Styxx started away then paused as a new threat went through him. He tended to forget that Acheron wasn't battle trained. Anyone could kill his brother.

"Guards!" he called out to another group that entered the hall-way. He gestured to his brother who stepped back in fear as if he thought Styxx might arrest him without cause . . . like their father had.

That fear made his heart clench. *I would never willingly hurt you, Acheron. Damn you, Ryssa, for the lies you tell against me.*

Heartsick, he pointed to Acheron. "Guard him. I want some-one at his back at all times."

Knowing his siblings didn't want him disturbing them, Styxx went to help search the rest of the palace.

As soon as he reached the stairs, he saw Galen bursting through the main doors as if Cerberus was on his heels. Relief spread across his grizzled features the minute he saw Styxx on the landing. Galen took the steps two at a time until he was in front of him.

Placing his hands on Styxx's shoulders, he scanned his body with a stern frown. "Good gods, son! You shouldn't be up. Where were you struck? Where is the physician for you?"

Tears choked him at Galen's concern. Out of a palace full of people, only Galen had bothered to ask after his welfare. He low-ered the neck of his cloak to show the wound. "I've had worse."

Galen snorted. "Yes and no. That needs stitching." He grabbed a young guard who was coming up the stairs. "Fetch the physician and send him to Prince Styxx's room. Fast, damn you, fast!" Then he took Styxx's arm and pulled him back down the hallway.

"I was searching for my assailant."

"Did you see him?" Galen asked.

"No. Not really."

"Then you're no good in a search, are you?"

"Yes, but—"

"No buts." Galen forced him into his room. "Your Bethany would have both our arses if she saw you searching with a wound like that. And you're covered in blood. Let's get you cleaned up."

Styxx had no choice as Galen hauled him to the bathing pool and helped him to wash the wound.

"Where's your father?"

"I left him in his rooms with his guards."

Galen glanced about the empty chamber. "Who's guarding *you*?"

Styxx held his sword up from where it rested on the floor beside Galen. "Me."

Galen scoffed as he glared at the wound and took the sword from Styxx's scarred hand. "And you're doing a mighty fine job of it, I must say. Why wasn't there a guard at your door?"

Styxx hissed as the warm water burned the injury. "You know I don't like people around me."

Galen arched a brow at that. "And yet you tolerate my sorry ass."

"You're entertaining."

"Keep insulting me and I'll stitch your wound myself. I know how much you enjoy that."

Styxx snorted as he remembered all the times he'd cursed Galen as the old man stitched his wounds after battle. "What can I say? Your delicate touch stings me."

Galen's gruff smile melted into a stern glower as he helped Styxx out of the water and to bed. "I don't want you to sleep again without at least two men on your door. I will be doing random checks and if I find your door unguarded again, I'm going to start standing at the foot of your bed at night. *All* night long."

Apollo would love that. Which was part of the reason Styxx hadn't wanted anyone at his door. That and he could hear their thoughts.

But Galen was right. After this, he couldn't afford to be stupid. "Yes, sir."

Galen growled as he looked about the room and especially at the huge bloodstain on his sheets and the floor next to the bed. "Where's that damned physician? You could have bled to death by now." Then his frown deepened as he realized that they were in the room alone. *Where's your father? What kind of man doesn't bother to check on his own son when he's damn near murdered in his sleep? No wonder he didn't care about killing my boy. He couldn't care less about his own.*

Stupid bastard.

When he glanced back, Styxx took care to keep his expression blank. "Can I get you anything?" Galen asked.

"I'm fine."

The physician came in. Galen stayed while Styxx was stitched then afterward Galen went to help search.

Hours later after Styxx, against Galen's dire threats, had rejoined the search for his attacker, it was obvious the culprit had escaped. Damn. It'd happened so fast and unexpectedly that he hadn't seen even the smallest detail as to who it'd been.

On his way back to his chambers, Styxx paused as he saw Acheron returning to his own room. Alone. Fully dressed and wearing a cloak and shoes, Acheron had obviously been outside the palace.

"Where have you been?"

Acheron glared at him. "You don't own me. I owe you nothing." *Bastard.*

Styxx held his temper in check. "No, you don't. But you should be careful. My attacker might come for you."

Thank the gods you didn't see me.

That unexpected thought slapped him harder than Ryssa had.

"I'll take care it doesn't happen to me," Acheron mumbled as he headed for the stairs.

"Acheron?"

He paused to look back at him.

Styxx wasn't sure what to say. He wanted to ask if Acheron had killed him. If his brother had discovered the truth Styxx had learned that afternoon when he'd first met Bethany. That he couldn't die unless Acheron did.

If Acheron knew, he gave nothing away while he waited for Styxx to speak.

"Sleep well."

Acheron scowled at him before he turned and continued on his way without responding.

FEBRUARY 23, 9527 BC

Bethany wanted nothing more than to see her prince. She'd had enough of Archon and the others raging over the fact that no one could find Apostolos, and that they only had a few more weeks until Apollymi came out of her jail, wanting their collective throats. If they kept this up, she was going to move to Egypt and be done with the lot of them.

She pushed open the cottage door. Dynatos ran ahead, barking happily. "Styxx?"

"Right here, sweet." He pulled her gently against him and held her close.

"What happened?"

"Nothing."

"Don't lie to me. I can feel it in the way you touch me. What's wrong?"

Styxx ground his teeth then smiled. He could never hide his feelings from her. She had an uncanny way of seeing his every emotion as if she could read his thoughts as well as he read everyone's but hers. "I think my brother tried to kill me while I slept."

"What?!"

"Don't breathe a word of it to anyone, please. I have no proof, and the last thing I want is to see him hurt over a suspicion that could be false."

Trembling for him, she ran her hands over his body, seeking an injury. "Were you hurt?"

"Stabbed."

"Where?"

He took her hand and led it to the stitches.

She sucked her breath in sharply at the location. "Your heart?"

"No. My heart is here." He placed her hand over her own chest. "You're not amusing."

He pulled her back into his arms and laid his head on her shoulder. "Just hold me for a little while. Please."

His humble, heartfelt request brought tears to her eyes. She sank her hands into his hair that was slowly growing longer and held him close. He'd needed her and yet again she hadn't been here for him because she'd been off with the others. It nauseated her that she'd let him down again. Yet he said nothing about it.

And as minutes went by and he didn't withdraw from her, she realized just how hurt he really was. Not physically, but emotionally. Who could blame him? If he was right, his own family had attempted to slaughter him while he slept. No wonder the man had so much trouble sleeping.

"Did you tell Galen your suspicion?"

"No. I was afraid to. As I said, I have no real proof and didn't really catch a look at my attacker."

Which meant he'd talked to no one about it, but rather had lived in silent torment. "When did this happen?"

"Four days ago."

She ground her teeth in anger that he'd been so long alone. "I'm sorry, Styxx."

"There's nothing for you to be sorry over. You didn't stab me, did you?"

She growled at his ridiculous question and ignored it. "You were hurt and I wasn't here."

"You were with your family. I understand."

He always said that to her, as if it was more important to him that she honor that obligation over the love she had for him. "You're my family, too."

"It's all right, Beth. Really."

Tears choked her as she held on to him. He *was* her family now . . . more than he knew. He was the father of her unborn son, but she couldn't tell him that yet. It was too soon.

She'd only realized it yesterday. For a couple of weeks now she hadn't felt well, which was extremely unusual for a goddess. Then, two nights ago, she'd dreamed of their son. He'd been fair-haired like his father with blue eyes and a precious smile, and he'd been dressed in a Greek helm ... a very small version of his noble father.

She'd conceived him when Styxx had been in her temple eight weeks ago, and their son would be born October fourth. She wanted to tell Styxx so badly that it was a physical pain. But she was terrified of how he might react. For too long Apollo and the other gods had played with his life. How would he react when he learned that his blind human fisherwoman was a goddess from two pantheons, far stronger than Apollo?

While Styxx might still love her, he'd be crushed that she'd lied to him. Or worse, he might blame her for not helping him combat Apollo or for fighting against Styxx and his people in their war with Atlantis.

Given the way he'd reacted in her temple when he'd discovered her emblem ...

It was possible he'd hate her forever. Not to mention what her mother's pantheon had done to him for the year she'd ignored him, and paid no attention to them. He had every right to hold that against her. Her undeniable stupidity deserved nothing less.

And eventually, she would have to tell him the truth, however today wasn't the day. Today, she wanted to focus on him and his needs.

In a few weeks, she'd tell him about their baby. Then later, she'd confess the rest. She just hoped he'd welcome the news of their son.

They'd never really spoken about children. And given the brutality of his own childhood, she'd stayed away from the topic out of respect for his pain. But he must have thought about it. As heir to Didymos, it was expected that he'd have children one day. Yet how strange that he never mentioned it to her.

Rising on her toes, Bethany pressed her cheek to his. "I love you, Styxx."

He cradled her head in his hand. "I love you. I always will."

She smiled and prayed that once he learned the full truth of her and what her carelessness had done to him that he continued to feel that way.

MARCH 10, 9527 BC

Apollo froze as he caught sight of Artemis in the woods outside her Olympian temple with Acheron. The two of them were laughing as they hunted deer in her sacred field. Fury ignited deep inside him. How dare his twin sister whore herself with a bastard byblow.

A prostitute, no less.

That was bad enough, but the fact that she would dare bring him here added to his indignation. It pained and infuriated him that Artemis had interfered with Eris's and Poena's plot to have the king punish her precious whore for treason. Every time he turned around, she was saving that bastard. The fact that both Didymosians continued to elude his wrath and plans was ever a vexation that ate at his gut.

No one defied him.

Ever.

Unable to stand it for another heartbeat, he teleported himself to Didymos where Styxx was leaving the weekly court sessions with his father. The prince walked behind the king with a grim countenance that said he was in need of more fiber in his diet.

"Styxx?"

He paused as his father turned to face him while their retinue continued on to give them privacy. "Sire?"

"Your sister is still angry at you. I was thinking you need to do something to placate her."

A tic started in Styxx's jaw. "What would you have me do?"

"Perhaps a gift? Surely, as intelligent as you are, you can think of something that would please her?"

"I shall have my heart cut out and delivered to her forthwith then."

The king curled his lip in revulsion. "I grow weary of your cheek, boy. You'd do well to curb it."

"Forgive me, Majesty." But his tone said he was anything other than contrite. It was the same tone that motivated Apollo to violence anytime the prince used it with him.

The king narrowed his eyes even more. "And speaking of your cheek . . . How go your reparations with Apollo?"

The tic picked up its rhythm as Styxx glanced away.

Before the prince could speak, Xerxes grabbed Styxx and slammed him back against the wall then growled in his ear. "I meant what I told you, boy. I am weary of your insolence and I will stomach no more of it. If I have to, I will put you down on your knees in front of Apollo myself to make sure you please him. Do you understand?"

"Yes, Majesty."

The king struck him hard in the middle of his chest then turned on his heel and left him.

Apollo waited until the king and his retinue had vanished before he materialized in front of Styxx who was still rubbing the area where his father had struck him.

Styxx cursed as Apollo trapped him in the dark corner. *Just what my lousy day needed . . .* "My sister's in her room."

Apollo tsked at him. "I think you know she's not the one I want."

Of course not. No one, other than Acheron and their drunken mother, could tolerate Ryssa for very long.

Styxx tried to step around the god he hated most. "I'm in no mood to entertain you." As he started past, Apollo backhanded him so hard, he hit the wall again.

Licking at the blood on his lips, Styxx almost retaliated then caught himself. While he could fight Apollo and even win, the god had already shown him how easy it was to rip him out of his life with no one being the wiser. How easy it was to put an imposter in as Prince Styxx, and, while he couldn't care less about his family, he did care about Bethany.

The imposter could hurt her or replace him in her bed. Worst of all, the imposter might make her hate him to the point she left him for good and never came back again.

Those were things he'd never take a chance on. No matter what, he had to bend to Apollo.

With no choice, Styxx reverted to what he'd been trained to do in Atlantis.

Survive.

Deadening himself, he lowered his gaze to the floor. "My will is your will, *akri*."

A smile curled Apollo's lips. "Better." He wrapped his hand around Styxx's neck and jerked him into his arms. Viciously, he sank his fangs into Styxx's jugular.

Styxx cried out as pain exploded through him. But Apollo had no mercy. For whatever reason, the Olympian was furious today and Styxx was his chosen scapegoat.

Think of Beth . . .

At least now, he'd have her arms to comfort him once it was over.

MARCH 12, 9527 BC

Styxx heard the knock on his door, but he was in too much pain to answer. He wasn't sure at what point Apollo had finished with him and teleported him home. Time on Olympus moved very differently than time here. Honestly, it felt like he'd been with Apollo for more than a month. He had no idea what had angered the Olympian, but whatever it was he'd taken every bit of it out on Styxx.

Someone jerked the drapes back from his windows, spilling harsh sunlight through his room. Hissing, Styxx moved to cover his eyes with his arm then groaned as more pain ravaged him.

"Get up! You worthless, whoreson, bastard!" his father growled before he threw a bucket of water over him.

Styxx gasped at the coldness that made his covers even heavier on his bruised body. He was shaking and hurting so badly, he could barely breathe, never mind move.

When his father stepped to pull him from the bed, he heard Galen's voice from the doorway.

"Majesty? Is something wrong?"

Now that they had a witness for his cruelty, his father pulled back. "What are you doing here?"

"His Highness was badly injured and I wanted to come by and check on his welfare."

Only then did his father look at him and see the bruises and cuts that covered his body. "What happened to you?"

"He fell from the stable loft," Galen said before Styxx could think of his own lie.

Finally, a modicum of compassion filled his father's eyes. "You should be careful . . . I'll have your morning appointments reset."

Styxx wiped at the blood and water on his face. "Thank you, Majesty . . . for your magnanimous kindness."

This time, his father caught the sarcasm in his tone. His glare promised later retribution. Without another word, he stormed from the room.

Shaking, Styxx tried to find a portion of his bed that wasn't wet.

Galen wrapped his cloak around his shoulders then stripped the wet linen from the mattress. "Lie still, boy." He piled the linens in a corner before he left the room.

A few minutes later, he came back with more blankets.

"Thank you, Master Galen . . . for everything."

Galen inclined his head to him. "I take it the king found out

549

you reduced the soldiers' yearly obligations or upped the pay for those who wanted longer ones?"

"That would be my guess for this assault."

Frowning, Galen inspected the bite marks on Styxx's neck and the bruises that covered him. "I thought Apollo released you."

"So did I. Apparently, we were mistaken."

Galen cursed under his breath. "I knew something was wrong when you missed practice yesterday and no one knew where you were."

"What day is it?"

"Middle of the week."

Styxx let out a relieved breath that he'd only been gone a day and a half. This time. Good.

Galen sighed wearily as he continued to inspect Styxx's injuries. "Have you eaten?"

He shook his head. "I have some apples in my table drawer."

His mentor went to retrieve two and handed them to him. "Munch on those, Highness, and I'll be back in a few minutes with something more substantial for you."

"Again, thank you, Galen."

Galen patted him gently on the shoulder before he left.

Leaning back with another groan, Styxx bit into his apple and grimaced at the teeth Apollo had knocked loose. He'd give the bastard credit, he could hit.

He tested his teeth with his fingers then winced. At least Apollo beat on him solely and left his sister alone. As far as he could tell, Apollo had never struck Ryssa. But he was getting really tired of being the Olympian's whipping boy.

There had to be some way to weaken the god and get out from under his thumb.

Whatever it took, he was going to find it and show the bastard what it felt like to be tied down and knocked around. Even if it took him ten thousand years, he was going to get back at Apollo.

One way or another.

MARCH 23, 9527 BC

Bethany kept her grip on Dynatos's collar as he guided her to the training arena where she knew Styxx would be with Galen. The moment they entered the area, she heard the clashing sounds of sword and shield as well as the men's good-natured insults for each other's abilities.

"You hit like an old woman."

"At least I am old. What's your reason, *boy*?"

Dynatos barked then jerked free of her grip and ran forward. Her heart stopped. "Dyna!"

She heard the sounds of Dynatos's attack. Galen cursed and hissed while Styxx barked as loud as the dog.

"Down, Dyna, down!" Styxx snapped.

Suddenly, Styxx was by her side with Dynatos. "Your dog doesn't like Galen hitting me."

"*I* don't like Galen hitting you."

Styxx kissed her lightly on the lips as Dynatos walked between them, while Styxx kept his left hand firmly on the dog's collar so that he wouldn't attack Galen again.

She sank her hand in Styxx's dripping-wet hair then grimaced. "Ew! You're all sweaty."

"You don't complain about my sweat when we're alone and naked."

"You don't smell like the back end of your horse when we're alone and naked."

Styxx laughed. "At least you didn't call me an old woman."

"Good day, Lady Bethany."

She smiled as she heard Galen approach from the side of them. "Hi, Galen."

"Would you like me to put your xiphos and hoplon away, my lord?"

She stopped Styxx as he moved to hand them over. "I actually came to listen to you two practice. Don't let me interrupt. I promise I'll keep Dyna off the field."

Galen snorted. "By the lovesick expression on Styxx's face, I daresay he'll be an even worse opponent than normal."

Styxx feigned laughter. "Thanks for making me look heroic to my woman, Galen. You could at least lie to her and tell her how fearless I am."

"Like a lion ... cub. All growl, with little baby teeth for biting."

She laughed at them and their gentle teasing then kissed Styxx on the cheek. "I know how fierce you are, my love."

Styxx handed his shield over to Galen and winked at him. "I think I'll give the old man a rest before he falls over from exhaustion."

"Don't listen to him. It's his own dignity he's trying to save, my lady. I shall put these away so as not to further embarrass him with his inferior skills. Good day."

Styxx took her hand and pulled her toward his dressing room. "Is something wrong?"

"Why would you think that?"

"You never come here, and I was supposed to meet you in a couple of hours at the cottage."

"True ... but I couldn't wait."

"For?" He released her hand and started disrobing.

She held her arms out and turned side to side. "Notice anything different about me?"

His body hardened at the sight of her playfulness that reminded him of one of her sensual Egyptian dances. "You're more beautiful than the last time I saw you?"

She smiled at him. "I love you ... but no. Try again."

Styxx frowned as he tried to discern it. Her hair was curled today, but she did that a lot, and it was the same ornate gold

552

diadem she always wore when she gathered it up to the crown of her head. She had on earrings, which she normally didn't wear, yet he'd seen those before, too. Someone had ringed her eyes with kohl, but again, she often wore Egyptian cosmetics. Her skin was as luminescent as ever. Her eyes every bit as golden tinged by green. Her lips hennaed and shiny with beeswax.

Unlike him, she smelled wonderful . . . but it was the same scent of lilies and eucalyptus.

For his life, he couldn't see a difference at all. Except . . . *maybe* she'd gained a tiny bit of weight, but he knew from Ryssa not to *ever* remark on a woman's weight fluctuations. He didn't own enough armor for that particular brand of stupidity.

He set his helm on the mannequin then went to unlace his greaves. "New dress?"

"Since you're having trouble with this, let's try a riddle. When do one and one make three?"

Styxx froze as he realized what she was trying to tell him. For a full minute, he couldn't breathe as her news slammed into him like an iron mallet.

She scowled. "Are you still here?"

"I am."

Fear creased her brow. "Are you not happy?"

He took her hand and led it to his face so that she could feel his smile then he kissed her palm. "I have never been happier in all my life." He kissed her other hand then knelt in front of her.

She scowled. "What are you doing?"

He held her hands in his and looked up at her beautiful face. "Marry me, Bethany."

"Your father . . . "

"I don't give a damn what my father or anyone else thinks, says, or does. You're all that matters to me. You and the baby you carry. And I know how you feel about marriage, I do, but I swear I will never, ever stifle your freedom or your thoughts . . . Marry me."

"Styxx—"

"Marry me . . . Please."

She bit her lip, and every heartbeat that passed without an answer was complete torture for him. Finally, she took mercy on his misery and spoke. "Yes."

He pulled her against him and kissed her stomach. Smiling even more, he splayed his hand out across her belly where their baby was safely nestled and nurtured. "She finally said yes to me, little one. Thank you both."

Bethany brushed her hand through his sweaty hair. "You're so silly." And yet she knew he wasn't like this with anyone else. Only she got to see this playful side of him.

"Oops, sorry. Didn't mean to interrupt."

"Galen, come back here!" Styxx rose to his feet then gently turned her to face him. "Bethany's pregnant."

Tears glistened in his gray eyes. "That's . . . that's incredible. Congratulations to both of you." He pulled Bethany into his arms for a hug and kissed her cheek. "How far along are you?"

"I'm told the baby is due *Boedromion*."

"Same as my blessed Antigone. Good month for babies. And now I shall leave you two to celebrate such wonderful news."

Styxx pulled her back against his chest and wrapped his arms around her. He leaned down to nuzzle her neck. "Does this mean that I finally get to meet your parents?"

She wrinkled her nose at him. "Probably not."

He gaped at her words. "Really? Admit it. You're ashamed of me, aren't you?"

She snorted in response. "Yes, *Highness.* I'm mortified of you and your humble origins that shame my status. My father shall find you completely unacceptable."

"Then why can't I meet them?"

"Because I love you and I don't want my father to spear your head to the wall for impregnating me. I know you're brave, but meeting my father wouldn't be as brave as it is stupid."

"I have a healthier than normal dose of stupid in me. You can ask anyone who knows me, especially Galen."

She laughed. "I know you do. And once the baby is here, I shall introduce you to my father. Then he'll have something else to focus on besides your defilement of me. And he'll be less likely to gut you for it."

Styxx cupped her face in his hand and kissed her forehead. "I'm glad he loves you so, and your mother, too."

But his family didn't love him like that and she knew it.

He spread his hand over her stomach again. "I still can't believe there's a little Bethany in there."

"And if it's a boy?"

"I shall love him, too . . . Should you be standing?"

She smiled at the sincere concern in his tone. "I'm pregnant, Styxx, not infirmed."

He laughed. "I know nothing of pregnant women or babies. I fear you'll have to educate me on both."

"Have you not practiced with your nephew?"

He tensed as if the question slapped him.

"Styxx?"

Sighing, he shook his head. "Ryssa doesn't want me around the baby."

"Why?"

"It's not important. We have our own little one to worry over." He lightly squeezed her stomach. "We should find a scribe to marry us."

"I would prefer an Egyptian wedding."

He hesitated as if the thought of waiting didn't appeal to him. But he relented without comment. "Very well."

"No argument?"

"Right now, Beth, you could ask me for the moon and I'd find some way to get it for you, even if I had to steal Apollo's chariot to bring it down for your touch."

She laid her hand against his cheek and savored the smile she felt there. "I will need a few weeks to put things in place and to work around my parents so as to keep you breathing."

His smile faded. "My father is likely to disinherit me. But we will be fine. I have some money of my own put away where he can't take it from us, and in spite of what he says and the damage that was done to my hand, I can still work as a soldier. There's always someone who needs a strong sword arm."

She shook her head at where his thoughts went. "Have no worries there. I assure you, should your father disinherit you, mine will welcome you like a son—"

"Or kill me."

"Or kill you. But if I manage to keep you out of his spear range, my father isn't a poor fisherman. He is quite wealthy, indeed. You won't have to war to feed us, and we will have a life equal to the means you've been raised with."

He scoffed. "I don't care where or how I live so long as you're with me."

"We'll see how you feel when I'm fat and cranky."

"I will still worship the ground you tread on."

She only prayed he continued to feel that way once he realized that his new father-in-law would be the Egyptian god Set, and his mother-in-law was one of the gods who'd gleefully tortured him in Atlantis.

APRIL 3, 9527 BC

Styxx froze as he came face-to-face with his brother in the hallway. Acheron held Apollodorus in his arms and it was obvious by the wet hair and droplets on his nephew's skin that Acheron had just bathed him. His nephew stood in Acheron's arms as he laughed and bounced happily.

A smile twitched at the edges of Styxx's lips as he saw the babe and thought of his own child he'd soon be able to hold like that and bathe. "He's grown a lot."

Apollodorus reached for Styxx. "*Ackee?*" Then he frowned in confusion as he looked back and forth between his matching uncles.

Acheron held the baby tighter while he glared at Styxx without comment.

Bitter regret thickened Styxx's throat as he realized how much his brother hated him. And that Acheron's and Ryssa's hatred would one day infect Apollodorus, too. It shouldn't hurt any worse than their rejection, and yet it did.

Styxx cleared his throat. "I still have the horse Ryssa gave you when we were boys . . . if you want, you could give it to Apollodorus."

Acheron curled his lip. "We don't need anything from you."

Ryssa came out of her room then paused as she saw them. She took her son from Acheron. "What's going on?"

"Styxx was offering me cast-offs I want no part of."

In that one moment, Styxx desperately needed to hate his brother as much as Acheron hated him. And yet . . .

"We were friends once."

Acheron sneered at him. "You were never my friend. You stole from me and you lied to me."

Styxx gaped at his unfounded accusations. "Name me one time in my life I stole from you."

"Your crown, for one. My parents' love . . . "

"And you can have them. Please, for the love of the gods, take them, if that's what you want. They've never brought me any kind of comfort or joy."

"Is that why you're plotting to kill Father?" Acheron asked.

Styxx's jaw went slack again. "Are you insane? Why would you accuse me of such a thing?"

"Because I know it's true. You're plotting against him, and you've tried to blame me for it."

Styxx shook his head at the ridiculous accusation. "When have I the time to plot against anyone?"

Ryssa snorted. "You're gone for days at a time and no one

knows where you are. Tell me, honestly, that you're not meeting with your coconspirators." She nodded at Acheron. "I believe you, little brother. It's just the sort of thing *he'd* do."

Styxx was aghast at them. Gods help him if they repeated that poison to his father. The king was just stupid enough he might believe them. "I've plotted against no one. *I* was the one stabbed in his sleep. Not Father."

Acheron went pale. *Does he know?*

Styxx turned his anger to his brother. "You did it, didn't you? You're the one who tried to kill me."

Ryssa stepped between them. "Don't be ridiculous. Acheron did no such thing. Why would he? If something happens to you, it would kill him, too."

"No," Styxx breathed as he glared at his brother. "And Acheron knows that. If he dies, *I* die. But my life has no impact on his at all. Is that not right, *brother?*"

Growling, Acheron ran at him and shoved him back so that he stumbled and fell to the floor. "I hate you! You should have died when I stabbed you and stayed dead!"

"What is this!"

Eyes wide, Acheron retreated at the sound of the king's roar. Ryssa put herself between them so that she could protect the one brother she loved against the brother she couldn't stand.

She might as well have gutted him herself. That was what it felt like.

"Answer me!" their father demanded as he looked from Ryssa and Acheron to Styxx.

"It's nothing, Father," Styxx said, making sure to keep his tone level and calm as he pushed himself up from the floor. "Just squabbling among siblings."

Ryssa narrowed her gaze on him. "Did you know Styxx is plotting your death, Father?"

Styxx gaped at her accusation.

His father turned a suspicious eye to Styxx. "Have you proof of your words, daughter?"

Then Styxx heard it. The speculation in her mind that she now had full rein to kill him and not harm her beloved Acheron.

If Styxx is gone, Father will have to love and accept my brother . . .

"It comes from a reliable source."

The look on his father's face said that the stupid bastard believed her. Shocked anger riveted him to the floor.

Ryssa would actually see him dead.

Narrowing his gaze on his sister, Styxx jerked the crown from his head and shoved it into his father's hands. "Take it. Ram it into whatever orifice you can manage. I really don't care. I've walked out on all of this before and will gladly do so again. The gods know being prince has never brought me anything but absolute fucking misery."

"We know the truth, Styxx!" Ryssa snarled.

Styxx curled his lip at her. "You don't know anything, you stupid bitch." He raked his father, her, and Acheron with a sneer. "None of you do, and I'm done with you all."

He just wanted Bethany. Turning away from them, he headed for the stairs to leave and never come back.

"Guards!" his father roared. "Seize the prince."

When they moved forward, Styxx glared at them. "Do you really think you can take me?"

Only one was dumb enough to try. Styxx had him disarmed and flat on his back before his father could blink. Bellowing in rage, he threw the guard's sword into the wall where it embedded into the stone.

His fury riding him hard, Styxx turned his lethal gaze to his gaping father. "If I wanted you dead, *Majesty,* you'd be dead by my hand already. And if I wanted your fucking crown, I'd have taken it when I marched my army through . . . " Styxx's voice trailed off as he had a profound flashback of having said this to his father before, and yet . . .

The memory was so vague. More like a dream than reality.

What in the name of Hades?

He locked gazes with his brother as Acheron's allegations rang

559

in his head. *I know you've tried to kill him. I know it! And you blamed me for it.*

Styxx wasn't sure what Acheron was thinking. None of it made sense.

And still suspicion darkened his father's eyes. So be it. It wasn't like he'd gone down any in the king's estimation.

Disgusted, Styxx looked at Apollodorus who was now distraught and crying from the chaos. "I'm so sorry, dear nephew. You deserved much better than to be born into this travesty of a family."

"Styxx!" his father roared, but Styxx ignored him as he met Acheron's fearful gaze.

Now he knew for certain that Acheron had tried to end his life. And his brother knew that he knew. But what difference did it make? Really? Whatever he did to retaliate against Acheron would rebound onto him and he'd be punished, too.

Perhaps the worst punishment of all was that Acheron would be saddled with Ryssa for a sister. Jealous, treacherous bitch that she was. *I just hope she never turns on you, brother.*

Tired of their crap, Styxx made his way out of the palace, to his horse. How he wished he could be with Beth today. He needed to see a set of eyes that didn't hate him. Feel a hand on his skin that didn't begrudge him anything, or wish him ill.

Five more days . . .

He'd had longer separations from her. But for some reason it hurt more today.

Soon, though. Soon they'd be married and no one would ever force him to be away from her for another heartbeat. Ever.

"Where have you been?"

Styxx paused on the palace stairs as he heard his father's voice. "I went riding."

"I wasn't sure you'd be back."

Not like he had any reason to return and honestly, he still wasn't sure why he bothered. Other than this was all he knew.

Styxx turned slightly on the steps to glare down at his father. The old man looked tired and, if he didn't know better, sad. "What do you want from me, Father?"

I wanted a son I could be proud of.

Styxx hid the pain his father's thought caused him as he waited for the king to speak.

"Your sister is convinced you plot against me. Is there any reason she should think that?"

"She has the mental capacity of an aged flea, and I refuse to be held accountable for her grotesque, unhinged stupidity."

His father closed the distance between them. "I wouldn't be so concerned if I didn't feel your hatred every time you look at me."

What was there to love?

"What do you want me to say, Father? I love you? Fine. I love you. Now, may I go to my room?"

"You don't love me the way you do that old man who serves you. You've never once looked at me the way you do Galen."

Styxx wanted to laugh at his jealousy . . . it was so ludicrous. "And you have never *once* tended me when I was sick. For that matter, you don't even check on me to ask after my health. You weren't there to fight against my enemies as they tried their damnedest to kill me then, wounded yourself, carry me off the field of battle and stitch my injuries. When you sent me too young to war, Galen was the one who stood by my side and defended me against the insults and jeers of my own people who thought *you* mocked them because I was there. For half my life and all my memory, Galen alone has picked me up when I've fallen. He is the only father I've ever known."

His father's head snapped back as if he'd slapped him. "You think he could give you what I have?"

"No, but when I was naked, he took his own cloak off his back to cover me. And he gave me the only thing that has ever mattered."

"And that is?"

"Love, Father. Even when I'm not at my best, even when I fail, he is proud of me, and he is there whenever I need him. He doesn't judge or condemn me for being human."

"Because he doesn't dare."

Styxx scoffed. His father knew nothing of Galen's fearless temerity. "I have no wish to argue with you on this." He turned to leave.

"Wait . . . you should know that I've entered into talks with the king of Ithaca for his daughter. I'm arranging a meeting for the two of you."

Sighing, Styxx turned back around. "And you can un-enter them, Father. I'm already betrothed."

Rage mottled his cheeks with color. "To whom?"

Styxx braced himself for the full force of his father's wrath. "My Bethany."

"A peasant! Are you out of your mind? You're my heir, boy! She's not even Greek!"

"Neither was Nefertari. But if you want the Ithacan princess, I suggest you marry her to Acheron or yourself. I am bound to my Bethany and I will take no other bride."

"I forbid it!"

Ignoring him, Styxx continued up the stairs. "Forbid it all you want. I care naught what you say or do. I will have her as my bride."

I will see you dead first!

Styxx winced at his father's threat. *Go on and try it, bastard.* Let him learn what Acheron had. So long as his brother lived, he was free and clear of death.

APRIL 6, 9527 BC

Styxx shook his head at the ring the jeweler held out to him. "Too small a stone."

"This is the one."

Styxx looked over at Galen's selection which appeared tiny in Galen's massive calloused paw. Even so, it was much larger than the one he'd been examining, and it would be large on Bethany's delicate hand. The stone was a deep celestial blue that glittered brightly even in the dim light of the store. "What stone is that?"

The jeweler smiled in approval. "Sapphire, Highness. It symbolizes purity, and is thought to protect against evil thoughts and wishes."

Styxx nodded at Galen. "You're right. It's perfect for her." He glanced back at the merchant. "I'll take this one."

While the merchant went to box it, Galen laughed. "Two men picking out a wedding ring is like two women shopping for swords. Both of us out of our element. Next thing you know, we'll be shopping for dresses and panas."

Styxx snorted. They had both amused the merchant to no end with their questions and comments. "Let's just hope the baby's a boy. After this travesty, I don't want to even contemplate trying to shop for a daughter."

Galen's laughter was deep and rich. "It's not so bad, really. I rather enjoy it, and unlike boys, daughters never hesitate to hug and kiss your old whiskered cheeks. There's a lot to be said for having a daughter. Then again there's a lot to be said for having a son. Either way, I'm sure you'll be very pleased."

He was sure about that, too.

The jeweler returned with his purchase. Styxx carefully tucked it into the pouch he carried.

Leaving the store, he started home then stopped with Galen by his side. "Is a ring enough?"

"For your Bethany? Aye, boy. She only wants you."

Still, he wasn't sure. He looked to the end of the street. "It just seems so insignificant to what I feel for her. Perhaps I should get—"

Galen shoved him back toward the store, cutting him off midsentence. Irritated, he opened his mouth to bark at Galen when he realized that something wet and warm was on his leg. Something bright red.

Blood.

His heart racing, Styxx caught Galen against his side as the old man staggered. "Galen?" he cried out, cradling him in his arms as Galen struggled to breathe.

Someone had cut his femoral artery. Deep and ragged, the wound shot blood everywhere.

No!

Who would have dared such?

"Someone fetch a physician!" Styxx called as he sank to the ground with his mentor in his arms. "Hold on, Galen." He tried his best to stanch the blood. But it was impossible.

And it kept coming and coming no matter how hard he tried to stop it.

Galen's gray eyes stared into his as the old man smiled and patted his blood-soaked hands. "This is how it should be, boy."

"How what should be?"

He swallowed hard. "No man should ever outlive his son. Never mind thrice in one lifetime. This time when I saw the assassin's blade, it ended the way it should have." He touched Styxx's cheek. "My beloved son is safe from harm."

Tears blinded Styxx as he bit back a sob. "Don't you die on me, Galen! You hear me? That's an order! You are not to die for me ... please ... please, don't leave me."

Galen licked his lips. "I couldn't love you more had I been lucky enough to sire you myself. It's been my greatest honor to fight with you, Styxx. To teach and protect you at home, and in battle. You are the greatest hero Didymos has ever bred. And I couldn't have asked for a better son ... you've done my old heart proud time and ..."

As he watched, the light faded from those gray eyes. Galen went limp in his arms.

Styxx couldn't breathe as tears fell down his face. He tried everything he could think of, but it was no use.

Galen was dead.

And it was his fault. He should have protected him. Why hadn't he been paying attention? Why?

It was so unfair.

"Damn you, gods! Damn you all!" Sobbing, he held Galen to his chest.

I can't die . . . why did you interfere, old man? Why?

Had the assassin's blade gone into him, it would have hurt. But it would have healed. Why had he never told Galen that secret?

Now, it was too late.

What have I done?

He'd killed the only father he'd ever known. Hating himself completely, Styxx rocked his mentor in his arms as his heart splintered into pieces.

"Why, Galen?" he whispered against Galen's grizzled cheek. "Why did you do this for something as worthless as me?" But he knew. Galen had loved him. For whatever stupid reason, the old man had.

"Highness?"

Styxx looked up to see the physician standing over them. "You're too late." Even so, he laid Galen down on the ground so that the man could examine him.

After a few minutes, the physician sighed. "I'm sorry, Highness. I shall fetch—"

"No. I'll take care of him." Styxx picked Galen up and carried him to the palace in his arms.

As he entered the foyer, his father came out of his study to scowl at him. "What is this?"

Styxx didn't speak to him. He couldn't. Instead, he carried Galen up to his room to make final preparations.

Bethany ran to the palace with Dynatos in front of her. Even now, she heard her great-grandfather's laughter as he announced Galen's death to the Atlantean gods. *They barely missed Prince Prick, but they got the old bastard who rode with him.*

Styxx would be absolutely devastated.

The doors opened and she stepped inside.

"May I help you?"

Holding on to Dynatos so that he wouldn't hurt or frighten anyone, she paused at the voice of a servant on her right. "I'm here for Prince Styxx. Please show me to him."

The servant started to lead her until a sharp female voice halted them.

"What are you doing?"

"The prince has a visitor."

"No, he doesn't. The prince doesn't receive commoners in our private quarters ... only in the throne room on designated days."

Bethany went ramrod stiff at Ryssa's haughty tone. She felt the air stir as the princess moved to stand in front of her.

"And in the future, we don't let whores through the front door. In fact, they are not to be admitted to the premises at all."

Unable to not respond in kind, Bethany arched her brow. "Then where do you plan to live?"

Ryssa sucked her breath in sharply. "Do you know who you're talking to?"

"Styxx's sister, I presume."

"That would be prince to you, peasant, and *princess* when you address me."

Bethany started past her, but Ryssa caught her by the arm and dug her nails into Bethany's skin.

"Did you not hear me?"

Bethany held Dynatos back as he growled angrily at the princess. "I heard you and I don't care. Styxx needs me."

"Get out before I have you whipped for your insolence. My brother has whores aplenty. I don't even know which one you are, and I don't care. I am not having him bring his whores under the same roof as my son ... the son of the god Apollo ... Guards! Throw this trash to the street where it belongs."

Bethany snatched her arm free. "I've always found it intriguing

566

how humans project their sins onto others. Your brother isn't the beast. And if you'd ever once in the last five years had a conversation with him, you'd well know my name."

Dynatos started barking and growling.

Bethany sank her hand into his fur to calm him. "I promise you, bitch. I will be back, and you will be very sorry for this."

Ryssa started for her, but Dynatos kept her away.

Without another word, Bethany left.

Styxx frowned as he heard something that sounded like a dog barking in the foyer. Leaving his room, he went to check.

Ryssa was coming up the stairs in a complete pique.

"Did I hear a dog downstairs?"

She raked him with a sneer that should have stripped the flesh from his bones. "Yes, your Nubian whore was here to see you and I threw her out."

Rage clouded his vision as he ran past his sister and went to find Bethany. He rushed through the doors and scanned the crowd on the street, but there was no sign of her or Dynatos.

Damn you, Ryssa. You selfish bitch.

Still, Bethany had come to him. That alone meant everything.

Furious and heartbroken, he returned inside to find Ryssa at the top of the stairs.

"In the future, tell your whores they are not welcome in the palace. And for the sake of the gods, wash yourself. You're disgusting."

Styxx ignored her as he walked past her.

"Did you hear me?"

He started to ignore her again, but he'd had enough. "Bethany is my fiancée, you stupid quim. She's not Nubian, she's Egyptian. And I've had enough of you insulting her. So help me, if you say one more word against her, I will have you exiled."

She started to slap him, but he caught her wrist. "How do you think Apollo will deal with your treatment of me when I tell him of this?"

"I don't know, but I'll ask him the next time he corners me for a grope."

"How dare you defame him!"

"Go fuck yourself, Ryssa." Releasing her arm, he headed back to where he'd been preparing Galen's body.

Alone.

He'd already sent an envoy to Antigone to escort her and her family here for the funeral. And while the task of preparing a body was normally reserved for women and priests, he didn't want anyone near Galen who didn't respect or love him. He owed him that much.

But it was so hard to be here. To do this.

Agony and regret mixed with his grief until he couldn't breathe. Shutting the door to his room, he went to finish.

"Maahes?" Bethany called as she entered her cousin's elaborate gold-encrusted temple in Thebes.

With his dark brown hair completely covered by his pschent headdress, and his bright green eyes gleaming, he appeared in front of her before she finished the last syllable of his name. The smile on his face faded the instant he saw how upset she was. "Baby, what is it?" At six foot six, he was a huge wall of muscle who dwarfed her, and yet he'd always been a cuddly pup with her.

Bethany sniffed back her tears. "I need twenty-four of the biggest, strongest, scariest men you have in your army for an envoy to Greece."

He arched a brow that had been darkened by cosmetics. "Are we going to war?" he asked hopefully.

As the Egyptian god of war, he was often too eager for battle.

"No," she said petulantly as the horror of what had just happened in Didymos replayed through her mind. She was furious, hurt, grief-stricken, and embarrassed. "A friend is dead and the bitch won't let me in to see Styxx. I want to terrify her and show them that I'm not a piece of trash to be thrown out!"

Maahes frowned as he tried to make sense of her rushed words. "What?"

"Nothing." She drew a ragged breath. "Please ... I need the most impressive envoy you can muster, right away."

"Anything for my dearest. You want elephants, too?"

She let out a pain-filled laugh at the thought of Ryssa's expression should they ride into town on those. "No, we'll be arriving by barge."

"I can have the elephants carry it or fly it in."

And this was why she loved her cousin so. Maahes was ever a gem.

"A little more believably subtle, please."

He kissed her forehead. "Okay, baby. How soon do you want it?"

"Twenty minutes?"

"Done. I'll meet you at the docks."

"Thank you." Bethany kissed his cheek then went to her aunt Ma'at's temple. Invisible to the priests, she walked through the sacred south wall into the antechamber the priests knew nothing about. It was here her aunt kept some of her choicest items.

"Aunt Ma'at?"

Her aunt appeared even faster than Maahes had. "Child, you're pregnant!"

Bethany cringed then brought her finger to her lips to silence her aunt. "Don't tell my father, or anyone, please?"

"Never." As tiny and delicate as Maahes was large, Ma'at wrinkled her nose. "I'm not that brave."

Bethany smiled then hugged her aunt for the kindness. "I need some help. May I borrow your most elaborate dress and jewelry?"

Ma'at arched a regal brow. "May I ask why?"

"To make a point to someone who was very rude to me. She treated me like a peasant and called me trash!"

Fury glittered in her green eyes. "In that case ... "

Bethany lifted her chin proudly as her aunt dressed her in Egyptian finery.

Ma'at manifested a bright bronze mirror for her to see herself.

Her aunt leaned against the mirror's side as she eyed Bethany with a smile of satisfaction. "Too much?"

In spite of her pain, Bethany laughed. Ma'at had put her in a solid black sheath with a muslin scarf threaded with gold draped around her hips and a golden jewel-encrusted sash that held it in place. Gold and turquoise bands held a matching gold muslin drape to her arms. Her huge ankh-embellished collar was made of coral, pearls, gold, and turquoise with matching earrings. But it was her headdress that was perfection. Elaborately sculpted, it was a large gold bird with a single gold feather at the back of it. The sides of the headdress were gold beads that fell down to her shoulders, overlapping the collar. Her eyes were heavily lined and she dripped with the wealth of Egypt.

No one would call her a peasant in this.

"It's perfect."

"Very well then. Whatever mischief you're up to, I wish you luck."

"Thank you." She kissed her aunt on both cheeks then went to see how Maahes was progressing.

A slow smile curled her lips as she saw the small army he'd assembled. Huge and well muscled, they were dressed in short shendyts made of leopard skins with jeweled collars and anklets. Even better, he'd brought along eight of his personal pet lions, which were lying next to her gold seat.

Maahes wore an elaborate headdress and mask in the shape of a lion's head that had a uraeus at the top of it. His shendyt was made of lion skin and covered with a gold drape and belt. Like hers, his ankh collar was massive and encrusted with rubies, and he had matching gold wristbands and armbands.

His dress surprised her. "You're coming?" she asked.

"Absolutely. No one insults my girl without a severe thrashing from me."

She tsked at him. "No bloodshed."

He poked his bottom lip out playfully. "Can I have a little, please?"

"Maahes . . ."

He pouted even more. "One eyeball? Or a testicle? Please give me something, Bet, my pet."

Laughing, she hugged him. "Please restrain yourself, cousin. This is a peace mission."

"Don't say that P word around me. It causes me great agony."

She shook her head then took her seat on the barge.

Maahes gave the signal and they were dropped in an area just in front of Didymos so that they could make a grand appearance at the docks without raising human suspicions.

As soon as they were moored, Maahes had his men bring an elaborate gold jewel–encrusted litter up from storage to carry her in.

Ryssa was about to get a severe lesson in manners she hoped the snotty bitch choked on.

Styxx jumped as someone pounded on his door.

Angry at being interrupted again, he answered it to find a guard there.

"His Majesty summons you, Highness. Immediately."

He started to tear the man's head off, but refrained. It wasn't the guard's fault he'd been sent on this errand, and Styxx didn't want to bring an innocent man into conflict with his king. However, his father would have the same reaction to Styxx's appearance that Ryssa had, since Styxx was still filthy.

And covered in Galen's blood.

Screw it . . .

He followed the guard downstairs to where his father and Ryssa were waiting in the foyer.

As expected, his father scowled at his bloodstained clothing.

"What?" Styxx asked irritably.

For once his father didn't comment on the disrespect. "We have an envoy here from Egypt. Judging from the report, I think it might be Nefertari."

Styxx rubbed at his forehead as he tried to understand what was going on. "Why would *she* be here?"

His father shrugged.

Styxx passed an irritated glance to Ryssa who was still angry at him over Bethany then he looked back at his father. "I really don't want to deal with this right now."

"You never want to deal with your duties," Ryssa sneered.

Their father stiffened. "And I will have words with you later over what you said earlier to your sister."

I really don't care.

Crossing his arms over his chest, Styxx hung back in the door-way as his father and sister went outside to greet the impressive envoy that came through the palace gates.

There was so much gold wrapped around the people and litter that it was hard to look at them directly. There were twenty-five men in all and one elaborately dressed woman. Six huge Nubian males set the litter down and a man dressed like a lion helped the tiny woman out of it. He tucked her hand into the crook of his elbow and led her up the stairs with eight massive lions leading the way for them.

It wasn't until the couple rudely bypassed his father and Ryssa that Styxx recognized the woman through the heavy eyeliner and makeup she wore.

"Bethany?" he breathed, rushing forward.

She let go of the man escorting her. "Styxx?"

Reaching her, he pulled her into his arms. "It's me, *akribos.*"

Bethany held him tight against her as Maahes and his men closed rank around them to keep anyone from approaching them. Styxx trembled in her arms as his tears fell against her neck. Her heart shattered at the loss she knew he felt. "I know, precious. I'm so sorry about Galen. I loved him, too."

"Excuse me?" the king demanded. "What is this?"

Maahes growled deep in his throat. "None of *your* business."

"Do you know who I am?"

Maahes gave a rude snort. "Not a clue. Don't care, either."

"But you might care about *us.*"

Styxx lifted his head as he heard Apollo's irate voice. Damn, he

572

thought that tone was only reserved for him whenever he defied the god. The Olympian stood beside Athena, and neither of them appeared pleased.

Apollo glared at Bethany and the men with her. "What are you doing here, Maahes?"

The man in the lion mask shrugged nonchalantly. "We're here on a mission of peace to pay respects to a fallen Greek hero. But if you want to start some shit ... " He stepped down toward Apollo. "It's been awhile since I had Greek for dinner."

Bethany put her hand on Maahes's shoulder. "Please, behave."

He gestured toward Apollo and Athena as if to say they were the problem then deflated with a sigh. "All right, Bet, my pet. But you're killing me."

Athena stepped around her brother to address Bethany. "Why are you *really* here?"

Bethany placed her hand on Styxx's arm. "For Styxx, who suffered a harsh tragedy today. I tried to come earlier and was very rudely insulted and denied entrance to the palace by Apollo's bitch-whore. And you're all *very* lucky I'm not calling out for her blood over the public embarrassment she maliciously and willfully caused me."

Maahes lifted his mask and bent down to Bethany. "Oh, I expect blood. I need that bitch beaten for any insult dealt to you."

Bethany touched his arm again and shook her head. "No war today."

Maahes screwed his face up as if in agony. "All right, pet. I really, really love you. Today I prove it. Next time, though, gut me. It'd be less painful."

Apollo started forward, but Athena caught his arm and shook her head.

Athena nodded to Maahes and Bethany. "Please, pay your respects. We are deeply honored by your presence and homage to one of our own." She gave her brother a harsh glare. "There will be no war today. Only peace."

Confused, but not wanting to cause any more of a spectacle in

573

public, Styxx led Bethany into the palace. Maahes and his men and lions followed after them.

As soon as they were inside and out of hearing range, Xerxes turned to Apollo. "Who is that?"

Athena answered for him. "The man in the mask is Maahes, Lord of the Massacre. He's the Egyptian god of war and serves his mother Bastet and aunt Ma'at. Bet is known by all as the Princess of Thebes. Her father is the Egyptian god Set, the embodiment of pure evil and chaos. Bringer of war and storms. And she is the light in his darkness. There is absolutely nothing Set would not do for his most cherished daughter and only child. Not to mention that the rest of the Egyptian pantheon is every bit as loyal and protective of her."

"*That* is Styxx's Bethany?" Xerxes glared at Ryssa who took a step back.

"How was I to know, Father? She was dressed as a peasant."

Apollo ignored them. "What should we do, sister?"

"Bet, I trust. Maahes ... he's not devious, just bloodthirsty. He loves war above all. We will stay and make sure he leaves without incident."

Bethany bit back a sob as she realized what Styxx had been doing on her arrival. "Is no one helping you with Galen?"

"No."

She opened the door and had four of the men come in to take over the body preparations. Styxx started to protest, but she placed her finger to his lips.

"You're too upset for this. Come, my love. Let me take care of you."

He kissed her hand. "Someone should be taking care of you."

"Shh," she breathed then she whispered, "Maahes doesn't know, and we can't risk him telling my father before I do."

Styxx frowned at the men and the wealth that dripped from every piece of expensive fabric and jewels they wore, and the elaborate outfit on Bethany. Even her sandals were made of gold and trimmed in coral, turquoise, and pearls. When she'd said her father was wealthy, she had greatly understated his means. "Who exactly is your father?"

She bit her lip. "I didn't want you to find out like this. Please promise you won't be angry at me."

"I could never be angry at you."

Still, she hesitated. "We're about to test that theory, my love."

He frowned at the fear and reservation on her face. Was he a famed pharaoh? "Beth . . . I won't be angry. I promise."

She pressed her lips together and put both her hands on his face to feel his expression. "My father is the god Set."

For a full minute, Styxx couldn't breathe as the room closed in on him. *That,* he had to admit, he hadn't seen coming.

Just what he needed. Another god screwing with his life and angry at him.

He should have known . . .

No wonder she'd been so reticent to tell him or let them meet. The daughter of a god.

Oh, but not just *any* god. One of the most violent, lethal, cruel gods imaginable.

"Styxx?" The tears in her voice cut him. "Honey?"

He took her hand and held it as he struggled to breathe. So many emotions slammed into him at once that he couldn't even identify them. Rage, betrayal, fear, irritation . . .

"I need a moment, Beth."

"Please don't hate me. I hid for the same reasons you did, and I didn't want to tell you because I know how you feel about the gods . . . How much you hate them. And my father's a really big one."

Who'd been known to cut the genitals off other gods—his own brothers—never mind a mortal man who dared to sleep with his beloved daughter. Having his head speared to the wall was the least of Styxx's concerns right now.

But the terror on her face as she dreaded his reaction made him feel like a complete shit.

He pulled her against him. "I don't hate you, Bethany. I can't afford to." Tears filled his eyes and choked him. "You're all I have left."

"And that's why I'm here. I knew you were alone and I couldn't stand it. Your sister wouldn't let me in. The only way I could think to bypass her was to fetch my cousin and force them to open the gates."

He cupped her head in his hands and pressed his cheek to hers. "Thank you for coming." Then he let out a half laugh as he saw four of the lions that were circling them while four more rested on the floor. "And here I bought you a dog to protect you . . . how stupid am I?"

"You're not stupid at all. It was wonderful and I adore Dyna."

But she didn't need a dog to protect her. No more than she needed him for a husband.

And yet here she was, for him, and willing to be bound to him in spite of her detestation of marriage. She could have had any man in the world. But he was the lucky bastard she'd claimed.

Never had he loved her more.

APRIL 8, 9527 BC

Styxx let go of Bethany's hand as he greeted the envoy that he'd sent after Galen's daughter. Even though he'd never met Antigone, he felt as if he knew her. Her dark hair was pulled back from a face that was every bit as beautiful as Galen had claimed. She had her youngest son, who was a year old, in her arms while six more children, two boys and four girls ranging in age from three to eighteen, were with her. Her husband carried their youngest daughter in his arms.

When Styxx had been at war, Antigone was the only one who'd

written a personal letter to him to ask how he was doing and to make sure her father hadn't lied about his own health for her sake. Styxx should have made a point of meeting her before now. But he'd stupidly thought he had plenty of time. "Antigone?"

Her eyes teared as she saw him. "Prince Styxx?"

When she started to bow, he stopped her. "I am the one who should be bowing to you, my lady. I am so sorry that he's gone. He loved all of you so very much."

Tears flowing down her face, she squeezed his hand. "Thank you, Highness, and I am so sorry for you, too. My father adored you like a son. I know him. He wasn't one to say it. But he talked about you endlessly, and it was obvious how much you meant to him. When our Philip died, a light went out in his eyes and never reignited until you kindled it again."

Styxx cleared his throat. "And he talked about nothing but you and your children when he was with me. I might have been the light in his eyes, but you were his heart and soul."

When she started away, he pulled her toward the royal dais. "Please sit with me for the funeral."

"Thank you."

Styxx helped her and her husband with their children. He gave them the choicest seats and took a seat behind them, with Bethany who held his hand throughout. Saying good-bye to Galen was the hardest thing he'd ever done. And as he watched the fires burn, his anger took hold of him. It was so unfair. If any human had ever deserved to die in his sleep at an ancient age, surrounded by the family he loved, it was Galen.

And he was dead because of him. Why had he not seen the attacker first?

Bethany laid her hand to Styxx's cheek as she felt his mood. She knew how much he hurt. How very much he'd loved Galen even though he stayed strong and said nothing. But what truly angered her was the fact that none of his family attended this with him.

Not a single member. Not even the king who had ordered Galen into battle to save his own crown.

How could they leave Styxx alone like this? But then why was she surprised? His father had sent him to war when he'd scarce been more than a child. Ryssa had no love for anyone but herself, and Bethany knew nothing of his brother—not even what he looked like. Though at this point, she didn't want to know anything about Acheron. Not if he could leave his brother to suffer alone. It was an act of complete cruelty.

A total lack of regard. Not just for Styxx, but for the man who'd once led an army for the royal house and defended all of them while they'd languished here at home in luxury paid for in Styxx's and Galen's blood and sweat. To this day, Styxx lacked the full use of his right hand from where a Greek assassin had pinned it to the ground with a dagger.

How dare they.

When the service was over, Styxx had Antigone and her family escorted to guest chambers in the palace. Bethany went with him to his room, where he sat in a chair for hours without speaking. Then he began pacing like a caged lion.

"What's on your mind, Styxx?"

"Nothing and everything."

She held her hand out for him. "Does your head ache? Would you like for me to rub it?"

Taking her hand, he sank down at her feet and laid his head in her lap then sighed as she ran her hands through his short blond hair. "I have such a bad feeling about things, Beth."

"You're just upset over Galen, and you have every right to be."

"No, it's more than that. Something bad is coming. I can feel it with every part of me. It's dark and it's dangerous, and it's out for blood."

She ran her hand over his cheek and jaw. "Have faith, my love."

"I don't know if I have any left. I'm not really sure if I ever had any at all." He lifted his head and placed his hand against her stomach. "If something were to happen to you and the baby, I don't know if I could survive it."

"Nothing will happen to us."

578

Yet Styxx couldn't shake the horrible dreams he'd been having. The feeling that pure evil stalked him.

Someone had killed Galen because of him and he had no idea who. It could have been a stranger or one of his family members or the bastard Apollo . . .

But it didn't matter who had struck the fatal blow. The assassin had been after *him*.

What if, in their desire to hurt him, they turned their sights to Bethany? How would he live with himself knowing that he'd caused her harm?

MAY 9, 9527 BC

Misery itself rained down on Katateros as Archon panicked. He'd fully expected Apostolos to come knocking on their door as soon as the day dawned.

Luckily, he'd been wrong.

At least so far.

"Relax," Epithymia told him as the Atlantean gods all huddled in their main hall, expecting Apollymi to escape at any moment and attack them. "It's not today that he hits his majority. Not until the anniversary of the human birth. We still have a handful of weeks to find him."

Archon cursed. "A slight stay of execution. It is imperative we stop this from happening!"

Bethany had had enough. She had no idea where Apostolos was, and honestly, she no longer cared. The only thing that mattered was the baby inside her, and the betrothed she wanted to marry more than anything else. She hadn't been here for the imprisonment of Apollymi and, no offense, given what they'd done to the goddess, they deserved her wrath.

Let Apollymi have them.

Unable to stand the arguments of the Atlanteans, she flashed herself to her aunt Ma'at's temple in Thebes.

Ma'at joined her immediately with a warm smile on her beautiful face. "To what do I owe this joyous visit?"

Bethany smiled and hugged her. "I have a favor to ask."

"Anything for you, you know that."

She was about to test those words. "Make me human."

Ma'at stepped back with a stern frown. "Excuse me?"

Bethany touched her stomach and thought of the life she carried and nurtured there. "I want to be fully human. I'm done with all the politicking and garbage that goes with godhood. I just want to raise my baby and live my life with Styxx, as a human, just like him."

"Oh, honey, think long and hard. If we do this, there's no way to undo it."

"I know, Mennie. But . . . " Bethany paused as she felt the lightest fluttering inside. Was that . . . ? Smiling wide, she gaped at her aunt. "What?"

Laughing, she took Ma'at's hand and led it to her stomach. "I just felt my son move!"

Ma'at smiled as she felt it, too. "Oh . . . He's a strong one."

"Like his father."

Ma'at cupped her cheek and gave her a stern scowl. "You think about this, long and hard, and I'll prepare the serum to make you and your baby human. But really, Bet'anya. Consider it well. Without your powers, you won't be able to protect them, and you of all creatures know the dangers that lurk for those who can't fight the gods."

Her aunt was right, but . . . "Those powers come with their own curse. As long as I have them, I'm torn between this pantheon and my mother's. I just want to be left alone with my husband and son, and not be pulled into drama I want no part of."

Ma'at nodded. "All right, sweetie. Go share this moment with your Styxx."

Bethany hugged her close then left to find him.

*

580

"Styxx?"

Cursing under his breath, Styxx tensed at the sound of his father's voice calling out to him as he came down the main stairs. What did the old man want?

Though to be honest, his father had been much more pleasant now that he knew Bethany was a wealthy princess and demigod, and the king was safely assured Styxx wasn't Ganymede or sterile.

"Father?" he asked as he entered the study.

The king looked up from his desk. "You've said nothing to me about your wedding plans."

They weren't his to make. Whatever his betrothed desired, he would do. "Bethany wants it in Egypt with her family."

"And you're fine with that?"

Styxx gave him a bland stare. "I would paint my skin blue and set myself on fire, Father, if she asked me to."

His father scoffed. "Now I know you're being ridiculous. I was thinking we should have at least a small ceremony here at home. Let everyone know that your heir is legitimate."

"No one will doubt the paternity of my son." *I'm not the cruel bastard you are.*

"You think it's a boy?" his father asked hopefully.

"Bethany assures me it is so, and I trust her judgment implicitly." Except for the sanity of loving him and her willingness to marry into this insane family. That he'd never understand.

"I can't tell you how proud I am of you, Styxx."

Then you should have said that to me when it mattered. Now, those words left him numb. Cold. He was long past the age of seeking his father's approval for anything. Honestly, he no longer cared.

Styxx was starting a new life with Beth and their son. Absolutely nothing else mattered to him.

He just wished Galen were here to see it.

But, unlike his family, he wasn't completely heartless and frigid. "Thank you, Father."

581

His father inclined his head to him. "Just wait for your birthday. I have an amazing feast planned."

Just what he didn't want. He'd never once in his life enjoyed the anniversary of his birth. He'd rather forget all about it.

Sighing, Styxx turned around and almost ran into Ryssa in the hallway. She glared at him.

"What did I do now, lamb-head?"

"You always have to outdo me, don't you? You can't let anyone have one thing better than *you*."

He scowled at her unreasoning anger. "What are you talking about?"

"I had Apollo. So what do you do? You run off to another pantheon to get an older, more powerful god's daughter. And then you *marry* her. It's ridiculous, Styxx. Really."

Yes, it was. But not for the reasons she thought. "Why are you so jealous of me?"

"I'm not jealous of *you*. I pity you. You're pathetic." Her eyes blazed with abject hatred. "And don't think I don't know how you went after Apollo. You even branded his mark on your back to get his attention."

He started to set her straight then stopped. What was the use? For whatever reason, she would always vilify him and whatever actions he took. Her heart had never been big enough to love both her brothers. And he knew why she was angry. His father was pulling out the stops for his birthday and in her mind, she was comparing it with hers.

That was what had her enraged.

"Prince Styxx?"

He looked past her to their servant. "Yes, Dorcas?"

"The Princess Bethany is here for you."

Grateful beyond measure for her appearance, he left his sister to glare in his general direction as he went to where Beth waited in the foyer. Dressed in her plain gray peplos, she was breathtaking. More so due to the slight bulge at her waist that was just really starting to show.

He walked up behind her and placed his hand on her stomach before he kissed her cheek.

She tsked at him. "You should be warned that my betrothed has a fierce temper and sword arm, and he'd be terribly upset to find a strange man molesting me."

Styxx laughed at her teasing. "Then we'd best meet . . ." He trailed off as he felt the subtlest of stirrings against his palm. "Is that—"

"Your equally fierce son?" She covered his scarred hand with hers. "It is indeed, my lord, which is why I came. I knew you'd want to feel him, too."

He splayed his hand wider, trying to feel it again. Then he cupped her stomach with both hands. "Where did he go?"

She moved his left hand lower so that he could feel the baby.

"That's . . . wow . . . We did that?"

She smiled at him. "We did."

Expelling a happy breath, Styxx looked up as he felt someone watching them. It was Ryssa and Acheron. Both of them glared at him as if the thought of his happiness repulsed them. Thankfully, with Bethany's presence, he couldn't hear their hatred in his head. He could only speculate at what ill wishes they had for him.

"What's wrong, love?" Beth asked as she laid her hand on his face to feel his expression.

"Nothing." He dropped his gaze from them to the only thing that was important to him.

Out of nowhere, his nose started bleeding. Releasing her immediately, he stepped away before any blood fell on her.

"Styxx?"

"It's all right, Beth. Just another nosebleed."

"I thought they'd stopped."

"They're not as frequent, but no . . . they haven't stopped." Taking her hand, he led her up the stairs.

As he reached the top, Acheron and Ryssa continued to glare at him and refused to make room for them. "Excuse us."

Bethany slowed as she heard him talking to someone. "Who's here?"

"My sister and brother."

"Acheron?" She paused. "It's a pleasure to finally meet you."

He mumbled something that might have been a greeting, but she wasn't sure as he quickly walked away from them.

"You'll have to forgive my brother. He has a bad history with Styxx's fiancées." Then Ryssa retreated, too.

Those words stunned her. "Plural?"

Sighing, Styxx led her to his room. "No, not plural. Just one. The year you were gone, my father betrothed me to Nefertari."

Her eyes widened in anger. "You agreed?"

His nosebleed worsened. "You'd left me, Beth. With no way to contact you, and I didn't think I'd ever see you again. I never touched her, and we only kissed once, briefly, on the day we met."

"Oh, fine," she snapped. "Just throw logic and guilt at me, why don't you?" Calming down, she sighed. "So what happened to her?"

"I sent her packing." At least that was what everyone had told him he'd done.

"And your brother and her?"

He used his cloth to pinch his nostrils together. "She said he tried to rape her."

Bethany arched her brow. "Did he?"

"I highly doubt it. While Acheron is an ass, raping women isn't his style. Besides, he's even less social than I am."

She let out a low whistle. "That's an impressive feat. I could have sworn you were the record holder."

Styxx sniffed back the blood as he checked the cloth then re-applied it. "If you don't mind, I'd rather not talk about my siblings." He sat down and leaned forward.

Bethany walked over to him. "I'm sorry, love. I didn't mean to stress you more."

He kissed her hand. "Honestly? You're the only one in my life who doesn't stress me at all."

584

But as he sat there, he had a bad feeling in his gut that Ryssa and Acheron were going to do something to try and ruin this for him. Both of them were still convinced he'd tried to kill their father and both lived in fear of his taking the throne. Which made no sense given the fact that he'd gladly cede them the entire palace if they'd just stop glaring their mutual hatred at him all the time.

MAY 15, 9527 BC

Styxx knew he was dreaming, but he couldn't wake up for anything. He saw himself in his battle armor, mounted on Troian, with his army stretching out for miles in three directions. Gaius was mounted on a white horse to his left and Galen was on his right with a brown stallion. His phoenix emblem was painted on every shield and the phoenix banners blew in a hot, desert wind.

They were on a hill, looking down on a field below where a blond woman, dressed in black, walked like a ghostly shade.

Across from them was the enemy. An army of demons who had swirling skin tones and wings, they were dressed in black armor and fought under a banner that held a sun symbol with three silver lightning bolts piercing its center.

From somewhere off in the distance, a cry sounded that spurred the enemy to ride down the hill to attack.

Styxx gave the order for his own troops to move forward.

He could hear and feel the thunder of the horses' hooves as the cavalry and charioteers rushed to engage the enemy. As his hoplites ran and locked their shields together. The air was completely and eerily still as the two armies collided. Screams, grunts, moans, and shouts filled the air and were punctuated by the sound of metal clashing and arrows and stones whizzing.

Troian went down under the onslaught. Styxx kept his hoplon

high as he cut through the demons, trying to protect Gaius and Galen.

All of a sudden, a shadow fell over him. He raised his hoplon in time to deflect a killing blow.

It was the enemy leader.

He was dressed in black armor that matched Styxx's, and his blue skin tone was covered with black and red blood. The two of them fought with equal skill. Every move he made, his opponent seemed to know.

Finally, Styxx swung a blow that knocked the helm from the demon's head. He froze at the sight of his brother with black hair and blue skin. It was the same form Acheron had held the time he'd gone to him on the balcony and fought. Acheron's swirling silver eyes turned red an instant before he drove his sword through Styxx's entire body. He buried the hilt just beside Styxx's navel and used the sword to pull Styxx into his arms.

"*Akri di diyum*," Acheron whispered in his ear, in Atlantean. *The lord and master will rule.* He twisted the grip, rotating the blade inside Styxx's body. "We were *never* brothers. And we will never know peace." Then he sank his fangs into Styxx's throat and drank from him as Apollo had done a thousand times . . .

Styxx woke up in a cold sweat with his heart racing.

"Sweetie?" Bethany's warm hand grounded him as she sat up and pulled him into her arms. "You're trembling."

He couldn't stop it.

"Another bad dream?"

"Yes."

She toyed with his hair. "More war?"

He nodded. Since the day of his first battle, he'd suffered horrendous flashbacks, both while awake and especially whenever he dreamed. But none of them had been like this. "I could feel it, Beth. Taste it. It was like I was there . . ."

She held his head to her breast and rocked with him in her arms. "You're home and you're safe."

He didn't feel safe. He barely felt sane. Closing his eyes, he

586

splayed his hand against her distended stomach where their son slept in a peace that forever eluded him. That and the scent of eucalyptus and her touch soothed him until he felt almost normal again. He kissed her cheek then moved to sit with his spine to the wall. Leaning back, he pulled her against his chest to hold her like he used to do whenever he'd visit her at the stream. Careful not to hurt her, he folded his arms over her stomach and below her breasts so that he could lose himself in this one moment of perfect bliss.

"You're scaring me, Styxx. Do you want to talk about it?"

"Not really. I don't want to dwell on nightmares while I have you with me."

Bethany ran her hand over his scarred forearm as she heard the voices of the Atlantean gods calling out for her. But for the first time in her life, she ignored them. She didn't care about any of that now. And she wasn't about to leave Styxx to go soothe their stupidity. Not when he needed her.

While he'd never slept a lot, he was sleeping even less now. Worse, he was growing even quieter around her . . . like he'd been when she first rescued him from Atlantis.

"You know, you never really told me what you did the year we were apart."

He leaned his head against hers. "I survived, and not well."

"And?"

He covered her hand with his scarred right one. "I don't want you to have anything but beautiful memories and thoughts. My job is to protect you and our son. It's not to burden you with things that can't be changed."

"I'm not weak, Styxx. I can handle your past."

He kissed her hand and held it to the whiskers on his cheek. "I've never thought of you as weak, my love. I know in my heart that you are far stronger than I am. And it's because of that that I can't tell you."

"I don't understand."

"In all my life, Beth, you are the only one who has always looked at me with love and respect."

"Galen loved and respected you."

"Not always. For years, he hated me, and even to the end, I could sometimes see it in his eyes. Not because he felt it for me at that time, but because I remembered what it felt like when he'd seen me as nothing but a piece of spoiled shit to be knocked around and despised for my birthright. You have never, ever looked at me that way, and I couldn't bear to see it if you did. I don't want you to judge me for things I did to survive. Things that I couldn't control."

"I would never judge you for that."

Styxx wished he could believe it. But he was afraid to take that chance. How could she look at a whore with love? How could anyone? "Words are easy to say, but emotions betray the best intentions. I have been used and hurt and degraded in ways no one should ever know, and I don't want you to see that worthless, pathetic victim whenever you look at me. I want you to see the warrior who would lay his life down to keep you safe."

She laced her fingers with his. "Very well, my heart. I won't push you, but I promise I would never judge you for things you couldn't help."

But Styxx judged himself for them, and as it drew closer to his birthday, it was getting harder and harder for him. The voices in his head screamed louder until he feared he was going insane. The only time he had any solace was when she was with him.

They are all coming for me.

He just hoped that whatever planned to destroy him didn't touch Bethany.

MAY 16, 9527 BC

Bethany carefully picked through the fruit that was laid out in bowls on the dining room buffet. Even though she'd eaten only an hour ago, she was starving again. And at times like this, she really missed her eyesight. It was aggravating to play "name the mystery item" when she had no idea what she was touching.

"When Aara was pregnant with Styxx, she always craved apples and figs."

Bethany paused at the sound of the king's voice. Xerxes had never really spoken to her before. And even though he was not her favorite person, he was the grandfather of her son. "Styxx still has a preference for both."

"Does he?"

Shouldn't you, his father, know? But she didn't want to be openly rude to the man, especially since he was trying. "He does, indeed."

"Hmmm . . . I know he also favors cheese."

"You mean, he did. He hasn't had a taste for it for quite some time now."

"Why is that?"

She had to bite back her anger over the fact that not one member of Styxx's family knew the most basic thing about him. "Cheese, onion, garlic, black soup, and bitter vetch are the staples of a soldier's diet, my lord. Many times at war, it was all he had to eat for months on end. Since his return, he rarely touches any of them."

"I had no idea he'd ever tasted bitter vetch."

That was because it was deemed peasant or famine food by the rich and aristocratic.

Or left for the cattle to eat.

It definitely was not something a prince should have had knowledge of.

"And what is this black soup?" he asked. "I've never heard of it."

"It's made with blood and barley."

When he spoke, his tone was laden with disgust. "How could he eat such?"

"In war one doesn't complain about what's fed to them. Soldiers are merely glad they have anything with which to slake their hunger."

"You seem to know a great deal about the matter."

Because she actually cared about Styxx. "My father is known for the wars he starts and fights, and I know that since his return, Styxx has a tendency to hoard apples in a drawer in his room. Though he rarely eats them, he's always checking to make sure they're still there."

"I had no idea war had left such an impression on him."

It took everything she had not to lash out at the man and his lack of regard for his own son.

"Should I be worried to find the two of you conspiring?"

She smiled at the sound of Styxx's deep, husky voice that never failed to send a shiver over her. Until him, she'd never found a Greek accent appealing. But she could listen to his all day.

"Not conspiring, my love. I fear your son is ever trying to ruin my figure."

He came up behind her and wrapped his arm around her before nuzzling her neck. Closing her eyes, she laid her hand against his cheek and savored the sensation of him holding her. She brushed her thumb against the goatee he was growing again. For some reason, it came and went at various times of the year.

"There are olives and mashed beans," Styxx said, knowing they were among her favorites.

"Mmmm, that could be good with apples." She felt his grimace.

"Seriously?" he asked in disbelief.

His father laughed. "Never argue with a pregnant woman, boy. They eat all manner of strangeness."

Styxx placed a kiss to her cheek before moving away. "All right, odd food it is." He made her a plate, and sliced her apples while his father watched them with an intensity he found disturbing.

"You look tired, boy. Have you not been sleeping?"

Styxx set the plate on a table then helped Bethany to sit. "I'm fine, Father." He went to get her some milk to drink while his father sat beside her.

"Styxx tells me it's your wish to marry in Egypt?"

He glared at his father.

Bethany shrugged. "The Greek gods would take issue with my family attending here. Gods tend to frown on other gods intruding into their territory."

"So your father really is Set?"

Styxx ground his teeth at his father's question. "Are you questioning my betrothed's integrity?"

She placed her hand on his arm to calm him. "Yes, my father is Set. If you like, I can summon him, but I doubt you'd enjoy the visit. While he dotes incessantly on me, he is a beast to everyone else. Even his own family. It's why he lives alone in the desert most of the year."

The old man's gaze went to Styxx. "How do you think he'll deal with the fact that you have a Greek husband?"

She wiped her lips with her napkin. "He won't care." She flashed a sweet smile at Styxx. "Rather, he'll want to gut any man who touches me, regardless of where he comes from."

Styxx laughed. "The more you speak of your father, the more worried I become."

"Don't fear, love. I've already spoken to the rest of my family. Maahes, Horus, and Osiris have sworn to join forces and keep him from tearing you into pieces. But I would recommend you attend the wedding in your armor . . . just to be safe."

His father snorted. "I'm glad to see my son marrying well. He's been so reticent to go near women that I'd begun to despair there was something lacking with him."

Styxx opened his mouth to respond, but Bethany squeezed his hand.

"Thank you, Majesty," she said with a smile.

"For what?"

"Confirming Styxx's loyalty. Not that it was needed. I've never once doubted his faithfulness to me."

Styxx kissed her cheek. "You are the only women I've ever touched, and I will have no other."

She smiled at his declaration. "And you are the only man I'd ever marry. The only man I've ever trusted to hold and not break my heart." She turned back toward his father. "We've been together since Styxx was scarce more than a boy. But even then, he was more of a man than any ancient I've ever known." She set aside her plate. "Now if you'll excuse us, all this talk of your son's loyalty and fidelity has made me feel a sudden urge to go riding."

His father scowled. "You shouldn't ride in your condition. You could fall from the horse and lose or injure the babe you carry."

Holding Styxx's hand in hers, she paused to smile graciously at him. "I never said anything about a horse, Majesty. It's your son I intend to mount and ride. Good day." With Styxx in tow, she headed for the door.

Styxx didn't make a sound until they were out in the hall then he burst into laughter. "I wish you could have seen the expression on his face. I can't believe you said that to him. *He* can't believe you said that."

Bethany finally let her irritation show, which was good, as she couldn't have withheld it a moment longer. "He deserves that and worse. Ugh, he makes me so angry. I just don't understand how you come from him!"

He didn't respond as he pulled her against him so close that she could feel his hard cock against her hip while he nibbled at her neck.

"What are you doing?"

He teased her earlobe with his teeth. "I'm going to take you upstairs and make an honest woman of you. You do still want that ride, don't you?"

Biting her lip, she reached down to cup and stroke him. He hardened even more. "It would be a shame to let this go to waste, wouldn't it?"

"It would, indeed." He kissed her lightly on the lips then swung her up in his arms and carried her upstairs, where he intended to make love to her until neither of them could walk.

JUNE 19, 9527 BC

"So it is true."

Inside her Theban temple, where she'd been unpacking baby clothes, Bethany looked up at her father's stern tone. She straightened instantly and tried to block them from his view then wondered why since her distended belly betrayed her pregnancy much more effectively than the baby clothes did.

Her heart thumped wildly as she met his light gold eyes that held more hurt in them than anger. Not to mention their color spoke volumes about his mood . . . his eyes were an even darker blue than Styxx's whenever he was happy.

Gold was not good in the case of the god Set.

"I was going to tell you, Papas."

"When?"

"When I was sure you wouldn't kill the father."

Sighing, he moved forward so that he could place his hand on her stomach and feel the baby moving inside her. "He's strong."

"Like his grandfather."

Set scoffed at her flattery. He was so much taller than her that he pulled her next to him until she was nestled under his arm with her head resting against his shoulder. He cupped her cheek in his large hand and kissed the top of her head. "You are my only child, Bet'anya. Have you any idea how precious you are to me?"

She touched her stomach and smiled. "I do now."

He shook his head and sighed. "Do you love his father?"

"More than my life . . . " She looked up to meet his gaze. "Please don't kill him."

He laughed. "But for you, I'd be thrashing him already. I can't stand the thought of any man touching you."

"I know, but he is quite remarkable and extremely kind to me."

"He better be more than that." Releasing her, he stepped away and gave her a harsh stare. "I want to meet him."

"Papas . . ."

"Take me to him. Now." There was a tone she'd seldom heard him use with her. It was one that brooked no delay or question.

Afraid for Styxx, she bit her lip in indecision. "What are your intentions?"

"To inquire about his."

Sure they were . . .

So she answered for her beloved. "He is going to marry me here in Thebes, in just under three weeks."

That didn't placate her father even a tiny bit. "I still want to meet him before you make any commitments."

She wasn't too sure about that. She rather liked having Styxx in one unbroken piece. "Only if you promise me you won't spear his head to a wall or tear off a vital part of his anatomy."

"Define *vital*. As in something he *can* live without or something you don't want him to be without?"

Unamused, she narrowed her gaze to let him know how serious she was. "Papas!"

He held his hands up in surrender. "Can I have a small testicle ripping?"

She gaped at him.

And then he tsked at her reaction. "Come, daughter . . . just one ball. He won't even miss it. Neither will you."

She smirked.

He let out another tired sigh. "Fine then. I promise I won't hurt your betrothed . . . today. I make no promises about the future should he do you or the baby harm."

For her father, that was quite a sacrifice, and it would be the best she could get out of him. But that being said, she had no doubt he'd love Styxx as much as she did once they met. "All right. But you should know before we go that he's Greek."

He twisted his face up into a look of supreme disgust. "Not even Egyptian . . . I blame your mother for this."

"That's fine, as she blames you for most of my bad habits. And speaking of Mom, he doesn't know who she is yet. I'd like to keep it that way, too."

Her father gave her an arch stare.

"He's Greek, Papas," she reiterated. "He was also the one who invaded Atlantis."

Her father let out a most evil laugh. "Styxx of Didymos?" The fact he knew the name said it all.

"Yes."

He sucked his breath in sharply. "The maternal side of your family will be even less pleased with your choice than I am."

She was well aware of that fact, which was why she'd delayed the wedding. Hopefully by then, all the mess with Apostolos would be behind them and her maternal side would be a little more accepting of her husband.

"I know, and neither will Styxx." His aversion was really the only thing that concerned her, especially given what her family had done to him while they'd held him in Atlantis. She prayed Styxx would be able to let the past go and learn to forgive her family in time. "I'm hoping the baby will help to bridge everything."

Her father released an elongated breath. "Secrets are never a good thing, child. Especially between lovers. But I won't tell him. That is your place, not mine."

"Thank you." She held her hand out for him. The moment he took it, she used her powers to flash them into Styxx's private receiving room. "I'm tucking my powers in to keep from upsetting the Greek pantheon."

"Probably for the best. So where do we go?"

She shrugged. "I'm not exactly sure. He's usually here this time of day."

No sooner had she finished speaking than Styxx walked in from the bathing room ... completely naked.

Gaping, Styxx sputtered at the unexpected sight of Bethany and her gigantic guest. Horrified, he quickly reversed direction and grabbed the towel he'd left on the floor by the pool. *Please tell me that's not her father . . .*

"Um, Styxx?"

He flinched at her sweet voice that could have warned him before he'd embarrassed himself by walking about with all his business hanging loose. Granted, he was in his private chambers . . . That didn't really matter to him at the moment. "I'll be right out, *akribos*."

"At least he speaks Egyptian. Mixed with Greek, but . . . "

Styxx cringed inwardly at that deep rumbling voice that shook the walls around him. This was so not how he'd wanted to meet his future in-laws.

Have I not suffered enough degradations in my life? Really?

Aggravated and humiliated, he returned with the towel wrapped around his hips to find Bethany standing next to a man who didn't look that much older than either of them . . . Still, he bore enough resemblance to Bethany that Styxx knew his death was imminent.

Especially since the well-muscled man towered over Styxx by a good foot. Crap. She'd neglected to tell him just how large a man her father was.

"Hmmm," the man said, narrowing his stern gaze on Styxx. "He's not a coward. That's a plus."

She laughed. "Papas, stop teasing him."

With that confirmation of the man's identity, Styxx wanted to melt into the floor and vanish. This was definitely not the way he'd envisioned meeting her father.

Clothes would have been a nice option.

"Forgive me, Lord Set, I wasn't expecting company."

"I should hope not, given your state of undress. While I've often said the Greeks are uncivilized, as a rule you do generally have enough manners not to walk around bare-assed with company present."

Bethany scowled at him. "Please, stop. I'm sure Styxx is mortified enough." She approached Styxx. "I'm so sorry we didn't

596

warn you. My father found out about the baby, and insisted he meet you immediately."

Without thinking, Styxx started to wrap his arms around her as he normally would then caught himself as he remembered her father's proclivity for slicing off parts of male anatomy, and that was from men who hadn't impregnated his only daughter. "Um . . ."

Set laughed. "And he appears to be housebroken, otherwise he'd have made a mess just now when he reached to touch you, daughter." He stepped forward and offered his hand to Styxx. "Relax, son. The way your entire face lit up when you first saw my girl tells me everything I need to know about how you feel where she's concerned . . . and I know how she feels about you. So long as I love my daughter, you are safe from harm."

When Styxx went to take his hand, Set jerked him into a fatherly embrace. He tightened his grip around Styxx to show him just how inhumanly strong he was. "But should you ever break her heart, I will dine on yours."

"Papas!"

He kissed Styxx's cheek before he released him. "I'm merely having fun with him, Bet. Surely you can allow me that much. It's not every day I get a new child, never mind two of them at once." He stepped back then frowned.

Before Styxx could ask what had him upset, Set turned Styxx around to examine his back. Clenching his teeth, Styxx knew exactly what had him irritated.

"You're marked by Apollo?"

Styxx had to force himself not to growl over something that was still a huge sore spot for him. "I was. He released me."

Set's eyes turned to a deep gold color that matched Bethany's. "You should know, I hate that bastard. Passionately."

"Then we are united, my lord. I hold no love of him either. He marked me against my will, and I haven't forgiven it."

That immediately relaxed the older god and changed his eyes back to a deep blue. "You are even more welcomed to my family,

597

Styxx. I extend my protection to you. Should he ever come at you again, let me know."

"I appreciate it, my lord. Thank you."

Set inclined his head then turned toward Bethany. "While I'm still not thrilled he's Greek, at least you chose a prince and a champion who speaks our language." He glanced back at Styxx and smiled. "And I can pretend his towel is a shendyt."

Styxx visibly cringed this time. "I hope I haven't overly offended you."

"By your lack of dress? Not at all. Impregnating my daughter—"

Bethany slapped him in the stomach, causing him to cut off his words mid-sentence. "Stop, Papas. He doesn't know you're teasing him."

"Who said I was teasing?"

"He's teasing you, my love, and now he's going."

Set opened his mouth to protest then clamped his jaw shut as if he knew better than to try. "Fine. I shall leave you two alone. But I will see you at dinner tonight, daughter. We have a wedding to discuss. Whatever plans you've made, I am sure they're inadequate."

He vanished instantly.

Bethany held her hand out toward Styxx. "You are still alive, right?"

Styxx laughed nervously. "For the moment."

"Are you completely embarrassed?"

"To the core of my being. But I'm too grateful to have survived the encounter with all my body parts intact to complain." Now that they were alone, he wrapped his arms around her and splayed his hands against her stomach to feel their baby. "Little Galen is extremely active today."

"I think he knows the sound of your voice. Anytime you speak, he immediately starts moving."

"Really?"

She nodded and pulled his hand lower to where their son was really thrashing about.

"Does that hurt you?"

"No. Not at all. Though he does wake me occasionally at night when he stirs."

"I can't wait to meet him." And yet Styxx couldn't shake the bad feeling that stayed in his own stomach.

She kissed his cheek. "Are you ready for your birthday celebration?"

Sighing, he pulled away from her. "I've been wanting to talk to you about that."

Bethany scowled at the odd note in his voice. "What?"

"There's no way for me to say this without it sounding bad so I'm just going to say it and please don't be offended."

With every word he spoke, her panic mounted. "What?" she repeated.

"I don't want you here for it."

She was definitely offended. "Why?"

"I have a terrible feeling, Beth. One that won't go away. I would just rather you be safe and away from here."

She winced at the needless fears that constantly plagued him. Especially since Galen's death. He was terrified the gods would rob him of anyone he cared for. "I'll be fine, love. It's just your war nerves again, and I understand. You've had too many vicious attacks. But no one's going to hurt me or the baby."

"Beth—"

"Styxx . . . it will be fine. Trust me. You've spent too many birthdays with people who don't love you. The baby and I want to be here for this one."

Closing his eyes, Styxx wanted to curse her love for him. But how could he? It was too rare a commodity for him to spurn it. "Fine, but promise me that we will leave as soon as it's done. We will go to Egypt and stay there where your family can protect you until after the baby's born."

"If that is what you want then I'm agreeable. But it's not necessary."

"For my sanity, it is."

"All right. For the sake of your sanity." She kissed his cheek again.

He left her to dress and only then did Bethany feel a twinge of his fear.

But she dismissed it. After his birthday, she intended to drink Ma'at's serum and become fully human. In four days, they would be headed to Egypt and no one would ever be able to harm them again.

She would put his fears to rest and all would be right in the world.

JUNE 22, 9527 BC

Styxx raked his hands through his hair as the voices of a thousand people screamed in his head. Because of the number of people his father had invited, he'd been in pain all day. So much so that his nose had poured blood throughout the morning. Honestly, he couldn't stand it.

The only person he wanted to see wasn't here yet, and a part of him hoped that Bethany would heed his fear and not show up at all.

His only saving grace was the fact that neither Acheron nor Ryssa had come near him. Rather they were sequestered in her rooms, no doubt wishing for his brutal demise.

Perhaps he should assign more tasters for his food tonight . . .

Smoothing his hair down, he returned his hated golden-leaf crown to his head.

Even worse than the feeling of dread that refused to go away was the grief he had over the absence of Galen. This was the first time in over a decade that he hadn't spent at least part of his birthday with the old man.

"You want an award for being born? What's wrong with you, boy? The world don't give out awards for births." For five years, that had been Galen's rant.

Tears choked him as he remembered the next anniversary.

His father had been a complete ass as Styxx had been forced to listen to court sessions all morning while trying to hide a vicious nosebleed. As for his "gift" from his father, it'd been a "personal" donation to the city for a monument to honor the king.

By the time Styxx had gone to practice, with his mother's and Ryssa's insults ringing in his ears, he'd been completely deflated and morose.

Until he'd gone in to change his clothes. Sitting on the shelf had been a pair of black and bronze vambraces that matched his armor.

Awed by the sight, he'd assumed they were put there by mistake.

"They don't bite, boy. Try them on. See if they fit."

Frowning, he'd turned to see Galen standing in the doorway with a wide grin on his face. "Who do they belong to?"

Galen had laughed. "You, Highness. They're my gift to you. Happy birthday, *gios*. I hope they always protect you in battle."

His eyes tearing from the memory, Styxx went to his chest and pulled them out. He wasn't sure who'd been prouder of them. Galen for the giving or him for the receiving. And they had served him well in battle.

"I miss you, Galen," he breathed, wishing he could see his mentor one more time.

But then he had a lot of regrets.

Sighing, he wrapped the vambraces back in their protective oiled cloth and tucked them in beside the wooden horse that Acheron wanted nothing to do with. He would give it to his own son to play with one day.

"Happy birthday, little brother," he whispered, knowing Acheron's perfect gift would be Styxx's head on a platter.

Suddenly, he heard a loud fanfare outside.

His rapid heartbeat pounded more pain through his head as he went to the windows to see who was arriving.

Bethany.

"I could strangle you for not listening to me." But the rest of him didn't agree with his brain. In spite of his common sense, he was thrilled she'd come.

He left his room to greet her and with every step, he prayed that she was right. That it was just his stupidity that made him dread this day so much.

JUNE 23, 9527 BC

Bethany was laughing in bed with Styxx when she heard an ear-splitting scream that echoed through the ether, which only the gods and a few others could hear ... The horrified agony of utmost heartache. She knew the source of the sound in an instant.

Apollymi.

Had they finally found her son and killed him? That was the kind of grief that would explain it. Surely nothing else could warrant so much pain.

Styxx went rigid around her as if he'd heard it, too, but as a mortal, he shouldn't have any way to access those voices. Though he continued to be hard inside her, he was completely still in her arms.

"Are you all right?" she asked him.

He cursed under his breath. "Nosebleed."

It was the first time he'd had one while making love to her. He pulled back and left her to tend it.

She sat up and pulled the sheets to cover her.

After a few seconds, he returned to bed and sat down by her side, holding a cloth to his nose.

"Sorry, love. Really bad timing."

She sat up to brush her hand through his hair, which was finally

602

long enough to have curls again. "I'm more worried about you. Have you any idea what caused it?"

Styxx fell quiet as he continued to hear the voice of a goddess in his head. It was one he'd heard many times while growing up. He didn't know her name, but when he'd been a small child, her voice had soothed him like a mother's lullaby.

Today, she was shrieking and furious, and he had no idea why. Worse, she was cursing and threatening him as if he'd done something to her.

I will find you and rip out your heart, you Greek whoreson! I'm coming for you and everything you hold dear. There is no place you can hide that I won't discover, and when I do, you will wish to your Greek gods that you had died at birth as you should have! How dare you not protect my son! I will bathe in your putrid entrails!

He had no idea what he'd done to deserve her hatred. *Maybe it's not directed at you . . .*

But it felt personal.

More than that, it felt like the same mood his mother had been in right before she'd stabbed him. And as Bethany brushed the hair back from his eyes, an image of Galen dying in his arms hit him like a vicious blow. Only this time, it was Bethany he saw dying.

"I need you to leave."

She froze instantly. "Excuse me?"

"Not permanently, *akribos*. You promised you'd go right after my banquet. Yet you're still here. I need you to get to Egypt as fast as you can so that your father and family can keep you safe for me."

"I don't want to leave you."

"I'll be right behind you. I'll probably catch up before you make it there."

Bethany hesitated. She started to tell him that she was a goddess and that he had no need to fear for her, but since she was giving it up in a few days to be with him, there was no need to mention it and risk his anger and condemnation. "I'm sure I'll be there first."

"Good. Now, please ... let's get you packed and out of here."

"Your nose is still bleeding. I can smell it."

"I've fought many battles with it bleeding worse than this. It's nothing. I'll be fine."

She curled up beside him with her belly resting against his ribs. Closing his eyes, Styxx savored the warmth of her there while his son kicked them both. She took his hand into hers and led it to her lips so that she could nibble his knuckles.

"You are the most important thing in my world, Styxx of Didymos, proud Ariclean prince. In my heart, I am your wife, and I need no contract or witness to validate it."

She placed his hand to her heart so that he could feel the soothing, strong beat of it. "In all my life, there has never been another man who has made me feel what I feel whenever I think of you. Your pleasure is my pleasure and your agony is a thousand times worse for me to bear than any I have ever felt on my own, because you are so much more important to me than I am. Every time you leave, I cannot breathe again until I know you're safe and back in my arms." She kissed his hand. "Against my wishes, I will go to please you, but know that I will live in absolute misery until I'm with you again." She bit his knuckle. "Don't make me wait, my love."

Realizing that she had started her Egyptian wedding vows by stating her devotion to him, and as such was asking him to marry her before she left, he pulled the cloth from his nose then brought her hand to his lips so that he could kiss her palm. "And you, sweet Bethany of Egypt, Princess of Thebes, are my *kunosoura*—"

"Your what?" She frowned. "Sorry, love. Not a native speaker and Greek is a very difficult language."

Laughing, he kissed her hand again then used the Egyptian word for the brightest star in the sky that soldiers and sailors used to navigate with at night to guide them to safety and home. "*Thuban*. On the worst day of my life, when I was lost and beyond hope or redemption, you came out of the darkest tempest unexpectedly. I was but an empty shell wandering the banks of the Phlegethon, trapped between Tartarus and the Fields of Punishment with nothing but reasons to die, and yet your kiss alone breathed life into my deadened heart and darkened soul. Until that moment when you first laid your gentle hand to my cheek, I knew nothing of kindness. Nothing of happiness. And absolutely nothing of love. That soft, tender touch that meant nothing to you, as it is in your nature to be thus, went far deeper than just my skin. It reached into the deadest part of me and set beating a heart I had never known existed. I can count every happy year of my life on one hand and all of them I owe to you. Without you, my precious Bethany, I have nothing. I am nothing. And all I ask is that you never send me back to the stygian hell you pulled me from. It was hard enough to suffer it before I knew you existed, but now that I know the face of Theia, I cannot go back to dwell in darkness alone. I need you, my love. Always."

He kissed her forehead. "You are not just my wife. You are what sustains me, and my only prayer is that I never bring even a shadow of hurt to your beautiful eyes or heart."

Bethany frowned as he placed a ring on her finger. "What is this?"

When he spoke, his voice was thick with pain. "It's the wedding ring Galen and I picked out for you right before he died."

Tears flowed down her cheeks as she smiled proudly. "And it will never leave my finger."

"And you will never leave my heart."

She pulled him into her arms and held him close. "How do you expect me to go when you speak to me like this? When I know how much pain you're in without me?"

He cupped her cheek. "Because you are taking the most important parts of me with you, Bethany ... My heart." He kissed her lips. "And my soul." He kissed her belly then he kissed away her tears. "Please, for my sanity. Every time in my life when things were going well, something horrific happened. I've already lost Galen. I cannot lose you and our son."

"All right. I will go. But not happily."

"And I will be counting down every beat of my heart until we're together."

Reluctantly, she left the bed and started dressing and packing.

His heart aching, Styxx helped her. In truth, he wanted to keep her by his side. But Thanatos was stalking him. He could feel the bastard's breath on his neck, and he knew if she stayed, she'd be caught in whatever storm was coming.

Too soon and not soon enough, he had her surrounded by men and on her way to Egypt. "I will leave tomorrow. I promise."

Bethany nodded. "I will be waiting for you. Do not tarry."

Styxx kissed her lips then held her hand to his heart while he kept his other hand on the area of her stomach where his son kicked. He was terrified of letting her go. Terrified he'd never see her again. But worse was the fear of her staying behind and being harmed because of his selfishness.

Smiling sadly, she breathed an Egyptian blessing in his ear. "May Ra be between you and harm in all the empty places where you walk."

He pressed her hand to his lips. "And I'd rather your grand-father walk with you and keep you safe every step of this journey."

She leaned down from her chariot to kiss his cheek. "Tomorrow."

"I will be hot on your heels. I swear." Styxx nodded to the driver, but he held her hand until they rolled too fast for him to keep pace.

As he watched her leave, it felt as if his heart was being ripped out of his chest. But he knew she had to go. It was the only hope they had.

JUNE 24, 9527 BC

Styxx paused in his packing to glance around the palace he'd assumed would one day be his. In just a few hours, he'd be long gone from here and would hopefully never see it again.

Let Acheron or Ryssa have it, or share it happily for the rest of their lives.

I should feel something other than relief.

But he didn't. In truth, he couldn't get away from here fast enough.

As he was taking his laurel crown down to his father's office to leave it there, the front door opened and Acheron strode in with a confidence his brother had never before exhibited. Acheron normally skulked about like a beaten dog that didn't want to be seen by anyone.

Styxx frowned at the change, wondering what had caused it. Was his brother drunk?

Boldly, Acheron approached him with his chest puffed out. It was the kind of posturing soldiers had sometimes used when they wanted to dare Styxx to fight them. But those who had held that kind of stupidity had been quickly schooled that Styxx didn't play well with others, and most importantly . . .

He didn't lose.

"Are you ill, brother?"

Acheron curled his lip. "Just sick of *you,* and the way you parade around like you own the world."

Styxx sighed heavily. *If I only lived the life other people think I do.* "I don't do that."

"Yes. You do. I see it every time I look at you."

His frown deepened as Styxx realized that he couldn't hear Acheron's thoughts anymore. How strange.

Not that it mattered. He had other things on his mind. Like getting the Hades out of here.

Styxx started for his father's study, but Acheron grabbed his arm. "You fear me, don't you?"

Styxx bit back laughter at the ludicrous question. "No."

Acheron grabbed him again.

"Are you herbal, little brother?"

Laughing, Acheron shoved Styxx against the wall in the same manner as Apollo often did. Then he leaned to whisper in Styxx's ear. "I know you can't die, *brother*. Not unless I do. That means I can hold you down and cut out your heart over and over again and there's nothing you can do to stop me."

There, Acheron was wrong. The one thing Atlantis had taught him was how to fight against gods. But he wasn't in the mood to fight with his brother.

Not today.

"Is that really what you want to do?"

Acheron's hand tightened around his throat. "You're no better than me."

No shit. He'd never thought otherwise. "And you're no better than I am."

The hatred in those silver eyes seared him. But that wasn't what Styxx really saw. He saw the same bloodlust Acheron had held for him in Atlantis when his brother had helped Estes sell and torture him. Acheron had delighted in seeing him humiliated.

"You deserve it!"

His brother's angry voice still rang in his ears as his vision darkened.

"I have reached my majority, Styxx. Do you know what that means?"

"You can own property? Join the senate?"

Acheron's teeth elongated.

Styxx went cold as he finally understood all the bits and pieces of what had happened to him in Atlantis. Why he had held so much fascination for Archon who'd suspected this, but he'd held the wrong twin in custody . . .

"You're Apostolos."

Shock stole the hatred from Acheron's eyes. "How do you know that name?"

The two years he'd warred in Atlantis and the year he'd been with their gods passing him around had well schooled him on the knowledge of Apollymi's hidden son.

The Atlantean gods would give him anything for this information . . .

Anything.

Acheron's hand all but crushed his windpipe. "You tell anyone and I *will* kill you!"

Styxx laughed at the threat. "I don't want anything from you, *brother*. Except to be left the fuck alone." He broke Acheron's hold and ignored the pain it caused him. "I don't care what powers you think you hold, I can still beat you down."

"Acheron!" Ryssa gasped as she ran to his brother. "What are you doing?"

"We were talking. Right, Styxx?"

He rolled his eyes. "Sure."

Ryssa glared at Styxx then gently pulled Acheron away from him. "You know what Father would do if he caught you with him."

For the first time in his life, Styxx didn't begrudge his brother Ryssa's love. It made it easier for him to walk away from the entire family knowing Ryssa and Acheron had an unbreakable bond. "You two look after each other."

Ryssa paused on the stairs to give him a suspicious glower. "What's that supposed to mean?"

Could her tone be any more accusatory? "Nothing, Ryssa. Absolutely nothing."

Unwilling to deal with either of them, Styxx went to his father's study and placed his crown in the chest where his father kept his own. Intricately carved with images of the Fates, the gold chest was ancient in age. When he'd been a boy, he'd sometimes sneak into it to look at his father's ornate crown and imagine if he'd look so dignified wearing it as a man.

How long ago that seemed, and at the same time, it was yesterday. But sadly, neither crown would be a part of his future. And for that, he hated his brother and the Atlantean gods all the more.

To protect Acheron, Apollymi had thoroughly screwed up Styxx's life.

Damn them all!

But then the gods who'd been searching for Apostolos had been looking for a single child. Not twins. How ironic that Acheron had spent much of his life right under their noses while they tore the world apart trying to find him.

"I smell divinity on you, Greek. Whose byblow are you?" Archon's angry words as the god had tried to beat information out of him that Styxx hadn't been given still caused a shiver to run down his spine.

I should have recognized their voices when I met them. But then he'd heard so many different ones over the years that it was hard to break them apart and identify them when he didn't have a personal relationship with the thinker. Like the Atlantean gods, Styxx had assumed himself born of an Olympian. Why else would Athena and Apollo have taken an interest in him? He'd attributed it to nepotism.

Now, he suspected they had sensed whatever had attracted Archon and Asteros to him. Whatever Apollymi had done to protect her son must have lured them to him, too.

However, none of that mattered now. He had an Egyptian demigoddess to worry over and meet up with.

Closing the lid, he practically ran up to his room to collect his things and go. It'd already taken him longer to pack than he'd meant for it to.

It wouldn't be that long until nightfall. But he'd travel through it. They'd done many marches at night so as to hide their numbers and protect their troops. Plus it saved water not to travel during the heat of the day. The soldiers and horses had a lot less exhaustion.

Styxx turned to leave then froze as Apollo appeared in his room. He cursed under his breath at the god's inconvenient timing. "What?"

Apollo let out a bitter laugh. "Tone, prince. You still haven't learned the proper tone."

Grinding his teeth, Styxx really wanted to punch the bastard. "Aren't you bored with me yet?"

Apollo gave him a lopsided grin. "If you were your mewling,

610

obsequious sister, yes. I'd be bored with you. But it's the fact that you continue to fight me even after all I've done to punish you for it that fascinates me. Most humans learn their lessons ... You don't. Why is that?"

Styxx reached for his saddlebags. "I'm dumber than most."

Moving faster than Styxx was prepared for, Apollo grabbed him and turned him around so that Styxx could see himself in the mirror with Apollo standing behind him. The Olympian didn't touch Styxx. Rather he locked gazes in the mirror. "If only you were, I could forgive you. But it's knowing how intelligent you are that fascinates me." Apollo touched his cheek.

Styxx jerked away, but Apollo refused to let him leave their reflection. He yanked Styxx back to the mirror.

"See what I mean? Why do you continue to fight me?"

"I have no stomach for men in general and you in particular. Your touch reviles me." How many times did he have to say it before Apollo got the message?

Apollo jerked Styxx against him. "And yet you're so beautiful ... even scarred as you are, I crave you."

Styxx cringed. "You gave your word to all that I was free."

"And I've never regretted anything more. Yield to me once ... just once ... Come to me as you would your betrothed, and bend to my will, and then I will leave you in peace. Forever."

Sure he would.

"I don't believe you."

Apollo tried to grab him, but Styxx caught his hand and jerked it away. It didn't deter the Olympian at all. He wrapped his arms around him and tried to kiss him. "I can't get you out of my mind. How many more people do I have to take from you before you bend to me?"

Styxx fought hard for his freedom. "You killed Galen?"

"Not personally, but yes. And I'll kill the rest if you don't give me what I want."

Styxx cried out as Apollo sank his fangs deep into his neck to feed.

The door to his room opened.

A sharp, feminine gasp froze him instantly. Eyes wide, Ryssa stared at them with horror etched into her fragile features. Styxx could only imagine the sight they made with Apollo's hand still pressed against his slave's brand on his groin and the god feeding from this neck.

Completely unperturbed, Apollo laughed and lifted his head then kissed Styxx's cheek while he cupped him in plain sight of his sister. "Would you care to join us, Ryssa?"

That set her off into one of her legendary shrieking fits as she began grabbing things in the room and hurling them at him and Apollo. Ducking the first clay vase, Styxx broke away from Apollo and glared at him.

Apollo sneered at Ryssa. "I am not putting up with this. I'll be back when you calm down." He flashed out of the room, leaving Styxx alone with the termagant.

She continued to scream out in a tone that rendered her words unintelligible as she sought to strip his room bare of projectiles.

"What in the name of Zeus is going on in here?" his father roared as he snatched the clay wine jug from her hand before it became another pile of broken fragments on the floor.

Sobbing in hysteria and ignoring the question, Ryssa kept her fury concentrated solely on Styxx. "How dare you! You disgust me! I wish you were dead!" She whirled about and stormed from the room.

His father returned the jug to the table as Styxx pushed himself up from the floor. "What did you do to her?"

"Nothing, Father. I didn't do anything to her at all."

His father moved to go after her. But Ryssa met him at the door. Without a word to their father, she crossed the room with a tranquility that concerned him. Expecting her slap, Styxx caught her left hand as she tried to deliver it. But the moment he did, he felt something sink painfully into his abdomen.

Stunned, he stumbled back to see the large bloody knife she'd hidden in the folds of her gown.

She lunged to stab him again.

Styxx grabbed her wrist and held it tight as his father finally realized what was going on.

Instead of calling for the guards, his father pulled Ryssa back and took the knife out of her hand. "What have you done, daughter?"

Styxx's knees buckled as the room spun around. While it never felt good to be stabbed, gut wounds had to be the worst. Breathing raggedly, he lay down and tried to focus.

"He's sleeping with Apollo! Selfish bastard! He's taken everything from me! Everything!"

Flat on his back, Styxx felt a tear slide from the corner of his eye as pain racked him while his father comforted Ryssa on the other side of the room. In spite of the agony, he laughed in bitter amusement.

Every member of his family, except his father and Bethany, had stabbed him.

But I'm young still. There's plenty of time for that to change.

Blood rushed between his fingers as he applied as much pressure as he could to the wound. Yet it was hard. His hands were shaking and he felt like he was about to vomit.

Still his father ignored him while the king dealt with Ryssa's hysterics.

"Father?" he breathed.

"Oh dear gods . . . Guards!" His father finally left Ryssa to check on him. "Fetch the physician!" Swallowing hard, his father started to touch Styxx's blood-covered hands then refrained. "Does it hurt much?"

No, it feels fucking wonderful. I live for my family to stab me.

Was the man insane? Of course it hurt. His sister had just tried to gut him.

"However much it hurts, it doesn't hurt enough for what he's done. He's humiliated me for the last time! I wish you could die like a normal person, you bastard! You've been nothing but misery to everyone since the day you were born. If you died tomorrow no one would miss you except that Egyptian whore you found. And even she wouldn't care for long. You're nothing!" She ran for him.

His father stood up to catch her before she reached Styxx again. As his father pulled her back, she spat in Styxx's face.

He wiped it away with the back of his scarred, bloodied hand.

Why didn't I leave here sooner?

He shouldn't have wasted five seconds of time on his brother. The gods knew Acheron wouldn't waste it on him. *I should have left that damned crown in my room and been on my way to Egypt.*

Maybe he could still ride later tonight. He just needed someone to stitch the wound. As Ryssa had pointed out, it wasn't like he could physically die from it. Though to be honest, he died a little inside every time they attacked him.

The physician gasped as he saw him on the floor. "Highness?"

Styxx opened his eyes. He moved his hands aside for the man to examine the gaping hole. The physician pulled Styxx's chiton up so that he could tend it.

The physician sucked his breath in sharply at the amount of damage. Mostly because on anyone else, the wound would be fatal. Blood loss wasn't the problem. But Styxx had seen enough injuries like this in battle to know the inevitable outcome. Within a few days, the soldier always died in extreme and utter agony. Because of that, the soldiers with these wounds were often killed just to put them out of their misery. It was something that still haunted him. But during war they couldn't afford to waste their limited supplies on someone who wouldn't live anyway, and it was cruel to let them die slowly in agony when there was no help or hope for them.

His father finally returned. The horror in his eyes confirmed Styxx's dire prediction.

"It's bad, Majesty," the physician said as he worked to stop the blood flow. "Most don't survive a wound like this."

His father sank to his knees by his side. Tears welled in his eyes. "Styxx?"

He bit back a groan. "I'll live, Father. I've had worse in battle."

The physician appeared skeptical.

Styxx brushed his hand across the scars he bore. "Trust me."

For the first time, the physician nodded. "So it appears, Highness. I need to stitch this and I can't give you wine to drink."

Styxx turned his head toward the chest by the window. "Bring me that."

His father frowned as the physician complied. "What is in it?"

Styxx didn't answer as the physician returned with it and Styxx dug out the Morpheus root he hadn't used since Bethany had come back into his life. "Do you know how to prepare this?" he asked the old bald man.

"You heat it, but I don't know how much to use."

Styxx pulled out the right amount and handed it off to him so that he could begin the preparations while his father watched with an even deeper frown. Hissing in pain, Styxx clenched his teeth. "It's a drug, Father. One that won't take the pain away, but it'll make me not care that I feel it."

"How do you know about such things?"

Your perverted brother.

The words hovered on his lips, and were hard to bite back. His father had been blind to Estes, and while it angered him, what good would it do to scream at his father over his abuse now?

He'd killed the bastard and the eternal damage was done. No need to worsen it.

Luckily, the physician returned. Styxx inhaled the herbs and gave them a few minutes to take effect before he nodded at the man to start closing the wound.

Trying to distract himself, Styxx locked gazes with his father whose countenance was a mask of total disbelief.

"It dawns on me that I know very little about your life and even less about you."

615

What? Did his father want to play catch-up now? Given the amount of blood loss and pain, Styxx really wasn't in the mood for a lengthy father-son conversation.

But what really hurt were the memories of Galen standing by him whenever he'd been wounded. In his mind, he saw himself on that day when the wooden spike had torn through his side in Atlantis. Cocky and stupid, Styxx hadn't been paying attention. But the moment the spike went in, he'd cried out in utter agony. Galen had pulled him back and protected him from their enemies. Too weak to even hold a dagger, Styxx had been completely defenseless.

"I've got you, mou gios. Don't worry. Nothing's getting through me."

Even though Styxx was taller, Galen had carried him off the field of battle and held his hand the whole time they'd closed the wound. *"Squeeze when it hurts, and don't worry about breaking anything, Highness. Trust me, if my deceptively strong Thia wasn't able to break it during her childbirths, there's no damage you can do. And at least you're not threatening to cut off my balls, fry them up, and feed them to me."* Only Galen could have made him laugh while in that kind of pain and misery.

Afterward, the old man had gotten him drunk.

Gods, how he missed him.

Damn you, Apollo! Was it not enough that he'd killed Galen? Why torture Ryssa, too? She already held more than her fair share of hatred for him—why would Apollo worsen it?

I should have just fucked him and got it over with.

Not that it would have mattered. Had he given in, Ryssa would have seen a lot more than him trying to fight Apollo off. Maybe in time she'd calm down and realize what was really going on.

Who are you kidding? Ryssa would *never* take his side in any matter.

Once the physician was finished and had cleaned Styxx's wound thoroughly, his father called for the guards to help him to bed.

"It's not necessary," Styxx said, amazed that his speech wasn't slurred. "I can do it." Grinding his teeth against the pain that came through in spite of his drug, he pushed himself up and stumbled into bed. His head reeling, he lay there, trying to get the room to stop spinning.

He heard the sound of his father nearing his bed. "Is any of what Ryssa said about you and Apollo true?"

Opening his eyes, Styxx gave him a vacuous stare. His father really wanted to go into this right now?

What the Hades? Why not? It wasn't like Styxx was suffering in agony or anything.

Too high to care or hold back, he blinked at his father. "Yes, Apollo has buggered me. Repeatedly. No, I didn't instigate it. I damn sure never enjoyed it. And I really wish she'd keep him inside her so the bastard would leave me alone."

For once, his father didn't remark on his crudity. "Why didn't you tell me about this?"

If he didn't know better, he'd swear his father was on something, too. "I believe your exact words were for me to suck his balls and cock, and to bend over and take it wherever Apollo wanted to shove it so long as I kept him happy for *you*."

His father looked as horrified and ill as Styxx had been when the bastard had said it to him. *I didn't mean it.*

Little late for that thought.

"How long has it been going on?" his father asked.

"Since you put me in the Dionysion when I was a boy."

The color faded from his father's face. "I don't understand."

"They invoked the gods, Father," he said bitterly. "So they came for me ... in more ways than one."

"Is that why you hate me so?"

"It certainly didn't endear you to me, and neither is this fucking conversation. For the love of Olympus, Father, I've been stabbed by your daughter and it hurts. I just want to bleed and suffer in peace and silence, if that's not too much to ask? So please, have mercy on me for once in my wretched life."

"Forgive me." He finally left.

Drawing a ragged breath, Styxx stared at his saddlebags and cursed the Fates who'd forced him to stay another night.

"And you believe that lie, Father? Really?" He flinched at Ryssa's strident tone that carried plainly through his walls.

His father's reply was an unintelligible rumble.

"He's a liar. How can you not see that? He's always been a covetous liar since the day he was born. He couldn't stand that I had Apollo so he threw himself at him. You didn't see what I saw when I walked in on them. He was pressing Apollo's hands against his body parts. It was disgusting!" Her accusations went on, gaining ludicrousness with every one.

"I wish you'd let me kill him. It's what he deserves. How am I supposed to be with Apollo now, knowing he's slept with my *brother*? The brother I hate with every part of my being! How can I ever sit down at a table again with either of them, knowing what they've done to me behind my back? If this were in reverse and I'd slept with his whore, you'd have me whipped and exiled for it. Yet you intend to let him get away with this like he's gotten away with everything else in his spoiled rotten life. It's not fair!"

Was it too much to ask that his father pull the bitch to the other end of the palace so that he didn't have to listen to her jealous stupidity?

Unable to cope with any more insults and accusations that burned to the core of his soul, he reached for his chest and pulled out a sack full of herbs then he dumped them into a goblet of wine. He wasn't supposed to be drinking with this wound, but fuck it. Let him die. And if his stomach hurt, maybe that pain would be enough to distract his thoughts from his sister's extremely loud and ridiculous condemnation.

Gulping it down, he grimaced the moment the wine and herbs hit his stomach and made it cramp and burn in protest. For a second, he feared he'd be ill.

Yet within a few moments, it had him so disoriented that his sister's diatribe and screams became meaningless words that eventually lulled him to sleep.

But as he started dozing, his mind tried to fight it. For some reason, it wanted him alert. His instincts were trying to tell him something. Unfortunately, he was too far gone to comprehend the warning.

JUNE 25, 9527 BC

Just After Midnight

Styxx opened his eyes, but he was still too disoriented to make sense of what had awakened him.

Several seconds later, he heard his nephew crying. Then silence. That must have been what had jerked him from his sleep. Apollodorus still wasn't sleeping through the night. It was nothing for his nephew to wake him up at strange intervals.

And soon that would be the sound of his own son waking him. He couldn't wait.

But he knew better than to try to help out with Ryssa's child. Especially after today's fiasco.

Only Acheron had those privileges.

Forget it. Don't waste time thinking about them and their hatred. Tomorrow he'd be on his way to Bethany and nothing would stop him.

Bethany woke up in a cold sweat. Her stomach burned with indigestion while her son played and bounced happily inside her. Rolling to her left side, she placed her hand over him. "You have got to stop kicking me, little bit. I can't sleep with you frolicking so."

He brushed a foot or hand against her touch as if he knew she was talking to him.

"You're smarting back to me already . . . What am I going to do with you, boy?"

But she knew. She'd love him with every part of her being.

An instant later, sadness stole her smile as she missed having Styxx beside her in bed. If he were here, he'd be pressed up against her back and cradling her with his long hard naked body. He'd have his arm draped across her hip so as not to hurt her or the baby, and his muscled masculine thigh would be resting between hers. Best of all, his face would be buried in her hair. She still didn't know how he could sleep like that and not feel suffocated by it. Yet he never complained.

Bethany!

She jerked at her mother's shrill call.

Please, daughter! I need to see you.

Tempted to ignore her, she felt her son kick again. How could she turn her back on her own mother now that she understood motherhood more than she ever had before? Besides, after tomorrow, she'd be human and she wouldn't have any way whatsoever to go to her mother on her own.

Sighing, she summoned clothes for her body and teleported herself from her Egyptian temple to the main hall on Katateros where her mother waited with the others.

Complete silence rang out at her appearance as every pair of eyes stared at her distended stomach.

She gave them all a droll smirk, irritated that they'd only just now realized her condition. "Yes, gods, I'm pregnant. Now what do you need?"

Her jaw completely slack, her mother approached her slowly. "Why didn't you tell me?"

"I was planning to once this mess blew over. Since all of you were so concerned about Apollymi, I didn't want to distract you."

Archon glared at her. "Who's the father?"

"A mortal. Not that it's any of *your* concern."

Their collective derision didn't endear them to her.

Bethany curled her lip. "Hence why I didn't want to come here.

Now, if you'll excuse me, I'd rather be with my family members who aren't such snobs."

Her mother gently touched her arm before she could leave. "Pay them no attention, child. I, for one, am thrilled to be a grandmother, immortal or not. Especially to such a strong boy."

Tears welled in her eyes. "Thank you, Matera. Now why did you call me?"

"Apollymi is summoning her army and expanding it. We know she's about to attack and we wanted everyone to be prepared."

Chara nodded grimly. "We've been told she's planning to move in three days. We're fortifying, and now that we know you're expecting, you'd best stay in Egypt where your father and the others can protect you from her."

"But before you leave . . . " Her mother took her hand and led her from the hall to the temple her mother was sharing with Agapa while Apollymi was confined to the palace her mother used to call home. "I would like a few more details about my grandson and his father."

Thus the real reason Bethany had gone into hiding once she could no longer disguise her pregnancy. How could she tell her family that Styxx of Didymos was the father? Especially since she was the only member of the entire Atlantean pantheon who didn't want to plant a sword through his heart.

And whenever she thought about that, she wanted their blood over what they had done to him.

"There's not much to tell, Matera. He's the Greek I've been in love with for several years now."

"Hector?"

Bethany was surprised her mother remembered the name. Then again . . .

Symfora was her mother, and she did love her.

Bethany rubbed her hand over her stomach. She'd never be able to forget anything about her child either. "Yes, it's my Hector."

Which wasn't a lie.

Her mother smiled. "I'm so happy for you. There is nothing

621

sweeter than holding your baby for the first time. And then to watch it grow . . . " Tears glistened in her eyes as she brushed a strand of hair back from Bethany's face. "You've no idea how much love I have for you, Bet. How proud I am of you. I know you're centuries old and yet, whenever I look at you, I still see this adorable little baby with curls flying everywhere and chubby cheeks and gold eyes that melt my heart every time I look into them. And what I miss most are those times when you'd be afraid and you'd run to me and hide your little face in my shoulder." She touched Bethany's stomach. "And now you'll know that feeling, too. So have you thought of a name for him?"

She barely caught herself before she answered. They planned to name him Galen, but if she said the name, her mother might recognize it. "We're not sure yet."

"Well whatever you decide, I'm sure it'll be perfect."

She paused as she watched her mother gathering her weapons. "Matera? I've been thinking. Since I'll be in Egypt for a while, why don't you use my temple here?"

Her mother kissed her brow without answering. "I have missed you so, my heart."

"Me, too."

She put her hands on Bethany's shoulders. "May I be selfish? Would you spend tonight with me? You can always go back to Egypt in the morning."

Bethany hesitated. Tomorrow she needed to visit Ma'at about the serum and she wanted to watch over Styxx as he made his way to her.

But what would it hurt to stay one last night with her mother? Had she not been pregnant, she might have left. As it was, she couldn't bring herself to go. Not while her mother looked at her like that and she understood a mother's love. "All right, but what about Apollymi?"

"You'll be long gone before she launches her plans. For one night, let's be as we used to. Just the two of us and our teas."

Bethany smiled. It'd been a ritual since she was a child. Whenever she'd returned home from her father's, her mother would sequester her for two days of uninterrupted "girl time." As much as she loved and adored her father, she'd treasured those times most of all. It was always so nice to not have to share her mother with anyone. Her father had done a similar thing whenever she'd go to visit him. He'd drive her across the desert, straight into the heart of his domain, and they'd hunt in his private preserve. Just the two of them and no one else. It was why her bow meant so much to her. Her father had given her that bow the first time she'd visited him in Egypt.

Unlike Styxx, she'd been fortuitous with her parents. The only thing they'd competed over was trying to show her how much they loved and supported her. How much they missed her whenever she was gone from them.

It was something she was going to spend the rest of eternity teaching to Styxx and their son, and all their future children.

Taking her mother's hand, she led her to her temple. "Matera? Would you be upset if I told you something?"

"You can tell me anything. You know that."

"Promise you won't tell anyone else?"

"Of course."

"I have Aunt Ma'at working on a concoction that will make me mortal."

Her mother froze. "What?"

She nodded. "I've thought about it long and hard. I don't want to live eternity without my husband."

"You love him that much?"

"He is everything to me."

"And you are everything to me, child. Could we not make him immortal?"

"I don't think that would please him. And I don't want us to be torn apart by pantheon politics. I'm through with it."

Her mother closed her eyes and winced. "I can't say that your decision pleases me. But it doesn't displease me either. I just want you happy."

"This will make me very happy."

623

"Can I be there when you transform?"

And this was why she loved her mother so. "Absolutely."

"Then come, Bet. Let us celebrate your new life and your new baby."

JUNE 25, 9527 BC

Styxx woke up to a vicious headache. His stomach pitched, but settled as soon as he sat up. However, the room spun like a whirlwind around him. He leaned back against the wall then pulled the bandage back from his stomach to examine the wound Ryssa had given him. While it continued to sting and was extremely sore, it was much better.

Once he washed and dressed, he'd be able to leave. Thank the gods for some small favors.

On unsteady feet, he quickly prepared himself for his trip. Not even his nosebleed was going to stop him. He only paused long enough to grab his saddlebags and a cloth for his nose.

"*Antio*," he said with bitter sarcasm to the room and palace, bidding them all his final adieu. He would say good-bye to his family, if he'd had some to leave. As it was, the sooner he got out of here, the happier he'd be.

But as he walked toward the stairs, he saw something strange leaking out from beneath Ryssa's door. He started to ignore it then stopped.

Something wasn't right.

Ryssa should still be screaming over the injustice done to her. Yet there wasn't a single sound and it was close to midday. Not even Apollodorus seemed to be awake.

And as he neared the door to see the red liquid, he realized he couldn't hear their thoughts either.

He stood outside the door, staring at the blood on the floor, as a thousand emotions speared him at once. Panic, trepidation, anger, but it was grief that overwhelmed him. Because he knew what had to be on the other side of the closed door.

"Please, Ryssa, no," he breathed as tears stung his eyes. It would be so like her to kill herself and the baby as a way of punishing them all. That was just the kind of dramatics she specialized in.

For a moment, he thought Acheron would be with her, but if he were dead, Styxx wouldn't be here.

Styxx set down the saddlebags and reached with a trembling hand for the latch. *Please, please, let me be wrong.*

Terrified, he pushed open the door.

He was wrong, all right. But not in a better way. His head spun even more as he saw a scene that slammed him back into battle-field memories. For a full minute, he couldn't move as he took in the slaughtered remains of his sister, her nurse, and his nephew. Someone had torn them apart and tried to make it appear as if an animal had done it. But he'd been a soldier long enough to know human brutality when he saw it. Animals wouldn't have slunk off and left this behind.

Tears scalded his cheeks as he remained frozen in the doorway. Who would have done such a thing? But more than that, how could this have happened with him and Acheron just rooms away?

And where were her guards?

Why hadn't his stupid, bastard brother been here to fight for the sister who'd loved him above all things? Even though she hated him, Styxx would given his life to defend her and the baby. How could Acheron not have heard them? His room was right here. Surely, she'd screamed and cried for help.

Guilt racked him that he hadn't heard her. *How could I have slept through* this? He never slept through a night. Ever. Why had he not been prowling the hallways last night as had been his custom since childhood?

Damn you, gods . . . damn you!

"Styxx?"

He didn't react to his father's voice at all. He was completely catatonic from the emotions that assailed him. By images of battle and soldiers laid out in broken pieces like this.

But they hadn't been his defenseless, frail sister and her infant son.

His father screamed in agony as he saw them, and ran past Styxx to gather her remains into his arms and rock her as if she were a baby. "What did you do! How could you!"

Styxx stumbled back at the accusation. He gasped for breath. "You think I could do this?"

"You're a soldier. She stabbed you."

So?

"But I didn't retaliate on my own sister. Dear gods, is this really what you think of me?"

His father didn't answer as he wailed and rocked her. His screams were loud enough to rouse the dead. And still his brother didn't come.

Baffled, Styxx went to find him.

He threw open the doors to Acheron's room to see his brother flinching in bed as if he'd just awakened. "Not so loud," he whispered.

Un-fucking-believable. Ryssa was slaughtered just a few feet away while Acheron had laid up drunk and hadn't protected her. Fury and his own guilt over the fact he'd been high, too, ravaged his heart. He'd only been out of it because she'd stabbed him and tried to kill him.

But Acheron . . .

He was the one she loved. The one she trusted. Why hadn't he been with her, soothing her as she condemned Styxx? Why had Acheron left her alone last night?

Yet the worse sting was the fact that she'd died hating him and now he would never be able to explain the matter to her. Never have a chance to make amends.

Wanting blood for the injustice of it all, Styxx grabbed his brother by the throat. He shoved Acheron back on the bed to straddle him. "Are you drunk?"

626

Acheron shook his head. But it was painfully obvious Acheron was still under the effects of something. He reeked of it.

Blind with grief, guilt, and fury, Styxx backhanded him. He pulled the chest of herbs from the table next to the bed and flung them into Acheron's face. "You worthless whore. You lie in here on your drugs and drunk while my sister was murdered!"

Styxx punched him again and again. Yet it wasn't really Acheron he was beating. It was himself and he knew it. His allegations toward his brother were the same ones he had in his head for himself.

How could I have done to this to her?

Because I'm a worthless whore, too . . .

Acheron shoved him back. "What did you say?"

Styxx glared at him. "Ryssa's dead, you bastard!"

Completely naked, Acheron shot from his bed and staggered down the hallway to Ryssa's rooms.

His heart splintered and his emotions ragged, Styxx followed him.

Just before the bed, Acheron fell to his knees as he cried out in agony. "I heard them," he whispered.

His side bleeding, Styxx winced as more rage clouded his vision. *Why didn't you do something? Why, Acheron?*

Then he heard Acheron's thoughts in his head. *Damn you, Artemis! I have the powers of a god and couldn't save the two people I loved most. Because of you, bitch!*

And I heard them. I heard Ryssa crying out for help. Apollodorus screaming for me to come to him . . .

Those words exploded in Styxx's heart and mind. Acheron had heard them and done nothing.

Nothing!

They had begged him for help . . . How could he?

Unable to stand it, Styxx kicked him in the ribs, knocking him to his side. Ignoring the pain it caused him, he stomped Acheron in the stomach. But it wasn't enough. It didn't even begin to assuage the agony inside him. Growling, he straddled Acheron and slammed his head against the stone floor over and over again until his own vision was blurred from it. "Why wasn't it you, you worthless maggot!"

Then they both would have been dead and Ryssa alive.

Roaring, Acheron shoved Styxx away from him. Styxx lay in a heap as the stitches were torn open and he bled anew.

Suddenly, a bright light exploded in the room. Styxx looked away as Acheron lifted his arm to shield his eyes.

Apollo appeared before them. Total silence descended as the god looked slowly around the room, taking in every single bloody detail. Even his father had stopped crying in expectation of the god's reaction.

The Greek god didn't speak as he saw Ryssa lying dead in her father's arms, and his son's lifeless body still in the arms of his savaged nurse.

"Who did this?" Apollo demanded through clenched teeth.

Tears stinging his eyes, Styxx pointed to Acheron as his brother's thoughts rang out in his head. "He *let* them die."

Apollo spun on his brother and hit him with his fist so hard that it lifted Acheron from the ground and slammed him into the wall ten feet above the floor. Then he was thrown to the ground.

Styxx hit the deck as physical agony overrode his mental anguish. It hurt so badly, he couldn't breathe. More blood gushed from his wound.

Apollo grabbed Acheron by the hair and wrenched his head. His brother tried to fight the god, but Styxx knew from experience it was futile unless you were extremely well-trained. Apollo was so much stronger there was nothing they could do except bleed.

Even so, he wanted to help Acheron fight against the Olympian who had never loved their sister, but Styxx couldn't move. It felt as if every bone in his body was broken.

The god backhanded his brother. Blood and pain exploded as both their noses were broken and their lips split. The god set on Acheron with the same ruthless fury he'd used the first time he'd attacked Styxx after battle. There was no way to defend against Apollo's onslaught. Acheron was just as helpless as Styxx had been.

"Artemis!" Acheron shouted.

"Don't you dare say my sister's name, you filthy whore!" Apollo grabbed a dagger from his waist and snatched at Acheron's tongue. He sliced it off.

Styxx choked on blood as he lost his own. Tears streamed from his eyes as unimaginable pain throbbed. *We're going to die.*

Apollo wasn't about to let them live. And he knew it wasn't because the god had loved Ryssa. It was because he viewed this as a personal slap to him.

Just like their father.

Styxx panicked as he realized he would never see Bethany again. Never breathe in the precious scent of her body. Or be there when his son was born.

I won't get to say good-bye.

Acheron tried to crawl away from Apollo. But Apollo grabbed him by the throat in a grip so searing it burned the god's handprint into his skin.

Styxx arched his back as he felt it on his own flesh.

"*Akri*! No!" Suddenly a demon appeared and dove for Apollo. With dark wings and swirling skin, she knocked the god back from Acheron and put herself between them.

"Out of my way, demon," Apollo demanded.

Her response was to launch herself at the god. The two of them tangled in a flurry of light and feathers as they pounded each other.

Styxx fought against unconsciousness. He didn't want to die. Not like this. And not now when Bethany needed him most.

She would be devastated. He didn't want to leave her with the legacy of birthing a child while knowing he would never see his son. Most of all, he didn't want to leave them unprotected in such a brutal world that would never take mercy on either of them.

Please don't let me die . . .

Not for him, but for them. He had to live.

Styxx tried to rise so that he could join the fight while Acheron crawled to where the god's knife had fallen.

Apollo blasted Styxx back.

Acheron seized the knife and spun on the combatants. The moment he touched it, the blade of the knife began to glow. His brother raced toward them.

Styxx pushed himself to his feet just as Acheron reached Apollo. The god knocked the demon back, into Acheron, impaling her on the knife in Acheron's hands. Eyes wide, the demon stared down at the knife then staggered away with a small cry of pain.

Acheron grabbed her against him as she struggled to breathe.

She lifted a bloodied hand to place it to his cheek. "Apollymi loves you," she whispered in Charonte—a language Styxx somehow understood even though he'd never heard it before. "Protect your mother, Apostolos. Be strong for her and for me ..." And then the light faded from her eyes as her final breath left her body.

Acheron threw his head back and let out a strangled cry. Grabbing the knife, he spun on Apollo.

Apollo caught his brother's hand and wrested the knife from him. The god seized Acheron again by the throat and threw him down to the ground. Acheron kicked him back and rolled to his side.

Styxx felt another Olympian presence in the room. Expecting Athena, he was stunned to see Artemis cowering in the shadows.

The bitch who'd played with his brother wouldn't even stand up for him now.

Yet he knew if Bethany was here, she'd fight for them both. Him and Acheron. She would never be able to stand back and watch this.

I'm sorry, Acheron. Artemis's thought repulsed him.

In spite of everything that had happened, his brother deserved more than this betrayal. Just as Styxx deserved to see his son born.

Acheron reached a hand out toward the only woman Styxx knew his brother had ever loved.

She shook her head no and stepped back.

Oh, bitch, you better be glad I can't fight. For that alone he'd have cut Artemis's throat if he could get to her.

No one deserved to be annihilated and denied like that. Not by the woman they loved. It was beyond cruel.

And with that action, Styxx knew she'd condemned them both to die. He saw the fight go out of his brother as Acheron rolled over onto his back at the same time Apollo appeared before him. Blithely, Acheron met the god's angry glare and made no further move to protect himself.

Styxx lunged at them, but slipped on blood and fell.

Growling in rage, Apollo sank his dagger deep inside Acheron's heart and sliced him open all the way to his navel.

Unmitigated agony burned through Styxx as the god slowly and methodically gutted his brother on the floor, no more than three feet from Ryssa's body. His own body registered every brutal cut and slice.

As his vision swam, Styxx's last thought was of the day Bethany had told him she was pregnant, and the happiness he'd held in that one perfect moment as he'd laid his cheek to her stomach and felt her gentle touch in his hair.

I'm so sorry, Beth. I should have been the man you deserved me to be.

Tears fell as the light and pain began to fade for the last time.

JUNE 25, 9527 BC

Tartarus

Hades, the Greek god of death and the Underworld, stood in the center of his throne room, staring in disbelief at their newest arrival who lay in one of the darkest cells of Tartarus.

And he hadn't put his "guest" there . . .

Which was one of the more disturbing facts about this whole scenario.

He looked down at the timepiece on his wrist and ground his teeth. It was still three months before his wife would be returned to the Underworld to be with him. But honestly, he had to speak with her.

And, mother-in-law be damned, it couldn't wait.

"Persephone?" he called, hoping her mother wasn't close enough to hear him. The old bitch would have a stroke if she caught them together during her visitation time. Not that it would be a bad thing for her to have one ... if only it would kill her.

An image of his beautiful wife flickered in the darkness by his side. Blond and petite, she was the only light in his darkness. "Butterbean!" she breathed. "I was just missing you something terrible."

He really hated the nicknames she came up with for him. Thank the gods that she only used them when the two of them were alone. Otherwise, he'd be the most mocked of all gods. "Where's your mother?"

"Off looking over some fields, why?"

Good. The last thing he needed was for Demeter to come in and catch them talking.

But that brought him back to his current "dilemma." Anger swept through him as he gestured toward the wall that showed the cells where his prisoners were kept. "I'm getting really sick of cleaning up the messes of the other gods, and right now I'd love to know whose ass I need to bust over this latest fiasco."

She solidified before him. "What's happened?"

Taking her hand, he led her to the cell where they could see inside, but the occupant was completely unable to see them.

At least that was the normal case. In this one, who knew what the occupant could and couldn't see?

He pointed to the blue-fleshed god who lay in a fetal position on the floor. "Any idea who killed that and sent it here?"

Eyes wide, Persephone shook her head. "What is it?"

"Well, I'm not completely sure. I think he's a god ... Atlantean ... maybe. But I've never seen anything like him before. He came in a short time ago and hasn't moved. I'd try to destroy his soul and send him into complete oblivion, but I don't think I have the powers to do it. In fact, I'm pretty sure that just by trying all I'd do is piss him off."

Persephone nodded. "Well, sweetie, my advice to you is if you can't defeat it, befriend it."

"Befriend it how?" As the god of the dead, he wasn't exactly sociable.

Persephone smiled at her husband. Tall and muscular with black hair and eyes, he was gorgeous, even when befuddled and angry. "Wait here." She opened the door to the cell and made her way slowly to the unknown god.

The closer she moved toward him, the more she understood Hades's concern. There was so much power emanating from the god that the air was rife with it. She'd been around the gods her whole life, but this one was different. His marbled blue skin was strangely attractive as it covered a body of perfect proportions. Long black hair fanned out. He had two black horns on top of his head and black lips and claws.

But more frightening than his appearance, he wasn't a god of creation. He was one of ultimate destruction.

Seph, get out of there.

She held her hand up to signal her husband that she was fine. Her legs trembling in trepidation, she reached out to touch the god.

He opened his eyes, which were a yellow-orange encircled by red. They flashed from that to a swirling silver color. And they were filled with raw anguish.

"Am I dead?" he asked, his voice demonic.

"You want to be dead?" She actually dreaded his answer, because if he didn't desire his current location, there could be serious consequences.

"Please tell me I've finally made it. That you're not going to send me back."

Those desperate words tugged at her heart. Reaching out to comfort him, she brushed the black hair back from his blue cheek. "You're dead, but as a god you live."

"I don't understand. I don't want to be any different than anyone else. I just want to be left alone."

Persephone smiled at him. "You can stay here as long as you want." She summoned a pillow for him and tucked it under his head then she covered him with a warm, thick blanket.

"Why are you being so nice to me?"

"Because you seem to need it." She patted him on the arm before she got up. "If you need anything else, I'm Persephone. My husband, Hades, is the one in charge here. You call for us and we'll come."

He gave a subtle nod before he closed his eyes and returned to lying quietly in the darkness.

Mystified by him, she returned to her husband. "He's harmless."

"Harmless, my ass. Seph? Are you insane? Can you not feel the powers he holds?"

"Oh, I feel them. Go near him and you'll have nightmares. But he doesn't desire anything. He's hurt, Hades. Badly. All he wants is to be left alone."

"Yeah, right. Left alone here in my Underworld? Another god whose powers rival mine? How stupid would I have to be? You know there's a reason pantheons don't mix."

"You can ally him," she said, trying to calm him down. "Having a friend is never a bad thing."

"Until the friend takes your hand off."

She shook her head. "Hades . . . "

"I'm a lot older than you, Seph. I've seen what can happen when one god turns on another."

"And I think he poses no harm to either of us." She lifted herself up on her toes to kiss his cheek. "I have to go before my mother finds me missing. You know how she gets when I see you during her time with me."

"Yeah, and a pox on the—"

She playfully pinched his lips together before he could let fly the insult. "I love you both. Now behave and take care of your guest."

Only his wife could get away with treating him like this and being so cavalier with his body. But then she held his heart and he'd give her anything.

He kissed her finger. "I miss you."

"I miss you, too. I'll be home soon."

Soon. Yeah, right . . .

But there was nothing to be done about that.

Hades nodded glumly then cursed as she faded away from him. Damn the bitch, Demeter, for cursing them to live apart half the year. But right now he had bigger problems than his wife's mother.

And at about six foot eight, that god-killer in his cell was definitely a *big* problem.

Apollymi gasped as she felt the weight in her chest lift. Without being told, she knew that she now had the ability to leave Kalosis.

Leave . . .

"No!" she screamed as she realized the significance of that. There was only one way for her to gain her release.

Apostolos is dead.

Those three words chased themselves around in her head until she was nauseated by them.

Unwilling to believe it, she ran to her pond and summoned the universal eye. There in the water, she saw Xiamara, her best friend and protector, lying dead on the palace floor, and Apostolos . . .

"No!"

From the deepest part of her being, a scream of rage and grief swelled, and when she gave vent to it, it shattered the pool and rocked the garden around her.

"I am Apollymia Thanata Deia Fonia!" she screamed until her throat was raw.

She was the ultimate destruction.

And she was going to bring her son home.

May the gods have mercy on each other because she was going

to have none for them. Every single member of her pantheon would pay for this!

Once she finished, *none* would be left standing.

Bethany gasped as an unexpected, unmitigated pain racked her.

"Bet? Is it the baby?"

She shook her head at her mother. "No. It feels more like my heart's been snatched out of my body and crushed. Something's wrong. I can feel it. I have to get to my husband ... He needs me."

Something had happened to Styxx. She knew it with every part of her being. Her heart was destroyed. She could feel it.

Her mother rubbed her back. "Breathe. Just breathe, daughter. There's nothing wrong. You're pregnant. It does strange things with our powers. I once sneezed while I carried you and set fire to your grandfather."

She laughed at the thought. "Did you really?"

"I did." Her mother kissed her brow. "But I also know nothing will calm you down until you visit your mortal and make sure he's all right. So let us go say good-bye to the family and then I'll send you on your way."

"I love you, Matera."

"And I love you, too."

Apollymi staggered on the rocks of the sea where Apostolos's broken body rested. Her precious son had been dumped here as if he were nothing but garbage. After all the bastard Greeks had done to him, they couldn't even provide a decent funeral.

Weak from her unshed tears, she made her way to him. His body was as cold as her heart. His beautiful silver eyes that matched hers were open and glazed, yet for all the horror of his death, his features were serene.

He looked so beautiful and perfectly formed. So tall and strong ...

Choking on a sob, she ran her hand over the long gash in his chest to seal it closed. And then her tears broke. This was the first time she'd held him since the moment she'd cut him from her womb.

Agony ripped her apart as she cradled his head to her breasts and screamed out so loud that the sound was carried on the wind all the way to the halls of Atlantis. "Damn you, Archon! Damn you!"

She buried her face in her son's wet blond hair and cried until her sobs were spent. How could her precious Apostolos be dead? How?

Why?

But she knew those answers and they cut her all the way to her soul. They'd both been betrayed by the very ones who were supposed to love and honor them.

Their worthless family.

Now there would be Kalosis to pay.

Heartbroken, Apollymi clothed her son in the black formesta robes of his godhood. As the son of the Destroyer, his symbol was that of the golden sun that represented her, pierced by the three silver lightning bolts of his power.

Picking him up from the surf, she took them both home to Katateros.

This was the home of the Atlantean gods. She had claimed this area aeons ago and had allowed her family to settle here with her. Similar to Atlantis, it was an island surrounded by islands. The tallest of them belonged to her personally. One of them housed the paradise lands where the souls of their Atlantean people went to rest until reincarnation. Another had been held by the Charonte before her banishment, and one had been intended as the home of her son.

But this one where she currently stood, the second-largest and tallest of the islands, was the main one where the hall that ruled and united all of the islands stood.

Archon's.

Music from the hall drifted out to her. Oblivious to what had come to pass, they were having a party.

A party!

She could feel the presence of every Atlantean god inside. *All of them.*

And her precious son was dead.

Holding him close, she ascended the stairs and slung the doors wide with her powers. The white marble foyer was circular with statues of the gods taking up station every four feet against the pristine walls.

She walked through the center of the foyer where her emblem of the sun had been etched into the floor. And as she crossed over it, she changed it to that of Apostolos's.

The colors, now red and black, represented her grief and his spilled blood.

Without hesitating, she walked straight for the set of gold doors that led to Archon's throne room. To the room where the gods made merry while her son lay dead from their treachery.

She opened those doors with the full force of her fury. A resounding crash resonated as the heavy doors snapped against the marble walls.

The music stopped instantly.

Every god in the hall turned to look at her and one by one, their faces blanched white. As well they should.

Without a word to her betrayers, Apollymi cradled her son in her arms and walked with a calmness she didn't feel toward the dais where her throne was set beside her husband's. Archon stood up at her approach and moved to the side as if to speak to her.

But it was too late for that. There were no words that could save any of them from her wrath. Not after every degradation and abuse her son had suffered in his human lifetime.

Apollymi ignored Archon as she placed Apostolos in Archon's throne where he belonged. Her hands shaking, she sat him up and carefully placed each of his arms on the railings. She lifted his head and brushed the blond hair back from his bluish face until he looked as if he would blink and move at any moment.

Only he would never blink again.

And it was all their fault.

Her heart beat with fury as her powers mounted. A feral wind exploded through the hall, sweeping her hair up and out as her eyes glowed red. She turned on the gods then and leveled a malevolent glare at each one in turn as they held a united breath in expectation of her wrath.

One that was going to be fierce indeed.

She didn't pause until she came to Archon. Only then did she speak in a voice that was deceptively calm. "Your bastard daughters deprived my son of his life. Those little whores damned him. And *you*," she snarled the word, "dared to protect them instead of my son."

"Apollymi—"

"Don't you ever speak my name again." She sealed his mouth shut with her powers. "You had every right to be afraid. But your bastard bitches were wrong. It won't be my son who destroys this pantheon. It is I. Apollymia Katastrafia Megola. Pantokrataria. Thanatia Atlantia deia oly!" *Apollymi the Great Destroyer. All powerful. Death to the gods of Atlantis.*

It was then they scrambled for the doors or tried to teleport out, but Apollymi would have none of it. Drawing from the darkest part of her soul, she sealed the hall closed. No one was going to leave here until she was appeased.

Archon fell to his knees, trying to plead for her mercy. But there was nothing left inside of her except a hatred so potent and bitter that she could actually taste it. She kicked him back and blasted him until he was nothing more than a statue remnant of a god.

Basi screamed out as Apollymi turned toward her. "I helped you."

"You didn't do shit, except whine and piss me off." Apollymi blasted her into oblivion.

One by one, she went to the gods she'd once considered family and turned them into stone as her relentless fury demanded appeasement. The only one she hesitated at was her beloved step-grandson, Dikastis—the god of justice. Unlike the others, he didn't cower or beg. He stood with one hand braced on the back of a chair, meeting her gaze as an equal.

But then he understood justice. He understood her wrath had been earned by all of them.

Inclining his head respectfully, he didn't move as she blasted him.

And then there was Epithymia. Her half sister. The goddess of desire. She was the bitch Apollymi had trusted more than the others.

With tears of crystal ice in her eyes, Apollymi confronted her. "How could you?"

Tiny and frail in her ethereal appearance, Epithymia stared up at her from where she cowered on the floor. "I did what you asked. I made sure he was born into a royal family. Why would you destroy me?"

Apollymi wanted to claw out her eyes for what she'd done. "You touched him, you slut! You knew what that would do to him. To be touched by the hand of desire and to have no god powers to countermand it ... You made it so that every human who saw him was driven mad with their lust to have him. How could you be so careless?"

And it was then she saw the truth in her sister's eyes.

"You did it on purpose!"

Epithymia swallowed. "What was I supposed to do? You heard the girls when they spoke. They proclaimed him to be the death of us all."

"And you thought the humans would kill him in their efforts to possess him?"

A tear slid down Epithymia's cheek. "I was only trying to protect all of us."

"He was your nephew," Apollymi spat.

"I know and I'm sorry."

Not as sorry as she was going to be.

Apollymi curled her lip. "So am I. I'm sorry I ever trusted you with the one thing you knew I loved above all others. You ungrateful bitch. I hope your actions haunt you into eternity."

She blasted her sister.

"What have you done?"

Apollymi turned at the sound of Symfora's question. She sent the force of her winds to knock both Symfora and her daughter back into the foyer. She flashed herself outside to stalk them like the predator she was. "What did *you* do? You hunted my son! And you killed him. All of you!"

"We didn't kill him. He still lives."

Apollymi shook her head. "He was slaughtered this morning by the Greek god *you* invited into *my* lands."

Symfora's eyes widened in terror. "I *never* welcomed Apollo here. That was a decision made by you and Archon."

"Shut up!" Apollymi blasted her for speaking a truth that speared her with guilt.

Bethany pulled every bit of power she could from her mother and from her Egyptian blood as she faced the older, primal goddess.

Apollymi hesitated as she realized Bethany was pregnant.

"I did not incarcerate you or hunt your son, Apollymi. You know this. The one time I thought I'd stumbled upon him, I came to you with that information and not the others. I never breathed a word to them against either of you." Tears choked her. "You know it's true. I came here today to leave this pantheon forever so that I could have my own baby in peace. Please, do not do to me what I did not do to you."

Apollymi hesitated. No matter how much she wanted Bet'anya's blood, she couldn't kill another innocent baby. Not when she understood how much it hurt to lose one. "Who among the gods is the father?"

"The father's mortal. Human."

Human. There was something Apollymi would have never suspected from a goddess she knew hated humans even more than Apollymi did. "His name?"

"Styxx of Didymos."

Uncontrolled fury consumed her. Of all the mortals, *that* was

641

not the name to give her. Not after she'd seen through her son's own eyes the life he'd lived and what had been done to him because of Styxx.

Bethany held her breath as she saw Apollymi's eyes turn from silver to red. "Please, Apollymi . . . don't hurt me. My baby's innocent."

"So. Was. Mine!" The goddess lunged at her then and ripped Bethany's son out of her.

Bethany staggered back as unmitigated pain tore through her. Gasping, she stared at her unmoving son in Apollymi's cruel hand. The very image of his father, he was so tiny and defenseless . . .

And far too young to survive on his own.

Blinded by tears, she reached to touch him. Just once.

The older goddess blasted her back then everything went completely dark.

Styxx stood on the human side of the River Acheron in the Underworld, watching as Charon took Ryssa and Apollodorus across to their final resting place in the Elysian Fields. Unable to speak as shades, he'd tried his best to get her attention. But she'd refused him even in death.

She wouldn't even look at him.

Alone now, he wandered along the banks, hoping that his father would soon place an obolos coin in the mouth of his corpse so that he could pay to cross, too. Otherwise, he'd be damned to wander the banks here as a dismal shade, trapped between this world and the human one.

And as long as he was on this side, he wouldn't be able to drink from the Lethe and forget the pain of having lost Bethany and his son. He wouldn't be able to take his place with Galen and all the others who'd fought under his banner and died for Didymos.

He glanced back as Charon's skiff holding Ryssa and Apollodorus vanished into the mists. His father had given them coins. Was it possible that his father had intentionally withheld his as a final punishment?

Surely not even his father would be so cold.

Who are you kidding? Of course he would. It'd been Styxx's fault that his sister and nephew had died. Like Acheron, he'd been too drunk and high to help them.

This is the best I deserve. But what hurt most was the knowledge that Bethany would never join him here. She would go to Anubis when she died. Most likely his son would, too.

So here he would stay, alone, unable to forget them, with the knowledge that even in the end, his father hadn't cared enough to tend his corpse.

Styxx was so cold his hands shook, but there was no way to warm himself. So he sat down to wait and to hope. But as more time passed and more and more people were ferried across, he had no choice except to accept the fact that he would never cross over.

And he would never forget.

JUNE 25, 9527 BC

Mount Olympus

Thin and small in stature with dark hair and eyes, Hermes flew through the hall of the gods until he stood before his father, Zeus. Hermes wasn't sure what was going on here, but most of the gods were gathered and lounging about as if the world was not about to end.

They ignored Hermes until he spoke. "You know the saying, don't kill the messenger? Hold that thought, really, really close to your hearts."

Zeus scowled at him as he stood up from the chair where he'd been playing chess with Poseidon. Dressed in a flowing white stola and chlamys, Zeus had short blond hair and vividly blue eyes. "What's going on?"

Hermes gestured toward the wall of windows that looked down onto the human realm. "Have any of you taken a look out at Greece in the last, say, hour or so?"

Sitting at a banquet table with Aphrodite, Athena, and Artemis, Apollo rolled his eyes and waved his hand dismissively at Hermes's panic. "What? Are they reacting to the fact I cursed the Apollites for murdering my mistress and son? It's none of *their* business."

Hermes shook his head in a gesture of sarcastic denial. "I don't think that bothers them nearly as much as the fact that the island of Atlantis is now gone and the Atlantean goddess Apollymi is cutting a swathe through our country, laying waste to everyone and everything that she comes into contact with."

The messenger god turned a smug look to Apollo. "And in case you're curious, she's headed straight for us, screaming your name. I could be really wrong here, but I'm guessing the goddess of destruction is extremely pissed . . . at *you*."

Apollo gaped at that disclosure. Why should Apollymi be gunning for him?

Zeus turned on Apollo. "What have you done?"

Sputtering, Apollo blanched. "I cursed my people, not hers. I didn't do anything to the Atlanteans, Papa. Unless their blood was mixed with my Apollites, they were unharmed by my curse. This is not *my* fault."

Suddenly, he had a bad feeling as he faced his twin sister who sat across from him.

Artemis covered her mouth as she realized what pantheon Acheron must have belonged to. While she'd known he'd received god powers on his twenty-first birthday, she'd had no idea where they'd come from.

Terrified of what she and Apollo had unknowingly set into motion, she left the hall while the gods prepared for war, and went to her temple so that she could think through this without their angry shouts in her ears.

"What can I do?" She had absolutely no idea.

Just as Artemis was about to summon her koris to her, the three

Fates appeared in her room. As triplets in the height of youthful beauty, their faces were perfect duplicates of each other. But that was the only thing they shared. The eldest, Atropos, had red hair, while Clotho was blond and the youngest, Lachesis, had dark hair. Daughters of the goddess of justice, no one was sure who their father was, but many suspected Zeus.

Not that their father mattered. The one thing every god on Olympus knew was that these three girls were the most powerful of their entire pantheon. Even Zeus didn't try to circumvent them.

Since the moment of their arrival a decade ago when they'd moved in with their mother, everyone had given them a wide berth. When the three of them held hands and made a statement, it became the law of the universe and no one was immune to it.

No one.

Artemis couldn't imagine why they'd be here in her temple. They certainly weren't friends or even friendly. "If you don't mind, I'm a little busy right now."

Lachesis grabbed her arm. "Artemis, you must listen to us. We've done something terrible."

That was why the gods lived in fear of them. They were always doing something terrible to someone. "Whatever it is, it'll wait."

"No," Atropos said grimly, "it won't. Apollymi is coming here to kill *us*. We're the ones she's after."

Stunned by that proclamation, Artemis scowled at them. "What?"

Atropos stepped forward. "You must never breathe a word to anyone what we're about to tell you. Do you understand? Our mother made us swear to keep it a secret."

"Keep what secret?"

"Swear to us, Artemis," Clotho demanded.

"I swear. Now tell me what's going on." And most importantly, why it involved *her*.

Atropos swallowed before she spoke in a hushed whisper as if terrified someone outside of the temple might overhear her. "Our father is Archon—the king of the Atlantean gods. He had an affair with our mother, Themis, and we were born of it. As soon as we were born, our mother sent us to Atlantis to live and our father took us in. Apollymi is our stepmother and we unknowingly cursed our half brother when we learned of his coming birth."

"It was an accident," Clotho blurted out. "We didn't mean to curse him."

Lachesis nodded. "We were just children and didn't understand our powers yet. We never meant to hurt our brother. We didn't, we swear!"

Artemis went cold inside. "Acheron? Acheron is your brother?"

Clotho nodded. "Apollymi barely tolerated us while we lived with them. We were a reminder of our father's infidelity and she hated us for it."

That didn't make sense, any more than their fear did. Artemis tried to sort through what they were telling her. "But everyone knows that Archon has never been unfaithful to his wife."

Lachesis snorted. "That's a lie the Atlantean gods keep so that Apollymi won't harm them. You don't understand just how powerful she is. She can kill us without even blinking. All the gods fear her power. Even Archon, and he's as faithless as most men, and so here we are."

"She wants us dead," Clotho interjected.

Still, Artemis was trying to make sense of it all. However, she was missing some vital pieces. "How exactly did you curse Acheron?"

"We were so stupid," Atropos said. "When Apollymi began to show her pregnancy, we spoke out of turn and gave Apostolos the power of final fate. We said he'd be the death of us all, and it seems today we are about to see our demise met."

Artemis was even more confused. "But he's not the one threatening us. It's his mother."

Clotho nodded. "And she will kill all of us for our part in his curse. Including *you*."

Artemis gaped at them. "Why? I did nothing!"

Atropos scoffed as the young women encircled her. "We know

646

what you've done, Artemis. We see everything. You hurt Acheron even more than we did. You turned your back on him while Apollo gutted him on the floor and Apollymi *knows* it. She saw it with her own eyes."

Fear tore through her. If what they said was correct, there would be no mercy from Apollymi. Truthfully, she didn't deserve any, but on the other hand, Artemis really didn't want to die, and definitely not by the means Apollymi would use on her. "What can we do? How do we defeat her?"

Atropos sighed heavily. "*We* can't. She's all-powerful. The only one who could check her powers is her son."

Who was dead.

Great. They were screwed. Couldn't someone have told her this *before* she'd left Acheron to Apollo? This information was just a little late in coming, and would have been much more beneficial earlier in the day.

"We're dead," Artemis breathed as images of herself being gutted by Acheron's mother went through her head. Apollymi was going to make what Apollo did to Acheron seem kind.

"No." Clotho shook her arm to get her full attention. "*You* can bring him back from the dead."

Artemis scowled at the woman. "Are you insane? I can't bring him back. I don't have those powers. Only Hades does, and since Acheron's not Greek, that won't help us at all."

Lachesis grabbed her other arm. "Yes, *you* can, Artemis. You're the only one who has the power."

"No, I don't."

Atropos growled at her. "You drank of Acheron's blood. You absorbed his powers when you did that."

Clotho nodded. "He can resurrect the dead, which means you can, too."

Artemis scowled at them. "Are you sure?"

They nodded in unison.

Even so, Artemis was uncertain. Granted, she'd tasted Acheron's powers when she drank from him, but that particular one was reserved for only a very select group of gods, and if they failed to bring him back . . .

It would only get worse from her having tried.

Atropos pushed her sisters aside. "The Atlantean gods used their powers to bind Apollymi with one condition. So long as Apostolos is alive in the human realm, she's locked in Kalosis."

"That's our loophole," Lachesis said. "We bring him back to the mortal realm, and she's interred again. Forever."

"We'll be safe," Clotho added. "*All* of us."

"You will be the savior of the pantheon," they said in unison, holding hands.

Did she really have a choice? Drawing in a deep breath for courage, Artemis nodded. "What do I have to do?"

"You will have to get him to drink your blood," Atropos said, as if it would be the easiest thing in the world to accomplish.

"And just how do I do that? In case you didn't notice, I let him die. I don't really think he's going to be happy to see me."

"With our help, you can do it."

Alone, Acheron lay on a cold stone floor in calm serenity, finally numb to everything from his past and present. He was at peace in a way he'd never been before. The walls of his cave shielded him from the voices of others. Not even the gods were in his head now.

For the first time in his life, he had total silence. And it was wonderful. There was no aching in his body, no grief. Nothing. And he loved this feeling of blissful tranquility.

"Acheron?"

He tensed at Artemis's voice. Of course the bitch was going to disturb his haven. She could never leave him in peace.

Damn her.

He tried to tell her to go away, but nothing other than a hoarse croak left his lips. Coughing, he tried to clear his throat to speak.

Still no words would come. What was going on? What had taken his voice?

Artemis gave him a tender, concerned look. "We need to talk."

He shoved her back, but she refused to go.

"Please," she begged with a look that would have weakened his resolve only a few days ago. But that concern for her was now long gone. He would never forgive her for turning her back on him and letting her brother gut him on the floor. "Just a few words and I'll leave you. Forever if you wish."

How could they talk when he couldn't speak?

She held a cup out to him. "Drink this and I'll be able to talk to you."

Furious with her, he grabbed the cup and downed the contents without tasting them. "Go to Tartarus and rot," he snarled at her, grateful that this time she could hear the venom in his voice.

And then something happened. Pain and fire ripped through his body as if something was setting his internal organs aflame. Panting, he looked up at Artemis. "What have you done to me now?"

There was no mercy or remorse in her gaze. "What I had to."

One moment he was in the quiet darkness of Hades's domain and in the next, he was standing on the banks of Didymos, not far from the palace.

Or rather what was left of it.

Confused, he looked around, trying to make sense of what had happened to him, and to the land. Before he could figure it out a searing pain tore through him with such ferocity that it drove him to his knees in the surf.

Acheron cried out, wanting it to stop.

Suddenly, Artemis was there before him. Gathering him into her arms, she held him close as the waves crashed against them. "I had to bring you back."

He shoved her away from him as he looked around at the smoldering remains of Didymos. "What have you done?"

"I didn't do this. Your mother did. She's destroyed everything and everyone who ever went near you. And she was coming to kill us on Olympus. It's why I had to bring you back. She would have killed us all had I not."

He glared so hard at her, he was sure his eyes were red. "You think I give a fuck about that?" He started away from her, only to be frozen in place by the pain tearing at his stomach. The agony of it caused him to double over as he struggled to breathe.

Artemis approached him slowly. She stood above him, looking down. "I'm the one in control here, Acheron. I've bound you to me with my blood. I own you."

Those three words set fire to his wrath. He felt the familiar heat ripple over him as his human appearance gave way to that of his god form. Rising against the pain, he held his hand out and brought Artemis into his grasp. "You seriously underestimate my powers, bitch."

She clutched at his hand, trying to loosen his feral grip. "Kill me and you'll become the worst sort of monster imaginable. You need my blood to maintain any sort of sanity. Without it, you will become a mindless killer, seeking only to destroy any and everyone you come into contact with . . . just like your mother."

Acheron roared with frustration. The bitch had thought of everything. Even as a god, he was still a slave. "I hate you."

"I know."

He shoved her away from him and turned his back on her.

"Acheron, did you not hear what I said? You will have to feed from me."

He ignored her as he made the long trek from the beach to the hill where the royal palace had once stood. There was nothing left but smoldering ashes and busted stones. There were hundreds and hundreds of bodies of servants, citizens, and merchants everywhere. Innocent victims of his mother's wrath.

Tears filled his eyes as he ran through the debris, seeking a sign of Ryssa or Apollodorus.

Aching and broken, he used his powers to move stone and marble until he uncovered the room that had been hers.

There in the wreckage he found three of the diaries she'd so meticulously kept. They were a little scarred by fire, but miraculously, they'd somehow survived intact. He opened the first one and stared at her childish writing as she described the very day he'd been born and the joy she'd felt at having twin brothers. Wiping his tears, he closed it and held it to his heart as he heard her voice in her words.

Styxx had been right. His precious sister was gone and it was all his fault. Devastated from the truth of it, he saw one of the silver hair combs he'd given her on her last birthday, just days ago.

He crawled over to it and placed it against his lips. "I'm so sorry, Ryssa. I'm so sorry."

And in that moment it hit him how pathetic it was that all he had to show for a life so vibrant was such minuscule things. Three diaries and a broken hair comb. Leaning his head back, he sobbed from the agony of her loss.

"Apostolos . . . please don't cry."

He felt his mother's presence. "What have you done, Matera?"

"I wanted them to pay for hurting you."

Did it even matter? What they'd done to him was nothing compared to what had been done this day because of his mother's actions. "And now Artemis owns me."

His mother's scream mirrored his own. "How?"

"To stop you, she's bound me to her with her blood."

He could feel his anger mirrored through his mother's voice. "Come to me, Apostolos. Free me and I will destroy that bitch and those bastards who cursed you."

Acheron shook his head. He should do it. He should. They all deserved nothing better, and yet he couldn't bring himself to destroy the world.

To kill innocent people . . .

He looked around at the bodies and winced. No. In spite of it all, he couldn't do this to the world.

His mother appeared before him as a translucent shade. Acheron sucked his breath in sharply as he saw her for the very first time. She was the most beautiful woman he'd ever seen. Hair as white as new-fallen snow fell from a crown that shimmered with diamonds. Her pale, silver eyes swirled just as his did. Her black dress flowed over her body as she held one hand out to him.

He tried to touch her, but his hand passed through hers.

"You are my son, Apostolos. The only thing in my life that I've ever truly loved. I would give my life for yours. Come to me, child. I want to hold you."

He treasured every word she spoke. "I can't, Matera. Not if that means sacrificing the world. I refuse to be so selfish."

"Why would you protect a world that turned its back on you and abused you?"

"Because I know what it's like to be punished for things not my fault. I know what it's like to have things forced on me that were wrong and against my will. Why would I ever serve that to someone else?"

"Because it would be justice!"

He glanced around at the scattered bodies of those who hadn't deserved to die like this and rot out in the open. "No. It would only be cruel. Justice to the humans has been more than served."

Her eyes flashed angrily. "What of Apollo and Artemis?"

He ground his teeth at the mere mention of their names. "They hold the power of the sun and the moon. I can't destroy them."

"*I* can."

And thus she'd destroy the entire earth and all who lived here. It was why he couldn't free her. "I'm not worth the end of the world, Matera."

Her eyes burned him with her sincerity. "To me you are."

In that moment, he would have sold his soul to be able to hold her. "I love you, Mama."

"Nowhere near as much as I love you, *m'gios.*"

M'gios. My son. He'd waited his entire life for someone to claim him. But as much as he wanted his mother, he wouldn't end the world for it.

Suddenly a cold wind whipped around him, tearing at his clothes and hair, yet not hurting him. The world around him faded as he found himself on unfamiliar ground. His mother's image flickered by his side. "This is Katateros. Your birthright."

He frowned at the pile of rubble. "It's in ruins."

She cast a sheepish look toward him. "I was a little upset when I came here."

A little?

"Close your eyes, Apostolos."

Trusting her completely, he did.

"Breathe in."

He took a deep breath and then he felt his mother inside him. Her powers merged with his and in the blink of an eye, the ruins reunited to form a beautiful palace of gold and black marble. His mother's presence pulled out of him.

"Welcome home, *palatimos*." *Precious one*.

The doors opened and as Acheron passed through them, his clothing changed. His hair grew long and black and a flowing robe fanned out behind him as he walked over the white marble floor. He paused at the sign of the sun that was pierced by three bolts of lightning.

His mother slowed as she noted him studying it. "The sun is my symbol and it represents the day. The silver of the lightning bolts is for the night. The bolt to the left is for me and the past, and the one on the right is your father and the future. Yours is the bolt in the middle that unites and binds the three of us together and stands for the present. That is the sign of the Talimosin and represents your dominion of the past, the present, and the future."

He frowned at the Atlantean word. "The Harbinger?"

She nodded. "You, Apostolos. You are the Talimosin. The final Fate of all. Your words are law and your wrath absolute. Be careful as you speak, for whatever you will, even in carelessness, will determine the fate of the person you're speaking to. It's a burden I would never have wished upon you. And it's one I hate those bitches for. But I can't undo what they've given you. No one can."

"What exactly are my powers?"

"I don't know. I took them from you and never looked at them for fear of exposing you to the others. I only know what Archon's daughters cursed you to. But you will learn them all in time. I only wish you'd come to me so that I could help you until you grow stronger."

"Matera—"

"I know." She held her hand up. "I respect you for being the man you are and I'm proud of you. However, should you get your fill of this world and change your mind, you know where I am."

He smiled at her.

"In the meantime, this is all yours now."

Acheron looked around at the statues and somehow he knew who each and every one of them were. As he approached the set of gold doors, he saw the image of his mother to the left and Archon to the right.

The doors opened and there he saw the remains of the gods where his mother had attacked them. They were frozen in the horror of their last moments.

His mother didn't show even the tiniest bit of remorse for what she'd done to her family. "If the sight of them bothers you, there is a room below the throne room where you can store them. While I'm locked in Kalosis, my powers won't let me put them there, but you shouldn't have that problem."

Closing his eyes, he wished the statues gone. In an instant, they were. He had no desire to see the images of people who'd wanted him dead.

His mother smiled approvingly. "You should have the ability to come and go from the human realm to this one at will. You'll find that Katateros is a large place with areas unexplored. The mountaintops are windy . . . and it's on the northernmost point that you can hear the sound of your grandmother, the North Wind. Zenobi will whisper to you and succor you in my absence. Any time you need to be comforted, go there and let her hold you."

"Thank you, Matera."

"I will leave now and give you time to adjust. If you need me, call and I will appear."

He inclined his head to her as she faded away and left him alone in this unfamiliar place.

It was so strange to be here and it would take some getting used to. Closing his eyes, he could see the gods as they'd been. Hear their voices echoing in the faintest of whispers. And when he opened them, they were all gone and he heard nothing.

As he moved around the room, he realized he wore some kind of leather leggings.

Pants.

How very odd to know the names of everything and everyone without even trying. Whatever information he needed was there instantly.

Crossing the room, he approached the single black and gold throne . . . Archon's. An image of his own dead human body in it appeared in his mind. And in the next, Acheron was sitting in it, looking out on the gleaming, empty room. Though ornate and gilded, it was sterile.

There was no life to the palace. No comfort here.

He stood and as he did so a large staff appeared by his side. Over seven feet tall, it held his emblem in gold and silver on the top. Atlantean words were inscribed down the smooth wood.

By this the Talimosin will be known. He will fight for himself and for others. Be strong.

Be strong. Acheron flinched as the demon Xiamara's words whispered through his mind. He teleported himself to the top of the northernmost mountain. The sun was just beginning to set as the winds whipped his formesta out behind him. He gripped his staff tight, looking back over his shoulder to see where the palace stood below.

Then he heard it.

Apostolos . . . feel my strength. It will be yours when you need it.

He smiled sinisterly as he felt his grandmother's caress against his skin. Closing his eyes, he took comfort and strength.

And when he opened his eyes, he could tell they glowed red now. His vision saw so much more than it had as a human. He felt the pulse of the universe in his veins. Felt the power of the primal source, and for the first time he realized his place in the cosmos.

I am the god Apostolos. I am death, destruction, and suffering. And I will be the one who brings forth Telikos—the end of the world.

That was if he could ever figure out how to use his powers. Acheron laughed at the truth of it.

Turning, he headed down the mountain and back to the throne room in Archon's palace. No . . . it was his now. Sadness hung deep inside him as he realized that though he had his grandmother and mother with him in spirit, he was still alone in the world.

Completely alone.

He froze as he heard something moving behind his throne. It was a soft scurrying sound . . . like a large rodent. Frowning, he teleported toward it, prepared to kill whatever dared defile his new home.

What he found there stunned him completely.

It was a small demon with marbled red and white skin and long black hair. Small red horns poked through the tangles of her curls as she looked up at him with red eyes that were rimmed in orange.

"Are you my akri?" she asked in a childish lilt.

"I'm no one's akri."

"Oh . . . " She looked about. "But akra sent me here. She said my akri would be waiting. The Simi is confused. I lost my mama and now the Simi needs her akri." She sat down and started crying.

Acheron laid down the staff to pick up the toddler. "Don't cry. It'll be all right. We'll find your mother."

She shook her head. "Akra said the Simi's matera is dead. Them evil Greek people killed the Simi's mama. Now the Simi needs her akri to love her."

Acheron rocked her gently in his arms as his mother's shade appeared before him.

Simi stopped crying. "Akra, he says the Simi's akri isn't here."

His mother smiled at them. "He is your akri, Simi."

Acheron scowled at her declaration. "What?"

"Her mother was your protector, Xiamara. Like you, Simi is all

656

alone in the world with no one to care for her. She needs you, Apostolos."

He looked down at those large eyes that swallowed the demon's small round face. Blinking, she stared up at him with the same trust and innocence of Apollodorus. And he was lost to that loving gaze that didn't judge or condemn him.

"Bond with him, Simi, protect my son as your mother protected me."

The thought of tying someone to him terrified Acheron. He didn't want anyone enslaved to him. "I don't want a demon."

"Would you cast her out alone in the world?"

"No."

"Then she's yours."

Before he could protest again, his mother faded away.

Simi snuggled against him and laid her head against his shoulder. "I miss my mama, akri."

Guilt over what had happened with his mother's demon he'd accidentally killed instead of Apollo, slammed into him at her whispered words as he held her close to him. But for him, her mother would still be alive to love her. "Where's your father, Simi?"

"He died before the Simi was born."

"Then I will be your father."

"Really?" she asked hopefully.

He nodded, smiling at her. "And I swear to you that you'll never want for anything."

Her innocent smile warmed his heart. "Then the Simi has the best akri-papa in the world." She hugged him tightly. "Simi loves her akri." As soon as the words were spoken, she faded like his mother had done. But as she faded, his skin just above his heart burned.

Hissing, Acheron jerked up his tunic to find a small colorful dragon emblazoned on his skin. He touched it gingerly, and heard Simi's laughter in his head. The tattoo inched its way up, toward his neck. Her motion on his skin tickled until she settled over his collarbone.

"Simi is a part of you now, Apostolos. While on your body, she won't be able to hear you unless you call for her. But she will be able to monitor your vital signs. Should she sense you're in danger, she will appear to you in demon form to protect you."

"But she's only a baby."

"Even as a baby, she's deadly. Never mistake that. The Charonte are by their very nature killers. She will be hungry and you'll have to feed her often. If you fail to, she'll eat whatever is near her ... even you. Make sure she doesn't get overly hungry. And the last thing you should know is that her kind age very slowly. Roughly one year of a human's development equals a thousand years of theirs."

That did not sound good. "What are you saying?"

"The Simi you have is over three thousand years old."

Acheron gaped at the information. "Shouldn't she be with another demon who can train her?"

"She's the last of her kind. You are all she has in this world, *m'gios*. Take care of her. As you have said, you are her father now. You'll be the one to teach her everything she knows."

Acheron placed his hand over the tattoo on his shoulder. He was a father ...

But then how could he train and protect a demon daughter when he didn't even know how to use his own powers?

JUNE 26, 9527 BC

Styxx hissed as he was jerked off the banks of the River Acheron and slammed back into his body in Didymos. For a full minute, he couldn't move. But once his eyes focused, he realized he was trapped beneath rubble. It felt as if every bone in his body was broken.

After a few more minutes, he was able to crawl out from beneath it and see the devastation that had been done to his homeland.

Just a few inches away from where he'd awakened was his father's body. Frowning, he dug him out and saw the small silver obolos still clutched in his hand.

His father must have been in his room about to give it to him when he'd been killed. Grief choked him. He didn't know why he hadn't seen his father in the Underworld. But it didn't matter.

His father hadn't withheld the coin, after all.

"I'm sorry, Father," he whispered. "I should have been able to do something to stop this." He had no idea what, but still . . .

Burning in utter agony, Styxx took the coin and placed it in his father's mouth so that if he was on the banks of the river, he'd be able to cross and find Ryssa and Apollodorus.

"May Hades grant you both a palace in the Elysian Fields." And as he rocked his father, he realized what had happened.

Acheron was alive again.

There was no other explanation. It was the only way he could be returned to life.

I have to bury my father.

And probably Ryssa and Apollodorus, too. He got up to find them and paused as he saw Artemis standing in what was once the hallway.

"What are you doing here?"

"You've done enough harm to Acheron. I will not allow you to hurt him further."

Styxx laughed incredulously. "*I* have harmed *him*? Are you out of your mind? Look around you." He gestured to the smoldering remains of his once great city. "Acheron caused the death of my sister, my father, my—"

"Enough! I refuse to allow you to wander the earth, looking for vengeance against him."

Strangely, Styxx felt no desire for vengeance. There was only one thing he wanted. Only one thing left for him. And honestly, he was all right with that. "Fine, let me go to my wife and neither of you will ever have to worry about seeing me again."

"Your wife?"

"The Princess of Thebes. Bethany."

Artemis's face blanched at the name.

Gods, no . . . anything but that.

Tears choked Styxx to the point he could no longer breathe. "She's in Egypt," he said firmly.

Artemis slowly shook her head. "Apollymi killed her, too."

A full wave of tears blinded him at the news. "Apollymi!"

She nodded.

Throwing his head back, he roared in agony. His vision swam with the ferocity of his loss. *No, no, no!* "She's not dead. Not my Beth. Not her. You're lying to me!"

"I would never lie about that. I'm sorry, Styxx."

But she wasn't. She didn't care. Why should she?

Raking his hands through his hair, Styxx did want blood, after all. He wanted to bathe in the blood of every god on Olympus. But none more than Acheron's.

His fury overtaking him, Styxx ran at Artemis, intending to carve out her heart. But before he could reach her, he was snatched away by angry, shredding winds.

Everything went dark.

The next thing he knew, he was slammed against the white sands of a foreign beach. Stunned, Styxx turned around in the sand on his knees.

What the fuck is this?

Artemis appeared before him. "You're on a Vanishing Isle in the Elysian Fields. I can't afford for anyone to know about you or Acheron. You have everything you need here and people will come with food for you from time to time." She dropped the chest from his room in front of him. "That should comfort you."

Then she was gone.

Aghast, Styxx stared at that stupid chest. *That* was supposed to comfort him for the loss of his entire family and country?

For the loss of Bethany and their son?

Styxx bellowed with rage until his throat was raw and could produce no more sounds. He hadn't screamed out like this since they'd tortured him in the Dionysion. And honestly, he'd rather go back to that than to live through this.

How could they take everything from him?

"I should have let the fucking Atlanteans beat you and the rest of the Olympians into the ground!"

He cursed the day he'd ever fought for Greece and her gods. Most of all, he cursed the day he'd been born twin to Acheron Parthenopaeus. That bastard . . .

Styxx stared out onto the horizon as he made a solemn vow. "You better pray, brother, that I never get off this island. If do . . . you will bleed for every tear you've given me. And I will rip out your heart and shove it down your throat for your mother taking my wife and son from me. Damn every single one of you!"

In all his life, he'd only ever wanted one thing.

Bethany.

And now all he wanted was death so that he could be with her in the next lifetime. But there was nothing left for him except eternity in isolated hell.

Eleven Thousand,
Five Hundred
and Thirty-One
Years Later. . .

AD JANUARY 3, 2004

Exhausted and sweating, Styxx sighed as he dug in the wet sand to uncover his lunch. He'd already found two clams. One more and he'd be done for the meal. As he tried to lift the heavy sand, the wooden handle on his handmade shovel broke. He knelt down to finish digging it out with the rock blade then added the clam to the small handmade leather pouch where he'd placed the other two.

He washed the sand off his hands in the surf then headed back to the thatched hut he'd built centuries ago for shelter from the winds and harsh, unforgiving sunlight.

Tossing the shovel pieces by the door so that he could repair it later, he wiped the sweat from his forehead and went in and grabbed his last coconut. He'd need to gather more after he finished eating.

Styxx returned outside to start a fire for his meager meal.

But just as he reached his cooking pit, something bright flashed. With reflexes honed by thousands of years of unexpected and extremely vicious animal attacks, Styxx grabbed his spear and readied it for the fight.

Only it wasn't a fur-covered predator.

This one walked on two legs.

Dionysus. Though he was a bit different from the last time Styxx had seen him, he remembered the bastard well from his brief imprisonment in Apollo's temple on Olympus. The god of wine and excess had cut his long brown hair short and put streaks of blond through it. Dressed in clothes the likes of which Styxx had never seen before, Dionysus wore a well-trimmed goatee.

Styxx scowled at the god's sudden and unexpected appearance. Was he hallucinating? Had something poisoned him while he'd been clamming? He hadn't been bitten in a while, but . . .

It'd been thousands and thousands of years since anyone had come to his island for any reason.

Dionysus spoke, but he couldn't understand him. The god stepped closer.

Suspicious as hell, Styxx backed up and angled the spear for the god's heart.

The Olympian stopped moving and held his hands up. "Sorry. I forgot to use ancient Greek. I'm a little rusty with it. Can you understand me now?"

Ironically, it took Styxx a few heartbeats to remember it, too. He'd long stopped thinking with words. With no one to talk to and no more voices in his head, only pictures had kept him company for countless centuries.

He nodded.

Again the Olympian said something Styxx didn't understand. He took a step.

Styxx pressed the point of the spear against his chest in warning.

Frustrated, Dionysus flung his hands out and sent a blast through him. Styxx dropped the electrified spear as he was lifted off his feet and thrown against the ground so hard it jarred every bone in his body.

His ears rang to the point of pain.

"Now can you comprehend what I'm saying?" the god growled.

"I hear you."

Dionysus closed the distance between them.

"Don't come near me!" Styxx snarled, shooting away from him. He was done with all of them.

Dionysus's eyes turned a dark, sinister red. "I'm trying to help you."

Styxx snorted. "No god has ever helped me. Go fuck yourself."

He arched an arrogant brow at that. "Wow ... that's mighty brave of you. But you know, rather than fuck myself, I could tell Apollo where *you* are. He thinks you're long dead. After all this time, you'd be like a new toy to him again. And I'm sure he'd love that loincloth look on you, especially combined with those incredibly defined muscles. Damn, you were hot before. Now ... " He bit his lip as he raked a lecherous smile over Styxx's body. "You grew up well, boy."

Styxx's blood ran cold at the threat.

"Or," Dionysus continued, "you could hear me out, and put an end to your hell completely. Which would you rather?"

"I'm listening."

Dionysus folded his arms over his chest. "The world has changed a great deal since you were last in it. One of the things that peeves me most is that the Greek pantheon has basically fallen into absolute obscurity. We're such a joke that even Disney makes cartoons about us. We have a few believers left, but by and large, we are forgotten. And I'm a bit nostalgic for the old days when people made sacrifices and fed my powers ... A little over a month from now, the portal between the human world and Kalosis will be thin enough to breach."

Styxx was well aware of a prophecy he'd been hoping would come to pass. It was the only hope he had of ever leaving this repulsive prison. "The Destroyer can be freed from captivity."

If Apollymi was free again, she'd end the world and Styxx with it. Or better yet, he could drive his Atlantean dagger straight into that bitch's black heart for what she'd done to his wife and child. He always knew there'd been a reason he'd hung on to the one he'd taken during his war there. As a human, it'd been his paranoia of Archon or one of the others coming after him that had prompted him to keep it.

Now it was the promise of revenge. An Atlantean dagger was the only weapon he knew that could kill one of their gods.

But he didn't understand why Dionysus was here. For him. "What's that got to do with me?"

"To open the portal, we need the blood of a true Atlantean. Not an Apollite, but one born of Apollymi's people and her blood. And there's only one left on the planet."

"Acheron." It was the only explanation.

Dionysus inclined his head to him. "See why I need you?"

Yeah, no one else could fight or defeat Acheron. Only his twin had that ability.

"I still don't see how any of this helps me."

"What's the one thing you want more than any other, prince?"

"My wife."

Dionysus rolled his eyes. "Okay, what's the second thing you want?"

"My son."

This time the god expelled a long exasperated breath. "Third? And if you name another family member, I will leave you here with Apollo, so help me, Zeus."

Sadly, Styxx had no other family to name and only one other thing he craved. "To die."

"Ah, you *can* be taught. Yah! And yeah, death. You kill Acheron and you die. I get to rule the world of man and everyone's happy." Hands on hips, Dionysus arched a brow. "So what do you say?"

"I say get me the fuck out of here."

Styxx flinched as Dionysus wrenched him from his island to a . . . room of some kind. One that held chairs and tables unlike any he'd ever seen before. There were numerous other items in it he couldn't even begin to identify or name.

"And before you do something stupid and embarrass us all with your backward, barbarian ways . . . " Dionysus placed his hand on Styxx's shoulder.

Pain exploded through his skull as the god planted eleven thousand years of history into his head. It was so foul, his nose bled for everything it was worth.

Dionysus pulled away from him as Styxx pressed his hand to his nostrils. And the gods wondered why he hated them.

Great to be back in the mortal world. Bastards.

"Bathroom?" he asked Dionysus.

"Door behind you."

Styxx went to it and grabbed a handful of toilet paper. As he held it to his nose, he frowned at all the new things around him that he'd never even dreamed of. He closed the lid on the toilet and sat down as his head reeled from sensory overload. Sounds, sights, smells . . .

Those damned voices that screamed in his head.

It was so overwhelming.

While he'd known he'd been isolated for a long time, he'd never have guessed this many centuries had passed.

Eleven thousand years.

It was mind-boggling. But what really, really hurt was the fact that Acheron had known he was alive, and had completely ignored him the entire time.

His brother had walked away from him and never looked back. Not once.

Don't I feel like the complete asshole? Styxx had never fully abandoned his brother. As a boy, he'd risked everything to help him. Meanwhile, Acheron had gone on with his life and with Artemis, and acted as if Styxx was dead and buried.

Out of sight. Out of mind.

Why was he even surprised?

So what if Styxx had put his ass on the line for Acheron when Acheron had been imprisoned in Atlantis and Didymos? *I at least brought you fresh food and wine, brother.* Even when Acheron had chosen a slow starvation suicide, Styxx had given him something to eat.

And unlike him, Acheron wasn't a mortal boy who had to jockey around a father who hated and threatened him. One who would have beaten the shit out of him if he'd learned what Styxx was doing behind his back. Acheron had enough powers that even their old gods had feared his brother's wrath.

He looked down at his scarred hands. Artemis had left him on that island without so much as a single spoon. Everything he'd had over these countless centuries, he'd been forced to make or find.

How could his twin brother leave him to suffer like this?

I hate you, Acheron.

Styxx brushed aside the leopard skin he wore to see the whore mark Acheron had helped brand on him.

Yeah . . .

There was no love lost between them.

He had no reason to be surprised by his brother's total lack of regard where he was concerned. Still, Acheron's neglect and utter absence of humanity for him burned deep in a place that should be used to being kicked by now.

So much for being twins.

But that wasn't true and he knew it. They might share the same features, but Acheron had been shoved into Aara's womb long after Styxx had been conceived. Apollymi had forced her bastard into his life and screwed him over royally in the process.

And maybe this was all part of being a god. A total disregard for what you did to humans. An inability to have even a modicum of compassion for them.

You could have at least come back and killed me. Acheron had that power. Three seconds. Three little heartbeats and Acheron could have put him out of his misery.

Instead, he'd left him to suffer. Eternally. Alone in an isolated hellhole.

Styxx winced as memories tore through him. Endless days of loneliness and self-loathing. Even centuries back, when Artemis had actually sent servants with food for him, they'd been blind, deaf, and mute . . . a precaution of hers to make sure they didn't tell anyone of his solitary existence.

Or more to the point, that she had a boy-toy pet who looked just like him.

He'd had no one. Nothing except bittersweet memories of his wife and the son he'd never met. Memories that hurt as much, if not more, than they comforted.

But what did it matter? He couldn't change the past. It was done and he'd somehow survived it. Damned if he knew how.

Rising, he washed the blood off his face, beard, hands, and chest then returned to the room with Dionysus.

"Better?" the god asked sarcastically.

"Not really. However, the bleeding's stopped." Externally, anyway. Internally, the arterial hemorrhaging never ceased.

"Good gods, he does look like him."

Styxx turned to find a god he couldn't identify approaching them. Nowhere near as tall as they were, he had long black hair pulled back into a ponytail. There was something evil, yet mischievous about him.

"Meet Camulus. Celtic-Gallic war god."

Styxx started to ask what "Celtic-Gallic" meant, but as soon as the question formed, his mind kicked up the answer from the information Dionysus had implanted into his head. They were two races that hadn't existed until long after his country had been destroyed and then rebuilt from the ashes of Apollymi's fury.

Camulus raked him with a snide grin. "He doesn't dress like him though. Or stand like him. Think he can pass?"

Dionysus shrugged. "Dark-Hunters are pretty stupid. They shouldn't be too hard to fool."

Styxx frowned at the unfamiliar term. "Dark-Hunters?"

"Ah, crap. Did I forget to do a full upload?" Dionysus put his hand on Styxx's shoulder again.

In an instant, he saw events unfolding. Apollo had taken credit for the destruction of Atlantis, claiming it as retaliation for what had been done to Ryssa. Since Apollymi wasn't around to contradict him, that was the most retold myth.

Apollo had cursed his Apollite race to feed on nothing except each other's blood. But the worst, they were condemned to die painfully on their twenty-seventh birthday . . . The age Ryssa had been on her death.

Kind of. His father had shaved a year off her age to make her more appealing on the marriage market and had never told Apollo the truth. Stupid bastard deserved that lie.

Then Apollymi, angered over Apollo's mutilation and murder of Acheron, had taken in Apollo's heir, Strykerius whom the god had accidentally cursed along with his people.

Ironically, the sun god had never been all that bright. Why the Greeks had ever designated Apollo as the god of prophecy, Styxx couldn't fathom.

Needless to say, Strykerius bore as much love for his father as Styxx did. But Stryker had yet to kill Apollo. Not for lack of effort on his part. He routinely made attacks on his progenitor and humanity.

Stryker and his army of Daimons were still around because Apollymi had taught them how to circumvent Apollo's curse by stealing human souls and living on those—her retribution on humanity for abusing her son. But from the moment an Apollite pulled a human soul into his or her body, it forever changed them physiologically, and many of them mentally. They were no longer Apollites, but so-called Daimons. Evil spirits who lived solely to feed off mankind's souls.

Then two thousand years after Apollo's curse, Artemis had created the Dark-Hunters to chase and kill the Daimons before the human souls within them died and were lost forever in painful limbo.

At least, that was Artemis's public story. Like her brother, she lied. The real purpose of the Dark-Hunters was to give her leverage against Acheron, and a tool she could use to manipulate and control him.

Styxx laughed bitterly at the irony. *You're still a whore, little brother. Still enslaved.*

Some things never changed.

"Are you caught up?" Dionysus asked.

"Yeah. You want me to run interference with my brother's men and use them against him until the night I finally get to return the favor he once paid me."

Camulus scowled. "What favor?"

Styxx flicked his hand over the scar in the center of his chest. "He drove a dagger through my heart while I slept. Only I'm not the coward Acheron is. I want him to know it's me when I slide the blade in."

Camulus let out a low whistle. "No wonder the Greeks are known best for their tragedies. You bastards wrote the book on dysfunctional families."

Dionysus scoffed. "Really? Do you want me to pull out *your* pantheon history?"

He held his hands up in surrender. "I cede, but don't get used to that. Not in my nature."

Dionysus conjured a set of modern clothes for Styxx and held them out to him. "Don't forget to bathe first."

Fighting the urge to make an obscene gesture, Styxx took the clothes and headed to the shower. He quickly climbed into it and sighed at how incredible it felt. He hadn't bathed in warm water since the day he'd died. Even though his head was way above the showerhead, the hot water still felt good sliding over his skin. And as he showered, he clenched his teeth at all the scars marring him from head to foot. But the two that still stung most were the one across his heart from Acheron and the one on his stomach from Ryssa. He didn't know why they bothered him more than the ones from his mother, yet they did.

And the scar that always brought tears to his eyes was one he'd carved himself into his left forearm with an obsidian knife he'd made.

Βηθανία.

Γαληνός.

Bethany above the scar his father had given him. Galen below it. And Galen not just for his mentor, but for the son who'd never been born to them. His permanent tribute to the people who'd meant everything to him.

To the ones he'd never see again. His scar was all he had left of them.

"I miss you," he breathed. Time had not made their deaths any easier to bear. In some ways, it seemed to make it worse.

Blinking back his tears, he shoved those thoughts out of his mind. There was nothing he could do. They were gone, and with luck, he wouldn't have to endure much longer without them.

He kissed their names then turned off the water and stepped out. The moment he touched the towel, his breath caught. It was so incredibly soft. There had been no cloth on the island. No towels of any kind. And the scent . . .

Like flowers.

What an incredible luxury. He froze as he caught a look at himself in the huge mirror that was a much higher quality than anything they'd ever possessed in his mortal days. His mother and Ryssa would have gone blind staring at themselves in this.

His gaze dropped to the horrendous scars that marked his flesh. He curled his lip in disgust. He was hideous. Had Bethany not been blind, she would have thrown him aside in a heartbeat had she ever seen these.

Sighing, he dressed quickly, shaved then left the room to find the two gods plotting Acheron's death and their rise to power. He should have guilt for participating, but honestly . . .

Screw Acheron. His brother had shown him no mercy, so why should he have any for him?

Styxx frowned as he caught a whiff of . . .

"Is that food?"

Camulus nodded. "I ordered steaks from room service. You want one?"

His jaw went slack as he positively salivated. "Beef?"

"Well yeah, ain't no vegetarians here." Camulus flexed his biceps. "Soy don't give you these."

Styxx ignored him as he pulled the silver cover off the plate and bit his lip. He hadn't seen steak in so long that he'd forgotten what it looked like.

Smelled like.

"Damn, Dion. I think the steak just gave your boy a hard-on."

"I imagine everything will give him a hard-on for a few weeks until he gets used to being in the world again."

"Just make sure you don't give him any chocolate cake. He might die from an orgasm."

Styxx's frown deepened as he sat down to eat. "Chocolate cake?"

Camulus snorted. "We'll order some later. Now be quiet and let the gods talk."

Styxx had to force himself not to throw his knife straight

through Camulus's skull for that. But he didn't want to waste the blade when there was real meat to be eaten. And he hadn't had to kill it first.

It took everything he had to eat civilly, as a human, and not shovel it into his mouth like the animal he'd become. Gods, it was *so* good. Forget the cake . . . nothing could be better than this.

He reached for the wine then paused at the container it was in. It looked so frail and delicate.

Camulus let out a heavy sigh. "This isn't going to work." He gestured at Styxx. "He's staring at the glass like it's some alien invader."

"He's never seen glass like that."

"My point. He'll never pass for Acheron."

Too used to criticism and mockery to react to it, Styxx's frown deepened. "What do I dilute this with?"

Camulus started to respond, but Dionysus cut him off. "You don't." He held his hand up to stifle Styxx's protest. "I know in your time period it was uncivilized to drink wine without dilution. However, that was a very long time ago. Drink it as it is. Trust me, it's good, and it won't make you rape and pillage the village." Then he returned to his conversation.

Well, if anyone should know how to drink wine, it was the Greek god of the vine.

Hoping for the best, Styxx took a tentative sip. It pained him to admit it, but Dionysus was right. It was delicious. And very different from what he'd known in Didymos.

As Styxx listened in on their conversation, he learned that Dionysus had been banned from Olympus and sent to live in the mortal realm . . . The real reason for his planned hostile takeover. Dionysus wanted to return to Olympus and throw his father from the mountain.

Likewise, Camulus's godhood was all but gone and he wanted the heart carved out of someone named Talon.

In the middle of their conversation, they stopped talking to stare at him. "Human?" Dionysus asked.

Don't I wish.

"God of drunken lunatics?" he shot back at Dionysus.

Camulus laughed.

Dionysus not so much. "Can you feign an Atlantean accent?"

Styxx wiped his mouth with his napkin. "It's been a while since I heard one, but I think I have it."

The Olympian actually appeared impressed. "Where did you get that?"

"I spent three years in Atlantis. I heard it a lot."

"Ah, well, just so you know, your brother's accent comes and goes."

"Noted."

Dionysus swirled his wine around in his . . . glass. That was the correct word for it. "I might live to regret this comment, but I think we're going to pull this off."

Styxx only wished he shared their optimism. *I better enjoy my limited freedom.* Because sooner or later, something was going to happen and he'd be relegated back to hell soon.

He was sure of it.

FEBRUARY 17, 2004

Styxx sat alone in the Cafe Pontalba at a table near one of the large doors that opened onto the street where tourists thronged in the midst of pre–Mardi Gras celebration. The waitress had just taken away his plate and card.

Drinking his beer, he stared at the foreign people who made no sense to him. They were all very odd.

Like you're not?

True. He was so out of place, he couldn't stand it. And he hated playing with people's lives. At first, he hadn't minded his assignments.

Get close to the Dark-Hunters who worked with his brother and report back to Dionysus and Camulus. Play with their heads and confuse them a little.

Something made infinitely easier because he could hear their thoughts. But what had stunned him was how much love and respect the Dark-Hunters bore his brother.

No matter how hard he tried, he couldn't reconcile the Acheron they knew with the cowardly brother who'd stabbed him. The brother who'd ruthlessly oiled his body and held him down so that Estes could brand "whore" on his groin and laugh while it was done to him.

The brother whose greatest wish was to pay money to see Styxx violently raped.

His twin had never been caring about other people. Justifiable given Estes's abuse, Acheron had been bitter and angry.

Hurt.

Maybe people did change. The gods knew Acheron had had plenty of time for it while he'd left Styxx to rot in isolation.

Still . . . why wouldn't such an altruistic, "decent," and benevolent person check on his own brother?

At least once in eleven thousand years?

As the waitress returned his card, Styxx rubbed at his temples. He had a splitting headache from the voices that echoed all around him. That had been the only good thing about being on the island. The only voice in his head had been his own. And even it had faded and gone quiet after a few thousand years.

Not even the keepers Artemis had sent at odd intervals had verbal thoughts. Rather their thoughts had been pictures so vivid, he'd drawn them in the sand after they left. Then the tide would come and wash them away and leave him with a new slate to draw on.

His phone rang. Styxx checked the number and was grateful it wasn't one of the Dark-Hunters Dionysus had been rerouting to his cell. Since he couldn't hear their thoughts over the phone, it made talking to them even more difficult than normal.

"What do you need?" he asked Camulus.

"Did you find out about the woman? Does Talon know she's his wife reincarnated?"

Yes, he did, but Styxx refrained from sharing that. He wasn't sure why. Just that the hopeful delight in Camulus's tone made him wary. Besides, he understood the pain of losing the woman he loved. He wasn't callous enough to torture another man with something like that.

Not even for his own freedom and sanity.

"I don't know," he lied.

Camulus cursed. "Find out!" He hung up.

"You look like you're about to splinter that thing."

Styxx glanced up to see Nick Gautier in front of his table. He'd bumped into the kid a few days ago while he'd been helping to set up one of the Dark-Hunters. This man was a Squire—modern day servant or employee, rather—to Talon, the Dark-Hunter Camulus wanted to torture most. Apparently, Talon had killed Camulus's son in battle, back in the Dark Ages, and the god ached for vengeance over it.

And yet they all thought that Styxx should be willing to forgive Apollo for all his transgressions that had cost Styxx's son *his* life . . .

Yeah.

"Hey, kid." Styxx slid the phone into his pocket. Standing at six foot four, Nick was physically older than Styxx and yet he seemed like an infant to him. There was an innocence to the Cajun boy that Styxx wasn't sure he'd ever possessed. If he had, he must have still been in a pana.

Nick took the chair in front of him, turned it around, and straddled it. "Are you sure you're all right? You seem a little off."

There was an understatement. Nick was the only one in town who really concerned him when it came to discovering he wasn't Acheron. Apparently, his brother had a tight-knit relationship with Nick that Acheron didn't have with other people.

"It's the Daimons. Too much shit going on."

Nick laughed. "I hear you. And on top of everything else,

school is kicking my a–s–s. I wish I could pay one of you to take my finals and write my papers. I don't know what it is about them, but every time I have to sit down to a test, I choke and can't remember how to do anything right."

Styxx snorted at his words. "So what you're telling me is that you're having performance anxiety issues?"

"What . . . ? No! Hell to the no!"

Styxx laughed at Nick's righteous indignation. He could see why Acheron took a liking to Nick, and it went a long way in explaining why Galen had befriended him.

There's a fire inside you, boy. Even though you walk around like Atlas with the weight of the world on your young shoulders, you do it and still hold on to your dignity.

He'd never understood those words until he met this kid. It was a perfect description of Nick Gautier. And Styxx admired the way the boy watched after his mother and protected her. Theirs was a very special bond, and he liked to think that had his son Galen grown up, he'd be a lot like Nick.

"Ah, crap." Nick dug his phone out.

Styxx held his breath, hoping that wasn't his brother on the phone. If it was, he was busted.

"Hey, Ma. Nah, I'm sitting with Ash at the Cafe P. You need something?" He pulled a pen out of his pants pocket and grabbed a napkin. "Skim milk. Sliced cheese. Bread." He paused and frowned. "Ah, Ma . . . do I got to?" He absolutely cringed. "Fine. Girly things I don't want to know about. Gah! No, Ma, don't go there. I am your son, you know? I don't want to know that, either. Love you. Bye." He hung up the phone and sighed. "You don't know how lucky you are that you were born before women had tampons. I swear they were invented for no other purpose than to cause endless hours of shame, humiliation, and torture to men. 'Cause nothing says whipped better than a man in the grocery store holding a giant pink flowered shrink wrapped monstrosity. Least they could do is put them in a plain brown wrapper or unmarked black box or something ubiquitous."

Styxx had no idea what tampons were, but the expression on Nick's face told him that he better not ask. Chalk it up to another thing Dionysus had forgotten to give him the definition to.

Nick shoved the paper into his pocket while he continued to rant. "And why do they always wait until they're down to the last one before they restock? Not like they don't get it once a month on a fairly regular schedule . . . If I did that with the toilet paper, she'd slaughter me in my sleep." He growled then got up. "I've gotta make an emergency run. See you later."

Laughing as he ascertained the definition of "tampon," Styxx inclined his head to Nick and watched as the kid disappeared into the crowd. He got up and left a twenty-dollar bill on the table as a tip then headed out.

Nick had no idea how lucky he was to have a mother who loved him the way his did. It was all too rare in the world.

Styxx wandered back to the hotel where they were staying. He'd barely closed the door to their room before Camulus appeared and backhanded him so hard, he broke the sunglasses Styxx had been wearing.

Pain exploded through his head. "What the hell?"

"You lie to me again and I will gut you."

Styxx wiped the blood away with the back of his hand. "You'll have to pick a better threat. I've already had a god gut me. Really don't give a shit about it now."

"Fine. I'll geld you."

He laughed. "Been there and done that, too. Want to try three for three?"

Camulus scowled at him. "You're insane, aren't you?"

At this point, it was a good bet.

But he didn't speak. Rather, he pushed his way past the god and went to get another bottle of beer from the small fridge. He popped the top and sat down on the couch to silently wait for his next assignment.

Something that was growing harder by the day. He was tired of screwing with people's lives. His own had been toyed with enough by the gods that he was getting more and more resentful of what Camulus and Dionysus wanted of him. At the rate they were going, he was about to demand to be returned to his island.

Apollo or no Apollo.

FEBRUARY 21, 2004

Styxx gaped as Camulus appeared with an unconscious, bleeding woman draped over his shoulder. He recognized her as Sunshine Runningwolf, the woman who was Talon's reincarnated wife.

"What did you do?"

Camulus didn't respond as he tossed her down on the bed then used his powers to heal her bullet wound. Next, he tied her, spread-eagle, to the bed.

Fury ripped through Styxx at the sight. "What are you doing." It wasn't a question. It was a demand.

"Making sure she doesn't leave."

"You don't have to tie her up like that."

"Why not?"

It's degrading. But Styxx couldn't say that as memories shredded him. It set off a panic within him so ragged that he could barely breathe for it. He remembered the way he'd been tortured and violated, over and over, while tied down like that.

Unable to stand it, he jerked the knife out of his boot and cut her loose.

Camulus arched a brow. "What do you think you're doing?"

"She won't escape."

"You are overstepping your place, human."

Styxx curled his lip. Apparently he couldn't learn his lesson with the gods, because the next words out of his mouth were extremely stupid. "Fine, Apollo. Do your worst to me."

"What's going on here?" Dionysus asked as he joined them.

Camulus glared at Styxx. "Your pet was about to get his ass kicked."

Styxx snorted. "And yours was about to have his ass handed to him."

Dion made a sound of disgust deep in his throat. "I'm really getting tired of separating you two. Now stop it!" He turned his attention to the unconscious woman on the bed. "Why is she here?" he asked Camulus.

With smug satisfaction, the Gallic war god folded his arms over his chest. "To torture Talon. He has no idea what we're doing to her and it will make him crazy. I literally ripped her out of his arms while he was powerless to stop me."

Styxx could only imagine how nasty the expression was on his own face. Because the minute those words were out of Camulus's mouth, Dionysus zapped him out of the room and into his bedroom so that he couldn't hear their conversation.

Or so they thought.

"Now that's he's gone, Cam, explain yourself. What have you done?"

"I broke in and took her from Talon so that he'd know who holds her. You wanted him out of commission. I assure you, he's going insane from the fear of what I might be doing to her. I'm sure by now he's contacted Acheron. We need them as riled as possible, is that not right?"

"It is. So what are we going to do with her?"

"Rape the shit out of her."

Styxx's sanity told him to stay out of it, but he couldn't. The thought of Camulus doing that to her or anyone . . .

He wanted the god's heart in his fist. Before his common sense could prevail, he barged back into the room. "Touch her and I'll tear both your arms off and beat you with them."

Dionysus caught the Gaul before he could attack, and glared at Styxx. "Do I have to put you back in Hades?"

Styxx held Camulus's gaze with his. If he didn't come up with an alternate plan, fast, that bastard would have his way, and as Styxx knew firsthand, while Dionysus might not participate in raping

682

someone, he damn sure wouldn't stop it. He'd merely walk away and leave the human to the perversity of their captor.

No matter what, he wouldn't stand for it.

"I have another idea."

Camulus started for Styxx, but Dionysus caught him again and pushed him back.

"Stay in your corner, Gaul. Let's hear him out." He turned his attention back to Styxx. "Go on."

Styxx forced himself to stay calm. "You want to mind-fuck all of them. Right? That is why I'm here?"

"Yes."

Styxx hesitated. It was the last thing he wanted to do to anyone. But if he didn't, something a lot worse would happen to the woman. "There's a chest in my hut that contains Eycharistisi."

Dionysus's jaw went slack. "How the hell did you get that?"

"It was a gift." Those words stuck in his craw. Estes had left it as a reminder of what he could do to Styxx whenever he wanted and Styxx had kept it to remember why he'd been justified in killing his uncle in cold blood.

Dionysus narrowed his gaze on him in disbelief. "Why do you still have it?"

"I was on a deserted island for the last eleven thousand years. Unless I wanted to screw a wild goat, there wasn't a lot of use for it. And unlike you gods, screwing animals doesn't appeal to me."

Indignant, Dionysus straightened. "For the record, I never did that."

Yeah, right. "Ampelos?"

"Satyrs are half human."

Styxx let out a bitter laugh at Dionysus's answer. "And why are they half human?"

"Fine, it was just the one time, and I was really tore up drunk when it happened, and Phobos dared me into it."

One time? Really?

"Ismarius?" Styxx taunted with another famous reminder of the Olympian's perversity.

683

"What are you? My effing biographer?"

Camulus laughed. "So the goat remark hit a little close to home, huh?"

"Shut up." Dionysus turned back to Styxx. "If you don't want her raped, why give her a potent aphrodisiac?"

Because you leave me with no choice. If I don't do this, the other bastard will hurt her for real. Better to make her horny than have her violated by a pig.

But he knew better than to give them the real reason. "Mess with their heads. It will stress out Talon to know it was given to her, but most of all, it will send Acheron a potent message that I'm here, and it will upset him to a level you can't even begin to imagine."

"Why would he care?" Camulus asked.

"I'm the only one alive who knows all his secrets and every detail of his past. Trust me, he doesn't want me to share any of it with his friends. Fear of what I might expose will paralyze him. And he'll be after me with his thoughts so scrambled he won't know if he's coming or going."

Dionysus glared at him. "This had better work."

"Believe me. No one knows my twin better than I do. Now, we need to take her somewhere to give it to her then let them find her under its influence." *And make damn sure Talon is the one who finds her and the Gallic pig keeps his hands to himself.*

Dionysus nodded. "I'll get some Daimons to set up a distraction and to protect her until the Dark-Hunters get to her."

After returning Styxx to the spartan hole that had been his home for centuries, Dionysus frowned at him. "You made this place?"

Nodding, Styxx hesitated in the doorway of his hut. "I originally had a stone cottage here, but after a few centuries, it crumbled to dust."

"Couldn't you fix it?"

He gave the Olympian a droll stare. "Too time intensive to find the stones and make mortar by hand. I was dropped here with no tools or any supplies. I had to make everything I needed to survive, including weapons and tools, and kill or gather whatever I ate and wore." Had Styxx not been a war veteran who'd been forced to scrounge with his army when supplies ran low, and a boy whose father had demanded he work the hardest, most menial jobs he could find, he'd have been completely shit out of luck here.

Dionysus scowled. "I thought you had caretakers?"

A tic started in Styxx's jaw at the memory. "For a little while people would bring some food, from time to time. Maybe a hundred years or so. Then never again."

"How did you not go insane from the solitude?"

"Who says I didn't?" Styxx glanced around and winced at the animal pelts on the sand floor where he'd slept for thousands of years. The stone tools he'd had to make to survive—something twice as hard as usual since his right hand had been left partially paralyzed from the Thracian attack on his return to Greece after the Atlantean war.

There had been nothing comfortable or comforting about his stark, harsh existence.

Had he not hated Acheron before Dionysus had freed him, he would definitely hate him now, having seen the luxury his brother had lived in all these centuries past. The friends who surrounded Acheron and loved him like family.

Styxx still didn't understand how the selfish bastard couldn't have bothered to check in on him. Just once. Brought him a burger.

One effing pillow or blanket. Really? Would that have been so much for Mr. Atlantean God?

Disgusted, Styxx went to his chest and picked it up. "I'm ready."

"Yeah. I imagine you've seen enough of this place."

You have no idea. Styxx didn't say anything, but he was glad Dionysus didn't drag his feet leaving.

At least that was the thought until they returned to the hotel suite and Apollo was there, waiting for them.

What the hell?

A slow smile spread across the Olympian's face as he saw Styxx, while Styxx's stomach shrank with each additional heartbeat.

Camulus slid his gaze to Dionysus. "He came here looking for you. I hope you don't mind. I told him to wait."

That was what his mouth said, but Styxx could hear that Camulus had done it intentionally to get back at him. And all because of Styxx's slip . . .

Damn it. He knew better than to ever expose a nerve to anyone, for any reason. Especially a vengeful god. Total misery and pain consumed every molecule of his body. Honestly, he'd rather be back on the island than subjected to that bastard's custody.

He turned on Dionysus. "Our deal's off. Send me back."

Dionysus actually had pity in his eyes as he shook his head at Styxx. "It won't matter. He knows you're alive now. He can track you there the same way I did."

Of course he could. And on that island, Styxx would be at Apollo's mercy any time, day or night. It would be even worse than it'd been in Didymos.

Apollo wouldn't have to worry about anyone disturbing them or . . .

Styxx slammed the chest down on the table. "I don't give a fuck. I'm out." He stormed to Sunshine's room and opened the door.

Her eyes widened as soon as she saw him. Fury spurring him, he pulled out his knife and went to free her.

Roaring, Camulus shoved him away from the bed.

Styxx turned on him with a feral gleam in his eye. He'd had enough of them all. "Bring it, bitch!"

Camulus lunged at him and Styxx feinted to the left then shot back right and buried his dagger into the god's side. The Gaul bellowed with fury.

Styxx caught him and flipped him to the floor. Camulus shot a bolt at him, but he dodged it and slammed Camulus's head down to stun the older being.

"Stop!" Dionysus ordered.

Styxx ignored him.

"I'll kill the woman if you don't stop. I mean it, Styxx."

He hesitated in debate. On the one hand, why should he care? But as he glanced at her and the terror in her dark eyes, he knew he couldn't hurt her. He'd seen too many innocents pay. Even though he didn't know her at all, he didn't want her or Talon to live with the nightmares he knew so intimately.

No one should bury his wife . . .

Never mind do it twice in one lifetime.

Furious, Styxx drove the knife into the floor next to Camulus's head then got up and left the room.

"I should have let him kill you," Dionysus sneered to Camulus, unaware that Styxx could hear them.

"I didn't know he could do that."

Apollo laughed. "You have no idea. For a human, he has incredible skills . . . in more than one event."

"Stop it!" Dionysus snapped at his brother. "Haven't you tormented him enough? Really?"

Styxx grabbed his coat and left the hotel. He had no destination in mind, he just had to get some fresh air as a thousand emotions ripped him apart. He should have known better than to agree to this.

The gods always screwed him.

One way or another.

I just want out. Was it not time for his torment to end? Really? How much more could they put him through?

Unable to stand it, he headed down Canal, toward the river. There were groups of people laughing all around him in carefree abandon. How he wished he could be one of them. But he'd never been free to hang out with friends and party. His whole human life had been nothing but responsibility.

Duty.

And he'd failed everyone he'd ever loved.

He pulled the sleeve of his jacket and shirt back so that he could touch the names of his wife and son. If he closed his eyes, he could sometimes catch a whiff of Bethany's scent from the bowels of his memory. But what he hated was the fact that he couldn't remember the sound of her voice anymore. He could remember inflections of it as she said his name or laughed. Yet not the exact sound.

She'd left him entirely.

I can't take another day of this . . .

And yet there was no way out. None. Strange how as a child forever had seemed like a long time, but it wasn't until you lived it that you fully grasped the horror of eternity.

The magnitude.

The insanity.

Although the Dark-Hunters he'd spoken to seemed to have adapted to the concept. As had his brother. But then, they weren't alone. They had a brotherhood where they looked out for each other.

The only one of the Dark-Hunters who seemed to even remotely understand Styxx's pain was the one named Zarek. In his dark, tortured eyes, Styxx had recognized a kindred spirit.

Styxx paused along the walkway that ran parallel to the river and leaned against the steel rail. His gaze dropped to the two clear plastic cups someone had carelessly tossed over the railing.

Discarded garbage . . .

Like him.

At home in Didymos and on the island in Hades, the water had always been the most luscious shade of clear turquoise. Here it was a murky greenish-brown. Still, it reminded him of the sounds of home on hot summer nights when he'd slept with all the windows open and listened to the sea outside.

There was a child screaming behind him while an irate mother tried to soothe her, and was fast losing patience with the girl. He glanced at them over his shoulder. The woman had no idea just how lucky she was to have that child with her. But he wouldn't pass judgment on her for her irritation. His father had been perpetually annoyed with him, and maybe if he'd been blessed enough to raise his son, he'd have been the same with Galen.

But he couldn't imagine ever being cross with his child, for any reason.

If only I could have held him.

Just once.

Sighing, he gripped the rail and tried to calm the rage and grief inside him as seagulls cried out over his head, temporarily drowning out the sound of Zydeco and people in the background.

"Styxx?"

Silently, he cursed at the sound of Dionysus's voice calling out to him. He didn't say a word until the god came to stand by his side.

"You promised me an end to my hell," Styxx whispered.

"I know. I'm sorry."

"No, you're not." Dionysus didn't care any more about Styxx than anyone else did. He was nothing to the god and he knew it.

Dionysus turned so that he could lean back against the railing and face Styxx. "Yes, I am. For everything. Believe it or not, even the gods can have remorse. I should have never shown you to Apollo. I was young and stupid. Trying to impress my big brother. It wasn't until I was cast into this putrid world that I began to fully understand the consequences of what we do . . . what we did."

"And yet you want to take it over. Rule it all again."

"I don't like being a pawn any more than you do. I've choked on my pride long enough. Like you, I want out."

Styxx snorted. "We're not friends or women. Why are you talking to me?"

"Because we need you to kill Acheron. You're the only one who can get close enough to him to do it. There's just a handful of days left to Mardi Gras. Help me finish this and you won't have to worry about Apollo. I'll make sure he stays away from you until then, and once you're dead . . . "

Styxx pushed himself away from the rail. "I better be dead, Dionysus. If not, yours is the first ass I'll be coming after." He headed back to the hotel with Dionysus trailing him the whole way. "If you're banned from Olympus, how were you able to free me?"

"Hades isn't part of Olympus. I wasn't banned from his domain."

That made sense.

Styxx held the door open and let Dionysus lead the way to the elevator. "I want full control of the woman. If Camulus goes near her again, I will gut him."

"I think he might have figured that out."

"I doubt it. He's even slower to learn than I am." Styxx stepped out of the elevator and headed back to the suite where Apollo and Camulus waited.

Dionysus cornered his brother without a word while Styxx grabbed a bottle of wine and went to his chest on the table. He mixed the wine with a very small amount of the Eycharistisi. As he worked, he felt Apollo's eyes on him to the point it made the hair at the back of his neck rise.

Glancing up, he caught the lecherous leer on Apollo's face, and it ignited his temper.

I hate you.

Doing his best to ignore him, Styxx poured the mixture into the thermos Dionysus had provided then handed it to the god of wine. "We're ready. I'll get the woman."

Camulus started to protest, but Dionysus stopped him.

Styxx's fury doubled as he saw Sunshine tied down again on the bed. Gods, he couldn't stand it. Grinding his teeth, he cut her free.

She immediately ran at him and shoved him back. Stunned, he didn't react for several heartbeats. But then he bolted to catch her before she could open the door where Camulus waited.

"Stop!" he snarled in her ear. "It's me or them, and believe me, you don't want them to touch you."

That made her fight even harder.

"Stop it!" he repeated. "I'm not going to rape you."

She tried to speak through her gag.

No doubt he should remove it, but knowing her, she'd scream. "Just calm down and everything will be fine." Taking her arm, he led her to the others.

Immediately, Dionysus flashed them from the hotel to an old, run-down warehouse of some kind. There were large paned windows, many of which had boards over them.

Using his powers, Dionysus conjured a small bed for the woman. Styxx pulled the gag from her lips as Dionysus unscrewed the Thermos lid. "I need you to drink this."

"You drink it, you bastard!" She ran for the door.

Styxx caught her then picked her up. On the one hand, he admired her bravery. On the other, it was seriously starting to piss him off. If she didn't cooperate, Camulus would insist on doing this his way. And she would be raped.

"C'mon," he said in her ear. "Swallow this. It's much better than what's going to happen to you if you don't."

Guilt stabbed him hard as she drank it, and he remembered what it'd been like when Estes had given it to him the first time on their hunting trip. How it'd felt when the Atlantean gods had forced him to drink it for their perverse pleasure. His anger mounted until he shook with its weight.

Once she was finished, he left her to Dionysus. He didn't want any part of tying her up or seeing her like that.

"Have you made your call?" Styxx snarled at Camulus.

"I took care of it. Did you write your note?"

He handed it to him then left. Since Acheron would be with the others who came to rescue the woman, he couldn't risk being here when they arrived.

But the problem was, he didn't know how to get back to the hotel from here.

"Styxx?"

He glanced over his shoulder to Dionysus. Before he could blink, the god blasted him and sent him back to their hotel suite.

That could have been a little more pleasant.

Of course, it could have been a lot more unpleasant, too.

However, the real unpleasantness was about to begin. As soon as his brother read the note Styxx had left for him, Acheron would come after his blood full throttle.

And who could blame him? The note was terse. Just a handful

of words designed to make Acheron insane enough to meet them and guarantee that soon Styxx wouldn't have to worry about Apollo or anything else ever again . . .

I know you, little brother. I know all you've done. I know how you live.

Most of all, I know the lies you tell yourself so that you can sleep.

Tell me, what would your Dark-Hunters think of you if they ever learned the truth of your past?

Keep them out of my way or I'll see them all dead.

And you I'll be seeing on Mardi Gras.

It was Styxx's declaration of war against Acheron, and it was one his brother would not let go unanswered.

FEBRUARY 24, 2004

Styxx kept checking the time as they waited for Zarek to bring Sunshine back to them. In less than an hour, if everything went as planned, Styxx would be dead.

Finally.

Please let this work. He didn't know if he could take another day of this putrid life he'd been cursed with.

The two gods moved in to flank him.

"He should be here any second," Dionysus said.

Suddenly, they heard footsteps outside. The metal door scraped against the concrete as Zarek pulled it open and came inside, pushing Sunshine in front of him. The woman's eyes widened at the sight of them then she turned to run.

Zarek closed the door and blocked it. All the fingers of his hand on the door were covered with lethal silver claws ... this Dark-Hunter's weapon of choice. He liked to feel the blood of his enemies on his hands when he took their lives.

Styxx could respect that.

Tall and barely one step this side of crazy, Zarek had been born a Greek slave to a Roman master. And from the tormented hell Zarek's eyes betrayed, Styxx suspected they shared a lot more than their mutual disdain and hatred of Acheron, and the world they lived in.

Camulus grinned at Sunshine. "Come in, come in, said the spider to the fly."

Styxx hated this game and his part in it. Terrorizing innocents had never been his tactic. He left that to assholes like Camulus.

And Apollo.

Sunshine lifted her chin as she bravely faced them then she spoke to the god of wine. "I'm going to take a wild guess that you are Dionysus."

He smiled as if flattered she knew him. "Guilty."

Camulus let out a long breath. "She's so bright. It's almost a shame to kill her. But ... oh well."

"You can't hurt her." Zarek stepped forward from the door. "You promised me she wouldn't be harmed if I brought her here."

"So I lied," Dionysus said. "Sue me."

Styxx ground his teeth at those words, which didn't bode well for any of them. What else had the bastard lied about? Was he planning to throw him to Apollo after this?

He tightened his hand on the dagger.

Styxx wouldn't go down again without a vicious fight that would cost Dionysus a lot more than just his dignity.

Zarek started for the god, but Sunshine stopped him. She turned back to Camulus. "I'm not going to let you kill me in front of Talon."

They all laughed. All except for Zarek, and Styxx who was extremely unamused by this turn of events.

Camulus postured like an idiot. "You can't stop us."

Zarek glanced down at her then did a double take as his gaze fell to her necklace. "Uh, gods, I think you've forgotten something."

Dionysus curled his lip. "We forget nothing."

"Oh, okay." Zarek's sarcasm was the only thing in this that amused Styxx. They definitely were kindred spirits. "Then you must already know that she wears a Marking Medallion."

They sobered instantly as recognition hit Styxx. He knew all about divine markings, courtesy of Apollo.

"What?" Camulus snarled.

Sunshine pulled a necklace out of her shirt and held it up to them. "My grandmother said that the Morrigán would always protect me."

Her amulet was similar to the one Beth had given him so long ago. A necklace he wished he'd kept. But he'd returned it to her for her protection when he'd sent her to Egypt to wait for him.

He hoped Sunshine's trinket held more power to protect her than Beth's had.

Camulus cursed. "Oh, this ain't right." He cursed again.

"This thing really works?" she whispered to Zarek.

"More than you know," he whispered back. "He can't kill you without making the Morrigán angry."

Amazed, she grinned. "Well, who knew?" She wrinkled her nose. "Cool."

"Yup." Zarek's dark eyes glittered with smug satisfaction that the gods had been quelled. "Better than a cross with Dracula."

Styxx frowned at a reference that had absolutely no meaning for him.

Sunshine beamed even more. "Does it work against Dionysus, too?"

Zarek nodded.

She stood even taller. "Okay, then let's talk."

"Talk about what?" Dionysus snarled.

"Not you. Him." She indicated Camulus with a jerk of her chin. "I want to talk about Talon's curse."

Camulus's eyes blazed at her. "What about it?"

"I want you to lift it."

"Never."

She held her medallion out to him. "Do it or . . ." She gave Zarek a sideways stare. "Does this have any power to hurt him?"

"Only if he hurts you first."

Disappointment was written all over her face.

A calculating glint lightened Camulus's eyes. He sighed as if bored. "Oh well, since I can't kill you, I guess I'll have to content myself with killing Talon instead."

Terror flashed across her brow. "What?"

Camulus shrugged nonchalantly. "It's rather pointless to let him live happily ever after with you when my intent was to make him suffer. Since you can't die, he'll have to."

Her hand shook. "Won't Artemis be mad if you kill one of her soldiers?"

Camulus looked at Dionysus who burst out laughing. "Artemis, darling that she is, would most definitely care. However, she won't start a war with the Celtic pantheon over it. Unlike me, Cam is safe from her wrath."

"Doesn't it just reek?" Camulus asked. His happy smile belied his dire words.

Styxx winced as he heard her confusion and pain in his head.

This can't be happening. How could I save myself and condemn Talon to die?

No, I can't. I have to do something.

"Okay," she said firmly, "there has to be another way."

Camulus narrowed his eyes as if thinking about the matter. "Perhaps there is. Tell me, Sunshine. How much does Talon's happiness mean to you?"

"Everything," she said sincerely.

Styxx cringed at that particular stupidity. Poor thing had no idea on how to negotiate. Especially not with a god.

"Everything. Well, that certainly is a lot." Camulus's look turned steely cold . . . frightening. "Does it mean as much to you as your own soul?"

"Sunshine," Zarek said. "Don't."

"You, heel," Dionysus snarled at the Dark-Hunter.

Zarek cracked his knuckles. "Don't tell me what to do. I don't like it."

Sunshine ignored them. "What are you saying to me, Camulus?"

He tucked his hands into his pockets and acted as cool as someone chitchatting about the weather, not sealing the fate of her immortal destiny. "A simple trade. I lift his curse. You give me your soul."

Sunshine hesitated. "That seems easy."

"It is."

Styxx cringed in fear for her. *Don't do it, girl . . .*

Sunshine bit her lip in indecision. "So what are you going to do with my soul once you have it?"

"Nothing at all. I'll keep it with me, just like Artemis keeps Talon's."

"And my body?"

"A body doesn't need a soul to function."

Zarek put a hand on her shoulder. "Don't do it, Sunshine. You can't ever trust a god."

Styxx couldn't agree more. *Listen to the Dark-Hunter, woman.*

Dionysus pierced Styxx with a glare. *Say something to seal this, or I'll bring you back from the dead and turn Apollo loose on you. And believe me, I can do it. You'll spend the rest of eternity chained to my brother's bed and we'll all take turns with you again.*

If the words weren't bad enough, the memories he conjured for Styxx were truly horrifying. He flinched in reflex.

Styxx didn't want to do this, but no one would stop his torture. He knew that for a fact.

The only one who had ever saved him was the Atlantean goddess of the hunt who was long dead.

I won't go back. I won't. It was time he looked out for himself.

Swallowing, Styxx met Sunshine's gaze. "Sure you can," he said, hating himself for the lie. "Trusting them is the best thing I ever did."

"I don't know," she breathed. Then he saw the determination

clouding her eyes before she nodded. "All right. You lift the curse and I'll give you my soul."

Styxx winced as she condemned herself.

Camulus let out an evil laugh. "Done. Talon has no curse. He can find love all day long."

She smiled.

"But you, my sweet . . . " He blasted her. "Have to die for me to take your soul."

The shot knocked her back into Zarek's arms. He gaped as her blood ran all over the two of them. "You bastard!"

Styxx started to go to her, but Dionysus held him back.

Apollo, he mouthed then dropped his gaze pointedly to Styxx's groin and licked his lips.

Styxx really wanted to kill them both. But before he could even move, Zarek lifted the woman and ran with her.

A smile curled Styxx's lips. *Run, Dark-Hunter. Get her to safety.*

If Zarek could make it to Acheron, his brother, who wouldn't piss on him if he were on fire, would save her. He knew it.

No sooner had they left than a bright light flashed through the room, temporarily blinding Styxx. Screams rang out. A wind whipped his clothes and hair around his body as a cloud appeared in the center of the room. In the next second, winged demons came pouring out. With rust-colored flesh and three barbed tails that they wielded like whips, they were a terrifying sight to behold.

Camulus grinned at them. "Go get them, my babies. Kill them all!"

The Celtic demons went after Zarek and Sunshine.

And so did the gods.

Styxx hesitated as he felt Acheron's presence on the premises. He'd forgotten about that ability. As a boy, he'd always been able to tell whenever his brother was nearby.

His throat tightened as he checked his watch and saw that it was almost time.

Strange . . . he'd killed hundreds of men in battle. As a boy, he'd killed his own uncle. But the prospect of stabbing Acheron . . .

It was harder than he'd have thought possible. But what choice did he have? Especially now that Apollo knew he was alive. If he didn't see this through . . .

He couldn't bear to contemplate the alternative.

Acheron had already shown him that he didn't care how Styxx was treated or what happened to him. That Acheron would gladly sit back, ringside, and watch others rape him, and laugh while they did it.

No, it was time to end his own hell. Determined to see this through, Styxx followed the gods down to a locked door. He heard Acheron and Talon on the other side talking to Zarek and Sunshine as they tried to save her life.

The demons began battering the door while Styxx stood back to watch. And listen to Acheron's kindness toward others, like Styxx had done with Ryssa through the walls of his room. A kindness Acheron hadn't shown Styxx since they were seven years old.

It seemed to take forever before they finally broke through. The demons spilled into the room, followed by the gods.

Styxx hung back for just a moment more as Talon jumped up and put himself between them and Sunshine. The tall, blond Celt did love his wife, and Styxx definitely sympathized with that.

Ash rose to his feet, ready to fight.

"It's midnight," Dionysus said with a laugh. "Let the show begin."

Taking a deep breath, Styxx headed in. Camulus's demons moved aside to allow him to walk through them to reach his brother.

Time froze as he finally saw Acheron for the first time since their deaths at Apollo's hands. Acheron looked better, healthier, than he ever had. No one would ever know this proud man was the whipped dog he'd once been. There was no trace of the Acheron who used to hug shadows and glare his hatred at Styxx. No trace of the boy who'd been so abused and tortured that he'd been terrified of trying to escape his uncle's hell.

And yet Styxx knew the truth.

They were both nothing more than used whores . . .

Bought, sold, and degraded for coin and entertainment.

"Hello, Acheron." He made sure to keep his voice completely steady and devoid of the hate and grief that surged inside him. "It's been a while, hasn't it? Eleven thousand years or so?" The Dark-Hunter, Talon, gaped at the sight of him and Acheron together.

Ignoring him, Styxx approached Acheron, slowly and steadily.

Acheron's eyes narrowed with warning. "Stand down, Styxx. I don't want to hurt you, but I will if I have to. I won't let you release her."

His brother didn't want to hurt him? Since when? Acheron had spent the whole of their human lives doing him harm. Wishing the worst sorts of ills on him.

Why would that change now? Or was it nothing more than empty words used so that Acheron's precious Dark-Hunters wouldn't learn how cruel their leader could truly be?

Styxx's gaze went to Talon who kept turning his head from him to Acheron and back again. He laughed bitterly at a reaction that had once been quite common. "It's like some bad soap opera, isn't it? Good twin, bad twin." He returned his glare to his brother. "But then, we're not really twins, are we, Acheron? We just happened to have shared the same womb for a while." He paused behind Acheron, who tensed noticeably as if he knew what Styxx intended.

He was so close to his brother now that barely a hand separated them. They didn't touch. They didn't have to.

Grief racked Styxx at the memory of their childhood together. At how they would lie, back to back, united against the world. United against everyone.

Brothers, forever and always . . .

Now they were enemies.

Forever and always.

How he wished things were different. That Acheron could have found the compassion for him that he'd given to everyone else.

Even Artemis.

But Styxx was too tired now. Too used and too battered. And

Acheron had made it abundantly clear that, unlike Styxx, he held no love or memory of them as brothers. That Styxx meant absolutely nothing to him.

He wasn't even worth a passing thought.

Angry and heartbroken, Styxx leaned forward to speak in a low tone near Acheron's ear. "Shall we tell him who the good one is, Acheron? Should I tell him which of us lived his life with dignity? Which of us was respected by the Greeks and Atlanteans and who was laughed at?"

Yeah, it was a harsh lie, but Acheron believed it, and Styxx needed to keep his brother upset and unbalanced so that he could finish this. Acheron was the god. He was not. And while Styxx was stronger than most, he was still just a human man with human strength.

And they were about to unleash Acheron's real mother into the world. She would rip him apart for this. But hopefully he'd die before she completely gutted him.

Expelling a deep breath, Styxx reached his hand around Acheron's throat and placed it to the exact spot Apollo had used when he'd held his brother to the floor of Ryssa's room.

Acheron whimpered and Styxx hated himself for causing that sound. But war had taught him well that the best way to win against a stronger opponent was to demoralize them. Put them mentally into a weakened position.

Styxx pulled Acheron back against him so he could whisper in their language into Acheron's ear and no one else would understand the cruelty of what he was about to say. It was bad enough to kill his brother. He refused to publicly shame him first.

If only Acheron had been so kind to him in Atlantis.

"You told me once that you would pay to see me fucked in my throat, little brother. But I wasn't the one who willingly whored myself for other men. The one who sold myself into eternal slavery to a bitch-goddess. I was the one who tried to help you, and instead of taking my hand, you lopped it off and fucked me worse than anyone. You laughed at my pain. And you laid up drunk while my sister and nephew were slaughtered just a few feet from you. First you stole her from me emotionally and then you let her brutally die, calling your name. Just as you would let me take your beatings for you when we were little and never utter a single word in my defense. You've never been anything but a worthless piece of shit."

Acheron panted as if in the throes of a nightmare. His eyes were haunted and glazed. He didn't even bother to fight him, which let Styxx know that his brother was ready for him to finally end this.

"That's it, Acheron," he said between clenched teeth, switching back to English. "Remember the past. Remember what you were. I want you to relive it all. Relive every foul thing you ever said or did. Every tear you made my parents weep for you. Every time I had to look at you and feel ashamed that you bore my face."

Tears filled his brother's eyes and they wrung his heart. He wanted to hate Acheron. He did.

No, he needed to hate him.

Yet he couldn't. No matter how hard he tried. All he could see was the two of them as boys. Feel Acheron's hand in his as his brother sought to comfort him when no one else would.

You have to do this . . .

Acheron doesn't love you. He never loved you.

No more than his parents had.

"Let him go," Talon ordered.

Ignoring him, Styxx tightened his grip on Acheron's throat and pressed his brother one more time. "Do you remember when Estes died? The way my father and I found you? I have never been able to forget it. Every time I have ever thought of you, it's the image I have. You're repulsive. Disgusting."

"Kill him," Dionysus ordered, "and open the portal."

Camulus started for them with a dagger. Talon rushed him and they fought for the weapon.

"Kill him, Styxx," Dionysus ordered again. "Or we'll miss the portal."

Styxx pressed his forehead against Acheron's cheek, aching over the tragic enemies they'd become. "Good-bye, Acheron. May we both finally sleep in peace." He pulled the dagger out from underneath his coat then sent it straight into Acheron's heart, burying it in all the way to its hilt.

Just as his brother had done to him in Didymos while he slumbered.

Acheron gasped and arched his back as if something had possessed him. The dagger shot through the air, bouncing off a wall above Dionysus's head. Light poured out of the wound then seared it closed.

In the next instant some sort of shock wave went through the room, knocking everyone off their feet. Styxx was hurled to a far corner while the gods were pinned to the ground.

Acheron rose from the floor, to hover spread-eagle several inches above it.

No one could stand. Not even the gods.

Lightning bolts shot through Acheron's body, blowing out the windows and the lights. Electrical energy snapped and hissed all around them. Acheron laid his head back as bolts of lightning pierced his eyes and mouth. They seemed to shoot through him and then out into the room giving bright flashes of light.

The Daimons and the demons exploded in one bright flash.

Suddenly, some kind of winged dragon came out from under Acheron's sleeve and wrapped itself around him as if it were protecting him.

It was a Charonte . . . Styxx remembered those from his time in Atlantis.

"What the hell is that?" Camulus asked. "Styxx, what did you do?"

He had no idea. "Nothing. Is this from the portal opening?"

Dionysus shook his head. "This is something else entirely. Something no one told me about." He looked up at the ceiling and shouted, "Artemis!"

Artemis appeared and was immediately pinned to the floor with the rest of them. She took one look at Acheron and her face went flush with anger. "Who's the idiot who pissed off Acheron?" she demanded.

The two gods pointed to Styxx, hurling his ass right under the bus.

"You fools!" she snarled. "What were you thinking?"

Dionysus glared at her. "We needed to kill an Atlantean to raise the Destroyer, and Acheron's the only one left."

Artemis growled at him. "Oh, you are so stupid! I knew your plan had to be a bad one. You can't just kill him with a dagger. In case you haven't noticed, he's not human. Where was your bonehead?"

Dionysus curled his lips at her. "How was I to know your pet was a god-killer? What kind of idiot ties herself down to one of his kind?"

"Well, gee, what was I supposed to do? Hook up with Mr. All-Powerful God-killer, or get myself a Mardi Gras float and hang out with him." She pointed to Camulus, who looked extremely offended by her comment. She sneered at Dionysus. "You're such a moron. No wonder you're the patron god of drunken frat boys."

"Excuse me," Talon snapped at them. "Could you gods focus for a sec? We have a bit of a situation here."

"Oh shut up," Dionysus snarled. "I knew I should have backed up when I ran you over."

Talon's jaw went slack at his words. "That was you who hit me with the float?"

"Yes."

"Damn, boy," Camulus laughed at Dionysus. "You've fallen a long way down. Yesterday Greek god . . . today incompetent float driver. Sheez, and I hooked up with you? What was I thinking? Artemis is right, what kind of idiot picks a float to mow a guy down so that he can go home with his dead wife? You're lucky you didn't kill him then, and blow the entire plan."

"Hey, have you ever tried to drive one of those things? It's not exactly easy. Besides, he's a Dark-Hunter. I knew it wouldn't kill him. I just needed something that would hurt him enough to make her take him home, and need I remind you it did work."

Artemis curled her lip. "You're so pathetic. I can't believe we share a common gene between us." Shooting one nasty glare at her brother, she struggled against the invisible force that held them down.

But like the rest of them, she couldn't reach Acheron. "Acheron!" she called. "Can you hear me?"

Disembodied laughter filled the room.

Styxx clenched his teeth at the sound. *What have I done?*
Besides screwed myself again.

Acheron wouldn't die tonight. And neither would he.

Great . . . just great.

He could only imagine how he'd pay for this.

Acheron leaned his head forward and more lightning flowed through him. The Charonte tightened its grip around him and hissed a fiery breath at the goddess.

Artemis tried to climb up Acheron's leg, but she was forced back, away from him.

"You know, folks," Camulus shouted. "The idea was to kill Acheron, free Apollymi, and reclaim our god status. Not piss him off and end the world. Personally, I don't want to be ruler of nothing. But if someone doesn't stop this guy, that chant he's making is going to undo life as we know it and un-create the world."

"What are we going to do?" Sunshine asked Talon.

Talon kissed her lips then moved away from her. Against all odds, he rose slowly to his feet.

Acheron shot a lightning bolt at him.

Talon deflected it. He moved slowly through the maelstrom until he reached Acheron's side. "Let it go, T-Rex."

Acheron spoke to him in Atlantean. By the expression on Talon's face, it was obvious he didn't understand.

"He says to back off or die," Styxx translated. "He's summoning the Destroyer."

Talon shook his head. "I can't let you do that."

Evil laughter echoed again.

Talon rushed him. He caught Acheron about the middle and knocked him to the floor. The Charonte arched up, shrieking.

The Celt ignored it as he slugged Acheron. Hard. Which woke his brother up, and the two of them started pounding each other even worse than the fight they'd had when Styxx had found Ryssa dead.

The floor beneath them shook.

Zarek came through the door, bleeding, and was immediately thrown backward, against a wall.

Artemis tried again to reach Acheron and again he tossed her back while he fought with Talon.

"I'll give the boy credit," Camulus said. "He always was a fighter."

Talon stopped fighting as he heard those words.

Styxx scowled as he heard Talon's thoughts in his own head. *You never could learn your place, Speirr. You never knew when you should just lay down the sword and play nice. You're right, Camulus. I've never known when to fight and when to withdraw. It's what got me cursed.*

I have to be calm now.

The next words in Talon's head stunned Styxx, as they had come from Acheron. *"I can show you how to bury that pain so deep inside you that it will prick you no more. But be warned that nothing is given freely and nothing lasts forever. One day something will come along to make you feel again, and with it, it will bring the pain of the ages upon you. All you have hidden will come out and it could destroy not only you, but anyone near you."*

Talon looked up at Acheron and saw the fury of the man who was attacking him.

Acheron rushed him again.

This time instead of fighting, Talon embraced him like a brother then he cupped Acheron's face in his hands and tried to make his old friend see him.

Acheron's features were no longer human. They were those of the twisted demon that had haunted Styxx's nightmares. The demon he fought in battle. His brother's eyes were bloodred and yellow, and there was no mercy in them. They were cold. Vicious.

The colors in his eyes swirled and danced like fire.

They were actually similar to what Apollo's eyes did right before his worst attacks on Styxx. Archon's, too.

"Acheron," Talon said calmly, slowly. "Enough."

At first Styxx didn't think Acheron had heard Talon. Not until his brother turned his head to see Sunshine on the floor.

"Talon," he rasped hoarsely. Acheron's eyes flickered then he looked back at Talon.

Suddenly, another shock wave shot through the room, this one in the reverse direction from the first. It was as if the unleashed power was drawing back into Acheron's body.

Still in dragon form, the Charonte shot up toward the ceiling then vanished.

Acheron's features transformed from a demon's back into those of a man. His brother blinked his now swirling silver eyes, and looked around as if he were waking up from a nightmare. Without a single comment, Acheron stepped away from Talon, wrapped his arms around his chest, and walked across the room as if nothing had happened.

As Acheron passed by Artemis, she reached for him, but he dodged her touch and kept walking.

Artemis turned on her own brother with a snarl. "Just you wait till Dad gets his hands on you."

"Me? He knew what I had planned tonight. Wait until I tell him about Acheron!"

Artemis curled her lip. "Oh shut up, whiney-boy." She held her hand out and zapped him out of the room.

Styxx braced himself as Artemis turned her angry gaze to him. He knew what was coming.

Back to his hell.

"You," she said, her tone thick with loathing.

I am so screwed. But maybe if he pissed her off enough, she might yet kill him rather than send him back. "How can you protect something like him? After I died, I was sent to the Elysian Fields while he was—"

"No concern of yours," she said, interrupting him. "You and

your precious family, you turned your backs on him and condemned him for something that wasn't his fault."

Styxx was aghast at her words. He'd never held anything against Acheron except what Acheron had done to hurt him. "Not his fault? Please." He tried to say something more, but his voice vanished.

"That's better." Artemis simpered. "Funny, the two of you sound alike and yet you whine. Thank Zeus, Acheron doesn't have that repugnant quality. But then he was always a man and not some sniveling little child."

Oh yeah, that so described his brother and him.

The bitch really was crazy.

She backed him against the wall. "I can't believe you. I gave you a perfect existence. Your own island, filled with everything you could ever desire, and what did you do? You've spent eternity hating Acheron, plotting ways to kill him. You don't deserve mercy."

Perfect island? Everything he could desire?

Yes, she was insane. She had to be if she thought his life on a desolate island was perfect.

As for Acheron . . . the last thing on Styxx's mind had been payback. He'd been too occupied by his own grief for his wife and son, and by trying to survive to even contemplate getting back at a brother he didn't think he'd ever see again.

"You can't kill me," Styxx squeaked out the erroneous thoughts in her head. "If you do, Acheron dies, too." He choked as she tightened the hold on his throat, cutting off his correction of her misinformation.

"I curse the day the Fates bound your life force to his."

That was not the Fates, bitch. It was his mother. Get your story straight. How stupid could one goddess be?

Oh wait. It was Artemis, after all. The twin sister of Apollo. Intelligence was not their forte.

Artemis narrowed her eyes at him as if she wanted nothing more than to splinter him where he stood. "You're right. I can't kill you, but I can make living a worse hell than anything you can imagine."

He laughed. "What are you going to do me?" *Turn me over to your perverted brother?*

That was the worst thing imaginable.

She smiled evilly. "You'll see, little human, you'll see."

One moment he was in the factory, and in the next . . .

Screams surrounded him, piercing the blackness. He tried his best to see something. Anything. But all he saw were the strange pinpoint ghost-lights made by eyes that were desperate to be of use.

This place was cold. Icy. He felt his way along a craggy rock wall only to learn he was encased in a small, six-feet-by-six-feet cell. There wasn't even enough room for him to lie down completely.

All of a sudden, a light appeared beside him. It faded to form a young, beautiful woman with dark red hair, fair skin, and the green, swirling eyes of a goddess. He knew her instantly.

She was Mnemosyne, or Mnimi for short, the goddess of memory. He'd seen her likeness countless times in temples and on scrolls. She held an old-fashioned oil lamp in her hand as she studied him closely.

"Where am I?" he asked her.

Her voice was faint and gentle, like a breeze whispering through crystal eaves. "You are in Tartarus."

Of course he was.

What the hell? He'd lived here his entire life.

Styxx swallowed his outrage and hurt. When he'd died aeons ago in ancient Greece, he should have been placed in the paradise realm of the Elysian Fields with Galen and his men . . . and not alone on a deserted island that vanished if anyone happened to look in its direction.

Tartarus was where Hades banished the evil souls he wished to torture. But hey, in theory it was a step up from where he'd been these last eleven thousand years. At least in hell he had company in his misery.

"I don't belong here."

"Where do you belong?" she asked.

He touched the names on his arm and thought about his wife and son. "I belong with my family."

Her eyes were tinged by sadness as she regarded him. "They have all been reborn. The only family you have left now is the brother you hate."

Reborn? Pain tore him apart. He'd never see his precious Bethany again. Never hear her or hold her . . .

Why can't I just die already?

But no. The one person he was left with was one who'd done nothing but hurt and humiliate him all his life. A man who would never even acknowledge him. The injustice of it made him want to slice open his own throat.

"He is not my brother. He was *never* my brother."

She cocked her head as if listening to something far away from them. "Strange. Acheron never felt that way about you. No matter the times you were cruel to him, he never hated you."

Bullshit! How could a goddess be so blind?

Or worse . . . if she was right and Acheron had done all he had without hating him then Acheron was exactly the monster their father had said he was.

But at the end of the day, it didn't matter. "I don't care what he feels."

"True," she said as if she knew his innermost thoughts, as if she knew him better than he knew himself.

"Honestly, I don't understand you, Styxx. For centuries, you were given the Vanishing Isle as your home. You had friends and every luxury known. It was as peaceful and beautiful there as the Elysian Fields, and yet all you did was plot more vengeance against Acheron. I gave you memories of your beautiful home and family, of your peaceful and happy childhood to comfort you, and instead of gaining pleasure from them, you used them to fuel your hatred."

He gaped. Friends? What friends? The stupid dolphins he talked to out of desperation? His brother's wooden horse? And it wasn't like she'd put him on the Vanishing Isle with the Dream-Hunters. No . . . his had been completely deserted.

Oh gee, bitch, thanks.

As for his memories, they had been the worst sort of hell, because they'd reminded him of the brother he'd lost. Of Bethany and Galen, and the life they'd planned and never had.

Those had been a dagger in his heart.

But most of all, those memories had shown him the father who despised him, the mother who tried to kill him, his sister whose heart had only been big enough to love Acheron, and all the people who had mocked and debased him because of his brother.

No, not his brother.

Apollymi's bastard seed!

"Do you blame me? Acheron stole everything from me. Everything I ever hoped for or loved. Because of him, my family is dead, my kingdom gone. Even my life ended because of him."

But for Acheron keeping him that day, he would have been in Egypt to protect Bethany when Apollymi came for her.

"No," she said softly. "You can lie to yourself, Styxx, but not to me. It was you who betrayed your brother. You and your father. You let your fear of him blind you. It was your own actions that condemned not only him, but yourself as well."

What fear? Never, ever once in his life had he feared Acheron!

Memories of Atlantis tore through him. He saw Acheron smirking as he secured Styxx's limbs to the bed so that Estes could violate him instead of Acheron.

"How can you do this to me? I came here to save you!"

"You are saving me, Styxx. Tonight I'm not the one getting fucked in my ass. You are. Just remember not to clench. It hurts a lot less when you stop fighting them."

He could still see the mocking gleam in his brother's eye as Acheron oiled and "prepared" Styxx's naked body for Estes and the others.

Yes, his brother had been beaten down and drugged to the point he'd possessed no mind of his own. Even so, Styxx couldn't understand how Acheron could have done such a thing to him.

The betrayal burned deep in his heart.

"What do you know of it? Acheron is evil. Unclean. He defiles everything he touches."

She danced her fingers through the lamp's flame, making it flicker eerily in the darkness of the small cell. All the while her eyes burned him with their intensity. "That is the beauty of memory, isn't it? Our reality is always clouded by our perceptions of truth. You remember events one way and so you judge your brother without knowledge of how things were to him."

Mnimi placed a hand on his shoulder. The heat of it seared his skin and when she spoke, her low tone sounded evil, insidious. "I am about to give you the most precious of gifts, Styxx. At long last, you will have understanding."

Styxx tried to run, but couldn't.

Mnimi's fiery touch held him immobile.

His head spun as he rushed back in time to the last place he wanted to go. He saw his beautiful mother lying on her gilded bed, her body covered in sweat, her face ashen as an attendant brushed her damp, blond hair from her pale blue eyes. He'd never known his mother to appear more joy-filled than she did that day.

Dear gods, she was even sober.

The room was crowded with court officials and his father, who stood to the side of the bed with his head of state. The long windows were open, letting the fresh sea air offer relief from the heat of the summer day.

"It is another beautiful boy," the midwife happily proclaimed, wrapping the newborn infant in a blanket.

"By sweet Artemis's hand, Aara, you've done me proud!" his father said as a loud jubilant shout ran through the room's occupants. "Twin boys to rule over our twin isles!"

Laughing, his mother watched as the midwife cleaned the firstborn.

It was then Styxx learned the true horror of Acheron's birth, learned the dark secret his father had hidden from him the whole of his life.

Acheron was the firstborn son.

Styxx, who was now in Acheron's infant body, struggled to breathe through his newborn lungs. He had finally taken a deep, clear breath when he heard a cry of alarm.

"Zeus have mercy, the eldest is malformed, Majesties."

His mother looked up, her brow creased by worry. "How so?"

The midwife carried him over to his mother, who held the second-born babe to her breast.

Scared, the baby wanted comfort away from the fear he sensed and the unfamiliar loud noises. He reached for the brother who had shared the womb with him. If he could just touch his brother, all would be right. He knew it.

Instead, his mother pulled his brother away, out of his sight and reach. "It cannot be," his mother sobbed. "He is blind."

"Not blind, Majesty," the eldest wise woman said as she stepped forward, through the crowd. Her white robes were heavily embroidered with gold threads, and she wore an ornate gold wreath over her faded gray hair. "He was sent to you by the gods."

Xerxes narrowed his eyes angrily at the queen. "You were unfaithful?"

"Nay, never."

"Then how is it he came from your loins? All of us here witnessed it."

The room as a whole looked to the wise woman who stared blankly at the tiny, helpless baby that cried out for someone to hold him and offer him solace. Warmth.

"He will be a destroyer, this child," she said, her ancient voice loud and ringing so that all could hear her proclamation. "His touch will bring death to many. Not even the gods themselves will be safe from his wrath."

"Then kill him now." Xerxes ordered his guard to draw his sword and slay the baby.

"Nay!" The wise woman halted the guard before he could carry out the king's will. "Kill this infant and your son dies as well, Majesty. Their life forces are combined. 'Tis the will of the gods that you should raise him to manhood."

The baby sobbed, not understanding the fear he sensed from those around him. All he wanted was to be held as his brother was. For someone to cuddle him and tell him that all would be fine.

Xerxes was emphatic. "I will not raise a monster."

"You have no choice." The wise woman took the baby from the midwife who'd delivered him and offered it to the queen. "He was born of your body, Majesty. He is your son."

The baby squalled even louder, reaching again for his mother. She cringed away from him, clutching her second-born even tighter than before. "I will not suckle it. I will not touch it. Get it away from my sight."

The wise woman walked the child to his father. "And what of you, Majesty? Will you not acknowledge him?"

"Never. That child is no son of mine."

The wise woman took a deep breath and presented the infant to the room. Her grip was loose, with no love or compassion evident in her touch.

"Then he will be called Acheron for the river of woe. Like the river of the Underworld, his journey shall be dark, long, and enduring. He will be able to give life and to take it. He will walk through his life alone and abandoned—ever seeking kindness and ever finding cruelty."

The wise woman looked down at the infant in her hands and uttered the simple truth that would haunt both twins for the rest of their existence. "May the gods have mercy on you, little one. No one else ever will."

DECEMBER 1, 2007

Acheron stopped at a doorway that was covered with an iridescent slime. It shimmered like a rainbow oil slick in the dim light. To his surprise, there was no sound coming from inside. No movement. It was as if the occupant was dead.

But unlike the others who lived in Tartarus, this particular person couldn't die.

At least not until Ash did, and since he was a god ...

He used his powers to open the door without touching it.

It was completely black inside the small, dingy room. Horrifying images of his human past slammed into him at the sight. Long-buried emotions ripped at him with daggers of pain that lacerated his heart.

Acheron wanted to run from this place.

He knew he couldn't.

Grinding his teeth, Ash forced himself to take the six steps that separated him from the man who was curled into a ball in one corner. An identical replica of himself, the man had long blond hair that was gnarled from the time he'd spent here and hadn't brushed it or bathed.

But then Ash never willingly wore his hair blond. It was a wretched reminder of a time in his past that he was desperate to forget.

Dressed in rags and his face covered with a long, matted beard, the man on the floor wasn't moving. He clenched his eyes shut like a child who thought that if he made no sound, no moves, the nightmare would end.

Ash had lived a long time in just such a state, and like the man before him, he had prayed for death repeatedly. But unlike his prayers that had gone unanswered, he was here to release Styxx from his prison.

"Styxx," he said, his low tone echoing off the walls.

His brother didn't react.

Ash knelt down and did something that had disgusted Styxx when they had been human brothers in Greece. He touched his brother's shoulder.

"Styxx?" he tried again.

Styxx screamed as Ash broke through the brutal memories of

horror that Mnimi had given to Styxx as punishment for trying to kill him. It was a punishment Ash had never agreed with. No one needed the memories of his human past. Not even him.

He could hear Styxx's thoughts as they left Ash's past and returned slowly to Styxx's control.

Knowing his brother would be disgusted by him, Ash let go and stepped back.

As humans, he and Styxx had never been close. Styxx had hated him with an unreasoning logic. For his own part, he had purposefully aggravated that hatred.

Ash's human rationale had been that if his family was going to hate him anyway, then he would give them all good cause for it. He'd gone out of his way to repulse them. Out of his way to antagonize his brother and father.

Only their sister had ever given him kindness.

And in the end, Ash had betrayed her and not been there to protect her when she'd died . . .

Styxx struggled to breathe as he became aware of the fact that he wasn't Acheron.

I am Styxx of Didymos. Heir to . . .

No, he wasn't the rightful heir to anything. Acheron had been. He and his father had stolen that from Acheron.

They had taken everything from him.

Everything.

For the first time in eleven thousand years Styxx understood that reality. In spite of what his father had convinced him, they had greatly wronged Acheron.

Mnimi had been right. The world as Prince Styxx had seen it had been whitewashed by lies and by hatred.

The world of Acheron had been entirely different. It had been steeped in loneliness and pain, and decorated with terror. It was a world he'd never dreamed existed. Sheltered and protected all his life, Styxx had never known a single insult. Never known hunger or suffering.

But Acheron had ...

His body shook uncontrollably as Styxx looked around the dark, cold room. He had seen such a place in Acheron's memories.

A place they had gleefully left Acheron in to face alone. Only this place was cleaner. Less frightening.

And he was a lot older than Acheron had been.

Styxx covered his eyes and wept as the agony of that tore through him anew. He knew Acheron's thoughts. Felt Acheron's emotions. His hopelessness. His despair. He heard Acheron's screams for death. His silent pleas for mercy—silent because to voice them only made his situation worse.

They echoed and taunted him from the past.

How many times had he hurt his own brother? Guilt gnawed at him, making him sick from it.

"I'll take them away from you."

Styxx flinched at the voice that sounded identical to his own, except for the soft lilting quality that marked Acheron's from the years he had spent in Atlantis.

Years Styxx wished to the gods that he could go back and change. Poor Acheron. No one deserved what had been handed to him.

"No," Styxx said quietly, his voice shaking as he gathered himself together. "I don't want you to."

He glanced up to see the surprise on Acheron's face.

It was something Acheron hid quickly behind a mask of stoicism. "There's no reason for you to know all that about me. My memories have never served good to anyone."

That wasn't true and Styxx knew it. "If you take them from me, I will hate you again."

"I don't mind."

No doubt. Acheron was used to being hated.

Styxx met that eerie swirling gaze of his levelly. "I do."

Ash couldn't breathe from the raw emotions he felt as he watched Styxx push himself to his feet.

They were so much alike physically and yet polar extremes when it came to their past and their present.

All they really had in common was that they were both longed-for heirs. Styxx was to inherit his father's kingdom while Acheron had been conceived to destroy the world for his mother.

It was a destiny neither of them had fulfilled.

Instead, Ash had been born human against his will and against the delight of his human surrogate family that had somehow sensed he wasn't really one of them.

And they had hated him for it.

"How long have I been here?" Styxx asked, looking around his dark prison.

"Three years."

Styxx laughed bitterly. "It seemed like forever."

It probably had. Ash didn't envy Styxx having to suffer the memories of Ash's human past. Then again, he envied himself even less for having lived them.

He cleared his throat. "I can return you to the Vanishing Isle again, or you can stay here in Tartarus. I can't take you into the Elysian Fields, but there are other areas here that are almost as peaceful."

"What did you have to bargain with Artemis and Hades for that?"

Ash looked away, not wanting to think about it. "It doesn't matter."

Styxx took a step toward him then stopped. "It does matter. I know what it costs you now . . . what it cost you then."

"Then you know it doesn't matter to me."

Styxx scoffed. "I know you're lying, Acheron. I'm the only one who does."

Ash flinched at the truth. But it changed nothing. "Make your decision, Styxx. I don't have any more time to waste here."

Styxx took another step forward. He stood so close now that Ash could see his reflection in Styxx's blue eyes. Those eyes pierced him with sincerity. "I want to go to Katateros."

Ash frowned at him. "Why?"

"I want to know my brother."

717

Ash scoffed at that. "You don't have a brother," he reminded him. It was something Styxx had proclaimed loud and clear throughout the centuries. "We only shared a womb for a very short time."

Styxx did something he had never done before. He reached out and touched Ash's shoulder. That touch seared him as it reminded him of the boy he'd been who had wanted nothing more than the love of his human family.

A boy they had brutally spat on and denied.

"You told me once, long ago," Styxx said in a ragged tone, "to look into a mirror and see your face. I refused to then. But now Mnimi has forced me to look at my own reflection. I've seen it through my eyes and I've seen it through yours. I wish to the gods that I could change what happened between us. If I could go back, I would never deny you. But I can't. We both know that. Now I just want the chance to know you as I should have known you all those centuries ago."

Angered at his noble speech and at a past that no mere handful of words could ease, Ash used his powers to pin Styxx back to the wall, away from him. Styxx hovered spread-eagle, above the floor, his face pale as Ash showed him his true god powers. He could tell by Styxx's thoughts that he was aware of exactly what he could do to him. Even though they were linked together, Ash could kill him with a single thought. He could shred him into pieces.

Part of him wanted to. It was the part of him they had turned vicious. The part of him that belonged to his real mother, the Destroyer.

"I am not a god of forgiveness."

Styxx met his gaze without flinching. "And I'm not a man used to apologizing. We are linked. You know it and I know it."

"How could I ever trust you?"

Styxx wanted to weep at that question. Acheron was right. He'd done nothing but hurt his brother.

He'd even tried to kill him.

"You can't. But I have lived inside your memories for the last three years. I know the pain you hide. I know the pain I caused. If

718

I stay here, I will go mad from the screams. If I return to the Vanishing Isle, I'll languish there alone and in time I will probably learn to hate you all over again."

Styxx paused as grief swept through him at the truth he could no longer deny. "I don't want to hate you anymore, Acheron. You are a god who can control human fate. Is it not possible that there was a reason why we were joined together? Surely the Fates meant for us to be brothers."

Ash looked away as those words echoed in his head. It was a divine cruelty that he could see the fate of everyone around him except for those who were important to him, or those whose fates were intertwined with his own. He held the fate of the entire world in his hand and yet he couldn't see his own future.

How screwed-up was that?

How unfair?

He looked at his "brother." Styxx was more likely to skewer him than he was to speak to him.

And yet he sensed something different about him.

Forget it. Erase his memory of you and leave him here to rot.

It was kinder than anything Styxx had ever done for him. But deep inside, down in a place that Ash hated was that little boy who had reached out for his brother. That little boy who had cried out repeatedly for his family only to find himself alone in Atlantis.

What should he do?

He set Styxx back on the ground.

Ash didn't move as memories and the emotions they reawakened assailed him. He could sense Styxx was approaching. He tensed out of habit. Every time Styxx had ever drawn near, he had hurt him.

"I can't undo the past," Styxx whispered. "But in the future, I will gladly lay my life down for you, brother."

Before he realized what Styxx was doing, Styxx pulled him close.

Ash didn't move as he felt Styxx's arms around him. He'd dreamed of this moment as a child in Atlantis. He'd ached for it.

The angry god inside him wanted to splinter Styxx into pieces for daring to touch him now, but that innocent part of him ... that human heart, shattered. It was the part that he listened to.

Ash wrapped his arms around his brother and held him for the first time in his memory.

"I'm so sorry," Styxx said in a ragged tone.

Ash nodded as he pulled away. "To err is human, to forgive divine."

Styxx shook his head at the quote. "I don't ask for your forgiveness. I don't deserve it. I only ask for a chance to show you now that I'm not the fool I was once."

Ash only hoped he could believe it. The odds were against them both. Every time Styxx had been given an opportunity to assuage their past, he had used it to hurt him more.

Closing his eyes, Ash teleported them out of Tartarus and into Katateros.

Stunned, Styxx pulled back to gape at the grand black marble foyer, he'd never ...

Styxx blinked slowly.

For a full minute, he was confused as his own memories finally surged past Acheron's. At first, he'd thought this room new. But he'd been here before. Centuries ago, the Atlantean gods had held him here.

Don't think about it.

Ironically, had he told them then where his brother was, the old gods would have ended an aeon of suffering for him.

As he glanced around the huge marble fountain and columns, he realized nothing had changed. It was all as perfectly preserved as it'd been when they tortured him here. A part of him swore he could even hear their laughter and jeers.

"So this is where you live," Styxx breathed, trying to keep his tone level as pain lacerated his heart.

"No." Acheron folded his arms over his chest, and indicated the tall, gilded windows that looked out over the tranquil water that stretched toward the horizon. "I live across the River Athlia, on the

720

other side of the Lypi Shores. There is no Charon to ferry you across the river to my home so don't bother looking."

He was completely baffled by that. "I don't understand."

Acheron took a step back from him and Styxx was puzzled by the suspicion he saw in his brother's silver eyes. "I will see to it that you have servants and all you could ever desire here."

"But I thought we were going to be together."

Acheron shook his head. "You made your choice and you wanted to come here. So here you are."

But this wasn't what he wanted.

Styxx tried to approach him only to find his pathway cut off by an invisible wall. "I thought you said to err is human, to forgive divine."

Those swirling, silver eyes burned him. "I'm a god, Styxx, not a saint. I do forgive you, but trusting you is another matter. As you said, you shall have to prove yourself to me. Until then, you and I will take this one step at a time and then we shall see what is to become of us."

As soon as those words were spoken, Styxx found himself alone. And the instant Acheron vanished, every single memory of Styxx's came back to him.

Full force and with complete clarity.

Contrary to his brother's thoughts, Styxx had not lived a perfect, happy life. He had not lived in luxury.

He had known pain . . .

Isolation.

Starvation and suffering.

Throwing his head back, he roared in fury. *"Damn you, Acheron!"*

He was the one who'd had pity on his brother, and now he knew exactly what Acheron had always thought of him. The horrid truth. And how wrong Acheron's thoughts were where Styxx was concerned. For three fucking years that bitch had made him live his brother's life and hold Acheron's memories of their world and past as if they were his own.

"Oh, this is rich . . . You stupid punk!"

Styxx was not the one who needed a dose of reality. Rather it was the petulant bitch-brother of his who refused to remember their childhood. At all. But then that was Estes's fault. He'd filled Acheron's mind with hatred and twisted it to the point his brother had forced himself to remember nothing other than Estes's lies.

Just as Acheron had once hated Ryssa for abandoning him. Yet somehow, Acheron had managed to forgive her and see the real truth of her actions.

But Acheron would never forgive him. He had no intention of looking any deeper than his own twisted and erroneous facts.

While Styxx had held on to those early memories of their friendship that had allowed him to feel for his brother, Acheron had locked out every one of them. He remembered nothing of the kindness Styxx had given him. Ever. None of his attempts to free him.

And now . . .

Acheron had abandoned him again. Because his brother refused to look at Styxx's life as it had really been.

Instead, Acheron judged him as everyone else had. On an assumed reality that had never existed anywhere other than inside their own jealous minds.

You are a prince and your father's beloved heir. You're rich. What problems could you possibly have?

How dare you complain, Styxx. You don't know what real suffering is. You can't imagine what the world is really like . . . .

His brother knew nothing of the years they'd lived apart. Nothing of Styxx's war career. Or Galen.

Nothing of Bethany.

Pressing the heels of his hands to his eyes, Styxx laughed as insanity claimed him.

His brother was across the river with his demon daughter and friends, and here Styxx was locked away again. With no one and nothing but memories that tore out his heart.

Take your sanctimonious indignation, Acheron, and shove it up your ass.

But all of his anger changed nothing.

Yet again, Acheron had made Styxx's situation worse. Strange how Acheron thought he could see Styxx's sins so clearly and yet he was blind to his own. In the end, Acheron was a god. He acted like all the others. He chose his pets, and the rest of humanity could burn for all he cared.

And worse, like Apollo, Apollymi, and Artemis, Acheron was capable of incredible acts of cruelty against anyone when he felt justified, right or wrong, for hating them.

That was bad enough when it was done by a human. Acheron had the powers to look into the hearts and pasts, and to see the truth. He had done it for others ... for all of his Dark-Hunter brethren.

Yet not his own brother.

Unlike a human who couldn't, Acheron *chose* not to see Styxx. That was what made it worse. That total lack of regard.

But then, Acheron was surrounded by people who kissed his ass and adored him. He had his daughter who loved him ...

And I am the king of hell.

With no one and nothing.

Οὖτις εμοί γ' ὄνομα ...

I am Nobody.

Sighing, Styxx sat on the floor and closed his eyes and thought of the only person who had ever given him comfort and love. One of only two people in his entire life who had seen him as he really was.

His Bethany.

And she had been murdered by Acheron's mother on the day the two of them were supposed to leave all this bullshit behind. If one brother had reason to hate the other, he believed he had a few legs up on Acheron.

Not that it mattered. Acheron was with his family again. Cradled next to their loving bosoms.

Meanwhile, Styxx was in his hole where Acheron would soon

forget his existence—if he hadn't already. A hole that was a lot crueler than the Vanishing Isle, because here, Styxx saw nothing but Acheron's real family using and abusing him, and laughing as they did so. It would be the same as locking Acheron back in Estes's home for eternity.

Thanks, brother. I hate you, too.

MAY 4, 2008

Styxx sighed as he secured the last plank on the small raft he'd made. Over the last few months, he'd learned that when Acheron had said Styxx had to earn his trust, what he really meant was "get out of my face and don't let me see you again."

Acheron must have reconsidered the servants and supplies because nothing had arrived since he'd been confined here.

Not a damn thing.

The only difference between this island and the Vanishing Isle was that this one didn't have predators to eat him. And while that made his world a bit safer, it also left him without much meat, and no way to make blankets or have sinew to use for bowstring and ties. Of course the twisted palm leaves could be used on his hammers and spears, but that wasn't nearly as strong or durable as leather cords.

Styxx grimaced at the blood on his hand. The really bad thing about palm leaves and trees was that they had sharp blades and spines, and he had no way to make leather gloves to protect his skin. His hands were so swollen from previous cuts that had gone to infection that he'd lost even more dexterity, especially in his right hand.

Not to mention both hands throbbed constantly.

The other thing this island lacked . . . castor beans. He had no way of making castor oil to draw out the infection. Then again, there were no beans or nuts here of any kind. His diet had been extremely limited to shellfish and coconuts. He hadn't even seen a bird, which meant no eggs.

The only good thing he could say about being here was that Apollo couldn't get to him.

Woo-fucking-hoo. At this point, he'd gladly whore himself for just a single bite of steak . . .

A drink of untainted water.

Cursing, Styxx jerked his hand back as another spine bit into the pad of his finger and left it bleeding. He put it in his mouth and sucked on it while he inspected his raft. On the Vanishing Isle, his rafts would only circle the lagoon. Any time he tried to go out farther or launch from another spot . . . or even swim out . . . winds would blow him straight back to shore.

That would probably happen here, too. But he had to find out. Besides, it wasn't like he had anything else to do . . . other than draw in the sand and watch the waves erase it.

Styxx grabbed the raft and hauled it toward the water. Grunting from the effort, he pulled against the hull. It took a few minutes to launch. Then he scrambled onto the back and grabbed his pole so that he could push it across the river. A lack of sail had never stopped him from being shoved back in Hades, but maybe here it would keep him from being turned over.

He left the lagoon and kept his gaze on the opposite shore, where Acheron made his home. At this point, he didn't care what his brother did. He just wanted to hear the sound of another human voice, even if that voice was cursing him.

To his shock and delight, he actually made it across the river. Bracing himself for the worst, he jumped into the water and pulled the raft onto the shore, out of the reach of the tide. He stored his pole then wiped the sweat from his brow. There was a huge mountain in front of him. It was Karnus, the mountain where the majority of the Atlantean gods had placed their temples.

Damn, that was a long climb.

Yeah, well, at least it's something to do that won't cut your hands. He laughed bitterly at that single truth then commenced his journey.

He didn't reach the top until well after nightfall. All the temples were dark except for the main hall where Apollo had first dumped him in front of Archon's throne.

Completely naked, Styxx had been bound in gold chains and gagged.

Archon had frowned at Apollo. "What is this?"

"My present to you. Styxx of Didymos. I was told by Athena to remove him from Olympus, and as I was doing so, I remembered you telling me during your war with Greece that you'd give anything to have him bound and tied at your feet for five minutes."

A slow, sickening smile had spread across Archon's face. "What reward do you want for this service?"

"Only the right to come and take possession of him whenever it suits me. The rest of the time, he's yours to do with as you please so long as you don't kill him."

Archon inclined his head to Apollo. "Your rights are granted."

Apollo had pulled Styxx up from the floor by his hair and forced him to kneel in submission to Archon. "In that case, have fun. Oh, you should be warned that he bites unless drugged. And if you fill him with Eycharistisi first, you'll see why he's branded as a tsoulus. He's remarkably talented when he has no control of himself." Then he'd leaned over to smell Styxx's hair.

Styxx had jerked away and glared at him.

Laughing, Apollo had sobered then licked his lips. "Don't worry, precious. I'll be back for my turn with you later." After one last grope, the god had vanished and left Styxx to the tender custody of the gods who had relished his total degradation and torture.

In that moment, Styxx truly hated Artemis and Acheron for having removed his own memories and replaced them with Acheron's while he'd been in Tartarus. If he'd been in possession of his own mind, he'd have never chosen to live here.

For Acheron, Katateros was a haven.

For him it was utter hell.

Had his thoughts not been wrapped up in Acheron's selfishness, he would have remembered how bad it'd been for him here.

How much he hated it.

But Acheron had no idea that Styxx had ever lived in this cursed place. That he knew Acheron's family much better than Acheron did.

Ready to confront his brother, Styxx started for the main doors, but the sound of laughter pulled him to the side of the building where lights shined with the brilliance of a sun. It took him a few minutes to climb up so that he could look inside and see his brother's steward, Alexion, and his wife Danger along with the Charonte demons Simi and Xirena. The four of them sat on cushions that lined the floor in front of a large-screen television, watching some show he couldn't name.

Acheron entered the room and moved to sit next to Simi while he and Alexion bantered. They looked so happy together. There had never been a time in Styxx's life when he'd been like that with his family. So relaxed and open. Laughing unrestrained.

In that moment, he remembered all the times he'd listened to Ryssa and Acheron laughing through the walls of his room while he'd been left alone.

Or worse, while he'd been forced to "entertain" Apollo to the sounds of their friendly reverie.

Climbing down, he leaned back against the stone building and tried to calm his ragged breaths. A part of him wanted to go in just to disturb their happiness. One look at him and they'd all stop laughing.

But he didn't want to intrude.

He didn't belong there. He wasn't part of Acheron's family.

Bending his knees, Styxx braced his arm across them so that he could see Bethany and Galen's names in the moonlight. How he missed sitting with her while she told him stories about her own family and how much they loved her. How her father would take her hunting, and how her mother lived for their girl-time excursions.

Styxx closed his eyes and let the agony of her loss keep him company for a little while as their laughter continued to reach his ears. He brushed his fingers against his cheek and pretended it was Bethany's delicate, beautiful hand that touched him. But his hands were coarse, cut, and swollen. Callused. They weren't the refined, soft hands of his gentle wife.

Tears filled his eyes as he missed her with every part of his being.

Trying to distract himself from something he couldn't change, Styxx glanced about the dark temples until he saw the one that had belonged to the goddess of wrath and misery. He still didn't know what all she'd done to him while he'd been there with her. Those memories had never returned.

But she had been nicer to him than the rest of her pantheon. Unlike the other buildings around him, that one held no horrible reminders of his time here.

Before he realized what he was doing, he headed for it. Though it was dark, the full moon cast enough light that he could see a great deal. Like the hall Acheron had dumped him in, it was pristine. It appeared as if she'd return any moment to reclaim it.

He went straight to the back, where the bathing pool was. The room was just as he remembered. He glanced to the white chaise where she had sat, watching him. As he headed toward it, he saw the tray of salts and lotions she'd place by the side of the pool for his use.

Kneeling down, he lifted the lids and froze as he caught a whiff of Bethany's eucalyptus and lilies. But then this had been her patron goddess. It made sense that she'd use fragrances sacred to Agriosa.

He started to put it back, but he couldn't. He wanted to keep it with him for a little while.

His gaze went to the room where the goddess had taken him to sleep. Cradling the small urn that smelled like Bethany, he headed for it and pushed the door open to see the same huge bed with red curtains that she'd tucked him into. Her symbol—a woman holding a bow—hung on the wall above it.

Against his will, he crossed the room and set the urn on the small table by the bed. He wondered if Agriosa had died at the same time Bethany had. Or if Apollymi had killed the blond god-dess of wrath before then.

Not that it mattered. Both were gone and neither had deserved what Apollymi had done to them.

Styxx pulled the covers back and slid into the soft bed ... it'd been years since he last slept on a mattress. He buried his face into the pillow that smelled so much like Bethany that it made his eyes water all over again. *I would give anything to wake up in your arms.*

To feel her hand in his hair.

A sad smile curved his lips as he remembered her irritation when he'd all but shaved his head after Apollo and his father had used his hair to savage him one time too many. If not for her, he'd have never grown it out again.

But as much as he hated his hair, she'd loved to play in it and would spend hours at night twirling the strands around her fingers. Even when she slept, she reached out for it.

"Why do you enjoy my hair so?"

"It fascinates me. You're so hard everywhere else, but your lips and hair are like the down of a duckling. And I love the waves in it, and how good it smells. Grow it to your knees and I'll knit a sweater from it. Then I could have it with me all the time."

"If I did that, Beth, you'd have no use for me. I might never see you again."

She'd let out a heavy sigh. *"Damn, you're on to me. Guess I'll never get that sweater now. I shall be stuck with you forever. Oh, the absolute horror of it all."*

He'd laughed at her teasing.

Styxx clutched at the pillow as a sob choked him. It ever seemed his fate to lose the ones he loved, and then be stuck with something unsubstantial to hold on to that reminded him of them. Closing his eyes, he let the agony of it all wash over him. All he'd ever wanted was what Acheron had always taken for granted.

A single family member who loved him.

One.

As a boy, Acheron had held Styxx's love and loyalty, as well as

729

Ryssa's. Acheron had always had Ryssa's heart, for that matter. While Styxx had been left with her wrath and rancor.

Over the centuries while Styxx had languished alone, Acheron had raised his Charonte daughter and been protected by Savitar, and Acheron's army of Dark-Hunters who loved and adored him. For almost eight thousand years, Acheron had Alexion here as his steward and brother.

It was so unfair.

"Listen to me, boy. Fair has no place in this world. Only infants whine about fairness. Men have more important battles to fight . . . And life, like war, is neither right nor wrong. It just is. And rather than worry over a philosophy you can't change, you should just try to live through it as best you can."

Galen was right and he knew it. But it didn't make it easier to bear.

"I can't keep living like this."

After all the sins he'd committed, Acheron had found his place in the world and managed to have a decent life . . .

Other than having to continue to deal with Artemis and her tantrums. Styxx didn't envy his brother that. But at least it wasn't as demeaning and brutal as Styxx's relationship with Apollo. While Artemis was difficult, she did love Acheron. She'd birthed him a daughter she treasured above all others. Yes, she was harsh on Acheron, but she could also be kind. She had never treated his brother with the same acrimony, disdain, and cruelty that Apollo had shown Styxx.

Never once had she passed Acheron around or shared him with others. She didn't hold him down and choke him until he was almost dead and then revive him so that he'd know how fragile he was compared to a god.

Worse, Apollo took out his hatred for Acheron and Artemis's relationship on Styxx, too. Every time Acheron had offended Apollo, he'd come straight to Styxx to beat him for it as if it was somehow his fault.

And since he'd been given Acheron's memories, he knew all that for a fact. Ironically, he didn't see Artemis the same way his brother did. She attacked Acheron out of fear.

Apollo attacked him out of rage and utmost hatred.

While they both sucked, Styxx could have handled Artemis's wrath a lot easier since it only came out whenever Acheron said or did something to scare her. There was no way to gauge Apollo's trigger. He was angry when Styxx fought him and he was twice as angry when he didn't. Unlike Artemis, there was no love in Apollo to mitigate his attacks. No guilt that came later that made him want to make amends.

Apollo was simply a bully. He loved his power over others and he savored every ounce of pain he could wring out of someone.

Indeed, Artemis had never joyfully laughed in Acheron's ear when she hurt him or punched him with her fists.

"That's it, prince. Scream out for me. Let me hear your agony! Beg me for my mercy!"

The first lesson he'd learned when dealing with Apollo—don't do what he said. The more he begged for mercy, the less the god gave it to him.

Just like Acheron. His brother had never intended for him to be free any more than Artemis had.

Out of sight, out of mind.

That was all Styxx was left with.

OCTOBER 1, 2008

"Who are you?"

Styxx paused at the angry male voice that was thick with an ancient Delphian accent. He turned around in the pool to see an extremely tall, well-built man with white blond hair he wore pulled back into a queue.

Urian.

He remembered him from Acheron's memories. This was Stryker's son who would have died by Stryker's hand had Acheron not saved his life. At one time, Urian had been the most vicious of killers and an enemy to Acheron and his Dark-Hunters. A Daimon, he had stood to the right-hand of his father and helped slaughter countless humans. But now, thanks to Acheron, Urian no longer needed human souls to survive.

These days, Urian was Acheron's second-in-command, and one of his best friends.

And as Styxx watched the man, there was something strangely familiar about him. Something he knew intimately.

That's because he's the direct grandson of Apollo.

Yeah, that would probably be it.

"I asked you a question," Urian snarled. "Do you not understand me?"

"I heard you."

"And?"

Styxx climbed out of the pool and reached for a towel. He quickly dried himself off then wrapped it around his hips before he closed the distance between them. "Ask me when you find a new tone. One with respect in it."

The way Urian arched his brow and cocked his head froze him to the spot. It was similar to a movement Bethany used to make whenever she was really cross with him. How weird to see that expression on a stranger, and a male one at that.

"You must be Styxx."

"So you're not as stupid as you look."

Urian started to comment until his gaze focused on Styxx's body. "Damn, you're scarred up."

"Aren't we all?"

Urian didn't comment on that. "I was told you'd been put on one of the other islands."

"I was."

"Then why are you here?"

732

Styxx picked up another towel to dry his hair. "I liked this one better."

"Are you always this big an asshole?"

"Are you?"

"Basically, yes. However, I thought I'd tempered it for you. Guess I'm an even bigger ass than I knew."

Styxx laughed at Urian's unexpected honesty. "Then I'd hate to see you on a bad day if this is a good one."

"Yeah, well, according to Ash I pretty much get on his nerves every ten minutes."

"It takes you an entire ten minutes? I'm impressed. All I have to do is enter his line of sight to wreck his whole year."

Urian smiled then indicated Styxx's scars with a tilt of his head. "You must have been a soldier who saw a lot of combat for those."

"I was . . . and I did."

"Cavalry?"

"Protostratelates."

Urian's eyes bugged. "At your . . . ? Oh wait, wait a minute. Styxx . . . Styxx of Didymos, Styxx?"

He nodded.

Urian sputtered incredulously. "How stupid do I feel? I never put the two names together before. Mostly because I assumed the protostratelates who damn near defeated Atlantis was an old man. Oh wow . . . " he breathed. "You were a legend. When I was a kid, I extensively studied your surviving war notes, and reports, and everything written about you. Your tactics fascinated me, but there was so much left out."

"I didn't want someone to use my strategies against me."

"As I said, brilliant, and if you knew me, you'd know I gush over no one." Urian held his arm out. "This is really an honor."

Styxx hesitated then shook it. "So how old are you . . . really?"

"I was born a few weeks before you and Acheron died. And before you condemn me, I mostly lived on people who deserved to die."

"Mostly?"

733

Urian shrugged. "Sometimes you can't be picky. But I never fed from a human woman or child. Or anyone who couldn't fight back."

Styxx held his hands up. "I'm in no position to judge anyone for how they survive."

A deep scowl furrowed Urian's brow. "It's strange though."

"What is?"

"How much you and Acheron favor not to be related at all."

Sighing, Styxx dropped his second towel then finger-combed his short blond hair. "Trick of his mother's to throw off the gods looking for him."

"She did well. I had a fraternal twin brother myself."

"Had?"

"He was killed a long time ago by a Dark-Hunter."

"Oh, I'm very sorry."

Urian inclined his head to him. "Thanks. Me, too. It's hard to lose a brother, and twice as hard when you're born together. Kind of like losing a limb."

Styxx would definitely agree with that. "In my case, more like losing a sphincter."

Urian laughed. "What happened between you? I mean, damn, Acheron forgave me, and I definitely didn't deserve a second chance. You don't seem like an outright bastard, and you definitely didn't battle like one. Things you did ... you protected your enemy against your own troops. And you were barbecued for it by Greek historians and commanders."

"I was barbecued for it by many people."

Urian followed him from the pool into the bedroom. "So how old were you when you first went into battle? Five?"

"Sixteen." Styxx picked his clothes up and went behind a screen to dress.

"Damn, that was harsh. My father refused to let us near battle until we were past our majority. He waited so long, it was actually embarrassing." Urian took a step back and gestured toward the door. "Would you like to come up to the main hall with me? Dinner should be about ready."

He would love to, but he knew better.

Styxx shook his head as he came around the screen. "I'm not welcome there. Acheron would have a fit to find me in his temple."

Sadness darkened Urian's eyes. "Don't worry. I won't tell boss-man you're here. Stay as long as you want."

"Thanks, Urian." Styxx went to hang his towels up to dry.

"Hey?" Urian called. "Would you like me to bring you some dinner?"

"Gods, yes, I'd kill for some." Those rushed, heartfelt words were out before he could stop them. Embarrassed by the emotion he'd betrayed, he cleared his throat. "Yes, please. I'd appreciate it."

"I'll be back as soon as I can."

Styxx stared after him for a few minutes as it dawned on him that Urian was barely older than his son Galen would have been. The two of them could have played together and gone to war as friends.

That knowledge made him strangely protective of a man who was physically older than he was. And while Urian wasn't quite as tall as Styxx, he was more muscular. How weird. The boy would be highly offended if he ever learned Styxx was protective of him.

Trying not to think about it, Styxx went to finish his chores before it got too dark to see.

A few hours later, he was pulling out his dried clams to eat with coconut milk when Urian returned with a backpack that he set on the table beside Styxx.

He frowned at Styxx's dinner. "What *is* that?"

Styxx shrugged then returned the clams to the urn where he stored them.

Urian's scowl deepened as he tipped the chipped clay cup to see the coconut milk in it. "Ew! Really? You were really going to drink this shit?"

"ἀνάγκᾳ δ ' οὐδὲ θεοὶ ἄχονται," Styxx said simply.

Urian laughed. "Not even the gods fight necessity . . . nice. You said that to your men right before the battle for Ena."

"Did I?"

735

"You don't remember?" Urian paused as he set out a bowl of something Styxx had never seen before, but it smelled wonderful.

"Honestly, no, and I can't really take credit for it. It was something my mentor used to say to me all the time."

"And what would he say about this?" Urian held up a bottle of wine.

"Brôma theôn." Food of the gods.

Urian handed it to him then dug out the opener and two glasses. "I'm going to hazard a wild guess that you're a little short on supplies. Would you like me to bring you something?"

"I can make do, but some fresh water would be nice. It doesn't rain here, and it doesn't get quite hot enough to make a lot of condensation. It's been difficult to desalinate the river water, which I can't figure out why it's salty . . . " But it was. And there weren't any streams or ponds that he'd been able to locate.

Urian scowled. "Why didn't you stay where your supplies were?"

Styxx dug a fork out of the backpack and sat down to eat the . . . strangest food he'd ever seen. It was like white worms only really long and coated in some kind of red sauce. "I haven't received any."

Urian was aghast. "What have you been living on?"

Closing his eyes, Styxx savored the unfamiliar taste. It was even warm . . . He swallowed and wiped his mouth before he answered. "Clams mostly . . . whenever I can find them. Coconuts. Some greens I discovered out back." He took a drink of wine then sighed at how good it tasted. The last time he'd had this was years ago in New Orleans.

He felt Urian staring at him. "What?"

"Nothing."

It wasn't until then that Styxx realized Urian was one of the few people whose thoughts he couldn't hear. He had no clue what the man was thinking.

Urian grabbed the backpack up. "I'll be back in a few minutes, okay?"

Styxx nodded as he kept eating the ... "Urian? What's this called?"

"Spaghetti."

"It's really good. Thank you."

"Parakaló."

Once Styxx finished, he washed out the bowl and dried it then took his wine to the pool. He didn't know why he liked to stay in this room. There was just something about it that soothed him.

Rolling up his pants leg, he saw that the fabric was starting to fray. He needed to be more careful washing it and wearing it. Since there wasn't anything here to replace it with or animals to use for pelts, he'd have to make it last. He dipped his feet into the pool and sat alone in the silence.

He'd just finished off his wine when Urian returned.

"Is this what you do at night?"

Styxx got up and pulled his jeans down. "There's nothing else to do, really. Sometimes I go outside and stare at the moon."

"You must get a lot of sleep."

"Not really." Even now, he couldn't sleep through a night.

"How are you not crazy?"

Styxx snorted. "Who says I'm not?"

Urian released an elongated breath. "I couldn't take three days of this boredom without being stark-raving mad."

"As far as prisons go, trust me, this isn't so bad. No one's sticking hot brands on me or beating me, and I'm not chained to anything or drugged. Best of all, I don't have to bend myself in half to lie down."

"When were you a prisoner?"

Styxx laughed bitterly. "Honestly? In the whole of my extremely long life, I've only spent roughly a high grand total of fourteen years where I wasn't imprisoned for one reason or another."

"Imprisoned for what?"

"Being born Acheron's brother ... well, except for when Apollo and the Atlanteans held me here. That was entirely my fault. Turns out, gods don't like it when humans defeat them and invade their homelands. Who knew?"

Styxx swung his arm around the room. "Did you know this temple belonged to Bet'anya Agriosa ... the Atlantean goddess of misery and wrath? The next temple on the right belonged to Epithymia, their goddess of desire. She was a royal fucking bitch. Vicious. Cold. Lived to hurt others. It always made me wonder if Aphrodite was anything like her." Styxx paused as he caught the expression on Urian's face. "Sorry. I'm not used to having anyone to talk to."

Urian wasn't sure what to make of Styxx. From what little Acheron had mentioned of his brother, he'd expected some arrogant, demanding prick who looked at the people around him like they were dirt.

The man in front of him was definitely not the brother Acheron had described. There was no arrogance in him. He had a very quiet, suspicious nature. He reminded Urian more of the gators that called the swamps home in Louisiana.

Styxx kept his eyes on everything around him, assessing each corner and shadow as a possible threat. Though he seemed to be at ease, there was no doubt he could launch himself at your throat and roll you under for the kill before you even saw him move.

Yeah, Urian could easily see in Styxx the legendary general he'd read about. The one who didn't complain over anything and who had sacrificed and sold his own personal effects to buy supplies for his men. Just the physical scars on his body alone made a mockery of the person Acheron thought him to be.

This was not some pampered prince who'd been waited on hand and foot, and who expected the entire world to bow down to him. In over eleven thousand years, Urian had never seen any man more scarred. Even Styxx's fingers and the backs of his hands said he'd lived a hard and harsh life. For that matter, Styxx barely had the use of his right hand. Two of his fingers, the pinkie and ring, stayed curled against his palm. And the other two didn't fully extend.

More remarkably still, there were just four scars on his face. And one of them was only noticeable if you paid close attention. He had a faint scar beneath his left eye. One that ran along his hairline across his forehead that was covered by his hair most of the time. One that slashed across his right eyebrow, and the one in the center of his upper lip where it'd been forcefully busted open so many times that it'd left a permanent divot and thick vertical line.

The awful condition of Styxx's body verified what he'd said about captivity. As did his knowledge of the temples. There was nothing left inside any of the buildings to say who they belonged to and not even Acheron knew.

But Styxx did.

And what really screwed with Urian's head was the fact that Styxx had been imprisoned for more than eleven thousand years. Alone. It was mind-blowing. He would call the man a liar for that, but again, the scars and his calm acceptance of Acheron dumping him here and forgetting about him testified to the fact that Styxx was more than used to isolation and neglect. More than used to scrounging for scraps to eat.

And all Styxx had asked for was drinking water.

He still couldn't believe how humble a request that was.

"I brought you more food," Urian said, trying to break the sudden awkward silence.

"It wasn't necessary."

"Having seen the shit you had on your plate when I brought in the spaghetti, I'm going to respectfully disagree." Urian headed back to the other room and didn't miss the fact that Styxx kept a lot of empty space between them. He also walked at an angle so that he could see if Urian was reaching for a weapon.

The way Styxx did it, it was hardwired into him. That, too, made a mockery of the pampered prince bullshit.

Styxx froze as he saw the abundance of food Urian had brought in a large plastic box. "Bread?" he whispered, awed by the precious sight of it.

"Yeah, that's the white stuff in the plastic bag."

His mouth watered at the thought of tasting bread again . . .

Urian stepped back so that Styxx would look through the box and see what else it contained.

Styxx's heart raced in excitement at the glorious amount of food. It'd been thousands of years since he'd last had a surplus like this. A lot of it, he had no idea what it was. But it was food . . . Peanut butter. Beef jerky. Deviled ham . . .

Why would ham be possessed?

It didn't matter. He'd eat it anyway.

Styxx jerked his hand back as he touched a bag of apples. For a full minute, he couldn't breathe as he saw himself as a boy in his room.

"Here, brother." Then Acheron would roll one through the hole in the wall for him to catch it.

His throat tightened as he moved his hand away and put the items back into the box to cover the apples. "Thank you."

Urian picked up another box that he'd set on the floor. "I have your water and more wine in this one. And I put candles and a lighter in here, too."

Styxx placed the lid on top of the box. "Thank you, but I won't need those."

"It's really dark in here."

Styxx shrugged. "I'm used to it. Besides, if Acheron sees a light, there's no telling how he'll react, and I don't want to fight with him. Most of all, I don't want him to take away what little freedom I have."

Or confine me in a temple where they raped and beat me.

"Okay. I'll . . . um . . . I'll bring more food after tomorrow."

Styxx smiled at Urian. "Careful, you keep this up and I won't have anything to occupy myself with."

Urian's phone rang. Excusing himself, he pulled it out and turned it on. "Hey, Cass, is everything all right?"

Styxx heard a woman on the other end as she asked Urian to come stay for a few days in a place he'd never heard of before.

"Sure. I don't mind babysitting. You know that. I love your rugrats . . . Yeah, see you soon. Love you, too." He hung up.

"Your wife?" Styxx made the most natural assumption given the love he'd heard in Urian's voice as he spoke to her.

"My wife's sister."

"Ah. So does your wife live in the main temple with you?"

Urian reached to touch the necklace he wore in a manner that reminded Styxx of how he used to caress Bethany's necklace on his wrist. "No. She died."

"I am extremely sorry. I know how hard that is."

"I appreciate it, but I had a very special bond with my Phoebe. And she was killed when I should have been there to protect her."

Styxx swallowed hard as his own tears rose up to choke him. "I do know your pain, Urian. My wife was murdered by Acheron's mother while she was pregnant with our first child. And I have absolutely nothing left of them, except my memories."

Urian's gaze fell to his arm. "Bethany and Galen?"

He nodded. "I had no other way to honor them. I never even got to see their bodies." He cleared his throat. "You need to go to your family. Don't keep them waiting."

"What about you?"

Styxx laughed. "I assure you, I'll be here when you get back."

Urian gave him an ancient salute that Styxx quickly returned then left to head up the hill. But with every step he took, he had a strange feeling. Like he knew Styxx from somewhere. The man was so familiar to him.

He is Acheron's twin.

There was that.

And it wasn't like you didn't obsess over him as a kid or anything. He laughed as he remembered his father banning him from even saying Styxx's name in his presence.

"If I hear you speak of that Didymosian bastard one more time, Urian, I will beat you until you can't sit down. And stop dressing like him! He was an enemy to Atlantis and Apollymi."

For that matter, Urian had Styxx's phoenix emblem tattooed on his biceps. Best not to ever let him see that, though. It might freak him out. But then Urian was used to keeping it covered. It'd been another thing that had enraged his father.

Urian paused to look back at the dark temple. Had he not been out for a walk earlier and heard the faint splashing, he'd have never known Styxx was in there. And he'd almost ignored it and kept going. Only his centuries of heightened nerves and incessant need to check and lock down his perimeter had caused him to investigate the foreign noise.

As he resumed the path to the main hall, he couldn't understand Acheron's reasoning where Styxx was concerned. Having lost all his brothers, he'd give anything to see one of them again. Even Archimedes, who'd bullied and shoved him to the point Urian had wanted to rip his heart out. The two of them could barely be in a room that they didn't walk out bruised from the unfortunate event.

Yet even so, he'd welcome that asshole back if he could.

"Dang, Ash. Who in their right mind throws out a perfectly good brother?"

NOVEMBER 1, 2008

Styxx sighed in his sleep as he felt a gentle hand in his hair. Chills shook him while the scent of Bethany filled his head.

"Beth?" he breathed, opening his eyes. He rolled over then jumped away as he saw a very tiny auburn-haired woman who bore no resemblance to Bethany at all.

She pulled back with an equal amount of wariness.

It took Styxx a minute to find her in Acheron's memories. Her name was Danger. A former Dark-Hunter who'd died, she was the female spirit who had married Alexion. The two of them lived in Acheron's temple and kept it for him.

"You must be . . ."—*the monster*—"Styxx."

He'd heard her catch loud and clear. "You should be going."

She tsked at him. "I kept wondering where my food was vanishing off to. Any idea how hard it is to keep a Charonte stocked in Ding Dongs when half the stash gets confiscated?"

He pulled the blankets higher to keep himself covered from her curious gaze. Her eyes widened as she saw the scars on his arms, hands, and upper chest.

"I didn't mean to startle you. Who's Beth?"

"My wife . . . was my wife."

She frowned. "I didn't know you were married. Acheron never mentioned that. Beth isn't a Greek name, is it?"

"She was Egyptian."

Danger cocked her head to study his forearm. "And Galen?"

"You read Greek?"

"My husband's Greek. Not quite as old as you, but definitely not modern. Since he loves his native language so much, I learned it . . . So who's Galen?"

"Galen was my son."

Her frown deepened. "I thought Acheron's nephew was Apollodorus."

"He was Ryssa's son, not mine."

"Oh . . ." *Why did Ash never mention he had another nephew?*

Styxx barely caught himself before he responded to her thought.

"Why are you here?" she asked.

"I was sleeping."

She rolled her eyes. "You know what I mean."

Get out was what she meant. He'd overstayed his welcome. Besides, if Acheron learned of his presence, there was no telling what he might do to him given his hatred. "I'll go back to my island. Sorry I disturbed you. I'll tell Urian not to bring me any more food." He glanced meaningfully to his clothes that were set on the table behind her as he lifted his sheet higher. "But I can't leave until you allow me to dress."

"I wasn't telling you to leave or to stop getting food. I was teasing about that."

"Oh. I'm not used to being teased."

"Are you all right?"

No, he wasn't. Styxx choked on the grief and sadness that her kindness evoked. He hadn't interacted with a woman like this since Beth. Nor had any woman touched him like that since the day she'd left to go to Egypt. And as bad as the memories had been, having awakened to Danger rammed the full weight of his loss down his throat.

"Fine," he breathed. But he wasn't fine. He hadn't been for thousands of years.

She moved to touch him.

Styxx flinched away from her. "Please don't." It hurt too much for a woman to be this close to him, and for her to lay her hand on his skin . . .

He'd rather have the priests and their hot brands.

Finally, she stepped back from the bed. "Would you like for me to make you breakfast while you dress?"

"Thank you, but I don't want you to trouble yourself."

"It's no trouble. Trust me. You'll be a lot easier to feed than two Charonte. It'll be waiting on you when you finish." She vanished before he could thank her again.

Danger paused by the boxes of foodstuffs as she glanced back to the room where she'd found Styxx. Acheron had ordered her to stay away from him. He'd been emphatic that she not go near Styxx's island.

But why?

He wasn't the monster Acheron had made him out to be. He was actually rather polite and bashful. Hardly the cocky asshole Acheron and Alexion called him.

She smiled as she saw the way he'd organized his food. Everything was meticulously placed, but then that made sense since he didn't have a lot to occupy himself with.

What did he do all day? There were no books, instruments, or anything of that nature. He had a small collection of handmade weapons and tools. And one really lovely bowl that had been carved out of stone.

She let out a low whistle as she ran her hand over the smooth surface. "You are incredibly talented." He'd even chiseled out a Greek key pattern around the edge of it.

Her smile faded as she realized his food consisted of nothing but Doomsday prep items. Everything was designed to be reconstituted or was dried, with a few fresh vegetables and fruits.

And one box of Simi's Ding Dongs.

"This is not meal worthy." She flashed herself back to the kitchen where she and Alexion cooked for Simi and Xirena, and Urian whenever he was home. As quickly as she could, she fried Styxx two eggs and some bacon and made a small stack of pancakes. Grabbing a glass of milk, she returned to him.

She'd just set it out on the table when he came through the door and paused.

His eyes lit up like Simi's whenever they had Diamonique on QVC. "Eggs and bacon?"

"Yes."

Even though he didn't smile, the joy in those electric blue eyes warmed her. But he didn't come any closer. Curious about that, she stepped away from the table.

Only when she was out of reach did he move to sit.

"It smells delicious. Thank you. I can't remember the last time I tasted eggs or bacon."

When he went to eat the pancakes like bread, she stopped him. "They're pancakes."

"Okay." He folded it to eat.

She bit back her smile. "It's not a pita, sweetie. You put syrup on it and cut it up."

He frowned as if he had no idea what she was talking about. "Syrup?"

They must not have had that in his day. She lifted the small container.

His scowl deepened. "Dark honey?"

745

"No. It's sweet like honey, but it's maple syrup." She poured it over the pancakes for him.

He hesitated before he tried it then he flashed a grin at her. "Who wants Ding Dongs when they can eat this?"

She laughed at his unexpected enthusiasm.

Then he lifted the milk and sniffed it. "Cow?"

"Um ... yeah." What did he think it was?

His expression said it was ambrosia to him. He took a deep drink. "I haven't had cow milk since ... I can't even remember."

Danger watched him. It was so disconcerting to see someone who looked so similar to Acheron and yet was so different. And as she studied him, she realized his short hair was really butchered and uneven.

Like he cut it with one of his handmade stone knives.

"Do you cut your own hair?"

He set his fork down and touched it self-consciously. "I'm sorry if it offends you. I don't have shears."

"It doesn't offend me. If you like, I could even it up for you."

His mood was much more somber as he returned to eating. "It doesn't matter. No one will see it."

Tears gathered in her eyes at his stoic tone. "I really don't mind. I cut Alexion's all the time."

Styxx considered it. He could only imagine how awful his hair must look to her, but honestly, he didn't want her touching him. "It's all right. I don't want to be any more trouble." He got up to wash his plate.

"Here," she said, holding her hand out. "I'll take it."

He hesitated before he gave it to her. "Thank you for your kindness. The food was delicious, and I really appreciate the gift."

Her heart aching for him, Danger inclined her head. "You're very welcome." Gathering up the dishes, she returned to the main hall.

"Where have you been?"

She paused as Alexion joined her in the kitchen. "I met Styxx."

He growled deep in his throat.

She held her hand up to stop him from saying a word. "Have you ever met the man?"

"Of course not. He's an arrogant asshole."

"Before you start trash-talking his character, sweetie, you should meet him. Believe me, I understand loyalty to Acheron. I have it, too, and I know what I owe the big guy. However, Styxx isn't the three-horned demon you think he is either. Did you know he had a wife and child?"

Alexion looked as stunned as she'd been. "No."

"What are we talking about?" Urian asked as he joined them. "Do I smell bacon?"

She sighed irritably. "Teach a Daimon to eat real food and he's impossible." She went to make more for him. "We were talking about your houseguest you didn't mention feeding."

Urian's eyes widened. "Um . . . "

"Don't worry. You're not in trouble. I was just telling Alexion that I think there's a lot more to him than we've been told."

Urian nodded. "No shit, right? You know who he is?" he asked Alexion.

He gave Urian a droll stare. "Acheron's brother."

One Urian returned full force. "You ever heard of the Stygian Omada?"

"I'm Groesian. Of course I've heard of it. Who hasn't?"

Danger looked up from the frying bacon. "Well, I'm French and confused. What's the Stygian Armada—"

"Stygian O . . . mada," Urian repeated.

"They were a legendary army that waged war against Atlantis," Alexion explained. "In all of Greek history, it was the only army that ever fought on Atlantean soil and won. They were practically on the main steps of the palace when they were called back to Greece for peace talks."

"Yeah." Urian jerked his chin in the direction of the temple where Styxx was staying. "And brother Styxx was their general the army was named for."

"Bullshit!" Alexion roared in denial.

"No. Real. I saw the battle scars on him myself. Ash has always said he was from Atlantis. He's never mentioned the Greek city-state he was born in so I didn't know ... But Styxx is Styxx of Didymos."

Alexion gaped. "You're shitting me."

Urian shook his head sarcastically.

"Again, French Revolution here. *Les Mis,* I get. This ... " She wagged the spatula. "My extent of Greek history is *Troy* with Brad Pitt and," she looked over at Alexion, "Mr. Luscious in his armor."

Alexion went bug-eyed. "Please don't call me that in front of Urian."

Urian laughed then sobered and explained it to her. "Didymos was the Athens of its day, and Athens was not much more than a big village back then. The largest and strongest of the Greek city-states, Didymos was two border islands that buffered the rest of Greece from Atlantis. And Styxx was the greatest, most successful general in their long and prestigious military history. His battle tactics and the way he ran his army were studied extensively by the soldiers of my time. We all wanted to grow up and be him. In fact, the way he trained, and the principles his mentor taught him were the foundation of the Spartans and their military ethics. That's how good he was. But in all my readings about Didymos and Styxx, I never saw more than one prince mentioned ... Him. And nothing of a princess in anything, not that that was unusual." He held his hand up to Danger to stop her before she spoke. "And don't lecture me on ancient stupidity and their treatment of women ... I am not personally responsible for misogynistic ancient writers just because I happen to be male."

He looked back at Alexion and resumed their discussion. "Because of that, and the fact that he and Ash were babies when they died, I never made the connection that Acheron's brother Styxx was the leader of the famed Stygian League."

Alexion snorted. "That explains his arrogance."

"But he's not arrogant," Urian and Danger said simultaneously.

"Yeah," Urian said, grabbing a slice of bacon, "what she said."

748

She put more bacon on a plate for Urian. "He's sweet, Alexion. Really sweet."

Swallowing his bacon, Urian snorted. "I would not use that word myself for him. He's lethal and you can't miss it, but I'll be honest. I'd call Ash arrogant before I would Styxx."

Alexion sucked his breath in sharply. "Don't let Acheron hear you say that."

"I know. Believe me." Urian sighed heavily. "Man, I don't know what happened between them, but it's a damn shame. Can you imagine having Styxx of Didymos train you to fight?"

"Be like taking lessons from Achilles or Alexander the Great."

"That settles it then," Danger said as she put the uncooked bacon back in the refrigerator.

"What?" Urian asked.

"We've got to reconcile them."

Alexion burst out laughing. "That is a pipe dream, honey. I've known Acheron for over nine thousand years. And it will be freezing on the equator before Acheron forgives Styxx for what he did."

She shrugged. "Well, you know what they say—"

Urian passed a knowing stare to Alexion. "We who are about to die, salute you?"

She rolled her eyes. "No. Over, under, around, or through, there's always a way."

Urian scoffed at her optimism. "Unless the rock falls on you while you're trying to go under it. Then you're toast."

Alexion laughed. "Well, she is French."

NOVEMBER 2, 2008

Styxx lay in bed, staring up at the ceiling. One of the neatest parts about Agriosa's temple was the way moonlight reflected in through the windows to cast shadows around the room. Or maybe he was so bored as to see images where there weren't any.

The one on the ceiling right now reminded him of his phoenix emblem.

Yeah, he was definitely imagining things.

Sighing, he reached over to the table and pulled the bath salts to him. He took a small amount and rubbed them across his face so that he could smell Bethany's scent and pretend for one moment that she was by his side. In his mind, he could see her in her white dance outfit as she twirled and danced for him with her veils.

She'd tried to tie one to his wrist once, and he'd panicked so badly that it had scared her. But if he could have that one afternoon back, he'd gladly let her chain him to her bed.

His breathing ragged, he was so hard and aching—so damn horny, he couldn't stand it. He pressed his hand to his swollen cock, wishing he could go back in time and change things.

He should have thrown her over his shoulder and run away with her like a caveman on the first day they met.

"I need you, Beth," he whispered. She had always been the better part of him.

No, the best part.

Holding on to an image of her, he slowly thrust himself against his hand. But as he tried to find release, other memories surged to replace the tender ones of Bethany.

Fucking Greek whore!

Piece of Ariclean shit!

Tell me how much of a hero do you feel like now that you're facedown with my cock in your ass, huh, prince?

Styxx bellowed in agony as he shot from the bed. Why couldn't the voices of the past leave him alone? Why?

Unable to stand it, he ran to the pool and threw himself into it, hoping to drown out the voices that haunted him. As fast and furious as he could, he swam laps until his body was exhausted. Only when he was on the verge of collapse did he find any kind of peace.

His arms trembling from overuse, he pulled himself out of the water and lay on the frigid marble floor. Breathing heavily, he looked up at the ceiling where he saw the image of an Atlantean soldier in armor standing next to a woman who held his hoplon. She had her hand on his arm as they gazed silently at each other.

As he stared at it, he remembered the story of Bathymaas and Aricles that he'd been told in Atlantis. Perhaps that was the curse of his family. Their entire house had been founded on pain. On a woman's broken heart.

Now that he thought about it, none of his paternal relatives had ever had a happy marriage. After birthing his father, uncle, and aunt, his grandmother had taken her daughter and returned to her native Athens to never set foot again in Didymos, or see her husband.

He didn't even want to contemplate the misery of his parents' marriage. The death of his father's first wife while in the middle of labor . . .

It made him wonder why his ancestor had assumed his brother's name for their royal house. Surely he'd known the curse that name carried.

The House of Aricles had been founded on tragedy and they'd ended in tragedy. Condemned by the gods from beginning to end. But at least Bathymaas's father had been kind. He'd taken her memories and had allowed her to live without the knowledge of her loss.

Turning his head, Styxx stared at the scar on his right hand where the Thracian had speared it to the ground. He could still see the insane, inhuman hatred in the man's eyes. "For all the lives you've taken . . ."

Maybe Galen had been right when he talked about the death of his son, Philip. Styxx didn't deserve to be happy after all the men he'd killed in battle. He'd deprived them of their futures and families.

Just as he'd deprived Acheron of his place as firstborn.

Perhaps this was justice, after all.

NOVEMBER 2, 2008

Artemis gasped as Apollo appeared in her temple on Olympus. "What are you doing here?"

"What do you think?"

She had no idea. Other than he was an ass and she was tired of dealing with him. "I've already fed you." Her neck still throbbed from his vicious bite. "You should be sated for a while."

He gave her a peeved glare. "Not what I'm here for. What is the disturbance I'm feeling from Atlantis?"

Oh, that . . .

"I have it under control. There was a group of archaeologists who uncovered a few items. But I've had them arrested and my Atlantikoinonia are on it to make sure they find nothing else."

Apollo arched a brow. "And what did they find?"

Artemis sighed as she stood up from her chaise. "Eleven thousand years later and your human whore is still causing grief for us. It's one of those stupid journals she kept."

Apollo cursed. "Which one?"

"One that details a few secrets about you and me that neither of us wants exposed." She rubbed at her bruised neck to illustrate her point. The other held the true identity of their mother and origins.

Anger flared in his eyes, flashing them to red. "And where is your pet?"

"Acheron? He's off pouting . . . and seeking the journal himself. He doesn't want his secrets exposed any more than we do."

"Where's his human half? And don't tell me Styxx is dead. I'm still furious with you for having hidden the prince from me for so long."

Artemis shrugged nonchalantly. "He's on Katateros, and I don't think you want to go there to get him, brother." Acheron hated Apollo as much as she did. If her brother dared to step one foot in Acheron's home, he'd tear him apart.

Rage darkened his eyes. "The prince is my property and I want him returned."

She growled at her brother. "You need to lay on him before it's too late."

Apollo snorted. "I'm trying to lay on him, precious sister. That's why I need him back."

It took her a second to realize she'd screwed down the colloquial phrase. "Lay *off* him. You've been extremely lucky Styxx has yet to remember who he was and what you did to him originally. I don't understand why you can't just walk away. Why you didn't walk away the first time."

Apollo shrugged. "Thanks to you and Apollymi messing with his memories and life, I don't have to worry about that. He'll never know how to defeat me. But need I remind you that we're approaching another perilous time when certain doorways will open and unleash things none of us want to deal with?"

"Which is why I'm getting that damn book back. Have no fear. I have it over control."

"Under control, Artemis. And see to it that you do." He snatched her against him and held her arm in a bruising grip. "Remember, sister, if you think I've been cruel to you, you've seen nothing yet. Get me that journal!" Then he was gone.

Artemis grimaced at the purple handprint he'd left on her arm. "I hate you!" she snarled. Most of all, she hated having to protect him.

But she had no choice. If he died, she died, too.

She rubbed at her arm and sighed. There were two places on Earth where no one ever needed to venture. The Aegean and the Sahara. Both locations held the keys that could not only destroy her and her twin, but the entire world.

And she would do whatever she had to to protect them all.

NOVEMBER 3, 2008

Drawing a picture in the sand, Styxx paused as he felt something strange . . . like he was being watched. He narrowed his gaze, and searched for the source of it, but saw nothing. Even so, the skin on the back of his neck crawled.

For a minute, he thought it might be Urian or Danger, but they would have called out a greeting.

As he reached for his knife, something slammed into him and knocked him sprawling. Pain exploded through his entire body.

He'd barely recovered before he was bashed again and again. Claws dug into his flesh and shredded him. Gasping, he couldn't move as his back was torn open. The pain and rapid blood loss made him light-headed and dizzy.

Finally, his attacker sank its claws into his hair and jerked his head up from the ground. "You tried to kill my akri!"

Styxx could barely make out Simi in her demonic form with that red and white swirling skin. Her eyes blazed with fury.

"No," he breathed.

She shrieked at him. "The Simi was there. She saw you stab him in the heart!"

Simi was the dragon Charonte he'd seen that had come off Acheron to protect him.

"No one attacks my akri and lives! No one!" She sank her fangs into his throat and ripped it open.

Styxx watched as his blood ran over his shoulder and down his arm, onto the sand. Too weak to move, he had no choice but to lie there and let death take him.

If only the putrid bastard would keep him for once.

NOVEMBER 4, 2008

Styxx stared down at the healing wounds that still stung like crazy. Simi had literally shredded his entire body. But then that was her job.

Protect Acheron.

I can't stay here. Once his brother's demon daughter learned he was alive again, she'd be back. And he wasn't Prometheus to have his liver ripped out every day and devoured. He'd been there, done that, and had no interest in the T-shirt.

The whole reason he'd wanted to come here was to get to know his brother and finally build a relationship with him. While Styxx was a slow learner, even he had to admit that their relationship was a lost cause at this point. Acheron had no interest in him at all.

Time to bury it and move on.

Resigned to the inevitable, Styxx headed for the main temple. But what he hadn't counted on were the horrific memories that tore into him once he entered it. They were so potent, he was shaking.

Or maybe that was the pain from his injuries.

Either way, he winced as he saw an image in his mind of his being dragged, while bound in chains, across Apollymi's seal. Even now, he heard Archon's angry growls echoing through this temple as Styxx fought to free himself from the gods who'd laughed and mocked his "pathetic" human efforts.

"Styxx?"

He turned to see Danger entering the foyer from a side door he knew led to Archon's private bedroom.

"What are you doing here?" she whispered.

"I wanted to speak to Acheron."

"He's not home."

"Do you know when he'll be back?"

"No." She sighed. "Sorry. But if you want, you can wait for his return in the throne room."

The good news was that Simi should be with Acheron. He was safe for a little while.

"Thanks." Styxx headed to the room before she had a chance to tell him where to go. There was no way he'd ever forget the layout of this temple. Every corner was seared violently into his memory.

Closing the doors behind him, he shook his head at the sight of Acheron's black throne. Finally, his brother had one. If only Acheron knew the reality of what being the heir to Didymos was really like. But then most princes didn't have Xerxes for their father. Maybe those princes did have a great, pampered life . . .

"Who the fuck let him out?" Acheron's angry voice outside the door interrupted his thoughts.

Missed you, too, brother.

Urian's tone was filled with mischievous humor. "The girl ghost who wants the two of you to kiss and make up."

"I'd rather be hit in the head with the tack hammer Tory threw at me."

"Tory?" Urian asked.

"Long story." Acheron let out a tired sigh. "Thanks for the warning. I'll go deal with him."

Deal with me . . . yeah. The coward had never dealt with him. He just tossed Styxx into his next prison and put him out of his thoughts.

The doors flew open in a staunch show of power much like Archon used to do when he reigned here. Dressed in an Atlantean formesta that bore Acheron's sun symbol and a pair of black leather pants, his brother walked toward him like a predator. As if such a move would ever intimidate a man who'd been forced to fight every day for his life.

And as Acheron approached, Styxx heard the voice that was tormenting Acheron at the sight of him.

Estes's.

How dare you make me want you like you do. I hate you for what you do to me, you disgusting whore. I. Hate. You.

Yeah, Estes had fucked them both in so many ways.

"I'm really not in the mood to deal with you, Styxx. What little patience I have was eaten alive about two minutes ago."

That explained some of the throbbing pain Styxx had. It worsened as Acheron neared. So, everything he felt wasn't all from Simi's attack. Figured.

Styxx forced himself to be submissive even though it went completely against his nature. "I know. I can sense your moods . . . it was a gift," he said sarcastically since Acheron couldn't remember the fact that he'd been the one who gave it to Styxx when their life forces were joined together by Acheron's mother, "from Artemis when she threw me into Tartarus. I'm only here to ask you one favor."

Acheron sneered at him. "You would dare ask another favor of me?"

When the hell had he ever asked Acheron for a first one?

Oh yeah . . . that's right. He remembered now.

Please, brother, please, send me to Katateros and let me starve alone in the temple where the gods passed me around like a bitch and beat me. That was the favor Acheron spoke of. And how magnificent was his brother's benevolence . . .

Don't open your stupid mouth.

A fight wouldn't get him out of here. Acheron was just like dealing with Apollo. Cater to the bastard's arrogant ego and he was pliable. "I ask as your brother and as a supplicant to a god."

There it was. That smug glower in those swirling silver eyes he knew so well from the others of Acheron's ilk. The ancient gods enjoyed their power and they lived to hold it over all humans. "As a supplicant, what sacrifice do you offer for this favor?"

Styxx had to force himself to stand perfectly still and not react to his brother's obvious baiting. At least he wasn't naked in a room full of Didymosian citizens with his father glaring while Ryssa laughed at his degradation.

I have nothing, thanks to you and your whore mother.

He could only think of one last commodity that he'd never need again. "My heart."

Acheron scowled. "I don't understand."

Of course he didn't. He didn't have one himself so how could he comprehend what Styxx meant?

Disgusted, he explained it. "I offered you my loyalty and it wasn't enough. So in this, I offer my heart to you. If I lie or betray you, you can rip it out over and over again. Chain me next to Prometheus on his rock." *And hopefully when you rip it out, mine won't grow back.*

That seemed to finally appease the bastard. "And what favor do you ask?"

"Let me go." Styxx had to pause to steady his voice and remove the pain and anger he held from it. "I can't live here anymore, isolated from people. I just want to have some kind of peace that neither of us ever had a chance to experience."

It took Acheron forever before he finally answered. "Fine. You'll have everything you need to start over."

Before Styxx could finish expelling a relieved breath, he was sucked out of the throne room and slammed facedown into the center of an apartment.

Loud sirens screamed above a dull roar. Styxx pushed himself up. The walls and ceiling were a stark white, as were the floor-to-ceiling curtains. A small black leather sofa was set against the wall with two matching armchairs facing it. A large, rectangular ottoman rested between them and under it all was a massive zebra-skin rug. Between the two armchairs was a granite fireplace, and a giant TV hung above it.

Where am I now?

Styxx was almost afraid of finding out as he crossed the room. He pushed the curtains aside to discover a large sliding glass door that looked out over some kind of park. None of it told him anything about his location. Not that it really mattered. The only time he'd been in the human world in the last eleven thousand years was the few weeks he'd spent in New Orleans over four years ago.

Opening the doors, he walked out to discover a huge rooftop patio that was even bigger than the apartment. Huge shrubs were in granite planters so that they provided privacy to the area. A travertine table was set in the center of it, along with six iron chairs.

Wow, someone seriously overestimated his social skills to assume he'd ever have six people sitting at a table at the same time.

He returned inside to search for a clue about his new home. Finally, in a kitchen drawer, he found an envelope with the address. 444 Central Park West. New York, New York.

That meant nothing to him. For that matter, he had no idea where Old York was, never mind the new one. But it was written in English. Still not that helpful.

As he searched for more clues, he found a driver's license with his name listed as Styxx Didymos, and his apartment information on it. A couple of credit cards, a bankbook, and other things he wasn't sure about. One of them was a small burgundy red booklet that had his picture inside. What was a passport? Why would he need it? Certificate of Naturalization? None of it made sense to him.

"Thanks, Acheron."

Once again, his brother had dumped him somewhere with no instructions or guidelines. Not even Dionysus had been this cruel.

Styxx took a deep breath and slid the drawer shut. Fine. He'd figured out how to lead an army into war as a child—he could certainly figure this out, too.

But honestly, it was worse here than finding himself alone on the islands. At least those had made sense to him. He'd known how to live there. How to function.

Here . . . not so much.

He laughed bitterly. Leave it to his brother to find a place where he was surrounded by people and still totally isolated.

Sitting at his bedroom desk, Styxx was busy on his PC playing the "New Atlantis" campaign for *Age of Mythology*. Yeah, it was weird to him, too, but strangely he found it almost comforting.

He was seriously gaining ground when he felt a strong presence behind him. Assuming it was Apollo, he jumped up, ready to fight.

It wasn't Apollo.

Urian stood there, looking sheepish. That alone made his trepidation worsen. There was only one reason he could think of for Urian to look like that . . .

"What does he think I've done now?"

Urian scowled. "Huh?"

"Acheron. Is he not the one who sent you for me?"

Urian shook his head. "He actually didn't send me. I came to ask a favor."

That shocked him completely. While he and Urian had kept in touch since Styxx had been put here, Urian wasn't the type of man to ask for a favor. "What do you need?"

"Acheron's woman, Tory, has been kidnapped and taken into Kalosis where his mother is. Ash is ready and willing to go get her." Which would free his mother from her prison and end the world.

Styxx stood completely stoic at the news. *I don't have a dog in this fight. What do I care?*

At least that was what he tried to tell himself. But it was obvious that Urian cared and didn't want to see his sister-in-law or his niece and nephews harmed.

Hesitating, Styxx knew better than to help his brother. Every time he'd ever tried had cost him dearly.

"Is Tory immortal?" he asked Urian.

"Completely human. She's being held by my aunt Satara, who

is unstable at best. Viciously brutal at worst." Since Satara was the daughter of Apollo, Styxx could well imagine her cruelty.

Don't do it. Acheron wouldn't do it for you . . .

"You're going in with him, aren't you?"

Urian nodded.

Grandson of Apollo. One of Apollymi's former chief Daimons. Acheron's right-hand. Styxx should hate the man in front of him with everything he had. But Urian had been kind to him and something about the boy brought out the protector in Styxx. It made no sense whatsoever. And no matter how hard he tried to fight it, he couldn't send Urian on a suicide mission alone.

Damn it.

Styxx sighed at the most obvious reason why Urian would be here. "You want me to pretend to be Acheron?"

"You did it once to help an enemy. Would you do it again to help a friend?"

Styxx laughed bitterly. "How would I know? I've only had two friends in my life and both were brutally murdered."

"You don't consider me a friend?"

"No, I consider you a hemorrhoid."

Urian grinned, flashing his fangs at Styxx. "Ah now, that's just mean."

"Yeah, yeah . . . Fine. But I am doing this for you and the innocent woman, not Acheron."

"Well, on behalf of myself and Tory, I can't thank you enough. By the way, how are your battle skills?"

Styxx snorted. "According to my father, I never had any. I shoved my men out in front of me, and hid behind their fallen bodies for cover."

Scowling, Urian didn't comment as he teleported Styxx to a small room.

Styxx froze as he saw Acheron beside a huge Chthonian named Savitar. This had been the man who'd trained his brother after death on how to use his god powers. In short, Savitar was Acheron's Galen . . . only Savitar was immortal and bloodthirsty.

Every bit as tall as they were, Savitar had dark hair and a perfect goatee. His eyes were an iridescent lavender and strangely reminded Styxx of something . . .

He couldn't put his finger on it, but in the back of his mind was some hidden message his brain was trying to give him.

His jaw slack, Savitar looked back and forth between Acheron and Styxx. "Holy Were-shit. This messes with my head."

Acheron glared at Styxx. "What is he doing here?"

"You can't go in," Urian reminded him. "Styxx can."

"No." Acheron was emphatic.

"Stop," Savitar snapped. "The kid has a point. Think about it. You can get Tory out of there and not end the world. Win-win."

The hatred in Acheron's eyes was searing. "I'm not leaving him alone with Tory. I don't trust him with her."

Styxx was aghast. "What do you think I'm going to do?"

"Rape her, kill her . . . with you there's no telling."

Now that infuriated him. He'd never done anything for Acheron to hold those suspicions about his character. "With me? Really?" He shoved Acheron.

Acheron ran at Styxx, but Savitar caught him and pushed him back a step. "Stop thinking with your emotions. Calm down." Then Savitar turned to glare at Styxx. "And you, punk, lay off him or I'll fry your greasy ass where it stands. I know I can kill you and not kill Acheron. So don't push me."

Styxx snorted in derision. "That is not the way to motivate me to leave him alone, Chthonian. But it's a hell of a one to make me attack." He met Acheron's swirling silver gaze. Gods, he wanted to bury a dagger right between his brother's traitorous eyes. He really, really did.

Instead, he snatched his sleeve back to show his brother his forearm. "I know what it's like to lose the only thing you love, and to be forced to live without her for eternity. As bad as I want to cut your throat and watch you bleed out at my feet for the insult you just dealt me, I won't see your woman dead for it. Unlike your fucking whore mother, I don't kill innocents."

Both Savitar and Acheron blasted him for that comment. Styxx hit the wall behind him so hard, he broke through part of it. The air left his lungs while pain temporarily paralyzed him. Blood ran from his lips, ears, and nose.

Before Styxx could breathe again, Urian was by his side. His face was a mask of rage as he glared at Acheron. "What are you doing? I asked him here to help you and you kill him? Good job. Both of you. Congrats, you stupid assholes."

"He insulted my mother," Acheron roared.

"No offense, boss, your mother killed his wife and his son. Instead of putting him through a wall, I want you both to take one second and imagine his loss. I have buried almost every member of my family. And the one thing that truly tore my heart out was losing Phoebe. You mourn your sister, Ash? So did I. Trust me, it ain't shit till you lose your wife, especially when you know you should have been at home protecting her, and not leaving her to die brutally by the hand of your enemies." He turned and helped Styxx extricate himself from the wall.

Styxx stumbled then caught himself. It was so hard to breathe. Every rib felt broken.

"I'm sorry," Urian said. "I shouldn't have asked you to come."

Styxx spat the blood in his mouth on the floor. "Trust me, they're pussies compared to the real Atlanteans I fought."

They went to blast him again.

Holding his arms out, Urian shielded Styxx with his body.

Styxx stepped around Urian then patted him on the shoulder. "I'm not afraid of them. Hits, I can take. After all, I was slapped on the ass the minute I was born, and not a damn thing has changed since."

Acheron curled his lip. "Don't listen to him, Urian. He's a liar and a thief. He was never married. He was only engaged, and he never had a son."

Bitterness choked Styxx as those words infuriated him all the more. "You know nothing about me, brother. After all, I'm just a liar and a thief to you."

Styxx paused as the harsh reality of Acheron's misconceptions slapped him hard. "By the way, tell Artie thanks for the memories. 'Cause now I not only know everything about what really happened to you, I know what you honestly think of me. I would say that one day I would love to return the favor, but truthfully the only person I hate that much is your putrid mother."

Still bleeding inside and out, Styxx wiped his hand across his face and spoke the words to his brother that he used to say to Apollo to drive the god into a murderous fury. "Now either use me, or send me home. I'm in no mood to play."

Savitar took a deep breath as he faced Acheron. "Urian's right. Styxx is the best shot we have at getting her out alive. We don't know what going into Kalosis will do to you, Ash. It could rip out your human soul and leave you nothing but your mother's tool for destruction. If that happens, you're as likely to kill Tory as they are."

Acheron shook his head. "It'll never work. His voice is hoarser than mine. And no one's going to believe I cut my hair off and bleached it blond."

Savitar snapped his fingers. Instantly, Styxx's hair was an exact copy of Acheron's. Long and black. He even had fangs and matching clothes. "I can't mess with his voice. But they can assume you've been screaming insults at them. It would account for the difference."

"That is creepy," Urian said, running his gaze up and down Styxx's body and then Acheron's. "Really creepy."

"He still doesn't move like me."

Styxx scoffed. "People aren't that observant. As you saw in New Orleans."

Savitar inclined his head to Urian and Styxx. "Let's do this, ladies. And Styxx ... for the record, you let anything happen to Tory and I will hand-deliver you to Apollymi for her eternal enjoyment."

Styxx laughed out loud at the impotent threat, which made both Acheron and Savitar scowl at him. "What's she going to do, Savitar? Drag me out into an arena butt-ass naked, make me fight elite

Atlantean champions until I can barely stand, set her starving dogs or leopards on me, and then have me publicly fucked for her entertainment? Or better yet, gut me on the floor ... or how about this ... murder my wife and child, and make me live with that for eternity in a dark hole by myself? Sure ... threaten me. Go ahead and make me live in total fear and terror." Flipping Savitar off, he turned to Urian. "Get me out of here."

Urian scowled at him. "You're really not sane, are you?"

"No, Urian. I'm not. A sane man would have told you to go to hell and meant it."

Shaking his head, Urian opened something that appeared to be a giant swirling gold ball. "Walk this way." He stepped into it and vanished.

Without so much as glancing at Savitar or Acheron, Styxx followed. Then wished he hadn't as he fell and was twisted through a bright, pulsing light.

When he finally stopped falling, he was inside a main room that was filled with Daimons and demons.

Beautiful.

Styxx let out a severely annoyed groan. "Great location, Uri," he said under his breath. "Think one of them is willing to sell us a summer home here?"

Urian grinned at him. "You can always ask."

Every demon and Daimon was frozen into place by their sudden appearance in the middle of their hall. It probably wasn't often that dinner was delivered in such a high-handed manner.

Styxx cut a sideways glance to Urian. "What are they waiting for?"

Urian winked at him. "Armageddon."

Styxx narrowed his eyes on Stryker. He was the only Daimon who dyed his hair black. Even in height with Styxx, Stryker looked enough like Apollo that Styxx really wanted to punch him for it.

Stryker glared at his son with an expression that was best defined as pained hatred. "You dare to stand with my enemy?"

"Against you, Father, I'd stand with Mickey Mouse."

765

Styxx had no idea who this Mickey was, but it was obvious from Stryker's expression Mickey was a lowly person.

Stryker curled his lip. "You worthless son of a bitch. You should have never been anything more than a cum stain."

Urian scoffed. "I could definitely say the same thing about you. It would have saved the world and all of us a lot of misery now, wouldn't it?"

Styxx and Urian braced themselves to fight as the Daimons started forward, but they were thrown back by some unseen force.

Not sure what had happened, Styxx turned to Stryker and growled. "Enough of the family reunion bullshit. Where is Soteria?"

Out of nowhere, Apollymi appeared a few feet from him. There was no doubt about her identity. Her features were the same ones Styxx saw every time he looked in a mirror. And those swirling silver eyes haunted his nightmares.

This was the selfish whore who had killed his precious Bethany.

It took everything Styxx had not to attack her.

Think of Soteria . . . She's innocent and wherever she is, she's terrified. Don't leave her to suffer.

Get her out first then beat the shit out of Apollymi.

That was his mission, and soldiers always followed orders. Even when they stunk to Mount Olympus.

Apollymi indicated a door behind him with an imperious jerk of her chin. "She's over there." Then Apollymi crossed the short distance to embrace him.

Styxx's breathing turned ragged at her touch. He clenched his fists tight to keep from lashing out at her and shoving her across the room. Something that would let everyone know he wasn't Acheron.

"At last, *m'gios*." Atlantean for *my son*. "You've come to set me free." She placed a kiss on his cheek and then whispered in his ear. "For my son's sake, you better embrace me, Greek whoreson. If I can touch something as vile and repugnant as you, you can touch divinity."

His lips quivered with fury as he forced himself to hug her close even though he wanted to spit in her face. *What kind of pathetic dog am I that I embrace my son's and wife's killer for a man who hates me?*

And still he did it.

Nodding to her, Styxx stepped back before he gave in to his need for vengeance.

He turned the angry sneer he wanted to give Apollymi to Stryker then headed for the door.

Before Styxx reached it, a tall, thin woman with brown hair and very pretty features came running out of the room. She wore a black jacket that was much too large for her and clutched it over her shirt, which had been torn open for only one thing Styxx could think of. His rage mounted even more.

All of a sudden, she threw herself into his arms and held him close. Too startled by the unexpected action, he gaped and she kissed the hell out of him. It took everything he had not to shove her away, but if he did, they'd know he wasn't his brother.

She stiffened and pulled back slowly to stare up at him suspiciously.

Swallowing hard, Styxx glanced past her to see an older Nick Gautier approaching them. Only now Nick had eyes that matched Acheron's and Apollymi's, and a bow-and-arrow mark on his left cheek that made it look like Artemis had bitch-slapped him when she marked him.

What all did I miss in captivity?

His eyes dark with rage and madness, Nick ran at Styxx as if he intended to kill him. But before he could reach him, Urian grabbed Nick and shoved him back into the room where they'd been.

Styxx pulled Tory in after them. He drew up short as he saw a woman's dead body on the floor.

"We have to go," Urian said to Styxx and Soteria. Then he looked at Nick. "And you need to come with us."

Nick curled his lip in obvious hatred. "I'm not going anywhere with him. I'd rather be dead."

Nice . . . someone who hated Acheron as much as he did. *What the hell did he do to you, kid?* It must have been bad because Nick had loved Acheron dearly the last time they met.

But then so had Styxx once upon a time.

Urian forced Nick to look down at the woman's body. "I'm going to make the wildly founded assumption that Satara's dead by your hand and not Tory's."

Gripping Nick's chin, Urian forced him to meet his gaze. "Now, stay with me on this, Cajun. My father slit my throat and murdered my wife because he thought I'd betrayed him by getting married. Before that, he loved me more than his life and I was his last surviving child. His second-in-command. Now what do you think he's going to do to you once he sees her body? I can assure you, it won't be a fun-filled trip to Chuck E. Cheese. For all their animosity toward each other, Satara is his sister and she's served him well over the centuries. If you really want to stay here and have some fun with Stryker, I won't stop you. But I really wouldn't recommend it."

That seemed to get through to Nick. Sanity returned to his eyes. "Fine. I'll go with you."

While they argued, Styxx cracked open the door to check on their restless enemies. "Urian," he said between clenched teeth. "I think they're catching on."

"Catching on to what?" Nick asked.

Tory rolled her eyes at Nick. "That this isn't Ash."

The words had barely left her lips before they faded out of the room.

Zolan, Stryker's third-in-command and the leader of his personal Illuminati attack force, cleared his throat in the silent room. "Um . . . boss, I don't mean this disrespectfully, but why are we still here? I mean, if Acheron has come to free Apollymi shouldn't there be an explosion or something?"

The Daimons and demons looked around as if waiting for an opening to the outer world to appear or for Apollymi to burst into song and dance, or for something else unnatural to happen.

Meanwhile, Apollymi just stood there completely stoic, appearing almost angelic and sweet, as she watched Stryker closely.

His second-in-command, Davyn, scratched the back of his neck nervously. "I agree, *kyrios,*" he said to Stryker, using the Atlantean term for lord. "It doesn't feel like the end of the world."

Stryker turned a cold sneer to Apollymi. "No, it doesn't, does it?"

Apollymi arched a taunting brow. "How does the song go, 'it's the end of the world as we know it, and I feel fine'?"

In that moment, Stryker knew exactly what had happened. Launching himself from his throne, he ran to the room just as Urian, Tory, Nick, and what had to be Ash's twin brother Styxx vanished.

His anger over the obvious trick mounted until he saw Satara lying on the floor in a pool of blood. Fear washed away his rage as he ran to her to find her dead. Her eyes were glazed and her skin tinged with blue.

His heart shattered as he pulled her into his arms and held her close, fighting against the tears of grief and pain. "You stupid psychotic bitch," he growled against Satara's cold cheek. "What have you done now?"

Apollymi stood in the doorway, aching for Strykerius as he rocked his dead sister in his arms, reminding her of the day she'd found her son's body left dumped on the cliffs of Didymos. Sympathy and a newfound respect for Stryker tore through her.

The fact that he could love someone as broken as Satara had been said much for him. Yes, he could be cold-blooded, but he wasn't heartless. Closing her eyes, she remembered him the day they'd first met. Stryker had been young and bitter over his father's curse.

"I gave up everything I ever cared about for him and this is how he repays my loyalty? I'm to die in agony in only six years? My young children are now banished from the sun and are cursed to drink blood from each other instead of eating food, and to die in pain at only twenty-seven? For what? For the death of a Greek whore killed by soldiers I've never even seen? Where's the justice in that?"

Understanding his agony and wanting to exact her own revenge on Apollo, Apollymi had pulled Stryker into her ranks and taught him how to circumvent his father's curse by absorbing human souls into his body to elongate his life. She'd given him and his children shelter in a realm where the humans couldn't harm them and where there was no danger of his children accidentally dying by sunlight. Then she'd allowed him to convert others and bring them here to live.

In the beginning, she'd pitied him and she'd even loved him as a son.

But he wasn't her Apostolos, and the more he was around her, the more she wanted to have her own child with her no matter the cost. She admitted it was her own fault that she'd put a wall between her and Strykerius. And the two of them had used each other to get back at the people they hated.

Now it all had come to this . . .

The death of his beloved sister.

"I'm so sorry, Strykerius."

He looked up at her, his silver eyes swirling in pain. "Are you? Or are you gloating?"

"I never gloat over death. I may relish it, from time to time, when it's justified. But I never gloat."

"And I don't let challenges like this go unanswered. There will be payback."

"But you owe it to Styxx and Nick, not my Apostolos or his Soteria. Remember that."

Styxx caught himself against a wall as they reappeared in a large room he didn't recognize. One filled with a huge group of ex-Dark-Hunters and friends of his brother's. A couple he remembered from his brief time in New Orleans. Others he knew only from Acheron's memories.

Acheron launched himself at Soteria and gathered her into his arms. Ironically, it was identical to the way Styxx had once embraced Bethany. Like she was the air he needed to live, and if he loosened his hold even a little bit, he would breathe no more.

But he had foolishly let his Beth go . . .

Unable to stand the sight and the memories that butchered him, Styxx turned away from them.

"Are you all right?" Acheron asked her.

"I'm fine. Really."

"But we're not," Urian said drily from the other side of the room. "Nick killed Satara while they held Tory."

"He did it to protect me," Tory interjected.

Urian snorted. "We'll put that on the headstone for you. In the meantime Stryker's going to want blood for this. A lot of blood."

Nick scoffed at his dire tone. "No offense, your father doesn't scare me, especially given how bad I want a piece of his hide. Come get some."

Urian looked less than impressed. "I know you think you share powers with him, Nick, but trust me, he didn't give you anything but the leftovers. Not to mention one small thing. No one gets a piece of him until after I do."

Acheron let out a shrill whistle. "Down, children. We have more important things to focus on right now. Save your machismo."

Styxx had to bite back his sarcasm at Acheron's hypocrisy. Funny how his brother didn't see that when it was the two of them fighting.

But then it was always easier to see other people's sins than it was to see your own.

Acheron leveled his glare at Nick. "We have a battle to prepare for. I'm not letting Stryker take Nick."

Nick laughed bitterly. "I don't need your fucking help. I can fight on my own."

Acheron didn't flinch at the hatred in his tone. "I know why you hate me, Nick. I get it. But your mother wouldn't want you to kill yourself again. Hate me tomorrow. Tonight, tolerate me as a necessary evil." His brother slid his gaze to him to let Styxx know that that was all he was to Acheron, too.

A necessary evil he tolerated.

So be it.

Nick shoved Acheron away from him. "This doesn't make us friends."

Acheron held his hands up. "I know." He turned back to Tory and took her hand in a tight grip. Indecision hung there before he spoke and shocked Styxx to the core of his being. "Styxx, take her out of here. Keep her safe."

His jaw went slack. *Who are you and where's my psychotic brother?*

Tory gaped, too, as she skimmed Styxx with a horrified expression and her thoughts blasted him. *You! You're the one I read about who tortured and castrated my Acheron. You're an animal. I hate you!*

Styxx couldn't believe they still blamed him for that. Unlike Acheron, he'd die before he ever willingly touched another man's junk. Even to castrate him.

Damn you, Apollo!

But then why damn him for it? Styxx had told the god to do his worst. Apollo had only obliged him. While Estes had begun the hatred Acheron had for him, Apollo had cemented it.

Suddenly, a bright flash of light blinded them. And out of it stepped dozens of Daimons. All of them open for business as they fell into an ancient Greek phalanx.

Stryker came through and his gaze went straight to Urian. "You've betrayed me for the last time." Flicking his wrist, he sent a leaf-shaped dagger right at Urian's heart.

Before it could reach its target, Acheron caught it in his hand. "Take your girls, scream, and run away now, Stryker. It'll save you time later. Believe me, you don't want a taste of me in the mood I'm in."

Stryker took that the same way Styxx would have. With flippant disregard. He ran his tongue over his fangs as if he was savoring the idea of feeding on Acheron. "There's nothing I crave more than the taste of blood." He looked around at the men who stood with Acheron and laughed in derision. "Tonight we feast, Spathi. Attack!"

Urian pulled Tory behind their group as the Daimons swarmed them. Unlike the rest of the men in the room, Styxx was at a serious disadvantage as their enemies attacked with god bolts and psychic powers. His head splitting with pain from all of their thoughts hitting him at once, he shrugged off the heavy overcoat he wore and picked up the nearest blade.

"Stab them in the heart," Urian said to Styxx before he demonstrated how to kill the Daimons.

Another blast of light in the room left them with a huge group of enemy reinforcements. Styxx stabbed the first one to reach him. Only he didn't explode into dust like the Daimon had. "Urian? A little instruction please."

"Demons ... eyes." Urian stabbed a demon between the eyes before he turned and ducked the fangs of a Daimon. "And whatever you do, don't let the demons bite you or they can control you."

See Acheron, it's so much easier when you give me a few important guidelines.

Styxx disarmed a Daimon who held a sword then he spun around and caught him with his dagger. The Daimon exploded all over Styxx.

Stryker went for Nick, but Acheron caught him and the two of them went to the ground, punching with a fury Styxx knew all too well. *Glad I'm not the only one you hate that much.*

More men arrived. Since they were neither Daimons nor demons, Styxx pulled back until he could determine if they were friends or foes.

A demon launched itself at Soteria. She tried to kick him back, but failed epically. Just as it would have reached her, Julian of Macedon, a longtime friend of Acheron's, was there with a xiphos. He severed the demon's head with one well-placed swing.

Balancing the leaf-shaped blade on his shoulder, Julian turned to face her. "Can you handle a sword?"

"Yes."

"Kyrian!" Julian shouted to his best friend, another blond Greek. "My kingdom for a sword."

Kyrian tossed what appeared to be only a hilt. In one fluid move, Julian caught it and pressed a button on the cross hilt. The blade shot out to just under three feet in length. He handed it over to Soteria. "Daimons have to be stabbed through their hearts. Demons between their eyes, and if you cut the heads off any of us, we all die."

"How do I tell the difference?"

"Most of the Daimons are blond and they explode into dust when you pierce their hearts. Hit the heart and if that doesn't work, try the eyes. If you stab someone who whimpers then hits the ground, you attacked a good guy. Just FYI."

Styxx snorted. *The girl gets a tutorial.* The one who could actually fight them off was just fodder.

Lovely.

Styxx kept fighting, but the numbers against them were gruesome and the sound of swords clashing brought back horrific images in his mind. Even though they were indoors, he could feel the sticky ground that was saturated with blood. The blood-soaked mud caked in his toes . . . The heat of the sun as it mercilessly beat down on his armor to the point that it burned his skin whenever he accidentally brushed against it.

Another flash of light heralded an even larger group of demons and Daimons.

Styxx sighed at the familiar sight. The Atlanteans would drop numbers on them like this. Just when you thought you were thinning them, a thousand more who weren't exhausted from the fight magically appeared.

All he could do was stay focused on the ones who were coming for him—both in front and behind—and make sure they didn't get away to attack someone else.

One of the demons made for Urian's back. Styxx pulled a smaller knife out of the demon body closest to him and used it to pin the new demon between his eyes.

Urian turned to fight as it fell to his feet. He met Styxx's gaze and inclined his head to him.

Styxx whirled and, forgetting he didn't have a hoplon, raised his arm to catch a sword down across it. Hissing, he stumbled back then lunged with the sword in his right hand. His opponent spun and came back immediately with another blow. Styxx narrowly jerked his head away in time. The blade came so close, he felt its breath over his Adam's apple.

He kicked the Daimon back then used his sword to pierce his heart. As he pulled away, he caught a glimpse of Stryker, and the expression on his face was one of controlled fury. He was locked on his target, and in his hand was the one weapon that could kill Acheron.

An Atlantean dagger imbued with the blood of Apollymi and with poisonous ypnsi sap from the darkest trees grown in the forests of Kalosis.

For a moment Styxx didn't react. If Stryker killed his brother, it was over. All of it.

He would finally have peace.

But then he made the fatal mistake of looking at Soteria who saw what he did.

Acheron's imminent death.

The horrified agony on her face and the tears in her eyes undid him. Love like that didn't deserve to be separated. There was no worse hell than being one half of an eternally separated whole.

Twice in his life, he'd been dealt that blow. He wouldn't let his hatred crush Soteria.

Damn me . . .

Styxx ran at Stryker. He caught the Daimon lord right before he reached Acheron who had stupidly closed his eyes while he fought.

Yeah, you didn't have Galen for an instructor.

Because Styxx still wore sunglasses, Stryker lost focus on Acheron and mistook him for his brother.

Stryker laughed in satisfaction as he buried the knife deep into Styxx's stomach. His vision dimmed while that familiar pain spread through him. It felt like Stryker had caught him in the same exact place Ryssa had.

Trying to catch his breath, Styxx stumbled back and fell into someone. His sunglasses went flying.

Time hung still as he realized he'd fallen against Acheron and his brother had stepped aside to let him go down hard on the floor. He laughed bitterly at that. Their father would have been proud.

Ryssa, too.

Growling at the fact he'd missed Acheron, Stryker reached for the dagger in Styxx's stomach. Styxx held it inside him with one hand while he tried to beat Stryker back with his other. But his blood made the hilt too slippery and the pain and scar weakened his grasp. Against his best effort, Stryker yanked the dagger out.

Styxx gasped as excruciating pain tore through him. "Acheron!" he shouted, warning his brother.

Turning in time, Acheron caught the Daimon overlord with the blunt end of his staff and shoved him back. "Flee or die," he snarled.

Stryker curled his lip. "Fuck you."

Narrowing his gaze on Stryker, Acheron shoved him back then slammed the staff to the ground. A wave of raw, unfettered power shot out from it to the demons and Daimons around them. Every one of them turned to dust.

Except for Stryker. He hovered above the ground in a dragon's form, snarling and flapping. Bellowing in rage, Stryker spewed fire at Acheron.

Acheron lifted his arm, barely in time to keep it from burning him. He shot another god bolt at Stryker who dodged it.

"This isn't over, Acheron. Next time you won't be able to use your powers." With another blast of fire, Stryker vanished.

Trembling with pain, Styxx laid his head on the ground and stared up at the ceiling. The others were talking, but his ears buzzed so loudly, he couldn't understand them.

Styxx laughed then groaned. It was just like the day before he died. He lay bleeding and no one even noticed. Rolling over, he tried to stand then slipped on blood and crashed back to the floor. There was no Galen here to render aid to him.

No friend whatsoever.

Yet Acheron was surrounded by people who were joking with him.

I've got to stop the bleeding. While he couldn't die from it, the last thing he needed was to be weak from blood loss. It would still make him sick, and there was no one to tend him at home.

His head pounded even more, blurring his vision. Unable to stand, Styxx rolled to his back and kept as much pressure on the wound as he could. He started shaking uncontrollably.

Great. I'm going into shock. He should have kept the coat on.

How was I to know I'd be gutted again?

He felt someone kneeling down beside him. Opening his eyes, he was stunned to see Acheron. There wasn't a bit of concern or compassion in his brother's cold expression.

Styxx panted in sheer agony. "You know, brother, you're never supposed to close your eyes in battle."

Ash laughed. "I wasn't the one training to be a general."

Good thing, too. You'd have sucked at it and caused everyone to die. But that was only part of being a leader and he knew it.

Styxx glanced around at the men surrounding them. He heard their thoughts and he knew their faces and histories from Acheron's memories. They loved his brother.

They'd never once mocked Acheron as Styxx's men had done him in the beginning. All of them looked to Acheron with respect and adoration.

None of them had ever paid to screw him.

Acheron's men knew nothing of his past.

A vengeful part of him wanted to tell them what Acheron had been. But then, that cruelty wouldn't hurt Acheron. Not really. Because these men cared about his brother and even if they knew everything, they wouldn't hold it against Acheron. His brother was stupid for even thinking that.

And Acheron had done something with them that Styxx had never done for his own men. Acheron had taken in these shattered creatures, such as Vane and Fang whose pack of werewolves had turned on them and tried to feed them to the Daimons—Kyrian whose wife had handed him over to his enemies to be tortured and crucified—Zarek who'd been a Roman whipping boy wrongfully

777

tortured and executed—and Talon who'd watched his sister murdered before his eyes after his clan, his own blood, had betrayed him—and with a patience he'd never shown Styxx, Acheron had healed them.

All of them.

It was amazing, really. But then, Acheron didn't hate them the way he hated Styxx.

Styxx sighed. "Perhaps. But you do a much better job of leading than I ever did. I definitely think Father trained the wrong one of us."

Without a word, Acheron placed his hand over Styxx's wound. It stung like a hot brand against his skin. And he should know, since it was just like being in the Dionysion. He glared at Acheron. "Fine, then you're a stupid fucking asshole. Get your hands off me," he snarled through gritted teeth.

Ignoring his outburst, Acheron held him down until Styxx was ready to whimper. Only then did Acheron pull away.

"Am I dead yet?" Styxx asked sarcastically.

"Not yet. You still have a few years left to seriously piss me off."

Styxx snorted. "I look forward to it."

I'm sure you do, Acheron thought silently. He inclined his head to Styxx. "You did a good job for me. Thank you."

That must have choked you to say, brother.

"Yeah, well, next time you need someone to descend into a Daimon sanctuary, pick one of your other assholes to do it. I don't have the powers of a god when they come at me, and it puts me at a definite disadvantage."

Grinning, Acheron helped Styxx to his feet then left him and went to be with his men.

In one heartbeat, Acheron had put Styxx out of his mind and forgotten he was here.

For this I left my computer games? Styxx sighed wearily.

"You want me to take you home?"

Styxx nodded at Urian. "Thanks."

"No problem."

In the blink of an eye, Styxx was back in his condo. He'd started for the couch when his knees buckled.

Urian caught him against his side and helped him to his bed. "Are you still wounded?"

"It's the poison from the dagger Stryker used. Acheron healed the wound, but he didn't draw the poison out." Whether that was intentional or not, he had no idea.

"How do you get it out?"

"You draw it out before you stitch the wound closed." Styxx looked down at the sealed scar. "Oops, too late." He started shaking again as sweat beaded on his forehead.

"Do you want me to call Ash?"

"I'll be fine." Acheron wouldn't come anyway. And Styxx couldn't blame him. If he had Bethany with him, he wouldn't bother with his brother either. "Not like I can die. I just need to rest." Styxx had barely slurred those words before he passed out.

NOVEMBER 21, 2008

Styxx came awake facedown in a thick forest. Birds sang out as the sun streaked through the foliage around him. His ribs hurt like Galen had kicked them. And as he lay there, trying to get his bearings, he heard a beautiful contralto singing an ancient Egyptian lullaby. Tears filled his eyes as the Egyptian words reminded him of Bethany.

Unable to resist the siren's lure, he pushed himself up and headed toward the sound. He broke into a clearing, where he found Bethany on her blanket, cuddling a boy around the age of five in her arms. She saw Styxx and smiled a smile that set fire to every part of him.

"Look, little Galen, Daddy's finally home." She set the boy down and he ran for Styxx.

"Daddy! Daddy!"

Styxx couldn't breathe as the boy latched on to his leg and held it tight. His hand trembling, he brushed it through the short, wavy blond hair and stared in awe at the bright blue eyes that looked at him with total adoration and love.

Swinging the boy up in his arms, he melted as Galen laid his head on his shoulder and hugged him tight. "I missed you, Daddy. Did you bring me something?"

"He brought you himself," Bethany teased their son. "Is that not enough?"

Laughing, Galen fell back into his mother's arms. Bethany held him on her hip before she rose on her tiptoes to place a scorching kiss to Styxx's lips. "Just so you know, I'm furious at you."

"Why?"

"You made me miss you. But I'm so glad you're back that you're completely forgiven."

His heart pounded as she laid her head against his chest and held him with one arm. He wrapped both of his around the two of them and choked on a wave of tears. The scent of eucalyptus and lilies warmed him. He never wanted to move or let them go.

I must be dead.

But he didn't mind. This was the only place he'd ever wanted to be. Held tight in her arms.

Bethany handed Galen back to him then took his hand to lead him toward their tiny stone cottage. Inside, Galen's toys were strewn across the floor. His son kicked his short legs to let Styxx know he wanted down. After obliging him, Styxx gently pulled Bethany into his arms so that he could bury his face in her hair and inhale her sweet scent while she ran her hands down his back. Every hormone in his body roared to life.

"Galen?" she called.

"Mama?"

"Why don't you go play with Dynatos outside for a little while?"

Galen grabbed a ball and ran to the door.

"Don't go far! Stay so that I can hear you."

"Okay, Mama."

As soon as the door closed, she claimed his lips with a scorching kiss. Styxx couldn't think straight as she dropped his chlamys to the floor then untied his chiton so that she could touch him all over.

He loosened the rope belt around her waist and let it fall to the floor before he pulled her peplos over her head. His starving gaze scanned every inch of her beautiful naked body. He pulled her against him.

Laughing playfully, she jumped into his arms and wrapped her legs around his waist while she nipped his lips and chin with her teeth. "I'm so glad you're home."

"Oh, Beth, so am I. I feel like I've been gone for an eternity."

"Every heartbeat you're away is an eternity for me."

He savored those words as much as the sensation of her soft skin sliding against his.

She took his hand into hers and frowned. "You've new scars."

"They're not important."

"They are to me. I don't like for you to get hurt."

He hardened even more at the sound of love in those words. Needing to be inside her, he carried her to the bedroom. Though to be honest, he didn't want to wait to be inside her. But she was his heart and soul and the mother of his son. He didn't want to rut with her like her comfort meant nothing to him when all he desired in this world was for her to love him with one-tenth the intensity he felt for her.

Gently placing her on the bed, he recaptured her lips and slowly lowered himself between her legs. Trembling, he kissed his way down her neck and shoulders so that he could taste her taut, perfect areola.

"I love you, Beth," he whispered, rubbing his chin against her breast.

"It's a pittance compared to what I feel for you, my heart . . . What kept you so long from us?"

"The gods I hate."

"You shouldn't hate the gods, Styxx."

How could he not? They had robbed him of everything. Even his dignity. But as he stared into the greenish-golden depths of her eyes, his hatred didn't matter anymore. "Then kiss me, Beth. Breathe your faith and love into me and I will hate no more."

She kissed him passionately then reached down between their bodies to slide him into her.

His breath left him in a gasp as he felt her cradling him. For a full minute, he couldn't move for fear of coming immediately.

"It's all right, love," she whispered in his ear. "I know how long it's been for you. Don't worry about me right now. We have the rest of the night for you to take your time pleasuring me." She thrust against him.

Pure bliss exploded through his entire body. Grinding his teeth, he roared with the force of it as he drove himself in as deep as he could and shuddered while she held him to her.

"That was worthless for you," he breathed raggedly into her ear.

She brushed her hand through his hair and toyed with it. "No, it wasn't. I have you in my arms and inside me. I'm happy as I can be. Besides, I know you'll make it up to me later."

Yes, he would.

Sighing, he listened to her heart beating against his ear while Dynatos barked outside and Galen laughed in play. Those sounds brought tears to his eyes.

"Dad!" Galen came running inside.

Styxx had barely pulled his chiton back on and covered Bethany before his son pounded on their door. Making sure he wouldn't scar the boy for life, he cracked open the door and knelt down. "What is it?"

"There's a turtle! Come see!"

Styxx belted his chiton then stepped into the kitchen and took Galen's hand so that Bethany could dress in peace. "Where is it?"

Galen ran with him outside to show it stuck in the mud by a tree. "I tried to free her, but couldn't reach it without getting dirty and I promised Mama I would stay clean for your home-coming."

Styxx knelt in the mud and pulled his son close as he remembered all the times his father had been a bastard to him because Styxx had wrinkled a garment or allowed a hem to sag. "You can roll around in it like a happy piglet for all I care, Galen. The only thing that matters to me is that you wear a smile when I come home to you. And that is the only thing I don't want tarnished." He held Galen out so that he could grab the turtle and pull her to safety.

He brushed his son's hair back and kissed his cheek. "Do you know where the khelone gets her name?"

"The gods!"

Smiling, Styxx helped Galen take the turtle to the pond and wash her off. "That's right. Khelone was a nymph who refused to attend Zeus and Hera's wedding feast, even though Hermes himself had gone to fetch her. Furious, Zeus went to the khelone and demanded to know why she would dare defy and disregard his authority. And do you know what she said?"

Galen shook his head.

"She said, and I quote . . . be it ever so humble, there's no place like home."

"Is that why she carries her home on her back?"

"It is, indeed." Though the tale claimed Hermes and Zeus had done it as punishment for her refusal to leave her house. But that wasn't a punishment to Styxx. "If I could, I would carry you and your mother on my back with me everywhere I go."

"You'd look very silly, Daddy."

"Some things are worth looking silly for."

Screwing his face up, Galen shook his head vigorously. "I hate looking stupid."

"To make you and your mother laugh or smile, I'd paint myself pink and walk naked around the world."

Galen laughed then freed the turtle into the pond. He threw himself against Styxx and smeared mud all over him. Pulling back, Galen stiffened. "Uh-oh."

"What?"

Galen leaned in to whisper against his ear. "Mama's here and she doesn't look happy that we're covered in mud. You might want to get your sword and shield, Daddy."

"Don't worry," he whispered back. "I'll protect you."

"I don't see how."

Styxx's heart swelled at the sight of Bethany approaching them. "The secret is not to lop the head off the gorgon, son. It's to make her smile."

Galen's eyes grew even wider. "I think it would be easier to lop off her head."

"Only as the last resort." He kissed Galen's cheek then rose to his feet with Galen in his arms. Slowly, he approached Bethany who frowned at them.

"My two heroes mired in mud. What am I to do with you?"

"Oh, Beth, that answer's simple."

She arched a brow at him.

"Love us." He dipped his head to kiss her then playfully wiped his mud-covered hand down her cheek, leaving a long smear of it. Laughing, he cuddled Galen and stepped out of her reach.

Shrieking in mock anger, she ran at them.

Galen's laughter mixed with theirs as she and Dynatos chased them until the traitorous dog tripped him. Styxx hit the ground with his shoulder, making sure he kept Galen from harm. He rolled to his back so that Galen was straddling his chest. Bethany fell down on top of him and straddled his waist. She grabbed Galen in her arms and hugged him till he protested. Then she hugged him even harder.

"Daddy! Help! The gorgon's trying to squeeze the breath out of me."

"Help? Very well." He rose up to wrap his arms around Bethany and trap Galen between them.

Galen protested even more. "I meant help me, not the gorgon!"

Laughing, he cradled his son to his chest and laid his head on Bethany's shoulder. Yet even as he savored this happiness with them, he knew it wouldn't last.

It never did for him.

The thought of it ending tore through his soul with talons. *Please, grant me this one wish. Please, just let me stay here with them.*

But he knew the truth. Acheron had spoken it to him long ago. Styxx was damned and happiness never came to the damned.

JANUARY 19, 2009

Urian ground his teeth as he led Savitar into Styxx's bedroom. "He's been like that for over a month."

Savitar gave Urian an arch stare.

"I know, right? It's like his whole body has shut down. He hasn't eaten or drank or even moved. Every now and again, he whispers in ancient Greek or Egyptian, but I can't make it out."

Frowning, Savitar pulled the blanket back to examine the wound Acheron had sealed. The moment he saw Styxx's extensive scarring he gaped in horror. "What the hell?"

Urian sighed as he understood Savitar's reaction. "Aside from being a war hero who fought in dozens of battles, he spent a year as a POW in Atlantis. He never really says much about it other than it sucked, but from the scars I'd say they tortured him the whole time he was there."

Savitar expelled a heavy breath. "I had no idea. Does Acheron know about this?"

"I don't know. Given his extreme hatred of Styxx, though, I'd say he doesn't care. He'd probably say Styxx deserved it."

Savitar felt Styxx's forehead. "How long has his fever been this high?"

"Since the fight with Stryker. He had it when I brought him home and it hasn't broken or gone down at all."

Savitar placed his hand to Styxx's throat. "He barely has a pulse."

"Yeah. I didn't know what to do. Not like I can call a doctor. I tried to tell Ash, but he said Styxx was probably faking it for attention. He told me Styxx couldn't die and would be fine. Not to concern myself with it. But he doesn't look fine. He looks like a corpse."

"All right. Stand back. I'm going to shock him out of this."

Urian moved to the doorway as Savitar placed his hand over Styxx's chest. A slight hum filled his ears a few seconds before what appeared to be a sledgehammer-like bolt shot from Savitar's hand into Styxx's chest.

Styxx's eyes flew open. Panting, he frowned at Savitar and then Urian as if he didn't recognize them at first. As soon as he did, his eyes filled with panic and tears.

"No!" Styxx breathed raggedly, sweeping the room with his gaze. "Beth! Galen!"

Styxx wanted to scream as he found himself not in his cottage, but back in hell. Desperate and hysterical, he rushed from his bed to frantically search his condo for his family.

They weren't here. They were gone.

All gone.

Treacherous agony tore him apart as he fell to his knees and bellowed. "Why did you bring me back here? Why? I was with them and we were happy! I was with them . . ." Styxx buried his head in his hands and tried to come to terms with the reality he despised. "Beth, don't leave me again . . . please . . . please come back to me . . . I can't live without you anymore." And he couldn't stand the thought of being here alone.

Urian choked at the sight of a profound grief he knew better than anyone. For a long time, he'd hated Ash for bringing him back to life. Every day he lived without Phoebe was a day he despised with fury.

Why didn't I leave him alone?

Had he known Styxx was in a coma with his family, he'd have left him there forever.

His heart breaking for his newfound friend, Urian knelt down

786

beside Styxx and gathered him into his arms. "I'm sorry, Styxx. We didn't know."

Savitar came up to them and placed his hand on Styxx's shoulder, knocking him out again. "Unfortunately, he won't stay that way."

"Help me put him back in bed."

Instead of helping, Savitar picked Styxx up as if he weighed nothing and carried him to the bedroom. There was something weird about how Savitar was acting now. But Urian didn't know him well enough to even hazard a guess about his thoughts.

"It's disturbing, isn't it?" Savitar asked him as Urian entered the bedroom.

"What?"

"How much he favors Ash."

Urian shrugged. "They're identical twins. I had two sets of brothers who were, too. But while they may share looks and some tendencies, they are usually very different people."

Savitar swept his gaze around the room then opened the closet where Styxx had two pairs of jeans folded neatly on the top shelf. One sweater, a jacket, two long-sleeved button-downs, and three short-sleeved shirts. One pair of shoes. Frowning, Savitar continued searching all six rooms of the condo.

Curious, Urian followed him around. "What are you looking for?"

"What's your impression of this place?"

Urian answered with the first word that popped into his head. "Spartan."

Savitar nodded. "Not exactly the kind of place a spoiled prince would be happy in, is it?" He handed a bankbook to Urian. "Acheron gave him plenty of money. And you can tell by the lack of dishes, he doesn't do much, if any, entertaining. The only thing he appears to have splurged on is the computer."

"Only because I ordered it for him. He didn't know anything about them and asked my advice."

Savitar picked up Styxx's phone, looked at it then handed it to

Urian. "Yours is the only number he has, and it's the only one he's called."

And not often, and even then not for very long. Their longest conversation had been about the computer and that had probably been no more than twenty minutes, tops.

Urian sighed. "I assumed he had other people he hung out with."

"Has he said anything to you about being alone?"

"He really doesn't talk much. He mostly asks questions about modern things he can't figure out. Or customs and phrases he's unfamiliar with."

Savitar scowled. "Does he ever mention Ash or their sister?"

"Only if I bring them up, and then he quickly deflects the conversation to another topic. Tonight notwithstanding, or when he and Ash went at each other, he's usually quiet and reserved. Unassuming. But he does have a wicked sense of humor."

"How so?"

Urian smiled at the memories of their brief conversations. "One of my personal faves . . . he made a snarky remark over a random online encounter and then apologized by saying that he was so allergic to stupidity that it caused him to break out into rampant sarcasm. Another time, I made the comment that he was a leader and not follower. He corrected me by saying if it was a dark place with loud growls then fuck that shit, he'd gladly follow me in to investigate it."

Savitar laughed.

Urian continued, "He also wanted to know why sour cream, buttermilk, and blue cheese have expiration dates. Why boxing rings are always square. Why buildings burn up as they're burning down." He paused to laugh. "And my two favorites, he asked why we have doctors now and not physicians."

Savitar screwed his face up. "They're the same."

"That's what I said, but then he pointed out to me that back in the so-called barbarian days, we didn't have doctors who practiced medicine, but rather physicians who healed you . . . or killed you, just like now. He asked me how modern man could trust someone with so little confidence of knowledge of their field that they told you right up-front that they were still in the learning process."

Savitar snorted. "I never thought of it that way."

"Yeah, and a few months ago, he was in a grocery store and wanted to know why lemon juice was artificially flavored, but dish-washing soap contained real lemons. And what did modern people have against turkeys? He could find turkey masquerading as bacon, steak, and burgers, but no plain turkeys. Needless to say, I never thought about any of that. Probably because the only time I was ever in a grocery store I was shopping for humans."

Savitar ignored those last comments. "It must be hard for him to adjust."

"He doesn't complain. He just tries to understand modern mind-sets, such as how can he be a chauvinist pig if he opens a door for a woman and then he's an insensitive pig if he doesn't."

"The day he figures that one out, tell him to write a book and we'll all be rich."

"He already has. He stays back until she goes in and then he runs for it before another one comes along."

Savitar laughed, then sobered. "Tell me honestly, Urian. What do you think of him?"

"I like him, and it's not because I idolized him as a military hero when I was a kid. He was a fierce old fart to me then. Kind of like you."

Savitar arched a censoring brow then smiled and heh'ed.

"You know me, Chthonian, I don't play well with others, and I basically hate everyone, all the time, but I would actually cross the street to have a conversation with him . . . In fact, I have."

"Coming from you, that's the highest endorsement I can think of."

Urian nodded. "I just don't understand their mutual hatred. I mean, I had brothers I couldn't stand to be around for more than five minutes, but I didn't really hate them. We were just different. While I might deck one from time to time, I never really tried to kill one."

"I get why Acheron hates him, and it is justified. Believe me. Apollymi herself has told me about their bad blood, and I know she's not lying. I'm just having a hard time reconciling the stories I've been told with the man who lives here. Of course, eleven thousand years can change someone ... I don't know." Savitar sighed. "Keep an eye on him and let me know if he slips back into another coma." He vanished.

Urian started to leave, too, but given how distraught Styxx had been, he didn't want Styxx to be alone when he woke up.

Sighing, he glanced around for something to occupy himself with. His gaze fell to a sketchbook on the end table. Curious what it contained, he walked over to it and flipped it open.

His jaw went slack at what he found inside. The majority of the book was filled with drawings of an absolutely stunning woman who had to be Bethany. Some of them were so real, she looked like she could step off the page and touch him. But the ones that were truly haunting were drawings of Styxx and her. He'd perfectly captured their smiles and laughs, but most of all he'd caught the anguish and love on his own features as he held her. There were also pictures of Bethany with a son, and of the boy by himself. A boy Styxx had never met. It wrung Urian's heart.

Damn, Styxx was talented. Who'd have ever guessed it?

What he found most telling was that while a couple of the drawings of Bethany had her seductively clad in Greek gowns, none of them showed her naked. Even though Styxx had never intended for anyone else to see this, he'd kept his wife's honor sacred and respected her.

Urian stopped on the next page as he found one of a toddler boy dressed in a hoplite's Corinthian helm. It was hilarious and adorable. Beside it, Styxx had written the name "Galen" in Greek ... He also had a few of an adult Galen, one of a woman named Tig, a horse and dog, and a few scenes from what must have been Didymos.

And then the ones that really floored him ... images of Acheron in his modern Goth wear and long black hair, as well as pictures of them together with a bolt of lightning coming down between them.

When Urian turned to the next page, his heart stopped. Styxx had drawn Urian with Phoebe. Even though Styxx had never seen her, he'd penned her perfect likeness from Urian's descriptions. It was absolutely eerie that Styxx could do that, and it showed him just how true to life his drawings of Bethany must be.

Incredible.

The love Styxx had for his wife and son bled onto every page. Since Styxx had nothing left of her to hold on to, he must have created this. And it was like looking into Styxx's soul.

Urian set the sketchbook back right where he'd found it. But honestly, what disturbed him the most about that book . . .

He saw his own future. Phoebe had only been a dead a handful of years and it still burned inside him like a raging furnace. For Styxx, it'd been over eleven thousand and he still ached as much now as he had then.

That did not bode well for Urian.

Maybe that was why he was so drawn to Styxx. They were bound by similar tragedies and had been born virtual contemporaries in ancient Greece. Well, not quite, Styxx was the same age as his father, but close enough.

Urian glanced back at the sketchbook and cringed. *So that's what I have to look forward to. Insanity.*

Great.

JANUARY 21, 2009

Just after midnight, Styxx woke up covered in sweat. He was so cold, his teeth chattered. Someone pulled another blanket over his shoulder. For the merest heartbeat he thought it might be Bethany.

It wasn't.

Urian stepped into his field of vision. "How are you?"

Broken. Completely. But there was no need in saying it. He still didn't know how a dream could seem so very real. He'd felt Beth's skin . . . her breath on his cheek. His son's early morning demands for breakfast and entertainment as he tried to pull Styxx out of bed.

"Come Daddy, come!"

If only he could . . .

When he didn't respond, Urian squatted down next to the bed until their gazes met. "I know," he whispered. "I still wake up and expect to find Phoebe beside me. I haven't even deactivated her cell phone. I keep it so that I can call and hear her voice on those hours when I feel like I can't take it anymore. It's not fair that we're forced to live without them while the world goes on oblivious to the fact that it's missing the most vital part of it." He let out a bitter laugh. "It's why I'm here with your hairy ass. I don't want to see Tory and Ash. Not because I hate him like you do, but because they remind me of what I no longer have. And while I don't begrudge them their happiness, it makes my loneliness burn even deeper."

Styxx finally blinked. "Why do you talk to me, Urian?"

"I don't know. You're entertaining when you're not catatonic or in a coma. Or in a homicidal rage. Why do you talk to me?"

The answer slipped out before he could stop it. "Because I can't hear your thoughts."

"Excuse me?"

Styxx sighed. "It's something I've been able to do from birth. With a tiny handful of exceptions, one of whom is you, I hear every thought in someone's head."

"That has to suck."

"It does, indeed. That was what made me so lethal on the battle-field. I knew what my enemies were going to do and I could cut them off."

"Yeah, okay, that would not suck." Urian had meant to make him laugh, but if anything, it darkened Styxx's mood, so he changed the subject. "You think you could eat something?"

"I don't know."

Urian handed him a bottle of water. "You need to sip this. While I know you can't die from hunger or thirst, you still feel both. I'll go recon the fridge while you take a shower." He rose to his feet then left the room.

Wishing himself dead, Styxx sat up slowly and leaned back on his arms to survey his bedroom as sirens rang outside above the steady hum of traffic. How he hated it here.

Yeah, Acheron had given him millions of people in this city, but Styxx didn't relate to any of them. The handful of women he'd talked to had rammed home how out of synch he was with this time period. While he was hornier than hell, he couldn't bring himself to sleep with any of them. The minute they opened their mouths and started ranting about trivial things, he lost interest.

He missed discussing philosophy, ideas, and politics with Bethany. Listening to her hum and sing when she wasn't even aware she was doing it . . .

No other woman could touch her beauty or grace.

With a heavy sigh, he forced himself to get up and shower. As he caught sight of himself he grimaced. He still had Acheron's long black hair. He curled his lip. How could Acheron stand it? It made Styxx feel like a woman. Not to mention it was unsanitary and got all over the place. For that matter, how could Acheron fight with it?

Unable to tolerate it any longer, he went back into his bedroom to get his shears from his desk drawer then returned to the bathroom to cut it off. As he moved to throw out the ponytail, he remembered seeing ads for Locks of Love that made wigs for cancer victims. He coiled the hair up and left it on the counter before he started the shower.

Once he was cleaned and clothed, he headed for the kitchen to find Urian eating a sandwich.

"You know, food still tastes weird to me. It's hard to get used to eating when I lived on blood for eleven thousand years."

Styxx grimaced at the reminder of what Apollo had done to his own people. "I'm surprised you haven't filed down your fangs."

"I've thought about it. But I've never seen myself without them. Too old to change now. Might throw off my bite and I have enough trouble chewing as it is. You probably don't realize chewing is a skill. And the first time I bit my tongue . . . be glad you weren't there for it."

Styxx sat down to eat his own ham sandwich. "What made you decide to go Daimon?"

"Rage mostly. My best friend was a couple of years older than me and he refused to fight the curse. So I watched him age to an old man in less than twenty-four hours, screaming in utter agony the entire day until he decayed into nothing but dust. All I could think about was that he'd never harmed anyone. Never even been in a fistfight, and all because of my own grandfather over something that happened before I could walk. It pissed me off. But after losing Phoebe, I can understand why Apollo was so upset and cursed us. I'd have done as much, if not more, if they'd murdered my son and beloved, too."

Styxx released a painful sigh. "He didn't love Ryssa."

Urian arched a brow. "What?"

"She was a possession. Nothing more. Most of the time, he bitched about her whining and complaining . . . which she did all the time, about everything."

"That's not what Ash says."

"He and I had two entirely different sisters. She coddled him and hated me."

"Why?"

Styxx swallowed his bite of food. "What can I say? I'm an asshole. As for Acheron, she felt sorry for him. In her mind, she was convinced that I stole our father's throne and his love from my brother."

"Is that why he calls you a thief?"

Styxx shrugged. "I don't know. Ironically, I didn't even want the throne. I just wanted a family that didn't hate me."

Urian finished off his sandwich. "I'd have gladly given you some brothers. Man, there was so much testosterone in that house, I don't

794

know how my mother and sister stood us. But we were mostly happy. Although my older brothers said that my father was a very different man before Apollo cursed us."

"How so?"

Urian shrugged. "He was happier and much more easygoing." He picked up the pickle from his plate. "The only thing I really hated was not seeing sunlight." He laughed bitterly. "My father used to get so mad at me when I was kid. I'd stand in the door at dawn, trying to catch a glimpse of the sunrise. And he'd start screaming that if I wanted to burst into flames then he was willing to begin the process by setting my ass on fire if I didn't get to safety."

Styxx laughed. "He loved you."

"Yeah, to the day he cut my throat. I've never understood it. After Darius died, I adopted his son and daughter who were toddlers at the time. When Ida and Mylinus died, it about killed me. I can't imagine ever getting so mad at them that I'd do something like that, and they weren't technically mine." The anguish in his eyes pierced Styxx's heart. "How do you cut your own son's throat?"

"I don't know, Uri. I've never understood it, either. When I was just a boy, my own mother tried to kill me for giving her a birthday present. She stabbed me I don't know how many times."

Urian's eyes widened with incredulity. "Your mother?"

He nodded. "Ryssa, too."

"Stabbed you?"

Styxx took a drink of his milk before he responded. "Ryssa gutted me the day before she died."

"What'd you do?" The way Urian asked the question, it was almost comical.

Unfortunately, he'd done nothing to them. "She attacked me over your grandfather."

"Apollo? Why?"

Styxx flinched at the memory. "Jealousy." A shiver of revulsion ran through him. "She stupidly thought I was trying to seduce him as a lover to take his attention from her."

"Ew!"

"Believe me, I couldn't agree more. No offense, but I hate your grandfather with every part of me. Just being in a room with him makes my skin crawl and my stomach turn."

"Don't worry. I'm not going to defend him. I personally think he's a rank, sorry, selfish son of a whore." Urian's phone rang. He looked down and checked the ID. "Excuse me, I need to take this." He got up and left the room while Styxx finished off his food. By the sudden exit, he assumed the call must be from Acheron.

Urian came back a few minutes later while Styxx was cleaning up. "I have to head out. *AOM* later?"

"Sure."

Urian held his hand out to him. When Styxx took it, he pulled him into a brotherly embrace with their hands between their chests. Without another word, Urian vanished.

Styxx finished his chores then went to get his sketchbook. He flipped through the pages, touching the faces of his past that always haunted him. He stopped on the image of Bethany with their baby. It was just like his dream. She sat in a field, on a blanket, cuddling his son. And now he knew these images were what had fed his hallucination.

The boy he'd held wasn't real.

And Bethany was gone. He should have known it was all a dream by the mere fact that Bethany had been able to see them. But he'd been so grateful and happy that he hadn't questioned that small miracle.

A single tear slid from the corner of his eye. Styxx brushed it away and sighed. He was so tired now. More tired than he'd ever been before.

He remembered a time, long, long ago, when he'd known his destiny. Known who and what he was.

Now . . .

I belong nowhere.

Worse, he belonged to no one.

In that moment, he knew what he needed to do. It was time he took his life back, such as it was. He might have lost sight of things for a while, but at the end of the day, he was a fighter. It was all he knew. And he was tired of other people making decisions about his existence. From this moment forward, he was on his own. And he was going to find some place where no one would ever again control or imprison him. Some place where he was comfortable. Some place where he belonged.

JANUARY 24, 2009

Urian tried to call Styxx again, and again it rolled to voicemail. Afraid Styxx might have slipped into another coma, Urian flashed himself to Styxx's condo.

He knew the minute he materialized that something wasn't right. Everything about the condo felt off. But glancing around, he saw nothing out of place.

"Styxx?"

No one answered.

He quickly searched the condo, to find it empty. This time when he went into Styxx's bedroom, he saw that Styxx had pulled out the sketchbook page of him and Phoebe, and left it on top of his desk with a folded note. Fear cinched his gut as he opened it and read.

Urian,
You're the only one who will notice that I'm not here. Don't worry, I'm not doing anything particularly stupid. I just don't want to live in a world I don't understand anymore.
When I find my place and the peace I need to function, I'll be in touch. Until then, take care, my brother. And thank you for being my friend.
S

Grinding his teeth, Urian wanted to find him and beat the shit out of Styxx for the pain he felt right now, and he didn't know why he felt it. Why should he care? He barely knew Styxx.

It must be that they were kindred spirits. Styxx was the only one who really understood about Phoebe. After six years, everyone else had lost patience with his unwillingness to move on and find someone new to love.

But it wasn't that easy. Not when you had a past that was so hard to share with another person. One that left you bleeding and vulnerable. It was difficult to open up to anyone because the moment you did, you knew you ran the risk of being hurt worse, and humiliated should they ever tell your secrets, and when you'd been hurt all your life by others . . .

There was only so much bravery in any given soul.

To finally find the courage to trust and to dare lay your heart in the hands of another and then to lose them was the ultimate cruelty. And it was not something you got over. Ever.

Six years was just a blink of the eye. And apparently so was eleven thousand.

Urian cleared his throat. "Good luck, brother. I hope when you find a way to sleep through the night and breathe again, you'll share the secret with me."

JANUARY 16, 2011

"This . . . seriously sucks."

Styxx laughed at the sound of Urian's disgusted voice from outside his tent as his dog started barking to warn him they had a visitor. He calmed the huge brown dog down before he got up. Throwing back the flap, he came out to greet him. "Depends on your vantage point, little brother."

Arms akimbo, Urian turned in a circle as he surveyed Styxx's small black tent and the vast desert that surrounded them as far as the eye could see in all directions. "From mine . . . you found hell, buddy, except I doubt hell is this hot."

Still laughing, Styxx closed the distance between them. "It's not hot. This is winter. Come back in July or August."

"Yeah, no thanks." Urian hugged him then stood back with a severe frown. "Damn, you've gone native. But for the blue eyes, I'd have no idea it was you."

Styxx lowered the black veil from his face. "Better?"

"Not really. Weirds me out more." He shook his head. "When you called last week and told me you'd been living in the desert for the last two years, I thought you meant Morocco or another city. But you really live out in the middle of Nowhere, Sahara."

Styxx shrugged. "This place makes sense to me."

"You might like it, but it's bringing back bad childhood memories. Life before toilet paper was not worth living."

"Again, a matter of perspective."

Urian appeared doubtful that anyone could like it in the desert. "You look good, by the way. Healthy."

"Thanks." Styxx held the flap open so that Urian could go inside where he had nothing but his bedroll and saddlebags of necessary supplies. "I feel better than I have in a very long time."

The big brown dog came bounding in and curled up on Styxx's bedroll to chew his rawhide bone. Urian arched a brow. "What's his name?"

"Skylos."

He scowled at Styxx. "You named your dog . . . Dog? Seriously?"

Again, Styxx shrugged. "He doesn't seem to mind."

"Probably because he doesn't speak Greek."

Grinning, Styxx pulled out a bottle of wine and the only two cups he had and poured drinks for them.

Urian took a sip. "So what do you call the horse and camel? Alogo and Kamila?"

Styxx rolled his eyes. "No, they had names when I bought them. Jabar and Wasima. The dog just started following after me one day."

Urian sighed heavily. "I'd go insane here. How do you cope with the solitude?"

"That was what I had to make peace with. All my life, I hated being alone. After we freed Soteria, it dawned on me that I had to make a choice. Either be part of the modern world or not."

"You chose poorly, my friend."

"No, this I understand. It's the existence I willingly chose on my own. No one incarcerated or dropped me here against my will. Not to mention, I really like not having solid walls that confine me." And he'd finally come to terms with the fact that he would never be part of a family or group. So long as he was in the vicinity of other people, Styxx had held out hope that Acheron would change his mind or that he'd find a group that would accept him.

Out here, he'd stopped being one half or part of a whole and had learned to be whole by himself. "But what about you? How have you been?"

Urian reached for the can of cashews. "Same old, same old. Someone's always trying to take over the world or end it. Really not looking forward to dealing with 2012 and the crap that's coming out to play with us." He laughed as he scanned Styxx from the top of his agal-wrapped black keffiyeh to his desert boots. "It's really messing with my head how natural you look dressed like a Bedouin. The scimitar and dagger just add to the whole cosplay, *Assassin's Creed* thing you got going."

Styxx laughed. "I also have a handgun tucked at my back, and a rifle." He inclined his head over to where it rested near his bedroll. "But the sword doesn't run out of bullets when bandits attack."

"Another thing I tend to forget. You're human."

"There are many who would argue that."

Urian didn't respond. Instead, he opened the backpack he'd brought and handed a dark blue box to Styxx. "I got you something I thought you might like."

Styxx set his cup aside to take it and open it. A slow smile curled his lips as he saw four new sketchbooks and a pencil set. "Thank you, very much."

"Hey, someone with your talent should never be without. That picture you drew of me and Phoebe . . . incredible. You nailed her looks and you've never even seen her, and I can't thank you enough for leaving that for me. The only pictures I had of her were the ones in my head. Is that why you started drawing?"

He carefully tucked his gift away. "I actually started as a kid. It was one of my favorite things to do until Ryssa saw me and thought I was copying her journals. She had one of her more legendary hissy fits and then when she opened it and saw my feeble attempts at drawing, she laughed and ridiculed them, and ran straight to my father to tell him I'd been wasting my study time and precious parchment on stupidity. He didn't take it well. He made me burn my sketches and had me whipped. Then he made me earn back all the money I'd squandered on wasting good parchment for foolishness. After that wonderful experience, I had such an aversion to art, I didn't even want to look at figured pottery."

"Then how did you learn to draw like that?"

"Vanishing Isle. I didn't have paper or pencil, but I did have a lot of sticks and a lot of wet sand, and a shit ton of time. You think I can draw? You should see my sand cities."

"You mean sand castles?"

"Nah, anyone can build a sand castle. I do entire cities, complete with armies and aqueducts."

Urian laughed even harder. "I hate to admit it, but I have missed your twisted sense of humor. And I'm stunned you get cell reception out here."

"I don't. I was in a town a week ago buying supplies when I called."

"Ah. So how do you charge the phone?"

"Bribe a store clerk to use their outlet for an hour while I shop."

"You've thought of everything."

Styxx leaned over to his backpack and pulled out a roll of toilet paper then chucked it at Urian. "I try."

"That's so messed up." Sobering, Urian cleared his throat. "You haven't asked me about Acheron."

Styxx forced himself not to react. Or to care. That had been the hardest thing to do . . . to let go of and bury a relationship that had died a long, long time ago. "I assume he's doing fine. The world hasn't ended and I'm not dead."

"He's expecting a baby in April."

Styxx snorted. "That should make medical news then, and I'm sure Soteria is grateful she doesn't have to go through labor."

"Wha . . . ah, gah. Yeah. You knew what I meant."

He did, indeed. "Do they know what it is?"

"A boy."

Styxx's breath caught in his throat at the injustice. But he forced his anger down. It wasn't Acheron's fault that his mother had murdered Styxx's son.

His brother's life and happiness had nothing to do with his . . . another thing he'd come to terms with. They may have been born twins, but they were two different people who'd always led two separate lives.

And Acheron didn't want him in his.

Styxx smiled. "I'm happy for them. I'm sure his son will be handsome and strong."

Just as his son would have been, had Galen lived.

Styxx had never been quite sure what had bothered him most about losing Bethany and their baby. The fact that they were gone or that he hadn't been there to at least try and protect them. He could only imagine the horror Bethany must have felt when she faced the Destroyer.

Alone.

He swallowed hard at the eternal pain that never lessened. "So how's Davyn?" he asked, switching the topic to Urian's best friend.

"Insane. I seem to attract that personality type for some reason."

Styxx smirked. *"Aeì koloiòs parà koloiôi hizánei."*

Urian scowled at the old Greek saying. "A jackdaw is always with a jackdaw?"

"Birds of a feather."

Urian laughed. "Hey now, I resent that remark."

Styxx leaned back so that he could peep through the crack in the tent flap to see that it was now completely dark outside. He set his cup aside. "If you really want to know why I love it here, follow me."

Skylos lifted his head, but since Styxx didn't call him outside with them, he went back to sleep.

As soon as they were out of the tent, Styxx looked up at the sky and started opening the sides of the tent so that they could take advantage of the much cooler night air. "You don't have a view like that in New York."

Urian gaped at the sight of the vivid night sky. "I'd forgotten how beautiful and bright they are."

"Yeah. When I was a kid, I'd sit out on my balcony for hours staring at them." He and Acheron would make up stories about the heroes whose constellations they could identify. "Most of the time, I don't pitch the tent. I sleep out here on the sands, watching them. It was one of the things I missed over the centuries. They don't exist on the Vanishing Isle or Katateros."

"Again, I never think about the fact Katateros only has a moon. Alexion said the stars faded when Apollymi killed Astors, I think his name was."

"Asteros."

Urian cocked a brow at his answer. "I'm amazed you remember any of their names."

Honestly, Asteros was one he'd like to forget. But some memories were just too brutal to die no matter how much time passed.

"Are you hungry?" Styxx asked. "I have dried scorpion, nuts, figs, dates, and apples."

Urian twisted his face up in distaste. "I really hope the scorpion offer is just to screw with me."

"No, it's actually quite good. Tastes like chicken."

"Ar, ar, ar." Urian feigned laughter. "I'd rather live on blood . . . or my shoes."

Styxx tsked. "I might have some beef jerky left."

"That I could be talked into."

Styxx went back inside. "It's good to have you here, Urian. I'd forgotten what it was like to actually carry on a real conversation with someone outside of my head."

"Well, now that I know where you are, I might occasionally bother you. As long as you don't feed me grasshoppers, ants, scorpions, or other nasty multi-legged things the gods never intended us to eat."

"Stop being a baby. Eat your meat or you can't have any pudding. How can you have any pudding if you don't eat your meat?"

Urian laughed. "I am stunned you know Pink Floyd."

Styxx shrugged as he opened Skylos's dinner first and poured it into a small metal bowl. "Modern music is the only thing I miss about your world."

"Next time I come, I'll bring you a solar battery charger for your phone. Not like you don't have an abundant supply of sunlight here."

"That I do have. Definitely." Styxx paused as his gaze fell to his small chest near his rifle that had reappeared one day while he'd been in Katateros. He'd thrown out all the herbs long ago, but there were still four things in it that had belonged to him as a man.

Opening it, he pulled out the oiled cloth and handed it to Urian. "My gift to you, little brother."

Urian frowned. "Thank you." He unwrapped the cloth to find Styxx's black and bronze vambraces. "Wow . . . how old are these?"

"They were mine back in the day. Galan gave them to me, and I wore them into every battle I fought."

Urian's jaw went slack then he shook his head. "I can't take these."

Styxx pushed them back toward him. "I have no use for them anymore. They're just something else I have to pack and carry, or worry about losing."

Urian let out a long, appreciative breath. "These are incredible. I can't believe how pristine they are. Thank you. I'll cherish them always."

His gratitude made Styxx extremely uncomfortable. "I know how much you like to collect antiques. And they don't get much older than those." He went to start the campfire so that he could cook their dinner.

Urian carefully wrapped the vambraces back into their cloth and tucked them into his backpack as he watched Styxx. His heart broke for his friend who'd felt so out of place in the world that he'd had to come to the remotest place on it to find some sense of belonging. Urian hadn't been joking when he said that he'd go insane with this kind of isolation. This was truly a desolate, hard way to live.

But sadly, it was all Styxx knew.

All he'd ever known.

MAY 14, 2012

Acheron brushed his hand through his son's blond hair while Sebastos napped on his chest. There was nothing in the world more soothing to him, and the older Bas got, the less Ash was able to understand how his family could have turned their backs on him the way they had. He'd rather have his arm cut off than hit his son.

And the other acts of cruelty against him . . .

Never. He wouldn't be able to put his worst enemy through the things they'd forced him to endure.

Closing his eyes, Ash listened to Tory complaining in Greek as she graded papers in her green armchair across from him.

"I'm sure they're paying attention in class, love."

"Really?" She looked up with a peeved grimace. "'Cause I never knew either of the Thebes was in Yugoslavia."

He cringed at that mistake. "Ouch."

805

"Yes, ouch. I don't even teach that subject. And did you know that one of the heroes in *Seven Against Thebes* was named ... not Parthenopaeus like the last name of the professor who teaches this Ancient Civ class ... oh no, no. Parthenon was his name. Parthenon ... I thought that one was a gimme. Dang. How can anyone get that wrong when Dr. Soteria Parthenopaeus is your professor? Really?" She scribbled a grade on the paper. "One big fat F for you, my lovely." She screwed her face up then erased the grade. "Okay, a D ... no, C. I can't stand to fail a student."

Ash laughed at her kind heart that had saved him from the hell his life had been. "I don't know, *akribos*. That one sounds like she's on her knees, begging to fail."

"And this is why I don't have you help me grade my papers. You'd flunk everybody."

Ash kissed the top of his son's head. "I wouldn't flunk Bas."

"He's only a year old. Even with his superlative gene pool, he won't be taking this class for at least ten years."

"Still planning to have him graduate college by age twelve, huh?"

"Yes. With a name like Sebastos Eudorus Parthenopaeus he does not need to attend high school for very long."

Ash laughed again. She had a valid point, however Bas came with his own guard demon and a father who was a god. "I don't think he's going to have any problems with bullies."

At least not for long.

Smiling, she picked her phone up from the end table and snorted.

"Pam and Kim texting more puppy photos?"

She shook her head. "Your brother has an extremely twisted sense of humor."

His entire body went cold at the mention of Styxx. Ash arched a brow as every bit of his humor was sucked out of him. "What are you talking about?"

"I asked him for his mailing address and this is what he sent back." She held her phone out to him.

Styxx Anaxkolasi
13 Phlegethon Way
Tartarus, Hades 88888

Lightly smiling in spite of the fact it aggravated him, Acheron rolled his eyes. "I particularly appreciate his surname."

"Yeah, king of hell. I thought you would. And I love that his zip code is unhappiness repeated. Oh, and the thirteen for Hades and his river of fire. Even Lord Darkness would find that hysterical. Think I should forward it over to Persephone?"

Fighting against the surge of anger he felt, Ash cupped Bas's head with his hand. "Sure. Why not?"

Tory paused at the look on Ash's face. "What's wrong? I thought you'd be amused."

Those swirling silver eyes burned with a torment she couldn't begin to fathom. "I'm just wondering why you asked him for it."

She was aghast at his words. "Tell me you're not jealous."

He dropped his gaze down to Bas and wouldn't even look her in the eye.

"Acheron . . ." she chided. "Really?"

This time when he met her gaze, the anger and hatred in those swirling silvers set her aback. "We have a bad history, Sota. And you've no idea really how bad. You've only been given bits and pieces. Suffice it to say, I'd rather you keep your distance from him . . . Eleven thousand years later, his paybacks still burn and make me want to draw his blood. It's why I haven't brought him in any closer. I'd love to give him a chance, I really would, but I don't dare. You two are too precious to me to take such a chance with your safety."

Her heart lurched at the agony he tried so hard to conceal. No one else would hear it in his voice, but she did. She was well aware of every nuance of her husband's moods.

Since Ash had always refused to talk about his brother, or to him even when they'd been in close proximity, she'd known their past had to be brutal. But this was such an innocent contact that she

807

hadn't considered how much it would bother him, especially since Styxx had been kind enough to rescue her, and then had quietly gone his way and never bothered them again. "I am so sorry, Achimou. I didn't mean to hurt you. I only wanted to send him a thank-you note."

His eyes turned red, letting her know he was furious. "Thank you for what? Making my life miserable?"

She swallowed as she reconsidered showing him what Styxx had sent for Sebastos's birthday. Would it upset him even more? But there was no missing the suspicion Ash had over her e-mailing his brother.

Better to allay it before it grew. The imagination was far deadlier and more destructive than the simple truth.

Taking her phone back, she went to Bas's room then returned with the ancient box. She took the baby from him before she handed the box over. "He sent that to my office at work for Bas's birthday. There was no return address on it. Just the small note wishing him a happy birthday. It wasn't even signed."

"Then how do you know it was from Styxx?"

"Open it."

Ash wasn't sure what to expect. Severed head ... statue of an obscene gesture ... live cobra. He had no idea, but when he pushed the tissue paper aside and found an old hand carved horse, his heart stopped.

No. It couldn't be ...

Completely stunned, he picked it up and turned it over. Etched on the bottom, in ancient Greek were the words

To Acheron
From Ryssa.
Love always.

Tears filled his eyes as he remembered his beloved sister giving it to him for his fifth birthday. He'd been so thrilled ... And Styxx had gifted him the matching soldier that their father had later burned in a fit of rage. It was that uncalled-for action that had prompted Ash to ask Styxx to keep the horse for him in Styxx's room where, unlike Ash, it'd be safe from harm.

Tory smiled as she fingered the horse in his hands. "I figured it had to come from Styxx. Who else would have had it?"

Ash had to force himself not to splinter the horse as he heard Styxx's angry voice in his head from the past. *I would pay to see you fucked in the ass until you bleed from it.* "The bastard mocks me."

Tory scowled at him. "How so?"

"Why else would he send this if not to hurt me?" Of all men, Styxx had to know how badly those memories burned.

"I don't know, Ash. Maybe he sent it because he thought you'd like to have it for your son. He has to know how much you love Ryssa and he probably thought that you'd like to have the gift she gave you."

Still unsure, Ash returned the horse to the box. "You give him too much credit."

"Maybe. And maybe you don't give him enough."

To have his own wife defend the bastard who'd tried to kill him made him seethe with fury. One good deed Styxx had been forced into committing did not make up for the years and years of abuse he'd suffered at Styxx's hands. "Do not ever defend him to me," he growled. "He was born a selfish bastard and he remains one to this day."

She held her hands up in surrender. "Fine. I'll lose his e-mail and block the account. Not that I think he'll ever use it. As you can see, his response was quite terse, and . . . obviously he doesn't mean for me to contact him again."

"Thank you."

Tory inclined her head then started to leave. Yet she couldn't help adding one last thing. "I swear I'm going to drop the subject and never mention this again, but I have to ask . . . Why would he hang on to that for almost twelve thousand years and keep it so pristine if he truly hated you and is as selfish as you claim? It looks brand new, and I of all people know how hard it is to maintain something that old in that condition for this amount of time. That just doesn't strike me as a labor of hatred, Acheron, but rather one of love."

I shouldn't be doing this ...

Acheron had sworn to himself that he'd never look at Ryssa's journals again. He couldn't stand seeing her handwriting and hearing her voice in his head. But after what Tory had said and the memories she'd stirred, he wanted to know something about Styxx's life all the years they'd been apart.

Because the one thing that damned horse had done was make him remember what Styxx had received as gifts that same year ...

A fighting instructor who'd gleefully blackened his eye and busted his nose during their first practice, and the "pleasure" of attending court sessions with his father. When Styxx had asked about a toy present, his father had sneered at him. *"I'm not raising a boy. You're to be a king, and kings don't play with toys. You're too old for play. It's time for you to start assuming your royal duties, and stop being selfish and thoughtless."*

Styxx had only been five years old.

Ryssa had given Styxx nothing. *"Why waste my money on something he won't appreciate? He has more than enough toys for one boy."* But really, he hadn't. His father had used them as a source of punishment. Whenever Styxx displeased him, he made Styxx burn them.

The only times he could ever remember Styxx playing was when he'd sneak away to be with Ash.

Ash fell silent as those long forgotten memories surged and he focused on his sister's writing. Most of the entries were innocuous. Many chronicled whatever Styxx had been given ...

Today, Father gave Styxx an incredible black horse. It would easily cost four to five times the price of my pony. Father said it's because Styxx will one day ride it into battle. But I don't think so. I'm sure Styxx will be safely tucked in a chariot, behind a driver and two bodyguards.

Acheron flipped forward a few more pages.

For the Dionysian Festival tomorrow, Father gave me a simple gold necklace. Styxx was given an impressive leaf crown. He didn't even say thank you for it. But then why should he? Father gives him everything. I tried to speak to Father earlier and he couldn't be bothered with my idle prattle. Not while he had his precious Styxx to coach about politics.

Acheron frowned at the date. Politics? Styxx was only eight. What kind of political discussion could his father have had with an eight-year-old?

"What are you doing?"

He jumped at the sound of Tory's voice. "Dang, woman, make some noise when you walk. You startled me."

"Now you know how I feel living with Captain Never-make-a-peep." She came forward to peer over his shoulder. "Why are you looking at those up here all alone?"

"Because I have this really annoying wife who made a lot of sense to me earlier, and I didn't want her to know that she had me thinking about things."

"Aw, in that case, I won't tell her I caught you snooping."

"I would definitely appreciate it."

Smiling, Tory leaned against his back and wrapped her arms around his waist. Acheron closed his eyes and savored the sensation of her there. She was the only person alive he'd allow at his back. She rested her chin on his shoulder. "What are you looking for?"

Unlike him, she'd read through them all.

"Information about Styxx."

"Oh, I call those the Jealous Rant Series."

Ash frowned. "How so?"

"Granted, I don't know Ryssa. I know you love her and I would never, ever say anything against her, but when you read her entries as an objective outsider, they come off as very mean-spirited whenever she mentions Styxx. It's as if she's bipolar. Anything to do with

811

you is sweet and complimentary. Filled with love and compassion and devotion. But everything with Styxx is, kill the obnoxious little beast I hate. Like the one you're looking at."

Tory flawlessly read the ancient Greek he'd taught her. "Today Styxx left for war. I still can't believe how he embarrassed Father when he took off his prince's signet ring in front of everyone and shoved it at him. I could buy a fleet of horses for the cost of that ring and he treated it as if it was nothing. He's so spoiled. Nothing has any value to him at all. I told Father he should melt it down and make me one. I would at least appreciate it."

She sighed. "Makes you wonder why a prince would take off the one thing that was guaranteed to get him home should he be taken by his enemies. Without that ring, he would have been treated as any prisoner and put to death or sold into slavery, especially given his age and physical beauty at the time. I mean that was a pretty big 'Screw you, Dad.' I know he was young, but still he'd have to be mentally defective to risk what slavery meant for a handsome teenager in those days."

Ash swallowed as he noted the date. "Damn, he was too young to go to war." Barely sixteen . . .

"Mmm, and speaking of, I wanted to ask you about . . . " She flipped through the pages.

"Wait." Ash stopped her then flipped back and started reading.

June 23, 9529 BC
It was midday before I finally found Acheron's whereabouts. I knew better than to ask my father for his location—that would only invite his anger toward me . . .

Acheron shook his head as he reread it. "This can't be right."
"How so?"
"Ryssa brought me food well before this date."
"Are you sure?"
"Believe me, I wouldn't forget it. Acts of kindness toward me were rare enough that they tended to stand out."

"Not what I meant. Are you sure it was Ryssa and not Styxx who brought the food?"

Ash grimaced as he considered it. "Styxx hated me. Tory, he castrated me. Brutally. You have no idea the shit he put me through."

"And I ask you again ... Are you sure? How many times has Artemis pretended to be someone else to get to you? Or any of the gods, for that matter. Remember in the *Odyssey* when Athena walks around disguised as Mentor? Or the *Iliad*? The gods were forever masquerading as others, for all kinds of reasons."

She was right.

Tory picked up another journal and opened it. "And you never told me that Styxx was with you in Atlantis."

"That's because he wasn't."

"No?" She flipped to a page and pointed to the entry. "Read that one."

October 28, 9533 BC
Styxx returned from Atlantis today and you would have thought that Zeus himself had come down from Olympus to grace us with His golden presence. Instead of being cross with Styxx for selfishly abandoning his duties and vanishing without notice or word, and worrying Father sick, Father rewarded the beast for it! He placed him in a suite of rooms that make a mockery of mine. How is Styxx to learn to be considerate of others when Father dotes on him so for his rudeness? It sickens me to see him so spoiled.

And when I asked him for news of Acheron, Styxx sounded just like Estes. "He's fine, Ryssa. Just fine." Nothing else. Not a single word about how Acheron looked or anything. Styxx didn't even want to discuss it. He very rudely told me to leave him alone when I pressed him for more details about my brother.

He acts like he's drugged or drunk or something. It's disgusting, and he smells. The scent is fruity and cloying and repugnant. If I smelled like that, Father would make me bathe it off.

I should go to Atlantis and vanish for over two months, too, and see how Father likes that.

The letters Estes sent Father said he enjoyed his time with Styxx immensely, and that they had great fun riding with Estes and his friends and Acheron. He said that he loved teaching Styxx new things, and seeing the twins together, night and day. Of course, he lavished praise all over Styxx at Acheron's expense.

"He's an even quicker learner and has a very gifted tongue that we greatly took advantage of," Estes wrote. As if Styxx could be better at anything than my Acheron is.

What I really don't understand . . . How can Styxx be so sullen after having such a long and fun-filled visit? He's been locked in his room since his return and growls if anyone approaches him. When he comes out, he looks awful. Shakes all the time and cringes if you go near him. He won't even look at Father. I don't understand my beastly brother's mind.

Father hasn't even noticed. He's just so glad to have him back, he couldn't care less how shameful Styxx behaves.

Since I received the servant's letter asking me to Atlantis, I think I shall go, too. After all. If Styxx can have fun there, so can I.

Yes, that's what I'll do. I'll show Father. I'll visit Acheron and Estes and have my own adventure. Then I can see how Acheron is and make sure he's happy.

Acheron's head reeled as he read that. "I have no memory of Styxx ever being there with me."

"For two months?"

Ash shut the journal and pushed it aside. From what Ryssa described, and what his sister claimed Estes had written, he could only imagine what had been done to Styxx. Estes had loved his double entendres. Entendres he used to publicly humiliate and hurt his victims. And Ash had received more than his fair share of that cruelty when he lived with his uncle.

And as Ash sat there, he remembered some of the things Styxx had mentioned to him in anger and in passing, but never elaborated on.

The night Styxx had tried to free him after his father had ordered him returned to Atlantis . . .

Styxx hadn't been lying when he'd buried the dagger in the ground. He must have gone to Atlantis on his own to free him. And somehow he'd been captured, too.

Damn you, Estes. You sick bastard. It would be just like his twisted uncle to take those memories from Ash and leave them with Styxx to torture him with. There was nothing Estes loved more than playing with people's heads and scrambling their thoughts.

Turning and using them against each other.

Estes had done that with Ryssa. He'd convinced Ash that she hated him and wanted nothing to do with him at all, while telling his sister that Ash was fine and happy. If Styxx had cared enough to go after Ash to free him, Estes would have definitely kept Ash from remembering it so that he wouldn't ever try to leave, and he would have made sure Styxx was punished severely enough that he never tried to free him again.

Tears filled his eyes as he stared at the closed journals and pulled Tory into his arms for comfort.

"What is it, sweetie?"

"Tory, if I've done what I think I have, I don't know how I'll live with it."

JUNE 23, 2012

Styxx froze as he entered his tent to find a Charonte demon sitting on his bedroll, staring at him with big red eyes. The last time he'd seen Simi, she'd shredded him and left him . . . dead.

Moving as slowly as he could, he put his hand on the .38 he kept in a holster at the base of his spine. It wouldn't kill her, but it would give him time to get away from her should she attack again. He also made sure to keep Skylos outside where the demon couldn't hurt him either.

To his complete shock, she smiled warmly. "Hello, akri-copy."

Wary as hell, Styxx eyed her. "What do you want?"

She sighed heavily. "The Simi come to say she sorry for what she did to you. But see, you hurt my akri and the Simi loves her akri so anyone who attacks her akri gets eat, even those who look like akri, see?"

Not really.

She stood up.

Tightening his grip on the gun, Styxx immediately backed away.

The demon cocked her head and frowned. "You look so strange like that. Why you wear eye makeup, akri-copy?"

He shrugged. "Protects my eyes from the sun."

"That's why yous gets sunglasses, silly. Don't nobody tell you that?" She bent down and picked up her red heart-shaped backpack that had black demon wings spanning out from it. She wrinkled her nose at him. "Itn't it cute? Akra-Danger gived it to me at Christmas. Now less see ..." She rummaged around until she pulled out a bottle of barbecue sauce with a ribbon tied around it. "Happy birthday, akri-copy!"

When he didn't move to take it, her smile faded. She stepped toward him and he quickly took two steps back.

Her shoulders and wings dropped as she pouted. "Why you so skittish of the Simi?"

"I don't know. Call me stupid, but the last time we met, you killed me."

Her wings drooped even more. "I know. It was wrong to do that to you. But that was before you saved akri and akra-Tory and gave Baby Bas his horse he loves to play with. So the Simi glad you didn't stay dead, and I promise I won't kill you again. Friends?"

Styxx wasn't sure what to make of his brother's demon daughter. He knew from Acheron's memories that she was hopelessly devoted to his brother. Unlike a human, she wasn't devious or conniving or even complicated. Simi was very black-and-white. She either hated or she loved.

Letting go of the gun, he reached for the barbecue sauce. "Thank you, Simi."

Her wings shot back up as a smile curved her lips. "It the Simi's favorite that she only give to special quality people. See ... " She pointed to the label. "Hot, hot ... though it hot here, you might not need it. But it's good on everything." She beamed a giant smile at him.

He inclined his head to her. "I appreciate it. Thank you very much."

She cocked her head again and frowned. "Why you so sad, akri-copy? You got aches in your heart?"

"I'm fine, Simi."

Her frown deepening, she glanced around the tent. "Who you gots coming to celebrates with you?"

Styxx sighed. "I don't celebrate birthdays."

Eyes wide, she gaped. "No! Birthdays are always special cause they's the days when you were welcomed to the world and people be all happy when babies are born."

Yeah ... not in his experience.

Styxx set the barbecue sauce down next to his pack. "You should probably go back to Acheron before he misses you."

Instead, she sat down on his bedroll.

Now it was Styxx's turn to frown. "What are you doing?"

She opened her backpack. "Akri got lots of people who celebrate with him, and akri-copy got nobody. That makes Simi sad for akri-copy. Nobody should be alone on their birthday so ... " She pulled out a package of Ding Dongs and held them toward him. "We have birthday cake!"

Styxx smiled at the innocent gesture. "I've never had birthday cake before."

"Never?"

He shook his head.

She pressed her index finger to her lips in an adorable expression.

817

"We need candles, but you so old that we'd have to have cakes the size of a . . . battleship . . . Hmmm . . . that's okay." She reached into her pack and pulled out a glowstick. "Less pretend this is one. But you can't blow it out, but we pretend you do. How's that?"

"Sure."

"Okays. Now akri–copy sit."

Styxx sat down across from her while she carefully opened the package and left the cakes on the wrapper. Then she snapped the glowstick and shook it.

"Now you make your wish and blow out the candle." She held the glowstick up in front of his face.

Styxx blew on it.

She narrowed her eyes at him. "You didn't make a wish, did you?"

"I don't have anything to wish for." The things he wanted, he couldn't have, and nothing else really seemed important.

"Everybody has wishes, akri–copy."

"I'm not everybody."

Οὔτις ἐμοί γ' ὄνομα . . .

I am Nobody.

Simi took his hand into hers then placed a cake in it. "Then the Simi will make your wish for you. The Simi wishes you will be happy like the Simi and her akri."

He smiled at her childlike wonder and views. "Thank you, Simi."

She touched her cake to his then ate it. "You gots to eat yours all in one bites," she said with her mouth full. " 'Cause we gots no candles to blow out, you have to eat in one gulp for the wish to come true."

He laughed in spite of himself and shoved the cake into his mouth.

Simi licked her fingers and nodded. "Good, right?"

He swallowed the cake. "The best ever."

Simi got up on her knees and kissed his cheek then hugged him. "If you want, akri–Styxx, the Simi can love you, too. 'Cause hearts

818

are amazing things. They get lots bigger to make room for new people to love alongside the old people you love." She patted her chest. "The Simi gots lots of room to love you, too . . . if you want."

Styxx was amazed by her. His brother had been lucky to have Simi by his side for all these centuries. "I should like that very much."

She hugged him again, and patted his back. "Okay, the Simi have to go now, but she'll be back to see you soon. And remember akri-Styxx that wishes are powerful, powerful things that come true when you believe in them. And the Simi believes you will be very happy, very soon. Bye." Then she was gone.

Smiling over his unexpected visit, Styxx picked up the wrapper and threw it away. He let Skylos back into the tent and still wasn't sure what to make of Simi's appearance. No doubt his brother would have a fit if he ever learned she'd come to see him.

But it had been a nice surprise. No one had remembered his birthday since Bethany had been with him. He wouldn't have even known it was today had Simi not visited. Not that it mattered. At his age, really, what was the point in counting them?

JUNE 25, 2012

"Where the hell's my brother?"

Urian paused his game to stare blankly at Acheron. "You need to modulate that unwarranted ire, buddy. I'm not your 'ho and you ain't my pimp."

A tic started in Acheron's jaw. "Sorry." But his tone contradicted his apology. "Do you happen to know where Styxx is?"

Urian took a swig of his beer. "Am I your brother's keeper?"

"You gave Tory his e-mail. I assume that means you're keeping tabs on him."

Urian clicked back into play and had to bite his tongue to stop his causticity from saying something that would cause Ash to blast him through a wall. "Your point?"

"I've been to his condo three times this month and he's not there. As far as I can tell he hasn't been there for quite some time."

Nice powers of observation, Atlantean god. It only took you what? Three and a half years to realize your brother had moved out?

For that alone, he wanted to punch Ash.

Refraining from that particular level of stupid, Urian cleared his throat. "Maybe we should put his face on a milk carton, see if anyone has information on his location." He frowned. "Do they still have milk cartons? Now that I think about it, I haven't seen one in a while."

"I'm serious, Urian."

"I can hear that," he said, taking his anger out on his online opponent as opposed to his boss. "I mean, damn, how dare my eleven-thousand-year-old brother not be right where I put him three and a half years ago after he did me a huge favor and saved my life and that of my wife. Rank filthy bastard. Inconsiderate dog! Maybe we should take him out back and beat the shit out of him for worrying you so."

"What is your problem?"

Time to kiss the wall.

Urian signed off and removed his headset. Picking up his beer, he faced Acheron. "You know I'd die for you. I put my ass on the line for you all the time without fail or hesitation. Hell, sometimes I'm even grateful you saved my life. But you're not perfect, Ash. None of us are, and when it comes to your brother, you're a fucking prick."

Rage mottled Acheron's cheeks as his eyes darkened. "You don't know my brother like I do."

"Really?" His voice dripped with sarcasm. "When was the last time you sat down and had an actual conversation with Styxx? Oh wait . . ." Urian feigned a laugh as he slapped his thigh. "I know this." He sobered and those blue eyes pierced Ash with contempt.

"You were seven years old at the time. So that's what? You're the same age as my dad ... so that would make you older than shit and shit's great-grandfather ... it would have been only about eleven thousand five hundred and fifty-three years ago, give or take a few hours ... Yeah, you're right, that makes you one hell of an expert on everything to do with Styxx. Why did I even question it? Stupid me."

Ash's cheeks mottled with even more color. "Don't you dare judge me on something you know nothing about."

"Why not? You judge Styxx all the time on things you know nothing about."

"I'm warning you, Urian."

"And I'm suicidal, boss. Fear factor really doesn't play in with a man who doesn't give a shit about life. But ... you know your brother, you say? Fine, expert, then answer me one basic, easy question about him."

Urian paused for effect. "What was the name of his wife? You know, the one you didn't even know he had? He had a five-year committed relationship with her before he died, while you lived in the same house with him and gained all your expertise where he was concerned ... and you know him so well. She's the only woman he has ever loved. Not knowing her name is like claiming to know me and not knowing Phoebe's. For that matter, it's not like he didn't carve her name and that of his son into his arm eleven thousand five hundred and thirty-six years ago."

Ash's eyes turned vibrant red. "He tried to kill me," he growled.

"Yeah, I know, because I do talk to him. About a decade ago in New Orleans. Surrounded by Dark-Hunters, you were wide awake and an Atlantean god with all his powers available to him when Styxx attacked you out of desperation to escape the eternal hell he was damned to. Not quite the same as being a human boy in bed, sound asleep when someone plunges a dagger through your heart and leaves you on the floor, in a pool of your own blood to die alone."

"He was trying to kill his own father. Did he tell you that? Plotting a conspiracy against him and blaming me for it."

"Was he? 'Cause you know, people never lie about shit like that. Ever."

Ash stiffened. "Yes, they do lie, Urian. So why are you believing Styxx when I know what a liar he is?"

Glaring his rage, Urian set his beer aside. "How do you know? You still haven't answered the easiest question on the planet about him . . . if you know nothing else about your brother, you should know his wife's name."

Acheron glanced away.

Urian shook his head. When he spoke, his tone was low and chiding. "All those powers you hold and you can't answer it. It was Bethany, just so you know. They were going to name their son Galen, after his mentor who died in his arms when he was a kid. A mentor who gave his life to save Styxx's when someone other than you tried to assassinate him while he was buying his wife's wedding ring. Now let me tell you about the man I know . . ."

Ash ground his teeth as he struggled not to hit Urian for his blatant stupidity. "I don't want to hear it. And for your information, I'm not the only one who hated him. You have no idea how many people wanted him dead in his human lifetime." *How many times I was beaten and grudge-fucked by men who despised every breath he took.* Ash flinched at the memories that still burned raw. Because Styxx was the prince, they couldn't touch him. But Acheron was a worthless whore and they paid top dollar to pretend he was their prince so that they could abuse him in Styxx's stead.

That kind of hatred had a basis in something.

Not to mention Ryssa. She was a kind, beautiful, and gentle soul and she'd hated Styxx with every part of her being. "Did Styxx ever tell you that he had no friends . . . because no one could stand the arrogant bastard?"

"Arrogant? My God, Ash, you are so blind where he's concerned. Have you ever once spoken to him?"

"I'm out of here," Ash growled.

Urian stepped forward to pin him with a merciless glare. "You leave, and I'll have Tory hold you down to hear what I have to say. Things you need to know."

"You wouldn't dare."

"Try me ... Because tonight when you lie down in your bed and your wife snuggles up to you and you smile with happiness, I want you to take a minute and imagine in the morning when you wake up in that same bed and reach for her warmth, it's gone. Forever. That you'll never know another minute of having her limbs tangled with yours. Never wake up and feel her body pressed against you. Then imagine going into Bas's room and finding it empty, too. All the plans you had for him, gone forever. Then, I want you to take a minute and imagine the kind of love and decency it took for Styxx to go with me into Kalosis and embrace the woman who murdered them. For you, Acheron. The brother who hates his guts."

Urian paused to let those words sink in. "Now I admit I'm not as big a man as you are, Ash. But I can tell you right now, I wouldn't piss on my father to save the world, never mind hug him to keep my brother from sharing the pain I have every time I think of Phoebe ... which is every other heartbeat. I'm a vindictive son of a bitch. Because after the fit you pitched where you blasted him through the wall just moments before we went down to Kalosis, I would have gutted your mother for what she took from me. And here's another thing you don't know. She whispered something to him before he hugged her, and I have no idea what she said, but knowing your mother as I do, it wasn't kind. Kindness just isn't something the goddess of destruction is known for."

Snorting, Urian crossed his arms over his chest. "And then, after he went down there to save your wife, to keep you from spending the rest of eternity in hell, he took a blade for you from my father. I was there, Acheron. I saw it. No lies. Truth. Yeah, you healed him, and then you turned around and put the man who had just saved your life, and your wife's, completely out of your mind. You turned your fucking back on him. I was the one who took him home that night and you never once asked about him again until today."

Urian sarcastically bit his lip. "Oh and by the way, you forgot to pull the poison out of him when you healed his wound. For two months he lay in a coma, burning with fever and delirium, and I had to get Savitar to come in and help him because when I asked you, you told me he was doing it for attention. So while I love you like a brother, I consider Styxx my family, too, and unlike you, Styxx has no one else in this world. Poor bastard got stuck with me alone. Can you imagine *that* nightmare?"

Drawing a ragged breath, Urian curled his lip in disgust. "He left that apartment a couple of days after Savitar brought him out of his coma, over three years ago. He saved your life and Tory's, and it took you three and a half years to realize he'd left." He applauded sarcastically. "Good job, brother. Good job."

Ash wanted to hold on to his hatred for Styxx. He needed it. But right now . . .

"And you know what I've always found fascinating, Ash? You never once asked me how I met your brother."

Ash looked away as shame filled him.

"It was in Katateros, just so you know. I went out for a walk on the beach and heard something in the temple down the hill from yours. I found him inside, alone in the dark, with scraps to eat, and when I asked him if there was anything I could bring him, do you know what your arrogant bastard brother asked me for?"

Ash shook his head.

"Fresh water. That's all Mr. Selfish wanted. He was having a hard time desalinating the river seawater to drink. Now I know you don't like to eat, but the next time you're home, I want you to take Tory and walk around your island and have her point out the edible foods she finds. There aren't many."

"I assumed one of you was taking food to him."

"You've assumed a lot of things about him that aren't true. Such as telling me that he was in the Elysian Fields for eleven thousand years. He wasn't. Artemis put him on a Vanishing Isle completely alone. No one to talk to, and again with no supplies whatsoever. Not even a hammer."

"That's not what she told me."

"Because Auntie Artemis never lies. Ever. About anything . . . such as having an eleven-thousand-year relationship with you that resulted in the birth of a daughter my age. Artemis is the fountain of absolute truth, especially where you're concerned. Her kind, benevolent care for all those centuries was why Styxx didn't complain when you dropped him in Katateros. It was how he knew how to survive there with nothing. But the real question is why did he leave?"

"I assumed he got bored."

"There you go again with the assumptions." Urian dropped his gaze down to the tattoo on Ash's body where his Charonte daughter slept. "Our precious little Simi demon attacked him unprovoked and . . . well, she did kill him. But he didn't stay dead, obviously. Now before you call him a liar for that, too, I want you to know he never told me that story. I overheard it from Simi when she was bragging to her sister about ripping apart the bad copy of you who tried to hurt her akri. In fact, Styxx never says a word against you. Ever."

"He told you I stabbed him."

"Yeah, one night when he was really tore up and drunk and I was asking him about some of the scars on his body. As many and as bad as most of them are, the huge jagged one in the center of his chest directly over his heart tends to stand out."

Ash frowned at his words. "What scars?"

"Dear gods, Ash . . . have you never looked at your brother? They're all over him. Even his face."

No, he'd never seen scars on Styxx. But as Urian pointed out, he never really looked at him.

Only through him.

"Where is he?"

Urian narrowed his gaze. "Why? So you can hurt him again?

Forget it. He's gone someplace safe so that you won't have to worry about him darkening your doorstep ever again."

"Yeah, he's so altruistic with his billion-dollar bank account."

"If you're talking about the money you set up for him when you dumped him off without a second thought? He transferred that back to your account before he left New York. That, too, has been closed for three years."

Sick of this game, Ash glared at him. "You know, I can find him without you."

"You hurt him, Acheron, and I swear to the gods I loathe that I will beat you down for it. For once in your lives, can you not think of him and just leave him alone. It's all he wants. You've already forgotten him for three years. What's another three hundred?"

Those words were harsh. But harsher still was the truth behind them.

Ash swallowed. "I want to talk to my brother."

Urian sighed. "Fine. He's in the Sahara. Literally. Living like a Bedouin. I had dinner with him a month ago and haven't heard anything since. That's all I know."

Inclining his head, Ash left Urian and went to locate Styxx.

Careful to stay invisible, Ash watched Styxx feed his horse and camel. Urian hadn't exaggerated the horrors of Styxx's meager existence in the least. But for the vivid blue eyes that were ringed in kohl, Styxx would easily pass for a Bedouin. Dressed all in black, he had his keffiyeh pulled over his mouth and nose, concealing his hair and features completely. The only color on his body was the brown sheath for his scimitar and the red agal wrapped around his black keffiyeh. And the two brown leather arm sheaths for the throwing knives they contained.

The horse nipped at the black leather pouch on Styxx's hip.

Styxx laughed. "Ah, you caught me." He scratched the horse's ears and patted her neck. "Yes, they're for you." He opened the pouch and pulled out apple slices that he fed by hand to his horse. "Good, right?" His horse actually nodded and snorted.

The camel made a sound of annoyance. "Don't worry, Jabar. I haven't forgotten you." Styxx went to share some with his other mount.

Once the animals were fed and secured, and after he'd washed off his hands in the small oasis, Styxx headed into a tiny black tent.

Ash followed him in and was stunned at what he found. The "prince" had a modest bedroll on top of a worn-out Persian rug where a big brown dog lay sleeping beside metal bowls of half-eaten dog food, and water. Next to the bedroll was an iPhone on the ground hooked to a small speaker that was playing Disturbed's "Criminal" low enough to be heard in the tent, but not so loud as to drown out the sound of someone approaching outside. A backpack, saddlebags, four medium-sized solar lanterns, one rifle, and nothing else.

Unaware of Ash's presence, Styxx stripped down to his akarbey.

Damn, Urian wasn't kidding. The scars on Styxx's body were horrifying to look at. When, where, and how had Styxx gotten those? And when Styxx squatted in the corner to search his backpack, Ash's breath caught in his throat as he saw Apollo's sun symbol that spanned the entire length of Styxx's shoulders.

As a god, Ash knew exactly what a mark like that meant and all the horrors it entailed . . .

Fierce ownership.

It was a warning to any god who saw it that Apollo would fight hard to keep Styxx as his slave. And Apollo didn't do that lightly. The Olympian god had never marked Ryssa as his property. He hadn't cared enough about her to do it. For that matter, Artemis had never officially marked Acheron, and they'd been together thousands of years before Tory had freed him.

And as Ash stared at the mark, Ryssa's last day, with her screams of how Styxx had seduced Apollo, took on an ominous tone. While Ash might have been wrong about many things to do with his brother, the one thing he knew for a fact was that Styxx was completely and staunchly heterosexual.

But Apollo wasn't. And if Styxx had fought his ownership,

Apollo would have retaliated with a vengeance. *Look what the bastard had done to his own people . . .*

His own son.

Acheron himself.

Tory's words about the gods in human form rang with a frightening possibility. He'd always wondered how Styxx could be so vicious to him. How his own twin brother could essentially assault himself whenever he attacked Acheron.

Apollo castrating him made a lot more sense than Styxx doing so. The Olympian would have wanted vengeance on Ash for having slept with Artemis and "defiling" her. The savagery of that attack over Artemis made a lot more sense than Styxx attacking for a woman he couldn't have cared less about.

Putting an apple in his mouth and holding it there with his teeth, Styxx stood up with two bottles of warm water, and a sketchbook and pencils. He sat down on the bedroll without disturbing the dog then opened the water to sip at it. While he ate the apple, he turned to a page in the book where there was a sketch of a woman who sat in a beautiful meadow, holding an infant in her arms. The baby's hand was on her lips as she smiled down at him. Even though it was only a drawing, the love in her expression was haunting.

Ash's gaze went to Styxx's left hand that held his apple and then down to the names of his wife and son that Styxx had meticulously carved into his own flesh.

An ultimate tribute. Not something a man would have done lightly.

The full magnitude of what Styxx had lost and how much his brother had loved his family slammed into him with such force that for a moment he thought he'd be sick.

Styxx set the apple aside and wiped his hand against his thigh then leaned over so that he could draw. Ash winced as he watched the way Styxx had to use his left hand to wedge the pencil into the grip of his damaged right hand so that he could use it. The way Styxx did it said that he was so used to making accommodations for his partially paralyzed hand that he didn't even think about it anymore.

Tears misted in Styxx's blue eyes as he lovingly brushed his fiercely scarred right hand across the page. "Miss you, Beth," he breathed before he began filling in more details. He pushed the book back a bit as he worked, and it was only then Ash realized why.

He was protecting it.

Every so often, a random tear would fall as Styxx worked. Silent and focused, he would wipe it away on his shoulder and keep drawing.

Awed by his brother's heart and talent, Ash sank to his knees to watch Styxx's precise, expert strokes. He'd had no idea that his brother could do such.

Once it was finished, Styxx sniffed back his quiet tears and flipped through the book that was filled with pictures of the same woman and the baby boy at various ages that ranged from newborn to adulthood. It was as if Styxx had created the memories of his wife and child that he'd wanted to have.

Memories that had been stolen from him.

By Acheron's mother.

But what tore out Ash's heart was how much the boy looked like Bas. And when Styxx paused on a drawing of Styxx holding his wife and child, Acheron had to leave.

Sobs tore through him as Urian's words came home to roost and he thought about trying to live without Tory and Bas for even one day. Never mind centuries.

How could I have asked him to save my wife's life and embrace the killer of his own?

Urian was right. He was a fucking prick. And he knew nothing about his brother.

Pressing the heels of his hands to his eyes, Ash fought for control as he saw the drawing Styxx had made of the boy holding a teddy bear. If he didn't know better, he'd swear his brother had met his son.

Now that he thought about it, even their wives favored enough to be related.

Was it possible that he'd allowed his hatred for Estes and Ryssa's jealousy toward Styxx to infect him so completely and color his own opinions? Surely he wouldn't have been so easily swayed.

Would he?

All the times in his life he'd preached to others that there were always three sides to every event—yours, theirs, and the truth that lay somewhere in the middle.

Yet when it came to his brother . . .

Emotions don't have brains. Ash knew that better than anyone.

And as he stood on the solitary dune, looking out at a hot, vast desert, he remembered how much Styxx had hated being alone as a child. How many times he'd sneak into Acheron's room and had been beaten for it. But Styxx hadn't cared. He'd come to Acheron regardless.

Brothers. Forever and always.

Styxx had tried to make amends. He'd reached out and Acheron had slapped him away. Repeatedly. Worse, Ash had walked away from Styxx for centuries and hadn't even given him a single, passing thought.

Not once.

It's amazing the damage we do to ourselves and others when all we're trying to do is protect ourselves from being hurt. How many times had he said that to a Dark-Hunter?

But then advice was always easier to give than to follow.

Needing to set this right, Ash returned to the tent. He stood outside for several minutes, debating the sanity of this.

But he wasn't a coward.

With a deep breath for courage, Acheron opened the tent flap. "Styxx?"

The dog crouched low and growled at him.

His brother was now sitting forward, holding a blood-soaked cloth to his pinched nose while he calmed the dog beside him. "I didn't fucking do it."

Baffled, Ash frowned. "Do what?"

"Whatever it is you're here to accuse me of. I am not a god. I cannot travel from here to wherever you live in the blink of an eye. It would take me a solid week to reach even a modest village." The anger and hatred seared him.

And Ash knew he deserved it. "I came to thank you for the present you sent to Sebastos."

"An e-mail would have sufficed."

"Would you have gotten it?"

"Eventually."

Ash narrowed his gaze as he saw the other two blood-soaked cloths on the ground. "You still get headaches, too?"

"Yes, and the biggest one of all just traipsed through my door." Styxx pulled the rag back to check the bleeding, which was still pouring. He folded the cloth and returned it to his nose. "What do you want?"

Forgiveness. Yet he had no right to ask this man for it. Urian had been right. Styxx had tried to kill him, but Styxx had come at him openly. Hell, he'd even warned him he was gunning for him.

He, on the other hand, had gone at Styxx's back. And both had struck for the same reason. They'd just wanted an end to their suffering.

"Can I ask you something?"

"Yes," Styxx snarled, "you're an asshole and I'm a bastard. What the fuck is wrong with the men of my family that they always want to interrogate me when I'm in pain and bleeding?"

Ash dropped his gaze to the row of brand scars that ran the length of Styxx's side. They started in his armpit where no hair could grow because of the burn-damaged flesh and vanished beneath his waistline. Even his nipple was severely disfigured. Those unique scars tweaked Ash's memory and brought out a long-suppressed act of stupidity on Ash's part. He cringed as he remembered when he'd seen the scars that covered his brother's groin and thighs in Atlantis.

What did you do? Masturbate with a hot poker?

831

Instead of punching him as he should have, Styxx had curled into a ball and said nothing. He'd just stared at the wall.

Ash wished he could go back in time and slap himself for that cruelty. It was obvious someone had tortured the hell out of his brother.

And Styxx would have had them as a kid.

Before he went into battle. Only back then, Ash hadn't cared. Lost in his own misery, he hadn't spared three seconds to consider Styxx's.

Just because you have it bad, Acheron, it doesn't mean I have it good. No wonder Styxx had snarled that at him.

Repeatedly. But the scar that really racked him was the one right over his heart. The one Ash had given his own brother . . .

"Why are you still here?" Styxx asked. "You wanted me out of your life. I'm out. I'm sorry I sent that damn horse that I didn't want to look at anymore. I won't ever bother any of you again. Just go!"

"Why did you send it?"

A tic worked in Styxx's jaw. "Because I promised you that I wouldn't let anything happen to it, and contrary to what you think of me, I don't break the promises I make."

Ash closed his eyes as pain overwhelmed him. *Why didn't I talk to you when you were in Katateros like you asked me to?*

Because he'd been angry. Hurt.

Mostly angry.

"I just wanted to say I'm sorry, Styxx."

Styxx gave him an astonished glare. "Oh, okay." His tone dripped with sarcasm. "Glad you got it all off your chest. Ta-ta!"

You are an asshole.

So what if it was justified?

Ash sighed. "Before I go, would you like to see a picture of Sebastos with your gift?"

When those searing blue eyes met his, the raw anguish in them hit Ash like a groin kick. "You think you know pain? You don't. Trust me. I lived your fucking life, remember? I know every single detail of it. And since Artemis had me locked in that hell and I saw why you hate me for no reason and for things I had no part in, it has taken everything I have to not hate you for it, and for what your mother did to me. For everything she stole from me. But if you show me a picture of your perfect, healthy son, I will not be responsible for what I do to you. And before you go Ryssa on me, and tell me how selfish I really am . . . I do not begrudge you your happiness or your family. I don't have room in my thoughts for it as I'm too busy grieving for mine. Now go!"

Nodding, Ash backed out of the tent.

He heard Styxx's anguished bellow of unleashed rage. It was the same sound of injustice that rang out whenever a Dark-Hunter had died as a human. It was the sound that summoned Artemis down from Olympus to ask them if they would like to sell their soul to her for an act of vengeance against the person or persons who'd wronged them.

Acheron had never once thought someone would make it because of his actions against them.

And never would he have dreamed it would come from the throat of his own brother. He'd been so wrapped up in his own pain and anger that he'd never once considered Styxx's. From the outside, Styxx's life had looked so perfect.

Beloved prince. Hero of Didymos. Heir to a vast empire.

But a house could look new on the outside and be riddled with termites that ate away at its foundations until it crumbled from the strain of trying to hold itself up under their brutal assault.

And a single smile could hide profound pain.

"I am sorry, Styxx." And this time, he really meant it.

Needing his own sense of peace, Acheron headed for Savitar's island home. Since it was dusk there, he found his old mentor and friend in a black wet suit sitting in the surf beside his surfboard, watching the sunset over the ocean. Leaning back on his arms, he had his legs stretched out and crossed at the ankles.

Savitar groaned the minute he saw him. "Grom coming to disturb my mellow. What up, my brother?"

Ash transformed his clothes into a wet suit so that he could join Savitar in the surf. He sat down. Bending his knees and wrapping his arms around his legs, he sighed heavily. "Urian said that you had to pull Styxx out of a coma?"

Savitar nodded.

"What do you know about his past?"

The ancient Chthonian shrugged nonchalantly. "You were his brother. You should know."

"Don't play with me, Sav. I'm not in the mood."

He glanced over at Ash. "I truly don't know more than a handful of details."

"Such as?"

"You know I was the Chthonian for Atlantis so I only know what happened there."

Sav was lying his ass off, but Ash wouldn't call him on it right now. "And?"

"I knew what you did ... that Styxx led his army to Atlantean shores and kicked the shit out of them to the point their gods were forced to make a pact with Apollo before Styxx completely defeated them."

Ash frowned at that. "It wasn't the gods who made the pact, though. It was the Greek kings. They offered Apollo my sister."

"Not exactly."

Ash hated whenever Savitar used those words. It was never good. "What do you mean?"

"It wasn't your sister Apollo really wanted. Styxx had the same unearthly beauty and sexual allure, courtesy of Epithymia, that you did, and Apollo was infatuated with Styxx from the moment he first saw him ... like you and Artemis. The Atlantean gods had to get Styxx off their shores before he overthrew them. They told Apollo what to do to accomplish that. But they all knew the Didymos king would never agree to publicly give his heir up to be Apollo's mister-ess. So Apollo used Ryssa as a ruse to get to and control Styxx."

Sadly, that explained a lot.

834

And it made Ash's stomach burn with guilt and pain. "Since you were the Atlantean Chthonian, do you know about the other time Styxx came to Atlantis?"

Savitar gave him a blank, cold stare. "Your brother was in Atlantis four times in his lifetime."

Ash gaped. No, it wasn't possible . . . "Four?"

Savitar nodded. "The first was as a boy to free you from your uncle. Estes caught him and took him into custody."

"And you didn't stop it?"

"I didn't know about that one at the time."

"What do you mean?"

His gaze tormented, Savitar leaned forward and raked his hand through his damp hair. "Your mother had my powers shielded when you were young so that I couldn't see you or your twin. I didn't know he'd tried to free you until I yanked him out of his coma."

"What made you look then?"

"I saw the word 'whore' in ancient Greek and the Atlantean 'tsoulus' along with your uncle's slave mark branded into his groin. I foolishly wanted to know how he'd gotten it. Let that be a lesson about looking into an abyss."

Ash closed his eyes as pain slammed into him so hard, he could barely think straight. "Please . . . tell me you're lying."

"You know better. That was why Styxx assaulted Atlantis like he had a grudge match. He did. Your uncle had kept him and sold him, just like he did you. He even pierced Styxx's tongue . . . as did Apollo."

Ash's breath left him in a bitter wave of sympathy. "Since you looked, how did my uncle capture him?"

"Do not ask questions you do not want the answers to."

But Ash didn't listen. "I want to know." He needed to know.

Savitar cut a harsh look toward him. "You should know already, Acheron. You were there when it happened."

"Bullshit!" Ash paused. "Show me."

Savitar shook his head. "There are some memories no one needs."

Still, Ash didn't listen. "Artemis punished Styxx with my memories. She forced him to live my life and instead of it making him forgive me, it's fueled his hatred of me and I want to know why. Please, Savitar. I need to see how he was taken."

"And I refuse to show you," he said harshly ... in a bitter tone he'd never used with Ash before. "Suffice it to say, he would have gotten away had you not dragged your feet, and called out to your uncle to tell him where you were. You could have voluntarily escaped with Styxx, but were too afraid to try. Worse, while Estes held him, you laughed and gloated over what they did to Styxx. Constantly. You threw it in his face the whole time he was in Atlantis with you and you helped to prep him to service the men your uncle sold him to. You even held him down while he was branded as a whore."

Ash panted as that reality slapped him. He choked on denial. "I didn't do that."

"Yes, you did."

Ash shook his head. "I'm not that kind of person, Savitar. I'm not."

"Every man, woman, and child is capable of extreme and utter prejudice and cruelty when they feel justified in their hatred. Right or wrong. We are all capable of lashing out when we're in pain. No one, not even you or I, is immune from that. As Plato said, be kind to everyone you meet for we are all fighting difficult battles. And yes, you thought it was funny to have the beloved prince and heir branded a whore and a slave and sold to the same men who'd paid to fuck you. In your defense, you were young, drugged, and lost in your own hell. "

"That's no excuse." Ash blinked back his tears.

"No, it's not an excuse. It's just harsh, biting reality." Savitar let out a bitter laugh. "Ever wonder why the gods created man, Grom? I personally think that we're the original reality show. They were so effing bored that they created us just so that they could feel better about themselves."

"You're not funny."

Savitar sighed. "No. Tragedy never is. Our lives are marked and shaped by our regrets. Things we all want to take back and can't. In a perfect world, we would never hurt the ones we love or cause hurt to befall them. But the world isn't perfect and neither are we."

Even so, Ash couldn't forgive himself for the way he'd treated Styxx all these centuries ago. "I'm almost afraid to ask about Styxx's second visit."

"You were there for that one, too."

"When they threw me out." And after he'd purposefully baited and mocked Styxx.

And his father.

Savitar nodded. "By the way, do you know how Estes died?"

"Stroke or heart attack in his sleep."

Slowly, Savitar shook his head again.

An awful sense of dread went through Ash as reality hit him hard. Something he had never thought to contemplate before . . .

His brother had been a soldier trained to kill. "Styxx?"

"Yeah," Savitar breathed. "Estes had been planning to sell your sister to an Atlantean prince. To protect her and you, after he'd been viciously gang-raped, Styxx pried loose his restraints to smother Estes in his sleep. And then, riddled with guilt, panic, and fear, he went with the father he hated to Atlantis to free you."

And I insulted him for it. "I didn't know."

"Of course not. Had Styxx breathed a word of it to anyone, he'd have been executed. Brutally. But can you imagine being a boy and carrying that amount of fear and guilt with you?"

No, he couldn't. No wonder Styxx had been so sullen and quiet. Something they had all mocked him for.

He's too good to even talk to anyone. Look at him, walking around like he's so important. Ryssa's harsh observations and condemnation were very different from Ash's new vantage point. With hindsight, he no longer saw his brother's vanity and arrogance as much as he saw Styxx's exhaustion, and wary sadness.

And he did remember Bethany. Vaguely. But those memories

stung hard as they reminded Ash of how much resentment he'd felt whenever he saw Styxx with her. Because Artemis had refused to publicly claim him, the fact that Bethany had smiled and embraced Styxx whenever she saw him had made Acheron hate them both all the more.

"And the other two times?" Ash asked, trying to find some sense of peace with himself.

"The next one wasn't quite so bad. Styxx had his army with him then. But they'd been short on supplies and hammered every step of the way by the Atlanteans who wanted them dead and burned. Even so, he was victorious."

And he'd been viciously attacked on his way home by jealous Greeks.

Savitar scratched at his cheek and pinned him with a cold stare. "It's the last time he was there that was the bad one."

"Worse than Estes?" Ash asked in stunned disbelief.

He nodded slowly. "You know about Apollo's mark on his back?"

"Yeah. I saw it before I came here."

"Your brother didn't take to slavery well. He fought Apollo bitterly, to the point Apollo decided to violently break him. When he couldn't do it by himself, he solicited others. Styxx spent a year in Atlantis as a prisoner of war. First the gods had their go at him, and then they turned him over to the Atlantean queen and her people in Aeryn."

Ash winced at that. "They tortured him."

"Oh, they did a lot more to him than that."

Ash cringed. Having been his brother's scapegoat in a brothel, he could only imagine how much worse others had been when they actually had Styxx in their hands. One thing about the ancient world, their cruelty had been creative.

And harsh.

But for the life of him, Ash couldn't remember a time when Styxx hadn't been accounted for. "Other than war, when was he gone for a year?"

"You already know the answer, Acheron. It was that last year when he kept acting so strange. When he actually mingled with people in public and partied. That wasn't Styxx."

Of course not. Even Ryssa had commented on how war must have changed him because he was acting so out of character. "The year he was engaged to Nefertari." The same year Acheron was gelded, tortured, and the conspiracy against his father had happened.

Savitar nodded. "Apollo was behind it all. Like I said, he wanted Styxx broken. So he yanked Styxx out of the palace and left one of his minions there to keep anyone from knowing what he'd done ... His goal was to ruin Styxx's life and reputation. To turn everyone against him."

And he had definitely succeeded.

"When did Styxx return to Didymos?"

"You know that, too."

Ash glanced away. When Styxx had been forced to kneel naked in front of Apollo in a temple filled with laughing citizens ...

You should have seen him, Acheron, Ryssa's voice echoed in his head as she'd recounted it to him later. *It serves him right after insulting Apollo with his hubris.*

Hubris ... fighting Apollo's ownership.

And like the others, Acheron had been amused by Styxx's public humiliation that had been similar to the one Acheron had been given, courtesy of Apollo and Artemis in her temple.

No wonder Styxx hated them all.

Savitar sighed again. "In case you haven't had enough guilt ladled on you, let me mind-fuck you one more time."

Ash's stomach shrank with dread. "What?"

"You know how all Chthonians are mortal born? None are supposed to ever come from the gods?"

"Yeah?" Ash was the only exception to that rule.

"Styxx didn't steal your birthright, Grom ... you stole his. He was the one who was supposed to be born a Chthonian. But when you were put into the womb with him, you sucked up all of his main powers from him and left him with some pretty crappy byproducts."

The nosebleeds and headaches and ability to hear other people's thoughts.

And no means to protect himself from it.

Shit.

Ash was so nauseated over it all, he wasn't sure how he kept from vomiting. "How do I make this right, Savitar?"

"That, my brother, is the question. And if I knew the answer, I'd play the lottery."

AUGUST 8, 2012

Styxx slowed his horse as he approached the modest-sized Bedouin camp where he came every year around this time to trade. Girls and women were tending goats and sheep, and cooking, along with other chores. They'd already donned their burquas since their scouts would have warned them of his approach long before he'd arrived. The men were tending horses and camels. Those men who could be easily seen, anyway. Styxx had noted the number of them who'd been hidden as guards and scouts on his way in. To most, they wouldn't be seen, but very little escaped Styxx's scrutiny.

As soon as the camp members could ascertain his gargantuan size, they knew who he was. With the exception of the Atlanteans and gods, Styxx had always towered over others. But since the Bedouins tended to be shorter than average, he felt even more like a freakish giant whenever he was around them.

Reaching the center of their camp, Styxx lowered the keffiyeh from his face and left it to trail down his shoulder then dismounted. He petted Skylos to calm him and nodded a welcome to several of the tribe members who greeted him.

A young boy came forward to take the reins of his horse and camel. "Hi, Sadur," Styxx said to the boy as he quietly handed him a Hershey's chocolate bar.

Sadur's face lit up. "Thank you, my lord!"

Styxx inclined his head to him. He'd bartered for the bar last week with a tour group that had passed by his own camp. While he would have enjoyed it, he knew the boy would love it more. Skylos ran after Sadur as he led Styxx's horse and camel to water.

Rahim, a cousin of Sheikh Saif, who ruled this tribe, came out of the largest tent with a smile on his face. Unlike Styxx's plain black garments, Rahim's held beautiful gold, red, and white embroidery to let others know which tribe, social class, and marital status he belonged to.

Styxx placed his hand over his heart as a sign of respect and humility. *"Salaam alaikum." Peace be with you.*

Smiling, Rahim hugged him then held his hand out. "Prince Styxx, it is so good to see you again."

Styxx took his hand and had to bend over so that they could touch noses three times. Rahim held on to his hand after they shook as a sign of friendship and welcome.

"I trust the Sahara has been good to you this year?" Rahim asked.

"Very good, indeed. I see you took a wife. Congratulations."

"Ah yes, my Yesenia. I finally won her and she told me only yesterday that she will be gifting me with a firstborn this coming November."

Styxx smiled at the news. "Again, congratulations, my friend."

Rahim moved his right hand like a scratching claw, beckoning Styxx to enter his cousin's tent. He took him into the mag'ad where the sheikh stood with important members of his tribe and family.

Saif came forward immediately to embrace him. "Prince Styxx! *Salaam alaikum!*"

While Styxx despised his title, social status was extremely important to the desert people, and it bought him a needed advantage when it came to trade and other necessities. It was the only thing his royal birth had ever been good for. "And with you, my friend."

Saif beckoned him to sit on one of the elaborate burgundy cushions on the Persian carpet–lined floor and to partake of the cardamom coffee and small feast that had been prepared when they'd been notified of a stranger's approach.

Placing his hand over his heart again, Styxx gave the sheikh a bow. "Thank you, Your Highness. I am honored."

With a bright smile, Rahim passed him a bowl of dates and fresh yogurt, which they knew were Styxx's favorites.

Saif took Styxx's cup and tasted the coffee first as a way of letting Styxx know it was safe then set it down for him to use. "My daughter wanted you to know that she prepared that yogurt especially for you."

"Dima?"

Saif nodded. "She is now old enough to marry and has a bit of a crush on you, I'm afraid. As it has been nearing the time of your bi-yearly visit, she has driven me mad, begging me to mention her to you while you're here."

Styxx swallowed his coffee. "I am truly honored and humbled by her affection, Your Highness. And while she is a very beautiful woman, it wouldn't be fair for her to share my heart with my first wife. Dima deserves a man who can love her with the whole of his being."

Saif smiled. "And that is why she regards you so highly. You are honest and forthright."

"I humbly try."

Rahim held a spit of lamb for Styxx so that he could cut some of the meat off to eat.

Styxx thanked him.

Saif sat back with his cup. There was a light in his dark eyes that didn't bode well for Styxx. "You have come just in time, prince."

"How so?"

"We have tourists who will soon invade our camp. If you will help us negotiate with them, I will be more than pleased to pay you for your services."

Styxx would rather be hit in the head with a sledgehammer, repeatedly. But he smiled, knowing he would do it anyway. Saif and his people had been very good to him over the last four years and he would do anything for them.

"It would be my honor and privilege to aid you and your people, Your Highness."

"Good. These tourists make my head crazy."

Styxx had just finished his third cup of coffee when he heard the gunshots that announced the arrival of the tourists who must be European or American for the sheikh to ask for his help.

The expression on Saif's face said he shared Styxx's enthusiasm for their arrival. However they were a necessary evil for the tribe. Rich tourists could pay a small fortune for the handmade wares and items that Styxx bartered hides for. And the tour companies loved camps such as this where they could safely bring their groups and know that no harm would come to them.

Saif quirked a wry grin at Styxx. "Today, you prove your friendship to my people, Your Highness."

Yes, he did.

Dreading it already, Styxx followed Rahim outside to find two busloads of gawkers who were making photos of the Bedouin camp and spectacles of themselves. Too late, Styxx remembered his face was showing.

Shit.

And because of his massive height, he stood out from the rest of the tribe. Cameras and phones turned toward him like he was the reigning celebutante at the hottest Hollywood club.

Covering his face, he slid his gaze to Rahim. "Tell your cousin, the price for my services just doubled."

Rahim laughed, knowing Styxx was joking.

One of the women squealed as she showed a photo on her phone to another woman who was with her. "Oh my God!" she said in English. "This goes to Facebook as soon as I have reception.

Do they sell their men like their women? How many camels would we have to buy for him?"

"Forget buying, can we just rent him out for an hour?"

Those were the least raunchy of their comments. And never mind the lechery going on inside their heads. It was enough to make him want to grab his rifle to hold the she-wolves off in case they attacked.

Styxx paused beside them. "Ladies, I speak English. Fluently."

They couldn't have turned any redder had they been walking naked in the Sahara for a month.

Ignoring them, Styxx went over to the tents where the tribe had laid out the wares they had for sale. As he was helping Farid haggle over the price of a carpet with a rich banker, he felt a slight tugging on his sleeve.

"Oh, Beth, don't do that!"

His heart clenched at the name. He looked down into a pair of wide, bright hazel eyes of a five-year-old girl whose face was framed with black pigtails.

"Are you a giant?" she asked, ignoring her mother's warning. "Do you eat little kids like a troll?"

Squatting down, Styxx exposed his face for her to see that he wasn't really scary. "No, little one. But do you want to know how I grew to such height?"

She nodded eagerly.

"I ate all my vegetables and drank a lot of milk."

"Really?"

Styxx glanced up to see her mother smiling down at them. "It's very true." Pushing his sleeve back to expose the small ribbons he used to secure his arm sheaths in place, he pulled a red one loose. "Where I grew up, it's customary to give a gift to the prettiest girl we've ever seen." He held the ribbon out to her and then tied it around her tiny wrist. "Beths are always counted among the most beautiful of all women."

"Thank you." She curtsied to him.

Styxx covered his heart with his hand and bowed his head.

"Thank you," her mother repeated. "I'm sorry she bothered you."

"It's all right. She's no bother at all. Children are our most precious gifts and should always be cherished." Styxx covered his face and returned to helping Farid.

After a few minutes, his nose started bleeding from the pain of their thoughts screaming in his head. Since he spent so much time alone, he was out of practice with protecting himself.

Styxx reached into his pocket and pulled out a handkerchief. He excused himself and went outside to the back of the tent to tend it.

"Are you all right?"

He turned slightly to find a young woman around the age of twenty. "Fine. I get them all the time."

"Yeah, me, too. Especially here with this really dry air." She reached into her bag and pulled out a cellophane-covered box of nasal saline spray then handed it to him. "It really helps prevent them. You can keep that one, I have three more. Yes, I'm that OCD."

Styxx smiled at her. "Thank you."

"No problem." She left him and rejoined her friends.

As soon as the nosebleed stopped, he returned to the tent to finish the transactions.

When the woman who'd given him the nose spray went to buy a bracelet, he told Farid in Egyptian to charge it to his account.

Farid smiled at the girl then responded in broken English. "For you . . . nothing. Take. Take."

She thanked him then turned a suspicious eye to Styxx. "Did you just buy this for me?"

"One good deed deserves another."

She shook her head. "It's too much. The spray isn't expensive."

"In my culture, the price of the gift isn't what's important. It's the heart behind it, which makes the nose spray very valuable to me."

"That's beautiful. Is that a desert custom?"

845

"Didymosian."

She frowned at the unfamiliar name. "Where's that?"

Unfortunately, it was currently at the bottom of the Aegean, courtesy of his brother. "A province of Greece."

"You're Greek?" She beamed in happiness. "My great-grand-mother was from there."

Styxx smiled in spite of himself. "What a coincidence. So was mine."

She laughed.

"Hey, Mindy? You think we could get a picture with your new friend?"

Styxx cringed at the question.

"Would you mind?" Mindy asked hopefully.

Like having my eyes gouged. "It's fine."

Squealing, her friends crowded around him to make photos.

"Can we take one with your face exposed? Please!"

Styxx had to force himself not to grimace. "Who needs a soul in this day and age?"

"Sweet!"

Rahim came up to laugh while the women took turns posing with Styxx. "You should be charging, my friend," he said in Egyptian.

Feigning laughter, Styxx folded his middle finger down and gestured back at him.

"Oh, very nice to teach the tourists. Very nice!"

"What are they saying?" Ana asked Mindy, who shrugged.

"He was correcting my behavior," Styxx explained, "and I gestured my displeasure of his censure."

"Ooo," one of the girls said, "he's like smart and stuff."

"I love your accent. Are you an Arab?"

"No."

"Are you a bandit?"

"He's a full-blooded prince." Their eyes widened at Rahim's random comment as he passed back by them.

Styxx growled low in his throat before he spoke in Egyptian.

"Thank you, Rahim. May all of the fleas of the desert roost in your most private places."

"And the same good wishes to you, my prince," he responded in English.

Now the women were bombarding him with questions and gropes.

"Guys!" Mindy snapped. "Stop acting like a bunch of slutty porn queens. Leave the poor man alone." She pulled him away from them. "Sorry. We're from Minnesota, which is in the—"

"I know where it is." Urian's sister-in-law lived there and it was where Urian spent part of every year.

"Oh. Sorry. Anyway, we don't get to meet princes where we live." *Especially not ones that look like you. Forget William, you make him look like a shriveled goat.*

The William comment, however, he had no clue about.

"No problem."

As he started away, Mindy took his arm. "What's your name?"

"Styxx."

"Like the band?"

A smile quirked at the edges of his lips. "Like the river in the Greek Underworld that the band and I are named after."

"Oh. That's cool ... anyway, we're flying back to the States in two days. Our fall classes start back next week. Um, if you'd like to have lunch or something before we leave ... " She bit her lip hopefully as she ran her hand along the edges of her lacy tank top that exposed the top swell of her large breasts.

For the first time in a long while, Styxx felt a stirring in his body. She was actually starting to arouse him.

Before he could stop himself, he dipped his head down to capture her lips. Groaning, she wrapped her arms around him and pulled him against her voluptuous body.

Styxx closed his eyes as he savored the sensation of being held again. It'd been so very long ...

But as the scent of her perfume hit him, it quelled his desire. This wasn't his Bethany. And while he savored the sensation of being physically touched, it wasn't what he craved. Not to mention the small fact that if Mindy saw the scars that covered him there would be questions he didn't want to answer. Memories he didn't want to deal with.

He pulled back and cupped her cheek in his hand. "It was nice meeting you, Mindy. Have a safe journey home." Heartbroken and lonely, he turned and walked away.

Damn you, gods. Between them and the cruelty of his parents and uncle, they'd not only taken his heart, they'd taken his soul.

And while he'd finally found peace in the desert, he'd never found happiness or acceptance anywhere other than in Bethany's arms.

SEPTEMBER 3, 2012

For hours now, Styxx had seen the vultures circling something. Since they continued to be airborne, he knew their victim was still breathing. But it wasn't until he neared the top of a dune and Skylos took off barking that he realized their intended meal was human.

He kicked his horse forward, pulling Jabar behind him as he closed the distance to see a body half buried in the sand.

After dismounting, he approached slowly. Sometimes bandits would use this as a ruse to trap victims. But since Skylos continued to be occupied by the man on the ground and wasn't running around to warn of others, it was a good bet the man was alone.

However, treachery and trickery were often a necessary part of desert survival. With one hand on the gun concealed at the base of his spine, Styxx closed the distance cautiously.

It was a tall, frail man whose pale skin had been ravaged by the harsh sun.

Carefully, Styxx placed his hand to the man's exposed, blistered shoulder. "Are you Egyptian?"

"Yes." The response was so low, he wasn't sure he heard it. No trickery here. The man was practically dead.

"I mean you no harm." Styxx pulled his aba off to cover the man's raw, sun-ravaged skin. "I'm going to slowly roll you over, okay?"

He didn't respond.

As gently as he could, Styxx dug the man's body out of the sand. He cursed as he saw the rusted stake and chains that had been used to secure his legs to the ground. Unsure if it'd been meant as tribal punishment or had been done by raiders, Styxx pulled his canteen off and opened it. He helped the man to drink. "Slow and easy." If he drank too fast in this condition, it'd only sicken him.

Styxx made him as comfortable as possible. "I'll be back. I need to get bolt cutters to free you."

His breathing ragged, the man said nothing as Styxx left him to go through his pack on Jabar. Just as he found the tool he was look-ing for, Skylos started barking again. He looked up to see the wall of rushing sand several miles away.

Crap . . .

Clicking his tongue to urge his camel forward, he pulled Jabar toward the man and had the camel sit so that both of them were on the leeward side of it. "Wasima!" he said sharply to his horse, call-ing her over so that he could have her lie down on the ground to prepare for the coming storm.

Panic was in the man's eyes as Styxx returned to him.

"Simoon," he explained as he covered the stranger's mouth and eyes to protect them from the sandstorm headed their way.

Skylos ran back and forth, barking to alert him.

"Here, boy!" Styxx shouted, trying to get the dog to calm down enough to sit by the man so that the camel could protect the dog, too.

He'd barely cut through the steel and pulled the man against the camel and covered him and Skylos with a blanket before the storm hit. Since there wasn't enough room for all of them under the blanket, Styxx kept his head down as the harsh wind and sand tore at his clothes and exposed skin.

Luckily, it was a short storm and was over in about twenty-five minutes. After shaking the sand off himself, Styxx dug the animals and man out. Jabar nipped angrily at his shoulder as Styxx helped him to stand. "I know. Sorry, old friend."

Wasima wasn't much happier, but Skylos didn't mind. He rolled over for Styxx to scratch his belly. He patted him gently on the ribs laughed at the dog's playfulness.

"Later, Skylos." He had the man to see about.

Gratitude shined in the man's eyes. "Thank you," he breathed.

"You're welcome." Styxx pulled out an energy bar and pressed it into his hands. "I'll get camp made as soon as I can."

He attacked the bar while Styxx went to unpack. Since Styxx was still on the move toward his usual campsite, he normally wouldn't have pitched the tent or stopped this early in the day, but the man needed care before he traveled or he wouldn't make it.

Once Styxx had the tent up and his bedroll out, he carried the man in to lie down while he finished preparations. "My name is Styxx," he said as he tucked the blanket around him.

The man placed his hand to his heart and bowed his head. "Seti."

Styxx covered his hand with his own. "Rest easy." He pulled his backpack over to Seti. "I have more food and water in here. Eat slowly and let me know if you need anything else. I have a few more things to do and the animals to care for then I'll be back."

"Thank you, Styxx."

He inclined his head before he left to tend the animals and unpack the rest of his supplies.

By the time he returned, Skylos was lying beside Seti who looked a lot better than he had earlier. He was still blistered and skeletal, but there was now life in his blue eyes.

Seti smiled as he saw him entering the tent.

Styxx pulled his keffiyeh down to expose his face. He set the medical pack next to his pallet and knelt by Seti's side. "What happened to you?"

"I was attacked by a vicious bastard and his she-bitch and left for dead. May they rot for all eternity."

Grimacing in sympathetic pain, Styxx handed him a bottle of aloe gel. "That'll help with the sunburn."

Seti caught his hand and frowned at the sight of the cuts on his skin the storm had given him. "I am sorry I caused you to be harmed."

"Don't worry about it. I'm just glad I got to you before the simoon hit."

"Me, too."

Styxx set up the lanterns, but didn't turn them on. He paused as he saw his sketchbook on the ground near Seti. It'd been inside the backpack with his food.

"Your drawings?"

"They are." Embarrassed that someone else had seen them, Styxx picked the book up and returned it to the backpack.

"You are very talented, my friend. The woman . . . is she yours?"

"My beautiful wife, Beth."

Seti inclined his head respectfully. "You're a very lucky man."

"I was, indeed."

"Was?"

His heart aching, Styxx glanced down at the names on his arm as he zipped his backpack closed. "She died a long time ago."

For a moment, Seti's eyes darkened as if he felt the pain of her death as deeply as Styxx did. "I am very sorry for your loss."

"Thank you."

"And the boy? Your son?"

With a ragged breath, Styxx stood up. "Yes, but I never met him. My wife was expecting him when I lost her."

"Again, I am very, very sorry."

Styxx pulled out a new stick of lip balm and handed it to Seti. "What of you? Have you a wife?"

Seti frowned at the balm as if he'd never seen anything like it before. "I've had many. And you . . . have you another?"

"No. Just the one."

"You're a young man. Why only one?"

851

Styxx smiled wistfully. "You can't improve perfection, Seti, and there will never be another woman equal to my precious Bethany. But I am sure your wives will be glad to have you back. And your children, too."

"Alas, I have no children. Not anymore." The sadness in Seti's voice said that they shared the same pain.

"I'm sorry." Styxx cleared his throat and changed the subject. "I have coffee and tea. Which would you prefer?"

"I would sacrifice a goat for coffee."

He let out a short laugh at the desperation in Seti's voice. He'd been there himself. "Coffee it is. I'll be back with it shortly."

It didn't take Styxx long to make the coffee and return to Seti, who was propped on his bedroll, rubbing Skylos's ears.

"So what has brought you to the desert, my young friend?"

Styxx handed him a cup of thick Greek coffee. "I'm at peace here." At least that was what he thought until the sign on his back started tingling . . .

"Are you all right?"

Styxx glanced around. Was Apollo nearby? He turned back toward Seti and smiled. "Fine. Just a . . . weird feeling I haven't had in a long time."

One that told him something evil was watching. He just didn't know what.

Or who.

SEPTEMBER 8, 2012

"Zakar!"

Styxx slowed down as Seti shouted. When Seti had told him where his brother lived, he'd expected a camp or small village. That was not where they were. "Your brother lives in a cave?"

"He does, indeed." Seti dismounted from Wasima and led Styxx toward the small opening.

There was something very peculiar about this place. Other than the fact it was ancient. While Seti went inside to look for his brother, Styxx watered the animals. They'd been traveling most of the morning, and on his own, he'd have never gone this long without a break for them. But Seti had been dying to let his brother know he lived.

A small group of goats came down the side of the hill to chatter at him. Actually, they wanted water, too.

Laughing at their eagerness, Styxx pulled out another bowl and poured them some. He'd just finished when Seti returned with a man who was almost the same height as Styxx. There was something he didn't see every day, especially with desert people.

"Styxx, meet my brother. Zakar . . . Styxx."

Much younger than Styxx expected, Zakar had curly black hair and eyes that were very different from Seti's red hair and baby blues. They looked nothing alike, but Styxx wasn't about to mention it. And now that he thought about it, Zakar reminded him a lot of Acheron's son-in-law, Sin.

"It's a pleasure to meet you, Styxx. Thank you for freeing my brother. I'd begun to despair of ever seeing him again."

"The pleasure is all mine. I'm merely grateful I got to him when I did."

The brothers exchanged an odd look and it wasn't until then that Styxx realized he couldn't hear either of their thoughts . . . Because he'd been alone for so long, it hadn't dawned on him that he couldn't hear Seti's until now.

Hmmm, peculiar.

Zakar gestured toward the cave. "I have fresh coffee and yogurt, as well as some fruit and hummus with crackers."

Even though he'd rather be on his way, Styxx smiled and yielded to desert custom and hospitality. "Thank you, that would be wonderful and much appreciated."

He followed them inside to find a surprising home. Outside, it looked meager and uninviting. Inside, it was a palace. He uncovered his face as he glanced around at the ornate and expensive furnishings. "You have a beautiful home."

"Thank you." Zakar went to get the coffee and refreshments while Seti led him to an actual couch and chairs.

Styxx sighed as he sank down into an extremely comfortable recliner.

"Good, eh?"

Completely amazed, Styxx nodded. "Not used to anything this luxurious." It felt so good, he had to struggle to stay awake and bite back a yawn.

Seti said something, but honestly he was too drowsy to understand it. Styxx tried to blink his eyes open, but the next thing he knew, he was out.

Zakar set the coffee down and arched his brow. "Is he an offering?"

"No!" Seti snapped.

"But he's marked by Apollo."

"He wasn't marked by choice and he's no friend of our enemy's."

Zakar frowned. "Is that why you brought him here?"

"No. I brought him here so that we could use him."

DECEMBER 21, 2012

"Simi . . . are you sure this is a good idea?"

"Absolutely." Simi grinned at her sister Xirena as they entered the basement of akri's temple on Katateros. "Now where's a light switch."

"There's not one." Xirena breathed fire onto an old spider web–covered torch. As soon as one lit, it spread light to all the others in the dark marble room. The flames danced along the wall, adding creepy shadows to the already creepy environment.

Simi stepped back at the number of statues that were housed here. While she'd known they'd been placed here centuries and centuries ago, she'd never actually visited them, especially since they made her akri very unhappy. "The Simi didn't remember there being so many ... Akra really broke bad on all these nonquality peoples."

"I remember." Xirena's tone was low and breathless. "It was not a pretty day."

Simi arched a brow. "You were there, Big Sissy?"

Xirena nodded. "Xedrix, too." Xedrix was their brother, who'd been Apollymi's most favored Charonte after their mother's death. But Xed had deflected ... no, defected when akri-Styxx opened the portal in New Orleans and let him out. Now he owned a club in New Orleans where the Simi got to eats lots of good seafood.

"Ooo, so what happened, Big Sissy?"

"The bitch-goddess Apollymi was furious. They all died screaming. Except for two."

"Who two?"

"Dikastis and Bet'anya. She tried to keep the bitch-goddess from killing her baby, but the bitch-goddess didn't listen. She yanked it right out of her belly, and then turned her into one of these."

Simi touched her own stomach in sympathetic pain. "Why was akra so mean?"

Xirena shrugged. "The bitch-goddess was always mean. She only likes you and her son ... and akra-Kat and Mia-Mia."

Simi climbed up on the woman closest to her and poked at her stone eyeball. "Which one is she?"

Xirena spat on the ground at the statue's feet. "Epithymia. She an even bigger bitch-goddess. She used to pull the wings off Charonte who made her mad."

Simi cringed then poked harder in the goddess's eye, hoping she could feel it. "Who the one who lost her baby? She's the one the Simi needs."

Xirena walked around them, looking at them, up and down, until she found one in the back. "This is Bet'anya."

Simi headed over then gasped. "She look just likes akri-Styxx's drawings. She the one he loved so much." Biting her lip, she met her sister's gaze. "Was she nice?"

Nodding, Xirena touched Bet'anya's hand. "She was always very sad though. Even when she was happy, she looked so sad. Like something wasn't quite right in her heart. Chara goddess used to say it's because they took something from her long ago they shouldn't have."

Simi gave her sister a knowing look. "That's cause she didn't have her akri-Styxx. He loves her and so this is the Simi's Christmas present to him. I told him on his birthday that wishes come true and his wish is for his akra to come home to him."

"Yeah, but Xiamara, this . . . " Xirena shook her head. "I don't think we should."

"We gots to, Big Sissy. This the only time them portals things open. If we don't do it now, akri-Styxx will have to wait a long, long time and he already waited a long, long time. The Simi don't like to see him so sad. He don't get prezzies and the Simi wants to get him the best prezzie ever."

The ground beneath their feet rumbled. Simi's eyes widened. "What's that?"

Bug-eyed, Xirena shrugged.

Simi's watch tingled, letting her know it was time. She had less than one minute to free the goddess. Using her wings, she hovered and placed the sacred anti-aima to the goddess's lips. When akri had been frozen that time in New Orleans, she and akra-Kat had used this to free him so she was hoping it would work on Styxx's akra, too.

Hmmm . . .

Another rumble went through the room. Something akin to a dark shadow shot out and flew past Simi's head.

Suddenly the other bitch-goddess Xirena didn't like opened her eyes. And so did Archon . . .

Uh-oh.

Simi ran to her sister. "Go get help. The Simi will hold them off!"

DECEMBER 23, 2012

Savitar paused as he watched Styxx, silhouetted by the setting sun, on top of a small dune. He'd stripped down to nothing but his loose pants and boots while he played Frisbee with his dog. Over and over, Styxx would laughingly take the Frisbee, praise the animal then wait for the dog to run out again so that he could toss it for the dog to jump, catch it, and return.

It was the first time he'd ever seen Styxx at ease. Unguarded. For that matter, it was the only time he'd known the prince to play.

Or laugh.

And as he watched Styxx with the dog, he didn't see the feral military commander who'd terrified a pantheon and nation, or the rigid prince who had to ooze decorum at all times. He didn't even see a man. He saw the boy who had never been given a chance to live. One who'd been cut down in the height of his youth and deprived of a normal, mortal life.

Because of the way Styxx and Acheron acted, the maturity, responsibility, and pain they held that went far beyond their years, it was easy to forget how young they'd been when they died. But Savitar saw it now.

And the injustice of it burned inside his heart.

I have no right to ask this of him.

None of them did. Remorse gutted him as he felt for the childhood and life Styxx would have had had they not interfered. Styxx would have been that beloved, cherished and spoiled prince that everyone thought he was.

And he would have been a proud Chthonian guardian for the world . . .

To save and protect Acheron, they all had taken a turn at ruining Styxx. Athena had said it best at their births. When Apollymi had joined their lives, she ordained that whatever ills were committed against Acheron would be done to Styxx. Only for Styxx, it would be so much worse . . . Savitar knew he should go and leave the boy in peace. Styxx wanted only to be alone and he'd certainly earned the right to it.

But he couldn't. Acheron was too important to the world.

Most of all, he was too important to Savitar personally.

Savitar waited until Styxx had poured water into a bowl for the dog before he appeared beside him.

Faster than he could blink, Styxx had a knife in one hand and gun in the other. Both angled at Savitar's head.

"Impressive." Savitar hadn't even known Styxx was armed.

Gone was any hint of the boy who'd been playing with his dog just moments before. This was the rigid general who had led armies, and fought gods and fiercely trained warriors in an arena with such strength and cunning that his enemies had been forced to resort to tricks and traps to defeat him.

Styxx glared his hatred. "What do you want?"

"You to point those somewhere else."

He lowered them to Savitar's groin.

"Cute."

Smirking, Styxx tucked the gun into the holster at his back and returned the knife to the sheath on his forearm. "Whatever it is you want, it has nothing to do with me."

"Some of the Atlantean gods have returned."

"As I said, it has nothing to do with me."

"They want vengeance."

Styxx bent down to pull his water out from under his aba. "So?"

"On Acheron."

Styxx took a swig of his bottled water before he capped it. "Nothing to do with me."

"So that's it then? You're just going to let your brother die? And he will . . . There's no way for him to survive this."

Styxx swallowed the pain inside him. "Are you deaf? The gods know, Acheron has said it enough. I don't have a brother."

"The world as you know it will end."

He laughed bitterly at that. "The world as I knew it ended the moment my wife was killed. And anything remotely related to the life I once lived ended while I was held in solitary confinement for over eleven thousand years. I know nothing of this place and I have no dog in this fight. It has nothing to do with me," he repeated. He headed toward his horse and camel.

"Tory's pregnant again."

Styxx froze as those words cut him to the quick. "Good for her . . . and Acheron."

"Are you really going to condemn an innocent woman and her two children to live without their husband and father?"

"That's not fair!" he growled, glowering at the Chthonian he wanted to shoot.

"Life, like war, isn't fair. It just is. Isn't that what Galen taught you?"

Styxx winced at the reminder of all he'd lost . . . because of his brother and the gods he'd hated since the moment of his birth. "You're not helping your case by reminding me of Apollo's treachery, Chthonian."

"Fine then. Stay here in your desert. At least you'll have the comfort of knowing Acheron's widow and fatherless children will be able to commiserate with your pain."

Whirling about in fury, Styxx threw the water bottle at him.

Savitar ducked. Had that hit him, it would have counted.

"I hate all of you!" Styxx growled deep in his throat. A throat that was still damaged because of Acheron and the gods who could never leave him alone.

Damn it all . . .

No, damn *them* all.

None of them had ever taken pity on him. He was thrown aside and forgotten like garbage.

Until they needed him.

All he'd ever wanted was a family. One person who treated him like he mattered to them. And all he'd gotten was disappointment.

Slapped in the face and stabbed in the heart.

By all of them. It'd taken him centuries to come to terms with the one single fact that no one could or would ever love him.

What the fuck does it matter? Really? He didn't have a life. He never had.

And he damn sure didn't have a wife or a child . . .

Never mind two kids.

Go ahead and die already. There was no one to mourn his passing.

Angry, hurt, and aching over a fact he'd never been able to change, Styxx pulled his aba on then jerked his backpack up from the ground. His breathing ragged, he glared his hatred at Savitar. "Can you make sure my animals and gear go to someone who needs them and that my dog doesn't get eaten by his new caretaker?"

Savitar was stunned. "You agree?"

Styxx averted his gaze as a thousand emotions pile-drived him to the point he didn't really know what he felt. Other than hurt and alone.

But that was nothing new for him.

He met Savitar's stoic lavender gaze. "I've never been quite the bastard all of you labeled me. You knew I couldn't let him die, otherwise you wouldn't have come here."

"Thank you, Styxx."

"For what?"

"Being the man I knew you were."

"Go fuck yourself, Savitar. Just take me wherever I need to go and stop with the sentimental bullshit you don't mean before I give in to my desire to punch the shit out of you."

*

Tory wanted to beat her husband into the ground. "I would give anything to have enough god powers for five minutes to Force choke you with. You can't do this."

"Sota—"

A bright flash in the corner cut his words off.

Tory sucked her breath in sharply as Savitar and Styxx appeared in the room on Savitar's island home where he'd taken them for safety until this latest threat was resolved. Alexion and Danger were in the back of the house, tending Sebastos while she'd tried to argue sanity with her obstinate husband.

Her jaw went slack as the two men joined them. The last time she'd seen Styxx had been very brief on the night he'd saved her from Satara. Then he'd been identical to Acheron.

Now . . .

Dressed all in black Bedouin clothing, he looked like something out of a Mummy movie. His wavy, short blond hair was faded by sunlight and his skin a deep, dark olive. While Acheron had never been pale, he appeared so in comparison to his twin. And with Styxx's eyes ringed in kohl, they were a vibrant, haunting blue like the deepest part of the Aegean. Shirtless beneath the aba, he was covered by horrifying scars that testified to how brutal a past he'd survived. The sight of them made her stomach clench in sympathy.

Ash growled at their unexpected appearance. "This has nothing to do with him."

Savitar snorted. "Ye gods, I don't know why you two fight all the time. You're just alike and not only in looks. You know what it tells me? You can't stand yourself and you both know what an asshole you are to deal with . . . that's why you don't get along."

Simultaneously, they gave him a matching droll stare that caused her to laugh.

Until they turned it to her.

That made her laugh harder. "They are like matching, moving bookends, aren't they?"

A tic started in Acheron's jaw. "You're not funny, Sota."

"I'm pleading Savitar on this."

Styxx's gaze fell to her distended belly. The utter grief and misery those eyes betrayed tightened her chest. To see that kind of agony on a face that was identical to the one person who meant everything to her . . .

She wanted to soothe him, but knew better than to try. Neither her husband nor Styxx would appreciate it.

Blinking, he blanked out his eyes and looked to Acheron. "Stop being stupid. Tell me what I need to do."

"Go home."

"Fine." Styxx shrugged. "I'll be more than happy to comfort your wife and raise your children in your absence. I'm sure after one night in my bed, Soteria will never remember you exist."

Bellowing in rage, Ash attacked him. He threw Styxx to the ground and started banging his head against the floor. Styxx rolled and slugged him then kicked Acheron back.

"Stop it!" Savitar roared, putting himself between them as Ash went in for more. He passed a peeved, almost fatherly expression to Tory. "Have you ever?" he asked her.

"No. Do they always do this?"

"Yes," the three men said simultaneously.

Styxx cursed as his nose started bleeding. He pulled a white handkerchief out of his pocket and used it to pinch his nostrils closed.

"Lean your head back," Tory instructed.

Styxx sighed. "Forward's better."

"You sure?"

"I've been getting them since birth."

And he'd ruined several of his sister's gowns with them. Something Ryssa had held against him the whole of her life. Tory wanted to cry for him. "Can I get you anything?"

"Where's the bathroom."

She pointed to the door right outside the room.

"Excuse me." He left them to tend it.

The moment he was gone, Tory stalked her husband. "What is wrong with you?"

Ash glared after his brother. "He always knows exactly what to say to thoroughly piss me off."

Tory folded her arms over her chest. "You know, my father had an old saying—the sharpest knives cut both ways."

"You're defending him?"

"No, baby. I would never defend anyone over you. I love you with every part of me. But I also know you better than anyone and this isn't about saving Styxx. It's about punishing yourself. Whenever you feel guilty, you lash out. And if you go to them and die, you won't be punishing yourself or helping Styxx. You'll be punishing me and Bas and this one." She took his hand and held it to her stomach so that he could feel their son moving inside her. "Is that really what you want to do?"

Ash looked past her as Styxx returned. The haunted, tormented look in Styxx's eyes as he stared at Ash's hand on Tory's stomach was heart-wrenching.

He locked gazes with Acheron. "You know, a long time ago, my mentor taught me that there's only one reason to go to war. To protect the ones you love. But life has taught me that sometimes protecting isn't about leaving them. It's about being here when they need you. It doesn't take courage to die, Acheron. It takes courage to live and to fight."

"And it takes a lot more to forgive." Ash left her to approach Styxx. He held his hand out to him. "Brothers?"

Styxx hesitated. Then he slowly shook his head. "I'm not going to let you do this to me."

"Do what?"

"Send me out to die in your stead with regret. How dare you. Don't you even try to be a brother to me now when it no longer matters. I needed my brother eleven thousand years ago. I begged for a brother then and in '07 and again even in '08, and you turned your back on me and walked away without a second thought. Every time. I have no forgiveness inside me for you. Not anymore."

Styxx paused then laughed. "You're right, Acheron. I am a selfish bastard. I had to be, because no one else ever gave a single shit about me except me."

Acheron winced. "You can hear my thoughts . . . I forgot you could do that."

"You forgot a lot of things I wish I could." He looked over at Savitar. "What do I need to do?"

"I need to take you to Apollymi so that you can fully pass for Acheron."

He went rigid as if he couldn't breathe. After a minute, he expelled a bitter sigh. "Of course you do. 'Cause my life just isn't miserable enough."

A tic worked in his jaw before he returned those cold blue eyes to his brother. "And yes, Acheron, I do know how much you would give to have your mother embrace you. The same amount I'd have given to have mine hold me. Not stab me in my heart because she birthed *you*." He pulled the aba tighter around his body. "Take me to her. Get it over with before I change my mind."

"Styxx—"

He held his hand up to silence Acheron. "If you thank me for this, I swear to the gods I loathe that I will put my fist through your face, and I don't care how much it hurts me when I do it."

Savitar took them out of the room.

Tory rubbed Ash's back. "You okay, baby?"

"Not really. I'm seriously hating myself right now as I remember things I'd forgotten on purpose. Things I should have never allowed myself to bury."

"Such as?"

Tears filled his eyes. "All the times when we were little and Styxx would try to protect me. There was this one time when we were playing and running around and I accidentally knocked over the bust of Styxx's grandfather. As his father came storming into the room, Styxx shoved me under a table and told him he was the one who'd bumped into it. He had the hell beat out of him for being reckless and thoughtless. And after he'd been sent to his room with no dinner, I snuck in to check on him. He was bruised from the middle of his back to the backs of his knees. Horrible welts that were four inches thick from the cane they'd used on him. I asked him why he hadn't told his father the truth. Do you know what he said to me?"

She shook her head.

"It's what big brothers do."

She pulled him into her arms as his silent tears fell. "Shh, baby, it's okay."

"It's not okay, Sota. I've seriously wronged him and I don't know how to make it right. How can I let him do this for me?"

"I don't know. And honestly, I'm too selfish for you to ask me ... I don't want Styxx hurt, I don't. But I can't live without you. So my vote is to sacrifice him to save your life."

"Yeah, but I'm the big brother now ... "

Styxx paused inside the courtyard doorway as he caught sight of Apollymi sitting on a stone bench that overlooked a dark fountain. The hair on the back of his neck rose as the old Didymosian adage went through him. *A silent man is a thinking man. A silent woman is an angry one ...*

And silent women had a nasty habit of stabbing him when he wasn't looking.

But this one didn't need a knife to stab him through the heart. Not to mention, Apollymi had never been that merciful to him.

The last time they'd met had been brief and with an audience who had intently watched their every move. Then he hadn't dared to allow himself to focus on her then for fear of what he might do that would get Urian killed.

This was the first time he'd ever actually looked at the woman who had taken his wife and son.

The woman who had taken everything from him.

And all to save the life of her own son.

He should probably hate her for that alone, but given the fact that he'd have sold his soul to have a mother who would just acknowledge his existence with something other than profound hatred, how could he? In spite of what Acheron thought, Apollymi's unconditional and unreasoning love for her son was the only thing Styxx had ever coveted.

That and Ryssa's.

Styxx swallowed hard as that old wound ripped open and flooded him with pain. Ryssa's last words to him had been so harsh and cutting—in more ways than one. He'd done everything he could to make his sister love him, but her unwarranted jealousy and love of Acheron had kept her from seeing him as anything other than worthless, spoiled, and selfish. An unwanted nuisance. While he'd done his absolute best to protect and shield Acheron, Ryssa had ruthlessly blamed him for things he had no control over.

For things he hadn't done.

But he wouldn't think about that. The past was ancient history. Literally.

This was the present, and once again, Acheron needed him. *What the hell? Not like I have anything to live for anyway . . .*

Wasima and Jabar couldn't care less who fed them. Dog either, for that matter.

Taking a deep breath, Styxx studied the goddess who despised him even more than his own mother and sister had.

Her pale blond hair was a stark contrast to her black gown, both of which flowed around her perfect body. Ironically, the Atlantean goddess of ultimate pain and destruction had to be the most beautiful woman who had ever lived.

The splashing water made a soothing sound in spite of the fact that they were both currently in Atlantean hell. Her isolation struck him hard as the memory of his own slammed into him and reawakened a horror he did his best every waking minute to forever bury. There was nothing worse than to exist in a tight hole where the only company you had was the sight of your own face in a cold reflection that showed you just how much you hated yourself.

But unlike him, Apollymi didn't sit alone in her prison.

His gaze went to the two Charonte who stood on opposite sides of her. While they didn't speak, they were at least another life form nearby. Not to mention, she had an entire Daimon army to serve her and keep her company.

He winced as he remembered all the centuries he'd screamed out for someone, anyone, to have mercy on him and just speak so that he could hear them. They didn't even have to talk to him. Just speak.

Eleven thousand years was hard to live through.

Eleven thousand years of utter solitude . . .

"So you're not a coward, after all."

He narrowed his gaze on Apollymi as his hatred rose to swallow every last remnant of his pain. "I've been many things in my life, but never a coward."

She rose with the same slow, graceful movements he was now trying to duplicate. As she turned to face him, her eyes flashed from swirling silver to a deep, vibrant red—another thing she shared with her son. "You don't fool me, dog. I see you for what you really are."

Styxx caught his bitter laughter out of habit. As a human, that kind of response would have caused his father to knock him through a wall. But then Apollymi couldn't kill him.

Only Acheron could, and the bastard had never been that merciful.

"I find that hard to believe." Not once in his entire existence had anyone other than Galen or Bethany ever seen the truth in him. And that was okay. He'd long ago grown used to being misjudged and despised.

Before he could blink, she vanished then reappeared right beside him . . . Just like Apollo used to do to him. She sank her hand deep into his short blond hair and wrenched it hard. "But for my son, I'd have your heart in my fist right now."

He didn't flinch or react to the pain at all. "But for my brother, I'd gut you where you stand."

She laughed at his threat then tightened the grip in his hair. "You are nothing but a second-rate copy of my Apostolos. A mere shadow of the man he has become. No one will ever mistake you for him. How could they?"

Strange to hear his own doubtful litany coming out of someone else's mouth. She might as well be his father, telling him how he'd never be good enough to rule. How he should have drowned him the moment he was born.

Or bashed in his head.

When he didn't respond, she hissed at him, baring her fangs. "I hate you."

Styxx smirked. "The feeling is entirely mutual."

She yanked his hair so hard, he was amazed she didn't draw out a fistful of bloody strands. Her eyes flashing again, she jerked him against her and sank her fangs into his neck.

He gasped at the raw, unrelenting pain of her bite. A pain she took pleasure in giving him. It was the same way Apollo used to do him, over and over again.

For the love of the gods, please rip out my throat. Maybe then, for a few minutes at least, he might actually be at peace.

But as she drank from him, her hold started to gentle and the pain lessened. Within a few seconds, it almost felt like a mother's embrace. Not that he remembered the sensation of being hugged. In fact, he could count on one hand how many times in his entire existence he'd been held by anyone.

And none of those had ever come from his own mother.

Apollymi pulled back to look up at him with a stern frown. His blood stained her lips. To his complete shock, she brushed a tender hand over the wound she'd left in his neck. "I had no idea," she said in a tight voice.

Styxx shrugged her arms away. He didn't want or need anyone's kindness or pity, and especially not hers. "Yeah, well, we all have shit to deal with, don't we?"

She reached out to him, but he stepped back. He wasn't a boy anymore begging for a modicum of kindness from someone. He'd learned as a toddler that he was alone in this world. And honestly, he now preferred it that way.

"Is it done?" he asked.

Apollymi gave a subtle nod.

Good. Now he could move into his next prison and be done with it . . . or, best of all, die. He wiped the blood off his neck and turned to leave.

"Styxx?"

He paused, but didn't speak. Ironically, it was the first time she'd ever called him by name and not an insult.

"Thank you for doing this for Apostolos," she whispered, her voice thick with emotion. "And for what it's worth, I am so sorry for what happened to you because of my actions."

Sorry . . . That one word caused his lip to curl.

This time he gave free rein to his disdainful snort. "Everyone's sorry for something." He pinned her with a heated glare. "And there are some things, my lady, that sorry doesn't fix."

"Wait!"

He started to ignore her, but stopped for some unknown reason.

Before he could say a word, Apollymi appeared at his back. Placing her hand on his forehead, she pulled his head against her shoulder and again sank her fangs deep into his jugular.

Styxx gasped as his head spun, not with pain but with an unbelievable surge of power. Everything became more vibrant, more vivid. He'd always been able to hear voices, but they were louder now.

Clearer.

Panting and weak, he couldn't breathe as she lifted her lips from his neck and held him in her arms. "What have you done to me?"

She stroked his hair as if he was the son she loved. "I have given you my powers. It's only temporary. But I don't want you hurt."

"I don't understand."

She kissed his cheek and tightened her hold on him. "You agreed to do this and you don't even know what it is we're asking you for. All you knew was that your brother would die if you didn't. That my grandchildren would be fatherless . . ." Her words broke off into a sob. "Come back from this, Styxx. Survive and I promise you, you will have what you crave most."

"I don't believe you."

He felt her hot tears on his cheek while she continued to hold on to him. "I know, baby. But I'm an Atlantean god. I have to keep my promises or I'll die. You can trust in that." She kissed his cheek one more time then released him.

Still dizzy, Styxx was afraid to move. He felt so strange . . . both weak and strong at the same time.

"You should know that it's Apollo who started this by awakening my pantheon with his mother's blood. His intent is to kill Apostolos, bring back the entire Atlantean pantheon, and then come for you. I originally marked you just enough that he would know it was you and leave my son alone. But as of right now, you are as much my son as Apostolos is. You draw the same powers he does. Apollo will never know the difference unless you tell him. No one will." Her eyes sad and tormented, she cupped his cheek in her hand. "Your courage and heart are duly noted, *m'gios*. And they will never be forgotten."

"Is he ready?"

Unsure of what to say to Apollymi, Styxx turned as Savitar rejoined them.

The instant the Chthonian looked at him, Savitar stepped back. "That's eerie as hell."

Styxx scowled at him. "What?"

Savitar manifested a mirror and held it up so that Styxx could see his wavy black hair that fell just past his jaw and swirling silver eyes. Yeah, that was eerie. His clothes had also been replaced with black jeans and a T-shirt and black leather jacket—the same exact outfit Acheron had been wearing at Savitar's. No wonder Apollymi had been so kind to him. Like this, he really was absolutely identical to Acheron. It must have touched her maternal instincts.

"Remember, it's only temporary," Apollymi repeated. "The more of my power you use, the quicker it will leave you exposed as to who you really are. So please, save it for when you absolutely need it."

Styxx inclined his head to her then spoke to Savitar. "Where are we going?"

"Katateros."

"Wait!"

Styxx arched a brow at the sound of Urian's fierce shout as he came running toward them with a blond man in tow.

Savitar growled. "We don't have time for this."

Urian snorted nonchalantly. "Take it up with the bossman. He's the one who sent me in with a time-out. Acheron has called a team huddle before we make our final play."

Savitar let out an exasperated sigh. "Remind me to cancel your ESPN subscription." He glanced to Styxx with an odd glimmer in his eyes that Styxx couldn't begin to define. "Fine."

The next thing Styxx knew, the four of them were back on Savitar's island with Acheron, and Tory who was feeding crackers to their son. Danger and Alexion, along with Simi, Xirena, and Acheron's daughter Katra and her husband Sin.

So his brother had decided to hold a family reunion while sending him off to die in his stead . . .

Really nice touch.

"They're not going to wait all day," Savitar warned Acheron.

"I know, but as I was reviewing the situation with everyone and trying to come up with an alternate plan that didn't leave Styxx hacked into little bloody pieces Urian reminded me that we were missing a most vital member of the team." Acheron pinned his gaze on Styxx. "The quarterback who actually went up against the Atlantean gods and beat the shit out of them."

Styxx scowled as all heads turned to him. Honestly, it scared him. He wasn't used to this many people looking at him like that unless they were about to throw him onto a live subway track.

He shrugged at the group. "Since no one has bothered to tell me what I'm heading into, I've got nothing."

Ash looked at Simi who blushed and grinned sheepishly.

"Well, see, akri-Styxx, it all started when the Simi decided she was gonna give you the promise for your birthday for Christmas. See?"

"Clear as a two-hundred-mile-an-hour sandstorm."

Ash gave a low, sinister laugh. "Simi decided to wake up the Atlantean gods for you."

Styxx frowned. "Why?"

Simi sighed heavily. "Well see, it wan't supposed to be all them gods. Is only supposed to be the one. But she won't get up. Lots of them others got up and got ugly, fast, and the Simi still don't know why the only one I tried to wake keeps sleeping when it's so important she get up and talk. It's so confusing."

Yes, yes, it was.

Before Styxx could comment, Sin turned to Savitar. "I have two gods and a demigod requesting permission to enter your home and join our powwow."

Savitar gave him a look that questioned his sanity. "Who?"

"My brother, Seth, and your least favorite god of all time."

"Noir?"

"Second least favorite," Sin quickly amended.

Savitar made a sound of supreme disgust. "I thought that bastard was dead."

"Apparently not."

A tic started in Savitar's jaw. "Why?"

Sin shrugged. "They say they can help with this."

Hands on his hips, Savitar glared at Acheron and then Kat. "Apollymi owes me. Big. And so do you." He he looked back at Sin and gave a curt nod.

Styxx was even more confused than before, especially when Set appeared beside Acheron with a man identical in looks to Sin— only with longer hair. The other newcomer bore a remarkable resemblance to the man Styxx had rescued in the desert.

Just what the hell was going on?

The Sin lookalike laughed and nudged Set to look at Styxx. "Now there's a photo op expression if ever there was one."

872

With a wry grin, Set transformed into the redheaded man Styxx had saved a few months back in the desert and Zakar into his "brother" then they quickly returned to their immortal appearances.

"Over four thousand years ago," Set explained, "Apollo and his whore mother used my son Seth," he indicated the red-haired man with them, "to trap me in the desert without his knowledge of what was being done to him and why, and restricted my powers so that the Greeks could take over my pantheon and hand my son over to my bitterest enemy. But for you, Styxx, I'd still be there, chained in the desert, fighting off vultures—human and animal." He glanced to his son and his gaze softened instantly. "And my son would still be hating me for something I tried my best to spare him."

Styxx's scowl deepened. "Why didn't you tell me it was you when I freed you?"

"You were in enough anguish over Bet. I didn't want to make it worse on you when I didn't think I could do anything to fix it or help you. Especially after you did me such a massive favor." Set inclined his head to Sin's brother. "Zakar and I were allies back in the day, which was why I had you take me to his place to recuperate. Since you left, we've been trying to find a way to revive my daughter without awakening the other Atlanteans."

The more they talked, the less clear all of this became. Why would they worry about another pantheon? "But Bethany was Egyptian, not Atlantean."

"From me, yes. Her mother is Symfora."

Styxx's stomach churned as an image of that cold-blooded bitch went through him and he had perfect clarity as to his wife's real name. "Bethany's Bet'anya Agriosa?"

Set nodded. "For an obvious reason, she was scared to tell you the truth. She was so afraid you couldn't forgive her for what they did to you without her knowledge or approval, that she was planning to give up her godhood entirely, in both pantheons, to live a mortal life with you in Didymos. Her aunt had already mixed the serum that would have stripped her of everything so she could be with you and not hurt you."

Tears clouded his vision as Styxx remembered Bethany telling him the truth after she'd freed him in Atlantis, and his steadfast. In his mind, it hadn't seemed feasible at the time. Now ...

"I wouldn't have cared." At least not after he'd had a chance to aborb it all.

"Good. Because if you want her back, you're going to have to bleed Apollo and battle the worst of the Atlantean gods for her."

"And you're not going to fight without us." Maahes and Ma'at flashed into the room, next to Savitar.

Savitar growled. "Anyone else you want to bring to the party?"

Maahes grinned insolently. "Mother, may I?"

The look on Savitar's face said that Maahes was barely a step away from becoming a lion throw rug on Savitar's floor.

Ma'at stood up on her tiptoes to place a kiss to Savitar's cheek. "Remember, you like me."

"I don't like anyone who barges into my home uninvited, Mennie."

"You'll get over it." She turned her attention to the group. "All right, children. Where are we?"

"From what I'm hearing ... screwed." Styxx crossed his arms over his chest as he considered everything they'd told him. "I'm going to be dense for a moment because I'm having trouble wrapping my head around this ... Bethany can be brought back. Yes?"

Ma'at and Set nodded.

Pain exploded inside him at the news. All these needless centuries he'd been forced to live without her ... He glared his fury at Acheron. "Why didn't anyone tell me this before?"

His brother held his hands up in surrender. "I had no idea your Bethany was Bet'anya or that she was in my basement garden of statues. That's the truth. I was a little distraught and disoriented eleven thousand years ago when my mother took me to Katateros the first time. After I teleported their statues to the basement, I locked the door and never went near that area again."

Even so, it took everything Styxx had not to punch Acheron where he stood. Had his brother ever bothered to meet her and speak to Styxx for five heartbeats this could have been resolved centuries ago.

You stupid bastard . . .

He looked at Set and Ma'at. Why hadn't *they* told him?

"Sugar, every one of us thought she was dead," Ma'at said gently. "Believe me, had we known she was frozen in Katateros, we'd have freed her for all of our sakes."

"Well, we would have tried." Set sighed. "Probably would have failed. It was the alignment on the twenty-first that made this possible . . . that and the demon." He turned his gaze to Simi.

Simi flashed a happy smile at Styxx that melted him on the spot. How something so lethal and cold could be so adorable and cute defied his best attempts to explain. Yet she succeeded. "I told you wishes can come true, and not just at Disney World. The real world does a good job, too, sometimes."

Acheron scowled at Simi's familiarity with him. "When did you two become friends?"

She wrinkled her nose. "On your birthdays, akri. Did you know akri-Styxx don't gots no one to spend his special day with? He all alone on it and so the Simi went to apologize and make him her friend, too, so he won't be alone on his special days anymore. But he done broke my heart so now he my other akri-baby like Baby Bas and akra-Kat. The Simi has officially adapted him . . . no . . . adopted him." She grinned so wide, her fangs flashed.

Instead of being angry, Acheron laughed and kissed her cheek. "All right, Styxx. Your show. How do we do this?"

Styxx glanced around at the gods and demons. "Still the sole human in the room. I don't know what we're up against or who we're fighting. I need more details."

Acheron spread his hands out and a schematic of his temple on Katateros appeared on the wall that showed the basement and the statues housed there. As he spoke, the animation illustrated his words. "A dozen gods woke up while Simi was in the basement with Xirena, looking for Bet'anya. Since I was in Vegas with Sin and Katra fighting off Ren's nightmare, and Tory was with my mother in Kalosis, the two demons were alone to create well-intentioned mischief. As soon as the gods began to stir, Xirena ran to tell Alexion and Danger. The three of them grabbed Simi and escaped here to Savitar to let him know what had happened."

"That's when they called me in Minnesota," Urian said. "And told me not to come home for a few days as we had ancient interlopers in Katateros who most likely would not host me a Welcome Back party."

Acheron sighed. "We're also flying blind." He motioned to his wall decoration. "We have that tidbit based on Simi's recollection. After Simi and crew vacated the premises, Archon and the others have blocked out our sforas. None of us can see where they are or anything inside the main temple."

Styxx nodded as he absorbed it all. "Do we know who we're up against?"

Acheron glanced to Simi before he answered. "We're not one hundred percent sure. Because Simi was an infant when they ruled, she's a little iffy on some of their identities and she was the only one who got a look at them. Best we can figure, it's ... " He again turned to the images on the wall—one of which looked more like Wreck-It Ralph than an actual god ... go Simi. "Dikastis, Ilos, Isorro, Asteros, Epithymia, Diafonia, Nyktos, Paidi, Teros, Phanen, Demonbrean, and we know for a fact Archon is with them as he's the one we've been talking to. And of course everyone's favorite dickhead, Apollo."

"Beautiful." Styxx ground his teeth as old memories churned. "My ideal guest list ... for a fête in hell." The Who's Who of the gods who had personal grudges against him and who'd gone out of their way to leave a scar on his soul. The Fates were definitely mocking him with this.

Letting out an exasperated sigh, Styxx went over them for the others so that they'd know who they were fighting. Unlike Simi, he knew the names and faces of every one of them ... even

Wreck-It Ralph aka Demonbrean. They were forever seared into his memories.

Styxx used Acheron's diagram of the gods he'd named to highlight each one. "Apollo's not a problem. He's an effing idiot when it comes to things like this. And he's a bully with no courage who will back down to someone more powerful." Which sadly wasn't him. "He won't be leading a charge, but will stay back until he can land a punch from safety. Unfortunately, Archon isn't any of that. He's sharp and deadly. Vindictive as hell. Brutal. But out of the list, Epithymia and Asteros"—he highlighted them—"are the two we have to neutralize immediately. Do not underestimate them, especially Epithymia."

He swept his gaze around the room's occupants. "And do *not* let that bitch touch you ... Demonbrean is even dumber than Apollo, but he's also the size of an effing house. His skin is armored and he lives to crush things. Treat him like a python and don't let him get his arms around you. Dikastis will hang back to get the lay of the situation and might not fight us at all. The rest are followers. Lethal, but pawns nonetheless. They were servants for Misos in war, and only did what they were told to do. You take out Archon and they will stand down ... Now what do we know of their demands?"

Savitar let out a bitter growl. "Because I was their Chthonian, Archon contacted me, not knowing my relationship with the Grom. They want Acheron as a sacrifice so that they can use his blood and heart to bring back the rest of their merry band, except for Bethany. Archon blames her for this, as if he wasn't the one who caused Acheron to be cursed ... what were you telling me about his intelligence?"

"Steadfast denial is not the same as intelligence." Styxx rubbed at his eyebrow as he digested the little gold nugget no one had bothered to tell him about when they'd asked him to be Acheron. "Just out of curiosity, what was the game plan you had once you sent me in to die and they discovered my blood and heart couldn't bring back their dead?"

Savitar shrugged nonchalantly. "Buy us time to gather enough Chthonians to take them down."

'Cause the Chthonians were such known people pleasers ... yeah. Their official motto—Does Not Play Well With Others. Do Not Mix With General Population or People. Period.

And whatever you do, don't feed them after midnight or any other time of the day as they would take the hand feeding them and shove it in an uncomfortable place on your body.

Styxx would be tempted to laugh if he wasn't so pissed. "Thank the gods none of you were among my military advisors. We'd have had our asses handed to us," he mumbled under his breath. Then louder, "Are they at full strength?"

Acheron shrugged. "No idea."

"Let's assume yes." Styxx ran over the facts. "So our numbers are basically even. The weakest link in our group is me ... What are our strengths?"

Simi opened her bag and pulled out her barbecue sauce. "Demons ready to eat, Sir Akri-Styxx! Gimme!"

Laughing at Simi's enthusiasm, Acheron jerked his chin toward his other daughter. "I don't want Katra in harm's way, but she's a siphon."

That was a good power to have, especially when it was on your side and not theirs.

"I'm also a trained soldier, Dad." Kat rolled her eyes at Acheron then looked at her husband, Sin, and warned him with her gaze not to say a word. She turned toward Styxx. "I was my mother's primary kori, and unlike my seriously overprotective father and husband, she—"

"Put her ass in harm's way all the damn time with a blatant disregard for her safety that still pisses me off," Sin growled.

Kat smiled and cupped his cheek. "Yes, baby, but had she not been so careless, I wouldn't have you. Now would I?"

He grumbled under his breath.

And like Bethany, Kat was born of the two pantheons they were up against. A definite plus.

"What else do we have that they won't know about?"

Set folded his arms over his chest. "For thousands of years, my son was the High Guardian for Noir in Azmodea."

Seth nodded. "I'm used to battling angry gods. I can also get us a bird's-eye view of anything you need. What I use, they can't block."

"And thanks to Davyn," Urian said, indicating the friend he'd brought with him out of Kalosis. "We have this." He held up a necklace that meant nothing to Styxx.

However, Set's eyes widened with recognition. "How did you get that?"

Urian snorted. "My enemy's enemy is my best damn friend. Davyn borrowed it from my father who was more than happy to lend it and wants us to tie it in a bow around Apollo's neck."

"What is it?" Styxx asked.

Set laughed, low and evil, and made no moves to touch it. "The Eye of Verlyn. That will deplete the powers of any god it comes into direct contact with."

Styxx looked at it with a new respect. "For how long?"

"As soon as it touches them, they're wiped. Then it depends on how long it's on their body and how strong they are. Too long, it'll kill them."

Styxx smiled and inclined his head to them. That was a nice toy. "Does it work on just full-bloods or any other species?"

Set shrugged. "I don't know."

Before anyone could react, Simi grabbed her sister and put her hand on it.

"Hey!" Xirena snapped at her sister.

"You still got power?"

Xirena shot a blast of fire at her.

Grinning and ducking, Simi looked at Styxx and let go of Xirena. "It don't work on us."

Urian laughed. "I'm only a quarter demigod, and it doesn't seem to affect me."

"I think I'm the only true demi then." Seth bravely took it into his hand and waited. After a couple of minutes, he shook his head. "No effect on me, either."

"Since my powers are borrowed from Apollymi, I'm not chancing it. We'll assume I need to stay clear of it. Urian, let's leave it in your custody." Styxx hesitated as another thought occurred to him. "Can the stone be broken apart or duplicated?"

Set shook his head. "Not without destroying it."

Styxx frowned at Acheron who was an unknown in all of this. "Would the stone just suck out your god powers and leave the rest intact?"

"That's what usually happens. Why? You thinking of giving me an early Christmas present?"

"Don't distract or tempt me." Styxx ran over the rest of their arsenal and the layout of Acheron's temple. They'd definitely use Seth to get a peek of what they were going into.

But first . . .

"My most important question of all . . . Where's my Bethany?"

As Styxx reached for the doorknob, Katra placed her hand on his arm. "I know this is the first time we've met, Styxx, but I'd rather you not go in there alone. Someone should be with you."

The compassionate concern in her green eyes shocked him. "How are you Artemis's daughter?"

Kat smiled. "She's not as bad as you think . . . Apollo, however, is probably worse."

Simi stood on his other side and leaned in to whisper in his ear. "We'll be super quiet. Akri-Styxx won't even know we're there."

Urian put his hand on Styxx's shoulder. "Don't worry. What happens happens and we won't think anything about it. We'll just be here for you if you need us."

Their kindness overwhelmed him. He wasn't used to anyone being concerned about him. Not since Bethany and Galen. "Thank you."

Taking a deep breath to steady his dizzying emotions, Styxx opened the bedroom door. The floor-to-ceiling windows were open, letting in the soft ocean breeze. But it was the huge canopied bed in the center of the room that held his attention. White linen drapes were pulled back with gold cords, obscuring most of the bed's contents.

All he could see was a bump beneath the stark white covers.

Right before the Atlanteans had attacked on Katateros, Simi had carried Bethany's body out and brought her here for safekeeping until they found some way to wake her.

He wasn't sure what he expected, but every step that took him closer to her made his heart pound harder.

And as soon as he saw Bethany's peaceful face, he froze as his entire body locked up with so many emotions, he couldn't even begin to define them. She looked just as she had the last time he'd seen her . . .

Flawless.

Except her stomach was flat. His hand trembling, he pulled the covers back and saw the blood that was still on her gown from where Apollymi had assaulted her. Throwing his head back, he roared in anger and pain at the sight of what the bitch had done to his heart. Unable to stand the guilt of not being there to protect her, he gathered her body into his arms so that he could finally hold her again.

She was ice-cold.

"Beth?" he breathed against her cheek as he cradled her head to his shoulder like he'd done all those centuries ago when it'd only been the two of them. "Please come back to me. Please. I need you so . . ."

But she didn't move or breathe. She merely lay in his arms in silence.

Tears fell down his cheeks as his heart shattered all over again. It was just like losing her the first time. He felt so lost and alone. Useless.

Broken.

Why were those other assholes up and around and not her? Why? It didn't make sense.

And it wasn't right.

He felt a large hand on his shoulder. Expecting Urian, he was stunned to find Acheron with him as the others quietly gave them the room. And the sight of his brother there hit him like a hot poker on his skin. He wanted the bastard's blood for this.

Gently, he laid Bethany back on the bed.

With a furious bellow, he turned on Acheron with a wide punch. Acheron blocked it and yanked him into his arms. Styxx tried to fight, but Acheron held him close against him in an iron grip.

"It's all right, Styxx. I know it hurts."

But Acheron didn't know. His children were all alive and well. Tory was healthy . . .

No one was going to kill her baby and leave her frozen and alone like this for centuries.

Yet something inside him splintered as he felt Acheron finally embracing him. Styxx didn't see them as men. He saw them as desperate, hated children who only had each other.

And it burned him to the core of his soul that Acheron would dare to embrace him now after all this time.

"I fucking hate you," he growled in Acheron's ear.

"I know, brother . . . I know." And still Acheron held him the way he used to when it was just the two of them against the world that begrudged them their very lives. When the only affection they could count on was a brother's love and respect. "I wish more than anything that I could take it all back. Everything," Acheron breathed. "That I'd listened to and followed the advice I gave to others. I hurt you and I abandoned you and it was wrong. I was wrong and I am so incredibly sorry."

Styxx wanted to rip him apart. He did. Deep inside, he needed to feel Acheron's blood on his hands.

And yet . . .

That piece of his heart that had only wanted his brother back savored this moment. Long before Bethany, this was what he'd craved. This was what he'd sought when he'd gone to Atlantis, sick, scared, and alone to free Acheron.

In spite of everything and everyone, even them and their own stupidity, he still loved his brother.

"Why can't I just hate you?"

Acheron's arms tightened around him. "Because you're a better man than I am. You always were."

But that wasn't true and Styxx knew it. He would never have been able to do for the Dark-Hunters what Acheron had done. While his brother had been a complete douche to him, Acheron had been the saving grace and sole champion for countless others. And he'd done it with a dignity and kindness that Styxx knew were hard-won given their brutal pasts.

They were both branded whores who'd been used, betrayed, and thrown away like garbage . . .

His brother had risen above it and built a life in spite of all the people who'd tried to destroy him. And Acheron still stood strong.

Acheron pulled back and placed his forehead to Styxx's just as he used to do when they were children. He gently fisted his hand in the hair at the nape of Styxx's neck and stared into his eyes. "I will never turn my back on you again, brother. I—"

Styxx covered his mouth with his hand, cutting off his words. "Don't make a promise you might not keep." It would kill him if he did. He wiped at the tears on Acheron's face. "Gah, we look like two old women." Styxx balled his fists in Acheron's hair, that no longer fell down his back. Rather, it hung now to just past his jaw. "But at least you finally got a decent haircut."

Acheron laughed.

Both he and Tory had cut their long hair and donated it to charity in honor of Sebastos's first birthday. While Tory's was now past her shoulders, Acheron had kept his to the same length Styxx had worn his before he'd first gone to war.

With a ragged breath, Acheron released him. "You've no idea how much I missed you when Estes took me away, Styxx. I couldn't stand it. Literally, I cried myself sick. It's why I had to bury it. The pain of being told you hated me and not having you was more than I could bear. And all Estes did was say over and over that you didn't want me with you. That you wanted our father's love for yourself and that you were the sole reason I'd been taken from home and given to him. That you never thought of me or asked about me at any time. I should have known better. But I burned with a furious shame and blind hatred you can't imagine. In my mind, you were given all the love, comfort and respect that was denied me."

Styxx snorted. "I do know your pain. I have not only my memories, but yours, too."

Acheron gave him a fierce, stern look. "And now I have yours." Tears welled in his eyes again. "And boy, don't I feel stupid. In my wildest nightmare, I never imagined Estes would dare whore you. Never mind what Apollo and the Atlanteans did . . . what I did." Styxx had been brutally used and sold three years longer than he had. "Honestly, I don't know how you could ever talk to me again."

But then Acheron did know. Styxx's guilt. He felt responsible for what had happened to him. For not being able to do something to spare him from his uncle and father.

For putting Bethany's safety and well-being before his.

"If it makes you feel better, Styxx, I would have chosen her over me, too." Especially given their pasts and what Acheron had said and done to him. Love was such a rare gift that both of them knew better than to squander it or take for granted the one person strong enough to give them what so few had. "You weren't wrong to protect her. And we will get her back for you. I swear it."

Styxx wiped at his eyes as he roped his emotions into submission. He wasn't sure he could believe in Acheron's words, but this was the closest they'd been to trust in centuries. "Just promise me one thing. If this doesn't work, you'll finally kill me."

"Is that really what you want?"

Styxx took Bethany's hand into his and nodded as he spun her wedding ring around on her finger. "She was so happy when I put this on her hand. I can still see her smiling . . . " He flinched in agony. "Gods, Beth, why didn't I go with you when you left?"

Acheron put his hand on Styxx's shoulder. "It wouldn't have mattered. Had she taken her serum, my mother still would have killed her. At least this way, we have a chance to bring her back."

Before Styxx could respond, something bright flashed.

They both turned, ready to fight, only to be stunned at the sudden appearance of Artemis in the room. Frowning, she made the strangest noise at the sight of them together.

Styxx leaned his head back to speak to Acheron. "I think we startled her more than she startled us."

Acheron sighed. "What are you doing here?"

She started to speak then closed the distance between them so that she could poke them each on the shoulder. "That's just . . . not right. Say something else so I know which of you is Acheron."

"What, Artemis?"

"There's that irritated tone I loathe." She turned her back to Acheron so that she could speak to Styxx. "I have brought you presents."

That scared him more than anything else.

Always beware a Greek bearing gifts, especially when it was a god.

"Why?"

"You're going up against my brother and the rest of those animals . . . I want you to win, and make him bleed. A lot. Buckets and buckets full until it gushes and fills the entire hall."

Styxx met Acheron's gaze over her shoulder. "Should I be afraid of the bloodlust?"

"I'm terrified." Acheron's frown deepened. "What did Apollo do?"

"He attacked Nicholas while he was weakened. I will not have it. Since I'm not powerful enough to harm him on my own, I want you two to kick his leg."

Acheron rolled his eyes. "You mean ass, Artie?"

"Whatever body part pleases you. You can't kill him, but you can make him suffer. Long. Hard. Pitifully. I gave Savitar an assortment of weapons I dipped in the River Styx. It will weaken Apollo to the point he'll be as a mortal." She glared her hatred for Apollo at Styxx. "If I were you, I'd castrate him slowly and with a great deal of—"

"Grammy! Grammy!" Out of nowhere, a dark-haired toddler around the age of four popped into the room and leapt into Artemis's arms.

Her rant instantly forgotten, Artemis gave the child a giant hug as she swung the child away from them. "Mia Bella! How is my precious today?"

The girl squealed. "Gamma, Gamma, Gamma, guess what? Guess what! The Simi gonna put hornays on my head like hers and Pappas's. And she said that I could pick any color I want and that they'd be on all the time and they can glow in the dark, too."

Bug-eyed, Artemis looked as horrified by the idea as Styxx felt.

Acheron laughed and rubbed Mia's back. "How about if Simi makes you a pair that can come off?"

Mia wrinkled her nose at him. "Pappas! No! I want real ones. Like you and Simi and Xireni."

Artemis blew out a burst of air. "You know Pappas only has those when he's mad, right?"

Mia's eyes widened. "Really?"

They both nodded.

Mia's attention finally went to Styxx. Her eyes widened. "Who cloned Pappas?" she whispered.

Acheron smiled. "He's my brother ... your uncle Styxx."

Before Styxx knew what the toddler was doing, she launched herself into his arms and kissed him.

"You look just like my Pappas." Then she put her hands on his cheeks and rubbed noses with him. "That's how Charonte say hello. But only if they like you. Otherwise they eat you with ketchup or barbecue sauce, or if they're like my uncle Xed, jalapenos which are really hot, too."

"Don't scare your uncle the first time you meet him, silly belle." Artemis pulled her back into her arms and tickled her.

The door opened. Kat and Sin came into the room making irritated, yet relieved parental sounds.

"Sorry." Kat took her daughter from Artemis. "She got off the chain when we took our eyes away from her for three seconds. She must have sensed you were here." Hugging her mother, she gave her a kiss on the cheek as Sin took his daughter from Kat.

Styxx bit back a smile at the way they passed the poor child around like a football. Yet she didn't seem to mind in the least.

Mia made an adorable face at her father. "Am I in trouble, Daddy?"

Sin had the same reaction Styxx would. He melted and grinned. "No, baby girl. But you shouldn't vanish like that without telling us where you're going." It was so incongruous to see a man as rugged and stern as Sin holding what basically amounted to a bright delicate fairy princess. The top of her dress was even bulging with pink and white cloth flowers, some of which decorated the long poofy yellow tulle skirt. Her legs were covered with matching pink leggings and pink patent leather shoes. The child was even wearing a pair of munchkin-sized pink tulle fairy wings. "You do have to go back to Aunt Tory and Aunt Danger and Uncle Kish and stay with them for a bit, okay?"

She pouted adorably and nodded.

Artemis stopped Sin before he could leave with Mia. "Grammy will be by in a little bit to read her baby belle a story, okay?"

Mia grinned and bounced. "Can we ride in your deer chariot, too?"

"Only if Mommy and Daddy say it's okay . . . and you'll have to put on a sweater." Artemis gave her a big hug and kiss. "I'll be there as soon as I can."

She nodded then went rigid in Sin's arms. "Wait! Wait! Pappas!"

Smiling, Acheron gave her a tight squeeze. "I, too, will be back as soon as I can."

"Then we'll watch *Megamind*?"

"Sure, baby."

She planted a loud, wet kiss on Acheron's cheek. Then Kat took her back from Sin. "I'll return her to her closet and lock her in."

Sin kissed the top of Mia's head before he turned back to them. "Really sorry for the intrusion." He followed after his wife and daughter.

Alone now with Artemis, Acheron met Styxx's gaze. "Are you all right?"

Not really.

Styxx swallowed hard against the pain inside him. "You have a beautiful granddaughter and I truly don't begrudge you your family, Acheron." He glanced to Bethany and felt tears prick the back of his eyes. "I just want mine."

"That's not going to be easy."

They both frowned at Artemis. The way she said that told them she knew something they didn't.

"What do you mean?" Styxx asked.

"You do know my brother was in love with her, right?"

Styxx gaped at something no one had ever mentioned. "Bethany?"

"Bathymaas," Artemis amended. "He and my mother are the ones who moused you out."

He had the hardest time understanding her. "Moused you out?"

"Ratted . . . you out," Acheron corrected in a pain-filled tone.

She sighed. "Whatever. I just don't understand modern idiots."

Styxx bit back a laugh as he silently agreed.

Acheron cleared his throat. "I think she means idioms."

She turned a peeved glare at Acheron. "No, this time, I got it right. Modern idiots. Anyway, my mother hated her because she coveted Bathymaas's powers and because Bathymaas didn't stop Hera from being such a bitch to us and leaving us with the blood-sucking curse I really want to claw Hera's eyes out over . . . and when Apollo fell in love with Bathymaas and she refused to have anything to do with him, he was furious. He couldn't stand it. So when he found out she was not only in love with the Atlantean Aricles, but sleeping with him, he went crackers."

"Nuts."

"Whatever." She growled at Acheron and his continued corrections. "Apollo's the one who tricked her into killing you, just like he did me with Orion. Bastard bitch that he is. It destroyed her. But you swore to her if it took you ten thousand lifetimes, you'd find your way back. And I'm glad you did, but Apollo won't be so happy once he realizes you're you."

Styxx was starting to get one of his "better" migraines. "I'm completely lost again. Bethany isn't Bathymaas. Bathymaas was born of the primal source."

"Yes. Set."

"Set?" Styxx repeated.

Artemis nodded. "She went . . . " she passed an evil grimace toward Acheron, "insane. Rather similar to what Apollymi did when Apollo killed Acheron. But her off knob—"

"Button or switch?" Acheron really didn't seem capable of stopping himself from correcting her. Styxx was beginning to think his brother did it just to get under her skin.

She wrinkled her nose and kept talking. "Off-switch was a lot harder than Apollymi's. The only way to stop Bathymaas was to have her reborn without the memory of Aricles. It's why her mother is Symfora—sorrow—and why Bethany wouldn't marry or really dabble much with men. But weirdly, she'd always go fishing where the two of you used to meet all those centuries before. Like she was waiting for you to come back to her, even though she had no memory of you or him."

Styxx had always wondered why Beth had chosen that fishing spot and why she'd been so loyal to it. Now it made sense. "In Didymos?"

"It wasn't called Didymos then, but yes. Aricles was born in a small stone cottage almost identical to the one you bought for Bet'anya, and it was where they first met when she went to recruit him for her Ēperon. Anyway, she set up their headquarters on the matching island where you, as Styxx, were raised. Bathymaas always wanted to stay close to Aricles, and she would often spy on him whenever he had free time. Even though he was the best warrior who ever held a sword in his hand, Aricles remained more farmer than soldier. Anytime he could, he'd seclude himself from his brethren and fish quietly by the same stream where you met her. Because she was a goddess, she'd never seen anyone do that before and was curious about it. As he taught her how to fish and they spent more time together, they fell in love."

"And that's why I didn't throw a fit the day we met."

Styxx turned toward Set who'd joined them in the room.

"As soon as I laid eyes on you, I knew you were Aricles. That somehow, you'd managed to keep your word and find her again, and I'm pretty sure it's what drew Apollo to you, too. Why he was so hellbent on making you suffer."

"No. That was my idiot other brother who pointed Styxx out to him. You give Apollo too much credit. He's like a spoiled toddler . . . pretty . . . shiny . . . gimme. Kind of like Acheron's demon." Artemis met Styxx's gaze. "Bathymaas was my brother's first love and her rejection crushed him—at least that's what he claims. Because of that, my mother cursed the two of you to never be together."

"Is that why Bethany can't wake up?"

"In part," Set said. "But mostly it's because she only has half her heart. To bring her back and allow her to be sane and not the soul of vengeance she'd became after Aricles died, I had to remove the part of her heart that had you in it and wipe all knowledge of you from her memory."

Acheron frowned. "That's biologically impossible."

"No. Bath wasn't human in any way, nor was she born of a womb. She was a gift to me to teach me compassion for others. Since the Mavromino had birthed the first Malachai, the Kalosum created her to keep me from turning my back on what I'd been born to do. It's why she was never supposed to know the love of any man. Her duty was to stay pure and remain the order to my chaos. She was justice. Cold and unyielding, without any personal interests or the ability to play favorites. Aricles changed all of that.

When her heart broke in half over his death, her tears are what transformed her into ruthless, uncaring vengeance. She lost all balance and nothing mattered except to make the world pay for the wrong it'd done her and Aricles. Ironically, it was that more than anything that showed me why I needed to keep a handle on my own powers. As bad as she was, I would be much worse should I ever let the Mavromino control me."

Styxx glanced back to Bethany. "So how do I wake her?"

"You have to return her heart to her."

"And that is where?"

Set sighed. "Last I heard it was given to Epithymia. The ugly side of desire is covetous jealousy. Epithymia wanted Apollo and thought that if she stole that part of Bet, it would help her seduce him."

Artemis scoffed. "Didn't work. She was too big a slut for my brother. He does have *some* standards."

"Then she's the one we use the necklace on." After kissing Bethany's hand, Styxx pulled the covers over her. He brushed the back of his fingers across her soft cheek. *I will not fail you, Beth.*

Whatever it took, he would reawaken her. Even if he had to die to do it.

He stepped back and swept them with a determined grimace. "Let's finish this."

DECEMBER 23, 2012

"You know this isn't going to work, right?" Styxx asked Acheron.

"I've had worse odds."

"So have I, but most didn't work out well for me." Dreading the fact he was about to be an ant under a magnifying glass, Styxx allowed Acheron to teleport them to his brother's bedroom in Katateros.

Before Acheron's marriage, the room had been sparsely decorated in black and brown. Now it was powder-puff blue with dancing circus animals on the walls and a canopied crib within easy reach of the large bed . . . a holdover from Acheron's paranoia and guilt about Apollodorus.

Acheron's son, Sebastos, was never left to sleep alone. The baby had been almost a year old before Acheron had allowed him to sleep anywhere other than his father's chest.

But Styxx couldn't fault him for that. He'd be as bad, if not worse with his own.

Styxx froze at that thought.

It was the first time in centuries that he'd thought about the prospect of having a child again. That it was suddenly a real possibility . . .

Yet he refused to be happy. Not until Beth was back in his arms and it was a done deal. Between now and then, anything could happen and he wasn't about to jinx himself.

Can you hear me?

He frowned as Acheron's thoughts intruded on his then nodded.

Good. I think it best if we communicate like this for a while.

Styxx nodded again. He went to the door and listened for the others. Seth's "bird" spirit had shown them that the gods were all gathered in the throne room, where they bragged about what they intended to do once they had Apostolos in their custody.

None of it was pretty and it made him rather glad that Acheron had reconsidered sending him in as his double.

Acheron joined him at the door. "They've sensed our powers." Something they wanted the Atlanteans to do since it would throw them off.

Ready? Styxx asked.

Absolutely not.

Styxx rolled his eyes at Acheron's warped humor.

Locking gazes, Acheron held his hand up in offering to Styxx. Styxx glanced to the crib and felt his stomach lurch. Acheron was as likely to hand him over to his enemies as he was to fight for him.

While his brother had stood strong and steadfast for his Dark-Hunter brethren, he'd never hesitated to throw Styxx under a bus.

But this was his only chance to get Bethany back. Like it or not, he had to trust Acheron to fight for and with him.

With a deep breath for strength, he took Acheron's hand and let his brother teleport them into the throne room.

Styxx let go of Acheron and took his position at his back. He faced Archon, Apollo, and Epithymia while Acheron faced the rest.

Archon rose to his feet. "Well, isn't this unexpected?" He smirked at Apollo. "We don't have to play chase for your pet, after all. How kind of them to save us time." He glared at Styxx. "Which of you is Apostolos?"

"I am," they said simultaneously.

Archon growled low in his throat.

"Their eyes," Apollo said quickly. "Styxx's are blue."

Acheron turned to stand beside his brother. When they spoke, it was as one. "Not anymore."

Archon narrowed his gaze on them. "Then we'll kill you both."

"No," Apollo snarled. "That wasn't the agreement."

Epithymia made a sound of supreme disgust. "Stand down, both of you. There's an easy way to get to the truth."

Styxx didn't like the sound of that. Where was Urian and their backup?

Epithymia tugged at the black cord around her neck to show them a small crystal vial. She pulled it over her head and placed it on the arm of Archon's chair then manifested a hammer. "This is the heart of Bathymaas. If the real Styxx doesn't step forward, I'll destroy her. Forever."

Cold panic erupted inside Styxx and when it did, it brought out his battle calm, which belied his volatile state. He knew better than to react.

Never let your enemies see your underbelly.

Styxx wouldn't even glance at Apollo who must have told them that he was Aricles. How else would they have known that Bathymaas's heart held any importance to him?

"So you don't love her?" She hovered the hammer over the vial. "Really?"

Styxx used Apollymi's powers to mask his voice. "You do that and you lose all leverage over both of us. Her life is the only thing keeping you alive right now."

A light flashed.

Expecting Urian, Styxx and Acheron had to force themselves not to react to Artemis's sudden appearance next to her brother.

"Oh my!" she exclaimed as she looked at them. "Am I interrupting?"

Apollo seized her arm. "What are you doing here?"

"I came to see Acheron. This is his house where he lives. I'm allowed to visit."

Archon bellowed in outrage. "This is not *his* home!"

Acheron and Styxx exchanged a puzzled frown. Neither of them had a clue what Artemis was doing here. She was not part of their plan. At all.

But she'd inadvertently found Archon's weakness. Don't refer to his home as Acheron's. Too bad the ancient god hadn't been tutored by Galen or he'd know better.

Blinking her eyes, Artemis gave the older Atlantean an innocent look. "No? Then why are you sitting on his throne? That's not yours, you know. I was with Acheron when he picked it out and brought it here."

No, she wasn't.

Styxx bit back a smile at Acheron's indignant thought. Go, Artemis. She was here to whip their emotions and frazzle them. And judging by the mottled color on Archon's face, she was doing an excellent job.

"Why is she here, Apollo?" Archon asked through clenched teeth.

"I have no idea."

Epithymia went rigid. "Something's not right . . . "

"That's because she's not my daughter."

Styxx and Acheron turned to see Leto, the mother of Apollo

and Artemis, entering from a side door. Dread cut through Styxx. If that wasn't Artemis . . .

It had to be Katra.

Crap.

"Mom," Apollo said irritably. "What are you doing?"

Ignoring Apollo's question, Leto smirked as she approached them. "Really, Katra? I'm so disappointed in you. But that's all right." She looked at Archon. "We don't need the twins now. Katra is the daughter of Artemis and Acheron. She has the Destroyer's bloodline and is actually stronger than her parents." She grabbed Kat and held a dagger to her throat. "So, Acheron, who do we kill? You or your daughter?"

Before they could blink, a sonic blast went through the room. One so fierce, it knocked everyone off their feet and slammed Leto against the wall.

Artemis appeared instantly and pulled Kat to safety. "How dare you," she enunciated each word slowly as she faced her mother. "No one threatens my baby ever! You cow!" She attacked her mother so ferociously, Kat had to pull Artemis away to keep her from killing Leto.

Acheron took advantage of the distraction to use his powers to jerk the vial from Epithymia's hand. He sent it to Styxx.

With a mutual nod, they attacked the Atlanteans closest to them. And Acheron quickly learned why pantheons didn't like to war within themselves. Since all of them pulled their powers from a mutual source, they were fighting in a weakened position and their powers weren't working properly. It was why gods who belonged to more than one pantheon were stronger. They could call on these additional powers and not be weakened.

Worse, it was playing havoc with his eyesight and his eyes kept tearing up.

"Katra!" Styxx called as he saw Epithymia going for her back.

She turned the instant Epithymia went to touch her. Instead of retreating, Kat pulled her close and sucked her powers out of her. "You won't be needing those, bitch."

And as she pulled Epithymia's powers, her teeth elongated and her eyes turned demonic red. Her skin began to swirl like Acheron's.

"Acheron!" Artemis screamed. "The demon's taking over Katra. Help!"

His face turning white, Acheron met Styxx's gaze.

"She's more important than I am. Get her out of here." Covertly, he handed Acheron the vial with Bethany's heart. *Free Beth even if I don't make it back.*

For the first time in his extremely long life, he saw the hesitation in Acheron's eyes as his brother debated on whether or not to leave him to fight without Acheron's help. That alone meant everything to Styxx.

But in the end, Acheron made the right decision.

He ran to his daughter to get her to safety.

Styxx manifested his hoplon and used it to deflect their godbolts as he covered Acheron's and Katra's retreat.

They teleported out with Artemis, leaving him alone to face the others.

A slow, lecherous smile curled Archon's lips. "It's like old times, isn't it, prince? And I have to say you're looking mighty tasty."

"What are you planning to do?" Apollo growled.

An evil smiled curled Archon's lips. "Tonight, we are going to have our fun of him again."

Refusing to react to those words, Styxx manifested his armor and sword. He would use Apollymi's powers as long as he had them, but at the end of the day, this was how he knew best to fight. Not as a god, but as a man. He narrowed his eyes on them, assessing each one's abilities . . . and weaknesses, which were too few to really matter.

Yeah, this was going to leave a mark.

And be bloodier than any battle he'd ever known.

So be it. Pain he was used to. And he wasn't going down without a vicious fight. Tonight he was taking his life back and agony to anyone who tried to stop him.

Lowering his chin, he smiled at them. "Come get some, bitches."

Acheron handed his unconscious daughter off to Sin. "Something from the old demon bite interacted with Epithymia's powers," he explained. "I drained her, but she needs to feed."

Sin nodded grimly as he took her and vanished.

Acheron was aghast at the others in the room, who were supposed to have been there to help them fight. "What happened?"

Set growled. "We're locked out. If you're not Greek or Atlantean, forget it. Only Katra had the ability to get to you. And even then it wasn't easy for her to teleport in."

Urian nodded. "I couldn't get in either. You're all he's got, boss."

"Simi, return to me."

She immediately laid herself over Acheron's heart as a dragon-shaped tattoo.

Xirena bit her lip. "Me, too, akri?"

"Absolutely."

That would get the demons in.

Acheron glanced around at his allies. "I'm weakened—every time I strike them, it drains a portion of my god powers—and the weapons Artemis brought might work on Apollo, but they're shite on the Atlanteans. We are in over our heads and I won't lie, it's ugly. So, who wants to try to go in with me and save my brother's life?"

They all stepped forward.

"All right. Here goes nothing." Closing his eyes, Acheron summoned everything he could and teleported them back to Katateros.

For several minutes, he, too, was locked out. When they finally broke through whatever Archon had done to shield the temple, Acheron was completely unprepared for the sight that awaited them. Blood was everywhere. It looked like the stage production of *Evil Dead*. But what scared him was the sight of Styxx's phoenix shield. Twisted and bent out of shape, it was in the middle of the largest pool of blood. Blood was smeared to the doors as if a struggling body had been dragged out through them.

Demonbrean and Ilios lay moaning on the ground near Apollo who wasn't in any better shape. Styxx must have beat the crap out of the Greek god before they'd overpowered him. Epithymia was still sobbing uncontrollably and hadn't moved from her spot where she'd fallen after Kat had drained her powers.

As Styxx had predicted, Dikastis stood calmly in the shadows and appeared to have not fought at all.

Not sure of the god's loyalties or intentions, Acheron went to him first. "Where's my brother?"

Raw anger flared in the god's eyes. "They took him to the temple arena."

"Why aren't you with them?"

"I'm a god of justice. I will not participate in something that's wrong and undeserved."

"Will you fight with us then?"

Dikastis nodded without hesitation.

His breathing ragged, Styxx was so battered and bruised at this point, he wasn't sure why he was still conscious. He'd managed to knock out three of them and weaken the rest, but in the end, he'd been outnumbered and was no match for a dozen gods who'd been asleep and resting for centuries.

Against Styxx's best efforts, Archon and Asteros had dragged him to the temple Acheron had confined him in years ago ... To the arena where they'd once made his life utter hell. Laughing all the while, they'd secured him to the rack they'd used for his beatings and other things that had left him bleeding internally for eternity.

Damn them.

Archon fisted his hand in Styxx's blood-soaked hair and jerked his head back. "You're not defeated so soon, are you, prince?"

As if. Ryssa had slapped harder than Archon hit. "Fuck you."

"How I wish, but unfortunately, we're making you a sacrifice." Archon gagged him then looked over to Leto. "Summon our lady vengeance."

Leto laughed as she neared Styxx. "You didn't really think

Epithymia had Bathymaas's heart, did you? Trust me, I kept that for myself. Now I'm going to finish what I started fourteen thousand years ago."

And when I'm done destroying what's left of the Greeks, I'm going to tear apart the Atlanteans as I did the Sumerians and Egyptians. No one is going to stop me. No one.

Styxx's eyes widened as he heard her thoughts loud and clear.

Leto pulled out a knife and sliced open Styxx's cheek so that she could fill a vial with his blood. She mumbled words he didn't understand as she blended his blood with another compound. And as she did so, his head began to spin.

All of a sudden, he remembered being Aricles.

He saw Bethany at his side as she held on to his biceps. "Do not fight Apollo for my honor. It's not worth one single drop of your blood. Run with me, Ari. Let's leave all this behind and never look back."

"I can't, and neither can you, Bathia. We have too many responsibilities. Too many to protect. We cannot abandon this world to their cruel hands."

"I no longer care about any of that. You are all I cherish now."

His blood racing with fury and pain, Aricles had pressed his cheek to hers and held her close. "And you're all that matters to me. I won't have your reputation tarnished by that pig. You've done nothing wrong." The two of them had secretly married and he wanted Apollo's throat for the lies the Greek god and his whore mother had told against Bathymaas. "I will beat that bastard down for you, my goddess. Have no fear."

She buried her hand in his hair as tears streamed down her beautiful face. "You are the heart they claim I was born without. It's why I can't be the soul of justice anymore. You've changed me forever . . . And you can't leave me in this awful world without you."

He kissed her forehead. "Let me win your honor and then we will go wherever you wish."

"Swear it to me."

"On my eternal soul. I will always be with you, Bathia. Nothing

899

will take me from you, ever. Not even the gods." He lifted the Egyptian ieb amulet from her chest and kissed it then tucked it back between her breasts.

Styxx gasped as he fully understood what Set had told him. Bathymaas had been created by the Source, not born of a mother . . .

With no heartbeat whatsoever, she'd been a complete stranger to any kind of emotion until Aricles had taught her how to love.

The Egyptian jug-shaped amulet was the heart Set had given her as a girl when she'd asked her father why she didn't have a heartbeat like others. It was part of the same amulet Bethany had given him to protect him in battle.

"This holds my love for you, child, and while you can't understand it, know that so long as you wear it, you carry a vital piece of me with you. My heart has great power and it will keep you safe and warm in my absence."

That was how Leto had destroyed the Egyptian pantheon and trapped Set in the desert. Once she'd stolen the half of Bathymaas's heart that Set had hidden in his domain, she'd used Set's DNA and Seth's blood to trap the primal god.

Lifting his head, Styxx saw the broken ieb shard on Leto's wrist that matched the one Bethany had given him. While his half had held Bethany's bow and arrow emblem, the one Leto wore had the phoenix symbol of Aricles. Two halves of one whole. It was so obvious now, but unless you knew what an Egyptian heart looked like, you'd never guess its origins.

Or its significance.

Leto poured the blood from the vial onto her fingers and waved the ieb over it. Then she wiped it down his other cheek. "History always repeats itself. Poor you to die twice by the hand of the woman you love. And once you're dead, she'll destroy the gods for me." Stepping back, she let out a sharp, piercing ololuge . . . a sound used in his time to summon a god's presence when a sacrifice was being offered to them.

All of a sudden, a fierce wind came tearing through the arena. It blew open doors and ripped at his body. Leto stumbled against it.

A baleful howl sounded an instant before a swirling specter joined them. Inhumanly large, it floated on the wind wearing a bloodred cloak. And when it neared Styxx, he realized this was the vengeful spirit of Bethany that had been born after Apollo had tricked her into killing her beloved.

With his gag in place, he couldn't say a word of warning to her. Just as they'd done fourteen thousand years ago, Apollo and Leto had set Bethany up to fall. And to suffer.

Leto pointed to him as she spoke to Bethany. "Behold the bastard son of your enemy who cost your prince his life and existence. Take your vengeance on them both! Rip out the heart of Apostolos!"

Bethany screamed in furious agony.

Styxx's eyes widened as he realized she was going to kill him and there was nothing he could do to stop her.

Acheron paused at the temple's entrance. It was the same one he'd confined Styxx to when he'd brought him here. "What is this place?"

"It's our arena," Dikastis answered. "It's where we held games and competitions, and where we brought those who needed to be punished and taught humility."

Ash winced as images from Styxx's memories mingled with his. *And I left him here to rot . . .*

For that alone, I deserve to have my name engraved in the lowest pit of hell.

How could he have allowed his own pain to blind him to Styxx's so completely? The knowledge that Styxx had tried to help him when Acheron had been held, and that he had never once reached out to his brother when Styxx had been in captivity, made him ill. How could he have been so cold? So callous?

What spoke highest of Styxx's character was that he'd never sought credit for his actions whenever he'd done something for Acheron or even Ryssa. He'd given simply because it'd been the right thing to do, and personal glory had never mattered to him. Not once.

Meanwhile both Acheron and Ryssa had slapped him for it. Repeatedly. No wonder Styxx had been so eager to kill him in New Orleans. He'd more than earned Styxx's hatred.

But he wouldn't fail Styxx this time.

Ash swept his gaze over Urian, Davyn, Dikastis, Seth, Set, Maahes, Ma'at, Zakar, and the demons. "I don't know what we're about to walk into, but let's move forward with Styxx's original plan. And whatever we do, save my brother."

They nodded in agreement, except Dikastis.

"What do you want from me?" the Atlantean asked.

"Help us any way you can."

But what concerned Ash the most was the fact that none of the Atlanteans had come out to challenge them on their arrival. They had to know they were here. So why were they so quiet while they had this many foreign gods in their domain?

His heart pounding in fear of what awaited them, he entered the building. Inside the dark hall, a feral wind howled and plastered their clothes against their bodies.

It took them several minutes to make it to the arena, and to fight the wind so that they could see what was happening. The Atlanteans were all pinned down.

The moment Ash located Styxx, his stomach hit the floor. A ghostly image dressed in red was wrapped around him and held a dagger over his heart.

"Bathymaas! No!" Set shouted.

Without the slightest hesitation, she sank the dagger deep into Styxx's chest, all the way to the hilt then threw her head back and roared in satisfaction. When she spoke, she used Atlantean only. "Take your bastard back, Apollymi. Now come and face me, you wretched bitch, so that I can bathe in your putrid blood! Taste my vengeance, whore, and choke on it!"

Horrified, Ash looked to Set whose expression was every bit as pain-filled as his own.

They were too late.

Again. Styxx was dead and it was final. The coating on that

dagger would kill anything with a heartbeat. Even Styxx. It didn't matter that their life forces were joined. It didn't matter that Styxx held Apollymi's powers. The sap of the ypnsi didn't discriminate. It was absolute.

Tears filled Acheron's eyes as he failed his brother for the last time. Now he would never be able to make amends and show Styxx just how sorry he truly was for the things he'd done to him. And it wasn't until this moment that he realized just how much he had loved his brother, after all. Styxx had been right. They were two halves of a single whole, and the pain of Styxx's loss slammed into him harder than he would have ever imagined possible.

Wishing with all the powers he had that he could bring his brother back, Ash felt a single tear slide down his cheek. *I'm so sorry, adelphos. I should have been the brother to you that you were to me.*

An image of his mother appeared. It was the same ethereal shade form she used whenever she visited Acheron. "What have you done?"

Bathymaas ran at her and then through her. "Are you afraid to face me?"

Her expression one of deep sadness, Apollymi shook her head. "You did not kill Apostolos." Tears filled her eyes as she looked at Styxx's body. "I am still trapped in Kalosis. The man you killed is Styxx of Didymos."

"No," Bathymaas breathed. Disbelief widened her eyes as she turned back toward Styxx and paled. "You lie!"

Blood dripped from the wound she'd given him and as it did so, it drained Apollymi's powers from Styxx. His hair returned to blond, his skin darkened, and the scars that had been hidden re-appeared on his body.

Leto's laughter filled the room. "Poor Bathymaas ... you are damned again by your own hand." She materialized behind Bathymaas and ripped the necklace from where Styxx had placed it before he sent her to Egypt to wait for him.

Set ran for them, but before he could close the distance, Leto put the two pieces together.

"Now I will be the soul of justice and you'll . . ." Leto frowned as the amulet refused to reunite. "What? Why isn't this working?"

Ash met Urian's gaze and jerked his chin toward the pinned gods.

Urian nodded in understanding and made his way toward them with Davyn in tow.

Ash had just started for Styxx when all of a sudden, Styxx gasped and arched his back as if something possessed him. The knife Bathymaas had buried in his chest shot through the air and landed harmlessly on the ground. Light streamed out of the wound, sealing it closed. In the next heartbeat, a shock wave went through the room, knocking everyone off their feet, except Ash, who'd seen this twice before.

The last time in New Orleans.

A slow smile spread across his face as he realized that Styxx had finally received his Chthonian powers that prevented any god from killing him. This was a Chthonian rebirth and it was painful as hell. But the drawback was that his brother would have no idea what those powers were or how to use them. Whenever they manifested, they took control over their master and were hard to use or to fight.

Especially the first time.

The chains that held Styxx in place shattered, sending shrapnel in all directions. Styxx rose to hover over the floor.

"What's happening?" Archon roared.

No one answered as lightning bolts shot from Styxx's body, blowing out the windows and ripping the doors from their hinges. Bolts of light pierced Styxx's eyes and mouth. They exploded through his body, strengthening him and bringing him back from his undeserved death.

Simi started to go to Styxx, but Ash held her back. Since she wasn't Styxx's Charonte, Styxx might unwillingly hurt her.

There was only one person in the room who could stop this and she was about to make the horrendous mistake of attacking Styxx.

Ash summoned as much of his powers as he could and teleported himself to where Styxx hovered. He knew it was an idiotic move, but he had no alternative.

The moment Bathymaas saw Ash, her nostrils flared with anger. "You!"

When she moved for him, Ash caught her with his powers. "Kill me and Styxx dies, too. Is that what you want?"

"Kill them both!" Leto shouted, still trying to put the two halves of the Egyptian heart together.

Bethany rose up as if she'd obey Leto, but then her gaze went to Styxx and she calmed instantly. "What do I do to save him?" she asked Ash in an anguished tone.

"You have to ground him. Make him aware of who and what he really is outside of his powers."

"How?"

Ash shook his head. "Damned if I know. I'll try and hold him, but you have got to reach him or those powers will rip him apart and destroy us all."

Nodding, she stepped back and cleared the way for Ash to launch himself at Styxx. When his brother went to hit him, Ash embraced him with everything he had.

Styxx bellowed furiously as he tried to break free.

In her Bethany form, she appeared in front of his brother and cupped his face in her hands. "Styxx? Can you hear me?"

Another blast went through the room as something like a hurricane swept through with enough force that it knocked Bethany back. Ash held on to Styxx and grabbed Bethany before it carried her away.

Bethany trembled as all her memories merged with Bathymaas's and she was fully restored. She saw herself with Styxx and with Aricles, and remembered everything the gods had done to them both to tear them apart and keep them from each other.

Anger rose up, but she forced it down. There would be a full accounting later. Right now, she had to save him. No matter what, she couldn't allow him to suffer another day or die for these bastards.

Or for her.

He shoved Acheron away and turned on her with a murderous glint in his blue eyes. Scared and unsure, she did the only thing she could think of.

She kissed him.

Styxx froze as the scent of eucalyptus and lilies invaded his head. As softness again filled his arms and he remembered what it was like to be part of a whole. That sweet, precious touch calmed him instantly.

Afraid he was dreaming, he pulled back ever so slowly to look down at the woman in his arms. Was it real? Was she real?

"Beth?"

She gave him a smile that harded him instantly. "Are you with me, *akribos*?"

"I'm not sure. Am I dead?"

She laughed. "I don't know. Am I?"

"No!" Leto screamed as she ran for them.

Without hesitating, Ash intercepted her. But as soon as he neared her, she stabbed him through his stomach with the same Atlantean dagger laced with ypnsi sap that Bethany had used to kill Styxx. While the poison was fatal to mortal beings, it was a potent miasma for the gods, and it was the same serum Apollymi had used on her family to lock them in deathlike limbo when she'd confronted them over Acheron's death.

Ash staggered back and fell to his knees.

Styxx ran to him. "Acheron?"

"Simi!" he called, ignoring his brother.

"Simi on it, akri!" She vanished.

Acheron's body was quickly turning gray as the poison spread from the wound to the rest of him. His eyes flared red as he cupped Styxx's cheek and pulled him into his arms.

Before Styxx realized what Acheron intended, his brother sank his fangs into his neck and handed over his powers for Styxx's use. As soon as it was done, Ash fell back and locked gazes with Styxx. "Kick their asses, brother."

"With pleasure." Laying Acheron on the floor, Styxx saw Urian fighting Phanen. "Urian, on deck."

Urian flashed over then cursed as he saw Acheron's condition.

"Watch and protect him." Styxx rose slowly to his feet as he let the weight of Acheron's power and his own newly acquired ones mingle. Damn ... Acheron's abilities made a mockery of Apollymi's. If Katra really was stronger than her father ...

That was a terrifying prospect.

"Styxx?"

He hesitated at the fear in Bethany's voice. She was the only person in this room he'd never willingly hurt. Taking her hand into his, he pulled her closer so that he could protect her, and she could keep him grounded in case his powers surged beyond his control again. "I'm fine," he assured her. "As long as you're with me."

All around him, the gods battled.

Leto came at them with the dagger raised. Styxx stepped in front of Bethany to confront the *kuna* who had twice tried to destroy his wife. It was time he ended this and her, once and for all. Leto leapt at him. The force of her attack unbalanced her. He jerked her forward and disarmed her with a single twist to her wrist.

But in spite of everything the bitch had done to them, he couldn't bring himself to strike her. It'd been hardwired into him by Galen that there was never, ever any reason for a man to hit a woman, no matter what she did to deserve it. Men were much too strong.

Leto laughed as she realized he wouldn't strike her.

Until Bethany came around him with a grim, determined glint in her eye. "I've got this bitch."

Styxx stepped back and let her take fourteen thousand years of vengeance out on the goddess they both hated. The goddess who had done her best to destroy them both.

And speaking of hatred and retribution ...

He turned toward Archon who was battling Zakar. Manifesting his sword and shield, Styxx headed for them.

"Zakar?"

The Sumerian looked past Archon then fell back as Styxx moved in to engage the Atlantean god.

Archon laughed. "Really? You think borrowed powers scare me, boy? I've wiped my ass on higher beings and better warriors than you."

"I'll concede the higher beings, but you should remember, Archon, there has never been born a better warrior than me. It's why you helped Apollo and Leto cheat in order to kill Aricles. You knew the debt I owed Apollymi for her favor and that I'd be coming for you eventually."

Scoffing, Archon brought his axe down across Styxx's shield. Styxx lunged at his feet with his sword. The older god danced away as Styxx twirled with an uppercut that nicked his arm.

Archon screamed out in pain.

Styxx drove him back as Archon struggled to keep up with his blows. And he saw the fear in Archon's eyes as the god realized he wouldn't win this round.

"Go ahead," Archon taunted, "put me back to sleep. I *will* get free again. And when I do, I'm coming for all three of you. There's nothing you can do to stop me. I will return."

"No," Styxx said firmly. "You won't." He feinted right and when Archon moved to defend, he shot back with a well-practiced swing that severed the god's head in one final stroke.

Everyone in the room froze as they realized what Styxx had done. And more to the point, they became aware of what he really was.

A Chthonian god-killer. They alone had the power to destroy a god and send his or her power back to the Source without destroying the fabric of the universe. And while killing a god weakened them, they were still the baddest asses in the Nether Realm.

The only things that could kill one of them was the Source, one of its servants, or serums or another Chthonian.

In that moment, the Atlanteans did what they'd done in Halicarnassus when they realized Styxx would not be defeated . . . they dropped their weapons immediately, and stood down.

Except Bethany and Leto who continued to battle. The blood-lust in his wife's eyes was a scary thing.

"Should we break them up?" Urian asked as he joined Styxx.

Before he could answer, Set intervened by grabbing Leto in a fierce sleeper-hold. As soon as she passed out, he tossed her over his shoulder. "While I respect your need to beat on her, daughter, I'm the one with a much larger grudge against her. Not just for what she did to you, but for what she did to your brother." He leaned forward to kiss Bethany's cheek. "I will be back very soon and never fear . . . while I wouldn't deign strike a lady, this bitch is open season." He paused to glance at Zakar, who smiled in wicked antici-pation.

Then the three of them were gone.

"Brother?" Bethany whispered in confusion as she turned to Styxx. "What brother?"

He pointed to Seth across the room. "Seth was born long after Apollymi had frozen you in Katateros."

Bethany went to meet him for the first time while Styxx knelt beside Acheron. He was stone gray from head to toe. Frowning, Styxx glanced to Urian. "What causes this?"

"Aima," Dikastis answered, kneeling next to Styxx.

Styxx started for Dikastis to finish him off, but Urian stopped him.

"He's on our side."

"You sure?"

"He stabbed that one." Urian pointed to Teros. "And saved my ass."

Maahes joined Seth and Bethany while Ma'at moved to stand by Styxx. She placed a comforting hand on his shoulder.

"Acheron will be fine. As soon as Simi brings the antidote, he'll wake up."

Styxx wanted to believe that. "Are you sure?"

She nodded. "Otherwise, Apollymi wouldn't be so quiet."

And she was quiet . . . eerily so. Even when Simi returned with three leaves from the Tree of Life that only grew in the Destroyer's temple in Kalosis, Apollymi remained extremely reserved and dubiously silent.

"What do I do with these?" Styxx asked Simi.

"Twist them until they're moist," Apollymi said. "Then drip nine drops into Apostolos's mouth."

Styxx hesitated. "What happens if I do ten by mistake?"

"Let's not find out."

Duly noted.

Bethany returned to his side as he carefully counted.

As soon as the ninth one hit Acheron's lips, the color slowly returned to the whole of his body. Groaning, Acheron opened his eyes then grimaced. "Next time, add peppermint flavoring, somebody. That is the nastiest tasting crap on the planet."

Styxx scoffed. "You're not seriously complaining that I brought you back. Are you?"

"Yes, and no. Taste it yourself and you'll bitch, too."

Snorting, Styxx held his hand out to his brother. Acheron took it and allowed him to pull him to his feet.

They stared at each other, fully united for the first time since the day Estes had taken Acheron to Atlantis. Brothers forever and always.

Even through mutual idiocy.

Acheron hugged him close then stepped back to leave him to Bethany.

Still expecting all this to be a twisted dream, Styxx turned and wrapped his arms around her. He leaned his head against hers and took a deep breath as her scent and warmth filled him in a way nothing else ever had. While he'd learned to be whole alone, it didn't compare to what he felt as one half of their whole. "I told you I'd come back for you, my goddess. That nothing would stop me."

"Yes, but did you have to drag your feet? Seriously?"

He laughed in spite of the pain her teasing wrung inside him as he tightened his arms around her. "I'm afraid you're going to have to get used to living with me right here. I will never again let you go. Just consider me a large exterior growth on your body."

Her lips trembling, she smiled up at him as her own tears flowed. "I am so glad to have you back. I just wish we had our son with us."

"I know, precious," he breathed.

"Um . . . about that."

Styxx glanced up at Apollymi's trepidatious voice that she had suddenly found again. Dread replaced his happiness as he feared that nervous tone. "What?"

"Remember my promise to you, Styxx?"

That she would make everything right if he survived. "Yes?"

"I didn't kill your son. I wanted to. Desperately. But as I looked down at that tiny, beautiful baby, I saw Apostolos and I couldn't bring myself to hurt him."

Bethany gasped. "He lives? Where is he?"

Apollymi's gaze went to Urian who turned around to look behind him.

Styxx's jaw dropped in understanding. "Urian is Galen?" And yet some part of him had known it the first time they met. He'd felt that connection and love. Now it made total sense.

Urian shook his head. "It's not possible. I was born before they died."

"No, you weren't." Apollymi smiled sadly. "Strykerius told you that because he didn't want you to know that you and your brother were the first Apollites born cursed. And that was my fault. I intentionally chose Strykerius's wife because I thought it the perfect revenge that Apollo should look after Styxx's child given what he'd done to him . . . in both lifetimes. I had no idea Apollo would curse all of you over the death of a woman he really couldn't stand. Like Apostolos and Styxx, your blood mingled with that of Strykerius's real son, and that made you a part of Strykerius, too. You, child, are the only being alive who is part human, Atlantean, and Apollite . . . and you carry in your veins the blood of three pantheons and gods."

Urian was aghast. "Does Stryker know?"

She nodded. "I told him long ago—after you were grown and

he wondered about some of your heightened abilities—that you were very special to this world, but not who your real parents were. Your unique bloodline was why the evil souls you once lived on didn't infect you at all. Why you could go longer between feedings than others of your kind, and how your blood sustained Phoebe while she lived. It's also why Strykerius cut your throat instead of stabbing you in the heart. Unlike other Daimons, you wouldn't have died from a heart wound. Only blood loss could have killed you back then."

Urian looked at Acheron. "Did you know this?"

"I knew it was odd that Stryker cut your throat instead of stabbing you, but no. I had no clue you were my nephew. My mother"—he passed a peeved glare at her—"never mentioned it to me."

Urian scowled. "Man, I'm messed up right now. My best friend is my father? The man I idolized as a kid . . . whose tattoo is on my arm . . . And he's younger than me. Yeah, I don't think I can handle this. Mindwipe me, somebody . . . please! Where's that dragon from Sanctuary? Simi, go get Max. I need him."

Biting her lip, Bethany approached Urian tentatively. Her heart pounded as she sought physical confirmation for what Apollymi said. While his hair was lighter than Styxx's, it was the same color as Aara's. He wasn't quite as tall as his father, but he had the same expression now that Styxx often wore whenever he was irritated or confused. She placed a gentle hand on his cheek as she stared up at him. "I see your father in you. My baby's beautiful. Just like I knew you'd be." She pulled him into her arms and held him tight as a thousand emotions ripped her apart. But the one thing she couldn't deny was the joy in her heart that they had him with them. That Apollymi had finally learned compassion and kindness. "I hate that I missed seeing you grow, but I do love you . . . Urian."

In spite of what Urian had said, he held on to her as if she'd raised him. Styxx wrapped his arms around both of them as he'd ached to do for centuries. He couldn't believe this was real. That they were really with him.

Finally.

A part of him was doubly furious that Apollymi hadn't told him about Urian years ago. But right now, he was so glad and grateful to have them that he didn't want to spend a single moment lamenting a past he couldn't change. Hell had already owned too many centuries of his life. All he wanted now was to forget what had happened and focus on the future, which was finally one of hope and love.

And family.

The only things that had ever really mattered to him.

Yeah, life was hard for everyone, but it was all the more so when you fought it alone. And though Styxx was powerful on his own, he was a lot stronger with his brother at his back and his wife and son by his side.

DECEMBER 24, 2012

Styxx pulled back from his family to realize that everyone had left the arena.

Except Apollymi. Her crystal tears glistened against her pale cheeks as she watched them. "What I did to all of you was inexcusable. I lashed out in anger and pain, and what I thought was vengeance was nothing more than selfish envy. Because I knew I'd never be able to hold my baby, I took that pleasure from both of you, and for that, I am truly sorry. But your son is why I saved the Apollites that I did. Once my anger cooled, and I realized how wrong I was to take him away from his mother and father, I kept him safe for you both."

Styxx glared at her. "I can't even begin to put into words how infuriated I am that I was alive and imprisoned, and missed seeing my son grow up—"

Apollymi nodded. "I know, Styxx."

And she did. She knew exactly how it felt. Only she had been able to see her son after twenty-one years.

For that matter, Acheron also shared his pain. Artemis and Apollymi had done the same thing to him. Until five years ago, Acheron hadn't known about Katra, and at times over the centuries, Acheron had even been in the same room with her while never knowing she was a part of him and Artemis.

That, too, was cold-blooded.

Styxx met Apollymi's gaze levelly. "Oddly enough, Apollymi, I can't find any hatred for you right now. I'm too grateful to have them with me to waste one minute thinking about anything else."

Bethany nodded. "I will probably hate you in the morning, Pol. But tonight, I'm with Styxx. I just want to be with my boys and forget everything else."

Apollymi inclined her head to them. "The others quietly made their way back to the main temple and left the three of you to your privacy. Know that if you ever need anything . . . I will be here for you." She returned to Kalosis.

Styxx smiled at his wife and son. "I would give anything to spend the night talking to both of you. But . . . "

"Shit to do," Urian said for him.

Bethany made a face at her son. "Who taught you how to speak?"

Urian visibly cringed. "She's going to be in for a rude awakening with all the modern changes and gadgets, isn't she?"

That deepened her frown. "How long have I been gone?"

Styxx checked his watch. "I let go of your hand eleven thousand five hundred and thirty-nine years, one hundred eighty-three days, and roughly ten hours, give or take a few minutes . . . ago."

Bethany was floored by the length of time. But more than that . . . "You really did count the heartbeats."

Styxx slid the sleeve back on his arm. "Oh Beth, you have no idea."

Tears choked her as she saw the scar where he'd carved their names into his own flesh so that he'd always have them with him. She kissed Galen's name then lifted her lips to his. She wouldn't have thought she could love him more, but right then ... all she wanted was to spend the rest of the night with him inside her, showing him exactly how much she adored her noble prince.

Urian whistled low. "You know, this would be awkward if you *weren't* my parents. The parental designation ups the ick factor exponentially."

Laughing, Bethany pulled away from the kiss to frown at him. "I am desperate to know you." She looked back at Styxx. "And you and I have a lot to talk about. But ... "

"We have gods to attend to," Styxx breathed.

She nodded. "I want to make sure they never threaten us again."

"I couldn't agree more."

Her heart swelling with pride and love, Bethany took their hands and teleported them to the main temple. She sucked her breath in sharply at the signs of battle and the amount of blood on the walls and floor. Horrified, she met Styxx's sheepish gaze. "Please tell me that's not yours."

"Some is, but a lot of it was Demonbrean. That bastard bleeds like a slaughtered pig."

When she started forward, Styxx refused to let go of her hand. She turned back with a frown.

The agonized fear in his eyes slashed across her heart. "I let go of your hand once when I didn't want to, and it was the biggest mistake of my life. One I never intend to make again."

She laced her fingers with his and pulled him toward Acheron who sat on Archon's black throne. That was shocking enough, but the presence of Artemis and the Sumerian god Sin really messed with her head.

I have missed a lot ...

Most of the gods were gone now. The only ones left were Ma'at, Urian, Sin, Artemis, Seth, two demons, and a man she didn't know.

She paused near the throne. Styxx pressed himself against her back and wrapped his arms around her waist then rested his chin on top of her head. There was a time when she'd have been irritated by the constriction.

Tonight, nothing could have pleased her more.

Acheron looked at them.

"Catch us up?" Styxx asked.

Simi blew out an irritated breath. "Akri won't let me eat any of them nasty gods. What's the world coming to when a demon gots to beg for tidbits ... not even a finger sandwich or a single knuckle. Tragic. Terribly tragic."

Laughing at Bethany's confusion, Styxx whispered in her ear. "I'll explain Simi later."

Acheron let out a "heh" sound over Simi's words then he spoke to Styxx. "Well, after the way you took Archon's head, the rest are more than happy to be returned to stasis. But I was thinking of allowing a couple of them to be siphoned off by Kat and transitioned into the human world."

Styxx hesitated. "Which ones?"

"I wasn't going to make the offer without conferring with you first. I know they were less than kind to you while you were here, and if you want to gut them, I'm going to help you."

Bethany tilted her head back to stare at Styxx with a frown. "When did you two become friends?"

Styxx kissed the tip of her nose. "About five minutes before you woke up."

Her scowl deepened. She definitely had a lot of questions for later.

"Dikastis," Acheron continued, "I was going to leave alone ... as long as you agree. He seems to be decent enough."

Bethany nodded. "He is extremely trustworthy and loyal so long as no rules are broken."

"Will Epithymia get her powers back?" Styxx asked.

Sin laughed uproariously. "Hell to the no. Trust me. When Kat removes your powers, they stay gone. Technically—in theory—Kat *could* give them back. And I hate speaking for my wife while she's not here, but I'm pretty sure Epi is going to learn to be without."

From the way he said that, Bethany suspected Sin had firsthand experience with losing powers to his wife.

Acheron continued. "Leto is with Set and I'm not about to step in on that. Especially given what Seth and Artemis have told me about her and what she's done to all of you."

Artemis lifted her chin proudly. "Yes, we threw her over the trolley."

Acheron rolled his eyes. "Under . . . bus, Artemis. You throw people under a bus."

"Whatever. My mother threatened my baby, and my loyalty is to Katra and Mia and no one else . . . until Katra has more children, and they have babies. But that's it!" She pursed her lips. "Oh wait, there is one more, but that really is all and it's not to the heifer who threatened to harm my girl. Either of them. Since I gladly cede my mother to Set, I want Epithymia for my personal collection."

Acheron met Styxx's gaze. "If anyone can make someone's life a living hell, I can personally attest to Artemis's expertise."

Styxx had to bite back a laugh at Acheron's understatement and the look Artemis gave him. His brother was right. Artemis definitely knew how to punish someone. Given some of the extreme things she'd done to Acheron whom she'd claimed to love, he couldn't imagine what she'd do to someone she actually hated. "I'm in accord."

"Me, too," Ma'at agreed.

"Which leaves us with Apollo." Acheron paused to sweep his gaze around the room. "Most of us have an equal grudge against him so I have no idea how to be fair about his fate."

Artemis sighed. "Even though I'd love it, you can't kill him."

All of a sudden, as an old memory and idea struck, Styxx started laughing in an evil tone.

Bethany frowned. "Why does that scare me?"

"Because I have the perfect gift for someone. Even Simi will approve."

*

917

Apollo shouted in outrage around his gag as he fought against Artemis's diktyon net that held him tighter than a fly in a spider web. If he had his regular powers, he'd be able to escape. But Urian's necklace kept them drained.

Urian chuckled like a bad cartoon villain. "Remind me to never, ever piss off my father. And I don't mean Stryker. Damn, Dad. This is soooo cold."

Artemis smiled. "Yes, well, payback's a cat."

Acheron sighed and rubbed his head. "I absolutely give up."

Ignoring his brother's exasperation, Styxx hauled Apollo to his feet. "All right. One long overdue special delivery on its way." He kissed Bethany before he glanced to Acheron. "Take care of my girl. I'll be right back." He turned to Urian. "You ready?"

"After you."

Even though he knew it wasn't "done," Styxx teleported them directly into Apollymi's garden where she sat at her fountain.

Gasping in indignation, she rose to her feet. "What is this?"

Styxx forced Apollo to kneel before her. Totally naked and bound up like Styxx had been when the bastard had handed him over to Archon for torture, Apollo had no choice except to obey. Styxx would feel sorry for the Olympian had the bastard ever shown him an ounce of mercy or compassion.

But as Artemis had said, payback's a cat. And this one had ferocious claws.

"I come bearing gifts, my lady. As Aricles, I promised you that I'd deliver Apollo to your custody once I had him defeated . . . Sorry it took so long to keep my word." He stepped back so that Urian could remove the necklace from Apollo.

"I'll return this to Davyn and be right back."

Apollymi gaped. "I don't understand."

"Acheron and I decided that Apollo had screwed with all our lives for far too long. And while you can't kill Apollo, we thought you might find him an amusing toy that can help you pass the time here."

A slow sadistic smile curled her lips as she savored the very idea.

"Oh, trust me, Styxx, I promise I won't kill him. That would be too kind an end. No, no, no ... I plan to enjoy every minute of this." She closed the distance between them and kissed Styxx on the cheek. "Thank you for my gift, *m'gios*. And please give your brother my deepest love and adoration."

The French doors opened, but instead of Urian, Stryker's wife Zephyra came in with hungry eyes. "Oh," she laughed greedily at the sight of Apollo. "I knew I felt him." She locked gazes with Apollymi. "Let me know when I can have a turn with your gift."

A chill went down Styxx's spine as Apollo screamed and struggled. For one single heartbeat, Styxx almost felt bad. But the sensation quickly passed.

Apollymi's smile widened as she ignored Apollo and spoke to Zephyra. "Don't worry, child. I'll make sure to return the kind favor Apollo once did for Styxx. Everyone who wants a go at him can have him. After all, we have plenty of time."

"Troo to peridromo" Eat a bellyful, Styxx said, using the exact words Dionysus had when he'd first offered Styxx to Apollo. He turned as Urian rejoined them.

Together, they teleported back to Bethany, who was holding Sebastos while talking to Tory and Ma'at. The sight of her with a blond baby boy hit him like a sledgehammer in the crotch. It was just like the dreams he'd had ... For a full minute, he couldn't breathe.

Until she glanced over and smiled at him. "There he is. Bas, say hi to Uncle Styxx."

"Hi, Unkie Six!" he said, laughing and bouncing in Bethany's arms.

She tickled his belly. Squealing, he kissed her while his little hand tangled in her long hair.

"Are you all right?" Acheron asked as he came up behind Styxx.

Styxx met Urian's gaze and nodded. "I am." And for the first time in centuries, he really was.

Closing the distance between him and his wife, Styxx brushed his hand over Sebastos's curls then helped to untangle the baby's hand from Bethany's hair. "Hi, Bas."

"You want to hold him?" Tory asked.

Terrified at the mere thought, Styxx shook his head. "I might break him and piss off Acheron."

Tory and Bethany laughed.

"You can't break him, sweetie," Bethany said.

"I don't know. The last time I held a child that age, I must have broken it 'cause it leaked all over me."

Bethany laughed so hard, she had to give Bas back to his mother before she dropped him.

Tory kissed Bas's head. "You're right, Bethany. He's hilarious."

"And now that he's back," Ma'at said, "we need to finish something. Will all of you excuse us?"

Unsure of what she needed, they allowed her to flash them to Savitar's home.

Bethany was baffled at the location. "Where are we?"

Ma'at answered by beckoning her into the same bedroom Simi had taken her body originally.

Styxx's breath caught as he saw Bethany's body still on the bed where he'd left her earlier. No wonder her dress was clean now. Still . . . "I don't understand . . . what's going on?"

"Set told you. He split her heart. She hasn't been whole since the day Apollo tricked her into killing you. When Leto summoned the vengeance part of her, she only had that portion of Bet that had loved Aricles." She gestured to the Bethany standing next to him. "This one."

"Is that why the amulet wouldn't join?"

Ma'at shook her head. "As a link to Bethany and Bathymaas, the amulet was worthless once it was broken by Aricles's death. Bathymaas told you herself, long ago. You are her heart. She gave it to you as Aricles and it was reborn with you and you alone. It's why she couldn't smile or laugh until she found you again. Set bound her heart to your soul to make sure you kept your word to return to her." She moved toward the bed. "Now come, Bet. Let's put you back together, for once and for all."

Bethany hesitated. "Will I be different?"

"No, precious." Ma'at gave her a kind smile. "Except you will be able to be fully happy again."

Biting her lip in trepidation, she looked up at Styxx.

He rubbed her shoulders. "I'm right here, Beth. I'm not going anywhere."

Reluctantly, she left him and went to the bed. "What do I do?"

"Just lie down on top of yourself."

"That's it?"

Ma'at nodded.

Hoping it worked, Bethany laid herself over her other body. At first, she felt nothing. Then a slow burn started. One that spread through her blood until she saw stars. In the next instant, she fell and opened her eyes.

She sat up and looked around. "What happened?"

"You're back." Ma'at kissed her cheek. "And I'm out of here. Savitar is on the beach and won't return until after dawn. There's no one to disturb you two at all and I know you both want some alone time." She flashed out.

Suddenly unsure and cautious, Styxx sat on the edge of the bed.

Bethany watched him staring at her. There was a light in his blue eyes that told her he was terrified that this wasn't real. That he'd wake up alone again.

In truth, she was disoriented by it all. It'd been one bizarre day. But now . . .

She reached out to finger the hole in his shirt where her knife had gone through it. Sickened over what Leto had caused her to do, she grimaced. "I'm so sorry, Styxx. Now every member of your family has tried to kill you."

"Except Urian."

She tried to suppress her smile and failed miserably. "The day's still young."

He laughed. "If it means getting you back, Beth, you can carve out my heart and serve it on a platter."

She gave him a suspicious stare. "Have you really not been with a woman in all these centuries?"

921

"Trust me, you're about to find out. If I even last long enough to make it inside you, it'll be a miracle ..." His haunted gaze burned her as he swallowed hard. "That is, if you'll have me."

And that was what she loved most about him. For all his confidence and power, he still had moments of profound shyness and uncertainty. Not many, but enough to be endearing and fallible.

She pulled his shirt off, and placed her hand over the scar in the center of his chest. "I feel so bad for you. To me, it seems like we were together only yesterday. I have no concept of how long I slept. But for you—"

He placed his fingers over her lips. "It doesn't matter."

Yet it did, and she knew it. While he'd been off delivering Apollo to Apollymi, Tory and Acheron had told her about his sketchbooks. About how tortured and miserable he'd been all these centuries without her. She had no idea how he could have kept his faith and troth. How he'd managed to find the strength to carry on and survive. But she was so glad that he had. Then again, her Styxx had never been a coward. He was, and would always be, a steadfast warrior hero. Imperfectly perfect. The keeper of her heart. Wanting to please him, she moved to straddle his hips.

Styxx sucked his breath in sharply at the sensation of her soft body against his. He trembled at the one thing he'd been most desperate for. And still, he couldn't believe she was really here in his arms. She sank her hands into his hair and gave him a kiss that set his entire being on fire. And when she trailed one hand down his chest to the button on his jeans, he thought he was going to die from the need to feel her hands on his bare skin.

Pulling back and sliding to his side, Bethany scowled as she tugged at his fly. "What is this thing?"

He laughed. "Zipper."

"What's a zipper?"

He smiled, remembering how confused he'd been when Dionysus had first taken him to New Orleans. "It secures clothes to the body." He untied his boots and dropped them to the floor then showed her how to work the zipper and button on his jeans.

922

"I miss your chiton. It was easy access." She pushed his jeans down until he was exposed to her questing hand.

His breathing rugged. Styxx did his best to think about anything other than her touching him. But when she brushed her hand down the length of his cock and cupped him, he lost the battle in one heartbeat. Against his wishes, he came in a blinding sweet moment of pure bliss.

His body still shuddering, he buried his head under the pillows and groaned in utter agony and embarrassment. He'd been right. Not only had he not made it inside her, he hadn't even gotten close. "I'm worthless!"

She continued to stroke and tease him as she pulled the pillow off his face. "No, Styxx. You're not. I didn't doubt you, but this shows me how much you love me, and the fact that you have been every bit as faithful as you promised me you would be." Wrinkling her nose playfully, she smiled down at him. "Besides, I know you. You'll spend the next twenty-four hours more than making up for it. You are nothing if not an overachiever."

He reached up to toy with a stray lock of her hair. "I am that, Beth, but only for you." Then he pulled her peplos off and rolled her over so that he could savor the sight of her naked in his bed. His heart pounded as indecision on where to begin paralyzed him. He wanted to devour her.

So he started with her lips then moved south to her breasts.

Bethany cradled his head against her as he meticulously tasted every inch of her while his fingers stroked and delved, and heightened the aching need she had for him. And when his mouth replaced his fingers at the center of her body, she cried out in ecstasy.

He laughed deep in his throat. "That's it, Beth. Come for me. I need to taste you."

Those words sent her over the edge. Throwing her head back, she screamed as pleasure ripped her apart and her body spasmed with pure rhythmic bliss. Still he nibbled and teased until he'd wrung every last bit of orgasm from her.

Then he slowly nibbled his way back to her lips. He lifted himself up on his arms to stare down at her while his long hard body lay between her legs.

Bethany cupped his face in her hands as she felt his cock already hardening against her stomach. "See, I knew you'd be back in business."

Smiling, he kissed her lips then slid himself inside her. They moaned in unison as she wrapped her body around his while he began thrusting against her hips.

"I have missed you so much," he breathed in her ear. "And not just this. I could drown myself in your scent and warmth."

"I am yours forever. Literally."

"And I am eternally yours."

This time, Styxx knew that nothing would ever to separate them again. And if anyone or anything was dumb enough to try, they were going to learn the lesson that he'd given both Archon and Apollo. Styxx of Didymos fought for what he wanted. He didn't back down. He didn't give up. He didn't lose.

Even when it meant coming back from the dead. He wouldn't be stopped and he would never again live without his most vital part. Bethany.

DECEMBER 28, 2012

Azura entered Noir's study without knocking to find him in the middle of entering one of their servants. "Put it away, love. I have business to discuss."

Noir growled at her intrusion. "What is so important that—"

"Rezar has returned."

He shoved the woman off his lap and quickly tucked himself back into his pants. "What?"

She nodded and watched as the servant made a quick exit. Crossing her arms over her chest, she faced her brother. "And Bathymaas is reunited with Aricles."

"Then the prophecy is true . . . "

"So it seems." Azura wrinkled her nose at him. "Right at this moment, Darkness is covering the Light."

"How do you know all this?"

"Our slave made a report."

Noir considered that. "Has he found Braith yet?"

"No. He's still looking. But with Bathymaas free . . . "

The Malachai wouldn't be far behind. The balance must always be maintained.

And they were about to rain hell itself down on the unsuspecting humans . . .

Noir couldn't wait.

FEBRUARY 9, 2013

Acheron was expecting his brother to meet him so when the door to his bedroom opened, he was surprised to find the former dream god, Arik, there. Since Arik was the husband of Tory's cousin Geary, it wasn't unusual for him to visit.

"Tory's not home. She went shopping for baby clothes with Bethany."

"I'm not here to see Tory. I wanted to ask you something."

Ash pulled the blanket up on Bas who was in the middle of his afternoon nap. "Sure. What do you need?"

"How old was Tory when her father died?"

Now that was an odd question. "Ten."

Arik shook his head in denial. "When I first met Tory in 1996, Geary told me that she was six when her father died."

He scowled at that. "I have photos of her with her father on her birthdays all the way up to ten. You must be mistaken."

"No. I'm not. Even Geary now has memories of him being with Tory longer than that ... and we have pictures that never existed until recently."

Ash cursed at the significance of what Arik was telling him. "Who's messing with the time sequence?"

"I don't know. But since it's affecting the one person nearest and dearest your heart ... "

It most likely involved Acheron somehow. He winced in apprehension. "So whatever was altered had to have occurred between 1996 when you met her and 2008 when I met her."

Arik nodded. "I'm thinking this time breach more than the cosmic alignment in December is what has unleashed Tiva and Zev." Tiva was the original goddess of untime and her brother Zev of time itself.

Chaos and Order ...

Ash wanted to curse. "I saw Tiva in December. She was after the Time Stone."

"Where's it now?"

"Safe. Back in the hands of its keeper." Neither Kateri nor Ren would allow anything happen to it. And Ren knew better than to let Tiva anywhere near the Stone.

"Glad to hear it. But with Order and Chaos unleashed ... "

And not just Zev and Tiva. Set and Bethany were also Order and Chaos. And they were now released, too.

Yeah ... this was looking bad.

"Something's coming, Acheron. And I don't know what it is."

"Neither do I. But at least we're forewarned about it. Let's see if we can find other breaches and fluctuations. Maybe we can undo whatever has been done."

Arik nodded. "I'll let you know what I find out."

"And I'll do the same."

As soon as Arik left, Ash turned back to watch his slumbering son as fear permeated every part of his being. Nothing good ever came when someone or something tampered with time. While Artemis had moments of profound lunacy, she wouldn't dare mess with that one.

Maybe one of the Were-Hunters ...

Or something a lot deadlier.

Whatever or whoever it was, Acheron would find them and he would make them pay for it. Most of all, he would stop them before they unleashed the one evil that nothing could ever defeat.

SEPTEMBER 21, 2013

"Look at them, Apollymi. Have you ever seen anything more pathetic than two grown, immortal warriors so terrified of something so small? I don't know who's more nervous about the birth ... dad or uncle."

In her shade form on Katateros, Apollymi couldn't agree more with Ma'at as they watched Styxx and Apostolos gather ice chips. "Should we have them boil water?"

Athena laughed. "Perhaps it's my presence they find most unsettling. After all, the last time I attended a birth was theirs and ... Well, thankfully this will turn out much better. I think."

Styxx pinned the three goddesses with a stern frown. "You do know we can hear you, right?"

Athena laughed. "Of course we do, love. Wouldn't be nearly as much fun if you couldn't."

"Styxx!" Acheron barked. "Get over here. Now!"

Ignoring the goddesses, Styxx ran to Bethany with the ice. "I'm right here, Beth."

Lying on their bed in her temple, she took his hand and squeezed it as she screamed out in pain. Styxx was shaking in fear while Simi held a catcher's mitt in expectation of their son's birth.

Artemis rolled her eyes at Simi as she motioned for Ma'at to take over the birthing process. "He's almost here. I'm sure you want to deliver this one."

Tory wiped at Bethany's brow. "Breathe, sweetie. Just a few minutes more."

Acheron tsked. "I'm so jealous, Styxx. This is usually when Tory starts calling out for the wrath of the Furies to geld me."

Tory passed a look to her husband that said he'd be spending the night on the couch.

Bethany laughed then groaned.

"One more push, child," Ma'at said.

Closing her eyes, she obeyed.

Happy and terrified beyond belief, Styxx held his breath as his son entered the world. He didn't breathe again until he heard the boy's healthy cry. Shaking as much as Bethany, he pressed his cheek to hers. They were both laughing through their tears.

Finally, they'd done it . . .

Before she even cleaned the baby, Ma'at wragged him in a light blue blanket and handed him to his mother. "I know better than to make you two wait a minute longer to hold your baby son."

He was the most beautiful thing Styxx had ever seen. Perfect and adorable, he had a mop of black hair like his mother and a set of golden eyes. Styxx placed a nervous hand on his son while he kissed Bethany's cheek. "What are we going to call him?"

Because of what had happened with Urian, they'd been too superstitious this time to name the baby before he arrived.

She laid her gentle hand over Styxx's jaw. "Aricles Galen?"

He hesitated as a wave of fear went through him. "Is that bad luck?"

Athena tsked at them. "Not this time, sweetie. He will do his namesakes proud."

A loud knock sounded on the door. "Is that my newest grandson I hear?"

They laughed at Set's impatient voice. He'd become so distraught

928

during Bethany's labor that Ma'at had banned him, Maahes and Urian from the room.

Opening the door, Athena let Set in. He flashed across the room to make sure Bethany and child were healthy.

Set kissed Bethany's cheek then cooed at his grandson. "There's a room full of beings who want to meet this little guy. Including his other aunt and uncle, and cousins, and older brother."

Ma'at laughed. "Let me get little Ari cleaned up and dressed then the extreme spoiling can commence."

Neither of them wanted to let go of their son, but they knew Ma'at was right. Sooner or later, they would have to let someone else hold him. Styxx stepped back so that Ma'at could reclaim Ari.

Styxx covered Bethany with a blanket. "What can I get for you?"

Her smile dazzled him. "Nothing. Just don't let Ari out of your sight."

He laughed. "Don't worry." He inclined his head to Simi who was micromanaging every step of the bathing process and driving Ma'at crazy. "This time he has his own demon mother hen who will eat anyone or anything that comes near him."

Soteria kissed her on the cheek, too. "We'll leave you to rest, but if you need anything, let us know."

Acheron gave a light squeeze to Bethany's hand then hugged Styxx. "Congratulations, brother. I can't wait to watch Theron and Bas play with him."

Neither could Styxx. Acheron's son Theron had been born this past May. Barely four months apart, their boys would be more like twins than cousins.

And their sons would all have the spoiled-rotten childhoods that he and Acheron should have had.

Once Ari was cleaned and dressed in a white cotton jumper, Ma'at returned him to them.

Her heart bursting with emotions she couldn't name, Bethany choked. And her gaze swam at the sight of her perfect, healthy baby as he stared up at his parents. "We finally get to raise our son."

Styxx returned her smile. "Poor thing. We're both going to smother him."

She laughed. "Absolutely. We'll make Acheron and Tory look neglectful." She kissed the top of their son's head then held him out to Styxx. "You better go make the rounds with him."

More petrified than he'd ever been before, Styxx hesitated. "I don't know about this. He's awful tiny."

She tsked at his fear. "You've got to learn to hold him at some point."

"I'd rather face an army of gods with nothing more than a knife and my bare hands." But she was right and he knew it. Taking a deep breath for courage, Styxx allowed her to place their son in his arms.

"See, you didn't break him."

Awed and amazed, Styxx stared down at his tiny, precious son. Never in all his long life had he seen a more incredible sight than his boy in his own arms. "Wish me luck."

Bethany kissed him then allowed Ma'at to pull him out of the room to show off his boy. The instant they opened the door, Skylos barked happily and ran past Styxx to jump on the bed and take his usual place beside Bethany. Laughing, she patted his head. He licked her twice then settled down to sleep.

Athena stayed behind to be with her. "How are you doing?"

"I've never been happier ... or more frightened."

She laughed. "That's called life."

No, Bethany thought as she watched her husband through the open door smiling proudly with both of their sons. It was called love. The hardest thing in the world to find and keep, but the one thing that made the worst imaginable hell tolerable. More than hope, it was truly the light that guided the lost to safety and kept them sane in the midst of utter chaos.

And never again would she choose any obligation over her sons and husband. They were her family, and for them alone, she would kill or die. The things in this world didn't matter. Only the people did. And that was the way life should always be.

Forever.

ACKNOWLEDGMENTS

As always, a very special thank-you to my friends, who are so forgiving when they don't hear from me for long periods of time while I'm working. One day, I know they're going to get together and put my face on a milk carton.

To my sons and hubby who tolerate my absentmindedness and bizarre work hours. I love you more than mere words can ever convey and I thank God every day for the gift that is you.

For the fans who visit and make my day online.

And especially to my editor and team at Macmillan for not strangling me when I handed in a 1600+ page manuscript. There aren't many publishers who would be so bold and supportive. You guys are the best!